Ellen Wood

Johnny Ludlow

Ellen Wood

Johnny Ludlow

ISBN/EAN: 9783337399276

Printed in Europe, USA, Canada, Australia, Japan

Cover: Foto ©Andreas Hilbeck / pixelio.de

More available books at **www.hansebooks.com**

BY

MRS. HENRY WOOD,

AUTHOR OF "EAST LYNNE," "THE CHANNINGS," ETC.

FIRST SERIES.

𝔉𝔦𝔣𝔱𝔦𝔢𝔱𝔥 𝔗𝔥𝔬𝔲𝔰𝔞𝔫𝔡.

LONDON:

RICHARD BENTLEY AND SON,

Publishers in Ordinary to Her Majesty the Queen.

1895.

CONTENTS.

CONTENTS.

JOHNNY LUDLOW.

I.

LOSING LENA.

We lived chiefly at Dyke Manor. A fine old place, so close upon the borders of Warwickshire and Worcestershire, that many people did not know which of the two counties it was really in. The house was in Warwickshire, but some of the land was in Worcestershire. The Squire had, however, another estate, Crabb Cot, all in Worcestershire, and very many miles nearer to Worcester.

Squire Todhetley was rich. But he lived in the plain, good old-fashioned way that his forefathers had lived ; almost a homely way, it might be called, in contrast with the show and parade that have sprung up of late years. He was respected by every one, and though hotheaded and impetuous, he was simple-minded, open-handed, and had as good a heart as any one ever had in this world. An elderly gentleman now, was he, of middle height, with a portly form and a red face ; and his hair, what was left of it, consisted of a few scanty, lightish locks, standing up straight on the top of his head.

The Squire had married, but not very early in life. His wife died in a few years, leaving one child only ; a son, named after his father, Joseph. Young Joe was just the pride of the Manor and of his father's heart.

I, writing this, am Johnny Ludlow. And you will naturally want to hear what I did at Dyke Manor, and why I lived there.

About three-miles' distance from the Manor was a place called the Court. Not a property of so much importance as the Manor, but a nice place, for all that. It belonged to my father, William Ludlow. He and Squire Todhetley were good friends. I was an only child, just as Tod was ; and, like him, I had lost my mother. They had christened me John, but always called me Johnny. I can remember many incidents of my early life now, but I cannot recall my mother to my mind. She must have died—at least I fancy so—when I was two years old.

One morning, two years after that, when I was about four, the servants told me I had a new mamma. I can see her now as she looked when she came home : tall, thin, and upright, with a long face, pinched nose, a meek expression, and gentle voice. She was a Miss Marks, who used to play the organ at church, and had hardly any income at all. Hannah said she was sure she was thirty-five if she was a day—she was talking to Eliza while she dressed me—and they both agreed that she would probably turn out to be a tartar, and that the master might have chosen better. I understood quite well that they meant papa, and asked why he might have chosen better; upon which they shook me and said they had not been speaking of my papa at all, but of the old black-smith round the corner. Hannah brushed my hair the wrong way, and Eliza went off to see to her bedrooms. Children are easily prejudiced : and they prejudiced me against my new mother. Looking at her with the eyes of maturer years, I know that though she might be poor in pocket, she was good and kindly, and every inch a lady.

Papa died that same year. At the end of another year, Mrs. Ludlow, my step-mother, married Squire Todhetley, and we went to live at Dyke Manor; she, I, and my nurse Hannah. The Court was let for a term of years to the Sterlings.

Young Joe did not like the new arrangements. He was older than I, could take up prejudices more strongly, and he took a mighty strong one against the new Mrs. Todhetley. He had been regularly indulged by his father and spoilt by all the servants ; so it was only to be expected that he would not like the invasion. Mrs. Todhetley introduced order into the profuse household, hitherto governed by the servants. They and young Joe equally resented it ; they refused to see that things were really more com-fortable than they used to be, and at half the cost.

Two babies came to the Manor ; Hugh first, Lena next. Joe and I were sent to school. He was as big as a house, compared with me, tall and strong and dark, with an imperious way and will of his own. I was fair, gentle, timid, yielding to him in all things. His was the master-spirit, swaying mine at will. At school the boys at once, the very first day we entered, shortened his name from Todhetley to Tod. I caught up the habit, and from that time I never called him anything else.

And so the years went on. Tod and I at school being drilled into learning ; Hugh and Lena growing into nice little children. During the holidays, hot war raged between Tod and his step-mother. At least *silent* war. Mrs. Todhetley was always kind to him, and she never quarrelled ; but Tod opposed her in many things, and would be generally sarcastically cool to her in manner.

We did lead the children into mischief, and she complained of
that. Tod did, that is, and of course I followed where he led.
" But we can't let Hugh grow up a milksop, you know, Johnny," he
would say to me ; " and he would if left to his mother." So Hugh's
clothes in Tod's hands came to grief, and sometimes Hugh himself.
Hannah, who was the children's nurse now, stormed and scolded
over it : she and Tod had ever been at daggers drawn with each
other; and Mrs. Todhetley would implore Tod with tears in her
eyes to be careful with the child. Tod appeared to turn a deaf ear
to them, and marched off with Hugh before their very eyes. He
really loved the children, and would have saved them from injury
with his life. The Squire drove and rode his fine horses. Mrs.
Todhetley had set up a low basket-chaise drawn by a mild she-
donkey : it was safer for the children, she said. Tod went into fits
whenever he met the turn-out.

But Tod was not always to escape scot-free, or incite the children
to rebellion with impunity. There came a day when he brought
himself, through it, to a state of self-torture and repentance.

It occurred when we were at home for the summer holidays, just
after the crop of hay was got in, and the bare fields looked as white
in the blazing sun as if they had been scorched. Tod and I were
in the three-cornered meadow next the fold-yard. He was making a
bat-net with gauze and two sticks. Young Jacobson had shown us
his the previous day, and a bat he had caught with it ; and Tod
thought he would catch bats too. But he did not seem to be
making much hand at the net, and somehow managed to send the
pointed end of the stick through a corner of it.

" I don't think that gauze is strong enough, Tod."

" I am afraid it is not, Johnny. Here, catch hold of it. I'll go
indoors, and see if they can't find me some better. Hannah must
have some."

He flew off past the ricks, and leaped the little gate into the
fold-yard—a tall, strong fellow, who might leap the Avon. In a
few minutes I heard his voice again, and went to meet him. Tod
was coming away from the house with Lena.

" Have you the gauze, Tod ! "

" Not a bit of it ; the old cat won't look for any; says she hasn't
time. I'll hinder her time a little. Come along, Lena."

The " old cat " was Hannah. I told you she and he were often
at daggers drawn. Hannah had a chronic complaint in the shape
of ill-temper, and Tod called her names to her face. Upon going
in to ask her for the gauze, he found her dressing Hugh and Lena
to go out, and she just turned him out of the nursery, and told him
not to bother her then with his gauze and his wants. Lena ran
after Tod ; she liked him better than all of us put together. She

had on a blue silk frock, and a white straw hat with daisies round it; open-worked stockings were on her pretty little legs. By which we saw she was about to be taken out for show.

"What are you going to do with her, Tod?"

"I'm going to hide her," answered Tod, in his decisive way. "Keep where you are, Johnny."

Lena enjoyed the rebellion. In a minute or two Tod came back alone. He had left her between the ricks in the three-cornered field, and told her not to come out. Then he went off to the front of the house, and I stood inside the barn, talking to Mack, who was hammering away at the iron of the cart-wheel. Out came Hannah by-and-by. She had been dressing herself as well as Hugh.

"Miss Lena!"

No answer. Hannah called again, and then came up the fold-yard, looking about.

"Master Johnny, have you seen the child?"

"What child?" I was not going to spoil Tod's sport by telling her.

"Miss Lena. She has got off somewhere, and my mistress is waiting for her in the basket-chaise."

"I see her just now along of Master Joseph," spoke up Mack, arresting his noisy hammer.

"See her where?" asked Hannah.

"Close here, a-going that way."

He pointed to the palings and gate that divided the yard from the three-cornered field. Hannah ran there and stood looking over. The ricks were within a short stone's throw, but Lena kept close. Hannah called out again, and threw her gaze over the empty field.

"The child's not there. Where can she have got to, tiresome little thing?"

In the house, and about the house, and out of the house, as the old riddle says, went Hannah. It was jolly to see her. Mrs. Todhetley and Hugh were seated patiently in the basket-chaise before the hall-door, wondering what made Hannah so long. Tod, playing with the mild she-donkey's ears, and laughing to himself, stood talking graciously to his step-mother. I went round. The Squire had gone riding into Evesham; Dwarf Giles, who made the nattiest little groom in the county, for all his five-and-thirty years, behind him.

"I can't find Miss Lena," cried Hannah, coming out.

"Not find Miss Lena!" echoed Mrs. Todhetley. "What do you mean, Hannah? Have you not dressed her?"

"I dressed her first, ma'am, before Master Hugh, and she went out of the nursery. I can't think where she can have got to. I've searched everywhere."

"But, Hannah, we must have her directly; I am late as it is."
They were going over to the Court to a children's early party at
the Sterlings'. Mrs. Todhetley stepped out of the basket-chaise to
help in the search.

"I had better fetch her, Tod," I whispered.

He nodded yes. Tod never bore malice, and I suppose he thought
Hannah had had enough of a hunt for that day. I ran through the
fold-yard to the ricks, and called to Lena.

"You can come out now, little stupid."

But no Lena answered. There were seven ricks in a group, and
I went into all the openings between them. Lena was not there. It
was rather odd, and I looked across the field and towards the lane
and the coppice, shouting out sturdily.

"Mack, have you seen Miss Lena pass indoors?" I stayed to ask
him, in going back.

No: Mack had not noticed her; and I went round to the front
again, and whispered to Tod.

"What a muff you are, Johnny! She's between the ricks fast
enough. No danger that she'd come out when I told her to stay!"

"But she's not there indeed, Tod. You go and look."

Tod vaulted off, his long legs seeming to take flying leaps, like a
deer's, on his way to the ricks.

To make short of the story, Lena was gone. Lost. The house,
the outdoor buildings, the gardens were searched for her, and she
was not to be found. Mrs. Todhetley's fears flew to the ponds at
first; but it was impossible she could have come to grief in either
of the two, as they were both in view of the barn-door where I and
Mack had been. Tod avowed that he had put her amid the ricks
to hide her; and it was not to be imagined she had gone away.
The most feasible conjecture was, that she had run from between
the ricks when Hannah called to her, and was hiding in the lane.

Tod was in a fever, loudly threatening Lena with unheard-of
whippings, to cover his real concern. Hannah looked red, Mrs.
Todhetley white. I was standing by him when the cook came up;
a sharp woman, with red-brown eyes. We called her Molly.

"Mr. Joseph," said she, "I have heard of gipsies stealing
children."

"Well?" returned Tod.

"There was one at the door a while agone—an insolent one,
too. Perhaps Miss Lena—— "

"Which way did she go?—which door was she at?" burst forth
Tod.

"'Twas a man, sir. He came up to the kitchen-door, and steps
inside as bold as brass, asking me to buy some wooden skewers
he'd cut, and saying something about a sick child. When I told

him to march, that we never encouraged tramps here, he wanted to answer me, and I just shut the door in his face. A regular gipsy, if ever I see one," continued Molly; "his skin tawny and his wild hair jet-black. Maybe, in revenge, he have stole off the little miss."

Tod took up the notion, and his face turned white. "Don't say anything of this to Mrs. Todhetley," he said to Molly. "We must just scour the country."

But in departing from the kitchen-door, the gipsy man could not by any possibility have made his way to the rick-field without going through the fold-yard. And he had not done that. It was true that Lena might have run round and got into the gipsy's way. Unfortunately, none of the men were about, except Mack and old Thomas. Tod sent these off in different directions; Mrs. Todhetley drove away in her pony-chaise to the lanes round, saying the child might have strayed there; Molly and the maids started elsewhere; and I and Tod went flying along a by-road that branched off in a straight line, as it were, from the kitchen-door. Nobody could keep up with Tod, he went so fast; and I was not tall and strong as he was. But I saw what Tod in his haste did not see—a dark man with some bundles of skewers and a stout stick, walking on the other side of the hedge. I whistled Tod back again.

"What is it, Johnny?" he said, panting. "Have you seen her?"

"Not her. But look there. That must be the man Molly spoke of."

Tod crashed through the hedge as if it had been so many cobwebs, and accosted the gipsy. I followed more carefully, but got my face scratched.

"Were you up at the great house, begging, a short time ago?" demanded Tod, in an awful passion.

The man turned round on Tod with a brazen face. I say brazen, because he did it so independently; but it was not an insolent face in itself; rather a sad one, and very sickly.

"What's that you ask me, master?"

"I ask whether it was you who were at the Manor-house just now, begging?" fiercely repeated Tod.

"I was at a big house offering wares for sale, if you mean that, sir. I wasn't begging."

"Call it what you please," said Tod, growing white again. "What have you done with the little girl?"

For, you see, Tod had caught up the impression that the gipsy *had* stolen Lena, and he spoke in accordance with it

"I've seen no little girl, master."

"You have," and Tod gave his foot a stamp. "What have you done with her?"

The man's only answer was to turn round and walk off, muttering to himself. Tod pursued him, calling him a thief and other names; but nothing more satisfactory could he get out of him.

"He can't have taken her, Tod. If he had, she'd be with him now. He couldn't eat her, you know."

"He may have given her to a confederate."

"What to do? What do gipsies steal children for?"

Tod stopped in a passion, lifting his hand. "If you torment me with these frivolous questions, Johnny, I'll strike you. How do I know what's done with stolen children? Sold, perhaps. I'd give a hundred pounds out of my pocket at this minute if I knew where those gipsies were encamped."

We suddenly lost the fellow. Tod had been keeping him in sight in the distance. Whether he disappeared up a gum-tree, or into a rabbit-hole, Tod couldn't tell; but gone he was.

Up this lane, down that one; over this moor, across that common; so raced Tod and I. And the afternoon wore away, and we had changed our direction a dozen times : which possibly was not wise.

The sun was getting low as we passed Ragley gates, for we had finally got into the Alcester road. Tod was going to do what we ought to have done at first : report the loss at Alcester. Some one came riding along on a stumpy pony. It proved to be Gruff Blossom, groom to the Jacobsons. They called him "Gruff" because of his temper. He did touch his hat to us, which was as much as you could say, and spurred the stumpy animal on. But Tod made a sign to him, and he was obliged to stop and listen.

"The gipsies stole off little Miss Lena!" cried old Blossom, coming out of his gruffness. "That's a rum go! Ten to one if you find her for a year to come."

"But, Blossom, what do they do with the children they steal?" I asked, in a sort of agony.

"They cuts their hair off and dyes their skins brown, and then takes 'em out to fairs a ballad-singing," answered Blossom.

"But why need they do it, when they have children of their own?"

"Ah, well, that's a question I couldn't answer," said old Blossom. "Maybe their'n arn't pretty children—Miss Lena, she is pretty."

"Have you heard of any gipsies being encamped about here?" Tod demanded of him.

"Not lately, Mr. Joseph. Five or six months ago, there was a lot 'camped on the Markis's ground. They warn't there long."

"Can't you ride about, Blossom, and see after the child?" asked Tod, putting something into his hand.

Old Blossom pocketed it, and went off with a nod. He was riding about, as we knew afterwards, for hours. Tod made straight for the police-station at Alcester, and told his tale. Not a soul was there but Jenkins, one of the men.

"I haven't seen no suspicious characters about," said Jenkins, who seemed to be eating something. He was a big man, with short black hair combed on his forehead, and he had a habit of turning his face upwards, as if looking after his nose—a square ornament, that stood up straight.

"She is between four and five years old; a very pretty child, with blue eyes and a good deal of curling auburn hair," said Tod, who was growing feverish.

Jenkins wrote it down—"Name, Todhetley. What Christian name?"

"Adalena, called 'Lena.'"

"Recollect the dress, sir?"

"Pale blue silk; straw hat with wreath of daisies round it; open-worked white stockings, and thin black shoes; white drawers," recounted Tod, as if he had prepared the list by heart coming along.

"That's bad, that dress is," said Jenkins, putting down the pen.

"Why is it bad?"

"'Cause the things is tempting. Quite half the children that gets stole is stole for what they've got upon their backs. Tramps and that sort will run a risk for a blue silk that they'd not run for a brown holland pinafore. Auburn curls, too," added Jenkins, shaking his head; "that's a temptation also. I've knowed children sent back home with bare heads afore now. Any ornaments, sir?"

"She was safe to have on her little gold neck-chain and cross. They are very small, Jenkins—not worth much."

Jenkins lifted his nose—not in disdain, it was a habit he had. "Not worth much to you, sir, who could buy such any day, but an uncommon bait to professional child-stealers. Were the cross a coral, or any stone of that sort?"

"It was a small gold cross, and the chain was thin. They could only be seen when her cloak was off. Oh, I forgot the cloak; it was white: llama, I think they call it. She was going to a child's party."

Some more questions and answers, most of which Jenkins took down. Handbills were to be printed and posted, and a reward offered on the morrow, if she was not previously found. Then we came away; there was nothing more to do at the station.

" Wouldn't it have been better, Tod, had Jenkins gone out seeking her and telling of the loss abroad, instead of waiting to write all that down ? "

" Johnny, if we don't find her to night, I shall go mad," was all he answered.

He went back down Alcester Street at a rushing pace—not a run but a quick walk.

" Where are you going now ? " I asked.

" I'm going up hill and down dale until I find that gipsies' encampment. You can go on home, Johnny, if you are tired."

I had not felt tired until we were in the police-station. Excitement keeps off fatigue. But I was not going to give in, and said I should stay with him.

" All right, Johnny."

Before we were clear of Alcester, Budd the land-agent came up. He was turning out of the public-house at the corner. It was dusk then. Tod laid hold of him.

" Budd, you are always about, in all kinds of nooks and by-lanes : can you tell me of any encampment of gipsies between here and the Manor-house ? "

The agent's business took him abroad a great deal, you know, into the rural districts around.

" Gipsies' encampment ? " repeated Budd, giving both of us a stare. " There's none that I know of. In the spring, a lot of them had the impudence to squat down on the Marquis's—— "

" Oh, I know all that," interrupted Tod. " Is there nothing of the sort about now ? "

" I saw a miserable little tent to-day up Cookhill way," said Budd. " It might have been a gipsy's or a travelling tinker's. 'Twasn't of much account, whichever it was."

Tod gave a spring. " Whereabouts ? " was all he asked. And Budd explained where. Tod went off like a shot, and I after him.

If you are familiar with Alcester, or have visited at Ragley or anything of that sort, you must know the long green lane leading to Cookhill ; it is dark with overhanging trees, and uphill all the way. We took that road—Tod first, and I next ; and we came to the top, and turned in the direction Budd had described the tent to be in.

It was not to be called dark ; the nights never are at midsummer ; and rays from the bright light in the west glimmered through the trees. On the outskirts of the coppice, in a bit of low ground, we saw the tent, a little mite of a thing, looking no better than a funnel turned upside down. Sounds were heard within it, and Tod put his finger on his lip while he listened. But we were too far off, and he took his boots off, and crept up close.

Sounds of wailing—of some one in pain. But that Tod had been three parts out of his senses all the afternoon, he might have known at once that they did not come from Lena, or from any one so young. Words mingled with them in a woman's voice; uncouth in its accents, nearly unintelligible, an awful sadness in its tones.

"A bit longer! a bit longer, Corry, and he'd ha' been back. You needn't ha' grudged it to us. Oh——h! if ye had but waited a bit longer!"

I don't write it exactly as she spoke; I shouldn't know how to spell it: we made a guess at half the words. Tod, who had grown white again, put on his boots, and lifted up the opening of the tent.

I had never seen any scene like it; I don't suppose I shall ever see another. About a foot from the ground was a raised surface of some sort, thickly covered with dark green rushes, just the size and shape of a gravestone. A little child, about as old as Lena, lay on it, a white cloth thrown over her, and just touching the white, still face. A torch, blazing and smoking away, was thrust into the ground and lighted up the scene. Whiter the face looked now, because it had been tawny in life. I would rather see one of our faces in death than a gipsy's. The contrast between the white face and dress of the child, and the green bed of rushes it lay on was something remarkable. A young woman, dark too, and handsome enough to create a commotion at the fair, knelt down, her brown hands uplifted; a gaudy ring on one of the fingers, worth sixpence perhaps when new, sparkled in the torchlight. Tod strode up to the dead face and looked at it for full five minutes. I do believe he thought at first that it was Lena.

"What is this?" he asked.

"It is my dead child!" the woman answered. "She did not wait that her father might see her die!"

But Tod had his head full of Lena, and looked round. "Is there no other child here?"

As if to answer him, a bundle of rags came out of a corner and set up a howl. It was a boy of about seven, and our going in had wakened him up. The woman sat down on the ground and looked at us.

"We have lost a child—a little girl," explained Tod. "I thought she might have been brought here—or have strayed here."

"I've lost *my* girl," said the woman. "Death has come for her!" And, when speaking to us, she spoke more intelligibly than when alone.

"Yes; but this child has been lost—lost out of doors! Have you seen or heard anything of one?"

"I've not been in the way o' seeing or hearing, master; I've been in the tent alone. If folks had come to my aid, Corry might not have died. I've had nothing but water to put to her lips all day ? "

"What was the matter with her?" Tod asked, convinced at length that Lena was not there.

"She have been ailing long—worse since the moon come in. The sickness took her with the summer, and the strength began to go out. Jake have been down, too. He couldn't get out to bring us help, and we have had none."

Jake was the husband, we supposed. The help meant food, or funds to get it with.

"He sat all yesterday cutting skewers, his hands a'most too weak to fashion 'em. Maybe he'd sell 'em for a few ha'pence, he said ; and he went out this morning to try, and bring home a morsel of food."

"Tod," I whispered, "I wish that hard-hearted Molly had—— "

"Hold your tongue, Johnny," he interrupted sharply. "Is Jake your husband?" he asked of the woman.

"He is my husband, and the children's father."

"Jake would not be likely to steal a child, would he?" asked Tod, in a hesitating manner, for him.

She looked up, as if not understanding. "Steal a child, master! What for ? "

"I don't know," said Tod. "I thought perhaps he had done it, and had brought the child here."

Another comical stare from the woman. "We couldn't feed these of ours ; what should we do with another ? "

"Well : Jake called at our house to sell his skewers ; and, directly afterwards, we missed my little sister. I have been hunting for her ever since."

"Was the house far from here ! "

"A few miles."

"Then he have sunk down of weakness on his way, and can't get back."

Putting her head on her knees, she began to sob and moan. The child—the living one—began to bawl ; one couldn't call it anything else ; and pulled at the green rushes.

"He knew Corry was sick and faint when he went out. He'd have got back afore now if his strength hadn't failed him ; though, maybe, he didn't think of death. Whist, then, whist, then, Dor," she added, to the boy.

"Don't cry," said Tod to the little chap, who had the largest, brightest eyes I ever saw. "That will do no good, you know."

"I want Corry," said he. "Where's Corry gone?"

"She's gone up to God, answered Tod, speaking very gently. " She's gone to be a bright angel with Him in heaven."

"Will she fly down to me?" asked Dor, his great eyes shining through their tears at Tod.

"Yes," affirmed Tod, who had a theory of his own on the point, and used to think, when a little boy, that his mother was always near him, one of God's angels keeping him from harm. "And after a while, you know, if you are good, you'll go to Corry, and be an angel, too."

"God bless you, master!" interposed the woman. "He'll think of that always."

"Tod," I said, as we went out of the tent, "I don't think they are people to steal children."

"Who's to know what the man would do?" retorted Tod.

"A man with a dying child at home wouldn't be likely to harm another."

Tod did not answer. He stood still a moment, deliberating which way to go. Back to Alcester?—where a conveyance might be found to take us home, for the fatigue was telling on both of us, now that disappointment was prolonged, and I, at least, could hardly put one foot before another. Or down to the high-road, and run the chance of some vehicle overtaking us? Or keep on amidst these fields and hedgerows, which would lead us home by a rather nearer way, but without chance of a lift? Tod made up his mind, and struck down the lane the way we had come up. He was on first, and I saw him suddenly halt, and turn to me.

"Look here, Johnny!"

I looked as well as I could for the night and the trees, and saw something on the ground. A man had sunk down there, apparently from exhaustion. His face was a tawny white, just like the dead child's. A stout stick and the bundles of skewers lay beside him.

"Do you see the fellow, Johnny? It is the gipsy."

"Has he fainted?"

"Fainted, or shamming it. I wonder if there's any water about?"

But the man opened his eyes; perhaps the sound of voices revived him. After looking at us a minute or two, he raised himself slowly on his elbow. Tod—the one thought uppermost in his mind—said something about Lena.

"The child's found, master?"

Tod seemed to give a leap. I know his heart did. "Found!"

"Been safe at home this long while."

"Who found her?"

"'Twas me, master."

"Where was she?" asked Tod, his tone softening. "Let us hear about it."

"I was making back ·for the town" (we supposed he meant Alcester), "and missed the way; land about here's strange to me.

A-going through a bit of a groove, which didn't seem as if it was leading to nowhere, I heard a child crying. There was the little thing tied to a tree, stripped, and——"

"Stripped!" roared Tod.

"Stripped to the skin, sir, save for a dirty old skirt that was tied round her. A woman carried her off to that spot, she told me, robbed her of her clothes, and left her there. Knowing where she must ha' been stole from—through you're accusing *me* of it, master —I untied her to lead her home, but her feet warn't used to the rough ground, and I made shift to carry her. A matter of two miles it were, and I be not good for much. I left her at home safe, and set off back. That's all, master."

"What were you doing here?" asked Tod, as considerately as if he had been speaking to a lord. "Resting?"

"I suppose I fell, master. I don't remember nothing, since I was tramping up the lane, till your voices came. I've had naught inside my lips to-day but a drink o' water."

"Did they give you nothing to eat at the house when you took the child home?"

He shook his head. "I saw the woman again, nobody else. She heard what I had to say about the child, and she never said 'Thank ye.'"

The man had been getting on his feet, and took up the skewers, that were all tied together with string, and the stick. But he reeled as he stood, and would have fallen again but for Tod. Tod gave him his arm.

"We are in for it, Johnny," said he aside to me. "Pity but I could be put in a picture—the Samaritan helping the destitute!"

"I'd not accept of ye, sir, but that I have a child sick at home, and want to get to her. There's a piece of bread in my pocket that was give me at a cottage to-day."

"Is your child sure to get well?" asked Tod, after a pause; wondering whether he could say anything of what had occurred, so as to break the news.

The man gazed right away into the distance, as if searching for an answer in the far-off star shining there.

"There's been a death-look in her face this day and night past, master. But the Lord's good to us all."

"And sometimes, when He takes children, it is done in mercy," said Tod. "Heaven is a better place than this."

"Ay," rejoined the man, who was leaning heavily on Tod, and could never have got home without him, unless he had crawled on hands and knees. "I've been sickly on and off for this year past; worse lately; and I've thought at times that if my own turn was coming, I'd be glad to see my children gone afore me."

"Oh, Tod!" I whispered, in a burst of repentance, "how could we have been so hard with this poor fellow, and roughly accused him of stealing Lena?" But Tod only gave me a knock with his elbow.

"I fancy it must be pleasant to think of a little child being an angel in heaven—a child that we have loved," said Tod.

"Ay, ay," said the man.

Tod had no courage to say more. He was not a parson. Presently he asked the man what tribe he belonged to—being a gipsy.

"I'm not a gipsy, master. Never was one yet. I and my wife are dark-complexioned by nature; living in the open air has made us darker; but I'm English born; Christian, too. My wife's Irish; but they do say she comes of a gipsy tribe. We used to have a cart, and went about the country with crockery; but a year ago, when I got ill and lay in a lodging, the things were seized for rent and debt. Since then it's been hard lines with us. Yonder's my bit of a tent, master, and now I can get on alone. Thanking ye kindly."

"I am sorry I spoke harshly to you to-day," said Tod. "Take this: it is all I have with me."

"I'll take it, sir, for my child's sake; it may help to put the strength into her. Otherwise I'd not. We're honest; we've never begged. Thank ye both, masters, once again."

It was only a shilling or two. Tod spent, and never had much in his pockets. "I wish it had been sovereigns," said he to me; "but we will do something better for them to-morrow, Johnny. I am sure the Pater will."

"Tod," said I, as we ran on, "had we seen the man close before, and spoken with him, I should never have suspected him. He has a face to be trusted."

Tod burst into a laugh. "There you are Johnny, at your faces again!"

I was always reading people's faces, and taking likes and dislikes accordingly. They called me a muff for it at home (and for many other things), Tod especially; but it seemed to me that I could read people as easily as a book. Duffham, our surgeon at Church Dykely, bade me *trust to it* as a good gift from God. One day, pushing my straw hat up to draw his fingers across the top of my brow, he quaintly told the Squire that when he wanted people's characters read, to come to me to read them. The Squire only laughed in answer.

As luck had it, a gentleman we knew was passing in his dog-cart when we got to the foot of the hill. It was old Pitchley. He drove us home: and I could hardly get down, I was so stiff.

Lena was in bed, safe and sound. No damage, except fright and the loss of her clothes. From what we could learn, the woman who took her off must have been concealed amidst the ricks; when Tod put her there. Lena said the woman laid hold of her very soon, caught her up, and put her hand over her mouth, to prevent her crying out; she could only give one scream. I ought to have heard it, only Mack was making such an awful row, hammering that iron. How far along fields and by-ways the woman carried her, Lena could not be supposed to tell: "Miles!" she said. Then the thief plunged amidst a few trees, took the child's things off, put on an old rag of a petticoat, and tied her loosely to a tree. Lena thought she could have got loose herself, but was too frightened to try; and just then the man, Jake, came up.

"I liked *him*," said Lena. "He carried me all the way home, that my feet should not be hurt; but he had to sit down sometimes. He said he had a poor little girl who was nearly as badly off for clothes as that, but she did not want them now, she was too sick. He said he hoped my papa would find the woman, and put her in prison."

It is what the Squire intended to do, chance helping him. But he did not reach home till after us, when all was quiet again: which was fortunate.

"I suppose you blame me for that?" cried Tod, to his step-mother.

"No, I don't, Joseph," said Mrs. Todhetley. She called him Joseph nearly always, not liking to shorten his name, as some of us did. "It is so very common a thing for the children to be playing in the three-cornered field amidst the ricks; and no suspicion that danger could arise from it having ever been glanced at, I do not think any blame attaches to you."

"I am very sorry now for having done it," said Tod. "I shall never forget the fright to the last hour of my life."

He went straight to Molly, from Mrs. Todhetley, a look on his face that, when seen there, which was rare, the servants did not like. Deference was rendered to Tod in the household. When anything should take off the good old Pater, Tod would be master. What he said to Molly no one heard; but the woman was banging at her brass things in a tantrum for three days afterwards.

And when we went to see after poor Jake and his people, it was too late. The man, the tent, the living people, and the dead child —all were gone.

II.

FINDING BOTH OF THEM.

WORCESTER ASSIZES were being held, and Squire Todhetley was on the grand jury. You see, although Dyke Manor was just within the borders of Warwickshire, the greater portion of the Squire's property lay in Worcestershire. This caused him to be summoned to serve. We were often at his house there, Crabb Cot. I forget who was foreman of the jury that time : either Sir John Pakington, or the Honourable Mr. Coventry.

The week was jolly. We put up at the Star-and-Garter when we went to Worcester, which was two or three times a-year; generally at the assizes, or the races, or the quarter-sessions; one or other of the busy times.

The Pater would grumble at the bills—and say we boys had no business to be there; but he would take us, if we were at home, for all that. The assizes came on this time the week before our summer holidays were up; the Squire wished they had not come on until the week after. Anyway, there we were, in clover; the Squire about to be stewed up in the county courts all day; I and Tod flying about the town, and doing what we liked.

The judges came in from Oxford on the usual day, Saturday. And, to make clear what I am going to tell about, we must go back to that morning and to Dyke Manor. It was broiling hot weather, and Mrs. Todhetley, Hugh, and Lena, with old Thomas and Hannah, all came on the lawn after breakfast to see us start. The open carriage was at the door, with the fine dark horses. When the Squire did come out, he liked to do things well; and Dwarf Giles, the groom, had gone on to Worcester the day before with the two saddle-horses, the Pater's and Tod's. They might have ridden them in this morning, but the Squire chose to have his horses sleek and fresh when attending the high sheriff.

"Shall I drive, sir?" asked Tod.

"No," said the Pater. "These two have queer tempers, and must be handled carefully." He meant the horses, Bob and Blister. Tod looked at me; he thought he could have managed them quite as well as the Pater.

"Papa," cried Lena, as we were driving off, running up in her white pinafore, with her pretty hair flying, "if you can catch that naughty kidnapper at Worcester, you put her in prison."

The Squire nodded emphatically, as much as to say, "Trust me for that." Lena alluded to the woman who had taken her off and stolen her clothes two or three weeks before. Tod said, afterwards, there must have been some prevision on the child's mind when she said this.

We reached Worcester at twelve. It is a long drive, you know. Lots of country-people had arrived, and the Squire went off with some of them. Tod and I thought we'd order luncheon at the Star —a jolly good one; stewed lampreys, kidneys, and cherry-tart; and let it go into the Squire's bill.

I'm afraid I envied Tod. The old days of travelling post were past, when the sheriff's procession would go out to Whittington to meet the judges' carriage. They came now by rail from Oxford, and the sheriff and his attendants received them at the railway station. It was the first time Tod had been allowed to make one of the gentlemen-attendants. The Squire said now he was too young; but he looked big, and tall, and strong. To see him mount his horse and go cantering off with the rest sent me into a state of envy. Tod saw it.

"Don't drop your mouth, Johnny," said he. "You'll make one of us in another year or two."

I stood about for half-an-hour, and the procession came back, passing the Star on its way to the county courts. The bells were ringing, the advanced heralds blew their trumpets, and the javelin-guard rode at a foot-pace, their lances in rest, preceding the high sheriff's grand carriage, with its four prancing horses and their silvered harness. Both the judges had come in, so we knew that business was over at Oxford; they sat opposite to the sheriff and his chaplain. I used to wonder whether they travelled all the way in their wigs and gowns, or robed outside Worcester. Squire Tod-hetley rode in the line next the carriage, with some more old ones of consequence; Tod on his fine bay was nearly at the tail, and he gave me a nod in passing. The judges were going to open the commission, and Foregate Street was crowded.

The high sheriff that year was a friend of ours, and the Pater had an invitation to the banquet he gave that evening. Tod thought he ought to have been invited too.

"It's sinfully stingy of him, Johnny. When I am pricked for sheriff—and I suppose my turn will come some time, either for Warwickshire or Worcestershire—I'll have more young fellows to my dinner than old ones."

The Squire, knowing nothing of our midday luncheon, was surprised that we chose supper at eight instead of dinner at six ; but he told the waiter to give us a good one. We went out while it was getting ready, and walked arm-in-arm through the crowded streets. Worcester is always full on a Saturday evening ; it is market-day there, as every one knows ; but on Assize Saturday the streets are almost impassable. Tod, tall and strong, held on his way, and asked leave of none.

" Now, then, you two gents, can't you go on proper, and not elbow respectable folks like that ? "

" Holloa ! " cried Tod, turning at the voice. " Is it you, old Jones ? "

Old Jones, the constable of our parish, touched his hat when he saw it was us, and begged pardon. We asked what he was doing at Worcester ; but he had only come oh his own account. " On the spree," Tod suggested to him.

" Young Mr. Todhetley," cried he—the way he chiefly addressed Tod—" I'd not be sure but that woman's took—her that served out little Miss Lena."

" That woman ! " said Tod. " Why do you think it ? "

Old Jones explained. A woman had been apprehended near Worcester the previous day, on a charge of stripping two little boys of their clothes in Perry Wood. The description given of her answered exactly, old Jones thought, to that given by Lena.

" She stripped 'em to the skin," groaned Jones, drawing a long face as he recited the mishap. " two poor little chaps of three years, they was, living in them cottages under the Wood—not as much as their boots did she leave on 'em. When they got home their folks didn't know 'em ; quite naked they was, and bleating with terror, like a brace of shorn sheep."

Tod put on his determined look. " And she is taken, you say, Jones ? "

" She was took yesterday, sir. They had her before the justices this morning, and the little fellows knowed her at once. As the 'sizes was on, leastways as good as on, their worships committed her for trial there and then. Policeman Cripp told me all about it ; it was him that took her. She's in the county goal."

We carried the tale to the Pater that night, and he despatched a messenger to Mrs. Todhetley, to say that Lena must be at Worcester on the Monday morning. But there's something to tell about the Sunday yet.

If you have been in Worcester on Assize Sunday, you know how the cathedral is on that morning crowded. Enough strangers are in the town to fill it : the inhabitants who go to the churches at other times attended it then ; and King Mob flocks in to see the show.

Squire Todhetley was put in the stalls; Tod and I scrambled for places on a bench. The alterations in the cathedral (going on for years before that, and going on for years since, and going on still) caused space to be limited, and it was no end of a cram. While people fought for standing-places, the procession was played in to the crash of the organ. The judges came, glorious in their wigs and gowns; the mayor and aldermen were grand as scarlet and gold chains could make them; and there was a large attendance of the clergy in their white robes. The Bishop had come in from Hartlebury, and was on his throne, and the service began. The Rev. Mr. Wheeler chanted; the Dean read the lessons. Of course the music was all right; they put up fine services on Assize Sundays now: and the sheriff's chaplain went up in his black gown to preach the sermon. Three-quarters of an hour, if you'll believe me, before that sermon came to an end!

Ere the organ had well played its Amen to the Bishop's blessing, the crowd began to push out. We pushed with the rest and took up our places in the long cathedral nave to see the procession pass back again. It came winding down between the line of javelin-men. Just as the judges were passing, Tod motioned me to look opposite. There stood a young boy in dreadful clothes, patched all over, but otherwise clean: with great dark wondering eyes riveted on the judges, as if they had been stilted peacocks; on their wigs, their solemn countenances, their held-up scarlet trains.

Where had I seen those eyes, and their brightness? Recollection flashed over me before Tod's whisper: "Jake's boy; the youngster we saw in the tent."

To get across the line was impossible: manners would not permit it, let alone the javelin-guard. And when the procession had passed, leaving nothing but a crowd of shuffling feet and the dust on the white cathedral floor, the boy was gone.

"I say, Johnny, it is rather odd we should come on those tent-people, just as the woman has turned up," exclaimed Tod, as we got clear of the cathedral.

"But you don't think they can be connected, Tod?"

"Well, no; I suppose not. It's a queer coincidence, though."

This we also carried to the Squire, as we had the other news. He was standing in the Star gateway.

"Look here, you boys," said he, after a pause given to thought; "keep your eyes open; you may come upon the lad again, or some of his folk. I should like to do something for that poor man; I've wished it ever since he brought home Lena, and that confounded Molly drove him out by way of recompense."

"And if they should be confederates, sir?" suggested Tod.

"Who confederates? What do you mean, Joe?"

"These people and the female-stripper. It seems strange they should both turn up again in the same spot."

The notion took away the Pater's breath. "If I thought that; if I find it is so," he broke forth, "I'll—I'll—transport the lot."

Mrs. Todhetley arrived with Lena on Sunday afternoon. Early on Monday, the Squire and Tod took her to the governor's house at the county prison, where she was to see the woman, as if accidentally, nothing being said to Lena.

The woman was brought in: a bold jade with a red face: and Lena nearly went into convulsions at the sight of her. There could be no mistake the woman was the same: and the Pater became redhot with anger; especially to think he could not punish her in Worcester.

As the fly went racing up Salt Lane after the interview, on its way to leave the Squire at the county courts, a lad ran past. It was Jake's boy; the same we had seen in the cathedral. Tod leaped up and called to the driver to stop, but the Pater roared out an order to go on. His appearance at the court could not be delayed, and Tod had to stay with Lena. So the clue was lost again. Tod brought Lena to the Star, and then he and I went to the criminal court, and bribed a fellow for places. Tod said it would be a sin not to hear the kidnapper tried.

It was nearly the first case called on. Some of the lighter cases were taken first, while the grand jury deliberated on their bills for the graver ones. Her name, as given in, was Nancy Cole, and she tried to excite the sympathies of the judge and jury by reciting a whining account of a deserting husband and other ills. The evidence was quite clear. The two children (little shavers in petticoats) set up a roar in court at sight of the woman, just as Lena had done in the governor's house; and a dealer in marine stores produced their clothes, which he had bought of her. Tod whispered to me that he should go about Worcester after this in daily dread of seeing Lena's blue-silk frock and open-worked stockings hanging in a shop window. Something was said during the trial about the raid the prisoner had also recently made on the little daughter of Mr. Todhetley, of Dyke Manor, Warwickshire, and of Crabb Cot, Worcestershire, "one of the gentlemen of the grand jury at present sitting in deliberation in an adjoining chamber of the court." But, as the judge said, that could not be received in evidence.

Mrs. Cole brazened it out: testimony was too strong for her to attempt denial. "And if she *had* took a few bits o' things, 'cause she was famishing, she didn't hurt the childern. She'd never hurt a child in her life; couldn't do it. Just contrairy to that; she gave 'em sugar plums—and candy—and a piece of a wig,* she did. What

* A small plain bun sold in Worcester.

was she to do? Starve? Since her wicked husband, that she hadn't seen for this five year, deserted of her, and her two boys, fine grown lads both of 'em, had been accused of theft and got put away from her, one into prison, t'other into a 'formitory, she hadn't no soul to care for her nor help her to a bit o' bread. Life was hard, and times was bad; and—there it was. No good o' saying more."

"Guilty," said the foreman of the jury, without turning round. "We find the prisoner guilty, my lord."

The judge sentenced her to six months' imprisonment with hard labour. Mrs. Cole brazened it out still.

"Thank you," said she to his lordship, dropping a curtsey as they were taking her from the dock; "and I hope you'll sit there, old gentleman, till I come out again."

When the Squire was told of the sentence that evening, he said it was too mild by half, and talked of bringing her also to book at Warwick. But Mrs. Todhetley said, "No; forgive her." After all, it was only the loss of the clothes.

Nothing whatever had come out during the trial to connect Jake with the woman. She appeared to be a waif without friends. "And I watched and listened closely for it, mind you, Johnny," remarked Tod.

It was a day or two after this—I think, on the Wednesday evening. The Squire's grand-jury duties were over, but he stayed on, intending to make a week of it; Mrs. Todhetley and Lena had left for home. We had dined late, and Tod and I went for a stroll afterwards; leaving the Pater, and an old clergyman, who had dined with us, to their wine. In passing the cooked-meat shop in High-street, we saw a little chap looking in, his face flattened against the panes. Tod laid hold of his shoulder, and the boy turned his brilliant eyes and their hungry expression upon us.

"Do you remember me, Dor?" You see, Tod had not forgotten his name.

Dor evidently did remember. And whether it was that he felt frightened at being accosted, or whether the sight of us brought back to him the image of the dead sister lying on the rushes, was best known to himself; but he burst out crying.

"There's nothing to cry for," said Tod; "you need not be afraid. Could you eat some of that meat?"

Something like a shiver of surprise broke over the boy's face at the question; just as though he had had no food for weeks. Tod gave him a shilling, and told him to go in and buy some. But the boy looked at the money doubtingly,

"A whole shilling! They'd think I stole it."

Tod took back the money, and went in himself. He was as proud a fellow as you'd find in the two counties; and yet he would do all sorts of things that many another glanced askance at.

"I want half-a-pound of beef," said he to the man who was carving, "and some bread, if you sell it. And I'll take one of those small pork-pies."

"Shall I put the meat in paper, sir?" asked the man: as if doubting whether Tod might prefer to eat it there.

"Yes," said Tod. And the customers, working-men and a woman in a drab shawl, turned and stared at him.

Tod paid; took it all in his hands, and we left the shop. He did not mind being seen carrying the parcels; but he would have minded letting them know that he was feeding a poor boy.

"Here, Dor, you can take the things now," said he, when we had gone a few yards. "Where do you live?"

Dor explained after a fashion. We knew Worcester well, but failed to understand. "Not far from the big church," he said; and at first we thought he meant the cathedral.

"Never mind," said Tod; "go on, and show us."

He went skimming along, Tod keeping him within arm's-length, lest he should try to escape. Why Tod should have suspected he might, I don't know; nothing, as it turned out, could have been farther from Dor's thoughts. The church he spoke of proved to be All Saints'; the boy turned up an entry near to it, and we found ourselves in a regular rookery of dirty, miserable, tumble-down houses. Loose men stood about, pipes in their mouths, women, in tatters, their hair hanging down.

Dor dived into a dark den that seemed to be reached through a hole you had to stoop under. My patience! what a close place it was, with a smell that nearly knocked you backwards. There was not an earthly thing in the room that we could see, except some straw in a corner, and on that Jake was lying. The boy appeared with a piece of lighted candle, which he had been upstairs to borrow.

Jake was thin enough before; he was a skeleton now. His eyes were sunk, the bones of his face stood out, the skin glistened on his shapely nose, his voice was weak and hollow. He knew us, and smiled.

"What's the matter?" asked Tod, speaking gently. "You look very ill."

"I be very ill, master; I've been getting worse ever since."

His history was this. The same night that we had seen the tent at Cookhill, some travelling people of Jake's fraternity happened to encamp close to it for the night. By their help, the dead child was removed as far as Evesham, and there buried. Jake, his wife, and son, went on to Worcester, and there the man was taken worse; they had been in this room since; the wife had found a place to go to twice a week washing, earning her food and a shilling each time. It was all they had to depend upon, these two shillings weekly; and the few bits o' things they had, to use Jake's words, had been taken by the landlord for rent. But to see Jake's resignation was something curious.

"He was very good," he said, alluding to the landlord and the seizure; "he left me the straw. When he saw how bad I was, he wouldn't take it. We had been obliged to sell the tent, and there was a'most nothing for him."

"Have you had no medicine? no advice?" cried Tod, speaking as if he had a lump in his throat.

Yes, he had had medicine; the wife went for it to the free place (he meant the dispensary) twice a week, and a young doctor had been to see him.

Dor opened the paper of meat, and showed it to his father. "The gentleman bought it me," he said; "and this, and this. Couldn't you eat some?"

I saw the eager look that arose for a moment to Jake's face at sight of the meat: three slices of nice cold boiled beef, better than what we got at school. Dor held out one of them; the man broke off a morsel, put it into his mouth, and had a choking fit.

"It's of no use, Dor."

"Is his name 'Dor'?" asked Tod.

"His name is James, sir; same as mine," answered Jake, panting a little from the exertion of swallowing. "The wife, she has called him 'Dor' for 'dear,' and I've fell into it. She has called me Jake all along."

Tod felt something ought to be done to help him, but he had no more idea what than the man in the moon. I had less. As Dor piloted us to the open street, we asked him where his mother was. It was one of her working-days out, he answered; she was always kept late.

"Could he drink wine, do you think, Dor?"

"The gentleman said he was to have it," answered Dor, alluding to the doctor.

"How old are you, Dor?"

"I'm anigh ten." He did not look it.

"Johnny, I wonder if there's any place where they sell beef-tea?" cried Tod, as we went up Broad Street. "My goodness! lying there in that state, with no help at hand!"

"I never saw anything so bad before, Tod."

"Do you know what I kept thinking of all the time? I could not get it out of my head."

"What?"

"Of Lazarus at the rich man's gate. Johnny, lad, there seems an awful responsibility lying on some of us."

To hear Tod say such a thing was stranger than all. He set off running, and burst into our sitting-room in the Star, startling the Pater, who was alone and reading one of the Worcester papers with his spectacles on. Tod sat down and told him all.

"Dear me! dear me!" cried the Pater, growing red as he listened. "Why, Joe, the poor fellow must be dying!"

"He may not have gone too far for recovery, father," was Tod's answer. "If we had to lie in that close hole, and had nothing to eat or drink, we should probably soon become skeletons also. He may get well yet with proper care and treatment."

"It seems to me that the first thing to be done is to get him into the Infirmary," remarked the Pater.

"And it ought to be done early to-morrow morning, sir; if it's too late to-night."

The Pater got up in a bustle, put on his hat, and went out. He was going to his old friend, the famous surgeon, Henry Carden. Tod ran after him up Foregate Street, but was sent back to me. We stood at the door of the hotel, and in a few moments saw them coming along, the Pater arm-in-arm with Mr. Carden. He had come out as readily to visit the poor helpless man as he would to visit a rich one. Perhaps more so. They stopped when they saw us, and Mr. Carden asked Tod some of the particulars.

"You can get him admitted to the Infirmary at once, can you not?" said the Pater, impatiently, who was all on thorns to have something done.

"By what I can gather, it is not a case for the Infirmary," was the answer of its chief surgeon. "We'll see."

Down we went, walking fast: the Pater and Mr. Carden in front, I and Tod at their heels; and found the room again with some difficulty. The wife was in then, and had made a handful of fire in the grate. What with the smoke, and what with the other agreeable accompaniments, we were nearly stifled.

If ever I wished to be a doctor, it was when I saw Mr. Carden with that poor sick man. He was so gentle with him, so cheery and so kind. Had Jake been a duke, I don't see that he could have been treated differently. There was something superior about the man, too, as though he had seen better days.

"What is your name?" asked Mr. Carden.

"James Winter, sir, a native of Herefordshire. I was on my way there when I was taken ill in this place."

"What to do there? To get work?"

"No, sir; to die. It don't much matter, though; God's here as well as there."

"You are not a gipsy?"

"Oh dear no, sir. From my dark skin, though, I've been taken for one. My wife's descended from a gipsy tribe."

"We are thinking of placing you in the Infirmary, Jake," cried the Pater. "You will have every comfort there, and the best of attendance. This gentleman——"

"We'll see—we'll see," interposed Mr. Carden, breaking in hastily on the promises. "I am not sure that the Infirmary will do for him."

"It is too late, sir, I think," said Jake, quietly, to Mr. Carden.

Mr. Carden made no reply. He asked the woman if she had such a thing as a tea-cup or wine-glass. She produced a cracked cup with the handle off and a notch in the rim. Mr. Carden poured something into it that he had brought in his pocket, and stooped over the man. Jake began to speak in his faint voice.

"Sir, I'd not seem ungrateful, but I'd like to stay here with the wife and boy to the last. It can't be for long now."

"Drink this; it will do you good," said Mr. Carden, holding the cup to his lips.

"This close place is a change from the tent," I said to the woman, who was stooping over the bit of fire.

Such a look of regret came upon her countenance as she lifted it: just as if the tent had been a palace. "When we got here, master, it was after that two days' rain, and the ground was sopping. It didn't do for *him*"—glancing round at the straw. "He was getting mighty bad then, and we just put our heads into this place —bad luck to us!"

The Squire gave her some silver, and told her to get anything in she thought best. It was too late to do more that night. The church clocks were striking ten as we went out.

"Won't it do to move him to the Infirmary?" were the Pater's first words to Mr. Carden.

"Certainly not. The man's hours are numbered."

"There is no hope, I suppose?"

"Not the least. He may be said to be dying now."

No time was lost in the morning. When Squire Todhetley took a will to heart he carried it out, and speedily. A decent room with an airy window was found in the same block of buildings. A bed and other things were put in it; some clothes were redeemed; and by twelve o'clock in the day Jake was comfortably lying there. The Pater seemed to think that this was not enough: he wanted to do more.

"His humanity to my child kept him from seeing the last moments of his," said he. "The little help we can give him now is no return for that."

Food and clothes, and a dry, comfortable room, and wine and proper things for Jake—of which he could not swallow much. The woman was not to go out to work again while he lasted, but to stay at home and attend to him.

"I shall be at liberty by the hop-picking time," she said, with a sigh. Ah, poor creature! long before that.

When Tod and I went in later in the afternoon, she had just given Jake some physic, ordered by Mr. Carden. She and the boy sat by the fire, tea and bread-and-butter on the deal table between them. Jake lay in bed, his head raised on account of his breathing. I thought he was better; but his thin white face, with the dark, earnest, glistening eyes, was almost painful to look upon.

"The reading-gentleman have been in," cried the woman suddenly. "He's coming again, he says, the night or the morning."

Tod looked puzzled, and Jake explained. A good young clergy-man, who had found him out a day or two before, had been in each day since with his Bible, to read and pray. "God bless him!" said Jake.

"Why did you go away so suddenly?" Tod asked, alluding to the hasty departure from Cookhill. "My father was intending to do something for you."

"I didn't know that, sir. Many thanks all the same. I'd like to thank *you* too, sir," he went on, after a fit of coughing. "I've wanted to thank you ever since. When you gave me your arm up the lane, and said them pleasant things to me about having a little child in heaven, you knew she was gone."

"Yes."

"It broke the trouble to me, sir. My wife heard me coughing afar off, and came out o' the tent. She didn't say at first what there was in the tent, but began telling how you had been there. It made me know what had happened; and when she set on a-grieving, I told her not to: Carry was gone up to be an angel in heaven."

Tod touched the hand he put out, not speaking.

"She's waiting for me, sir," he continued, in a fainter voice. "I'm as sure of it as if I saw her. The little girl I found and carried to the great house has rich friends and a fine home to shelter her; mine had none, and so it was for the best that she should go. God has been very good to me. Instead of letting me fret after her, or murmur at lying helpless like this, He only gives me peace."

"That man must have had a good mother," cried out Tod, as we went away down the entry. And I looked up at him, he spoke so queerly.

"Do you think he will get better, Tod? He does not seem as bad as he did last night."

"Get better!" retorted Tod. "You'll always be a muff, Johnny. Why, every breath he takes threatens to be his last. He is miles worse than he was when we found him. This is Thursday: I don't believe he can last out longer than the week; and I think Mr. Carden knows it."

He did not last so long. On the Saturday morning, just as we were going to start for home, the wife came to the Star with the news. Jake had died at ten the previous night.

"He went off quiet," said she to the Squire. "I asked if he'd not like a dhrink; but he wouldn't have it: the good gentleman had been there giving him the bread and wine, and he said he'd take nothing, he thought, after that. 'I'm going, Mary,' he suddenly says to me about ten o'clock, and he called Dor up and shook hands with him, and bade him be good to me, and then he shook hands with me. 'God bless ye both,' says he, 'for Christ's sake; and God bless the friends who have been kind to us!' And with that he died."

That's all, for now. And I hope no one will think I invented this account of Jake's death, for I should not like to do it. The wife related it to us in the exact words written.

"And I able to do so little for him" broke forth the Squire, suddenly, when we were about half-way home; and he lashed up Bob and Blister regardless of their tempers. Which the animals did not relish.

And so that assize week ended the matter. Bringing imprisonment to the kidnapping woman, and to Jake death.

III

WOLFE BARRINGTON'S TAMING.

THIS is an incident of our school life; one that I never care to look back upon. All of us have sad remembrances of some kind living in the mind; and we are apt in our painful regret to say, "If I had but done this, or had but done the other, things might have turned out differently."

The school was a large square house, built of rough stone, gardens and playgrounds and fields extending around it. It was called Worcester House: a title of the fancy, I suppose, since it was some miles away from Worcester. The master was Dr. Frost, a tall, stout man, in white frilled shirt, knee-breeches and buckles; stern on occasion, but a gentleman to the back-bone. He had several under-masters. Forty boys were received; we wore the college cap and Eton jacket. Mrs. Frost was delicate: and Hall, a sour old woman of fifty, was manager of the eatables.

Tod and I must have been in the school two years, I think, when Archie Hearn entered. He was eleven years old. We had seen him at the house sometimes before, and liked him. A regular good little fellow was Archie.

Hearn's father was dead. His mother had been a Miss Stock-hausen, sister to Mrs. Frost. The Stockhausens had a name in Worcestershire: chiefly, I think, for dying off. There had been six sisters; and the only two now left were Mrs. Frost and Mrs. Hearn: the other four quietly faded away one after another, not living to see thirty. Mr. Hearn died, from an accident, when Archie was only a year old. He left no will, and there ensued a sharp dispute about his property. The Stockhausens said it all belonged to the little son; the Hearn family considered that a portion of it ought to go back to them. The poor widow was the only quiet spirit amongst them, willing to be led either way. What the disputants did was to put it into Chancery: and I don't much think it ever came out again.

It was the worst move they could have made for Mrs. Hearn. For it reduced her to a very slender income indeed, and the world wondered how she got on at all. She lived in a cottage about three miles from the Frosts, with one servant and the little child Archibald. In the course of years people seemed to forget all about the property in Chancery, and to ignore her as quite a poor woman.

Well, we—I and Tod—had been at Dr. Frost's two years or so, when Archibald Hearn entered the school. He was a slender little lad with bright brown eyes, a delicate face and pink cheeks, very sweet-tempered and pleasant in manner. At first he used to go home at night, but when the winter weather set in he caught a cough, and then came into the house altogether. Some of the big ones felt sure that old Frost took him for nothing : but as little Hearn was Mrs. Frost's nephew and we liked *her*, no talk was made about it. The lad did not much like coming into the house : we could see that. He seemed always to be hankering after his mother and old Betty the servant. Not in words : but he'd stand with his arms on the play-yard gate, his eyes gazing out towards the quarter where the cottage was ; as if he would like his sight to penetrate the wood and the two or three miles beyond, and take a look at it. When any of us said to him as a bit of chaff, "You are staring after old Betty," he would say Yes, he wished he could see her and his mother ; and then tell no end of tales about what Betty had done for him in his illnesses. Any way, Hearn was a straightforward little chap, and a favourite in the school.

He had been with us about a year when Wolfe Barrington came. Quite another sort of pupil. A big, strong fellow who had never had a mother : rich and overbearing, and cruel. He was in mourning for his father, who had just died : a rich Irishman, given to company and fast living. Wolfe came in for all the money ; so that he had a fine career before him and might be expected to set the world on fire. Little Hearn's stories had been of home ; of his mother and old Betty. Wolfe's were different. He had had the run of his father's stables and knew more about horses and dogs than the animals knew about themselves. Curious things, too, he'd tell of men and women, who had stayed at old Barrington's place : and what he said of the public school he had been at might have made old Frost's hair stand on end. Why he left the public school we did not find out : some said he had run away from it, and that his father, who'd indulged him awfully, would not send him back to be punished ; others said the head-master would not receive him back again. In the nick of time the father died ; and Wolfe's guardians put him to Dr. Frost's.

"I shall make you my fag," said Barrington, the day he entered, catching hold of little Hearn in the playground, and twisting him round by the arm.

"What's that?" asked Hearn, rubbing his arm—for Wolfe's grasp had not been a light one.

"What's that!" repeated Barrington, scornfully. "What a precious young fool you must be, not to know. Who's your mother?"

"She lives over there," answered Hearn, taking the question literally, and nodding beyond the wood.

"Oh!" said Barrington, screwing up his mouth. "What's her name? And what's yours?"

"Mrs. Hearn. Mine's Archibald."

"Good, Mr. Archibald. You shall be my fag. That is, my servant. And you'll do every earthly thing that I order you to do. And mind you do it smartly, or may be that girl's face of yours will show out rather blue sometimes."

"I shall not be anybody's servant," returned Archie, in his mild, inoffensive way.

"Won't you! You'll tell me another tale before this time to-morrow. Did you ever get licked into next week?"

The child made no answer. He began to think the new fellow might be in earnest, and gazed up at him in doubt.

"When you can't see out of your two eyes for the swelling round them, and your back's stiff with smarting and aching—*that's* the kind of licking I mean," went on Barrington. "Did you ever taste it?"

"No, sir."

"Good again. It will be all the sweeter when you do. Now look you here, Mr. Archibald Hearn. I appoint you my fag in ordinary. You'll fetch and carry for me: you'll black my boots and brush my clothes; you'll sit up to wait on me when I go to bed, and read me to sleep; you'll be dressed before I am in the morning, and be ready with my clothes and hot water. Never mind whether the rules of the house are against hot water, *you'll have to provide it*, though you boil it in the bedroom grate, or out in the nearest field. You'll attend me at my lessons; look out words for me; copy my exercises in a fair hand—and if you were old enough to *do* them, you'd *have* to. That's a few of the items; but there are a hundred other things, that I've not time to detail. If I can get a horse for my use, you'll have to groom him. And if you don't put out your mettle to serve me in all these ways, and don't hold yourself in readiness to fly and obey me at any minute or hour of the day, you'll get daily one of the lickings I've told you of, until you are licked into shape."

Barrington meant what he said. Voice and countenance alike wore a determined look, as if his words were law. Lots of the fellows, attracted by the talking, had gathered round. Hearn, honest and straightforward himself, did not altogether understand what evil might be in store for him, and grew seriously frightened.

The captain of the school walked up—John Whitney. "What is that you say Hearn has to do " he asked.

"*He* knows now," answered Barrington. "That's enough. They don't allow servants here : I must have a fag in place of one."

In turning his fascinated eyes from Barrington, Hearn saw Blair standing by, our mathematical master—of whom you will hear more later. Blair must have caught what passed : and little Hearn appealed to him.

"Am I obliged to be his fag, sir?"

Mr. Blair put us leisurely aside with his hands, and confronted the new fellow. "Your name is Barrington, I think," he said.

"Yes, it is," said Barrington, staring at him defiantly.

"Allow me to tell you that 'fags' are not permitted here. The system would not be tolerated by Dr. Frost for a moment. Each boy must wait on himself, and be responsible for himself : seniors and juniors alike. You are not at a public-school now, Barrington. In a day or two, when you shall have learnt the customs and rules here, I dare say you will find yourself quite sufficiently comfortable, and see that a fag would be an unnecessary appendage."

"Who is that man?" cried Barrington, as Blair turned away.

"Mathematical master. Sees to us out of hours," answered Bill Whitney.

"And what the devil did you mean by making a sneaking appeal to *him*?" continued Barrington, seizing Hearn roughly.

"I did not mean it for sneaking ; but I could not do what you wanted," said Hearn. "He had been listening to us."

"I wish to goodness that confounded fool, Taptal, had been sunk in his horse-pond before he put me to such a place as this," cried Barrington, passionately. "As to you, you sneaking little devil, it seems I can't make you do what I wanted, fags being forbidden fruit here, but it shan't serve you much. There's to begin with."

Hearn got a shake and a kick that sent him flying. Blair was back on the instant.

"Are you a coward, Mr. Barrington?"

"A coward!" retorted Barrington, his eyes flashing. "You had better try whether I am or not."

"It seems to me that you act like one, in attacking a lad so much younger and weaker than yourself. Don't let me have to report you to Dr. Frost the first day of your arrival. Another thing—I must request you to be a little more careful in your language. You have come amidst gentlemen here, not black-guards."

The matter ended here; but Barrington looked in a frightful

rage. It was unfortunate that it should have occurred the day he entered; but it did so, word for word, as I have written it. It set some of us rather against Barrington, and it set *him* against Hearn. He didn't "lick him into next week," but he gave him many a blow that the boy did nothing to deserve.

Barrington won his way, though, as the time went on. He had a liberal supply of money, and was open-handed with it; and he would often do a generous turn for one and another. The worst of him was his roughness. At play he was always rough; and, when put out, savage as well. His strength and activity were something remarkable; he would not have minded hard blows himself, and he showered them out on others with no more care than if we had been made of pumice-stone.

It was Barrington who introduced the new system at football. We had played it before in a rather mild way, speaking comparatively, but he soon changed that. Dr. Frost got to know of it in time, and he appeared amongst us one day when we were in the thick of it, and stopped the game with a sweep of his hand. They play it at Rugby now very much as Barrington made us play it then. The Doctor—standing with his face unusually red, and his shirt and necktie unusually white, and his knee-buckles gleaming—asked whether we were a pack of cannibals, that we should kick at one another in that dangerous manner. If we ever attempted it again, he said, football should be stopped.

So we went back to the old way. But we had tried the new, you see: and the consequence was that a great deal of rough play would creep into it now and again. Barrington led it on. No cannibal (as old Frost put it) could have been more carelessly furious at it than he. To see him with his sallow face in a heat, his keen black eyes flashing, his hat off, and his straight hair flung back, was not the pleasantest sight to my mind. Snepp said one day that he looked just like the devil at these times. Wolfe Barrington overheard him, and kicked him right over the hillock. I don't think he was ill-intentioned; but his strong frame had been untamed; it required a vent for its superfluous strength: his animal spirits led him away, and he had never been taught to put a curb on himself or his inclinations. One thing was certain —that the name, Wolfe, for such a nature as his, was singularly appropriate. Some of us told him so. He laughed in answer; never saying that it was only shortened from Wolfrey, his real name, as we learnt later. He could be as good a fellow and comrade as any of them when he chose, and on the whole we liked him a great deal better than we had thought we should at first.

As to his animosity against little Hearn, it was wearing off. The lad was too young to retaliate, and Barrington grew tired of knocking him about : perhaps a little ashamed of it when there was no return. In a twelvemonth's time it had quite subsided, and, to the surprise of many of us, Barrington, coming back from a visit to old Taptal, his guardian, brought Hearn a handsome knife with three blades as a present.

And so it would have gone on but for an unfortunate occurrence. I shall always say and think so. But for that, it might have been peace between them to the end. Barrington, who was defiantly independent, had betaken himself to Evesham, one half-holiday, without leave. He walked straight into some mischief there, and broke a street boy's head. Dr. Frost was appealed to by the boy's father, and of course there was a row. The Doctor forbade Barrington ever to stir beyond bounds again without first obtaining permission ; and Blair had orders that for a fortnight to come Barrington was to be confined to the playground in after-hours.

Very good. A day or two after that—on the next Saturday afternoon—the school went to a cricket-match ; Doctor, masters, boys, and all ; Barrington only being left behind.

Was he one to stand this? No. He coolly walked away to the high-road, saw a public conveyance passing, hailed it, mounted it, and was carried to Evesham. There he disported himself for an hour or so, visited the chief fruit and tart shops ; and then chartered a gig to bring him back to within half-a-mile of the school.

The cricket-match was not over when he got in, for it lasted up to the twilight of the summer evening, and no one would have known of the escapade but for one miserable misfortune—Archie Hearn happened to have gone that afternoon to Evesham with his mother. They were passing along the street, and he saw Barrington amidst the sweets.

"There's Wolfe Barrington !" said Archie, in the surprise of the moment, and would have halted at the tart-shop ; but Mrs. Hearn, who was in a hurry, did not stop. On the Monday, she brought Archie back to school : he had been at home, sick, for more than a week, and knew nothing of Barrington's punishment. Archie came amongst us at once, but Mrs. Hearn stayed to take tea with her sister and Dr. Frost. Without the slightest intention of making mischief, quite unaware that she was doing so, Mrs. Hearn mentioned incidentally that they had seen one of the boys—Barrington —at Evesham on the Saturday. Dr. Frost pricked up his ears at the news ; not believing it, however : but Mrs. Hearn said yes, for Archie had seen him eating tarts at the confectioner's. The Doctor finished his tea, went to his study, and sent for Barrington. Barrington denied it. He was not in the habit of telling lies, was too fearless of consequences to do anything of the sort; but he denied it now to the Doctor's face; perhaps he began to think he might have gone a little too far. Dr. Frost rang the bell and ordered Archie Hearn in.

"Which shop was Barrington in when you saw him on Saturday?" questioned the Doctor.

"The pastrycook's," said Archie, innocently.

"What was he doing?" blandly went on the Doctor.

"Oh! no harm, sir; only eating tarts," Archie hastened to say.

Well—it all came out then, and though Archie was quite innocent of wilfully telling tales; would have cut out his tongue rather than have said a word to injure Barrington, he received the credit of it now. Barrington took his punishment without a word; the hardest caning old Frost had given for many a long day, and heaps of work besides, and a promise of certain expulsion if he ever again went off surreptitiously in coaches and gigs. But Barrington thrashed Hearn worse when it was over, and branded him with the name of Sneak.

"He will never believe otherwise," said Archie, the tears of pain and mortification running down his cheeks, fresh and delicate as a girl's. "But I'd give the world not to have gone that afternoon to Evesham."

A week or two later we went in for a turn at "Hare and Hounds." Barrington's term of punishment was over then. Snepp was the hare; a fleet, wiry fellow who could outrun most of us. But the hare this time came to grief. After doubling and turning, as Snepp used to like to do, thinking to throw us off the scent, he sprained his foot, trying to leap a hedge and dry ditch beyond it. We were on his trail, whooping and halloaing like mad; he kept quiet, and we passed on and never saw him. But there was no more scent to be seen, and we found we had lost it, and went back. Snepp showed up then, and the sport was over for the day. Some went home one way, and some another; all of us were as hot as fire, and thirsting for water.

"If you'll turn down here by the great oak-tree, we shall come to my mother's house, and you can have as much water as you like," said little Hearn, in his good-nature.

So we turned down. There were only six or seven of us, for Snepp and his damaged foot made one, and most of them had gone on at a quicker pace. Tod helped Snepp on one side, Barrington on the other, and he limped along between them.

It was a narrow red-brick house, a parlour window on each side the door, and three windows above; small altogether, but very pretty, with jessamine and clematis climbing up the walls. Archie Hearn opened the door, and we trooped in, without regard to ceremony. Mrs. Hearn—she had the same delicate face as Archie, the same pink colour and bright brown eyes—came out of the kitchen to stare at us. As well she might. Her cotton sleeves were turned up to the elbows, her fingers were stained red, and she had a coarse kitchen cloth pinned round her. She was pressing black currants for jelly.

We had plenty of water, and Mrs. Hearn made Snepp sit down, and looked at his foot, and put a wet bandage round it, kneeling before him to do it. I thought I had never seen so nice a face as hers; very placid, with a sort of sad look in it. Old Betty, that Hearn used to talk about, appeared in a short blue petticoat and a kind of brown print jacket. I have seen the homely servants in France, since, dressed very similarly. Snepp thanked Mrs. Hearn for giving his foot relief, and we took off our hats to her as we went away.

The same night, before Blair called us in for prayers, Archie Hearn heard Barrington giving a sneering account of the visit to some of the fellows in the playground.

"Just like a cook, you know. Might be taken for one. Some coarse bunting tied round her waist, and hands steeped in red kitchen stuff."

"My mother could never be taken for anything but a lady," spoke up Archie bravely. "A lady may make jelly. A great many ladies prefer to do it themselves."

"Now you be off," cried Barrington, turning sharply on him. "Keep at a distance from your betters."

"There's nobody in the world better than my mother," returned the boy, standing his ground, and flushing painfully: for, in truth, the small way they were obliged to live in, through Chancery retaining the property, made a sore place in a corner of Archie's heart. "Ask Joseph Todhetley what he thinks of her. Ask John Whitney. *They* recognize her for a lady."

"But then they are gentlemen themselves."

It was I who put that in. I couldn't help having a fling at Barrington. A bit of applause followed, and stung him.

"If you shove in your oar, Johnny Ludlow, or presume to interfere with me, I'll pummel you to powder. There."

Barrington kicked out on all sides, sending us backward. The bell rang for prayers then, and we had to go in.

- The game the next evening was football. We went out to it as soon as tea was over, to the field by the river towards Vale Farm. I can't tell much about its progress, except that the play seemed rougher and louder than usual. Once there was a regular skirmish: scores of feet kicking out at once; great struggling, pushing and shouting: and when the ball got off, and the tail after it in full hue and cry, one was left behind lying on the ground.

I don't know why I turned my head back; it was the merest chance that I did so : and I saw Tod kneeling on the grass, raising the boy's head.

"Holloa!" said I, running back. "Anything wrong? Who is it?"

It was little Hearn. He had his eyes shut. Tod did not speak.

"What's the matter, Tod? Is he hurt?"

"Well, I think he's hurt a little," was Tod's answer. "He has had a kick here."

Tod touched the left temple with his finger, drawing it down as far as the back of the ear. It must have been a good wide kick, I thought.

"It has stunned him, poor little fellow. Can you get some water from the river, Johnny?"

"I could if I had anything to bring it in. It would leak out of my straw hat long before I got here."

But little Hearn made a move then, and opened his eyes. Presently he sat up, putting his hands to his head. Tod was as tender with him as a mother.

"How do you feel, Archie?"

"Oh, I'm all right, I think. A bit giddy."

Getting on to his feet, he looked from me to Tod in a bewildered manner. I thought it odd. He said he wouldn't join the game again, but go in and rest. Tod went with him, ordering me to keep with the players. Hearn walked all right, and did not seem to be much the worse for it.

"What's the matter now?" asked Mrs. Hall, in her cranky way; for she happened to be in the yard when they entered, Tod marshalling little Hearn by the arm.

"He has had a blow at football," answered Tod. "Here"—indicating the place he had shown me.

"A kick, I suppose you mean," said Mother Hall.

"Yes, if you like to call it so. It was a blow with a foot."

"Did you do it, Master Todhetley?"

"No, I did not," retorted Tod.

"I wonder the Doctor allows that football to be played!" she went on, grumbling. "I wouldn't, if I kept a school; I know that. It is a barbarous game, only fit for bears."

"I am all right," put in Hearn. "I needn't have come in, but for feeling giddy."

But he was not quite right yet. For without the slightest warning, before he had time to stir from where he stood, he became frightfully sick. Hall ran for a basin and some warm water. Tod held his head.

"This is through having gobbled down your tea in such a mortal hurry, to be off to that precious football," decided Hall, resentfully. "The wonder is, that the whole crew of you are not sick, swallowing your food at the rate you do."

"I think I'll lie on the bed for a bit," said Archie, when the sickness had passed. "I shall be up again by supper-time."

They went with him to his room. Neither of them had the slightest notion that he was seriously hurt, or that there could be any danger. Archie took off his jacket, and lay down in his clothes. Mrs. Hall offered to bring him up a cup of tea; but he said it might make him sick again, and he'd rather be quiet. She went down, and Tod sat on the edge of the bed. Archie shut his eyes, and kept still. Tod thought he was dropping off to sleep, and began to creep out of the room. The eyes opened then, and Archie called to him.

"Todhetley?"

"I am here, old fellow. What is it?"

"You'll tell him I forgive him," said Archie, speaking in an earnest whisper. "Tell him I know he didn't think to hurt me."

"Oh, I'll tell him," answered Tod, lightly.

"And be sure give my dear love to mamma."

"So I will."

"And now I'll go to sleep, or I shan't be down to supper. You will come and call me if I am not, won't you?"

"All right," said Tod, tucking the counterpane about him. "Are you comfortable, Archie?"

"Quite. Thank you."

Tod came on to the field again, and joined the game. It was a little less rough, and there were no more mishaps. We got home later than usual, and supper stood on the table.

The suppers at Worcester House were always the same—bread and cheese. And not too much of it. Half a round off the loaf, with a piece of cheese, for each fellow; and a drop of beer or water. Our other meals were good and abundant; but the Doctor waged war with heavy suppers. If old Hall had had her way, we should have had none at all. Little Hearn did not appear; and Tod went up to look after him. I followed.

Opening the door without noise, we stood listening and looking. Not that there was much good in looking, for the room was in darkness.

"Archie," whispered Tod.

No answer. No sound.

"Are you asleep, old fellow?"

Not a word still. The dead might be there, for all the sound there was.

"He's asleep, for certain," said Tod, groping his way towards the bed. "So much the better, poor little chap. I won't wake him."

It was a small room, two beds in it; Archie's was the one at the end by the wall. Tod groped his way to it: and, in thinking of it afterwards, I wondered that Tod did go up to him. The most natural thing would have been to come away, and shut the door. Instinct must have guided him—as it guides us all. Tod bent over him, touching his face, I think. I stood close behind. Now that our eyes were accustomed to the darkness, it seemed a bit lighter.

Something like a cry from Tod made me start. In the dark, and holding the breath, one is easily startled.

"Get a light, Johnny. A light!—quick! for the love of Heaven."

I believe I leaped the stairs at a bound. I believe I knocked over Mother Hall at the foot. I know I snatched the candle that was in her hand: and she screamed after me as if I had murdered her.

"Here it is, Tod."

He was at the door waiting for it, every atom of colour gone clean out of his face. Carrying it to the bed, he let its light fall full on Archie Hearn. The face was white and cold; the mouth covered with froth.

"Oh, Tod! What is it that's the matter with him?"

"Hush, Johnny! I fear he's dying. Good Lord! to think we should have been such ignorant fools as to leave him by himself!—as not have sent for Featherstone!"

We were down again in a moment. Hall stood scolding still, demanding her candle. Tod said a word that silenced her. She backed against the wall.

"Don't play your tricks on me, Mr. Todhetley."

"Go and see," said Tod.

She took the light from his hand quietly, and went up. Just then, the Doctor and Mrs. Frost, who had been walking all the way home from Sir John Whitney's, where they had spent the evening, came in, and learnt what had happened.

Featherstone was there in no time, so to say, and shut himself into the bedroom with the Doctor and Mrs. Frost and Hall, and I don't know how many more. Nothing could be done for Archibald Hearn: he was not quite dead, but close upon it. He was dead before any one thought of sending to Mrs. Hearn. It came to the same. Could she have come upon telegraph wires, she would still have come too late.

When I look back upon that evening—and a good many years have gone by since then—nothing arises in my mind but a picture of confusion, tinged with a feeling of terrible sorrow ; ay, and of horror. If a death happens in a school, it is generally kept from the pupils, as far as possible ; at any rate they are not allowed to see any of its attendant stir and details. But this was different. Upon masters and boys, upon mistress and household, it came with the same startling shock. Dr. Frost said feebly that the boys ought to go up to bed, and then Blair told us to go ; but the boys stayed on where they were. Hanging about the passages, stealing upstairs and peeping into the room, questioning Featherstone (when we could get the chance of coming upon him), as to whether Hearn would get well or not. No one checked us.

I went in once. Mrs. Frost was alone, kneeling by the bed ; I thought she must have been saying a prayer. Just then she lifted her head to look at him. As I backed away again, she began to speak aloud—and oh ! what a sad tone she said it in !

·" The only son of his mother, and she was a widow ! "

There had to be an inquest. It did not come to much. The most that could be said was that he died from a kick at football. " A most unfortunate but an accidental kick," quoth the coroner. Tod had said that he saw the kick given : that is, had seen some foot come flat down with a bang on the side of little Hearn's head ; and when Tod was asked if he recognized the foot, he replied No : boots looked very much alike, and a great many were thrust out in the skirmish, all kicking together.

Not one would own to having given it. For the matter of that, the fellow might not have been conscious of what he did. No end of thoughts glanced towards Barrington : both because he was so ferocious at the game, and that he had a spite against Hearn.

" I never touched him," said Barrington, when this leaked out ; and his face and voice were boldly defiant. " It wasn't me. I never so much as saw that Hearn was down."

And as there were others quite as brutal at football as Barrington, he was believed.

We could not get over it any way. It seemed so dreadful that he should have been left alone to die. Hall was chiefly to blame for that ; and it cowed her.

" Look here," said Tod to us, " I have a message for one of you. Whichever the cap fits may take it to himself. When Hearn was dying he told me to say that he forgave the fellow who kicked him."

This was the evening of the inquest-day. We had all gathered in the porch by the stone bench, and Tod took the opportunity to

relate what he had not related before. He repeated every word that
Hearn had said.

"Did Hearn know who it was, then?" asked John Whitney.

"I think so."

"Then why didn't you ask him to name him!"

"Why didn't I ask him to name him," repeated Tod, in a fume.
"Do you suppose I thought he was going to die, Whitney?—or that
the kick was to turn out a serious one? Hearn was growing big
enough to fight his own battles: and I never thought but he would
be up again at supper-time."

John Whitney pushed his hair back, in his quiet, thoughtful way,
and said no more. He was to die, himself, the following year—but
that has nothing to do with the present matter.

I was standing away at the gate after this, looking at the sunset,
when Tod came up and put his arms on the top bar.

"What are you gazing at, Johnny?"

"At the sunset. How red it is! I was thinking that if Hearn's
up there now he is better off. It is very beautiful."

"I should not like to have been the one to send him there,
though," was Tod's answer. "Johnny, I am certain Hearn knew
who it was," he went on in a low tone. "I am certain he thought
the fellow, himself, knew, and that it had been done for the purpose.
I think I know also."

"Tell us," I said. And Tod glanced over his shoulders, to make
sure no one was within hearing before he replied.

"Wolfe Barrington."

"Why don't you accuse him, Tod?"

"It wouldn't do. And I am not absolutely sure. What I saw,
was this. In the rush, one of them fell: I saw his head lying on
the ground. Before I could shout out to the fellows to take care, a
boot with a grey trouser over it came stamping down (not kicking)
on the side of the head. If ever anything was done deliberately,
that stamp seemed to be; it could hardly have been chance. I
know no more than that: it all passed in a moment. I didn't *see*
that it was Barrington. But—what other fellow is there among us
who would have wilfully harmed little Hearn? It is that thought
that brings conviction to me."

I looked round to where a lot of them stood at a distance.
"Wolfe has got on grey trousers, too."

"That does not tell much," returned Tod. "Half of us wear
the same. Yours are grey; mine are grey. It's just this: While
I am convinced in my own mind that it was Barrington, there's no
sort of proof that it was so, and he denies it. So it must rest, and
die away. Keep counsel, Johnny."

The funeral took place from the school. All of us went to it.

In the evening, Mrs. Hearn, who had been staying at the house, surprised us by coming into the tea-room. She looked very small in her black gown. Her thin cheeks were more flushed than usual, and her eyes had a great sadness in them.

"I wished to say good-bye to you; and to shake hands with you before I go home," she began, in a kind tone, and we all got up from the table to face her.

"I thought you would like me to tell you that I feel sure it must have been an accident; that no harm was intended. My dear little son said this to Joseph Todhetley when he was dying—and I fancy that some prevision of death must have lain then upon his spirit and caused him to say it, though he himself might not have been quite conscious of it. He died in love and peace with all; and, if he had anything to forgive—he forgave freely. I wish to let you know that I do the same. Only try to be a little less rough at play—and God bless you all. Will you shake hands with me?"

John Whitney, a true gentleman always, went up to her first, meeting her offered hand.

"If it had been anything but an accident, Mrs. Hearn," he began in tones of deep feeling: "if any one of us had done it wilfully, I think, standing to hear you now, we should shrink to the earth in our shame and contrition. You cannot regret Archibald much more than we do."

"In the midst of my grief, I know one thing: that God has taken him from a world of care to peace and happiness; I try to *rest* in that. Thank you all. Good-bye."

Catching her breath, she shook hands with us one by one, giving each a smile; but did not say more.

And the only one of us who did not feel her visit as it was intended, was Barrington. But he had no feeling: his body was too strong for it, his temper too fierce. He would have thrown a sneer of ridicule after her, but Whitney hissed it down.

Before another day had gone over, Barrington and Tod had a row. It was about a crib. Tod could be as overbearing as Barrington when he pleased, and he was cherishing ill-feeling towards him. They went and had it out in private—but it did not come to a fight. Tod was not one to keep in matters till they rankled, and he openly told Barrington that he believed it was he who had caused Hearn's death. Barrington denied it out-and-out; first of all swearing passionately that he had not, and then calming down to talk about it quietly. Tod felt less sure of it after that: as he confided to me in the bedroom.

Dr. Frost forbid football. And the time went on.

What I have further to relate may be thought a made-up story, such as we find in fiction. It is so very like a case of retribution. But it is all true, and happened as I shall put it. And somehow I never care to dwell long upon the calamity.

It was as nearly as possible a year after Hearn died. Jessup was captain of the school, for John Whitney was too ill to come. Jessup was almost as rebellious as Wolfe; and the two would ridicule Blair, and call him "Baked pie" to his face. One morning, when they had given no end of trouble to old Frost over their Greek, and laid the blame upon the hot weather, the Doctor said he had a great mind to keep them in until dinner-time. However, they ate humble-pie, and were allowed to escape. Blair was taking us for a walk. Instead of keeping with the ranks, Barrington and Jessup fell out, and sat down on the gate of a field where the wheat was being carried. Blair said they might sit there if they pleased, but forbid them to cross the gate. Indeed, there was a standing interdiction against our entering any field whilst the crops were being gathered. We went on and left them.

Half-an-hour afterwards, before we got back, Barrington had been carried home, dying.

Dying, as was supposed. He and Jessup had disobeyed Blair, disregarded orders, and rushed into the field, shouting and leaping like a couple of mad fellows—as the labourers afterwards said. Making for the waggon, laden high with wheat, they mounted it, and started on the horses. In some way, Barrington lost his balance, slipped over the side and the hind wheel went over him.

I shall never forget the house when we got back. Jessup, in his terror, had made off for his home, running most of the way—seven miles. He was in the same boat as Wolfe, except that he escaped injury—had gone over the stile in defiance of orders, and got on the waggon. Barrington was lying in the blue-room; and Mrs. Frost, frightened out of bed, stood on the landing in her night-cap, a shawl wrapped round her loose white dressing-gown. She was ill at the time. Featherstone came striding up the road wiping his hot face.

"Lord bless me!" cried Featherstone when he had looked at Wolfe and touched him. "I can't deal with this single-handed, Dr. Frost."

The doctor had guessed that. And Roger was already away on a galloping horse, flying for another. He brought little Pink: a shrimp of a man, with a fair reputation in his profession. But the two were more accustomed to treating rustic ailments than grave cases, and Dr. Frost knew that. Evening drew on, and the dusk was gathering, when a carriage with post-horses came thundering in at the front gates, bringing Mr. Carden.

They did not give to us boys the particulars of the injuries; and I don't know them to this day. The spine was hurt; the right ankle smashed: we heard that much. Taptal, Barrington's guardian, came over, and an uncle from London. Altogether it was a miserable time. The masters seized upon it to be doubly stern, and read us lectures upon disobedience and rebellion—as though we had been the offenders! As to Jessup, his father handed him back again to Dr. Frost, saying that in his opinion a taste of birch would much conduce to his benefit.

Barrington did not seem to suffer as keenly as some might have done; perhaps his spirits kept him up, for they were untamed. On the very day after the accident, he asked for some of the fellows to go in and sit with him, because he was dull. "By-and-by," the doctors said. And the next day but one, Dr. Frost sent me in. The paid nurse sat at the end of the room.

"Oh, it's you, is it, Ludlow! Where's Jessup?"

"Jessup's under punishment."

His face looked the same as ever, and that was all that could be seen of him. He lay on his back, covered over. As to the low bed, it might have been a board, to judge by its flatness. And perhaps was so.

"I am very sorry about it, Barrington. We all are. Are you in much pain?"

"Oh, I don't know," was his impatient answer. "One has to grin and bear it. The cursed idiots had stacked the wheat sloping to the sides, or it would never have happened. What do you hear about me?"

"Nothing but regret that it—— "

"I don't mean that stuff. Regret, indeed! regret won't undo it. I mean as to my getting about again. Will it be ages first?"

"We don't hear a word."

"If they were to keep me here a month, Ludlow, I should go mad. Rampant. You shut up, old woman."

For the nurse had interfered, telling him he must not excite himself.

"My ankle's hurt; but I believe it is not half as bad as a regular fracture: and my back's bruised. Well, what's a bruise? Nothing. Of course there's pain and stiffness, and all that; but so there is after a bad fight, or a thrashing. And they talk about my lying here for three or four weeks! Catch me."

One thing was evident: they had not allowed Wolfe to suspect the gravity of the case. Downstairs we had an inkling, I don't remember whence gathered, that it might possibly end in death. There was a suspicion of some internal injury that we could not get to know of; and it is said that even Mr. Carden, with all his surgical skill, could not get at it either. Any way, the prospect of recovery for Barrington was supposed to be of the scantiest; and it threw a gloom over us.

A sad mishap was to occur. Of course no one in their senses would have let Barrington learn the danger he was in; especially while there was just a chance that the peril would be surmounted. I read a book lately—I, Johnny Ludlow—where a little child met with an accident; and the first thing the people around him did, father, doctors, nurses, was to inform him that he would be a cripple for the rest of his days. That was common sense with a vengeance: and about as likely to occur in real life as that I could turn myself into a Dutchman. However, something of the kind did happen in Barrington's case, but through inadvertence. Another uncle came over from Ireland; an old man; and in talking with Featherstone he spoke out too freely. They were outside Barrington's door, and besides that, supposed that he was asleep. But he had awakened then; and heard more than he ought. The blue-room always seemed to have an echo in it.

"So it's all up with me, Ludlow?"

I was by his bedside when he suddenly said this, in the twilight of the summer evening. He had been lying quite silent since I entered, and his face had a white, still look on it, never before noticed there.

"What do you mean, Barrington?"

"None of your shamming-here. I know; and so do you, Johnny Ludlow. I say, though it makes one feel queer to find the world's slipping away. I had looked for so much jolly *life* in it."

"Barrington, you may get well yet; you may, indeed. Ask Pink and Featherstone, else, when they next come; ask Mr. Carden. I can't think what idea you have been getting hold of."

"There, that's enough," he answered. "Don't bother. I want to be quiet."

He shut his eyes; and the darkness grew as the minutes passed. Presently some one came into the room with a gentle step: a lady in a black-and-white gown that didn't rustle. It was Mrs. Hearn. Barrington looked up at her.

"I am going to stay with you for a day or two," she said in a low sweet voice, bending over him and touching his forehead with her cool fingers. "I hear you have taken a dislike to the nurse: and Mrs. Frost is really too weakly just now to get about."

"She's a sly cat," said Barrington, alluding to the nurse, "and watches me out of the tail of her eye. Hall's as bad. They are in league together."

"Well, they shall not come in more than I can help. I will nurse you myself,"

"No; not you," said Barrington, his face looking red and uneasy. "I'll not trouble *you*."

She sat down in my chair, just pressing my hand in token of greeting. And I left them.

In the ensuing days his life trembled in the balance : and even when part of the more immediate danger was surmounted, part of the worst of the pain, it was still a toss-up. Barrington had no hope whatever : I don't think Mrs. Hearn had, either.

She hardly left him. At first he seemed to resent her presence ; to wish her away ; to receive unwillingly what she did for him : but, in spite of himself he grew to look round for her, and to let his hand lie in hers whenever she chose to take it.

Who can tell what she said to him? Who can know how she softly and gradually awoke the better feelings within him, and won his heart from its hardness? She did do it, and that's enough. The way was paved for her. What the accident had not done, the fear of death had. Tamed him.

One evening when the sun had sunk, leaving only a fading light in the western sky, and Barrington had been watching it from his bed, he suddenly burst into tears. Mrs. Hearn busy amongst the physic bottles, was by his side in a moment.

"Wolfe ! "

"It's very hard to have to die."

"Hush, my dear, you are not worse : a little better. I think you may be spared; I do indeed. And—in any case—you know what I read to you this evening : that to die is gain."

"Yes, for some. I've never had my thoughts turned that way."

"They are turned now. That is quite enough."

"It is such a little while to have lived," went on Barrington, after a pause. "Such a little while to have enjoyed earth. What are my few years compared with the ages that have gone by, with the ages and ages that are to come. Nothing. Not as much as a drop of water to the ocean."

"Wolfe, dear, if you live out the allotted years of man, three score and ten, what would even that be in comparison? As you say—nothing. It seems to me that our well-being or ill-being here need not much concern us : the days, whether short or long, will pass as a dream. Eternal life lasts for ever ; soon we must all be departing for it."

Wolfe made no answer. The clear sky was assuming its pale tints, shading off one into another, and his eyes were looking at them. But it was as if he saw nothing.

"Listen, my dear. When Archibald died, *I* thought I should have died ; died of grief and pain. I grieved to think how short had been his span of life on this fair earth ; how cruel his fate in being taken from it so early. But, oh, Wolfe, God has shown me my mistake. I would not have him back again if I could."

Wolfe put up his hand to cover his face. Not a word spoke he.

"I wish you could see things as I see them, now that they have been cleared for me," she resumed. "It is so much better to be in heaven than on earth. We, who are here, have to battle with cares and crosses; and shall have to do so to the end. Archie has thrown-off all care. He is in happiness amidst the redeemed."

The room was growing dark. Wolfe's face was one of intense pain.

"Wolfe, dear, do not mistake me; do not think me hard if I say that you would be happier there than here. There is nothing to dread, dying in Christ. Believe me, I would not for the world have Archie back again: how could I then make sure what the eventual ending would be? You and he will know each other up there."

"Don't," said Wolfe.

"Don't what?"

Wolfe drew her hand close to his face, and she knelt down to catch his whisper.

"I killed him."

A pause: and a sort of sob in her throat. Then, drawing away her hand, she laid her cheek to his.

"My dear, I think I have known it."

"You—have—known—it?" stammered Wolfe in disbelief.

"Yes. I thought it was likely. I felt nearly sure of it. Don't let it trouble you now. Archie forgave, you know, and I forgave; and God will forgive."

"How could you come here to nurse me—knowing that?"

"It made me the more anxious to come. You have no mother."

"No." Wolfe was sobbing bitterly. "She died when I was born. I've never had anybody. I've never had a chapter read to me, or a prayer prayed."

"No, no, dear. And Archie—oh, Archie had all that. From the time he could speak, I tried to train him for heaven. It has seemed to me, since, just as though I had foreseen he would go early, and was preparing him for it."

"I never meant to kill him," sobbed Wolfe. "I saw his head down, and I put my foot upon it without a moment's thought. If I had taken thought, or known it would hurt him seriously, I wouldn't have done it."

"He is better off, dear," was all she said. "You have that comfort."

"Any way, I am paid out for it. At the best, I suppose I shall go upon crutches for life. That's bad enough : but dying's worse. Mrs. Hearn, I am not ready to die."

"Be you very sure God will not take you until you are ready, if you only wish and hope to be made so from your very heart," she whispered. "I pray to Him often for you, Wolfe."

"I think you must be one of heaven's angels," said Wolfe, with a burst of emotion.

"No, dear ; only a weak woman. I have had so much sorrow and care, trial upon trial, one disappointment after another, that it has left me nothing but Heaven to lean upon. Wolfe, I am trying to show you a little bit of the way there ; and I think—I do indeed —that this accident, which seems, and is, so dreadful, may have been sent by God in mercy. Perhaps, else, you might never have found Him : and where would you have been in all that long, long eternity? A few years here . never-ending ages hereafter !—Oh, Wolfe ! bear up bravely for the little span, even though the cross may be heavy. Fight on manfully for the real life to come."

"If you will help me."

"To be sure I will."

Wolfe got about again, and came out upon crutches. After a while they were discarded, first one, then the other, and he took permanently to a stick. He would never go without that. He would never run or leap again, or kick much either. The doctors looked upon it as a wonderful cure—and old Featherstone was apt to talk to us boys as if it were he who had pulled him through. But not in Henry Carden's hearing.

The uncles and Taptal said he would be better now at a private tutor's. But Wolfe would not leave Dr. Frost's. A low pony-carriage was bought for him, and all his spare time he would go driving over to Mrs. Hearn's. He was as a son to her. His great animal spirits had been taken out of him, you see ; and he had to find his happiness in quieter grooves. One Saturday afternoon he drove me over. Mrs. Hearn had asked me to stay with her until the Monday morning. Barrington generally stayed.

It was in November. Considerably more than a year after the accident. The guns of the sportsmen were heard in the wood ; a pack of hounds and their huntsmen rode past the cottage at a gallop, in full chase after a late find. Barrington looked and listened, a sigh escaping him.

"These pleasures are barred to me now."

"But a better one has been opened to you," said Mrs. Hearn, with a meaning smile, as she took his hand in hers.

And on Wolfe's face, when he glanced at her in answer, there sat a look of satisfied rest that I am sure had never been seen on it before he fell off the waggon.

IV.

MAJOR PARRIFER.

HE was one of the worst magistrates that ever sat upon the bench of justices. Strangers were given to wonder how he got his commission. But, you see, men are fit or unfit for a post according to their doings in it; and, generally speaking, people cannot tell what those doings will be beforehand.

They called him Major: Major Parrifer: but he only held rank in a militia regiment, and every one knows what that is. He had bought the place he lived in some years before, and christened it Parrifer Hall. The worst title he could have hit upon; seeing that the good old Hall, with a good old family in it, was only a mile or two distant. Parrifer Hall was only a stone's throw, so to say, beyond our village, Church Dykely.

They lived at a high rate; money was not wanting; the Major, his wife, six daughters, and a son who did not come home very much. Mrs. Parrifer was stuck-up: it is one of our county sayings, and it applied to her. When she called on people her silk gowns rustled as if lined with buckram; her voice was loud, her manner patronizing; the Major's voice and manner were the same; and the girls took after them.

Close by, at the corner of Piefinch Lane, was a cottage that belonged to me. To me, Johnny Ludlow. Not that I had as yet control over that or any other cottage I might possess. George Reed rented the cottage. It stood in a good large garden which touched Major Parrifer's side fence. On the other side the garden, a high hedge divided it from the lane: but it had only a low hedge in front, with a low gate in the middle. Trim, well-kept hedges: George Reed took care of that.

There was quite a history attaching to him. His father had been indoor servant at the Court. When he married and left it, my grandfather gave him a lease of this cottage, renewable every seven years. George was the only son, had been very decently educated, but turned out wild when he grew up and got out of everything. The result was, that he was only a day-labourer, and never likely to be anything else. He took to the cottage after old

Reed's death, and worked for Mr. Sterling; who had the Court now. George Reed was generally civil, but uncommonly independent. His first wife had died, leaving a daughter, Cathy; later on he married again. Reed's wild oats had been sown years ago; he was thoroughly well-conducted and industrious now, working in his own garden early and late.

When Cathy's mother died, she was taken to by an aunt, who lived near Worcester. At fifteen she came home again, for the aunt had died. Her ten years' training there had done very little for her, except make her into a pretty girl. Cathy had been trained to idleness, but to very little else. She could sing; self-taught of course; she could embroider handkerchiefs and frills; she could write a tolerable letter without many mistakes, and was great at reading, especially when the literature was of the halfpenny kind issued weekly. These acquirements (except the last) were not bad things in themselves, but quite unsuited to Cathy Reed's condition and her future prospects in life. The best that she could aspire to, the best her father expected for her, was that of entering on a light respectable service, and later to become, perhaps, a labourer's wife.

The second Mrs. Reed, a quiet kind of young woman, had one little girl only when Cathy came home. She was almost struck dumb when she found what had been Cathy's acquirements in the way of usefulness; or rather what were her deficiencies. The facts unfolded themselves by degrees.

"Your father thinks he'd like you to get a service with some of the gentlefolks, Cathy," her step-mother said to her. "Perhaps at the Court, if they could make room for you; or over at Squire Todhetley's. Meanwhile you'll help me with the work at home for a few weeks first; won't you, dear? When another little one comes, there'll be a good deal on my hands."

"Oh, I'll help," answered Cathy, who was a good-natured, ready-speaking girl.

"That's right. Can you wash?"

"No," said Cathy, with a very decisive shake of the head.

"Not wash?"

"Oh dear, no."

"Can you iron?"

"Pocket-handkerchiefs."

"Your aunt was a seamstress; can you sew well?"

"I don't like sewing."

Mrs. Reed looked at her, but said no more then, rather leaving practice instead of theory to develop Cathy's capabilities. But when she came to put her to the test, she found Cathy could not, or would not, do any kind of useful work whatever. Cathy could

not wash, iron, scour, cook, or sweep; or even sew plain coarse
things, such as are required in labourers' families. Cathy could do
several kinds of fancy-work. Cathy could idle away her time at
the glass, oiling her hair, and dressing herself to the best advantage; Cathy had a smattering of history and geography and
chronology; and of polite literature, as comprised in the pages
of the aforesaid halfpenny and penny weekly romances. The aunt
had sent Cathy to a cheap day-school where such learning was
supposed to be taught: had let her run about when she ought to
have been cooking and washing; and of course Cathy had acquired
a distaste for work. Mrs. Reed sat down aghast, her hands falling
helpless on her lap, a kind of fear of what might be Cathy's future
stealing into her heart.

"Child, what is to become of you?"

Cathy had no qualms upon the point herself. She gave a laughing kiss to the little child, toddling round the room by the chairs,
and took out of her pocket one of those halfpenny serials, whose
thrilling stories of brigands and captive damsels she had learnt to
make her chief delight.

"I shall have to teach her everything," sighed disappointed Mrs.
Reed. "Catherine, I don't think the kind of useless things your
aunt has taught you are good for poor folk like us."

Good! Mrs. Reed might have gone a little further. She began
her instruction, but Cathy would not learn. Cathy was always
good-humoured; but of work she would do none. If she attempted
it, Mrs. Reed had to do it over again.

"Where on earth will the gentlefolks get their servants from, if
the girls are to be like you?" cried honest Mrs. Reed.

Well, time went on; a year or two. Cathy Reed tried two or
three services, but did not keep them. Young Mrs. Sterling at the
Court at length took her. In three months Cathy was home again,
as usual. "I do not think Catherine will be kept anywhere," Mrs.
Sterling said to her step-mother. "When she ought to have been
minding the baby, the nurse would find her with a strip of
embroidery in her hand, or buried in the pages of some bad story
that can only do her harm."

Cathy was turned seventeen when the warfare set in between her
father and Major Parrifer. The Major suddenly cast his eyes on
the little cottage outside his own land and coveted it. Before this,
young Parrifer (a harmless young man, with no whiskers, and sandy
hair parted down the middle) had struck up an acquaintance with
Cathy. When he left Oxford (where he got plucked twice, and at
length took his name off the books) he would often be seen leaning
over the cottage-gate, talking to Cathy in the garden, with the two
little half-sisters that she pretended to mind. There was no harm:

but perhaps Major Parrifer feared it might grow into it; and he badly wanted the plot of ground, that he might pull down the cottage and extend his own boundaries to Piefinch Lane.

One fine day in the holidays, when Tod and I were indoors making flies for fishing, our old servant, Thomas, appeared, and said that George Reed had come over and wanted to speak to me. Which set us wondering. What could he want with me?

"Show him in here," said Tod.

Reed came in: a tall, powerful man of forty; with dark, curling hair, and a determined, good-looking face. He began saying that he had heard Major Parrifer was after his cottage, wanting to buy it; so he had come over to beg me to interfere and stop the sale.

"Why, Reed, what can I do?" I asked. "You know I have no power."

"You wouldn't turn me out of it yourself, I know, sir."

"That I wouldn't."

Neither would I. I liked George Reed. And I remembered that he used to have me in his arms sometimes when I was a little fellow at the Court. Once he carried me to my mother's grave in the churchyard, and told me she had gone to live in heaven.

"When a rich gentleman sets his mind on a poor man's bit of a cottage, and says, 'That shall be mine,' the poor man has not much chance against him, sir, unless he that owns the cottage will be his friend. I know you have no power at present, Master Johnny; but if you'd speak to Mr. Brandon, perhaps he would listen to you."

"Sit down, Reed," interrupted Tod, putting his catgut out of hand. "I thought you had the cottage on a lease."

"And so I have, sir. But the lease will be out at Michaelmas next, and Mr. Brandon can turn me from it if he likes. My father and mother died there, sir; my wife died there; my children were born there; and the place is as much like my homestead as if it was my own."

"How do you know old Parrifer wants it?" continued Tod.

"I have heard it from a safe source. I've heard, too, that his lawyer and Mr. Brandon's lawyer have settled the matter between their two selves, and don't intend to let me as much as know I'm to go out till the time comes, for fear I should make a row over it. Nobody on earth can stop it except Mr. Brandon," added Reed, with energy.

"Have you spoken to Mr. Brandon, Reed?"

"No, sir. I was going up to him; but the thought took me that I'd better come off at once to Master Ludlow; his word might be of more avail than mine. There's no time to be lost. If once the lawyers get Mr. Brandon's consent, he may not be able to recall it."

"What does Parrifer want with the cottage ? "

" I fancy he covets the bit of garden, sir ; he sees the order I've brought it into. If it's not that, I don't know what it can be. The cottage can be no eyesore to him ; he can't see it from his windows."

" Shall I go with you, Johnny ? " said Tod, as Reed went home, after drinking the ale old Thomas had given him. " We will circumvent that Parrifer, if there's law or justice in the Brandon land."

We went off to Mr. Brandon's in the pony-carriage, Tod driving. He lived near Alcester, and had the management of my property whilst I was a minor. As we went along who should ride past, meeting us, but Major Parrifer.

" Looking like the bull-dog that he is," cried Tod, who could not bear the man. " Johnny, what will you lay that he has not been to Mr. Brandon's ? The negotiations are becoming serious."

Tod did not go in. On second thought, he said it might be better to leave it to me. The Squire must try, if I failed. Mr. Brandon was at home ; and Tod drove on into Alcester by way of passing the time.

" But I don't think you can see him," said the housekeeper, when she came to me in the drawing-room. " This is one of his bad days. A gentleman called just now, and I went in to the master, but it was of no use."

" I know ; it was Major Parrifer. We thought he might have been calling here."

Mr. Brandon was thin and little, with a shrivelled face. He lived alone, except for three or four servants, and always fancied himself ill with one ailment or another. When I went in, for he said he'd see me, he was sitting in an easy-chair, with a geranium-coloured Turkish cap on his head, and two bottles of medicine at his elbow.

" Well, Johnny, an invalid as usual, you see. And what is it you so particularly want ? "

" I want to ask you a favour, Mr. Brandon, if you'll be good enough to grant it me."

" What is it ? "

" You know that cottage, sir, at the corner of Piefinch Lane. George Reed's."

" Well ? "

" I have come to ask you not to let it be sold."

" Who wants to sell it ? " asked he, after a pause.

" Major Parrifer wants to buy it ; and to turn Reed out. The lawyers are going to arrange it."

Mr. Brandon pushed the cap up on his brow and gave the tassel over his ear a twirl as he looked at me. People thought him incapable ; but it was only because he had no work to do that he

seemed so. He would get a bit irritable sometimes; very rarely
though; and he had a squeaky voice: but he was a good and just
man.

"How did you hear this, Johnny?"

I told him all about it. What Reed had said, and of our having
met the Major on horseback as we drove along.

"He came here, but I did not feel well enough to see him," said
Mr. Brandon. "Johnny, you know that I stand in place of your
father, as regards your property; to do the best I can with it."

"Yes, sir. And I am sure you do it."

"If Major Parrifer—I don't like the man," broke off Mr. Brandon, "but that's neither here nor there. At the last magistrates'
meeting I attended he was so overbearing as to shut us all up. My
nerves were unstrung for four-and-twenty hours afterwards."

"And Squire Todhetley came home swearing," I could not help
putting in.

"Ah," said Mr. Brandon. "Yes; some people can throw bile
off in that way. I can't. But, Johnny, all that goes for nothing,
in regard to the matter in hand: and I was about to point out to
you that if Major Parrifer has set his mind upon buying Reed's
cottage and the bit of land attached to it, he is no doubt prepared
to offer a good price; more, probably, than it is worth. If so, I
should not, in your interests, be justified in refusing this."

I could feel my face flush with the sense of injustice, and the
tears come into my eyes. They called me a muff for many things.

"I would not touch the money myself, sir. And if you used it
for me, I'm sure it would never bring any good."

"What's that, Johnny?"

"Money got by oppression or injustice never does. There was
a fellow at school——"

"Never mind the fellow at school. Go on with your own argument."

"To turn Reed out of the place where he has always lived, out
of the garden he has done so well by, just because a rich man wants
to get possession of it, would be fearfully unjust, sir. It would be
as bad as the story of Naboth's vineyard, that we heard read in
church last Sunday, for the First Lesson. Tod said so as we came
along."

"Who's Tod?"

"Joseph Todhetley. If you turned Reed out, sir, for the sake
of benefiting me, I should be ashamed to look people in the face
when they talked of it. If you please, sir, I do not think my father
would allow it if he were living. Reed says the place is like his
homestead."

Mr. Brandon measured two tablespoonfuls of medicine into a

glass, drank it off, and ate a French plum afterwards. The plums were on a plate, and he handed them to me. I took one, and tried to crack the stone.

"You have taken up a strong opinion on this matter, Master Johnny."

"Yes, sir. I like Reed. And if I did not, he has no more right to be turned out of his home than Major Parrifer has out of his. How would *he* like it, if some rich and powerful man came down on his place and turned him out?"

"Major Parrifer can't be turned out of his, Johnny. It is his own."

"And Reed's place is mine, sir—if you won't be angry with me for saying it. Please don't let it be done, Mr. Brandon."

The pony-carriage came rattling up at this juncture, and we saw Tod look at the windows impatiently. I got up, and Mr. Brandon shook hands with me.

"What you have said is all very good, Johnny, right in principle; but I cannot let it quite outweigh your interests. When this proposal shall be put before me—as you say it will be—it must have my full consideration."

I stopped when I got to the door and turned to look at him. If he would only have given me an assurance! He read in my face what I wanted.

"No, Johnny, I can't do that. You may go home easy for the present, however; for I will promise not to accept the offer to purchase without first seeing you again and showing you my reasons."

"I may have gone back to school, sir."

"I tell you I will see you again if I decide to accept the offer," he repeated emphatically. And I went out to the pony-chaise.

"Old Brandon means to sell," said Tod, when I told him. And he gave the pony an angry cut, that made him fly off at a gallop.

Will anybody believe that I never heard another word upon the subject, except what people said in the way of gossip? It was soon known that Mr. Brandon had declined to sell the cottage; and when his lawyer wrote him word that the sum, offered for it, was increased to quite an unprecedented amount, considering the value cf the cottage and garden in question, Mr. Brandon only sent a peremptory note back again, saying he was not in the habit of changing his decisions, and the place *was not for sale*. Tod threw up his hat.

"Bravo, old Brandon! I thought he'd not go quite over to the enemy."

George Reed wanted to thank me for it. One evening, in passing his cottage on my way home from the Court, I leaned over the gate to speak to his little ones. He saw me and came running out. The rays of the setting sun shone on the children's white corded bonnets.

"I have to thank you for this, sir. They are going to renew my lease."

"Are they? All right. But you need not thank me; I know nothing about it."

George Reed gave a decisive nod. "If you hadn't got the ear of Mr. Brandon, sir, I know what box I should have been in now. Look at them girls!"

It was not a very complimentary mode of speech, as applied to the Misses Parrifer. Three of them were passing, dressed outrageously in the fashion as usual. I lifted my straw hat, and one of them nodded in return, but the other two only looked out of the tail of their eyes.

"The Major has been trying it on with me now," remarked Reed, watching them out of sight. "When he found he could not buy the place, he thought he'd try and buy out me. He wanted the bit of land for a kitchen-garden, he said; and would give me a five-pound bank-note to go out of it. Much obliged, Major, I said; but I'd not go for fifty."

"As if he had not heaps of land himself to make kitchen-gardens of!"

"But don't you see, Master Johnny, to a man like Major Parrifer, who thinks the world was made for him, there's nothing so mortifying as being balked. He set his mind upon this place; he can't get it; and he is just boiling over. He'd poison me if he could. Now then, what's wanted?"

Cathy had come up, with her pretty dark eyes, whispering some question to her father. I ran on; it was growing late, and the Manor ever-so-far off.

From that time the feud grew between Major Parrifer and George Reed. Not openly; not actively. It could not well be either when their relative positions were so different. Major Parrifer was a wealthy landed proprietor, a county magistrate (and an awfully overbearing one); and George Reed was a poor cottager who worked for his bread as a day-labourer. But that the Major grew to abhor and hate Reed; that the man, inhabiting the place at his very gates in spite of him, and looking at him independently, as if to say he knew it, every time he passed, had become an eyesore to him; was easily seen.

The Major resented it on us all. He was rude to Mr. Brandon when they met; he struck out his whip once when he was on horseback, and I passed him, as if he would like to strike me. I don't know whether he was aware of my visit to Mr. Brandon; but the cottage was mine, I was friendly with Reed, and that was enough. Months, however, went on, and nothing came of it.

. One Sunday morning in winter, when our church-bells were going for service, Major Parrifer's carriage turned out with the ladies all in full fig. The Major himself turned out after it, walking, one of his daughters with him, a young man who was on a visit there, and a couple of servants. As they passed George Reed's, the sound of work being done in the garden at the back of the cottage caught the Major's quick ears. He turned softly down Piefinch Lane, stole on tiptoe to the high hedge, and stooped to peep through it.

Reed was doing something to his turnips; hoeing them, the Major said. He called the gentleman to him and the two servants, and bade them look through the hedge. Nothing more. Then the party came on to church.

On Tuesday, the Major rode out to take his place on the magisterial bench at Alcester. It was bitterly cold January weather, and only one magistrate besides himself was on it: *a clergyman*. Two or three petty offenders were brought before them, who were severely sentenced—as prisoners always were when Major Parrifer was presiding. Another magistrate came in afterwards. .

Singular to say, Tod and I had gone to the town that day about a new saddle for his horse; singular on account of what happened. In saying we were there I am telling the truth; it is not invented to give colour to the tale. Upon turning out of the saddler's, which is near the justice-room, old Jones the constable was coming along with a prisoner handcuffed, a tail after him.

"Halloa!" cried Tod. "Here's fun!"

But I had seen what Tod did not, and rubbed my eyes, wondering if they saw double.

"*Tod!* It is George Reed!"

Reed's face was as white as a sheet, and he walked along, not unwillingly, but as one in a state of sad shame, of awful rage. Tod made only one bound to the prisoner; and old Jones knowing us, did not push him back again.

"As I'm a living man, I do not know what this is for, or why I am paraded through the town in disgrace," spoke Reed, in answer to Tod's question. "If I'm charged with wrong-doing, I am willing to appear and answer for it, without being turned into a felon in the face and eyes of folks, beforehand."

"Why do you bring Reed up in this manner—handcuffed?" demanded Tod of the constable.

"Because the Major told me to, young Mr. Todhetley."

Be you very sure Tod pushed after them into the justice-room: the police saw him, but he was a magistrate's son. The crowd would have liked to push in also, but were sent to the right-about. I waited, and was presently admitted surreptitiously. Reed was standing before Major Parrifer and the other two, handcuffed still; and I gathered what the charge was.

It was preferred by Major Parrifer, who had his servants there and a gentleman as witnesses. George Reed had been working in his garden on the previous Sunday morning—which was against the law. Old Jones had gone to Mr. Sterling's and taken him on the Major's warrant, as he was thrashing corn.

Reed's answer was to the following effect.

He was *not* working. His wife was ill—her little boy being only four days old—and Dr. Duffham ordered her some mutton broth. He went to the garden to get the turnips to put into it. It was only on account of her illness that he didn't go to church himself, he and Cathy. They might ask Dr. Duffham.

"Do you dare to tell me you were not hoeing turnips?" cried Major Parrifer.

"I dare to say I was not doing it as work," independently answered the man. "If you looked at me, as you say, Major, through the hedge, you must have seen the bunch of turnips I had got up, lying near. I took the hoe in my hand, and I did use it for two or three minutes. Some dead weeds had got thrown along the bed, by the children, perhaps, and I pulled them away. I went indoors directly: before the clock struck eleven the turnips were on, boiling with the scrag of mutton. I peeled them and put them in myself."

"I see the bunch of turnips," cried one of the servants. "They was lying—— "

"Hold your tongue, sir," roared his master; "if your further evidence is wanted, you'll be asked for it. As to this defence"— and the Major turned to his brother-magistrates with a scornful smile—"it is quite ingenious; one of the clever excuses we usually get here. But it will not serve your turn, George Reed. When the sanctity of the Sabbath is violated—— "

"Reed is not a man to say he did not do a thing if he did," interrupted Tod.

The Major glared at him for an instant, and then put out of hand a big gold pencil he was waving majestically.

"Clear the room of spectators," said he to the policeman.

Which was all Tod got for interfering. We had to go out: and in a minute or two Reed came out also, handcuffed as before; not in charge of old Jones, but of the county police. He had been sentenced to a month's imprisonment. Major Parrifer had wanted

to make it three months; he said something about six; but the
other two thought they saw some slightly extenuating circumstances
in the case. A solicitor who was intimate with the Sterlings, and
knew Reed very well, had been present towards the end.

"Could you not have spoken in my defence, sir?" asked Reed,
as he passed this gentleman in coming out.

"I would had I been able. But you see, my man, when the law
gets broken—— "

"The devil take the law," said Reed, savagely. "What I want is
justice."

"And the administrators of it are determined to uphold it, what
can be said?" went on the solicitor equably, as if there had been
no interruption.

"You would make out that I broke the law, just doing what I
did; and I swear it was no more? That I can be legally punished
for it?"

"Don't Reed; it's of no use. The Major and his witnesses swore
you were at work. And it appears that you were."

"I asked them to take a fine—if I must be punished. I might
have found friends to advance it for me."

"Just so. And for that reason of course they did not take it,"
said the candid lawyer.

"What is my wife to do while I am in prison? And the
children? I may come out to find them starved. A month's long
enough to starve them in such weather as this."

Reed was allowed time for no more. He would not have been
allowed that, but for having been jammed by the crowd at the
doorway. He caught my eye as they were getting clear.

"Master Johnny, will you go to the Court for me—your own
place, sir—and tell the master that I swear I am innocent? Perhaps
he'll let a few shillings go to the wife weekly; tell him with my duty
that I'll work it out as soon as I am released. All this is done out
of revenge, sir, because Major Parrifer couldn't get me from my
cottage. May the Lord repay him!"

It caused a commotion, I can tell you, this imprisonment of
Reed's; the place was ringing with it between the Court and Dyke
Manor. Our two houses seemed to have more to do with it than
other people's; first, because Reed worked at the Court; secondly,
because I, who owned both the Court and the cottage, lived at the
Manor. People took it up pretty warmly, and Mrs. Reed and the
children were cared for. Mr. Sterling paid her five shillings a
week; and Mr. Brandon and the Squire helped her on the quiet,
and there were others also. In small country localities gentlemen
don't like to say openly that their neighbours are in the wrong:
at any rate, they rarely *do* anything by way of remedy. Some

spoke of an appeal to the Home Secretary, but it came to nothing, and no steps were taken to liberate Reed. Bill Whitney, who was staying a week with us, wrote and told his mother about it; she sent back a sovereign for Mrs. Reed; we three took it to her, and went about saying old Parrifer ought to be kicked, which was a relief to our feelings.

But there's something to tell about Cathy. On the day that Reed was taken up, it was not known at his home immediately. The neighbours, aware that the wife was ill, said nothing to her—for old Duffham thought she was going to have a fever, and ordered her to be kept quiet. For one thing, they did not know what there was to tell; except that Reed had been marched off from his work in handcuffs by Jones the constable. In the evening, when news came of his committal, it was agreed that an excuse should be made to Mrs. Reed that her husband had gone out on a business job for his master; and that Cathy—who could not fail to hear the truth from one or another—should be warned not to say anything.

"Tell Cathy to come out here," said the woman, looking over the gate. It was the little girl they spoke to; who could talk well: and she answered that Cathy was not there. So Ann Perkins, Mrs. Reed's sister, was called out.

"Where's Cathy?" cried they.

Ann Perkins answered in a passion—that she did not know where Cathy was, but would uncommonly like to know, and she only wished she was behind her—keeping her there with her sister when she ought to be at her own home! Then the women told Ann Perkins what they had intended to tell Cathy, and looked out for the latter.

She did not come back. The night passed, and the next day passed, and Cathy was not seen or heard of. The only person who appeared to have met her was Goody Picker. It was about two o'clock in the afternoon, Tuesday, and Cathy had her best bonnet on. Mother Picker remarked upon her looking so smart, and asked where she was going to. Cathy answered that her uncle (who lived at Evesham) had sent to say she must go over there at once. "But when she came to the two roads, she turned off quite on the contrairy way to Evesham, and I thought the young woman must be daft," concluded Mrs. Picker.

The month passed away, and Reed came out; but Cathy had not returned. He got home on foot, in the afternoon, his hair cut close, and seemed as quiet as a lamb. The man had been daunted. It was an awful insult to put upon him; a slur on his good name for life; and some of them said George Reed would never hold up his head again. Had he been cruel or vindictive, he might have revenged himself on Major Parrifer, personally, in a manner the Major would have found it difficult to forget.

The wife was about again, but sickly: the little ones did not at first know their father. One of the first people he asked after was Cathy. The girl was not at hand to welcome him, and he took it in the light of a reproach. When men come for the first time out of jail, they are sensitive.

"Mr. Sterling called in yesterday, George, to say you were to go to your work again as soon as ever you came home," said the wife, evading the question about Cathy. "Everybody has been so kind; they know you didn't deserve what you got."

"Ah," said Reed, carelessly. "Where's Cathy?"

Mrs. Reed felt obliged to tell him. No diplomatist, she brought out the news abruptly: Cathy had not been seen or heard of since the afternoon he was sent to prison. That aroused Reed: nothing else seemed to have done it: and he got up from his chair.

"Why, where is she? What's become of her?"

The neighbours had been indulging in sundry speculations on the same question, which they had obligingly favoured Mrs. Reed with; but she did not think it necessary to impart them to her husband.

"Cathy was a good girl on the whole, George; putting aside that she'd do no work, and spent her time reading good-for-nothing books. What I think is this—that she heard of your misfortune after she left, and wouldn't come home to face it. She is eighteen now, you know."

"Come home from where?"

Mrs. Reed had to tell the whole truth. That Cathy, dressed up in her best things, had left home without saying a word to any one, stealing out of the house unseen; she had been met in the road by Mrs. Picker, and told her what has already been said. But the uncle at Evesham had seen nothing of her.

Forgetting his cropped hair—as he would have to forget it until it should grow again—George Reed went tramping off, there and then, the nearly two miles of way to Mother Picker's. She could not tell him much more than he already knew. "Cathy was all in her best, her curls 'iled, and her pink ribbons as fresh as her cheeks, and said in answer to questions that she had been sent for sudden to her uncle's at Evesham: but she had turned off quite the contrary road." From thence, Reed walked on to his brother's at Evesham; and learnt that Cathy had not been sent for, and had not come.

When Reed got home, he was dead-beat. How many miles the

man had walked that bleak February day, he did not stay to think —perhaps twenty. When excitement buoys up the spirit, the body does not feel fatigue. Mrs. Reed put supper before her husband, and he ate mechanically, lost in thought.

"It fairly 'mazes me," he said, presently, in local phraseology. "But for going out in her best, I should think some accident had come to her. There's ponds about, and young girls might slip in unawares. But the putting on her best things shows she was going somewhere."

"She put 'em on, and went off unseen," repeated Mrs. Reed, snuffing the candle. "*I* should have thought she'd maybe gone off to some wake—only there wasn't one agate within range."

"Cathy had no bad acquaintance to lead her astray," he resumed. " The girls about here are decent, and mind their work."

" Which Cathy didn't," thought Mrs. Reed. "Cathy held her head above 'em," she said, aloud. "It's my belief she used to fancy herself one o' them fine ladies in her halfpenny books. She didn't seem to make acquaintance with nobody but that young Parrifer. She'd talk to him by the hour together, and I couldn't get her indoors."

Reed lifted his head. "Young Parrifer!—what—*his* son?" turning his thumb in the direction of Parrifer Hall. "Cathy talked to him?"

"By the hour together," reiterated Mrs. Reed. "He'd be on that side the gate, a-talking, and laughing, and leaning on it; and Cathy, she'd be in the path by the tall hollyhocks, talking back to him, and fondling the children."

Reed rose up, a strange look on his face. "How long was that going on?"

"Ever so long; I can't just remember. But young Parrifer is only at the Hall by fits and starts."

"And you never told me, woman!"

"I thought no harm of it. I don't think harm of it now," emphatically added Mrs. Reed. "The worst of young Parrifer, that I've seen, is that he's as soft as a tomtit."

Reed put on his hat without another word, and walked out. Late as it was, he was going to the Hall. He rang a peal at it, more like a lord than a labourer just let out of prison. There was some delay in opening the door: the household had gone upstairs; but a man came at last.

"I want to see Major Parrifer."

The words were so authoritative; the man's appearance so strange, with his tall figure and his clipped hair, as he pushed forward into the hall, that the servant momentarily lost his wits. A light, in a room on the left, guided Reed; he entered it, and found himself face

to face with Major Parrifer, who was seated in an easy-chair before
a good fire, spirits on the table, and a cigar in his mouth. What
with the smoke from that, what with the faint light—for all the
candles had been put out but one—the Major did not at first distinguish his late visitor's face. When the bare head and the resolute
eyes met his, he certainly paled a little, and the cigar fell on to the
carpet.

"I want my daughter, Major Parrifer."

To hear a demand made for a daughter when the Major had
possibly been thinking the demand might be for his life, was un-
doubtedly a relief. It brought back his courage.

"What do you mean, fellow?" he growled, stamping out the fire
of the cigar. "Are you out of your mind?"

"Not quite. You might have driven some men out of theirs,
though, by what you've done. *We'll let that part be*, Major. I
have come to-night about my daughter. Where is she?"

They stood looking at each other. Reed stood just inside the
door, hat in hand; he did not forget his manners even in the
presence of his enemy; they were a habit with him. The Major,
who had risen in his surprise, stared at him : he really knew nothing
whatever of the matter, not even that the girl was missing; and he
did think Reed's imprisonment must have turned his brain. Perhaps Reed saw that he was not understood.

"I come home from prison, into which you put me, Major
Parrifer, to find my daughter Catherine gone. She went away the
day I was taken up. Where she went, or what she's doing, Heaven
knows; but you or yours are answerable for it, whichever way it
may be."

"You have been drinking," said Major Parrifer.

"*You* have, maybe," returned Reed, glancing at the spirits on the
table. "Either Cathy went out on a harmless jaunt, and is staying
away because she can't face the shame at home which you have put
there; or else she went out to meet your son, and has been taken
away by him. I think it must be the last; my fears whisper it to
me; and, if so, you can't be off knowing something of it. Major
Parrifer, I must have my daughter."

Whether the hint given about his son alarmed the Major, causing
him to forget his bluster for once, and answer civilly, he certainly
did it. His son was in Ireland with his regiment, he said; had not
been at the Hall for weeks and weeks; he could answer for it that
Lieutenant Parrifer knew nothing of the girl.

"He was here at Christmas," said George Reed. "I saw him."

"And left two or three days after it. How dare you, fellow,
charge him with such a thing? He'd wring your neck for you if
he were here."

" Perhaps I might find cause to wring his first. Major Parrifer, I want my daughter."

" If you do not get out of my house, I'll have you brought before me to-morrow for trespassing, and give you a second month's imprisonment," roared the Major, gathering bluster and courage. " You want another month of it : this one does not appear to have done you the good it ought. Now—go ! "

" I'll go," said Reed, who began to see the Major really did not know anything of Cathy—and it had not been very probable that he did. " But I'd like to leave a word behind me. You have succeeded in doing me a great injury, Major Parrifer. You are rich and powerful, I am poor and lowly. You set your mind on my bit of a home, and because you could not drive me from it, you took advantage of your magistrate's post to sentence me to prison, and so be revenged. It has done me a great deal of harm. What good has it done you ? "

Major Parrifer could not speak for rage.

" It will come home to you, sir ; mark me if it does not. God has seen my trouble, and my wife's trouble, and I don't believe He ever let such a wrong pass unrewarded. *It will come home to you, Major Parrifer.*"

George Reed went out, quietly shutting the hall-door behind him, and walked home through the thick flakes of snow that had begun to fall.

V.

COMING HOME TO HIM.

THE year was getting on. Summer fruits were ripening. It had been a warm spring, and hot weather was upon us early.

One fine Sunday morning, George Reed came out of his cottage and turned up Piefinch Lane. His little girls were with him, one in either hand, in their clean cotton frocks and pinafores and straw hats. People had gone into church, and the bells had ceased. Reed had not been constant in attendance since the misfortune in the winter, when Major Parrifer put him into prison. The month's imprisonment had altered him; his daughter Cathy's mysterious absence had altered him more; he seemed unwilling to face people, and any trifle was made an excuse to himself for keeping away from service. To-day it was afforded by the baby's illness. Reed said to his wife that he would take the little girls out a bit to keep the place quiet.

Rumours were abroad that he had heard once from Cathy; that she told him she should come back some day and surprise him and the neighbours, that she was "all right, and he had no call to fret after her." Whether this was true or pure fiction, Reed did not say: he was a closer man than he used to be.

Lifting the children over a stile in Piefinch Lane, just beyond his garden, Reed strolled along the by-path of the field. It brought him to the high hedge skirting the premises of Major Parrifer. The man had taken it by chance, because it was a quiet walk. He was passing along slowly, the children running about the field, on which the second crop of grass was beginning to grow, when voices on the other side of the hedge struck on his ear. Reed quietly put some of the foliage aside, and looked through; just as Major Parrifer had looked through the hedge in Piefinch Lane at him, that Sunday morning some few months before.

Major Parrifer had been suffering from a slight temporary indisposition. He did not consider himself sufficiently recovered to attend service, but neither was he ill enough to lie in bed. With the departure of his family for church, the Major had come trolling out in the garden in an airy dressing-gown, and there saw his gardener picking peas.

"Halloa, Hotty! This ought to have been done before."

"Yes, sir, I know it; I'm a little late," answered Hotty; "I shall have done in two or three minutes. The cook makes a fuss if I pick 'em too early; she says they don't eat so well."

The peas were for the gratification of the Major's own palate, so he found no more fault. Hotty went on with his work, and the Major gave a general look round. On a near wall, at right angles with the hedge through which Reed was then peering, some fine apricots were growing, green yet.

"These apricots want thinning, Hotty," observed the Major.

"I have thinned 'em some, sir."

"Not enough. Our apricots were not as fine last year as they ought to have been. I said then they had not had sufficient room to grow. Green apricots are always useful; they make the best tart known."

Major Parrifer walked to the greenhouse, outside which a small basket was hanging, brought it back, and began to pick some of the apricots where they looked too thick. Reed, outside, watched the process—not alone. As luck had it, a man appeared on the field-path, who proved to be Gruff Blossom, the Jacobsons' groom, coming home to spend Sunday with his friends. Reed made a sign to Blossom to be silent, and caused him to look on also.

With the small basket half full, the Major desisted, thinking possibly he had plucked enough, and turned away carrying it. Hotty came out from the peas, his task finished. They strolled slowly down the path by the hedge; the Major first, Hotty a step behind, talking about late and early peas, and whether Prussian blues or marrowfats were the best eating.

"Do you see those weeds in the onion-bed?" suddenly asked the Major, stopping as they were passing it.

Hotty turned his head to look. A few weeds certainly had sprung up. He'd attend to it on the morrow, he told his master; and then said something about the work accumulating almost beyond him, since the under-gardener had been at home ill.

"Pick them out now," said the Major; "there's not a dozen of them."

Hotty stooped to do as he was bid. The Major made no more ado but stooped also, uprooting quite half the weeds himself. Not much more, in all, than the dozen he had spoken of: and then they went on with their baskets to the house.

Never had George Reed experienced so much gratification since the day he came out of prison. "Did you see the Major at it?—thinning his apricots and pulling up his weeds?" he asked of Gruff

Blossom. And Blossom's reply, gruff as usual, was to ask what might be supposed to ail his eyes that he shouldn't see it.

"Very good," said Reed.

One evening in the following week, when we were sitting out on the lawn, the Squire smoking, Mrs. Todhetley nursing her face in her hand, with toothache as usual, Tod teasing Hugh and Lena, and I up in the beech-tree, a horseman rode in. It proved to be Mr. Jacobson. Giles took his horse, and he came and sat down on the bench. The Squire asked him what he'd take, and being thirsty, he chose cider. Which Thomas brought.

"Here's a go," began Mr. Jacobson. "Have you heard what's up?"

"I've not heard anything," answered the Squire.

"Major Parrifer has a summons served on him for working in his garden on a Sunday, and is to appear before the magistrates at Alcester to-morrow," continued old Jacobson, drinking off a glass of cider at a draught.

"No!" cried Squire Todhetley.

"It's a fact. Blossom, our groom, has also a summons served on him to give evidence."

Mrs. Todhetley lifted her face; Tod left Hugh and Lena to themselves: I slid down from the beech-tree; and we listened for more.

But Mr. Jacobson could not give particulars, or say much more than he had already said. All he knew was, that on Monday morning George Reed had appeared before the magistrates and made a complaint. At first they were unwilling to grant a summons; laughed at it; but Reed, in a burst of reproach, civilly delivered, asked why there should be a law for the poor and not for the rich, and in what lay the difference between himself and Major Parrifer; that the one should be called to account and punished for doing wrong, and the other was not even to be accused when he had done it.

"Brandon happened to be on the bench," continued Jacobson. "He appeared struck with the argument, and signed the summons."

The Squire nodded.

"My belief is," continued old Jacobson, with a wink over the rim of the cider glass, "that granting that summons was as good as a play to Brandon and the rest. I'd as lieve, though, that they'd not brought Blossom into it."

"Why?" asked Mrs. Todhetley, who had been grieved at the time at the injustice done to Reed.

"Well, Parrifer is a disagreeable man to offend. And he is sure to visit Blossom's part in this on me."

"Let him," said Tod, with enthusiasm. "Well done, George Reed!"

Be you very sure we went over to the fight. Squire Todhetley did not appear: at which Tod exploded a little: he only wished *he* was a magistrate, wouldn't he take his place and judge the Major! But the Pater said that when people had lived to his age, they liked to be at peace with their neighbours—not but what he hoped Parrifer would "get it," for having been so cruelly hard upon Reed.

Major Parrifer came driving to the Court-house in his high carriage with a great bluster, his iron-grey hair standing up, and two grooms attending him. Only the magistrates who had granted the summons sat. The news had gone about like wild-fire, and several of them were in and about the town, but did not take their places. I don't believe there was one would have lifted his finger to save the Major from a month's imprisonment; but they did not care to sentence him to it.

It was a regular battle. Major Parrifer was in an awful passion the whole time; asking, when he came in, how they dared summon him. *Him!* Mr. Brandon, cool as a cucumber, answered in his squeaky voice, that when a complaint of breaking the law was preferred before them and sworn to by witnesses, they could only act upon it.

First of all, the Major denied the facts. *He* work in his garden on a Sunday!—the very supposition was preposterous! Upon which George Reed, who was in his best clothes, and looked every bit as good as the Major, and far pleasanter, testified to what he had seen.

Major Parrifer, dancing with temper when he found he had been looked at through the hedge, and that it was Reed who had looked, gave the lie direct. He called his gardener, Richard Hotty, ordering him to testify whether he, the Major, ever worked in his garden, either on Sundays or week-days.

"Hotty was working himself, gentlemen," interposed George Reed. "He was picking peas; and he helped to weed the onion-bed. But it was done by his master's orders, so it would be unjust to punish him."

The Major turned on Reed as if he would strike him, and demanded of the magistrates why they permitted the fellow to interrupt. They ordered Reed to be quiet, and told Hotty to proceed.

But Hotty was one of those slow men to whom anything like evasion is difficult. His master had thinned the apricot tree that Sunday morning; he had helped to weed the onion-bed; Hotty,

conscious of the fact, but not liking to admit it, stammered and
stuttered, and made a poor figure of himself. Mr. Brandon thought
he would help him out.

"Did you see your master pick the apricots?"

"I see him pick—just a few; green 'uns," answered Hotty,
shuffling from one leg to the other in his perplexity. "'Twarn't to
be called work, sir."

"Oh! And did he help you to weed the onion-bed?"

"There warn't a dozen weeds in it in all, as the Major said to me
at the time," returned Hotty. "He see 'em, and stooped down on
the spur o' the moment, and me too. We had 'em up in a twinkling.
'Twarn't work, sir; couldn't be called it nohow. The Major, he
never do work at no time."

Blossom had not arrived, and it was hard to tell how the thing
would terminate: the Major had this witness, Hotty, such as he
was, protesting that nothing to be called work was done. Reed
had no witness, as yet.

"Old Jacobson is keeping Blossom back, Johnny," whispered
Tod. "It's a sin and a shame."

"No, he is not," I said. "Look there!"

Blossom was coming in. He had walked over, and not hurried
himself. Major Parrifer plunged daggers into him, if looks could
do it, but it made no difference to Blossom.

He gave his evidence in his usual surly manner. It was clear
and straightforward. Major Parrifer had thinned the apricot tree
for its own benefit; and had weeded the onion-bed, Hotty helping
at the weeds by order.

"What brought *you* spying at the place, James Blossom?"
demanded a lawyer on the Major's behalf.

"Accident," was the short answer.

"Indeed! You didn't go there on purpose, I suppose?—and
skulk under the hedge on purpose?—and peer into the Major's
garden on purpose?"

"No, I didn't," said Blossom. "The field is open to every one,
and I was crossing it on my way to old father's. George Reed
made me a sign afore I came up to him, to look in, as he was
doing; and I did so, not knowing what there might be to see. It
would be nothing to me if the Major worked in his garden' of a
Sunday from sunrise to sunset; he's welcome to do it; but if you
summon me here and ask me, did I see him working, I say yes, I
did. Why d'you send me a summons if you don't want me to
tell the truth? Let me be, and I'd ha' said nothing to mortal
man."

Evidently nothing favourable to the defence could be got out of
James Blossom. Mr. Brandon began saying to the Major that he

feared there was no help for it ; they should be obliged to convict him : and he was met by a storm of reproach.

Convict him ! roared the Major. For having picked two or three green apricots—and for stooping to pull up a couple or so of worthless weeds? He would be glad to ask which of them, his brother-magistrates sitting there, would not pick an apricot, or a peach, or what not, on a Sunday, if he wanted to eat one. The thing was utterly preposterous.

"And what was it *I* did?" demanded George Reed, drowning voices that would have stopped him. "I went to the garden to get up a bunch of turnips for my sick wife, and seeing some withered -weeds flung on the bed I drew them off with the hoe. What was that, I ask? And it was no more. No more, gentlemen, in the sight of Heaven."

No particular answer was given to this; perhaps the justices had none ready. Mr. Brandon was beginning to confer with the other two in an undertone, when Reed spoke again.

"I was dragged up here in handcuffs, and told I had broken the law; Major Parrifer said to me himself that I had violated the sanctity of the Sabbath (those were the words), and therefore I must be punished ; there was no help for it. What has he done? I did not do as much as he has."

"Now you know, Reed, this is irregular," said one of the justices. "You must not interrupt the Court."

"You put me in prison for a month, gentlemen," resumed Reed, paying no attention to the injunction. "They cut my hair close in the prison, and they kept me to hard labour·for the month, as if I did not have enough of hard labour out of it. My wife was sick and disabled at the time, my three little children are helpless: it was no thanks to the magistrates who sentenced me, gentlemen, or to Major Parrifer, that they did not starve."

"Will you be quiet, Reed?"

"If I deserved one month of prison," persisted Reed, fully bent on saying what he had to say, "Major Parrifer must deserve two months, for his offence is greater than mine. The law is the same for both of us, I suppose. He——"

"Reed, if you say another word, I will order you at once from the room," interrupted Mr. Brandon, his thin voice sharp and determined. "How dare you persist in addressing the Bench when told to be quiet!"

Reed fell back and said no more. He knew that Mr. Brandon had a habit of carrying out his own authority, in spite of his nervous health and querulous way of speaking. The justices spoke a few words together, and then said they found the offence proved, and inflicted a fine on Major Parrifer.

He dashed the money down on the table, in too great a rage to do it politely, and went out to his carriage. No other case was on, that day, and the justices got up and mixed with the crowd. Mr. Brandon, who felt chilly on the hottest summer's day, and was afraid of showers, buttoned on a light overcoat.

"Then there are *two* laws, sir?" said Reed to him, quite civilly, but in a voice that every one might hear. "When the law was made against Sabbath-breaking, those that made it passed one for the rich and another for the poor!"

"Nonsense, Reed."

"*Nonsense*, sir? I don't see it. *I* was put in prison; Major Parrifer has only to pay a bit of money, which is of no more account to him than dirt, and that he can't feel the loss of. And my offence—if it was an offence—was less than his."

"Two wrongs don't make a right," said Mr. Brandon, dropping his voice to a low key. "You ought not to have been put in prison, Reed; had I been on the bench it should not have been done."

"But it was done, sir, and my life got a blight on it. It's on me yet; will never be lifted off me."

Mr. Brandon smiled one of his quiet smiles, and spoke in a whisper. "He has got it too, Reed, unless I am mistaken. He'll carry that fine about with him always. Johnny, are you there? Don't go and repeat what you've heard me say."

Mr. Brandon was right. To have been summoned before the Bench, where he had pompously sat to summon others, and for working on a Sunday above all things, to have been found guilty and fined, was as the most bitter potion to Major Parrifer. The bench would never again be to him the seat it had been; the remembrance of the day when he was before it would, as Mr. Brandon expressed it, be carried about with him always.

They projected a visit to the sea-side at once. Mrs. Parrifer, with three of the Miss Parrifers, came dashing up to people's houses in the carriage, finer and louder than ever; she said that she had not been well, and was ordered to Aberystwith for six weeks. The next day they and the Major were off; and heaps of cards were sent round with "P.P.C." in the corner. I think Mr. Brandon must have laughed when he got his.

The winter holidays came round again. We went home for Christmas, as usual, and found George Reed down with some sort of illness. There's an old saying, "When the mind's at ease the body's delicate," but Mr. Duffham always maintained that though that might apply to a short period of time, in the long-run mind and body sympathized together. George Reed had been a very healthy man, and as free from care as most people; this last year care and trouble and mortification had lain on his mind, and at the beginning of winter his health broke down. It was quite a triumph (in the matter of opinion) for old Duffham.

The illness began with a cough and low fever, neither of which can labourers afford time to lie up for. It went on to more fever, and to inflammation of the lungs. There was no choice then, and Reed took to his bed. For the most part, when our poor people fell ill, they had to get well again without notice being taken of them; but events had drawn attention to Reed, and made him a conspicuous character. His illness was talked of, and so he received help. Ever since the prison affair I had felt sorry for Reed, as had Mrs. Todhetley.

" I have had some nice strong broth made for Reed, Johnny," she said to me one day in January; "it's as good and nourishing as beef-tea. If you want a walk, you might take it to him."

Tod had gone out with the Squire; I felt dull, as I generally did without him, and put on my hat and coat. Mrs. Todhetley had the broth put into a bottle, and brought it to me wrapped in paper.

" I would send him a drop of wine as well, Johnny, if you'd take care not to break the bottles, carrying two of them."

No fear. I put the one bottle in my breast-pocket, and took the other in my hand. It was a cold afternoon, the sky of a steely-blue, the sun bright, the ground hard. Major Parrifer and two of his daughters, coming home from a ride, were cantering in at the gates as I passed, the groom riding after them. I lifted my hat to the girls, but they only tossed their heads.

Reed was getting over the worst then, and I found him sitting by the kitchen fire, muffled in a bed-rug. Mrs. Reed took the bottles from me in the back'us—as they called the place where the washing was done—for Reed was sensitive, and did not like things to be sent to him.

" Please God, I shall be at work next week," said Reed, with a groan : and I saw he knew that I had brought something.

He had been saying that all along; four or five weeks now. I sat down opposite to him, and took up the boy, Georgy. The little shaver had come round to me, holding by the chairs.

." It's going to be a hard frost, Reed."

" Is it, sir ? Out-o'-door weather don't seem to be of much odds to me now."

" And a fall o' some sort's not far off, as my wrist tells me," put in Mrs. Reed. Years ago she had broken her wrist, and felt it always in change of weather. "Maybe some snow's coming."

I gave Georgy a biscuit; the two little girls, who had been standing against the press, began to come slowly forward. They guessed there was a supply in my pocket. I had dipped into the biscuit-basket at home before coming away. The two put out a hand each without being told, and I dropped a biscuit into them.

It had taken neither time nor noise, and yet there was some one standing inside the door when I looked up again, who must have come in stealthily; some one in a dark dress, and a black and white plaid shawl. Mrs. Reed looked and the children looked; and then Reed turned his head to look also.

I think I was the first to know her. She had a thick black veil before her face, and the room was not light. Reed's illness had left him thin, and his eyes appeared very large: they assumed a sort of frightened stare.

"Father! you are sick!"

Before he could answer, she had run across the brick floor and thrown her arms round his neck. Cathy! The two girls were frightened and flew to their mother; one began to scream and the other followed suit. Altogether there was a good deal of noise and commotion. Georgy, like a brave little man, sucked his biscuit through it all with great composure.

What Reed said or did, I had not noticed; I think he tried to fling Cathy from him—to avoid suffocation perhaps. She burst out laughing in her old light manner, and took something out of the body of her gown, under the shawl.

"No need, father: I am as honest as anybody," said she. "Look at this."

Reed's hand shook so that he could not open the paper, or understand it at first when he had opened it. Cathy flung off her bonnet and caught the children to her. They began to know her then and ceased their cries. Presently Reed held the paper across to me, his hand trembling more than before, and his face, that illness had left white enough, yet more ghastly with emotion.

"Please read it, sir."

I did not understand it at first either, but the sense came to me soon. It was a certificate of the marriage of Spencer Gervoise Daubeney Parrifer and Catherine Reed. They had been married at Liverpool the very day after Cathy disappeared from home; now just a year ago.

A sound of sobbing broke the stillness. Reed had fallen back in his chair in a sort of hysterical fit. Defiant, hard, strong-minded Reed! But the man was three parts dead from weakness. It lasted only a minute or two; he roused himself as if ashamed, and swallowed down his sobs.

"How came he to marry you, Cathy?"

"Because I would not go away with him without it father. We have been staying in Ireland."

"And be you repenting of it yet?" asked Mrs. Reed, in ungracious tones.

"Pretty near," answered Cathy, with candour.

It appeared that Cathy had made her way direct to Liverpool when she left home the previous January, travelling all night. There she met young Parrifer, who had preceded her and made arrangements for the marriage. They were married that day, and afterwards went on to Ireland, where he had to join his regiment.

To hear all this, sounding like a page out of a romance, would be something wonderful for our quiet place when it came to be told. You meet with marvellous stories in towns now and then, but with us they are almost unknown.

"Where's your husband?" asked Reed.

Cathy tossed her head. "Ah! Where! That's what I've come home about," she answered: and it struck me at once that something was wrong.

What occurred next we only learnt from hearsay. I said good day to them, and came away, thinking it might have been better if Cathy had not married and left home. It was a fancy of mine, and I don't know why it should have come to me, but it proved to be a right one. Cathy put on her bonnet again to go to Parrifer Hall: and the particulars of her visit were known abroad later.

It was growing rather dark when she approached it; the sun had set, the grey of evening was drawing on. Two of the Misses Parrifer were at the window and saw her coming, but Cathy had her veil down and they did not recognize her. The actions and manners and air of a lady do not come suddenly to one who has been differently bred; and the Misses Parrifer supposed the visitor to be for the servants.

"Like her impudence!" said Miss Jemima. "Coming to the front entrance!"

For Cathy, whose year's experience in Ireland had widely changed her, had no notion of taking up her old position. She meant to hold her own; and was capable of doing it, not being deficient in the quality just ascribed to her by Miss Jemima Parrifer.

"What next!" cried Miss Jemima, as a ring and a knock resounded through the house, waking up the Major: who had been dozing over the fire amongst his daughters.

The next was, that a servant came to the room and told the Major a lady wanted him. She had been shown into the library.

"What name?" asked the Major.

"She didn't give none, sir. I asked, but she said never mind the name."

"Go and ask it again."

The man went and came back. "It is Mrs. Parrifer, sir."

" Mrs. who? "

" Mrs. Parrifer, sir."

The Major turned and stared at his servant. They had no relatives whatever. Consequently the only Mrs. Parrifer within knowledge was his wife.

Staring at the man would not bring him any elucidation. Major Parrifer went to the library, and there saw the lady standing on one side of the fender, holding her foot to the fire. She had her back to him, did not turn, and so the Major went round to the other side of the hearth-rug where he could see her.

"My servant told me a Mrs. Parrifer wanted me. Did he make a mistake in the name?"

"No mistake at all, sir," said Cathy, throwing up her thick veil, and drawing a step or two back. " I am Mrs. Parrifer."

The Major recognized her then. Cathy Reed! He was a man whose bluster rarely failed him, but he had none ready at that moment. Three-parts astounded, various perplexities held him tongue-tied.

"That is to say, Mrs. Spencer Parrifer," continued Cathy. "And I have come over from Ireland on a mission to you, sir, from your son."

The Major thought that of all the audacious women it had ever been his lot to meet, this one was the worst : at least as much as he could think anything, for his wits were a little confused just then. A moment's pause, and then the storm burst forth.

Cathy was called various agreeable names, and ordered out of the room and the house. The Major put up his hands to "hurrish" her out—as we say in Worcestershire by the cows, though I don't think you would find the word in the dictionary. But Cathy stood her ground. He then went ranting towards the door, calling for the servants to come and put her forth. Cathy, quicker than he, gained it first and turned to face him, her back against it.

"You needn't call me those names, Major Parrifer. Not that I care—as I might if I deserved them. I am your son's wife, and have been such ever since I left father's cottage last year ; and my baby, your grandson, sir, which it's seven weeks old he is, is now at the Red Lion, a mile off. I've left it there with the landlady."

He could not put her out of the room unless by force ; he looked ready to kick and strike her ; but in the midst of it a horrible dread rose up in his heart that the calmly spoken words were true. Perhaps from the hour when Reed had presented himself at the house to ask for his daughter, the evening of the day he was discharged from prison, up to this time, Major Parrifer had never thought of the girl. It had been said in his ears now and again that Reed was grieving for his daughter ; but the matter was altogether too contemptible for Major Parrifer to take note of. And now to hear that the girl had been with his son all the time, his wife! But that utter disbelief came to his aid, the Major might have fallen into a fit on the spot. For young Mr. Parrifer had cleverly contrived that neither his father away at home nor his friends on the spot should know anything about Cathy. He had been with his regiment in quarters; she had lived privately in another part of the town. Mrs. Reed had once called Lieutenant Parrifer as soft as a tomtit. He was a great deal softer.

"Woman! if you do not quit my house, with your shameless lies, you shall be flung out of it."

"I'll quit it as soon as I have told you what I came over the sea to tell. Please to look at this first, sir?"

Major Parrifer snatched the paper that she held out, carried it to the window, and put his glasses across his nose. It was a copy of the certificate of marriage. His hands shook as he read it, just as Reed's had shaken a short time before; and he tore it passionately in two.

"It is only the copy," said Cathy calmly, as she picked up the pieces. "Your son—if he lives—is about to be tried for his life, sir. He is in custody for wilful murder!"

"How dare you!" shrieked Major Parrifer.

"It is what they have charged him with. I have come all the way to tell it you, sir."

Major Parrifer, brought to his senses by fright, could only listen. Cathy, her back against the door still, gave him the heads of the story.

Young Parrifer was so soft that he had been made a butt of by sundry of his brother-officers. They might not have tolerated him at all, but for winning his money. He drank, and played cards, and bet upon horses; they encouraged him to drink, and then made him play and bet, and altogether cleared him out: not of brains, he had none to be cleared of: but of money. Ruin stared him in the face: his available cash had been parted with long ago; his commission (it was said) was mortgaged: how many promissory notes, bills, I O U's he had signed could not even be guessed at. In a quarrel a few nights before, after a public-house supper, when some of them were the worse for drink, young Parrifer, who could on rare occasions go into frightful passions, flung a carving-knife at one of the others, a lieutenant named Cook; it struck a vital part and killed him. Mr. Parrifer was arrested by the police at once; he was in plain clothes and there was nothing to show that he was an officer. They had to strap him down to carry him to prison: between drink, rage, and fever, he was as a maniac. The next morning he was lying in brain fever, and when Cathy left he had been put into a strait-waistcoat.

She gave the heads of this account in as few words as it is written. Major Parrifer stood like a helpless man. Taking one thing with another, the blow was horrible. Parents don't often see the defects in their own children, especially if they are only sons. Far from having thought his son soft, unfit (as he nearly was) to be trusted about, the Major had been proud of him as his heir, and told the world he was perfection. Soft as young Parrifer was, he had contrived to keep his ill-doings from his father.

Of course it was only natural that the Major's first relief should be abuse of Cathy. He told her all that had happened to his son *she* was the cause of, and called her a few more genteel names in doing it.

"Not at all," said Cathy; "you are wrong there, sir. His marriage with me was a little bit of a stop-gap and served to keep him straight for a month or two; but for that, he would have done for himself before now. Do you think I've had a bargain in him, sir? No. Marriage is a thing that can't be undone, Major Parrifer: but I wish to my heart that I was at home again in father's cottage, light-hearted Cathy Reed."

The Major made no answer. Cathy went on.

"When the news was brought to me by his servant, that he had killed a man and was lying raving, I thought it time to go and see about him. They would not let me into the lock-up where he was lying—and you might have heard his ravings outside. *I* did. I said I was his wife; and then they told me I had better see Captain Williams. I went to head-quarters and saw Captain Williams. He seemed to doubt me; so I showed him the certificate, and told him my baby was at home, turned six weeks old. He was very kind then, sir; took me to see my husband; and advised me to come over here at once and give you the particulars. I told him what was the truth—that I had no money, and the lodgings were owing for. He said the lodgings must wait: and he would lend me enough money for the journey."

"Did you see him?" growled Major Parrifer.

Cathy knew that he alluded to his son, though he would not speak the name.

"I saw him, sir; I told you so. He did not know me or anybody else; he was raving mad, and shaking so that the bed shook under him."

"How is it that they have not written to me?" demanded Major Parrifer.

"I don't think anybody liked to do it. Captain Williams said the best plan would be for me to come over. He asked me if I'd like to hear the truth of the past as regarded my husband; or if I would just come here and tell you the bare facts that were known

about his illness and the charge against him. I said I'd prefer to
hear the truth—it couldn't be worse than I suspected. Then he
went on to the drinking and the gambling and the debts, just as
I have repeated it to you, sir. He was very gentle; but he said he
thought it would be mistaken kindness not to let me fully understand the state of things. He said Mr. Parrifer's father, or some
other friend, had better go over to Ireland."

In spite of himself, a groan escaped Major Parrifer. The blow
was the worst that could have fallen upon him. He had not cared
much for his daughters; his ambition was centred in his son.
Visions of a sojourn at Dublin, and of figuring off at the Vice-
Regal Court, himself, his wife, and his son, had floated occasionally in rose-coloured clouds before his eyes, poor pompous old
simpleton. And now—to picture the visit he must set out upon
ere the night was over, nearly drove him wild with pain. Cathy
unlatched the door, but waited to speak again before she opened it.

"I'll rid the house of me now that I have broke it to you, sir. If
you wan't me I shall be found at father's cottage; I suppose they'll
let me stay there: if not, you can hear of me at the place where
I've left my baby. And if your son should ever wake out of his
delirium, Major Parrifer, he will be able to tell you that if he had
listened to me and heeded me, or even only come to spend his
evenings with me—which it's months since he did—he would not
have been in this plight now. Should they try him for murder;
and nothing can save him from it if he gets well; I——"

A succession of screams cut short what Cathy was about to add.
In her surprise she drew wide the door, and was confronted by Miss
Jemima Parrifer. That young lady, curious upon the subject of the
visit and visitor, had thought it well to put her ear to the library
door. With no effect, however, until Cathy unlatched it. And then
she heard more than she had thought for.

"Is it you!" roughly cried Miss Jemima, recognizing her for
the ill-talked-of Cathy Reed, the daughter of the Major's enemy.
"What do you want here?"

Cathy did not answer. She walked to the hall-door and let herself out. Miss Jemima went on into the library.

"Papa, what was it she was saying about Spencer, that vile girl?
What did she do here? Why did she send in her name as Mrs.
Parrifer?"

The Major might have heard the questions, or he might not; he
didn't respond to them. Miss Jemima, looking closely at him in
the darkness of the room, saw a grey, worn, terror-stricken face,
that looked as her father's had never looked yet.

"Oh, papa! what is the matter? Are you ill?"

He walked towards her in the quietest manner possible, took her arm and pushed her out at the door. Not rudely; softly, as one might do who is in a dream.

"Presently, presently," he muttered in quite an altered voice, low and timid. And Miss Jemima found the door bolted against her.

It must have been an awful moment with him. Look on what side he would, there was no comfort. Spencer Parrifer was ruined past redemption. He might die in this illness, and then, what of his soul? Not that the Major was given to that kind of reflection. Escaping the illness, he must be tried—for his life, as Cathy had phrased it. And escaping that, if the miracle were possible, there remained the miserable debts and the miserable wife he had clogged himself with.

Curiously enough, as the miserable Major, most miserable in that moment, pictured these things, there suddenly rose up before his mind's eye another picture. A remembrance of Reed, who had stood in that very room less than twelve months ago, in the dim light of late night, with his hair cut close, and his warning: "*It will come home to you, Major Parrifer.*" *Had* it come home to him? Home to him already? The drops of agony broke out on his face as he asked the question. It seemed to him, in that moment of excitement, so very like some of Heaven's own lightning.

One grievous portion of the many ills had perhaps not fallen, but for putting Reed in prison—the marriage; and that one was more humiliating to Major Parrifer's spirit than all the rest. Had Reed been at liberty, Cathy might not have made her escape untracked, and the bitter marriage might, in that case, have been avoided.

A groan, and now another, broke from the Major. How it had come home to him! not his selfishness and his barbarity and his pride, but this sorrowful blow. Reed's month in prison, compared with this, was as a drop of water to the ocean. As to the girl—when Reed had come asking for tidings of her, it had seemed to the Major not of the least moment whither she had gone or what ill she had entered on: was she not a common labourer's daughter, and that labourer George Reed? Even then, at that very time, she was his daughter-in-law, and his son the one to be humiliated. Major Parrifer ground his teeth, and only stopped when he remembered that something must be done about that disgraceful son.

He started that night for Ireland. Cathy, affronted at some remark made by Mrs. Reed, took herself off from her father's cottage. She had a little money still left from her journey, and could spend it.

Spencer Gervoise Daubeney Parrifer (the Major and his wife had bestowed the fine names upon him in pride at his baptism) died in prison. He lived only a day after Major Parrifer's arrival, and never recognized him. Of course it saved the trial, when he would probably have been convicted of manslaughter. It saved the payment of his hundreds of debts too; post-obits and all; he died before his father. But it could not save exposure; it could not keep the facts from the world. Major and Mrs. Parrifer, so to say, would never lift up their heads again; the sun of their life had set.

Neither would Cathy lift hers yet awhile. She contrived to quarrel with her father; the Parrifers never took the remotest notice of her; she was nearly starved and her baby too. What little she earned was by hard work: but it would not keep her, and she applied to the parish. The parish in turn applied to Major Parrifer, and forced from him as much as the law allowed, a few shillings a week. Having to apply to the parish was, for Cathy, a humiliation never to be forgotten. The neighbours made their comments.

"Cathy Reed had brought her pigs to a fine market!"

So she had; and she felt it more than the loss of her baby, who died soon after. Better that she had married an honest day-labourer: and Cathy knew it now.

VI.

LEASE, THE POINTSMAN.

I r happened when we were staying at our other house, Crabb Cot. In saying " we " were staying at it, I mean the family, for Tod and I were at school.

Crabb Cot lay beyond the village of Crabb. Just across the road, a few yards higher up, was the large farm of Mr. Coney ; and his house and ours were the only two that stood there. Crabb Cot was a smaller and more cosy house than Dyke Manor ; and, when there, we were not so very far from Worcester : less than half-way, comparing it with the Manor.

Crabb was a large and straggling parish. North Crabb, which was nearest to us, had the church and schools in it, but very few houses. South Crabb, further off, was more populous. Nearly a mile beyond South Crabb, there was a regular junction of rails. Lines, crossing each other in a most bewildering manner, led off in all directions : and it required no little manœuvring to send the trains away right at busy times. Which of course was the pointsman's affair.

The busiest days had place in summer, when excursion trains were in full swing : but they would come occasionally at other times, driving the South Crabb station people off their heads with bother before night.

The pointsman was Harry Lease. I dare say you have noticed how certain names seem to belong to certain places. At North Crabb and South Crabb, and in the district round about, the name of Lease was as common as blackberries in a hedge ; and if the different Leases had been cousins in the days gone by, the relationship was lost now. There might be seven-and-twenty Leases, in and out, but Harry Lease was not, so far as he knew, akin to any of them.

South Crabb was not much of a place at best. A part of it, Crabb Lane, branching off towards Massock's brickfields, was crowded as a London street. Poor dwellings were huddled together, and children jostled each other on the door-steps. Squire Todhetley said he remembered it when it really was a lane, hedges

on either side and a pond that was never dry. Harry Lease lived
in the last house, a thatched hut with three rooms in it. He was a
steady, civil, hard-working man, superior to some of his neighbours,
who were given to reeling home at night and beating their wives on
arrival. His wife, a nice sort of woman to talk to, was a bad
manager; but the five children were better behaved and better
kept than the other grubbers in the gutter.

Lease was the pointsman at South Crabb Junction, and helped
also in the general business there. He walked to his work at six in
the morning, carrying his breakfast with him; went home to dinner
at twelve, the leisure part of the day at the station, and had his tea
taken to him at four; leaving in general at nine. Sometimes his
wife arrived with the tea; sometimes the eldest child, Polly, an intelligent girl of six. But, one afternoon in September, a crew of
mischievous boys from the brickfields espied what Polly was carrying. They set upon her, turned over the can of tea in fighting for
it, ate the bread-and-butter, tore her pinafore in the skirmish, and
frightened her nearly to death. After that, Lease said that the
child should not be sent with the tea: so, when his wife could not
take it, he went without tea. Polly and her father were uncommonly alike, too quiet to battle much with the world: sensitive, in
fact: though it sounds odd to say that.

During the month of November one of the busy days occurred
at South Crabb Junction. There was a winter meeting on
Worcester race-course, a cattle and pig show in a town larger than
Worcester, and two or three markets and other causes of increased
traffic, all falling on the same day. What with cattle-trains, ordinary and special trains, and goods-trains, and the grunting of
obstinate pigs, Lease had plenty to do to keep his points in
order.

How it fell out he never knew. Between eight and nine o'clock,
when a train was expected in on its way to Worcester, Lease forgot
to shift the points. A goods-train had come in ten minutes before,
for which he had had to turn the points, and he never turned them
back again. On came the train, almost as quickly as though it had
not to pull up at South Crabb Junction. Watson, the station-
master, came out to be in readiness.

"The engine has her steam on to-night," he remarked to Lease as
he watched the red lights, like two great eyes, come tearing on.
"She'll have to back."

She did something worse than back. Instead of slackening on
the near lines, she went flying off at a tangent to some outer ones
on which the goods-train stood, waiting until the passenger train
should pass. There was a short, sharp sound from the whistle, a
great collision, a noise of steam hissing, a sense of dire confusion:

and for one minute afterwards a dead lull, as if every one and every-thing were paralyzed.

"You never turned the points!" shouted the station-master to Lease.

Lease made no rejoinder. He backed against the wall like a man helpless, his arms stretched out, his face and eyes wild with horror. Watson thought he was going to have a fit, and shook him roughly.

"*You've* done it nicely, you have!" he added, as he flew off to the scene of disaster, from which the steam was beginning to clear away. But Lease reached it before him.

"God forgive me! God have mercy upon me!"

A porter, running side by side with Lease, heard him say it. In telling it afterwards the man described the tone as one of intense, piteous agony.

The Squire and Mrs. Todhetley, who had been a few miles off to spend the day, were in the train with Lena. The child did nothing but cry and sob; not with damage, but fright. Mr. Coney also happened to be in it; and Massock, who owned the brickfields. They were not hurt at all, only a little shaken, and (as the Squire put it afterwards,) mortally scared. Massock, an under-bred man, who had grown rich by his brickfields, was more pompous than a lord. The three seized upon the station-master.

"Now then, Watson," cried Mr. Coney, "what was the cause of all this?"

"If there have been any negligence here—and I know there have —you shall be transported for it, Watson, as sure as I'm a living man," roared Massock.

"I'm afraid, gentlemen, that something was wrong with the points," acknowledged Watson, willing to shift the blame from him-self, and too confused to consider policy. "At least that's all I can think."

"With the points!" cried Massock. "Them's Harry Lease's work. Was he on to-night?"

"Lease is here as usual, Mr. Massock. I don't say this lies at his door," added Watson, hastily. "The points might have been out of order; or something else wrong totally different. I should like to know, for my part, what possessed Roberts to bring up his train at such speed."

Darting in and out of the heap of confusion like a mad spirit; now trying by his own effort to lift the broken parts of carriages off some sufferer, now carrying a poor fellow away to safety, but always in the thick of danger; went Harry Lease. Braving the heat and steam as though he felt them not, he flew everywhere, himself and his lantern alike trembling with agitation.

"Come and look here, Harry; I'm afraid he's dead," said a porter, throwing his light upon a man's face. The words arrested Mr. Todhetley, who was searching for Lease to let off a little of his anger. It was Roberts, the driver of the passenger-train, who lay there, his face white and still. Somehow the sight made the Squire still, too. Raising Roberts's head, the men put a drop of brandy between his lips, and he moved. Lease broke into a low glad cry.

"He is not dead! he is not dead!"

The angry reproaches died away on the Squire's tongue: it did not seem quite the time to speak them. By-and-by he came upon Lease again. The man had halted to lean against some palings, feeling unaccountably strange, much as though the world around were closing to him.

"Had you been drinking to-night, Lease?"

The question was put quietly: which was, so to say, a feather in the hot Squire's cap. Lease only shook his head by way of answer. He had a pale, gentle kind of face, with brown eyes that always wore a sad expression. He never drank, and the Squire knew it.

"Then how came you to neglect the points, Lease, and cause this awful accident?"

"I don't know, sir," answered Lease, rousing out of his lethargy, but speaking as one in a dream. "I can't think but what I turned them as usual."

"You knew the train was coming? It was the ordinary train."

"I knew it was coming," assented Lease. "I watched it come along, standing by the side of Mr. Watson. If I had not set the points right, why, I should have thought surely of them then; it stands to reason I should. But never such a thought came into my mind, sir. I waited there, just as if all was right; and I believe I *did* shift the points."

Lease did not put this forth as an excuse: he only spoke aloud the problem that was working in his mind. Having shifted the points regularly for five years, it seemed simply impossible that he could have neglected it now. And yet the man could not *remember* to have done it this evening.

"You can't call it to mind?" said Squire Todhetley, repeating his last words.

"No, I can't, sir: and no wonder, with all this confusion around me and the distress I'm in. I may be able to do so to-morrow."

"Now look you here, Lease," said the Squire, getting just a little cross: "if you had put the points right you couldn't fail to remember it. And what causes your distress, I should like to ask, but the knowledge that you *didn't*, and that all this wreck is owing to you?"

"There is such a thing as doing things mechanically, sir, without the mind being conscious of it."

"Doing things wilfully," roared the Squire. "Do you want to tell me I am a fool to my face?"

"It has often happened, sir, that when I have wound up the mantel-shelf clock at night in our sleeping-room, I'll not know the next minute whether I've wound it or not, and I have to try it again, or else ask the wife," went on Lease, looking straight out into the darkness, as if he could see the clock then. "I can't think but what it must have been just in that way that I put the points right to-night."

Squire Todhetley, in his anger, which was growing hot again, felt that he should like to give Lease a sound shaking. He had no notion of such talk as this.

"I don't know whether you are a knave or a fool, Lease. Killing men and women and children; breaking arms and legs; putting a whole trainful into mortal fright; smashing property and engines to atoms; turning the world, in fact, upside down, so that people don't know whether they stand on their heads or their heels! You may think you can do this with impunity perhaps, but the law will soon teach you better. I should not like to go to bed with human lives on my soul."

The Squire disappeared in a whirlwind. Lease—who seemed to have taken a leaf out of his own theory, and listened mechanically—closed his eyes and put his head back against the palings, like one who has had a shock. He went home when there was nothing more to be done. Not down the highway, but choosing the field-path, where he would not be likely to meet a soul. Crabb Lane, accustomed to put itself into a state of commotion for nothing at all, had got something at last, and was up in arms. All the men employed at the station lived in Crabb Lane. The wife and children of Bowen, the stoker of the passenger-train,—dead—also inhabited a room in that noisy locality. So that when Lease came in view of the place, he saw an excited multitude, though it was then long after ordinary bed-time. Groups stood in the highway; heads, thrust forth at upper windows, were shouting remarks across the street and back again. Keeping on the far side of the hedge, Lease got in by the back-door unseen. His wife was sitting by the fire, trembling and frightened. She started up.

"Oh, Harry! what is the truth of this?"

He did not answer. Not in neglect; Lease was as civil indoors as out, which can't be said of every one; but as if he did not hear. The supper; bread and half a cold red-herring; was on the table. Generally he was hungry enough for supper, but he never glanced at it this evening.

Sitting down, he looked into the fire and remained still, listening perhaps to the outside hubbub. His wife, half dead with fear and apprehension, could keep silence no longer, and asked again.

"I don't know," he answered then. "They say that I never turned the points; I'm trying to remember doing it, Mary. My senses have been scared out of me."

"But *don't* you remember doing it?"

He put his hands to his temples, and his eyes took that far-off, sad look, often seen in eyes when the heart is troubled. With all his might and main, the man was trying to recall the occurrence which would not come to him. A dread conviction began to dawn within him that it never would or could come; and Lease's face grew damp with drops of agony."

"I turned the points for the down goods-train," he said presently; "I remember that. When the goods came in, I know I was in the signal-house. Then I took a message to Hoar; and next I stepped across with some oil for the engine of an up-train that dashed in; they called out that it wanted some. I helped to do it, and took the oil back again. It would be then that I went to put the points right," he added after a pause. "I *hope* I did."

"But, Harry, don't you remember doing it?"

"No, I don't; there's where it is."

"You always put the points straight at once after the train has passed?"

"Not if I'm called off by other work. It ought to be done. A pointsman should stand while the train passes, and then step off to right the points at once. But when you are called off half-a-dozen ways to things crying out to be done, you can't spend time in waiting for the points. We've never had a harder day's work at the station than this has been, Mary; trains in, trains out; the place has hardly been free a minute together. And the extra telegraphing!—half the passengers that stopped seemed to want to send messages. When six o'clock came I was worn out; done up; fit to drop."

Mrs. Lease gave a start. An idea flashed into her mind, causing her to ask mentally whether *she* could have had indirectly a hand in the calamity. For that had been one of the days when her husband had had no tea taken to him. She had been very busy washing, and the baby was sick and cross: that had been quite enough to fill incapable Mrs. Lease's hands, without bothering about her husband's tea. And, of all days in the year, it seemed that he had, on this one, most needed tea. Worn out! done up!

The noise in Crabb Lane was increasing, voices sounded louder, and Mrs. Lease put her hands to her ears. Just then a sudden interruption occurred. Polly, supposed to be safe asleep upstairs, burst into the kitchen in her night-gown, and flew into her father's arms, sobbing and crying.

"Oh, father, is it true?—is it true?"

"Why—Polly!" cried the man, looking at her, in astonishment. "What's this?"

She hid her face on his waistcoat, her hands clinging round him. Polly had awakened and heard the comments outside. She was too nervous and excitable for Crabb Lane.

"They are saying you have killed Kitty Bowen's father. It isn't true, father! Go out and tell them that it isn't true!"

His own nerves were unstrung; his strength had gone out of him; it only needed something of this kind to finish up Lease; and he broke into sobs. Holding the child to him with a tight grasp, they cried together. If Lease had never known agony before in his life, he knew it then.

The days went on. There was no longer any holding-out on Lease's part on the matter of points : all the world said he had been guilty of neglecting to turn them; and he supposed he had. He accepted the fate meekly, without resistance, his manner strangely still, as one who has been utterly subdued. When talked to, he freely avowed that it remained a puzzle to him how he could have forgotten the points, and what made him forget them. He shrank neither from reproach nor abuse; listening patiently to all who chose to attack him, as if he had no longer any right to claim a place in the world.

He was not spared. Coroner and jury, friends and foes, all went on at him, painting his sins in flaring colours, and calling him names to his face. "Murderer" was one of the least of them. Four had died in all ; Roberts was not expected to live ; the rest were getting well. There would have been no trouble over the inquest (held at the Bull, between Crabb Lane and the station), it might have been finished in a day, and Lease committed for trial, but that one of those who had died was a lawyer ; and his brother (also a lawyer) and other of his relatives (likewise lawyers) chose to make a commotion. Mr. Massock helped them. Passengers must be examined ; rails tried ; the points tested ; every conceivable obstacle was put in the way of a conclusion. Fifteen times had the jury to go and look at the spot, and see the working of the points tested. And so the inquest was adjourned from time to time, and might be finished perhaps something under a year.

The public were like so many wolves, all howling at Lease; from the aforesaid relatives and Brickfield Massock, down to the men and women of Crabb Lane. Lease was at home on bail, surrendering himself at every fresh meeting of the inquest. A few wretched malcontents had begun to hiss him as he passed in and out of Crabb Lane.

When we got home for the Christmas holidays, nothing met us but tales of Lease's wickedness, in having sent one train upon the other. The Squire grew hot in talking of it. Tod, given to be contrary, said he should like to have Lease's own version of the affair. A remark that affronted the Squire.

"You can go off and get it from him, sir. Lease won't refuse it; he'd give it to the dickens, for the asking. He likes nothing better than to talk about it."

"After all, it was only a misfortune," said Tod. "It was not wilfully done."

"Not wilfully done!" stuttered the Pater in his rage. "When I, and Lena, and her mother were in the train, and might have been smashed to atoms! When Coney, and Massock (not that I like the fellow), and scores more were put in jeopardy, and some were killed; yes, sir, killed. A misfortune! Johnny, if you stand there grinning like an idiot, I'll send you back to school: you shall both pack off this very hour. A misfortune, indeed! Lease deserves hanging."

The next morning we came upon Lease accidentally in the fields. He was leaning over the gate amongst the trees, as Tod and I crossed the rivulet bridge—which was nothing but a plank or two. A couple of bounds, and we were up with him.

"Now for it, Lease!" cried Tod. "Let us hear a bit about the matter."

How Lease was altered! His cheeks were thin and white, his eyes had nothing but despair in them. Standing up he touched his hat respectfully.

"Ay, sir, it has been a sad time," answered Lease, in a low, patient voice, as if he felt worn out. "I little thought when I last shut you and Master Johnny into the carriage the morning you left, that misfortune was so close at hand." For, just before it happened, we had been at home for a day's holiday.

"Well, tell us about it."

Tod stood with his arm round the trunk of a tree, and I sat down on an opposite stump. Lease had very little to say; nothing, except that he must have forgotten to change the points.

And that made Tod stare. Tod, like the Pater, was hasty by nature. Knowing Lease's good character, he had not supposed him guilty; and to hear the man quietly admit that he *was* excited Tod's ire.

"What do you mean, Lease?"

" Mean, sir ? " returned Lease, meekly.

"Do you mean to say that you did *not* attend to the points ?—
that you just let one train run on to the other ? "

"Yes, sir; that is how it must have been. I didn't believe it,
sir, for a long time afterwards : not for several hours."

"A long time, that," said Tod, an unpleasant sound of mockery
in his tone.

"No, sir; I know it's not much, counting by time," answered
Lease patiently. "But nobody can ever picture how long those
hours seemed to me. They were like years. I couldn't get the idea
into me at all that I had not set the points as usual; it seemed a
thing incredible; but, try as I would, I was unable to call to mind
having done it."

"Well, I must say that is a nice thing to confess to, Lease ! And
there was I, yesterday afternoon, taking your part and quarrelling
with my father."

" I am sorry for that, sir. I am not worth having my part taken
in anything, since that happened."

"But how came you to *do* it ? "

"It's a question I shall never be able to answer, sir. We had a
busy day, were on the run from morning till night, and there was a
great deal of confusion at the station : but it was no worse than
many a day that has gone before it."

"Well, I shall be off," said Tod. "This has shut me up. I
thought of going in for you, Lease, finding every one else was dead
against you. A misfortune is a misfortune, but wilful carelessness
is sin : and my father and his wife and my little sister were in the
train. Come along, Johnny."

"Directly, Tod. I'll catch you up. I say, Lease, how will it
end ? " I asked, as Tod went on.

"It can't end better than two years' imprisonment for me, sir;
and I suppose it may end worse. It is not *that* I think of."

"What else, then ? "

"Four dead already, sir ; four—and one soon to follow them,
making five," he answered, his voice hushed to a whisper. "Master
Johnny, it lies on me always, a dreadful weight never to be got rid
of. When I was young, I had a sort of low fever, and used to see
in my dreams some dreadful task too big to be attempted, and yet I
had to do it; and the weight on my mind was awful. I didn't think,
till now, such a weight could fall in real life. Sleeping or waking,
sir, I see those four before me dead. Squire Todhetley told me
that I had their lives on my soul. And it is so."

I did not know what to answer.

"So you see, sir, I don't think much of the imprisonment; if I
did, I might be wanting to get the suspense over. It's not any

term of imprisonment, no, not though it were for life, that can wash
out the past. I'd give my own life, sir, twice over if that could
undo it."

Lease had his arm on the gate as he spoke, leaning forward. I
could not help feeling sorry for him.

"If people knew how I'm punished within myself, Master Johnny,
they'd perhaps not be so harsh upon me. I have never had a
proper night's rest since it happened, sir. I have to get up and
walk about in the middle of the night because I can't lie. The
sight of the dawn makes me sick, and I say to myself, How shall I
get through the day? When bed-time comes, I wonder how I shall
lie till morning. Often I wish it had pleased God to take me before
that day had happened."

"Why don't they get the inquest over, Lease?"

"There's something or other always brought up to delay it, sir.
I don't see the need of it. If it would bring the dead back to life,
why, they might delay it; but it won't. They might as well let it
end, and sentence me, and have done with it. Each time when I
go back home through Crabb Lane, the men and women call out,
'What, put off again!' 'What, ain't he in gaol yet!' Which is the
place they say I ought to have been in all along."

"I suppose the coroner knows you'll not run away, Lease."

"Everybody knows that, sir."

"Some would, though, in your place."

"I don't know where they'd run to," returned Lease. "They
couldn't run away from their own minds—and that's the worst part
of it. Sometimes I wonder whether I shall ever get it off mine, sir,
or if I shall have it on me, like this, to the end of my life. The
Lord knows what it is to me; nobody else does."

You cannot always make things fit into one another. I was
thinking so as I left Lease and went after Tod. It was awful carelessness not to have set the points; causing death, and sorrow, and
distress to many people. Looking at it from their side, the pointsman was detestable; only fit, as the Squire said, to be hanged.
But looking at it side by side with Lease, seeing his sad face, his
self-reproach, and his patient suffering, it seemed altogether
different; and the two aspects would not by any means fit in
together.

Christmas week, and the absence of a juror who had gone out
visiting, made another excuse for putting off the inquest to the next
week. When that came, the coroner was ill. There seemed to be
no end to the delays, and the public steam was getting up in consequence. As to Lease, he went about like a man who is looking
for something that he has lost and cannot find.

One day, when the ice lay in Crabb Lane, and I was taking the

slides on my way through it to join Tod, who had gone rabbit-
shooting, a little girl ran across my feet, and was knocked down.
I fell too; and the child began to cry. Picking her up, I saw it
was Polly Lease.

"You little stupid! why did you run into my path like that?"

"Please, sir, I didn't see you," she sobbed. "I was running after
father. Mother saw him in the field yonder, and sent me to tell him
we'd got a bit o' fire."

Polly had grazed both her knees; they began to bleed just a little,
and she nearly went into convulsions at sight of the blood. I
carried her in. There was about a handful of fire in the grate. The
mother sat on a low stool, close into it, nursing one of the children,
and the rest sat on the floor.

"I never saw such a child as this in all my life, Mrs. Lease.
Because she has hurt her knees a bit, and sees a drop of blood, she's
going to die of fright. Look here."

Mrs. Lease put the boy down and took Polly, who was trembling
all over with her deep low sobs.

"It was always so, sir," said Mrs. Lease; "always since she was
a baby. She is the timorest-natured child possible. We have tried
everything; coaxing and scolding too; but we can't get her out of
it. If she pricks her finger her face turns white."

"I'd be more of a woman than cry at nothing, if I were you,
Polly," said I, sitting on the window-ledge, while Mrs. Lease washed
the knees; which were hardly damaged at all when they came to be
examined. But Polly only clung to her mother, with her face
hidden, and giving a deep sob now and then.

"Look up, Polly. What's this!"

I put it into her hand as I spoke; a bath bun that I had been
carrying with me, in case I did not get home to luncheon. Polly
looked round, and the sight dried the tears on her swollen face.
You never saw such a change all in a moment, or such eager, glad
little eyes as hers.

"Divide it mother," said she. "Leave a bit for father."

Two of them came flocking round like a couple of young wolves;
the youngest couldn't get up, and the one Mrs. Lease had been
nursing stayed on the floor where she put him. He had a sickly
face, with great bright grey eyes, and hot, red lips.

"What's the matter with him, Mrs. Lease?"

"With little Tom, sir? I think it's a kind of fever. He never
was strong; none of them are: and of course these bad times can
but tell upon us."

"Don't forget father, mother," said Polly. "Leave the biggest
piece for father."

"Now I tell you all what it is," said I to the children, when Mrs.

Lease began to divide it into half-a-dozen pieces, " that. bun's for Polly, because she has hurt herself: you shall not take any of it from her. Give it to Polly, Mrs. Lease."

Of all the uproars ever heard, those little cormorants set up the worst. Mrs. Lease looked at me.

" They must have a bit, sir: they must indeed. Polly wouldn't eat all herself, Master Ludlow; you couldn't get her to do it."

But I was determined Polly should have it. It was through me she got hurt; and besides, I liked her.

" Now just listen, you little pigs. I'll go to Ford's, the baker's, and bring you all a bun a-piece, but Polly must have this one. They have lots of currants in them, those buns, for children that don't squeal. How many are there of you? One, two, three,—— four."

Catching up my cap, I was going out when Mrs. Lease touched me. " Do you really mean it, sir?" she asked in a whisper.

" Mean what? That I am going to bring the buns? Of course I mean it. I'll be back with them directly."

" Oh, sir—but do forgive me for making free to ask such a thing —if you would only let it be a half-quartern loaf instead?"

" A half-quartern loaf!"

" They've not had a bit between their lips this day, Master Ludlow," she said, catching her breath, as her face, which had flushed, turned pale again. " Last night I divided between the four of them a piece of bread half the size of my hand; Tom, he couldn't eat."

I stared for a minute. " How is it, Mrs. Lease? can you not get enough food?"

" I don't know where we should get it from, sir. Lease has not broken his fast since yesterday at midday."

Dame Ford put the loaf in paper for me, wondering what on earth I wanted with it, as I could see by her inquisitive eyes, but not liking to ask; and I carried it back with the four buns. They were little wolves and nothing else when they saw the food.

" How has this come about, Mrs. Lease?" I asked, while they were eating the bread she cut them, and she had taken Tom on her lap again.

" Why, sir, it is eight weeks now, or hard upon it, since my husband earned anything. They didn't even pay him for the last week he was at work, as the accident happened in it. We had nothing in hand; people with only eighteen shillings a week and five children to feed, can't save; and we have been living on our things. But there's nothing left now to make money of—as you may see by the bare room, sir."

" Does not any one help you?"

" Help us!" returned Mrs. Lease. " Why, Master Ludlow

people, for the most part, are so incensed against my husband, that they'd take the bread out of our mouths, instead of putting a bit into them. All their help goes to poor Nancy Bowen and her children : and Lease is glad it should be so. When I carried Tom to Mr. Cole's yesterday, he said that what the child wanted was nourishment."

"This must try Lease."

"Yes," she said, her face flushing again, but speaking very quietly. "Taking one thing with another, I am not sure but it is killing him."

After this break, I did not care to go to the shooting, but turned back to Crabb Cot. Mrs. Todhetley was alone in the bow-windowed parlour, so I told her of the state the Leases were in, and asked if she would not help them.

"I don't know what to say about it, Johnny," she said, after a pause. "If I were willing, you know Mr. Todhetley would not be so. He can't forgive Lease for his carelessness. Every time Lena wakes up from sleep in a fright, fancying it is another accident, his anger returns to him. We often hear her crying out, you know, down here in an evening."

"The carelessness was no fault of Lease's children, that they should suffer for it."

"When you grow older, Johnny, you will find that the consequences of people's faults fall more on others than on themselves. It is very sad the Leases should be in this state ; I am sorry for them."

"Then you'll help them a bit, good mother."

Mrs. Todhetley was always ready to help any one, not needing to be urged ; on the other hand, she liked to yield implicitly to the opinions of the Squire. Between the two, she went into a dilemma.

"Suppose it were Lena, starving for want of food and warmth ?" I said. "Or Hugh sick with fever, as that young Tom is ? Those children have done no more harm than ours."

Mrs. Todhetley put her hand up to her face, and her mild eyes looked nearly as sad as Lease's.

"Will you take it to them yourself, Johnny, in a covered basket, and not let it be seen ? That is, make it your own doing ?"

"Yes."

"Go to the kitchen then, and ask Molly. There are some odds and ends of things in the larder that will not be particularly wanted. You see, Johnny, I do not like to take an active part in this ; it would seem like opposing the Squire." •

Molly was stooping before the big fire, basting the meat, in one of her vile numours, If I wanted to rob the larder, I must do it, she cried; it was my business, not hers; and she dashed the basting spoon across the table by way of accompaniment.

I gave a good look round the larder, and took a raised pork-pie that had a piece cut out of it, and a leg of mutton three parts eaten. On the shelf were a dozen mince-pies, just out of their patty-pans; I took six and left six. Molly, screwing her face round the kitchen-door, caught sight of them as they went into the basket, and rushing after me out of the house, shrieked out for her mince-pies.

The race went on. She was a woman not to be daunted. Just as we turned round by the yellow barn, I first, she raving behind, the Squire pounced upon us, asking what the uproar meant. Molly told her tale. I was a thief, and had gone off with the whole larder, more particularly with her mince-pies.

"Open the basket, Johnny," said the Squire: which was the one Tod and I used when we went fishing.

No sooner was it done than Molly marched off with the pies in triumph. The Pater regarded the pork-pie and the meat with a curious gaze.

"This is for you and Joe, I suppose. I should like to know for how many more."

I was one of the worst to conceal things, when taken-to like this, and he got it all out of me in no time. And then he put his hand on my shoulder and ordered me to say *who* the things were for. Which I had to do.

Well, there was a row. He wanted to know what I meant by being wicked enough to give food to Lease. I said it was for the children. I'm afraid I almost cried, for I did not like him to be angry with me, but I know I promised not to eat any dinner at home for three days if he would let me take the meat. Molly's comments, echoing through the house, betrayed to Mrs. Todhetley what had happened, and she came down the road with a shawl over her head. She told the Squire the truth then: that she had sanctioned it. She said she feared the Leases were quite in extremity, and begged him to let the meat go.

"Be off for ·this once, you young thief," stamped the Squire, "but don't let me catch you, at anything of this sort again."

So the meat went to the Leases, and two loaves that Mrs. Todhetley whispered me to order for them at Ford's. When I reached home with the empty basket, they were going in to dinner. I took a book and stayed in the parlour. In a minute or two the Squire sent to ask what I was doing that for.

"It's all right, Thomas. I don't want any dinner to-day."

Old Thomas went away and returned again, saying the master ordered me to go in. But I wouldn't do anything of the sort. If he forgot the bargain, I did not.

Out came the Squire, his face red, napkin in hand, and laid hold of me by the shoulders.

"You obstinate young Turk! How dare you defy me? Come along."

"But it is not to defy you, sir. It was a bargain, you know; I promised."

"What was a bargain?"

"That I should not have any dinner for three days. Indeed I meant it."

The Squire's answer was to propel me into the dining-room. "Move down, Joe," he said, "I'll have him by me to-day. I'll see whether he is to starve himself out of bravado."

"Why, what's up?" asked Tod, as he went to a lower seat. "What have you been doing, Johnny?"

"Never mind," said the Squire, putting enough mutton on my plate for two. "You eat that, Mr. Johnny?".

It went on so throughout dinner. Mrs. Todhetley gave me a big share of apple pudding; and, when the macaroni came on, the Squire heaped my plate. And I know it was all done to show he was not really angry with me for having taken the things to the Leases.

Mr. Cole, the surgeon, came in after dinner, and was told of my wickedness. Lena ran up to me and said might she send her new sixpence to the poor little children who had no bread to eat.

"What's that Lease about, that he does not go to work?" asked the Squire, in loud tones. "Letting folks hear that his young ones are starving!"

"The man can't work," said Mr. Cole. "He is out on probation, you know, waiting for the verdict, and the sentence on him that is to follow."

"Then why don't they return their verdict and sentence him?" demanded the Squire, in his hot way.

"Ah!" said Mr. Cole, "it's what they ought to have done long ago."

"What will it be! Transportation?"

"I should take care it was *not*, if I were on the jury. The man had too much work on him that day, and had had nothing to eat or drink for too many hours."

"I won't hear a word in his defence," growled the Squire.

When the jury met for the last time, Lease was ill. A day or two before that, some one had brought Lease word that Roberts, who had been lingering all that time in the infirmary at Worcester, was going at last. Upon which Lease started to see him. It was not the day for visitors at the infirmary, but he gained admittance. Roberts was lying in the accident ward, with his head low and a blue look in his face ; and the first thing Lease did, when he began to speak, was to burst out crying. The man's strength had gone down to nothing and his spirit was broken. Roberts made out that he was speaking of his distress at having been the cause of the calamity, and asking to be forgiven.

"Mate," said Roberts, putting out his hand that Lease might take it, "I've never had an ill thought to ye. Mishaps come to all of us that have to do with rail-travelling ; us drivers get more.nor you pointsmen. It might have happened to me to be the cause, just as well as to you. Don't think no more of it."

"Say you forgive me," urged Lease, "or I shall not know how to bear it."

"I forgive thee with my whole heart and soul. I've had a spell of it here, Lease, waiting for death, knowing it must come to me, and I've got to look for it kindly. I don't think I'd go back to the world now if I could. I'm going to a better. It seems just peace, and nothing less. Shake hands, mate."

They shook hands.

"I wish ye'd lift my head a bit," Roberts said, after a while. "The nurse she come and took away my pillow, thinking I might die easier, I suppose : I've seen her do it to others. Maybe I was a'most gone, and the sight of you woke me up again like."

Lease sat down on the bed and put the man's head upon his breast in the position that seemed most easy to him ; and Roberts died there.

It was one of the worst days we had that winter. Lease had a night's walk home of many miles, the sleet and wind beating upon him all the way. He was not well clad either, for his best things had been pawned.

So that when the inquest assembled two days afterwards, Lease did not appear at it. He was in bed with inflammation of the chest, and Mr. Cole told the coroner that it would be dangerous to take him out of it. Some of them called it bronchitis, but the Squire never went in for new names, and never would.

"I tell you what it is, gentlemen," broke in Mr. Cole, when they were quarrelling as to whether there should be another adjournment or not, "you'll put off and put off, until Lease slips through your fingers."

"Oh, will he, though!" blustered old Massock. "He had better try at it! We'd soon fetch him back again."

"You'd be clever to do it," said the doctor.

Any way, whether it was this or not, they thought better of the adjournment, and gave their verdict. 'Manslaughter against

Henry Lease." And the coroner made out his warrant of committal to Worcester county prison : where Lease would lie until the March assizes.

"I am not sure but it ought to have been returned Wilful Murder," remarked the Squire, as he and the doctor turned out of the Bull, and picked their way over the slush towards Crabb Lane.

"It might make no difference, one way or the other," answered Mr. Cole.

"Make no difference! What d'ye mean? Murder and manslaughter are two separate crimes, Cole, and must be punished accordingly. You see, Johnny, what your friend Lease has come to!"

"What I meant, Squire, was this : that I don't much think Lease will live to be tried at all."

"Not live!"

"I fancy not. Unless I am much mistaken, his life will have been claimed by its Giver long before March."

The Squire stopped and looked at Cole. "What's the matter with him? This inflammation—that you went and testified to?"

"That will be the cause of death, as returned to the registrar."

"Why, you speak just as if the man were dying now, Cole!"

"And I think he is. Lease has been very low for a long time," added Mr. Cole; "half clad, and not a quarter fed. But it is not that, Squire : heart and spirit are alike broken : and when this cold caught him, he had no stamina to withstand it; and so it has seized upon a vital part."

"Do you mean to tell me to my face that he will die of it?" cried the Squire, holding on by the middle button of old Cole's great-coat. "Nonsense, man! you must cure him. We—we did not want him to die, you know."

"His life or his death, as it may be, are in the hands of One higher than I, Squire."

"I think I'll go in and see him," said the Squire, meekly.

Lease was lying on a bed close to the floor when we got to the top of the creaky stairs, which had threatened to come down with the Squire's weight and awkwardness. He had dozed off, and little Polly, sitting on the boards, had her head upon his arm. Her starting up awoke Lease. I was not in the habit of seeing dying people; but the thought struck me that Lease must be dying. His pale weary face wore the same hue that Jake's had worn when he was dying : if you have not forgotten him.

"God bless me!" exclaimed the Squire.

Lease looked up with his sad eyes. He supposed they had come to tell him officially about the verdict—which had already reached him unofficially.

"Yes, gentlemen, I know it," he said, trying to get up out of respect, and falling back. "Manslaughter. I'd have been present if I could. Mr. Cole knows I wasn't able. I think God is taking me instead."

"But this won't do, you know, Lease," said the Squire. "We don't want you to die."

"Well, sir, I'm afraid I am not good for much now. And there'd be the imprisonment, and then the sentence, so that I could not work for my wife and children for some long years. When people come to know how I repented of that night's mistake, and that I have died of it, why, they'll perhaps befriend them and forgive me. I think God has forgiven me: He is very merciful."

"I'll send you in some port wine and jelly and beef-tea—and some blankets, Lease," cried the Squire quickly, as if he felt flurried. "And, Lease, poor fellow, I am sorry for having been so angry with you."

"Thank you for all favours, sir, past and present. But for the help from your house my little ones would have starved. God bless you all, and forgive me! Master Johnny, God bless *you*."

"You'll rally yet, Lease; take heart," said the Squire.

"No, sir, I don't think so. The great dark load seems to have been lifted off me, and light to be breaking. Don't sob, Polly! Perhaps father will be able to see you from up there as well as if he stayed here."

The first thing the Squire did when we got out, was to attack Mr. Cole, telling him he ought not to have let Lease die. As he was in a way about it, Cole excused it, quietly saying it was no fault of his.

"I should like to know what it is that has killed him, then?"

"Grief," said Mr. Cole. "The man has died of what we call a broken heart. Hearts don't actually sever, you know, Squire, like a china basin, and there's always some ostensible malady that serves as a reason to talk about. In this case it will be bronchitis. Which, in point of fact, is the final end, because Lease could not rally against it. He told me yesterday that his heart had ached so keenly since November, it seemed to have dried up within him."

"We are all a pack of hard-hearted sinners," groaned the Squire, in his repentance. "Johnny, why could you not have found them out sooner? Where was the use of your doing it at the eleventh hour, sir, I'd like to know?"

Harry Lease died that night. And Crabb Lane, in a fit of repentance as sudden as the Squire's, took the cost of the funeral off the parish (giving some abuse in exchange) and went in a body to the grave. I and Tod followed.

VII.

AUNT DEAN.

TIMBERDALE was a small place on the other side of Crabb Ravine. Its Rector was the Reverend Jacob Lewis. Timberdale called him Parson Lewis when not on ceremony. He had married a widow, Mrs. Tanerton: she had a good deal of money and two boys, and the parish thought the new lady might be above them. But she proved kind and good; and her boys did not ride roughshod over the land or break down the farmers' fences. She died in three or four years, after a long illness.

Timberdale talked about her will, deeming it a foolish one. She left all she possessed to the Rector, "in affectionate confidence," as the will worded it, "knowing he would do what was right and just by her sons." As Parson Lewis was an upright man with a conscience of his own, it was supposed he would do so; but Timberdale considered that for the boys' sake she should have made it sure herself. It was eight-hundred a year, good measure.

Parson Lewis had a sister, Mrs. Dean, a widow also, who lived near Liverpool. She was not left well-off at all; could but just make a living of it. She used to come on long visits to the Parsonage, which saved her cupboard at home; but it was said that Mrs. Lewis did not like her, thinking her deceitful, and they did not get on very well together. Parson Lewis, the meekest man in the world and the most easily led, admitted to his wife that Rebecca had always been a litttle given to scheming, but he thought her true at heart.

When poor Mrs. Lewis was out of the way for good in Timberdale churchyard, Aunt Dean had the field to herself, and came and stayed as long as she pleased, with her child, Alice. She was a little woman with a mild face and fair skin, and had a sort of purring manner with her. Scarcely speaking above her breath, and saying "dear" and "love" at every sentence, and caressing people to their faces, the rule was to fall in love with her at once. The boys, Herbert and Jack, had taken to her without question from the first, and called her "Aunt." Though she was of course no relation whatever to them.

Both the boys made much of Alice—a bright-eyed, pretty little girl with brown curls and timid, winsome ways. Herbert, who was very studious himself, helped her with her lessons: Jack, who was nearer her age, but a few months older, took her out on expeditions, haymaking and blackberrying and the like, and would bring her home with her frock torn and her knees damaged. He told her that brave little girls never cried with him; and the child would ignore the smart of the grazed knees and show herself as brave as a martyr. Jack was so brave and fearless himself and made so little of hurts, that she felt a sort of shame at giving way to her natural timidity when with him. What Alice liked best was to sit indoors by Herbert's side while he was at his lessons, and read story books and fairy tales. Jack was the opposite of all that, and a regular renegade in all kinds of study. He would have liked to pitch the books into the fire, and did not even care for fairy tales. They came often enough to Crabb Cot when we were there, and to our neighbours the Coneys, with whom the Parsonage was intimate. I was only a little fellow at the time, years younger than they were, but I remember I liked Jack better than Herbert. As Tod did also for the matter of that. Herbert was too clever for us, and he was to be a parson besides. He chose the calling himself. More than once he was caught muffled in the parson's white surplice, preaching to Jack and Alice a sermon of his own composition.

Aunt Dean had her plans and her plots. One great plot was always at work. She made it into a dream, and peeped into it night and day, as if it were a kaleidoscope of rich and many colours. Herbert Tanerton was to marry her daughter and succeed to his mother's property as eldest son : Jack must go adrift, and earn his own living. She considered it was already three parts as good as accomplished. To see Herbert and Alice poring over books together side by side and to know that they had the same tastes, was welcome to her as the sight of gold. As to Jack, with his roving propensities, his climbing and his daring, she thought it little matter if he came down a tree head-foremost some day, or pitched head over heels into the depths' of Crabb Ravine, and so threw his life away. Not that she really wished any cruel fate for the boy; but she did not care for him; and he might be terribly in the way, when her foolish brother, the parson, came to apportion the money. And he *was* foolish in some things; soft, in fact: she often said so.

One summer day, when the fruit was ripe and the sun shining, Mr. Lewis had gone into his study to write his next Sunday's sermon. He did not get on very quickly, for Aunt Dean was in there also, and it disturbed him a little. She was of restless habits,

everlastingly dusting books, and putting things in their places without rhyme or reason.

"Do you wish to keep out all *three* of these inkstands, Jacob?
It is not necessary, I should think.   Shall I put one up?"

The parson took his eyes off his sermon to answer.   "I don't
see that they do any harm there, Rebecca.   The children use two
sometimes.   Do as you like, however."

Mrs. Dean put one of the inkstands into the book-case, and then
looked round the room to see what else she could do.   A letter
caught her eye.

"Jacob, I do believe you have never answered the note old
Mullet brought this morning!   There it is on the mantelpiece."

The parson sighed.   To be interrupted in this way he took quite
as a matter of course, but it teased him a little.

"I must see the churchwardens, Rebecca, before answering it.
I want to know, you see, what would be approved of by the
parish."

"Just like you, Jacob," she caressingly said.   "The parish must
approve of what you approve."

"Yes, yes," he said hastily; "but I like to live at peace with
every one."

He dipped his pen into the ink, and wrote a line of his sermon.
The open window looked on to the kitchen-garden.   Herbert Tanerton had his back against the walnut-tree, doing nothing.   Alice
sat near on a stool, her head buried in a book that by its canvas
cover Mrs. Dean knew to be "Robinson Crusoe."   Just then Jack
came out of the raspberry bushes with a handful of fruit, which he
held out to Alice.   "Robinson Crusoe" fell to the ground.

"Oh, Jack, how good they are!" said Alice.   And the words
came distinctly to Aunt Dean's ears in the still day.

"They are as good again when you pick them off the trees for
yourself," cried Jack.   "Come along and get some, Alice."

With the taste of the raspberries in her mouth, the temptation
was not to be resisted ; and she ran after Jack.   Aunt Dean put
her head out at the window.

"Alice, my love, I cannot have you go amongst those raspberry
bushes; you would stain and tear your frock."

"I'll take care of her frock, aunt," Jack called back.

"My darling Jack, it cannot be.   That is her new muslin frock,
and she must not go where she might injure it."

So Alice sat down again to "Robinson Crusoe," and Jack went
his way amongst the raspberry bushes, or whither he would.

"Jacob, have you begun to think of what John is to be?"
resumed Aunt Dean, as she shut down the window.

The parson pushed his sermon from him in a sort of patient

hopelessness, and turned round on his chair. "To be?—In what way, Rebecca?"

"By profession," she answered. "I fancy it is time it was thought of."

"Do you? I'm sure I don't know. The other day when something was being mentioned about it, Jack said he did not care what he was to be, provided he had no books to trouble him."

"I only hope you will not have trouble with him, Jacob, dear," observed Mrs. Dean, in ominous tones, that plainly intimated she thought the parson would.

"He has a good heart, though he is not so studious as his brother. Why have you shut the window, Rebecca? It is very warm."

Mrs. Dean did not say why. Perhaps she wished to guard against the conversation being heard. When any question not quite convenient to answer was put to her, she had a way of passing it over in silence; and the parson was too yielding or too inert to ask again.

"*Of course*, Brother Jacob, you will make Herbert the heir."

The parson looked surprised. "Why should you suppose that, Rebecca? I think the two boys ought to share and share alike."

"My dear Jacob, how *can* you think so? Your dead wife left you in charge, remember."

"That's what I do remember, Rebecca. She never gave me the slightest hint that she should wish any difference to be made: she was as fond of one boy as of the other."

"Jacob, you must do your duty by the boys," returned Mrs. Dean, with affectionate solemnity. "Herbert must be his mother's heir; it is right and proper it should be so: Jack must be trained to earn his own livelihood. Jack—dear fellow!—is, I fear, of a roving, random disposition: were you to leave any portion of the money to him, he would squander it in a year."

"Dear me, I hope not! But as to leaving all to his brother—or even a larger portion than to Jack—I don't know that it would be right. A heavy responsibility lies on me in this charge, don't you see, Rebecca?"

"No doubt it does. It is full eight-hundred a year. And *you* must be putting something by, Jacob."

"Not much. I draw the money yearly, but expenses seem to swallow it up. What with the ponies kept for the boys, and the cost of the masters from Worcester, and a hundred a year out of it that my wife desired the poor old nurse should have till she died, there's not a great deal left. My living is a poor one, you know, and I like to help the poor freely. When the boys go to the university it will be all wanted."

Help the poor freely!—just like him! thought Aunt Dean.

"It would be waste of time and money to send Jack to college. You should try and get him some appointment abroad, Jacob. In India, say."

The clergyman opened his eyes at this, and said he should not like to see Jack go out of his own country. Jack's mother had not had any opinion of foreign places. Jack himself interrupted the conversation. He came flying up the path, put down a cabbage leaf full of raspberries on the window-sill, and flung open the window with his stained fingers.

"Aunt Dean, I've picked these for you," he said, introducing the leaf, his handsome face and good-natured eyes bright and sparkling. "They've never been so good as they are this year. Father, just taste them."

Aunt Dean smiled sweetly, and called him her darling, and Mr. Lewis tasted the raspberries.

"We were just talking of you, Jack," cried the unsophisticated man—and Mrs. Dean slightly knitted her brows. "Your aunt says it is time you began to think of some profession."

"What, yet awhile?" returned Jack.

"That you may be suitably educated for it, my boy."

"I should like to be something that won't want education," cried Jack, leaning his arms on the window-sill, and jumping up and down. "I think I'd rather be a farmer than anything, father."

The parson drew a long face. This had never entered into his calculations.

"I fear that would not do, Jack. I should like you to choose something higher than that; some profession by which you may rise in the world. Herbert will go into the Church: what should you say to the Bar?"

Jack's jumping ceased all at once. "What, be a barrister, father? Like those be-wigged fellows that come on circuit twice a year to Worcester?"

"Like that, Jack."

"But they have to study all their lives for it, father; and read up millions of books before they can pass! I couldn't do it; I couldn't indeed."

"What do you think of being a first-class lawyer, then? I might place you with some good firm, such as——"

"Don't, there's a dear father!" interrupted Jack, all the sunshine leaving his face. "I'm afraid if I were at a desk I should kick it over without knowing it: I must be running out and about.—Are they all gone, Aunt Dean? Give me the leaf, and I'll pick you some more."

The years went on. Jack was fifteen: Herbert eighteen and at Oxford: the advanced scholar had gone to college early. Aunt Dean spent quite half her time at Timberdale, from Easter till autumn, and the parson never rose up against it. She let her house during her absence: it was situated on the banks of the river a little way from Liverpool, near the place they call New Brighton now. It might have been called New Brighton then for all I know. One family always took the house for the summer months, glad to get out of hot Liverpool.

As to Jack, nothing had been decided in regard to his future, for opinions about it differed. A little Latin and a little history and a great deal of geography (for he liked that) had been drilled into him: and there his education ended. But he was the best climber and walker and leaper, and withal the best-hearted young fellow that Timberdale could boast : and he knew about land thoroughly, and possessed a great stock of general and useful and practical information. Many a day when some of the poorer farmers were in a desperate hurry to get in their hay or carry their wheat on account of threatening weather, had Jack Tanerton turned out to help, and toiled as hard and as long as any of the labourers. He was hail-fellow-well-met with everyone, rich and poor.

Mrs. Dean had worked on always to accomplish her ends. Slowly and imperceptibly, but surely ; Herbert must be the heir; John must shift for himself. The parson had had this dinned into him so often now, in her apparently frank and reasoning way, that he began to lend an ear to it. What with his strict sense of justice, and his habit of yielding to his sister's views, he felt for the most part in a kind of dilemma. But Mrs. Dean had come over this time determined to get something settled, one way or the other.

She arrived before Easter this year. The interminable Jack (as she often called him in her heart) was at home ; Herbert was not. Jack and Alice did not seem to miss him, but went out on their rambles together as they did when children. The morning before Herbert was expected, a letter came from him to his stepfather, saying he had 'been invited by a fellow-student to spend the Easter holidays at his home near London and had accepted it.

Mr. Lewis took it as a matter of course in his easy way; but it disagreed with Aunt Dean. She said all manner of things to the parson, and incited him to write for Herbert to return at once. Herbert's answer to this was a courteous intimation that he could not alter his plans ; and he hoped his father, on consideration, would fail to see any good reason why he should do so. Herbert Tanerton had a will of his own.

"Neither do I see any reason, good or bad, why he should not pay the visit, Rebecca," confessed the Rector. "I'm afraid it was foolish of me to object at all. Perhaps I have not the right to deny him, either, if I wished it. He is getting on for nineteen, and I am not his own father."

So Aunt Dean had to make the best and the worst of it; but she felt as cross as two sticks.

: One day when the parson was abroad on parish matters, and the Rectory empty, she went out for a stroll, and reached the high steep bank where the primroses and violets grew. Looking over, she saw Jack and Alice seated below; Jack's arm round her waist.

"You are to be my wife, you know, Alice, when we are grown up. Mind that."

There was no answer, but Aunt Dean certainly thought she heard the sound of a kiss. Peeping over again, she saw Jack taking another.

"And if you don't object to my being a farmer, Alice, I should like it best of all. We'll keep two jolly ponies and ride about together. Won't it be good?"

"I don't object to farming, Jack. Anything you like. A successful farmer's home is a very pleasant one."

Aunt Dean drew away with noiseless steps. She was too calm and callous a woman to turn white; but she did turn angry, and registered a vow in her heart. That presuming, upstart Jack! They were only two little fools, it's true; no better than children; but the nonsense must be stopped in time.

Herbert went back to Oxford without coming home. Alice, to her own infinite astonishment, was despatched to school until mid-summer. The parson and his sister and Jack were left alone; and Aunt Dean, with her soft smooth manner and her false expressions of endearment, ruled all things; her brother's better nature amidst the rest.

Jack was asked what he would be. A farmer, he answered. But Aunt Dean had somehow caught up the most bitter notions possible against farming in general; and Mr. Lewis, not much liking the thing himself, and yielding to the undercurrent ever gently flowing, told Jack he must fix on something else.

"There's nothing I shall do so well at as farming, father," remonstrated Jack. "You can put me for three or four years to some good agriculturist, and I'll be bound at the end of the time I should be fit to manage the largest and best farm in the country. Why, I am a better farmer now than some of them are."

"Jack, my boy, you must not be self-willed. I cannot let you be a farmer."

"Then send me to sea, father, and make a sailor of me," returned Jack, with undisturbed good humour.

But this startled the parson. He liked Jack, and he had a horror of the sea. "Not that, Jack, my boy. Anything but that."

"I'm not sure but I should like the sea better than farming," went on Jack, the idea full in his head. "Aunt Dean lent me 'Peter Simple' one day. I know I should make a first-rate sailor."

"Jack, don't talk so. Your poor mother would not have liked it, and I don't like it; and I shall never let you go."

"Some fellows run away to sea," said Jack, laughing.

The parson felt as though a bucket of cold water had been thrown down his back. Did Jack mean that as a threat?

"John," said he, in as solemn a way as he had ever spoken, "disobedience to parents sometimes brings a curse with it. You must promise me that you will never go to sea."

"I'll not promise that, off-hand," said Jack. "But I will promise never to go without your consent. Think it well over, father; there's no hurry."

It was on the tip of Mr. Lewis's tongue to withdraw his objection to the farming scheme then and there: in comparison with the other it looked quite fair and bright. But he thought he might compromise his judgment to yield thus instantly: and, as easy Jack said, there was no hurry.

So Jack went rushing out of doors again to the uttermost bounds of the parish, and the parson was left to Aunt Dean. When he told her he meant to let Jack be a farmer, she laughed till the tears came into her eyes, and begged him to leave matters to her. *She* knew how to manage boys, without appearing directly to cross them: there was this kind of trouble with most boys, she had observed, before they settled satisfactorily in life, but it all came right in the end.

So the parson said no more about farming: but Jack talked a great deal about the sea. Mr. Lewis went over in his gig to Worcester, and bought a book he had heard of, "Two Years before the Mast." He wrote Jack's name in it and gave it him, hoping its contents might serve to sicken him of the sea.

The next morning the book was missing. Jack looked high and low for it, but it was gone. He had left it on the sitting-room table when he went up to bed, and it mysteriously disappeared during the night. The servants had not seen it, and declared it was not on the table in the morning.

"It could not—I suppose—have been the cat," observed Aunt Dean, in a doubtful manner, her eyes full of wonder as to where the book could have got to. "I have heard of cats doing strange things."

"I don't think the cat would make away with a book of that size, Rebecca," said the parson. And if he had not been the least suspicious parson in all the Worcester Diocese, he might have asked his sister whether *she* had been the cat, and secured the book lest it should dissipate Jack's fancy for the sea.

The next thing she did was to carry Jack off to Liverpool. The parson objected at first: Liverpool was a seaport town, and might put Jack more in mind of the sea than ever. Aunt Dean replied that she meant him to see the worst sides of sea life, the dirty boats in the Mersey, the wretchedness of the crews, and the real discomfort and misery of a sailor's existence. That would cure him, she said: what he had in his head now was the romance picked up from books. The parson thought there was reason in this, and yielded. He was dreadfully anxious about Jack.

She went straight to her house near New Brighton, Jack with her, and a substantial sum in her pocket from the Rector to pay for Jack's keep. The old servant, Peggy, who took care of it, was thunderstruck to see her mistress come in. It was not yet occupied by the Liverpool people, and Mrs. Dean sent them word they could not have it this year: at least not for the present. While she put matters straight, she supplied Jack with all Captain Marryat's novels to read. The house looked on the river, and Jack would watch the fine vessels starting on their long voyages, their white sails trim and fair in the sunshine, or hear the joyous shouts from the sailors of a homeward-bound ship as Liverpool hove in view; and he grew to think there was no sight so pleasant to the eye as these wonderful ships; no fate so desirable as to sail in them.

But Aunt Dean had changed her tactics. Instead of sending Jack on to the dirtiest and worst managed boats in the docks, where the living was hard and the sailors were discontented, she allowed him to roam at will on the finest ships, and make acquaintance with their enthusiastic young officers, especially with those who were going to sea for the first time with just such notions as Jack's. Before Midsummer came, Jack Tanerton had grown to think that he could never be happy on land.

There was a new ship just launched, the *Rose of Delhi;* a magnificent vessel. Jack took rare interest in her. He was for ever on board; was for ever saying to her owners—friends of Aunt Dean's, to whom she had introduced him—how much he should like to sail in her. The owners thought it would be an advantageous thing to get so active, open, and ready a lad into their service, although he was somewhat old for entering, and they offered to article him for four years, as "midshipman" on the *Rose of Delhi.* Jack went home with his tale, his eyes glowing; and Aunt Dean neither checked him nor helped him.

Not *then.* Later, when the ship was all but ready to sail, she told Jack she washed her hands of it, and recommended him to write and ask his stepfather whether he might sail in her, or not.

Now Jack was no letter writer; neither, truth to tell, was the parson. He had not once written home; but had contented himself with sending affectionate messages in Aunt Dean's letters. Consequently, Mr. Lewis only knew what Aunt Dean had chosen to tell him, and had no idea that Jack was getting the real sea fever upon him. But at her suggestion Jack sat down now and wrote a long letter.

Its purport was this. That he was longing and hoping to go to sea; was sure he should never like anything else in the world so well; that the *Rose of Delhi*, Captain Druce, was the most magnificent ship ever launched; that the owners bore the best character in Liverpool for liberality, and Captain Druce for kindness to his middies; and that he hoped, oh he hoped, his father would let him go; but that if he still refused, he (Jack) would do his best to be content to stay on shore, for he did not forget his promise of never sailing without his consent.

"Would you like to see the letter, Aunt Dean, before I close it?" he asked.

Aunt Dean, who had been sitting by, took the letter, and privately thought it was as good a letter and as much to the purpose as the best scribe in the land could have written. She disliked it, for all that.

"Jack, dear, I think you had better put a postscript," she said. "Your father detests writing, as you know. Tell him that if he consents he need not write any answer: you will know what it means—that you may go—and it will save him trouble."

"But, Aunt Dean, I should like him to wish me good-bye and God speed."

"He will be sure to do the one in his heart and the other in his prayers, my boy. Write your postscript."

Jack did as he was bid: he was as docile as his stepfather. Exactly as Mrs. Dean suggested, wrote he: and he added that if no answer arrived within two posts, he should take it for granted that he was to go, and should see about his outfit. There was no time to lose, for the ship would sail in three or four days.

"I will post it for you, Jack," she said, when it was ready. "I am going out."

"Thank you, Aunt Dean, but I can post it myself. I'd rather: and then I shall know it's off. Oh, shan't I be on thorns till the time for an answer comes and goes!"

He snatched his cap and vaulted off with the letter before he

could be stopped. Aunt Dean had a curious look on her face, and
sat biting her lips. She had not intended the letter to go.

The first post that could possibly bring an answer brought one.
Jack was not at home. Aunt Dean had sent him out on an early
commission, watched for the postman, and hastened to the door
herself to receive what he might bring. He brought two letters—
as it chanced. One from the Rector of Timberdale; one from
Alice Dean. Mrs. Dean locked up the one in her private drawer
upstairs: the other she left on the breakfast-table.

"Peggy says the postman has been here, aunt!" cried the boy.
all excitement, as he ran in.

"Yes, dear. He brought a letter from Alice."

"And nothing from Timberdale?"

"Well, I don't know that you could quite expect it by this post,
Jack. Your father might like to take a little time for consideration. You may read Alice's letter, my boy: she comes home this
day week for the summer holidays."

"Not till this day week!" cried Jack, frightfully disappointed.
"Why, I shall have sailed then, if I go, Aunt Dean! I shall not
see her."

"Well, dear, you will see her when you come home again."

Aunt Dean had no more commissions for Jack after that, and
each time the postman was expected, he placed himself outside the
door to wait for him. The man brought no other letter. The
reasonable time for an answer went by, and none came.

"Aunt Dean, I suppose I may get my outfit now," said Jack,
only half satisfied. "But I wish I had told him to write in any
case: just a line."

"According to what you said, you know, Jack, silence must be
taken for consent."

"Yes, I know. I'd rather have had a word, though, and made
certain. I wish there was time for me just to run over to Timberdale and see him!"

"But there's not, Jack, more's the pity: you would lose the ship.
Get a piece of paper and make out a list of the articles the second
mate told you you would want."

The *Rose of Delhi* sailed out of port for Calcutta, and John
Tanerton with her, having signed articles to serve in her for four
years. The night before his departure he wrote a short letter of
farewell to his stepfather, thanking him for his tacit consent, and
promising to do his best to get on, concluding it with love to himself and to Herbert, and to the Rectory servants. Which letter
somehow got put into Aunt Dean's kitchen fire, and never reached
Timberdale.

Aunt Dean watched the *Rose of Delhi* sail by; Jack. in his bran-new uniform, waving his last farewell to her with his gold-banded cap. The sigh of relief she heaved when the fine vessel was out of sight seemed to do her good. Then she bolted herself into her chamber, and opened Mr. Lewis's letter, which had lain untouched till then. As she expected, it contained a positive interdiction, written half sternly, half lovingly, for John to sail in the *Rose of Delhi*, or to think more of the sea. Moreover, it commanded him to come home at once, and it contained a promise that he should be placed to learn the farming without delay. Aunt Dean tripped down to Peggy's fire and burnt that too.

There was a dreadful fuss when Jack's departure became known at Timberdale. It fell upon the parson like a thunderbolt. He came striding through the ravine to Crabb Cot, and actually burst out crying while telling the news to the Squire. He feared he had failed somehow in bringing John up, he said, or he never would have repaid him with this base disobedience and ingratitude. For, you see, the poor man thought Jack had received his letter, and gone off in defiance of it. The Squire agreed with him that Jack deserved the cat-o'-nine tails, as did all other boys who traitorously decamped to sea.

Before the hay was all in, Aunt Dean was back at Timberdale, bringing Alice with her and the bills for the outfit. She let the parson think what he would about Jack, ignoring all knowledge of the letter, and affecting to believe that Jack could not have had it. But the parson argued that Jack must have had it, and did have it, or it would have come back to him. The only one to say a good word for Jack was Alice. She persisted in an opinion that Jack could not be either disobedient or ungrateful, and that there must have been some strange mistake somewhere.

Aunt Dean's work was not all done. She took the poor parson under her wing, and proved to him that he had no resource now but to disinherit Jack, and made Herbert the heir. To leave money to Jack would be wanton waste, she urged, for he would be sure to squander it: better bequeath all to Herbert, who would of course look after his brother in later life, and help him if he needed help. So Mr. Hill, one of the Worcester solicitors, was sent for to Timberdale to receive instructions for making the parson's will in Herbert's favour, and to cut Jack off with a shilling.

That night, after Mr. Hill had gone back again, was one of the worst the parson had ever spent. He was a just man and a kind one, and he felt racked with fear lest he had taken too severe a measure, and one that his late wife, the true owner of the money and John's mother, would never have sanctioned. His bed was fevered, his pillow a torment; up he got, and walked the room in his night-shirt.

"My Lord and God knoweth that I would do what is right," he groaned. "I am sorely troubled. · Youth is vain and desperately thoughtless; perhaps the boy, in his love of adventure, never looked at the step in the light of ingratitude. I cannot cut him quite off; I should never again find peace of mind if I did it. He shall have a little; and perhaps if he grows into a steady fellow and comes back what he ought to be, I may alter the will later and leave them equal inheritors."

The next day the parson wrote privately to Mr. Hill, saying he had reconsidered his determination and would let Jack inherit to the extent of a hundred and fifty pounds a year.

Herbert came home for the long vacation; and he and Alice were together as they had been before that upstart Jack stepped in. They often came to the Squire's and oftener to the Coneys'. Grace Coney, a niece of old Coney, had come to live at the farm; she was a nice girl, and she and Alice liked each other. You might see them with Herbert strolling about the fields any hour in the day. At home Alice and Herbert seemed never to care to separate. Mrs. Dean watched them quietly, and thought how beautifully her plans had worked.

Aunt Dean did not go home till October. After she left, the parson had a stroke of paralysis. Charles Ashton, then just ordained to priest's orders, took the duty. Mrs. Dean came back again for Christmas. As if she would let Alice stay away from the Parsonage when Herbert was at home!

The *Rose of Delhi* did not come back for nearly two years. She was what is called a free ship, and took charters for any place she could make money by. One day Alice Dean was leaning out of the windows of her mother's house, gazing wistfully on the sparkling sea, when a grand and stately vessel came sailing homewards, and some brown-faced young fellow on the quarter deck set on to swing his cap violently by way of hailing her. She looked to the flag which happened to be flying, and read the name there, "The *Rose of Delhi*." It must be Jack who was saluting. Alice burst into tears of emotion.

He came up from the docks the same day. A great, brown, handsome fellow with the old single-hearted, open manners. And he clasped Alice in his arms and kissed her ever so many times before she could get free. Being a grown-up young lady now, she did not approve of unceremonious kissing, and told Jack so. Aunt Dean was not present, or she might have told him so more to the purpose.

Jack had given satisfaction, and was getting on. He told Alice privately that he did not like the sea so much as he anticipated, and could not believe how any other fellow did like it; but as he had chosen it as his calling, he meant to stand by it. He went to Timberdale, in spite of Aunt Dean's advice and efforts to keep him away. Herbert was absent, she said; the Rector ill and childish. Jack found it all too true. Mr. Lewis's mind had failed and his health was breaking. He knew Jack and was very affectionate with him, but seemed not to remember anything of the past. So never a word did Jack hear of his own disobedience, or of any missing letters.

One person alone questioned him; and that was Alice. It was after he got back from Timberdale. She asked him to tell her the history of his sailing in the *Rose of Delhi*, and he gave it in detail, without reserve. When he spoke of the postscript that Aunt Dean had bade him add to his letter, arranging that silence should be taken for consent, and that as no answer had come, he of course had so taken it, the girl turned sick and faint. She saw the treachery that had been at work and where it had lain; but for her mother's sake she hushed it up and let the matter pass. Alice had not lived with her mother so many years without detecting her propensity for deceit.

Some years passed by. Jack got on well. He served as third mate on the *Rose of Delhi* long before he could pass, by law, for second. He was made second mate as soon as he had passed for it. The *Rose of Delhi* came in and went out, and Jack stayed by her, and passed for first mate in course of time. He was not sent back in any of his examinations, as most young sailors are, and the board once went the length of complimenting him on his answers. The fact was, Jack held to his word of doing his best; he got into no mischief and was the smartest sailor afloat. He was in consequence a favourite with the owners, and Captain Druce took pains with him and brought him on in seamanship and navigation, and showed him how to take observations, and all the rest of it. There's no end of difference in merchant-captains in this respect: some teach their junior officers nothing. Jack finally passed triumphantly for master, and hoped his time would come to receive a command. Meanwhile he went out again as first mate on the *Rose of Delhi*.

One spring morning there came news to Mrs. Dean from Timberdale. The Rector had had another stroke and was thought to be near his end. She started off at once, with Alice. Charles Ashton had had a living given to him; and Herbert Tanerton was now his stepfather's curate. Herbert had passed as shiningly in mods and divinity and all the rest of it as Jack had passed before the Marine Board. He was a steady, thoughtful, serious young man, did his duty well in the parish, and preached better sermons than ever the Rector had. Mrs. Dean, who looked upon him as Alice's husband as surely as though they were married, was as proud of his success as though it had been her own.

The Rector was very ill and unable to leave his bed. His intellect was quite gone now. Mrs. Dean sat with him most of the day, leaving Alice to be taken care of by Herbert. They went about together just as always, and were on the best of confidential terms; and came over to the Coneys', and to us when we were at Crabb Cot.

"Herbert," said Mrs. Dean one evening when she had all her soft, sugary manner upon her and was making the young parson believe she had no one's interest at heart in the world but his: "my darling boy, is it not almost time you began to think of marriage? None know the happiness and comfort brought by a good wife, dear, until they experience it."

Herbert looked taken aback. He turned as red as a school-girl, and glanced half-a-moment at Alice, like a detected thief.

"I must wait until I have a living to think of that, Aunt Dean."

"Is it necessary, Herbert? I should have thought you might bring a wife home to the Rectory here."

Herbert turned the subject with a jesting word or two, and got out of his redness. Aunt Dean was eminently satisfied; his confusion and his hasty glance at Alice had told tales; and she knew it was only a question of time.

The Rector died. When the grass was long and the May-flowers were in bloom and the cuckoo was singing in the trees, he passed peacefully to his Rest. Just before death he recovered speech and consciousness; but the chief thing he said was that he left his love to Jack.

After the funeral the will was opened. It had not been touched since that long past year when Jack had gone away to sea. Out of the eight-hundred a year descended from their mother, Jack had a hundred and fifty; Herbert the rest. Aunt Dean made a hideous frown for once in her life; a hundred and fifty pounds a year for Jack, was only, as she looked upon it, so much robbery on Herbert and Alice. Out of the little money saved by the Rector, five hundred pounds were left to his sister, Rebecca Dean; the rest was to be divided equally between Herbert and Jack; and his furniture and effects went to Herbert. On the whole, Aunt Dean was tolerably satisfied.

She was a woman who liked strictly to keep up appearances, and she made a move to leave the young parson at the end of a week or two's time, and go back to Liverpool. Herbert did not detain her. His own course was uncertain until a fresh Rector should be appointed. The living was in the gift of a neighbouring baronet, and it was fancied by some that he might give it to Herbert. One thing did surprise Mrs. Dean; angered her too: that Herbert had not made his offer to Alice before their departure. Now that he had his own fortune at command, there was no necessity to wait for a living.

News greeted them on their arrival. The *Rose of Delhi* was on her way home once more, with John Tanerton in command. Captain Druce had been left behind at Calcutta, dangerously ill. Alice's colour came and went. She looked out for the homeward-bound vessels passing upwards, and felt quite sick with anxiety lest Jack should fail in any way, and never bring home the ship at all.

"The *Rose of Delhi*, Captain Tanerton." Alice Dean cast her eyes on the shipping news in the morning paper, and read the announcement amidst the arrivals. Just for an instant her sight left her.

"Mamma," she presently said, quietly passing over the newspaper, "the *Rose of Delhi* is in."

"The *Rose of Delhi*, Captain Tanerton," read Mrs. Dean. "The idea of their sticking in Jack's name as captain! He will have to go down again as soon as Captain Druce returns. A fine captain I dare say he has made!"

"At least he has brought the ship home safely and quickly," Alice ventured to say. "It must have passed after dark last night."

"Why after dark?"

Alice did not reply—Because I was watching till daylight faded—which would have been the truth. "Had it passed before, some of us might have seen it, mamma."

The day was waning before Jack came up. Captain Tanerton. Jack was never to go back again to his chief-mateship, as Aunt Dean had surmised, for the owners had given him permanent command of the *Rose of Delhi*. The last mail had brought news from Captain Druce that he should never be well enough for the command again, and the owners were only too glad to give it to the younger and more active man. Officers and crew alike reported that never a better master sailed than Jack had proved himself on this homeward voyage.

"Don't you think I have been very lucky on the whole, Aunt Dean? Fancy a young fellow like me getting such a beautiful ship as that!"

"Oh, very lucky," returned Aunt Dean.

Jack looked like a captain too. He was broad and manly, with an intelligent, honest, handsome face, and the quick keen eye of a sailor. Jack was particular in his attire too: and some sailors are not so: he dressed as a gentleman when on shore.

"Only a hundred and fifty left to me!" cried Jack, when he was told the news. "Well, perhaps Herbert may require more than I,

poor fellow," he added in his good nature; "he may not get a good
living, and then he'll be glad of it. I shall be sure to do well now
I've got the ship."

"You'll be at sea always, Jack, and will have no use for money,"
said Mrs. Dean.

"Oh, I don't know about having no use for it, Aunt. Anyway,
my father thought it right to leave it so, and I am content. I wish
I could have said farewell to him before he died!"

A few more days, and Aunt Dean was thrown on her beam-ends
at a worse angle than ever the *Rose of Delhi* hoped to be. Jack
and Alice discussed matters between themselves, and the result was
disclosed to her. They were going to be married.

It was Alice who told her. Jack had just left, and she and her
mother were sitting together in the summer twilight. At first Mrs.
Dean thought Alice was joking: she was like a mad woman
when she found it true. Her great dream had never foreshadowed
this.

"How dare you attempt to think of so monstrous a thing, you
wicked girl? Marry your own brother-in-law!—it would be no
better. It is Herbert that is to be your husband."

Alice shook her head with a smile. "Herbert would not have
me, mamma; nor would I have him. Herbert will marry Grace
Coney."

"Who?" cried Mrs. Dean.

"Grace Coney. They have been in love with each other ever
so many years. I have known it all along. He will marry her as
soon as his future is settled. I had promised to be one of the
bridesmaids, but I suppose I shall not have the chance now."

"Grace Coney—that beggarly girl!" shrieked Mrs. Dean. "But
for her uncle's giving her shelter she must have turned out in the
world when her father died and earned her living how she could.
She is not a lady. She is not Herbert's equal."

"Oh yes, she is, mamma. She is a very nice girl and will make
him a perfect wife. Herbert would not exchange her for the richest
lady in the land."

"If Herbert chooses to make a spectacle of himself, you never
shall!" cried poor Mrs. Dean, all her golden visions fast melting
into air. "I would see that wicked Jack Tanerton at the bottom
of the sea first."

"Mother, dear, listen to me. Jack and I have cared for each
other for years and years, and we should neither of us marry any
one else. There is nothing to wait for; Jack is as well off as he
will be for years to come: and—and we have settled it so, and I
hope you will not oppose it."

It was a cruel moment for Aunt Dean. Her love for other people had been all pretence, but she did love her daughter. Besides that, she was ambitious for her.

"I can never let you marry a sailor, Alice. Anything but that."

"It was you who made Jack a sailor, mother, and there's no help for it," said Alice, in low tones. "I would rather he had been anything else in the world. I should have liked him to have had land and farmed it. We should have done well. Jack had his four hundred a year clear, you know. At least, he ought to have had it. Oh, mother, don't you see that while you have been plotting against Jack you have plotted against me?"

Aunt Dean felt sick with memories that were crowding upon her. The mistake she had made was a frightful one.

"You cannot join your fate to Jack's, Alice," she repeated, wringing her hands. "A sailor's wife is too liable to be made a widow."

"I know it, mother. I shall share his danger, for I am going out in the *Rose of Delhi*. The owners have consented, and Jack is fitting up a lovely little cabin for me that is to be my own saloon."

"My daughter sail over the seas in a merchant ship!" gasped Aunt Dean. "Never!"

"I should be no true wife if I could let my husband sail without me. Mother, it is you alone who have carved out our destiny. Better have left it to God."

In a startled way, her heart full of remorse, she was beginning to see it; and she sat down, half fainting, on a chair.

"It is a miserable prospect, Alice."

"Mother, we shall get on. There's the hundred and fifty a year certain, you know. That we shall put by; and, as long as I sail with him, a good deal more besides. Jack's pay is settled at twenty pounds a month, and he will make more by commission: perhaps as much again. Have no fear for us on that score. Jack has been unjustly deprived of his birthright; and I think sometimes that perhaps as a recompense Heaven will prosper him."

"But the danger, Alice! The danger of a sea-life!"

"Do you know what Jack says about the danger, mother? He says God is over us on the sea as well as on land and will take care of those who put their trust in Him. In the wildest storm I will try to let that great truth help me to feel peace."

Alas for Aunt Dean! Arguments slipped away from her hands just as her plans had slipped from them. In her bitter repentance, she lay on the floor of her room that night and asked God to have pity upon her, for her trouble seemed greater than she could bear.

The morning's post brought news from Herbert. He was made Rector of Timberdale. Aunt Dean wrote back, telling him what had taken place, and asking, nay, almost commanding, that he should restore an equal share of the property to Jack. Herbert replied that he should abide by his stepfather's will. The living of Timberdale was not a rich one, and he wished Grace, his future wife, to be comfortable. "Herbert was always intensely selfish," groaned Aunt Dean. Look on which side she would, there was no comfort.

The *Rose of Delhi*, Captain Tanerton, sailed out of port again, carrying also with her Mrs. Tanerton, the captain's wife. And Aunt Dean was left to bemoan her fate, and wish she had never tried to shape out other people's destinies. Better, as Alice said, that she had left that to God.

VIII.

GOING THROUGH THE TUNNEL.

WE had to make a rush for it. And making a rush did not suit the Squire, any more than it does other people who have come to an age when the body's heavy and the breath nowhere. He reached the train, pushed head-foremost into a carriage, and then remembered the tickets. "Bless my heart?" he exclaimed, as he jumped out again, and nearly upset a lady who had a little dog in her arms, and a mass of fashionable hair on her head, that the Squire, in his hurry, mistook for tow.

"Plenty of time, sir," said a guard who was passing. "Three minutes to spare."

Instead of saying he was obliged to the man for his civility, or relieved to find the tickets might still be had, the Squire snatched out his old watch, and began abusing the railway clocks for being slow. Had Tod been there he would have told him to his face that the watch was fast, braving all retort, for the Squire believed in his watch as he did in himself, and would rather have been told that *he* could go wrong than that the watch could. But there was only me: and I wouldn't have said it for anything.

"Keep two back-seats there, Johnny," said the Squire.

I put my coat on the corner furthest from the door, and the rug on the one next to it, and followed him into the station. When the Squire was late in starting, he was apt to get into the greatest flurry conceivable; and the first thing I saw was himself blocking up the ticket-place, and undoing his pocket-book with nervous fingers. He had some loose gold about him, silver too, but the pocket-book came to his hand first, so he pulled it out. These flurried moments of the Squire's amused Tod beyond everything; he was so cool himself.

"Can you change this?" said the Squire, drawing out one from a roll of five-pound notes.

"No, I can't," was the answer, in the surly tones put on by ticket-clerks.

How the Squire crumpled up the note again, and searched in his breeches pocket for gold, and came away with the two tickets and the change, I'm sure he never knew. A crowd had gathered round, wanting to take their tickets in turn, and knowing that he was keeping them flurried him all the more. He stood at the back a moment, put the roll of notes into his case, fastened it and returned it to the breast of his over-coat, sent the change down into another pocket without counting it, and went out with the tickets in hand. Not to the carriage ; but to stare at the big clock in front.

"Don't you see, Johnny? exactly four minutes and a half difference," he cried, holding out his watch to me. "It is a strange thing they can't keep these railway clocks in order."

"My watch keeps good time, sir, and mine is with the railway. I think it is right."

"Hold your tongue, Johnny. How dare you ! Right? You send your watch to be regulated the first opportunity, sir ; don't *you* get into the habit of being too late or too early."

When we finally went to the carriage there were some people in it, but our seats were left for us. Squire Todhetley sat down by the further door, and settled himself and his coats and his things comfortably, which he had been too flurried to do before. Cool as a cucumber was he, now the bustle was over ; cool as Tod could have been. At the other door, with his face to the engine, sat a dark, gentleman-like man of forty, who had made room for us to pass as we got in. He had a large signet-ring on one hand, and a lavender glove on the other. The other three seats opposite to us were vacant. Next to me sat a little man with a fresh colour and gold spectacles, who was already reading ; and beyond him, in the corner, face to face with the dark man, was a lunatic. That's to mention him politely. Of all the restless, fidgety, worrying, hot-tempered passengers that ever put themselves into a carriage to travel with people in their senses, he was the worst. In fifteen moments he had made as many darts ; now after his hat-box and things above his head ; now calling the guard and the porters to ask senseless questions about his luggage ; now treading on our toes, and trying the corner seat opposite the Squire, and then darting back to his own. He wore a wig of a decided green tinge, the effect of keeping, perhaps, and his skin was dry and shrivelled as an Egyptian mummy's.

A servant, in undress livery, came to the door, and touched his hat, which had a cockade on it, as he spoke to the dark man.

"Your ticket, my lord."

Lords are not travelled with every day, and some of us looked up. The gentleman took the ticket from the man's hand and slipped it into his waistcoat pocket.

"You can get me a newspaper, Wilkins. The *Times*, if it is to be had."

"Yes, my lord."

"Yes, there's room here, ma'am," interrupted the guard, sending the door back for a lady who stood at it. "Make haste, please."

The lady who stepped in was the same the Squire had bolted against. She sat down in the seat opposite me, and looked at every one of us by turns. There was a sort of violet bloom on her face and some soft white powder, seen plain enough through her veil. She took the longest gaze at the dark gentleman, bending a little forward to do it ; for, as he was in a line with her, and also had his head turned from her, her curiosity could only catch a view of his side-face. Mrs. Todhetley might have said she had not put on her company manners. In the midst of this, the man-servant came back again.

"The *Times* is not here yet, my lord. They are expecting the papers in by the next down-train."

"Never mind, then. You can get me one at the next station, Wilkins."

"Very well, my lord."

Wilkins must certainly have had to scramble for his carriage, for we started before he had well left the door. It was not an express-train, and we should have to stop at several stations. Where the Squire and I had been staying does not matter ; it has nothing to do with what I have to tell. It was a long way from our own home, and that's saying enough.

"Would you mind changing seats with me, sir ? "

I looked up, to find the lady's face close to mine ; she had spoken in a half-whisper. The Squire, who carried his old-fashioned notions of politeness with him when he went travelling, at once got up to offer her the corner. But she declined it, saying she was subject to face-ache, and did not care to be next the window. So she took my seat, and I sat down on the one opposite Mr. Todhetley.

"Which of the peers is that?" I heard her ask him in a loud whisper, as the lord put his head out at his window.

"Don't know at all, ma'am," said the Squire. "Don't know many of the peers myself, except those of my own county: Lyttleton, and Beauchamp, and——"

Of all snarling barks, the worst was given that moment in the Squire's face, suddenly ending the list. The little dog, an ugly, hairy, vile-tempered Scotch terrier, had been kept concealed under the lady's jacket, and now struggled itself free. The Squire's look of consternation was good ! He had not known any animal was there.

"Be quiet, Wasp. How dare you bark at the gentleman? He will not bite, sir: he——"

"Who has a dog in the carriage?" shrieked the lunatic, starting up in a passion. "Dogs don't travel with passengers. Here! Guard! Guard!"

To call out for the guard when a train is going at full speed is generally useless. The lunatic had to sit down again; and the lady defied him, so to say, coolly avowing that she had hidden the dog from the guard on purpose, staring him in the face while she said it.

After this there was a lull, and we went speeding along, the lady talking now and again to the Squire. She seemed to want to grow confidential with him; but the Squire did not seem to care for it, though he was quite civil. She held the dog huddled up in her lap, so that nothing but his head peeped out.

"Halloa! How dare they be so negligent? There's no lamp in this carriage."

It was the lunatic again, and we all looked at the lamp. It had no light in it; but that it *had* when we first reached the carriage was certain; for, as the Squire went stumbling in, his head nearly touched the lamp, and I had noticed the flame. It seems the Squire had also.

"They must have put it out while we were getting our tickets," he said.

"I'll know the reason why when we stop," cried the lunatic, fiercely. "After passing the next station, we dash into the long tunnel. The idea of going through it in pitch darkness! It would not be safe."

"Especially with a dog in the carriage," spoke the lord, in a chaffing kind of tone, but with a good-natured smile. "We will have the lamp lighted, however."

As if to reward him for interfering, the dog barked up loudly, and tried to make a spring at him; upon which the lady smothered the animal up, head and all.

Another minute or two, and the train began to slacken speed. It was only an insignificant station, one not likely to be halted at for above a minute. The lunatic twisted his body out of the window, and shouted for the guard long before we were at a standstill.

"Allow me to manage this," said the lord, quietly putting him down. "They know me on the line. Wilkins!"

The man came rushing up at the call. He must have been out already, though we were not quite at a standstill yet.

"Is it for the *Times*, my lord? I am going for it."

"Never mind the *Times*. This lamp is not lighted, Wilkins. See the guard, and *get it done*. At once."

"And ask him what the mischief he means by his carelessness," roared out the lunatic after Wilkins, who went flying off. "Sending us on our road without a light!—and that dangerous tunnel close at hand."

The authority laid upon the words "Get it done," seemed an earnest that the speaker was accustomed to be obeyed, and would be this time. For once the lunatic sat quiet, watching the lamp, and for the light that was to be dropped into it from the top; and so did I, and so did the lady. We were all deceived, however, and the train went puffing on. The lunatic shrieked, the lord put his head out of the carriage and shouted for Wilkins.

No good. Shouting after a train is off never is much good. The lord sat down on his seat again, an angry frown crossing his face, and the lunatic got up and danced with rage.

"I do not know where the blame lies," observed the lord. "Not with my servant, I think: he is attentive, and has been with me some years."

"I'll know where it lies," retorted the lunatic. "I am a director on the line, though I don't often travel on it. This *is* management, this is! A few minutes more and we shall be in the dark tunnel."

"Of course it would have been satisfactory to have a light; but it is not of so much consequence," said the nobleman, wishing to soothe him. "There's no danger in the dark."

"No danger! No danger, sir! I think there is danger. Who's to know that dog won't spring out and bite us? Who's to know there won't be an accident in the tunnel? A light is a protection against having our pockets picked, if it's a protection against nothing else."

"I fancy our pockets are pretty safe to-day," said the lord, glancing round at us with a good-natured smile; as much as to say that none of us looked like thieves. "And I certainly trust we shall get through the tunnel safely."

"And I'll take care the dog does not bite you in the dark," spoke up the lady, pushing her head forward to give the lunatic a nod or two that you'd hardly have matched for defying impudence. "You'll be good, won't you, Wasp? But I should like the lamp lighted myself. You will perhaps be so kind, my lord, as to see that there's no mistake made about it at the next station!"

He slightly raised his hat to her and bowed in answer, but did not speak. The lunatic buttoned up his coat with fingers that were either nervous or angry, and then disturbed the little gentleman next him, who had read his big book throughout the whole commotion without once lifting his eyes, by hunting everywhere for his pocket-handkerchief.

"Here's the tunnel!" he cried out resentfully, as we dashed with a shriek into pitch darkness.

It was all very well for her to say she would take care of the dog, but the first thing the young beast did was to make a spring at me and then at the Squire, barking and yelping frightfully. The Squire pushed it away in a commotion. Though well accustomed to dogs he always fought shy of strange ones. The lady chattered and laughed, and did not seem to try to get hold of him, but we couldn't see, you know; the Squire hissed at him, the dog snarled and growled; altogether there was noise enough to deafen anything but a tunnel.

"Pitch him out at the window," cried the lunatic.

"Pitch yourself out," answered the lady. And whether she propelled the dog, or whether he went of his own accord, the beast sprang to the other end of the carriage, and was seized upon by the nobleman.

"I think, madam, you had better put him under your mantle and keep him there," said he, bringing the dog back to her and speaking quite civilly, but in the same tone of authority he had used to his servant about the lamp. "I have not the slightest objection to dogs myself, but many people have, and it is not altogether pleasant to have them loose in a railway carriage. I beg your pardon; I cannot see; is this your hand?"

It was her hand, I suppose, for the dog was left with her, and he went back to his seat again. When we emerged out of the tunnel into daylight, the lunatic's face was blue.

"Ma'am, if that miserable brute had laid hold of me by so much as the corner of my great-coat tail, I'd have had the law of you. It is perfectly monstrous that any one, putting themselves into a first-class carriage, should attempt to outrage railway laws, and upset the comfort of travellers with impunity. I shall complain to the guard."

"He does not bite, sir; he never bites," she answered softly, as if sorry for the escapade, and wishing to conciliate him. "The poor little bijou is frightened at darkness, and leaped from my arms unawares. There! I'll promise that you shall neither see nor hear him again."

She had tucked the dog so completely out of sight, that no one could have suspected one was there, just as it had been on first entering. The train was drawn up to the next station; when it stopped, the servant came and opened the carriage-door for his master to get out.

"Did you understand me, Wilkins, when I told you to get this lamp lighted?"

"My lord, I'm very sorry; I understood your lordship perfectly, but I couldn't see the guard," answered Wilkins. "I caught sight of him running up to his van-door at the last moment, but the train began to move off, and I had to jump in myself, or else be left behind."

The guard passed as he was explaining this, and the nobleman drew his attention to the lamp, curtly ordering him to "light it instantly." Lifting his hat to us by way of farewell, he disappeared; and the lunatic began upon the guard as if he were commencing a lecture to a deaf audience. The guard seemed not to hear it, so lost was he in astonishment at there being no light.

"Why, what can have douted it?" he cried aloud, staring up at the lamp. And the Squire smiled at the familiar word, so common in our ears at home, and had a great mind to ask the guard where he came from.

"I lighted all these here lamps myself afore we started, and I see 'em all burning," said he. There was no mistaking the home accent now, and the Squire looked down the carriage with a beaming face.

"You are from Worcestershire, my man."

"From Worcester itself, sir. Leastways from St. John's, which is the same thing."

"Whether you are from Worcester; or whether you are from Jericho, I'll let you know that you can't put empty lamps into first-class carriages on this line without being made to answer for it!" roared the lunatic. "What's your name! I am a director."

"My name is Thomas Brooks, sir," replied the man, respectfully touching his cap. "But I declare to you, sir, that I've told the truth in saying the lamps were all right when we started: how this one can have got douted, I can't think. There's not a guard on the line, sir, more particular in seeing to the lamps than I am."

"Well, light it now; don't waste time excusing yourself," growled the lunatic. But he said nothing about the dog; which was surprising.

In a twinkling the lamp was lighted, and we were off again. The lady and her dog were quiet now: he was out of sight: she leaned back to go to sleep. The Squire lodged his head against the curtain, and shut his eyes to do the same; the little man, as before, never looked off his book; and the lunatic frantically shifted himself every two minutes between his own seat and that of the opposite corner. There were no more tunnels, and we went smoothly on to the next station. Five minutes allowed there.

The little man, putting his book in his pocket, took down a black leather bag from above his head, and got out; the lady, her dog hidden still, prepared to follow him, wishing the Squire and me, and even the lunatic, with a forgiving smile, a polite good morning. I had moved to that end, and was watching the lady's wonderful back hair as she stepped out, when all in a moment the Squire sprang up with a shout, and jumping out nearly upon her, called out that he had been robbed. She dropped the dog, and I thought he must have caught the lunatic's disorder and become frantic.

It is of no use attempting to describe exactly what followed. The lady, snatching up her dog, shrieked out that perhaps she had been robbed too; she laid hold of the Squire's arm, and went with him into the station-master's room. And there we were: us three, and the guard, and the station-master, and the lunatic, who had come pouncing out too at the Squire's cry. The man in spectacles had disappeared for good.

The Squire's pocket-book was gone. He gave his name and address at once to the station-master: and the guard's face lighted with intelligence when he heard it, for he knew Squire Todhetley by reputation. The pocket-book had been safe just before we entered the tunnel; the Squire was certain of that, having felt it. He had sat in the carriage with his coat unbuttoned, rather thrown back; and nothing could have been easier than for a clever thief to draw it out, under cover of the darkness.

"I had fifty pounds in it," he said; "fifty pounds in five-pound notes. And some memoranda besides."

"Fifty pounds!" cried the lady, quickly. "And you could travel with all that about you, and not button up your coat! You ought to be rich!"

"Have you been in the habit of meeting thieves, madam, when travelling?" suddenly demanded the lunatic, turning upon her without warning, his coat whirling about on all sides with the rapidity of his movements.

"No, sir, I have not," she answered, in indignant tones. "Have you?"

"I have not, madam. But, then, you perceive I see no risk in travelling with a coat unbuttoned, although it may have bank-notes in the pockets."

She made no reply: was too much occupied in turning out her own pockets and purse, to ascertain that they had not been rifled. Re-assured on the point, she sat down on a low box against the wall, nursing her dog; which had begun its snarling again.

"It must have been taken from me in the dark as we went through the tunnel," affirmed the Squire to the room in general and perhaps the station-master in particular. "I am a magistrate, and have some experience in these things. I sat completely off my guard, a prey for anybody, my hands stretched out before me, grappling with that dog, that seemed—why, goodness me! yes he *did*, now I think of it—that seemed to be held about fifteen inches off my nose on purpose to attack me. That's when the thing must have been done. But now—which of them could it have been?"

He meant which of the passengers. As he looked hard at us in rotation, especially at the guard and station-master, who had not been in the carriage, the lady gave a shriek, and threw the dog into the middle of the room.

"I see it all," she said, faintly. "He has a habit of snatching at things with his mouth. He must have snatched the case out of your pocket, sir, and dropped it from the window. You will find it in the tunnel."

"Who has?" asked the lunatic, while the Squire stared in wonder.

"My poor little Wasp. Ah, villain! beast! it is he that has done all this mischief."

"He might have taken the pocket-book," I said, thinking it time to speak, "but he could not have dropped it out, for I put the window up as we went into the tunnel."

It seemed a nonplus for her, and her face fell again. "There was the other window," she said in a minute. "He might have dropped it there. I heard his bark quite close to it."

"*I* pulled up that window, madam," said the lunatic. "If the dog did take it out of the pocket it may be in the carriage now."

The guard rushed out to search it; the Squire followed, but the station-master remained where he was, and closed the door after them. A thought came over me that he was stopping to keep the two passengers in view.

No; the pocket-book could not be found in the carriage. As they came back, the Squire was asking the guard if he knew who the nobleman was who had got out at the last station with his servant. But the guard did not know.

"He said they knew him on the line."

"Very likely, sir. I have not been on this line above a month or two."

"Well, this is an unpleasant affair," said the lunatic impatiently; "and the question is—What's to be done? It appears pretty evident that your pocket-book was taken in the carriage, sir. Of the four passengers, I suppose the one who left us at the last station must be held exempt from suspicion, being a nobleman. Another got out here, and has disappeared; the other two are present. I propose that we should both be searched."

"I'm sure I am quite willing," said the lady, and she got up at once.

I think the Squire was about to disclaim any wish so to act; but the lunatic was resolute, and the station-master agreed with him. There was no time to be lost, for the train was ready to start again, her time being up, and the lunatic was turned out. The lady went into another room with two women, called by the station-master, and *she* was turned out. Neither of them had the pocket-book.

"Here's my card, sir," said the lunatic, handing one to Mr. Todhetley. "You know my name, I dare say. If I can be of any future assistance to you in this matter, you may command me."

"Bless my heart!" cried the Squire, as he read the name on the card. "How could you allow yourself to be searched, sir?"

"Because, in such a case as this, I think it only right and fair that every one who has the misfortune to be mixed up in it *should* be searched," replied the lunatic, as they went out together. "It is a satisfaction to both parties. Unless you offered to search me, you could not have offered to search that woman; and I suspected her."

"Suspected *her!*" cried the Squire, opening his eyes.

"If I didn't suspect, I doubted. Why on earth did she cause her dog to make all that row the moment we got into the tunnel? It must have been done then. I should not be startled out of my senses if I heard that that silent man by my side and hers was in league with her."

The Squire stood in a kind of amazement, trying to recall what he could of the little man in spectacles, and see if things would fit into one another.

"Don't you like her look?" he asked suddenly.

"No, I *don't,*" said the lunatic, turning himself about. "I have a prejudice against painted women: they put me in mind of Jezebel. Look at her hair. It's awful."

He went out in a whirlwind, and took his seat in the carriage, not a moment before it puffed off.

"*Is* he a lunatic?" I whispered to the Squire.

"He a lunatic!" he roared. "You must be a lunatic for asking it, Johnny. Why, that's—that's——"

Instead of saying any more, he showed me the card, and the name nearly took my breath away. He is a well-known London man, of science, talent, and position, and of world-wide fame.

"Well, I thought him nothing better than an escaped maniac."

"*Did* you?" said the Squire. "Perhaps he returned the compliment on you, sir. But now—Johnny, who has got my pocket-book?"

As if it was any use asking me? As we turned back to the station-master's room, the lady came into it, evidently resenting the search, although she had seemed to acquiesce in it so readily.

"They were rude, those women. It is the first time I ever had the misfortune to travel with men who carry pocket-books to lose them, and I hope it will be the last," she pursued, in scornful passion, meant for the Squire. "One generally meets with *gentle-men* in a first-class carriage."

The emphasis came out with a shriek, and it told on him. Now that she was proved innocent, he was as vexed as she for having listened to the advice of the scientific man—but I can't help calling him a lunatic still. The Squire's apologies might have disarmed a cross-grained hyena; and she came round with a smile.

"If any one *has* got the pocket-book," she said, as she stroked her dog's ears, "it must be that silent man with the gold spectacles. There was no one else, sir, who could have reached you without getting up to do it. And I declare on my honour, that when that commotion first arose through my poor little dog, I felt for a moment something like a man's arm stretched across me. It could only have been his. I hope you have the numbers of the notes."

"But I have not," said the Squire.

The room was being invaded by this time. Two stray passengers, a friend of the station-master's, and the porter who took the tickets, had crept in. All thought the lady's opinion must be correct, and said the spectacled man had got clear off with the pocket-book. There was no one else to pitch upon. A nobleman travelling with his servant would not be likely to commit a robbery; the lunatic was really the man his card represented him to be, for the station-master's friend had seen and recognized him; and the lady was proved innocent by search. Wasn't the Squire in a passion!

"That close reading of his was all a blind," he said, in sudden conviction. "He kept his face down that we should not know him in future. He never looked at one of us! he never said a word! I shall go and find him."

Away went the Squire, as fast as he could hurry, but came back in a moment to know which was the way out, and where it led to. There was quite a small crowd of us by this time. Some fields lay beyond the station at the back; and a boy affirmed that he had seen a little gentleman in spectacles, with a black bag in his hand, making over the first stile.

"Now look here, boy," said the Squire. "If you catch that same man, I'll give you five shillings."

Tod could not have flown faster than the boy did. He took the stile at a leap; and the Squire tumbled over it after him. Some boys and men joined in the chase; and a cow, grazing in the field, trotted after us and brought up the rear.

Such a shout from the boy. It came from behind the opposite hedge of the long field. I was over the gate first; the Squire came next.

On the hedge of the dry ditch sat the passenger, his legs dangling, his neck imprisoned in the boy's arms. I knew him at once. His hat and gold spectacles had fallen off in the scuffle; the black bag was wide open, and had a tall bunch of something green sticking up from it; some tools lay on the ground.

"Oh, you wicked hypocrite!" spluttered the Squire, not in the least knowing what he said in his passion. "Are you not ashamed to have played upon me such a vile trick? How dare you go about to commit robberies!"

"I have not robbed you, at any rate," said the man, his voice trembling a little and his face pale, while the boy loosed the neck but pinioned one of the arms.

"Not robbed me!" cried the Squire. "Good Heavens! Who do you suppose you have robbed, if not me? Here, Johnny, lad, you are a witness. He says he has not robbed me."

"I did not know it was yours," said the man meekly. "Loose me, boy; I'll not attempt to run away."

"Halloa! here! what's to do?" roared a big fellow, swinging himself over the gate. "Any tramp been trespassing?—anybody wanting to be took up? I'm the parish constable."

If he had said he was the parish engine, ready to let loose buckets of water on the offender, he could not have been more welcome. The Squire's face was rosy with satisfaction.

"Have you your handcuffs with you, my man?"

"I've not got them, sir; but I fancy I'm big enough and strong enough to take *him* without 'em. Something to spare, too."

"There's nothing like handcuffs for safety," said the Squire, rather damped, for he believed in them as one of the country's institutions. "Oh, you villain! Perhaps you can tie him with cords?"

The thief floundered out of the ditch and stood upon his feet. He did not look an ungentlemanly thief, now you came to see and hear him; and his face, though scared, might have been thought an honest one. He picked up his hat and glasses, and held them in his hand while he spoke, in tones of earnest remonstrance.

"Surely, sir, you would not have me taken up for this slight offence! I did not know I was doing wrong, and I doubt if the law would condemn me; I thought it was public property!"

"Public property!" cried the Squire, turning red at the words. "Of all the impudent brazen-faced rascals that are cheating the gallows, you must be the worst. My bank-notes public property!"

"Your what, sir?"

"My bank-notes, you villain. How dare you repeat your inso-lent questions?"

"But I don't know anything about your bank-notes, sir," said the man meekly. "I do not know what you mean."

They stood facing each other, a sight for a picture; the Squire with his hands under his coat, dancing a little in rage, his face crimson; the other quite still, holding his hat and gold spectacles, and looking at him in wonder.

"You don't know what I mean! When you confessed with your last breath that you had robbed me of my pocket-book!"

"I confessed—I have not sought to conceal—that I have robbed the ground of this rare fern," said the man, handling carefully the green stuff in the black bag. "I have not robbed you or any one of anything else."

The tone, simple, quiet, self-contained, threw the Squire in amaze-ment. He stood staring.

"Are you a fool?" he asked. "What do you suppose I have to do with your rubbishing ferns?"

"Nay, I supposed you owned them; that is, owned the land. You led me to believe so, in saying I had robbed you."

"What I've lost is a pocket-book, with ten five-pound bank-notes in it; I lost it in the train; it must have been taken as we came through the tunnel; and you sat next but one to me," reiterated the Squire.

The man put on his hat and glasses. "I am a geologist and botanist, sir. I came here after this plant to-day—having seen it yesterday, but then I had not my tools with me. I don't know anything about the pocket-book and bank-notes."

So that was another mistake, for the botanist turned out of his pockets a heap of letters directed to him, and a big book he had been reading in the train, a treatise on botany, to prove who he was. And, as if to leave no loophole for doubt, one stepped up who knew him, and assured the Squire there was not a more learned man in his line, no, nor one more respected, in the three kingdoms. The Squire shook him by the hand in apologizing, and told him we had some valuable ferns near Dyke Manor, if he would come and see them.

Like Patience on a monument, when we got back, sat the lady, waiting to see the prisoner brought in. Her face would have made a picture too, when she heard the upshot, and saw the hot Squire and the gold spectacles walking side by side in friendly talk.

"I think still he must have got it," she said, sharply.

"No, madam, answered the Squire. "Whoever may have taken it, it was not he."

"Then there's only one man, and that is he whom you have let go on in the train," she returned decisively. "I thought his fidgety movements were not put on for nothing. He had secured the pocket-book somewhere, and then made a show of offering to be searched. Ah, ha!"

And the Squire veered round again at this suggestion, and began to suspect he had been doubly cheated. First, out of his money, next out of his suspicions. One only thing in the whole bother seemed clear; and that was, that the notes and case had gone for good. As, in point of fact, they had.

———————

We were on the chain-pier at Brighton, Tod and I. It was about eight or nine months after. I had put my arms on the rails at the end, looking at a pleasure-party sailing by. Tod, next to me, was bewailing his ill-fortune in not possessing a yacht and opportunities of cruising in it.

"I tell you No. I don't want to be made sea-sick."

The words came from some one behind us. It seemed almost as though they were spoken in reference to Tod's wish for a yacht. But it was not *that* that made me turn round sharply; it was the sound of the voice, for I thought I recognized it.

Yes: there she was. The lady who had been with us in the carriage that day. The dog was not with her now, but her hair was more amazing than ever. She did not see me. As I turned, she turned, and began to walk slowly back, arm-in-arm with a gentleman. And to see him—that is, to see them together—made me open my eyes. For it was the lord who had travelled with us.

"Look, Tod!" I said, and told him in a word who they were.

"What the deuce do they know of each other?" cried Tod with a frown, for he felt angry every time the thing was referred to. Not for the loss of the money, but for what he called the stupidity of us all; saying always had *he* been there, he should have detected the thief at once.

I sauntered after them: why I wanted to learn which of the lords he was, I can't tell, for lords are numerous enough, but I had had a curiosity upon the point ever since. They encountered some people and were standing to speak to them; three ladies, and a fellow in a black glazed hat with a piece of green ribbon round it.

"I was trying to induce my wife to take a sail," the lord was saying, "but she won't. She is not a very good sailor, unless the sea has its best behaviour on."

"Will you go to-morrow, Mrs. Mowbray?" asked the man in the glazed hat, who spoke and looked like a gentleman. "I will promise you perfect calmness. I am weather-wise, and can assure you this little wind will have gone down before night, leaving us without a breath of air."

" I will go : on condition that your assurance proves correct."

" All right. You of course will come, Mowbray ? "

The lord nodded. " Very happy."

" When do you leave Brighton, Mr. Mowbray ? " asked one of the ladies.

" I don't know exactly. Not for some days."

" A muff as usual, Johnny," whispered Tod. " That man is no lord : he is a Mr. Mowbray."

" But, Tod, he *is* the lord. It is the one who travelled with us ; there's no mistake about that. Lords can't put off their titles as parsons can : do you suppose his servant would have called him ' my lord,' if he had not been one ? "

" At least there is no mistake that these people are calling him Mr. Mowbray now."

That was true. It was equally true that they were calling her Mrs. Mowbray. My ears had been as quick as Tod's, and I don't deny I was puzzled. They turned to come up the pier again with the people, and the lady saw me standing there with Tod. Saw me looking at her, too, and I think she did not relish it, for she took a step backward as one startled, and then stared me full in the face, as if asking who I might be. I lifted my hat.

There was no response. In another moment she and her husband were walking quickly down the pier together, and the other party went on to the end quietly. A man in a tweed suit and brown hat drawn low over his eyes, was standing with his arms folded, looking after the two with a queer smile upon his face. Tod marked it and spoke.

" Do you happen to know that gentleman ? "

" Yes, I do," was the answer.

" Is he a peer ? "

" On occasion."

" On occasion ! " repeated Tod. " I have a reason for asking," he added ; " do not think me impertinent."

" Been swindled out of anything ? " asked the man, coolly.

" My father was, some months ago. He lost a pocket-book with fifty pounds in it in a railway carriage. Those people were both in it, but not then acquainted with each other."

" Oh, weren't they ! " said the man.

" No, they were not," I put in, " for I was there. He was a lord then."

" Ah," said the man, " and had a servant in livery no doubt, who came up my-lording him unnecessarily every other minute.

He is a member of the swell-mob; one of the cleverest of the *gentleman* fraternity, and the one who acts as servant is another of them."

"And the lady?" I asked.

"She is a third. They have been working in concert for two or three years now; and will give us trouble yet before their career is stopped. But for being singularly clever, we should have had them long ago. And so they did not know each other in the train! I dare say not!"

The man spoke with quiet authority. He was a detective come down from London to Brighton that morning; whether for a private trip, or on business, he did not say. I related to him what had passed in the train.

"Ay," said he, after listening. "They contrived to put the lamp out before starting. The lady took the pocket-book during the commotion she caused the dog to make, and the lord received it from her hand when he gave her back the dog. Cleverly done! He had it about him, young sir, when he got out at the next station. *She* waited to be searched, and to throw the scent off. Very ingenious . but they'll be a litttle too much so some fine day."

"Can't you take them up?" demanded Tod.

"No."

"I will accuse them of it," he haughtily said. "If I meet them again on this pier——"

"Which you won't do to-day," interrupted the man.

"I heard them say they were not going for some days."

"Ah, but they have seen you now. And I think—I'm not quite sure—that he saw me. They'll be off by the next train."

"Who are *they?*" asked Tod, pointing to the end of the pier.

"Unsuspecting people whose acquaintance they have casually made here. Yes, an hour or two will see Brighton quit of the pair."

And it was so. A train was starting within an hour, and Tod and I galloped to the station. There they were: in a first-class carriage: not apparently knowing each other, I verily believe, for he sat at one door and she at the other, passengers dividing them.

"Lambs between two wolves," remarked Tod. "I have a great mind to warn the people of the sort of company they are in. Would it be actionable, Johnny?"

The train moved off as he was speaking. And may I never write another word, if I did not catch sight of the man-servant and his cockade in the next carriage behind them!

IX.

DICK MITCHEL.

I DID not relate this story by my own wish. To my mind there's nothing very much in it to relate. At the time it was written the newspapers were squabbling about farmers' boys and field labour and political economy. "And," said a gentleman to me, "as you were at the top and tail of the thing when it happened, and are well up in the subject generally, Johnny Ludlow, you may as well make a paper of it." That was no other than the surgeon, Duffham.

About two miles from Dyke Manor across the fields, but in the opposite direction to that of the Court where the Sterlings lived, Elm Farm was situated. Mr. Jacobson lived in it, as his father had lived before him. The property was not their own; they rented it : it was fine land, and Jacobson had the reputation of being the best farmer for miles round. Being a wealthy man, he had no need to spare money on house or land, and did not spare it. He and the Squire were about the same age, and had been cronies all their lives.

Not to go into extraneous matter, I may as well say at once that one of the labourers on Jacobson's farm was a man named John Mitchel. He lived in a cottage not far from us—a poor place consisting of two rooms and a wash-house ; they call it back'us there—and had to walk nearly two miles to his work of a morning. Mitchel was a steady man of thirty-five, with a round head and not any great amount of brains inside it. Not but what he had as much brains as many labourers have, and quite enough for the sort of work his life was passed in. There were six children ; the eldest, Dick, ten years old ; and most of them had straw-coloured hair, the pattern of their father's.

Just before the turn of harvest one hot summer, John Mitchel presented himself at Mr. Jacobson's house in a clean smock frock, and asked a favour. It was, that his boy, Dick, should be taken on as ploughboy. Old Jacobson objected, saying the boy was too young and little. Little he might be, Mitchel answered, but not

too young—warn't he ten? The lad had been about the farm for
some time as scarecrow: that is, employed to keep the birds away:
and had a shilling a week for it. Old Jacobson stood to what he
said, however, and little Dick did not get his promotion.

But old Jacobson got no peace. Every opportunity Mitchel could
get, or dare to use, he began again, praying that Dick might be
tried. The boy was "cute," he said; strong enough also, though
little; and if the master liked to pay him only fourpence a day,
they'd be grateful for it; 'twould be a help, and was wanted badly.
All of no use: old Jacobson still said No.

One afternoon during this time, we started to go to the Jacobsons'
after a one-o'clock dinner,—I and Mrs. Todhetley. She was fond
of going over to an early tea there, but not by herself, for part of
the way across the fields was lonely. Considering that she had
been used to the country, she was a regular coward as to lonely
walks, expecting to see tramps or robbers at every corner. In passing the row of cottages in Duck Lane, for we took that road, we
saw Hannah Mitchel leaning over the footboard of her door to look
after her children, who were playing near the pond in the sunshine
with a lot more; quite a heap of the little reptiles, all badly clad
and as dirty as pigs. Other labourers' dwellings stood within hail,
and the children seemed to spring up in the place thicker than
wheat; Mrs. Mitchel's was quite a small family, reckoning by comparison, but how the six were clothed and fed was a mystery, out of
Mitchel's wages of ten shillings a week. It was thought good pay.
Old Jacobson was liberal, as farmers go. He paid the best wages;
gave all his labourers a stunning big portion of home-fed pork at
Christmas, with fuel to cook it: and his wife was good to the women
when they fell sick.

Mrs. Todhetley stopped to speak. "Is it you, Hannah Mitchel?
Are you pretty well?"

Hannah Mitchel stood upright and dropped a curtsey. She had
a bundle in her arms, which proved to be the baby, then not much
above a fortnight old.

"Dear me! it's very early for it to be about," said Mrs. Todhetley, touching its little red cheeks. "And for you too."

"It is, ma'am; but what's to be done?" was the answer. "When
there's only one pair of hands for everything, one can't afford to lie
by long."

"You seem but poorly," said Mrs. Todhetley, looking at her.
She was a thin, dark-haired woman, with a sensible face. Before
she married Mitchel, she had lived as under-nurse in a gentleman's
family, where she picked up some idea of good manners.

"I be feeling a bit stronger, thank you," said the woman.
"Strength don't come back to one in a day, ma'am."

The Mitchel children were sidling up, attracted by the sight of the lady. Four young grubs in tattered garments.

"I can't keep 'em decent," said the mother, with a sigh of apology. "I've not got no soap nor no clothes to do it with. They come on so fast, and make such a many, one after another, that it's getting a hard pull to live anyhow."

Looking at the children; remembering that, with the father and mother, there were eight mouths to feed, and that the man's wages were the ten shillings a week all the year round (but there were seasons when he did over-work and earned more), Mrs. Todhetley might well give her assenting answer with an emphatic nod.

"We was hoping to get on a bit better, resumed the wife; "but Mitchel he says the master don't seem to like to listen. A'most a three weeks it be now since Mitchel first asked it him."

"In what way better?"

"By putting little Dick to the plough, ma'am. He gets a shilling a week now, he'd got two then, perhaps three, and 'twould be such a help to us. Some o' the farmers gives fourpence halfpenny a day to a ploughboy, some as much as sixpence. The master he bain't one of the near ones; but Dick be little of his age, he don't grow fast, and Mitchel telled the master he'd take fourpence a day and be thankful for't."

Thoughts were crowding into Mrs. Todhetley's mind--as she mentioned afterwards. A child of ten ought to be learning and playing; not working from twelve to fourteen hours a day.

"It would be a hard life for him."

"True, ma'am, at first; but he'd get used to it. I could have wished the summer was coming on instead o the winter—'twould be easier for him to begin upon. Winter mornings be so dark and cold."

"Why not let him wait until the next winter's over?"

The very suggestion brought tears into Hannah Mitchel's eyes. "You'd never say it, ma'am, if you knew how bad his wages is wanted and the help they'd be. The older children grows, the more they wants to eat; and we've got six of 'em now. What would you, ma'am?—they don't bring food into the world with 'em; they must help to earn it for themselves as quick as anybody can be got to hire 'em. Sometimes I wonder why God should send such large families to us poor people."

Mrs. Todhetley was turning to go on her way, when the woman in a timid voice said: "Might she make bold to ask, if she or Squire Todhetley would say a good word to Mr. Jacobson about the boy: that it would be just a merciful kindness."

"We should not like to interfere," replied Mrs. Todhetley. "In

any case I could not do it with a good heart : I think it would be so
hard upon the poor little boy."

"Starving's harder, ma'am."

The tears came running down her cheeks with the answer ; and
they won over Mrs. Todhetley.

Crossing the high, crooked, awkward stile—over which, in coming
the other way, if people were not careful they generally pitched
head first into Duck Lane—we found ourselves in what was called
the square paddock, a huge piece of land, ploughed last year.
The wheat had been carried from it only this afternoon, and the
gleaners in their cotton bonnets were coming in.   On, from thence,
across other fields and stiles; we went a little out of our way to
call at Glebe Cottage—a small white house that lay back amidst
the fields—and inquire after old Mrs. Parry, who had just had a
stroke.

Who should be at Elm Farm, when we got in, but the surgeon,
Duffham : come on there from paying his daily visit to Mrs. Parry.
He and old Jacobson were in the green-house, looking at the grapes :
a famous crop they had that year ; not ripe yet. Mrs. Jacobson sat
at the open window of the long parlour, making a new jelly-bag.
She was a pleasant-faced old lady, with small flat silver curls and
a net cap.

Of course they got talking about little Dick Mitchel. Duffham
knew the boy ; seeing that when a doctor was wanted at the Mitchels',
it was he who attended.   Mrs. Todhetley told exactly what had
passed : and old Jacobson—a tall, portly man, with a healthy colour
—grew nearly purple in the face, disputing.

Dick Mitchel would be of as good as no use for the team, he said,
and the carters put shamefully upon those young ones.   In another
year the boy would be stronger and bigger. Perhaps he would take
him then.

"For my part, I cannot think how the mothers can like their poor
boys to go out so young," cried the old lady, looking up from her
flannel bag.   "A ploughboy's life is very hard in winter."

"Hannah Mitchel says it has to be one of two things—early
work or starving," said Mrs. Todhetley.   "And that's pretty true."

"Labourers' boys are born to it, ma'am, and so it comes easy to
'em : as skinning does to eels," cried Duffham quaintly.

"Poor things, yes.   But it is very hard upon the children.   The
worst is, all the labourers seem to have no end of them.   Hannah
Mitchel has just said she sometimes wonders why God should send
so many to poor people."

This was an unfortunate remark. To hear the two gentlemen
laugh, you'd have thought they were at a Christmas pantomime.
Old Jacobson brought himself up in a kind of passion.

What business, in the name of all that was imprudent, had these poor people to have their troops of children, he asked. They knew quite well they could not feed them; that the young ones would be three-parts starved in their earlier years, and in their later ones come to the parish and be a burden on the community. Look at this same man, Mitchel. His grandfather, a poor miserable labourer, had a troop of children; Mitchel's father had a troop, twelve; *he*, Mitchel, had six, and seemed to be going on fair for six more. There was no reason in it. Why couldn't they be content with a moderate number, three or four, that might have a chance of finding room in the world? It was not much less than a crime for these men, next door to paupers themselves, to launch their tens and their dozens of boys and girls into life, and then turn round and say, Why does God send them? Nice kind of logic, that was!

And so he kept on, for a good half-hour, Duffham helping him. *He* brought up the French peasantry: saying our folks ought to take a lesson from them. You don't see whole flocks of children over there, cried Duffham. One, or two, or at most three, would be found to comprise the number of a family. And why? Because the French were a prudent race. They knew there was no provision for superfluous children; no house-room at home, or food, or clothing; and no parish pay to fall back upon: they knew that however many children they had they must provide for them: they didn't set up, of themselves, a regiment of little famishing mouths, and then charge it on Heaven; they were not so reckless and wicked. Yes, he must repeat it, wicked; and the two ladies listening would endorse the word if they knew half the deprivation and the sufferings these poor small mortals were born to; he saw enough of it, having to be often amongst them.

"Why don't you tell the parents this, doctor?"

Tell them! returned Duffham. He *had* told them; told them till his tongue was tired of talking.

Any way, the little things were grievously to be pitied, was what the two ladies answered.

" I have often wished it was not a sin to drown the superfluous little mites as we do kittens," wound up Duff.

One of the ladies dropped the jelly-bag, the other shrieked out, Oh!

"For their sakes," he added. " It's true, upon my word of honour. Of all wrongs the world sees, never was there a worse wrong than the one inflicted on these inoffensive children by the parents, in bringing them into it. God help the little wretches! man can't do much."

And so they talked on. The upshot was, that old Jacobson

stood to his word, and declined to make Dick Mitchel a ploughboy yet awhile.

We had tea at four o'clock—at which fashionable people may laugh; considering that it was real tea, not the sham one lately come into custom. Mrs. Todhetley wanted to get home by daylight, and the summer evenings were shortening. Never was brown bread-and-butter so sweet as the Jacobsons': we used to say it every time we went; and the home-baked rusks were better than Shrewsbury cake. They made Mrs. Todhetley put two or three in her bag for Hugh and Lena.

Old Duff went with us across the first field, turning off there to take the short-cut to his home. It was a warm, still, lovely evening, the moon rising. The gleaners were busy in the square paddock: Mrs. Todhetley spoke to some as we passed. At the other end, near the crooked stile, two urchins stood fighting, the bigger one trying to take a small armful of wheat from the other. I went to the rescue, and the marauder made off as fast as his small bare feet would carry him.

"He haven't gleaned, hisself, and wants to take mine," said the little one, casting up his big grey eyes to us appealingly through the tears. He was a delicate-looking pale-faced boy of nine, or so, with light hair.

"Very naughty of him," said Mrs. Todhetley. "What's your name?"

"It's Dick, lady."

"Dick—what?"

"Dick Mitchel."

"Dear me—I thought I had seen the face before," said Mrs. Todhetley to me. "But there are so many boys about here, Johnny; and they all look pretty much alike. How old are you, Dick?"

"I'm over ten," answered Dick, with an emphasis on the over. Children catch up ideas, and no doubt he was as eager as the parents could be to impress on the world his fitness to be a ploughboy.

"How is it that you have been gleaning, Dick?"

"Mother couldn't, 'cause o' the babby. They give me leave to come on since four o'clock: and I've got all this."

Dick looked at the stile and then at his bundle of wheat, so I took it while he got over. As we went on down the lane, Mrs. Todhetley inquired whether he wanted to be a ploughboy. Oh yes! he answered, his face lighting up, as if the situation offered some glorious prospect. It 'ud be two shilling a week; happen more; and mother said as he and Totty and Sam and the t'others 'ud get treacle to their bread on Sundays then. Apparently Mrs. Mitchel knew how to diplomatize.

"I'll give him one of the rusks, I think, Johnny," whispered Mrs. Todhetley.

But while she was taking it from the bag, he ran in with his wheat. She called to him to come back, and gave him one. His mother had taken the wheat from him, and looked out at the door with it in her hands. Seeing her, Mrs. Todhetley went up, and said Mr. Jacobson would not at present do anything. The next minute Mitchel appeared pulling at his straw hair.

"It is hard lines," he said, humbly, "when the lad's of a' age to be earning, and the master can't be got to take him on. And me to ha' worked on the same farm, man and boy; and father afore me."

"Mr. Jacobson thinks the boy would not be strong enough for the work."

"Not strong enough, and him rising eleven!" exclaimed Mitchel, as if the words were some dreadful aspersion on Dick. "How can he be strong if he gets no work to make him strong, ma'am? Strength comes with the working—and nobody don't oughtn't to know that better nor the master. Anyhow, if he *don't* take him, it'll be cruel hard lines for us."

Dick was outside, dividing the rusk with a small girl and boy, all three seated in the lane, and looking as happy over the rusk as if they had been children in a fairy tale. "It's Totty," said he, pausing in the work of division to speak, "and that 'un's Sam." Mrs. Todhetley could not resist the temptation of finding two more rusks, which made one apiece.

"He is a good-natured little fellow, Johnny," she remarked, as we went along. "Intelligent, too: in that he takes after his mother."

"Would it be wrong to let him go on the farm as ploughboy?"

"Johnny, I don't know. I'd rather not give an opinion," she added, looking right before her into the moon, as if seeking for one there. "Of course he is not old enough or big enough, practically speaking; but on the other hand, where there are so many mouths to feed, it seems hard not to let him earn money if he can earn it. The root of the evil lies in there being so many mouths—as was said at Mr. Jacobson's this afternoon."

It was winter before I heard anything more of the matter. Tod and I got home for Christmas. One day in January, when the skies were lowering, and the air was cold and raw, but not frosty, I was crossing a field on old Jacobson's land then being ploughed. The three brown horses at the work were as fine as you'd wish to see.

"You'll catch it smart on that there skull o' yourn, if ye doan't keep their yeads straight, ye young divil."

The salutation was from the man at the tail of the plough to the boy at the head of the first horse. Looking round, I saw little Mitchel. The horses stopped, and I went up to him. Hall, the ploughman, took the opportunity to beat his arms. I dare say they were cold enough.

"So your ambition is attained, is it, Dick? Are you satisfied?"

Dick seemed not to understand. He was taller, but the face looked pinched, and there was never a smile on it.

"Do you like being a ploughboy?"

"It's hard and cold. Hard always; frightful cold of a morning."

"How's Totty?"

The face lighted up just a little. Totty weren't any better, but she didn't die; Jimmy did. Which was Jimmy?—Oh, Jimmy was after Nanny, next to the babby.

"What did Jimmy die of?"

Whooping cough. They'd all been bad but him—Dick. Mother said he'd had it when he was no older nor the babby.

Whether the whooping-cough had caused an undue absorption of Mitchel's means, certain it was, Dick looked famished. His cheeks were thin, his hands blue.

"Have you been ill, Dick?"

No, he had not been ill. 'Twas Jimmy and the t'others.

"He's the incapablest little villain I ever had put me to do with," struck in the ploughman. "More lazy nor a fattened pig."

"Are you lazy, Dick?"

I think an eager disclaimer was coming out, but the boy remembered in time who was present—his master, the ploughman.

"Not lazy wilful," he said, bursting into tears. "I does my best: mother tells me to."

"Take that, you young sniveller," said Hall, dealing him a good sound slap on the left cheek. "And now go on: ye know ye've got this lot to go through to-day."

He took hold of the plough, and Dick stretched up his poor trembling hands to the first horse to guide him. I am sure the boy *was* trying to do his best; but he looked weak and famished and ill.

"Why did you strike him, Hall? He did nothing to deserve it."

"He don't deserve nothing else," was Hall's answer. "Let him alone, and the furrows 'ud be as crooked as a dog's leg. You dun' know what these young 'uns be for work, sir.—Keep 'em in the line, you fool!"

Looking back as I went down the field, I watched the plough

going slowly up it, Dick seeming to have his hands full with the well-fed horses.

"Yes, I heard the lad was taken on, Johnny," Mrs. Todhetley said when I told her that evening. "Mitchel prevailed with his master at last. Mr. Jacobson is good-hearted, and knew the Mitchels were in sore need of the extra money the boy would earn. Sickness makes a difference to the poor as well as to the rich."

I saw Dick Mitchel three or four times during that January. The Jacobsons had two nephews staying with them from Oxfordshire, and it caused us to go over often. The boy seemed a weak little mite for the place; but of course, having undertaken the work, he had to do it. He was no worse off than others. To be at the farm before six o'clock, he had to leave home at half-past five, taking his breakfast with him, which was chiefly dry bread. As to the boy's work, it varied—as those acquainted with the executive of a busy farm can tell you. Besides the ploughing, he had to pump, and carry water and straw, and help with the horses, and go errands to the blacksmith's and elsewhere, and so on. Carters and ploughmen do not spare their boys; and on a large farm like this they are the immediate rulers, not the master himself. Had Dick been under Mr. Jacobson's personal eye, perhaps it might have been lightened a little, for he was a humane man. There were three things that made it seem particularly hard for Dick Mitchel, and those three were under no one's control; his natural weakliness, his living so far from the farm, and its being winter weather. In summer the work is nothing like as hard for the boys; and it was a great pity that Dick had not first entered on his duties in that season to get inured to them before the winter. Mr. Jacobson gave him the best wages—three shillings a week. Looking at the addition it must have seemed to Mitchel's ten, it was little wonder he had not ceased to petition old Jacobson.

The Jacobsons were kind to the boy—as I can affirm. One cold day when I was over there with the nephews, shooting birds, we went into the best kitchen at twelve o'clock for some pea-soup. They were going to carry the basins into the parlour, but we said we'd rather eat it there by the big blazing fire. Mrs. Jacobson came in. I can see her now, with a soft white woollen kerchief thrown over her shoulders to keep out the cold, and her net cap above her silver curls. We were getting our second basinfuls.

"Do have some, aunt," said Fred. "It's the best you ever tasted."

"No, thank you, Fred. I don't care to spoil my dinner."

"It won't spoil ours."

She laughed a little, and stood looking from the window into

the fold-yard, saying presently that she feared the frost was going
to set in now in earnest, which would not be pleasant for their
journey.—For this was the last day of the nephews' stay, and she
was going home with them for a week. There had been no very
severe cold all the winter; which was a shame because of the
skating; if the ponds had a thin coating of ice on them one day, it
would all melt the next.

"Bless me! there's that poor child sitting out in the cold! What
is he eating?—his dinner?"

Her words made us look from the window. Dick Mitchel had
put himself down by the distant pig-sty, and seemed to be eating
something that he held in his hands. He was very white—as might
be seen even from where we stood.

"Mary," said she to one of the servants, "go and call that boy
in."

Little Mitchel came in; pinched and blue. His clothes were
thin, not half warm enough for the weather; an old red woollen
comforter was twisted round his neck. He took off his battered
drab hat, and put his bread into it.

"Is that your dinner?" asked Mrs. Jacobson.

"Yes 'm," said Dick, pulling the forelock of his light hair.

"But why did you not go home to-day?"

"Mother said there was nothing but bread for dinner to-day, and
she give it me to bring away with my breakfast."

"Well, why did you sit out in the cold? You might have gone
indoors somewhere to eat it."

"I were tired, 'm," was all Dick answered.

To look at him, one would say the "tired" state was chronic.
He was shivering slightly with the cold; his teeth chattered. Mrs.
Jacobson took his hand, and put him to sit on a low wooden stool
close to the fire, and gave him a basin of pea-soup.

"Let him have more if he can eat it," she said to Mary when she
went away. So the boy for once was well warmed and fed.

Now, it may be thought that Mrs. Jacobson, being a kind old
lady, might have told him to come in for some soup every cold day.
And perhaps her will was good to do it. But it would never have
answered. There were boys on the farm besides Dick, and no
favour could be shown to one more than to another. No, nor to
the boys more than to the men. Nor to the men on this farm more
than to the men on that. Old Jacobson would have had his brother
farmers pulling his ears. Those of you who are acquainted with
the subject will know all this.

And there's another thing I had better say. In telling of Dick
Mitchel, it will naturally sound like an exceptional or isolated case,
because those who read have their attention directed to this one

and not to others. But, in actual fact, Dick's was only one of a great many; the Jacobsons had employed ploughboys and other boys always; lots of them; some strong and some weak, just as the boys might happen to be. For a young boy to be out with the plough in the cold winter weather, seems nothing to a farmer and a farmer's men: it lies in the common course of events. He has to get through as he best can; he must work to eat; and as a compensating balance there comes the warmth and the easy work of summer. Dick Mitchel was only one of the race; the carter and ploughman, his masters, had begun life exactly as he had, had gone through the same ordeal, the hardships of a long winter's day and the frost and snow. Dick Mitchel was as capable of his duties as many another had been. Dick's father had been little and weakly in his boyhood, but he got over that and grew as strong as the rest of them. Dick might have got over it, too, but for some extraordinary weather that set in.

Mrs. Jacobson had been in Oxfordshire a week when old Jacobson started to fetch her home, intending to stay there two or three days. The weather since she left had been going on in the same stupid way; a thin coating of snow to be seen one day, the green of the fields the next. But on the morning after old Jacobson started, the frost set in with a vengeance, and we got our skates out. Another day came in, and the Squire declared he had never felt anything to equal the cold. We had not had it as sharp for years: and then, you see, he was too fat to skate. The best skating was on a pond on old Jacobson's land, which they called the lake from its size.

It was on this second day that I came across Dick Mitchel. Hastening home from the lake after dark—for we had skated till we couldn't see and then kept on by moonlight—the skates in my hand and all aglow with heat, who should be sitting by the bank on this side the crooked stile instead of getting over it, but little Mitchel. But for the moon shining right on his face, I might have passed without seeing him.

"You are taking it airily, young Dick. Got the gout?"

Dick just lifted his head and stared a little; but didn't speak.

"Come! Why don't you go home?"

"I'm tired," murmured Dick. "I'm cold."

"Get up. I'll help you over the stile."

He did as he was bid at once. We had got well on down the lane, and I had my hand on his shoulder to steady him, for his legs seemed to slip about like Punch's in the show, when he turned suddenly back again.

"The harness."

"The what?" I said.

Something seemed the matter with the boy: it was just as if he had partly lost the power of speech, or had been struck stupid. I made out at last that he had left some harness on the ground, which he was ordered to take to the blacksmith's.

"I'll get over for it, Dick. You stop where you are."

It was lying where he had been sitting; a short strap with a broken buckle. Dick took it and we went on again.

"Were you asleep, just now, Dick?"

"No, sir. It were the moon."

"What was the moon?"

"I were looking into it. Mother says God's all above there: I thought happen I might see Him."

A long explanation for Dick to-night. The recovery of the strap seemed to have brightened up his intellect.

"You'll never see Him in this world, Dick. He sees you always."

"And that's what mother says. He sees I can't do more nor my arms'll let me. I'd not like Him to think I can."

"All right, Dick. You only do your best always: He won't fail to see it."

I had hardly said the last words when down went Dick without warning, face foremost. Picking him up, I took a look into his eyes by the moonlight.

"What did you do that for, Dick?"

"I don't know."

"Is it your legs?"

"Yes, it's my legs. I didn't mean it. I didn't mean it when I fell under the horses to-day, but Hall he beated of me and said I did."

After that I did not loose him; or I'm sure he would have gone down again. Arrived at his cottage, he was for passing it.

"Don't you know your own door, Dick Mitchel?"

"It's the strap," he said. "I ha' got to take it to Cawson's."

"Oh, I'll step round with that. Let's see what there is to do."

He seemed unwilling, saying he must take it back to Hall in the morning. Very well, I said, so he could. We went in at his door; and at first I thought I must have got into a black fog. The room was a narrow, poking place; but I couldn't see across it. Two children were coughing, one choking, one crying. Mrs. Mitchel's face, ornamented with blacks, gradually loomed out to view through the atmosphere.

"It be the chimbley, sir. I hope you'll please to excuse it. It don't smoke as bad as this except when the weather's cold beyond common."

" It's to be hoped it doesn't. I should call it rather miserable if it did."

" Yes, sir. Mitchel, he says he thinks the chimbley must have frozed."

" Look here, Mrs. Mitchel, I've brought Dick home : I found him sitting in the cold on the other side of the stile, and my belief is, he thought he could not get over it. He is about as weak as a young rat."

" It's the frost, sir," she said. " The boys all feel it that has to be out and about. It'll soon be gone, Dick. This here biting cold don't never last long."

Dick was standing against her, bending his face on her old stuff gown. She put her arm about him kindly.

" No, it can't last long, Mrs. Mitchel. Could he not be kept in-doors until it gives a bit—let him have a holiday? No? Wouldn't it do?"

She opened her eyes wide at this. Such a thing as keeping a ploughboy at home for a holiday, had never entered her imagination.

" Why, Master Ludlow, sir, he'd lose his place!"

" But, suppose he were ill, and had to stay at home?"

" Then the Lord help us, if it came to that! Please, sir, his wages might be stopped.' I've heard of a master paying in illness, though it's not many of 'em as would, but I've never knowed 'em pay for holidays. The biting cold will go soon, Dick," she added, looking at him; " don't be downhearted."

" I should give him a cup of hot tea, Mrs. Mitchel, and let him go to bed. Good night; I'm off."

I should have liked to say beer instead of tea; it would have put a bit of strength into the boy; but I might just as well have suggested wine, for all they had of either. Leaving the strap at the blacksmith's —it was but a minute or two out of my road—I told him to send it up to Mitchel's as soon as it was done.

" I dare say!" was what I got in answer.

" Look here, Cawson : the lad's ill, and his father was not in the way. If you don't choose to let your boy run up with that, or take it yourself, you shall never have another job of work from the Squire if I can prevent it."

" I'll send it, sir," said Cawson, coming to his senses. Not that he had much from us : we chiefly patronized Dovey, down in Piefinch Cut.

Now, all this happened : as Duffham and others could testify if necessary; it is not put in to make up a story. But I never thought worse of Dick than that he was done over for the moment with the cold.

Of all days in remembrance, the next was the worst. The cold was more intense—though that had seemed impossible ; and a fierce wind was blowing that cut you in two. It kept us from skating— and that's saying a good deal. We got half-way to the lake, and couldn't stand it, so turned home again. Jacobson's team was out, braving the weather : we saw it at a distance.

"What a fool that waggoner must be to bring out the team to-day!" cried Tod. "He can't do any good on this hard ground. He must be doing it for bravado. It is a sign his master's not at home."

In the afternoon, when a good hot meal had put warmth into us, we thought we'd be off again ; and this time gained the pond. The wind was like a knife : I never skated in anything like it before : but we kept on till dusk.

Going homewards, in passing Glebe Cottage, which lay away on the left, we caught sight of three or four people standing before it.

"What's to do there?" asked Tod of a man, expecting to hear that old Mrs. Parry had had a second stroke.

"Sum'at's wrong wi' Jacobson's ploughboy," was the answer. "He has just been took in there."

"Jacobson's ploughboy! Why, Tod, that must be Dick Mitchel."

"And what if it is!" returned Tod, starting off again. "The youngster's half frozen, I dare say. Let us get home. Johnny. What are you stopping for?"

By saying "half frozen" he meant nothing. Not a thought of real ill was in his mind. I went across to the house ; and met Hall the ploughman coming out of it.

"Is Dick Mitchel ill, Hall?"

"He ought to be, sir ; if he bain't shamming," returned Hall, crustily. "He have fell down five times since noon, and the last time wouldn't get up upon his feet again nohow. Being close a-nigh the old lady's I carried of him in."

Hall went back to the house with me. I don't think he much liked the boy's looks. Dick had been put to lie on the warm brick floor before the kitchen fire, a blanket on his legs, and his head on a cushion. Mrs. Parry was ill in bed upstairs. The servant looked a stupid young country girl, seemingly born without wits.

"Have you given him anything?" I asked her.

"Please, sir, I've put the kettle on to bile."

"Is there any brandy in the house?"

"*Brandy!*" the girl exclaimed with wonder. No. Her missis never took anything stronger nor tea and water gruel.

"Hall," I said, looking at the man, "some one must go for Mr. Duffham. And Dick's mother might as well be told "

Bill Leet, a strapping young fellow standing by, made off at this, saying he'd bring them both. Hall went away to his team, and I stooped over the boy.

"What is the matter, Dick? Tell me how you feel. "

Except that Dick smiled a little, he made no answer. His eyes, gazing up into mine, looked dim. The girl had taken away the candle, but the fire was bright. As I took one of his hands to rub it, his fingers clasped themselves round mine. Then he began to say something, with a pause between each word. I had to bend close to catch it.

"He—brought—that—there—strap."

"All right, Dick."

"Thank—ee—sir."

"Are you in any pain, Dick?"

"No."

"Or cold?"

"No."

The girl came back with a candle and some hot milk in a tea-cup. I put a teaspoonful into Dick's mouth. But he could not swallow it. Who should come rushing in then but old Jones the constable, wanting to know what was up.

"Well I never!—why, that's Mitchel's Dick!" cried Jones, peering down in the candle-light. "What's took *him?*"

"Jones, if you and the girl will rub his hands, I'll go and get some brandy. We can't let him lie like this and give him nothing."

Old Jones, liking the word brandy on his own score, knelt down on his fat gouty legs with a groan, and laid hold of one of the hands, the girl taking the other. I went leaping off to Elm Farm.

And went for nothing. Mr. and Mrs. Jacobson being out, the cellar was locked up, and no brandy could be got at. The cook gave me a bottle of gooseberry wine; which she said might do as well if hotted up.

Duffham was stooping over the boy when I got back, his face long, and his cane lying on the ironing-board. Bill Leet had met him half-way, so no time was lost. He was putting something into Dick's lips with a teaspoon—perhaps brandy. But it ran the wrong way; out instead of in. Dick never stirred, and his eyes were shut. The doctor got up.

"Too late, Johnny," he whispered.

The words startled me. "Mr. Duffham! No?"

He looked into my eyes, and nodded YES. "The exposure to-day has been too much for him. He is going fast."

And just at that moment Hannah Mitchel came in. I have often thought that the extreme poor, whose lives are but one vast

hardship from the cradle to the grave, who have to struggle always,
do not feel strong emotion. At any rate, they don't show much.
Hannah Mitchel knelt down, and looked quietly at the white,
shrunken face.

"Dicky," she said, putting his hair gently back from his brow;
which now had a damp moisture on it. "What's amiss, Dicky?"

He opened his eyes at the voice and feebly lifted one hand
towards her. Mrs. Mitchel glanced round at the doctor's face;
and I think she read the truth there. She gathered his poor head
into her arms, and let it rest on her bosom. Her old black shawl
was on, her bonnet fell backwards and hung from her neck by the
strings.

"Oh, Dicky! Dicky!"

He lay still, looking at her. She gave one sob and choked the
rest down.

"Be he dying, sir?—ain't there no hope?" she cried to Mr.
Duffham, who was standing in the blaze of the fire. And the
doctor just moved his head for answer.

There was a still hush in the kitchen. Her tears began to fall
down her cheeks slowly and softly.

"Dicky, wouldn't you like to say 'Our Father'?"

"I—'ve—said—it,—mother."

"You've always been a good boy, Dicky."

Old Jones blew his nose; the stupid girl burst into a sob. Mr.
Duffham told them to hush.

Dick's eyes were slowly closing. The breath was very faint now,
and came at long intervals. Presently Mr. Duffham took him
from his mother, and laid him down flat, without the cushion.

Well, he died. Poor little Dick Mitchel died. And I think,
taking the wind and the work into consideration, that he was
better off.

Mr. Jacobson got back the next day. He sharply taxed the
ploughman with the death, saying he ought to have seen the state
the boy was in on that last bitter day, and have sent him home.
But Hall declared he never thought anything ailed the boy, except
that the cold was cutting him more than ordinary, just as it was
cutting everybody else.

The county coroner came over to hold the inquest. The jury,
after hearing what Mr. Duffham had to say, brought it in that
Richard Mitchel died from exposure to the cold during the recent
remarkable severity of the weather, not having sufficient stamina
to resist it. Some of the local newspapers took it up, being in
want of matter that dreary season. They attacked the farmers;
asking the public whether labourers' children were to be held as
of no more value than this, in a free and generous country like

England, and why they were made to work so young by such hard and wicked task-masters as the master of Elm Farm. That put the master of Elm Farm on his mettle. He retorted by a letter of sharp good sense; finishing it with a demand to know whether the farmers were expected to club together to provide meat and puddings gratis for the flocks of children that labourers chose to gather about them. The Squire read it aloud to every one, as the soundest letter he'd ever seen written.

"I am afraid their view is the right one—that the children are too thick on the ground, poor things," sighed Mrs. Todhetley. "Any way, Johnny, it is very hard on the young ones to have to work as poor little Dick did: late and early, wet or dry: and I am glad for his sake that God has taken him."

X

A HUNT BY MOONLIGHT.

THIS is another tale of our school life. It is not much in itself, you may say, but it was to lead to lasting events. Curious enough, it is, to sit down and trace out the beginning of things : when we *can* trace it ; but it is often too remote for us.

Mrs. Frost died, and the summer holidays were prolonged in consequence. September was not far off when we met again, and gigs and carriages went bowling up with us and our boxes.

Sanker was in the large class-room when we got in. He looked up for a minute, and turned his head away. Tod and I went up to him. He did shake hands, and it was as much as you could say. I don't think he was the sort of fellow to bear malice ; but it took time to bring him round if once offended.

Sanker had gone home with us to Dyke Manor when the holidays began. He belonged to a family in Wales (very poor they were now), and was a distant cousin of Mrs. Todhetley's. Before he had been with us long, a matter occurred that put him out, and he betook himself away from the Manor there and then. But I do not intend to go into that history now.

Things had been queer at school towards the close of the past term. Petty pilferings took place : articles and money alike disappeared. A thief was amongst us, and no mistake : but we did not know where to look for him. It was to be hoped that the same thing would not occur again.

"My father and Mrs. Todhetley are in the drawing-room," said Tod. "They are asking to see you."

Sanker hesitated ; but he went at last. The interview softened things a little, for he was civil to us when he came back again.

"What's that about the plants?" he asked me.

I told him what. They had been destroyed in some unaccountable manner. "Whether it was done intentionally, or whether moving them into the hall and back again did it, is not positively decided ; I don't suppose it ever will be. You ought to have come over to that ball, Sanker, after all of us writing to press it."

"Well," he said, coldly. "I don't care for balls. Monk was suspected, was he not?"

"Yes. Some of us suspect him still. He was savage at being accused of—— But never mind that "—and I pulled myself up in sudden recollection. "Monk has left, and we have engaged another gardener. Jenkins is not good for much."

"Hallo! What has *he* come back?"

' Ned Sanker was looking towards the door as he spoke. Two of them were coming in, who must have arrived at the same time—Vale and Lacketer. They were new ones, so to say, both having entered only last Easter. Vale was a tall, quiet fellow, with a fair, good-looking face and mild blue eyes; his friends lived at Vale Farm, about two miles off. Lacketer had sleek black hair, and a sharp nose; he had only an aunt, and was from Oxfordshire. I didn't like him. He had a way of cringing to those of us who were born to position in the world; but any poor friendless chap, who had nothing but himself and his work to get on by, he put upon shamefully. As for him, we couldn't find out that he'd ever had any relations at all, except the aunt.

I looked at Sanker, to see which he alluded to; his eyes were fixed on Vale with a stare. Vale had not been going to leave, that the school knew of.

"Why are you surprised that he has come back, Sanker?"

"Because I—didn't suppose he *would*," said Sanker, with a pause where I have put it, and an uncommonly strong emphasis on the "would."

It was just as though he had known something about Vale. Flashing across my memory came the mysterious avowal Sanker had made at our house about the discovery of the thief at school; and I now connected the one with the other. They call me a muff, I know, but I cannot help my thoughts.

"Sanker! was *he* the thief?"

"Hold your tongue, Ludlow," returned Sanker, in a fright. "I told you I'd give him a chance again, didn't I? But I never thought he would come back to take it."

"I would have believed it of any fellow rather than of Vale."

Sanker turned his face sharp, and looked at me. "Oh, would you?" said he, after a pause. "Well, then, you'd *better* believe it of any other. Mind you do. It will be safer, Johnny Ludlow."

He walked away into a group of them, as if afraid of my saying more. I turned out at the door leading to the playground, and came upon Tod in the porch.

"What was that you and Sanker were saying about Vale, Johnny?"

I was aware that I ought not to tell him; I knew I ought not:

but I *did*. Tod read me always as one reads a book, and I had never attempted to keep from him any earthly thing.

"Sanker says it was Vale. About the things lost last half. He told me, you know, that he had discovered who it was that took them."

"What, he the thief! Vale?"

"Hush, Tod. Give him another chance, as Sanker says."

Tod rushed out of the porch with a bound. He had heard a movement on the other side the trellis-work, but was only in time to catch a glimpse of a tassel disappearing round the corner.

We went in for noise at Worcester House just as much as they do at other schools; but not this afternoon. Mrs. Frost had been a favourite, and Sanker told us about her funeral. Things seemed to wear a mournful look. The servants were in black, the Doctor was in jet black, even to his gaiters. He wore the old style of dress always, knee breeches and buckles : but I have mentioned this before. We used to call him old Frost; this afternoon we said "the Doctor."

"You can't think what it was like while the house was shut up," said Sanker. "Coal-pits are jolly to it. I never saw the Doctor until the funeral. Being the only fellow at school, was, I suppose, the reason they asked me to go to it. He cried ever so much over the grave."

"Fancy old Frost crying!" interrupted Lacketer.

"I cried too," avowed Sanker, in a short sharp tone, as if disapproving of the remark; and it silenced Lacketer. "She had been ailing a long time, as we all knew, but she only grew very ill at the last, she told me."

"When did you see her?"

"Two days before she died. Hall came to me, saying I was to go up. It was on Wednesday at sunset. The hot red sun was shining right into the room, and she sat back from it on the sofa in a white gown. It was very hot these holidays, and she felt at times fit to die of it : she never bore heat well."

To hear Sanker tell this was nearly as good as a play. A solemn play I mean. None of us made the least noise as we stood round him : it seemed as if we could see Mrs. Frost's room, and her nice placid face, drawn back from the rays of the red hot sun.

"She told me to reach a little Bible that was on the drawers, and sit close to her and read a chapter," continued Sanker. "It was the seventh of St. John's Revelation; where that verse is, that says there shall be no more hunger and thirst; neither shall the sun light on them nor any heat. She held my hand while I read it. I had complained of the light for her, saying what a pity it was the room had no shutters. 'You see,' she said, when the chapter was read, 'how soon all discomforts here will pass away. Give my dear love to the boys when they come back,' she went on. 'Tell them I should like to have seen them all and said good-bye. Not good-bye for ever ; be sure tell them that, Sanker : I leave them all a charge to come to me *there* in God's good time. Not one of them must fail.' And now I've told you, and it's off my mind," concluded Sanker, in a different voice.

"Did you see her again ? "

" When she was in her coffin. She gave me the Bible."

Sanker took it out of his pocket. His name was written in it, " Edward Brooke Sanker, with Mary Frost's love." She had made him promise to read in it daily, if he began only with one verse. He did not tell us that then.

While we were looking at the writing, Bill Whitney came in. Some of them thought he had left at Midsummer. Lacketer shook hands ; he made much of Whitney, after the fashion of his mind and manners. Old Whitney was a baronet, and Bill would be Sir William sometime : for his elder brother, John, whom we had so much liked, was dead. Bill was good-natured, and divided hampers from home liberally. ;

"*I* don't know why I am back again," he said, in answer to questions; "you must ask Sir John. I shall be the better for another year or two of it, he says. Who likes grapes ? "

He was beginning to undo a basket he had brought with him : it was filled with grapes, peaches, plums, and nectarines. Those of us who had plenty of fruit at home did not care to take much ; but the others went in for it eagerly.

"Our peaches are finer than these, Whitney," cried Vale.

Lacketer gave Vale a push. "You big lout, mind your manners!" cried he. " Don't eat the peaches if you don't like 'em."

" So they were," said Vale, who never answered offensively.

"There ! that's enough insolence from *you*."

Old Vale was Sir John Whitney's tenant. Of course, according to Lacketer's creed, Vale deserved putting down for only speaking to Whitney.

" He is right," said Whitney, who thought no more of being his father's son than he would of being a shopkeeper's. " Mr. Vale's peaches this year were the finest in the county. He sent my mother some, and she said they ought to have gone up to a London fruit-show."

" I never saw such peaches as Mr. Vale's," put in Sanker, talking at Lacketer, and not kindly. "And the flavour was as good as the look. Mrs. Frost enjoyed those peaches to the last : it was almost the only thing she took."

Vale's face shone. "We shall always be glad at home that they were so good this year, for her sake."

Altogether, Lacketer was shut up. He stood over Whitney, who was undoing a small desk he had brought. Amidst the things, that lay on the ledge inside, was a thin, yellow, old-fashioned-looking coin.

"It's a guinea," said Bill Whitney. "I mean to have a hole bored in it and wear it to my watch-chain."

"I'd lock it up safely until then, Whitney," burst forth Snepp, who came from Alcester. "Or it may go after the things that were lost last half-year."

Turning to glance at Sanker, I found he had left the room. Whitney was balancing the guinea on his finger.

"Fore-warned, fore-armed, Snepp," he said. "Who the thief was, I can't think; but I advise him not to begin his game again."

"Talking of warning, I should like to give one on my own score," said Tod. "By-gones may be by-gones; I don't wish to recur to them; but if I lose anything this half and can find the thief, I'll put him into the river."

"What, to drown him?"

"To duck him. I'll do it as sure as my name's Todhetley."

Vale dropped his handkerchief and stooped to pick it up again. It might have been an accident; and the redness of his face might have come of stooping; but I saw Tod did not think so. Ducking is the favourite punishment in Worcestershire for a public offender, as all the county knows. When a man misbehaves himself on the race-course at Worcester, they duck him in the Severn underneath.

"The guinea would not be of much use to any one," said Lacketer. "You couldn't pass it."

"Oh, couldn't you, though!" answered Whitney. "You'd better try. It's worth twenty-one shillings, and they might give a shilling or two in for the antiquity of the coin."

"Gentlemen."

We turned to see the Doctor, standing there in his deep mourning, with his subdued red face. He came in to introduce a new master.

The time went on. We missed Mrs. Frost; and Hall, the crabbed woman with the cross face, made a mean substitute. She had it all her own way now. The puddings had less jam in them, and the pies hardly any fruit. Little Landon fell ill; and one day, after hours, when some of us went up to see him, we found him crying for Mrs. Frost. He was only seven; the youngest in the school, and made a sort of plaything of; an orphan with no friends to see to him much. Illness had been Mrs. Frost's great point. Any of us who were laid by she'd sit with half the day, reading nice stories, and talking to us of good things, just as our mothers might do. I know mine would if she had lived. However, we managed to get along in spite of Hall, hoping the Doctor would find her out and discharge her.

Matters went on quietly for some weeks. No one lost anything: and we had almost forgotten there had been a doubt that we might lose something, when it occurred. The loss was Tod's—rather curious, at first sight, that it should be, after his threat of what he would do. And Tod, as they all knew, was not one to break his word. It was only half-a-crown; but there could be no certainty that sovereigns would not go next. Not to speak of the disagreeable sense of feeling the thief was amongst us still, and taking to his tricks again.

Tod was writing to Evesham for some articles he wanted. Bill Whitney, knowing this, got him to add an order for some stationery for himself: which came back in the parcel. The account, nine-and-tenpence, was made out to Tod ("Joseph Todhetley, Esquire!"), half-a-crown of it being Whitney's portion. Bill handed him the half-crown at once; and Tod, who was busy with his own things and had his hands full, asked him to put it on the mantelpiece.

The tea-bell rang, and they went away and forgot it. Only they two had been in the room. But others might have gone in afterwards. We were getting up from tea when Tod called to me to go and fetch him the half-crown."

"It is on the mantelpiece, Johnny."

I went through the passages and turned into the box-room; a place where knots of us gathered sometimes. But the mantelpiece had no half-crown on it, and I carried the news back to Tod.

"Did you take it up again, Bill?" he asked of Whitney.

"I didn't touch it after I put it down," said Whitney. "It was there when the tea-bell rang."

They said I had overlooked it, and both went to the box-room. I followed slowly; thinking they should search for themselves. Which they did; and were standing with blank faces when I got in.

"It has gone after my guinea," Whitney was saying.

"What guinea?"

"My guinea. The one you saw. That disappeared a week ago."

Bill was not a fellow to make much row over anything; but Tod —and I, too—wondered at his having taken it so easily. Tod asked him why he had not spoken.

"Because Lacketer—who was with me when I discovered the loss—asked me to be silent for a short time," said Whitney. "He has a suspicion; and is looking out for himself."

"Lacketer has?"

"He says so. I am sure he has. He thinks he could put his

finger any minute on the fellow ; but it would not do to accuse him
without proof ; and he is waiting for it."

Tod glanced at me, and I at him, both of us thinking of Vale.

" Yesterday Lacketer lost something himself," continued Whitney.
" A shilling, I think it was. He went into a fine way over it, and
said now he'd watch in earnest."

"Who is it he suspects ?" asked Tod.

"He won't tell me ; says it would not be fair."

"Well, I shall talk about my half-crown, if you and Lacketer
choose to be silent over your losses," said Tod, decisively. "And
I'll be as good as my word, and give the reptile a ducking if I can
track him."

He went straight to the playground. It was a fine October
evening, the daylight nearly gone, and the hunter's moon rising in
the sky. Tod told about his half-crown, and the boys ceased their
noise to listen to him. He talked himself into a passion, and said
some stinging things. "He suspected who it was, and he heard
that Lacketer suspected, and he fancied that another or two suspected, and one *knew;* and he thought, now that affairs had come
to this pitch, when nothing, put for a minute out of hand, was safe,
it might be better for them all to declare their suspicions, and hunt
the animal as they'd hunt a hare."

There was a pause when Tod finished. He was about the biggest
and strongest in the school ; his voice was one of power, his manner
ready and decisive ; so that it was just as though a master spoke.
Lacketer came out from amongst them, looking white. I could see
that in the twilight.

"Who says I suspect? Speak for yourself, Todhetley. Don't
bring up my name."

"Do you scent the fox, or don't you?" roared Tod back again,
not at all in a humour to be crossed. "If you *do*, you must speak,
and not shirk it. Is the whole school to lie under doubt because
of one black sheep?"

Tod's concluding words were drowned in noise ; applause for him,
murmurs for Lacketer. I looked round for Vale, and saw him
behind the rest, as if preparing to make a run for it. That said
nothing : he was one of those quiet-natured fellows who liked to
keep aloof from rows. When I looked back again, Sanker was
standing a little forward, not far from Lacketer.

"As good speak as not, Lacketer," put in Whitney. "I don't
mind telling now that that guinea of mine has been taken ; and you
know you lost a shilling yourself. You say you could put your
finger on the fellow."

"Speak!" "Speak!" "Speak!" came the shouts from all
quarters. And Lacketer turned whiter.

"There's no proof," he said. "I might have been mistaken in what I fancied. I *won't* speak."

"Then I shall say you are an accomplice," roared Tod, in his passion. "I intend to hunt the fellow to earth to-night, and I'll do it."

"I don't suspect any one in particular," said Lacketer, looking as if he were run to earth himself. "There."

Great commotion. Lacketer was hustled, but got away and disappeared. Sanker went after him. Tod had been turning on Sanker, saying why didn't *he* speak.

"Half-a-crown is half-a-crown, and I mean to get mine back again," avowed Tod. "If some of you are rich enough to lose your half-crowns, I'm not. But it isn't that. Sovereigns may go next. It isn't *that.* It is the knowing that we have a light-fingered, disreputable, sneaking rat amongst us, whose proper place would be a reformatory, not a school for honest men's sons."

"Name!" "Proofs!" "Proofs!" "Name!" It was as if a torrent had been let loose. In the midst of the lull that ensued a voice was heard, and a name.

"*Vale.* Harry Vale."

Harding was the one to say it: a clever, first-class boy. You might have heard a pin drop in the surprise: and Harding went on after a minute.

"I beg to state that I do not accuse Vale myself. I know nothing whatever about the case. But I have reason to think Vale's name is the one that has been 'mentioned in connection with the losses last half."

"I know it is," cried Tod, who had only wanted the lead, not choosing to take it himself. "Now then, Vale, make your defence if you can."

I dare say you recollect how hotly you used to take up a cause when you were at school yourselves, not waiting to know whether it might be right or wrong. Mrs. Frost said to us on one of these occasions she wondered whether we should ever be as eager to take up heaven. They pounced upon Vale with an awful row. He stood with his arm round one of the trees behind, looking scared to death. I glanced back for Sanker, expecting his confirming testimony, but could not see him, and at that moment Lacketer appeared again, peeping round the trees. Whitney called to him.

"Here, Lacketer. Was it Vale you suspected?"

"As much as I did anybody else," doggedly answered Lacketer.

It was taken as an affirmative. The boys believed the thief was found, and were mad against him. Vale spoke something, shaking and ·trembling like the leaves in the wind, but his words were drowned. He was not brave, and they looked ready to tear him to pieces.

"My half-crown, Vale," roared Tod. "Did you take it just now?"

Vale made no answer; I thought he could not. His face frightened me; the lips were blue and drawn, his teeth chattered.

"Search his pockets."

It was a simultaneous thought, for a dozen said it. Vale was turned out, and half-a-crown found upon him; no other money. The boys yelled and groaned. Tod, with his great strength, pushed them aside, as the coin was flung to him.

"Shall I resume possession of this half-crown?" he asked of Vale, holding it before him in defiant mockery.

"If you like. I——"

Vale broke down with a gasp and a sob. His piteous aspect might have moved even Tod.

"Look here," said he, "I don't care in general to punish a coward; I regard him as an abject animal beneath me: but I cannot go from my word. Ducking is too good for you, Vale, but you shall have it. Be off to that tree yonder; we'll give you so much grace. Let him start fair, boys, and then hound him on. It will be a fine chase."

Vale, seeming to be too confused and terror-stricken to do anything but obey, went to the tree, and then darted away *in the direction of the river*. It takes time to read all this; but scarcely a minute appeared to have passed since Tod first came out with Whitney, and spoke of the half-crown. Giving Vale the fair start, the boys sprang after him, like a pack of hounds in full cry. Tod, the swiftest runner in the school, was following, when he found himself seized by Sanker. I had stayed behind.

"Have you been accusing Vale? Are you going to duck him?"

"Well?" cried Tod, angry at being stopped.

"It was not Vale who took the things. Vale! He is as innocent as you are. You'll kill him, Todhetley; he cannot bear terror."

"Who says he is innocent?"

"I do. I say it on my honour. It was another fellow, whose name I've been suppressing. This is *your* work, Johnny Ludlow."

I felt a sudden rush of repentance. A conviction that Sanker spoke nothing but the truth.

"You said it was Vale, Sanker."

"I never did. *You* said it. I told you you'd better believe it was any other rather than Vale. And I meant it."

But that Sanker was not a fellow to tell a lie, I should have thought he told one then. The impression, resting on my memory, was that he acknowledged to its being Vale, if he had not exactly stated it.

" You know you told me to be quiet, Sanker: you said, give him a chance."

" But I thought you were speaking of another then, not Vale. I swear it was not Vale. He is as honest as the day."

Tod, looking ready to strike me, waiting for no more explanation, was already off, shouting to the crew to turn, far more anxious now to save Vale than he had been to duck him.

How he managed to arrest them, I never knew. He did do it. But for being the fleetest runner and strongest fellow, he could never have overtaken, passed, and flung himself back upon them, with his arms stretched out, words of explanation on his lips.

The river was more than a mile away, taking the straight course over the fields, as a bird flies, and leaping fences and ditches. Vale went panting on, *for it*. It was as if his senses were scared out of him. Tod flew after him, the rest following on more gently. The school-bell boomed out to call us in for evening study, but none heeded it.

" Stop, Vale ! Stop ! " shouted Tod. " It has been a mistake. Come back and hear about it. It was not you; it was another fellow. Come back, Harry ; come back ! "

The more Tod shouted, the faster Vale went on. You should have seen the chase in the moonlight. It put us in mind of the fairy tales of Germany, where the phantom huntsman and his pack are seen coursing at midnight. Vale made for a part where the banks of the river are overshadowed by trees. Tod was only about thirty yards behind when he gained it ; he saw him leap in, and heard the plunge.

But when he got close, there was no sign of Vale in the water. Had he suddenly sunk ? Tod's heart stood still with fear. The boys were coming up by ones and twos, and a great silence ensued. Tod stript ready to plunge in when Vale should rise.

" Here's his cap," whispered one, picking it up from the bank.

" He was a good swimmer ; he must have been seized with cramp."

" Look here ; they say there are holes in the river, just above this bend. What if he has sunk into one ? "

" Hold your row, all of you," cried Tod, in a hoarse whisper that betrayed his fear. " Who's to listen with that noise ? "

He was listening for a sound, watching for the faintest ripple, that might give indication of Vale's rising. But none came. Tod stood there in his shirt till he shivered with cold. And the church clock struck seven, and then eight, and it was of no use waiting.

It was a horrible feeling. Somehow we seemed, I and Tod, to be responsible for Vale's death. I for having mistaken Sanker;

Tod for entering upon the threatened ducking, and hounding the boys on.

The worst was to come : going back to Dr. Frost and the masters with the tale; breaking it to Mr. and Mrs. Vale at Vale Farm. While Tod was dressing himself, the rest went on slowly, no one staying by him but me and Sanker.

"It's *your* doing more than mine," Tod said, turning to Sanker in his awful distress. "If you knew who the thief was last half, you should have disclosed it; not have given him the opportunity to resume his game. Had you done so this could not have happened."

"I promised him then I should proclaim him if he did resume it; I have told him to-night I shall do it," quietly answered Sanker. "It was Lacketer."

"Lacketer!"

"Lacketer. And since my eyes were opened, it has seemed to me that all yours must have been closed, not to find him out. His manner was enough to betray him: only, I suppose—you wanted the clue."

"But, Sanker, why did you let me think it was Vale?" I asked.

"*You* made the first mistake; I let you lie under it for Lacketer's sake; to give him the chance," said Sanker. "Who was to foresee you would go and tell?"

It had never passed my lips, save those few words at the time when Tod questioned me. Harding was the one outside the porch who had overheard it; but he had kept it to himself until now, when he thought the time had come for speaking.

What was to be done?—what was to be done? It seemed as if a great darkness had suddenly fallen upon us, and could never again be lifted. We had death upon our hands.

"There's just a chance," said Tod, dragging his legs along like so much lead, and beginning with a sort of groan. "Vale may have made for the land again as soon as he got in, and come out lower down. In that case he would run home probably."

Just a chance, as Tod said. But in the depth of despair chances are caught at. If we cut across to the left, Vale Farm was not more than a mile off: and we turned to it. Absenting ourselves from school seemed as nothing. Tod went on with a bound now there was an object, a ray of hope; I and Sanker after him.

"I can't go in," said Tod, when we came in front of the farm, a long, low house, with lights gleaming in some of the windows. "It's not cowardice; at least, I don't think it is. It's—— Never mind; I'll wait for you here."

"I say," said Sanker to me, "what excuse are we to make for going in at this time? We can't tell the truth."

I could not. Harry Vale stood alone; he had neither brother nor sister. I could not go in and tell his mother that he was dead. She was sitting in one of the front parlours, sewing by the lamp. We saw her through the window as we stole up to look in. But there was no time for plotting. Footsteps approached, and we only got back on the path when Mr. Vale came up. He was a tall, fine man, with a fair face and blue eyes like his son's. What we said I hardly knew; something about being close by, and thought we'd call on our way home. Sanker had been there several times in the holidays.

Mr. Vale took us in with a beaming face to his wife. They were the kindest-hearted people, liberal and hospitable, as most well-to-do farmers are. Mrs. Vale, rolling up her work, said we must take something to help us on our way home, and rang the bell. We never said we could not stop; we never said Tod was waiting outside. But there were no signs that Vale had gone home half-drowned.

Two maids put the supper on the table, and Mrs. Vale helped them; for Sanker had summoned courage to say it was late for us to stop. About a dozen things. Cold ducks, and ham, collared-head, a big dish of custard, and fruit and cake. I couldn't have swallowed a morsel; the lump rising in my throat would have hindered it. I don't think Sanker could, for he said resolutely we must not sit down because of Dr. Frost.

"How is Harry?" asked Mrs. Vale.

"Oh, he is—very well," said Sanker, after waiting to see if I'd answer. "Have you seen him lately?"

"Not since last Sunday week, when he and young Snepp spent the day here. He was looking well, and seemed in spirits. It was rather a hazard, sending him to school at all; Mr. Vale wanted to have him taught at home, as he has been until this year. But I think it is turning out for the best."

"He gets frightened, does he not?" said Sanker, who knew what she meant.

"He did," replied Mrs. Vale; "but he is growing out of it. Never was a braver little child born than he; but when he was four years old, he strolled away from his nurse into a field where a bull was grazing, a savage animal. What exactly happened, we never knew; that Harry was chased across the field by it was certain, and then tossed. The chief injury was to the nerves, strange though that may seem in so young a child. For a long time afterwards, the least alarm would put him into a state of terrible fear, almost a fit. But he is getting over it now."

She told this for my benefit; just as if she had divined the night's work; Sanker knew it before. I felt sick with remorse as I listened —and Tod had called him a coward! Let us get away.

"I wish you could stay, my lads," cried Mr. Vale; "it vexes me to turn you out supperless. What's this, Charlotte? Ah yes, to be sure! I wish you could put up the whole table for them."

For Mrs. Vale had been putting up some tartlets, and gave us each a packet of them. "Eat them as you go along," she said. "And give my love to Harry."

"And tell him that he must bring you both on Sunday, to spend the day," added Mr. Vale. "Perhaps young Mr. Todhetley will come also. You might have breakfast, and go with us to church. I'll write to Dr. Frost."

Outside at last; I and my shame. These good, simple-hearted people—oh, had we indeed, between us, made them childless? "Young Mr. Todhetley," waiting amid the stubble in the outer field, came springing up to the fence, his face white in the light of the hunter's moon.

"What a long while you have been! Well?"

"Nothing," said Sanker, briefly. "No news! I don't think we've been much above five minutes."

What a walk home it was! Mr. Blair, the out-of-school master, came down upon us with his thunder, but Tod seemed never to hear him. The boys, hushed and quiet as nature is before an impending storm, had not dared to tell and provoke it. I could not see Lacketer.

"Where's Vale?" roared Mr. Blair, supposing he had been with us. "But that prayers are waiting, I'd cane all four of you. Where are you going, Todhetley?"

"Don't stop me, Mr. Blair," said Tod, putting him aside with a quiet authority and a pain in his voice that made Blair stare. We called Blair, Baked Pie, because of his name, Pyefinch.

"Read the prayers without me, please Mr. Blair," went on Tod. "I must see Dr. Frost. If you don't know what has happened to-night, sir, ask the rest to tell you."

He went out to his interview with the Doctor. Tod was not one to shirk his duty. Seeing Vale's father and mother he had shrunk from; but the confession to Dr. Frost he made himself. What passed between them we never knew: how much contrition Tod spoke, how much reproach the Doctor. Roger and Miles, the man-servant and boy, were called into the library, and sent abroad: we thought it might be to search the banks of the river, or give notice for it to be dragged. The next called in was Sanker. The next, Lacketer.

But Lacketer did not answer the call. He had vanished. Mr. Blair went searching for him high and low, and could not find him. Lacketer had run away. He knew his time at Worcester House was over, and thought he'd save himself from dismissal. It was he who had been the thief, and whom Sanker suspected. As good mention here that Dr. Frost got a letter from his aunt the next Saturday, saying the school did not agree with her nephew, and she had withdrawn him from it.

Whether the others slept that night, I can't tell; I did not. Harry Vale's drowned form was in my mind all through it; and the sorrow of Mr. and Mrs. Vale. . In the morning Tod got up, looking more like one dead than alive : he had one of his frightful headaches. I felt ready to die myself; it seemed that never another happy morning could dawn on the world.

" Shall I ask if I may bring you some breakfast up here, Tod ? And it's just possible, you know, that Vale—— "

" Hold your peace, Johnny ! " he snapped. " If ever you tell me a false thing of a fellow again, I'll thrash your life out of you."

He came downstairs when he was dressed, and went out, waiting neither for breakfast nor prayers. I went out to watch him away, knowing he must be going to Vale Farm.

Oh, I never shall forget it. As Tod passed round the corner by the railings, he ran up against him. *Him*, Harry Vale.

My sight grew dim; I couldn't see; the field and railings were reeling. But it only lasted for a moment or two. Tod's breath was coming in great gasps then, and he had Vale's two hands grasped in his. I thought he was going to hug him; a loud sob broke from him.

" We have been thinking you were drowned ! "

Vale smiled. " I am too good a swimmer for that."

" But you disappeared at once."

" I struck back out of the river the instant I got into it; I was afraid you'd come in after me ; and crept round the alder trees lower down. When you were all gone I swam across in my clothes; see how they've shrunk ! "

" Swam across ! Have you not been home ? "

" No, I went to my uncle's : it's nearer than home : and they made me go to bed, and dried my things, and sent to tell Dr. Frost. I did not say why I went into the water," added Vale, lifting his kind face. " But the Doctor came round the ferry late, and he knew all about it. They talked to me well, he and my uncle, about being frightened at nothing, and I've promised not to be so stupid again."

" God bless you, Vale ! " cried Tod. " You know it was a mistake."

" Yes, Dr. Frost said so. The half-crown was my own. My uncle met us boys when we were out walking yesterday morning, and gave it me. I thought you might have seen him give it."

Tod linked his arm within Vale's and walked off to the breakfast-room. The wonder to me was how, with Vale's good honest face and open manners, we could have thought him capable of theft. But when you once go in for a mistake it carries you on in spite of improbabilities. The boys were silent for an instant when Vale went in, and then you'd have thought the roof was coming off with cheers. Tod stood looking from the window, and I vow I saw him rub his handkerchief across his eyes.

We went to Vale Farm on Sunday morning early: the four of us invited, and Harding. Mr. Vale shook hands twice with us all round so heartily, that we might see, I thought, they bore no malice; and Mrs. Vale's breakfast was a sight to do you good, with its jugs of cream and home-made sausages.

After that, came church: it looked like a procession turning out for it. Mr. and Mrs. Vale and the grandmother, an upright old lady with a China-crape shawl and white hair, us five and a man and maid-servant behind. The river lay on the right, the church was in front of us; people dotted the fields on their way to it, and the bells were ringing as they do at a wedding.

"This is a different sort of Sunday from what we thought last Thursday it would be," I said in Tod's ear when we were together for a minute at the gate.

"Johnny, if I were older, and went in for that kind of thing, as perhaps I shall do sometime, I should like to put up a public thanksgiving in church to-day."

"A public thanksgiving?"

"For mercies received."

I stared at Tod. He did not seem to heed it, but took his hat off and walked with it in his hand all across the churchyard.

XI.

THE BEGINNING OF THE END.

PERHAPS this might be called the beginning of the end of the chain of events that I alluded to in that other paper. An end that terminated in distress, and death, and sorrow.

It was the half-year following that hunt of ours by moonlight. Summer weather had come in, and we were looking forward to the holidays, hoping the heat would last.

The half-mile field, so called from its length, on Vale Farm was being mowed. Sunday intervened, and the grass was left to dry until the Monday. The haymakers had begun to rake it into cocks. The river stretched past along the field on one side; a wooden fence bounded it on the other. It was out of all proportion, that field, so long and so narrow.

Tod and I and Sanker and Harry Vale were spending the Sunday at the Farm. Since that hunt last autumn Mr. and Mrs. Vale often invited us. There was no evening service, and we went into the hay-field, and began throwing the hay at one another. It was rare fun; they might almost have heard our shouts at Worcester House: and I don't believe but that every one of us forgot it was Sunday.

What with the sultry weather and the hay, some of us got into a tolerable heat. The river wore a tempting look; and Tod and Sanker, without so much as a thought, undressed themselves behind the trees, and plunged in. It was twilight then; the air had began to wear its weird silence ; the shadows were putting on their ghastliness; the moon, well up, sailed along under white clouds.

I and Vale were walking slowly back towards the Farm, when a great cry broke over the water,—a cry as of something in pain ; but whether from anything more than a night-bird, was uncertain. Vale stopped and turned his head.

A second cry: louder, longer, more distinct, and full of agony. It came from one of those two in the water. Vale flew back with his fleet foot—fleeter than any fellow's in the school, except Tod's and Snepp's. As I followed, a startling recollection came over me, and

I wondered how it was that all of us had been so senseless as to forget it: that one particular spot on the river was known to be dangerous.

"Bear up; I'm coming," shouted Vale. "Don't lose your heads."

A foot-passenger walking on the other side the fence, saw something was wrong: if he did not hear Vale's words, he heard the cry, and came cutting across the field, scattering the hay with his feet. And then I saw it was Baked Pie ; which meant our mathematical master, Mr. Blair. They had given him at baptism the name of "Pyefinch," after some old uncle who had money to leave; no second name, nothing but that: and the school had converted him into "Baked Pie." But I don't think fathers and mothers have any right to put odd names upon helpless babies and send them out to be a laughing-stock to the world.

Blair was not a bad fellow, setting his name aside, and had gone in for honours at Cambridge. We reached the place together.

"What is amiss, Ludlow?"

"I don't know, sir. Todhetley and Sanker are in the water; and we've heard cries."

"In the water to-night! And *there!*"

Vale, already in the middle of the river, was swimming back, holding up Sanker. But Tod was nowhere to be seen. Mr. Blair looked up and down; and an awful fear came over me. The current led down to Mr. Charles Vale's mill—Vale's uncle. More than one man had found his death there.

"Oh, Mr. Blair! where is he? What has become of him?"

"Hush!" breathed Blair. He was quietly slipping off some of his things, his eyes fixed on a particular part of the river. In he went, striking out without more splash than he could help, and reached it just as Tod's head appeared above water. *The third time of rising.* I did not go in for such a girl's trick as to faint; but I never afterwards could trace the minutes as they had passed until Tod was lying on the grass under the trees. *That* I remember always. The scene is before my eyes now as plainly as it was then, though more time has since gone by than perhaps you'd think for: the treacherous river flowing on calmly, the quivering leaves overhead, through which the moon was glittering, and Tod lying there white and motionless. Mr. Blair had saved his life; there could be no question about that, saved it only by a minute of time; and I thought to myself I'd never call him Baked Pie again.

"Instead of standing moonstruck, Ludlow, suppose you make a run to the Farm and see what help you can get," spoke Mr. Blair. "Todhetley must be carried there, and put between hot blankets."

Help was found. Sanker walked to the Farm, Tod was carried; and a regular bustle set in when they arrived there. Both were put to bed: Tod had come-to then. Mrs. Vale and the servants ran up and down like wild Indians; and the good old lady with the white hair insisted upon sitting up by Tod's bedside all night.

"No, mother," said Mr. Vale; "some of us will do that."

"My son, I tell you that I shall watch by him myself," returned the old lady ; and, as they deferred to her always, she did.

When explanation of the accident was given—as much of it as ever could be given—it sounded rather strange. *Both* of them had been taken with cramp, and the river was not in fault, after all. Tod said that he had been in the water two or three minutes, when he was seized with what he supposed to be cramp in the legs, though he never had it before. He was turning to strike out for the bank, when he found himself seized by Sanker. They loosed each other in a minute, but Tod was helpless, and he sank.

Sanker's story was very much the same. He was seized with cramp, and in his fear caught hold of Tod for protection. Tod was an excellent swimmer, Sanker a poor one ; but while Sanker's cramp grew better, Tod's disabled him. Most likely, as we decided when we heard this, Sanker, who never went down at all, would have got out of the water without help; Tod would have been drowned but for Blair. He had sunk twice when the rescue came. Mr. Featherston, the man of pills who attended the school, said it was all through their having jumped into the water when they were in a white heat; the cold had struck to them. While Mrs. Hall, with her grave face, thought it was through their having gone bathing on a Sunday.

Whatever it was through, old Frost made a commotion. He was not severe in general, but he raised noise enough over this. What with one thing and another, the school, he declared, was being everlastingly upset.

Tod and Sanker came back from Mr. Vale's the next day; Monday. The Doctor ordered them into his study, and sat there with his cane in his hand while he talked, rapping the table with it now and again as fiercely as if it had been their backs. And the backs would surely have had it but for having just escaped coffins.

All this would not have been much, but it was to lead to a great deal more. To quite a chain of events, as I have said ; and to trouble and sorrow in the far-off ending. Hannah, at home, was fond of repeating to Lena what she called the sayings of poor Richard : " For want of a nail the shoe was lost ; for want of a shoe the horse was lost ; for want of a horse the rider was lost ; and all for the want of a little care about a horse-shoe nail." The horse-shoe nail and the man's loss seemed a great deal nearer each other than that Sunday night's accident, and what was eventually to come of it. A small mustard-seed, dropped into the ground, shoots forth and becomes in the end a great tree.

On the Wednesday, who should come over but the Squire, clasping Pyefinch Blair's hand in his, and saying with tears in his good old eyes that he had saved his son's life. Old Frost, you see, had written the news to Dyke Manor. Tod, strong and healthy in constitution, was all right again, not a hair of his head the worse for it ; but Sanker had not escaped so well.

As early as the Monday night, the first night of his return home from Vale Farm, it began to come on ; and the next morning the boys, sleeping in the same room, told a tale of Sanker's having been delirious. He had sat up in bed and woke them all up with his cries, thinking he was trying to swim out of deep water, and could not. Next he said he wanted some water to drink ; they gave him one draught after another till the big water-jug was emptied, but his thirst kept on saying "More! more!" Sanker did not seem to remember any of this. He came down with the rest in the morning, his face very white, except for a pinkish spot in the middle of his cheeks, and he thought the fellows must be chaffing him. The fellows told him they were not ; and one, it was Bill Whitney, said they would not think of chaffing him just after his having been so nearly drowned.

It went on to the afternoon. Sanker ate no dinner, for I looked to see ; he was but one amidst the many, and it was not noticed by the masters. And if it had been, they'd have thought that the ducking had taken away his appetite. The drawing-master, Wilson, followed suit with Hall, and said he was not surprised at their being nearly drowned, after making hay on the Sunday. But, about four o'clock, when the first-class were before Dr. Frost with their Greek books, Sanker suddenly let his fall. Instead of stooping for it, his eyes took a far-off look, as if they were seeking for it round the walls of the room.

"Lay hold of him," said Dr. Frost.

He did not faint, but seemed dull : it looked as much like a lazy fit as anything ; and he was sensible. They put him to sit on one of the benches, and then he began to tremble.

"He must be got to bed," said the Doctor. "Mr. Blair, kindly see Mrs. Hall, will you. Tell her to warm it. Stay. Wait a moment."

Dr. Frost followed Mr. Blair from the hall. It was to say that Sanker had better go at once to the blue-room. If the bed there was not aired, or otherwise ready, Sanker's own bedding could be taken to it. "I'll give Mrs. Hall the orders myself," said the Doctor.

The blue-room—called so from its blue-stained walls—was the one used on emergencies. When we found Sanker had been taken there, we made up our minds that he was going to have an illness. Featherston came and thought the same.

The next day, Wednesday, he was in a sort of fever, rambling every other minute. The Squire said he should like to see him, and Blair took him upstairs. Sanker lay with the same pink hue on his cheeks, only deeper; and his eyes were bright and glistening. Hall, who was addicted to putting in her word on all occasions when it could tell against us boys, said if he had stayed two or three days in bed at Vale Farm, where he was first put, he'd have had nothing of this. Perhaps Hall was right. It had been Sanker's own doings to get up. When Mrs. Vale saw him coming downstairs, she wanted to send him back to bed again, but he told her he was quite well, and came off to school.

Sanker knew the Squire, and put out his hand. The Squire took it without saying a word. He told us later that to him Sanker's face looked as if it had death in it. When he would have spoken, Sanker's eyes had grown wild again, and he was talking nonsense about his class-books.

"Johnny, boy, you sit in this room a bit at times; you are patient and not rough," said the Squire, when he went out to his carriage, for he had driven over. "I have asked them to let you be up there as much as they can. The poor boy is very ill, and has no relatives near him."

Dwarf Giles, touching his hat to Tod and me, was at the horses' heads, Bob and Blister. The cattle knew us: I'm sure of it. They had had several hours' rest in old Frost's stables while the Squire went on foot about the neighbourhood to call on people. Dr. Frost, standing out with us, admired the fine dark horses very much; at which Giles was prouder than if the Doctor had admired *him*. He cared for nothing in the world so much as those two animals, and groomed them with a will.

"You'll take care that he wants for nothing, Doctor," I heard the Squire say as he shook hands. "Don't spare any care and expense to get him well again; I wish to look upon this illness as my charge. It seems something like an injustice, you see, that my boy should come off without damage, and this poor fellow be lying there."

He took the reins and stepped up to his seat, Giles getting up beside him. As we watched the horses step off with the high step that the Squire loved, he looked back and nodded to us. And it struck me that, in this care for Sanker, the Pater was trying to make some recompense for the suspicion cast on him a year before at Dyke Manor.

It was a sharp, short illness, the fever raging, though not infectious; I had never been with any one in anything like it before,
and I did not wish to be again.   To hear how Sanker's mind
rambled, was marvellous; but some of us shivered when it came to
raving.   Very often he'd be making hay; fighting against numbers
that were throwing cocks at him, while he could not throw back at
them.   Then he'd be in the water, buffeting with high waves,
and shrieking out that he was drowning, and throwing his thin
hot arms aloft in agony.   Sometimes the trouble would be his
lessons, hammering at Latin derivations and Greek roots; and
next he was toiling through a problem in Euclid.   One night when
he was at the worst, old Featherston lost his head, and the next
day Mr. Carden came posting from Worcester in his carriage.

There were medical men of renown nearer; but somehow in extremity we all turned to him.   And his skill did not fail here.
Whether it might be any special relief he was enabled to give, or
that the disease had reached its crisis, I cannot tell, but from the
moment Mr. Carden stood at his bedside, Sanker began to mend.
Featherston said the next day that the worst of the danger had
passed.   It seemed to us that it had just set in; no rat was ever
so weak as Sanker.

The holidays came then, and the boys went home: all but me.
Sanker couldn't lift a hand, but he could smile at us and understand,
and he said he should like to have me stay a bit with him; so
they sent word from home I might.   Mr. Blair stayed also; Dr.
Frost wished it.   The Doctor was subpœnaed to give evidence
on a trial at Westminster, and had to hasten up to London.   Blair
had no relatives at all, and did not care to go anywhere.   He told
me in confidence that his staying there saved his pocket.   Blair was
strict in school, but over Sanker's bed he got as friendly with me
as possible.   I liked him; he was always gentlemanly; and I
grew to dislike their calling him Baked Pie as much as he disliked
it himself.

"You go out and get some air, Ludlow," he said to me the day
after the school broke up, "or we may have you ill next."

Upon that I demanded what I wanted with air.   I had taken
precious long walks with the fellows up to the day before yesterday.

"You go," said he, curtly.

"Go, Johnny," said Sanker, in his poor weak voice, which
couldn't raise itself above a whisper.   "I'm getting well, you
know."

My way of taking the air was to sit down at one of the schoolroom desks and write to Tod.   In about five minutes some one
walked round the house as if looking for an entrance, and then
stopped at the side-door.   Putting my head out of the window, I

took a look at her. It was a young lady in a plain grey dress and straw bonnet, with a cloak over her arm, and an umbrella put up against the sun. The back regions were turned inside out, for they had begun the summer cleaning that morning, and the cook came clanking along in pattens to answer the knock.

"This is Dr. Frost's, I believe. Can I see him?"

It was a sweet, calm, gentle voice. The cook, who had no notion of visitors arriving at the cleaning season, when the boys were just got rid of, and the Doctor had gone away, stared at her for a moment, and then asked in her surly manner whether she had business with Dr. Frost. That cook and old Molly at home might have run in a curricle, they were such a match in temper.

"Business!—oh, certainly. I must see him, if you please."

The cook shook off her pattens, and went up the back stairs, leaving the young lady outside. As it was business, she supposed she must call Mr. Blair.

"Somebody wants Dr. Frost," was her announcement to him. "A girl at the side door."

Which of course caused Blair to suppose it might be a child from one of the cottages come to ask for help of some sort; as they did come sometimes. He thought Hall might have been called to her, but he went down at once; without his coat, and his invalid-room slippers on. Naturally, when he saw the young lady, it took him aback.

"I beg your pardon, sir; I hope you will not deem me an intruder. I have just arrived here."

Blair stared almost as much as the cook had done. The face was so pleasant, the voice so refined, that he inwardly called himself a fool for showing himself to her in that trim. For once, speech failed him; a thing Blair had never done at mathematics, I can tell you; he had not the smallest notion who she was or what she wanted. And the silence seemed to frighten her.

"Am I too late?" she asked, her face growing white. "Has the, —the worse happened?"

"Happened to what?" questioned Blair, for he never once thought of the sick fellow above, and was all at sea. "Pardon me, young lady, but I do not know what you are speaking of."

"Of my brother, Edward Sanker. Oh, sir! is he dead?"

"Miss Sanker! Truly I beg your pardon for my stupidity. He is out of danger; is getting well."

She sat down for a minute on the old stone bench beyond the door, roughed with the crowd of boys' names cut in it. Her lips were trembling just a little, and the soft brown eyes had tears in them; but the face was breaking into a happy smile.

"Oh, Dr. Frost, thank you, thank you! Somehow I never thought of him as dead until this moment, and it startled me."

Fancy her taking him for Frost! Blair was a good-looking fellow under thirty, slender and well made. The Doctor stood out an old guy of fifty, with a stern face and black knee-breeches.

"My mother had your letter, sir, but she was not able to come. My father is very ill, needing her attention every moment; she strove to see on which side her duty lay—to stay with him, or to come to Edward; and she thought it must lie in remaining with papa. So she sent me. I left Wales last night."

"Is Mr. Sanker's a fever, too?" asked Blair, in wonder.

"No, an accident. He was hurt in the mine."

It was odd that it should be so; the two illnesses occurring at the same time! Mr. Sanker, it appeared, fell from the shaft; his leg was broken, and there were other injuries. At first they were afraid for him.

Blair fell into a dilemma. He wouldn't have minded Mrs. Sanker; but he did not know much about young ladies, not being accustomed to them. She got up from the bench.

"Mamma bade me say to you, Dr. Frost—— "

"I beg your pardon," interrupted Blair again. "I am not Dr. Frost; the Doctor went to London this morning. My name is Blair—one of the masters. Will you walk in?"

He shut her into the parlour on his way to call Hall, and to put on his boots and coat. Seeing me, he turned into the schoolroom.

"Ludlow, are not the Sankers connections of yours?"

"Not of mine. Of Mrs. Todhetley's."

"It's all the same. You go in and talk to her. I don't know what on earth to do. She has come to be with Sanker, but she won't like to stay here with only you and me. If the Doctor were at home it would be different."

"She seems an uncommon nice girl, Mr. Blair."

"Good gracious!" went on Blair in his dilemma. "The Doctor told me he had written to Wales some time ago; but he supposed Mrs. Sanker could not make it convenient to come; and yesterday he wrote again, saying there was no necessity for it, as Sanker was out of danger. I don't know what on earth to do with her," repeated Blair, who had a habit of getting hopelessly bewildered on occasions. "Hall! Where's Mrs. Hall?"

As he went calling out down the flagged passage, a boy came whistling to the door, carrying a carpet-bag: Miss Sanker's luggage. The coach she had had to take on leaving the rail put her down half-a-mile away, and she walked up in the sun, leaving her bag to be brought after her.

It seemed that we were going in for mistakes. When I went to her, and began to say who I was, she mistook me for Tod. It made me laugh.

"Tod is a great, strong fellow, as tall as Mr. Blair, Miss Sanker. I am only Johnny Ludlow."

"Edward has told me all about you both," she said, taking my hand, and looking into my face with her sweet eyes. "Tod's proud and overbearing, though generous; but you have ever been pleasant with him. I am afraid I shall begin to call you 'Johnny' at once."

"No one ever calls me anything else; except the masters here."

"You must have heard of me—Mary?"

"But you are not Mary?"

"Yes, I am."

That she was telling truth any fellow might see, and yet at first I hardly believed her. Sanker had told us his sister Mary was beautiful as an angel. *Her* face had no beauty in it, so to say; it was only kind, nice, and loving. People called Mrs. Parrifer a beautiful woman; perhaps I had taken my notions of beauty from her; she had a Roman nose, and great big eyes that rolled about, had a gruff voice, and a lovely peach-and-white complexion (but people said it was paint), and looked three parts a fool. Mary Sanker was just the opposite to all this, and her cheeks were dimpled. But still she had not what people call beauty.

"May I go up and see Edward?"

"I should think so. Mr. Blair, I suppose, will be back directly. He is looking very ill: you will not be frightened at him?"

"After picturing him in my mind as dead, he will not frighten me, however ill he may look."

"I should say the young lady had better take off her bonnet afore going in. Young Mr. Sanker haven't seen bonnets of late, and might be scared."

The interruption came from Hall; we turned, and saw her standing there. She spoke resentfully, as if Miss Sanker had offended her; and no doubt she had, by coming when the house was not in company order, and had nothing better to send in for dinner but cold mutton and half a rhubarb pie. Hall would have to get the mutton hashed now, which she would never have done for me and Blair.

"Yes, if you please; I should much like to take my bonnet off," said Miss Sanker, going up to Hall with a smile. "I think you must be Mrs. Hall. My brother has talked of you."

Hall took her to a room, and presently she came forth all fresh and nice, the travel dust gone, and her bright brown hair smooth and glossy. Her grey dress was soft, one that would not disturb a sick-room; it had a bit of white lace at the throat and

wrists, and a little pearl brooch in front. She was twenty-one last
birthday, but did not look as much.

Blair had been in to prepare Sanker, and his great eyes (only
great since his illness) were staring for her with a wild expectation.
You never saw brother and sister less alike; the one so nice, the
other ugly enough to frighten the crows. Sanker had my hand
clasped tight in his, when she stooped to kiss him. I don't think
he knew it; but I could not get away. In that moment I saw how
fond they were of each other.

"Could not the mother come, Mary?"

"No, papa is—is not well," she said, for of course she would not
tell him yet of any accident. "Papa wanted her there, and you
wanted her here; she thought her duty lay at home, and she was
not afraid but that God would raise up friends to take care of
you."

"What is the matter with him?"

"Some complicated illness or other," Mary Sanker answered, in
careless tones. "He was a little better when I came away. You
have been very ill, Edward."

He held up his wasted hand as proof, with a half smile; but it
fell again.

"I don't believe I should have pulled through it all, Mary, but
for Blair."

"That's the gentleman I saw. The one without a coat. Has he
nursed you?"

Sanker motioned with his white lips. "Right well, too. He,
and Hall, and Johnny here. Old Hall is as good as gold when any
of us are ill."

"And pays herself out by being tarter than ever when we are
well," I could not help saying: for it was the truth.

"Blair saved Todhetley's life," Sanker went on. "We used to
call him Baked Pie before, and give him all the trouble we could."

"Ought you to talk, Edward?"

"It is your coming that seems to give me strength for it," he
answered. "I did not know that Frost had written home."

"There was a delay with the letters, or I might have been here
three days ago," said Miss Sanker, speaking in penitent tones, as if
she were in the habit of taking other people's faults upon herself.
"While papa is not well, the clerk down at the mine opens the
business letters. Seeing one directed to papa privately, he neither
spoke of it nor sent it up, and for three days it lay unopened."

Sanker had gone off into one of his weak fits before she finished
speaking: lying with his eyes and mouth wide open, between sleeping and waking. Hall came in and said with a tone that snapped
Miss Sanker up, *it wouldn't do :* if people could not be there with-

out talking, they must not be there at all. I don't say but that she was a capable nurse, or that when a fellow was downright ill, she spared the wine in the arrowroot, and the sugar in the tea. Mary Sanker sat down by the bedside, her finger on her lips to show that she meant to keep silence.

We had visitors later. Mrs. Vale came over, as she did most days, to see how Sanker was getting on; and Bill Whitney brought his mother. Mrs. Vale told Mary Sanker that she had better sleep at the Farm, as the Doctor was away; she'd give her a nice room and make her comfortable. Upon that, Lady Whitney offered a spacious bed and dressing-room at the Hall. Mary thanked them both, saying how kind they were to be so friendly with a stranger; but thought she must go to the Farm, as it would be within a walk night and morning. Bill spoke up, and said the carriage could fetch and bring her; but Vale Farm was decided upon; and when night came, I went with her to show her the way.

"That's the water they went into, Miss Sanker; and that's the very spot behind the trees." She shivered just a little as she looked, but did not say much. Mrs. Vale met us at the door, and the old lady kissed Mary and told her she was a good girl to come fearlessly all the way alone from Wales to nurse her sick brother. When Mary came back the next morning, she said they had given her such a beautiful room, the dimity curtains whiter than snow, and the sheets scented with lavender.

Her going out to sleep appeased Hall;—that, or something else. She was gracious all day, and sent us in a couple of chickens for dinner. Mr. Blair cut them up and helped us. He had written to tell Dr. Frost in London of Miss Sanker's arrival, and while we were at table a telegram came back, saying Mrs. Hall was to take care of Miss Sanker, and make her comfortable.

It went on so for three or four days; Mary sleeping at the Farm, and coming back in the morning. Sanker got well enough to be taken to a sofa in the pretty room that poor Mrs. Frost sat in nearly to the last; and we were all four growing very jolly, as intimate as if we'd known each other as infants. I had taken to call her Mary, hearing Sanker do it so often; and twice the name slipped accidentally from Mr. Blair. The news from Wales was better and better. For visitors we had Mrs. Vale, Lady Whitney, and Bill, and old Featherston. Some of them came every day. Dr. Frost was detained in London. The trial did not come on so soon as it was put down for; and when it did, it lasted a week, and the witnesses had to stay there. He had written to Mary, telling her to make herself quite happy, for she was in good hands. He also wrote to Mrs. Vale, and to Hall.

Well, it was either the fourth or fifth day. I know it was on

Monday; and at five o'clock we were having tea for the first time
in Sanker's sitting-room, the table drawn near the sofa, and Mary
pouring it out.   It was the hottest of hot weather, the window was
up as high as it would go, but not a breath of air came in.   Therefore, to see Blair begin to shake as if he were taken with an ague,
was something inexplicable.   His face looked grey, his ears and
hands had turned a sort of bluish white.

"Halloa!" said Sanker, who was the first to notice him. "What's
the matter, sir?"

Blair got up, and sat down again, his limbs shaking, his teeth
chattering.   Mary Sanker hastily put some of the hot tea into a
saucer, and held it to his lips.   His teeth rattled against the china;
I thought they would bite a piece out of it; and in trying to take
the saucer from Miss Sanker, the tea was spilt on the carpet.

"Just call Mrs. Hall, Johnny," said Sanker, who had propped
himself up on his elbow to stare.

Hall came, and Mr. Featherston came; but they could not make
anything out of it except that Blair had had a shaking-fit.   He was
soon all right again (except for a burning heat); but the surgeon,
given naturally to croak (or he wouldn't have got so frightened
about Sanker when Mr. Carden was telegraphed for), said he hoped
the mathematical master had not set in for fever.   .

He had set in for something.   That was clear.   The shaking-fits
took him now and again, giving place to spells of low fever.
Featherston was not sure whether it had not a "typhoid character,"
he said; but the suspicion was quite enough, and our visitors fell
off.   Mrs. Vale was the only one who came; she laughed at supposing she could be afraid of it.   So there we still were, we four;
prisoners, as may be said; with some fever amongst us that perhaps might be of a typhoid character.   Mr. Featherston said (or
Hall, I forget which) that it must have been smouldering within
him ever since the Sunday night when he jumped into the river,
and Blair thought so himself.

Do not imagine he was as ill as Sanker had been.   Nothing of
the sort.   He got up every morning, and was in Mrs. Frost's sitting-
room with us until evening: but he grew nearly as weak as Sanker,
and wanted pretty nearly as much waiting on.   Sometimes his
hands were like a burning coal; sometimes so cold that Mary
would take them in hers to try and rub a little life into them.   She
was the gentlest nurse possible, and did not seem to think anything
more of waiting on him than on her brother.   Mrs. Hall would
stand by and say there was nothing left for her to do.

One day Lady Whitney came over, braving the typhoid suspicion, and asked to see Miss Sanker in the great drawing-room;
where she stood sniffing at a bottle of aromatic vinegar.

"My dear," she said, when Mary went to her, "I do not think this is at all a desirable position for you to be placed in. I should not exactly like it for one of my own daughters. Mr. Blair is a very gentleman-like man, and all that, with quite proper feelings no doubt; but sitting with him in illness is altogether different from sitting with your brother. Featherston tells me there's little or no danger of infection, and I have come to take you back to the Hall with me."

But Mary would not go. It was not the position she should have voluntarily chosen, but circumstances had led her into it, and she thought her duty lay in staying where she was at present, was the substance of her answer. Mr. Blair had nursed her brother through his dangerous illness, and it would be cruelly ungrateful to leave him, now that he was ill himself. It seemed a duty thrown expressly in her way, she added; and her mother approved of what she was doing.

So Lady Whitney went away (leaving the bottle of aromatic vinegar as a present for the sick-room) three parts convinced. Any way, when she got home, she said that Mary Sanker was a sweet, good girl, trusty to her fingers' ends.

I'm sure she was like sunshine in the room, and read to us out of the Bible just as Harry Vale's fine old grandmother might have done. The first day that Sanker took a drive in a fly, he was tired afterwards, and went to bed and to sleep at tea-time. Towards sunset, before I walked with her to the Farm, Mary took the Book as usual; and then hesitated, as if in doubt whether to presume to read or not, Sanker being away.

"Oh yes; yes, if you please," said Mr. Blair.

She began the tenth chapter of St. John. It is a passably long one, as every one knows; and when she laid the Book down again, Blair had his eyes shut and his head resting on the back of the easy chair where he generally sat. His face never looked more still and white. I glanced at Mary and she at me; we thought he was worse, and she went up to him.

"I ought not to have read so long a chapter," she gently said. "I fear you are feeling worse."

"No; I was only thinking. Thinking what an angel you are," he added in low, impassioned, yet reverent tones, as he bent forward to look up in her face, and took both her hands for a moment in his.

She drew them away at once, saying, as she passed me, that she was going to put on her bonnet, and should be ready in a minute. Of course it might have been the reflection of the red sun-clouds, but I never saw any face so glowing in all my life.

The next move old Featherston made, was to decide that the

fever was *not* of a typhoid character; and visitors came about us
again. It was something like opening a public-house after a spell
of closing; all the Whitneys flocked in together, except Sir John,
who was in town for Parliament. Mrs. Hall was uncommonly
short with every one. She had said from the first there was nothing
infectious in the fever, told Featherston so to his face, and resented
people's having stayed away. I wrote home to tell them there. On
the Saturday Dr. Frost arrived, and we were glad to see him. Blair
was getting rather better then.

"Well, that Sunday night's plunge in the water has had its
revenge!" remarked Dr. Frost. "It only wants Todhetley and
Vale to follow suit."

But neither of them had the least intention of following suit. On
the Monday Tod arrived to surprise us, strong as ever. The
Squire had trusted him to drive the horses: you should have seen
them spanking in at the gate of Worcester House, pawing the
gravel, as Tod in the high carriage, the ribbons in his hands, and
the groom beside him, brought them up beautifully to the door.
Some people called Tod ugly, saying his features were strong;
but I know he promised to be the finest man in our two counties.

He brought an invitation for the sick and the well. When the
two invalids were able to get to Dyke Manor, Mr. and Mrs. Todhetley expected to see them, for change of air. Mary Sanker and
I were to go as soon as we liked. Which we did in a few days, and
were followed by Sanker and Mr. Blair: both able to help themselves then, and getting well all one way.

It did not surprise people very much to hear that the mathematical master and Mary Sanker had fallen in love with one another.
He (as Bill Whitney's mother had put in) was gentleman-like; a
good-looking fellow to boot: and you have heard what *she* was.
The next week but one after arriving at Dyke Manor, Blair took
Mrs. Todhetley into his confidence, though he had said nothing to
Mary. They would be sure to marry in the end, she privately
told the Squire, for their likeness to each other had struck her at
first sight.

' "Mary will not have a shilling, Mr. Blair; she will go to her
husband (whenever she shall marry) with even a very poor outfit,"
Mrs. Todhetley explained, wishing Blair to fully understand things.
"Her father, Philip Sanker, was a gentleman bred and born, but
his patrimony was small. He was persuaded to embark it in a
Welsh mine, and lost all. Report said some roguery was at work,
but I don't know that it was. It ended in his becoming overlooker
on the very same mine, at a salary so small that they could hardly
have reared their family anywhere but in Wales. Mary does not
play, or draw, you see; she has no accomplishments."

"She has what is a great deal better; she does not want them," answered Blair, his pale face lighting up.

"In point of fact, the Sankers—as I fancy—have sacrificed the girls' interests to the boys; they of course must have a thorough education," remarked Mrs. Todhetley. "They are good people, both; you could not fail to like them. I sometimes think, Mr. Blair, that the children of these refined men and women (and Philip Sanker and his wife are that), compelled to live closely and to look at every sixpence before it is spent, turn out all the better for it."

"I am sure they do," answered Blair, earnestly. "It was my own case."

Taking Mrs. Todhetley into confidence meant as to his means as well as his love. He had saved a little money during the eight years he had been at work for himself—about two hundred pounds. It might be possible, he thought, to take a school with this, and set up a tent at once: he and Mary. Mrs. Todhetley shook her head; she could make as much of small sums as any one, but fancied this would scarcely be enough for what he wished.

"There would be the furniture," she ventured to say with some hesitation, not liking to damp him.

"I think that is often included in the purchase-money for the good-will," said Blair.

He had been acting on this notion before speaking to Mrs. Todhetley, and a friend of his in London, the Reverend Mr. Lockett, was already looking out for any schools that might be in the market. In a few days news came down of one to be disposed of in the neighbourhood of London. Mr. Lockett thought it was as good an investment as Blair was likely to find, he wrote word: only, the purchase-money, inclusive of furniture, was four hundred pounds instead of two.

"It is of no use to think of it," said Mr. Blair, pushing his curly hair (they used to say he was vain of it at Frost's) from his perplexed brow. "My two hundred pounds will not go far towards that."

"It seems to me that the first step will be to go up and see the place," remarked Mrs. Todhetley. "If what Mr. Lockett says of the school be true; that is, if the people who have the disposal of it are not deceiving him; it must be a very good thing."

"I suppose you mean that half the purchase-money should remain on it as a mortgage, to be paid off later," cried Blair, seizing the idea and brightening up.

"No; not exactly," said Mrs. Todhetley, getting as red as a rose, for she did not like to tell him what she did mean; it looked rather like a conspiracy.

"Look here, Blair," cried the Squire, taking him in the garden by the button-hole, "*I* will see about the other two hundred. You go up and make inquiries on the spot; and perhaps I'll go too; I should like a run up; and if the affair is worth your while, we'll pay the money down on the nail, and so have done with it."

It was Blair's turn to grow red now. "Do you mean, sir, that you—that you—would advance the half of the money? But it would be too generous. I have no claim on you——"

"No claim on me!" burst forth the Squire, in a passion, pinning him against the wall of the pigeon-house. "No claim on me! When you saved my son from drowning only a few weeks ago! And had an ague through it! No claim on me! What next will you say?"

"But that was nothing, sir. Any man, with the commonest feelings of humanity, would jump into the water if he saw a fellow-creature sinking."

"Commonest fiddlestick!" roared the Squire. "If this school is one likely to answer your purpose, you put down your two hundred pounds, and I will see to the rest. There! We'll go up to-day."

"Oh, sir, I never expected this. Perhaps in a year or two I shall be able to pay the money back again: but the goodness I can never repay."

"Don't you trouble your head about paying me back till you're asked to do it," retorted the Squire, mortally offended at the notion. "If you are too proud to take it and say nothing about it, I'll give it to Mary Sanker instead of you. I will, too. Mind, sir! that half shall be your wife's, not yours."

If you'll believe me, there were tears in old Blair's eyes. He was soft at times. The Squire gave him another thrust, which nearly sent Blair into the pigeon-house, and then walked off with his head up and his nankeen coat-skirts held out behind, to watch Drew give the green meat to the pigs. Blair got over his push, and went to find Miss Mary, his thin cheeks alight with a spot as red as Sanker's had worn when his illness was coming on.

They went up to London that day. The Squire had plenty of sense when he chose to exercise it; and instead of trusting to his own investigation and Blair's (which would have been the likeliest thing for him to do in general) he took a lawyer to the spot.

It proved to be all right. The gentleman giving up the school had made some money at it, and was going abroad to his friends, who had settled in Queensland. Any efficient man, he said to the Squire, able to *keep* pupils when once he had secured them, could not fail to do well at it. The clergyman, Mr. Lockett, had called on one or two of the parents, who confirmed what was asserted. Altogether it was a straightforward thing; but they wouldn't abate a shilling of the four hundred pounds.

The Squire concluded the bargain on the spot, for other applicants were after it, and there was danger in delay. He came back to Dyke Manor; and the next thing he did was to accompany Mary Sanker home, and tell the news there.

Mr. Blair stayed in London to take possession, and get things in order. He had only time for a few days' flying visit to Mr. and Mrs. Sanker in Wales before opening his new school. There was no opposition there: people are apt to judge prospects according to their own circumstances; and they seemed to think it a good offer for Mary.

There was no opposition anywhere. Dr. Frost found a new mathematical master without trouble, and sent Blair his best wishes and a full set of plated spoons and forks and things, engraved with the initials P. M. B. He was wise enough to lay out the sum he wished to give in useful things, instead of a silver tea-pot or any other grand article of that kind, which would not be brought to light once a year.

Blair cribbed a week's holiday at Michaelmas, and went down to be married. We saw them at the week's end as they passed through Worcester station. Mary looked the same sweet girl as ever, in the same quiet grey dress (or another that was related to it); and Blair was jolly. He clasped the Squire's hands as if he wanted to take them with him. We handed in a big basket of grapes and nectarines from Mrs. Todhetley; and Mary's nice face smiled and nodded her thanks to the last, as the train puffed on.

"Good luck to them!" said Tod.

Good luck to them. You will hear what luck they had.

For this is *not* the end of that Sunday night's work, or it would have hardly been worth relating, seeing that people get married every day, and no one thinks cheese of it but themselves. The end has to come.

XII.

"JERRY'S GAZETTE."

THE school, taken to by Mr. Blair, was in one of the suburbs of London. It may be as well not to mention which of them; but some of the families yet living there cannot fail to remember the circumstances when they read this. For what I am going to tell you of is true. It did not happen last year; nor the year before. When it did happen, is of no consequence to any one.

When Pyefinch Blair got into the house, he found that it had some dilapidations, which had escaped his notice, and would have to be repaired. Not an uncommon case by any means. Mr. Blair paid the four hundred pounds for the school, including the furniture and good-will, and that drained him of his money. It was not a bad bargain, as bargains go. He then had the house put into fair order, and bought a little more furniture that seemed necessary to him, intending that his boys should be comfortable, as well as the young wife he was soon to bring home.

The school did not profess to be one of those higher-class schools that charge a hundred a year and extras. It was moderate in terms and moderate in size; the pupils being chiefly sons of well-to-do tradesmen, some of them living on the spot. At first, Blair (bringing with him his Cambridge notions) entertained thoughts of raising the school to a higher price and standard. But it would have been a risk; almost like beginning a fresh venture. And when he found that the school paid well, and masters and boys got on comfortably, he dropped the wish.

More than two years went by. One evening, early in February, Mrs. Blair was sitting by the parlour fire after tea, with a great boy on her lap, who was forward with his tongue, and had just begun to walk with a totter. I don't think you could have seen much difference in *her* from what she was as Mary Sanker. She had the same neat sort of dress and quiet manner, the fresh gentle face and sweet eyes, and the pretty, smooth brown hair. Her husband told her sometimes that she would spoil the boys with kindness. If any one fell into disgrace, she was sure to beg him off; it was wonderful what a good mother she was to them, and only twenty-four years old yet.

Mr. Blair was striding the carpet with his head down, as one in perplexed thought, a scowl upon his brow. It was something unusual, for he was always bright. He was as slender and good-looking a fellow as he used to be. Mrs. Blair noticed him and spoke.

"Have you a headache, Pyefinch?" She had long ago got over the odd sound of his Christian name. Habit familiarizes most things.

"No."

"What is it, then?"

He did not make any answer; seemed not to hear her. Mrs. Blair put the boy down on the hearthrug. The child was baptized Joseph, after Squire Todhetley, whom they persisted in calling their best friend.

"Run to papa, Joe. Ask him what the matter is."

The young gentleman went swaying across the carpet, with some unintelligible language of his own. Mr. Blair had no resource but to pick him up: and he carried him back to his mother.

"What is the matter, Pyefinch?" she asked again, taking his hand. "I am sure you are not well."

"I am quite well," he said; "but I have got into a little bother lately. What ails me this evening is, that I find I must tell you of it, and I don't like to do so. There, Mary, send the child away."

She knew the nursemaid was busy; would not ring, but carried him out herself. Mr. Blair was sitting down when she returned, staring into the fire.

"I had hoped you would never know it, Mary; I had not intended that you should. The fact is——"

Mr. Blair stopped. His wife glanced at him; a serene calm in her eyes, a firm reliance in her loving tone.

"Do not hesitate, Pyefinch. The greater the calamity, the more need that I should hear it."

"Nay, it is no such great mischief as to be called a calamity. When I took to this house and school, I incurred a debt, and I am suddenly called upon to pay it."

"Do you mean Mr. Todhetley's?"

A smile at the question crossed the schoolmaster's face. "Mr. Todhetley's was a present; I thought you understood that, Mary. When I would have spoken of returning it, you may remember that he went into a passion."

"What debt is it, then?"

"I paid four hundred pounds, you know, for the school; half of it I had saved; the other half was given by Mr. Todhetley. Well

and good, so far. But I had not thought of one thing—the money
that would be wanted for current expenses, and for the hundred and
one odd things that stare you in the face upon taking to a new
concern. Repairs had to be done, furniture to be bought in; and
not a penny coming in until the end of the quarter: not much then,
for most of the boys pay half-yearly. Lockett, who was down here
most days, saw that if I could not get some money to go on with,
there would be no resource but to re-sell the school. He bestirred
himself, and got me the loan of a hundred and fifty pounds from
a friend, at only five per cent. interest. This money I am suddenly
called upon to repay."

"But why?"

"Because he from whom I had it is dead, and the executors have
called it in. It was Mr Wells."

She recognized the name as that of a gentleman with whom they
had been slightly acquainted; he had died suddenly, in the prime
of life.

"Has any of it been paid off?"

"None. I could have repaid a portion every half-year as it came
round, but Mr. Wells would not let me. 'You had a great deal
better use it in improving the school and getting things comfortable
about you; I am in no hurry,' was his invariable rejoinder. Lockett
thought he meant eventually to make me a present of the money,
being a wealthy man without near relatives. Of course I never
looked for anything of the sort; but I was as easy as to the debt as
though I had not contracted it."

"Will the executors not let you have the use of the money
still?"

"You should see their curt note, ordering its immediate repayment! Lockett seems more vexed at the turn affairs have taken
than even I am. He was here to-day."

Mrs. Blair sat in silent reflection, wishing she had known of this.
Many an odd shilling that she had thought justified in spending,
she would willingly have recalled now. Not that they could have
amounted to much in the aggregate. Presently she looked at her
husband.

"Pyefinch, it seems to me that there's only one thing to do. You
must borrow the sum from some one else, which of course will make
us only as much in debt as we are now; and we must pay it off by
instalments as quickly as we possibly can."

"It is what Lockett and I have decided on already as the only
course. Why, Mary, this worry has been on our minds for a fortnight past," he added, turning quickly. "But now that it has come
to borrowing again, and not from a friend, I felt that I ought to tell
you. Besides, there's another thing."

"Go on," she said.

"We have found a man to advance the money. Lockett and I picked him out from the *Times* advertisements. These fellows are awful rogues, for the most part; but this is not one of the worst. Lockett made inquiries of a parishioner of his who understands these things, and finds Gavity (that's his name) is tolerably fair for a professional money-lender. I shall have to pay him higher interest. And he wants me to give him a bill of sale on the furniture."

"A bill of sale on the furniture! What is that?"

"That is what I meant when I said there was another thing," replied Mr. Blair. "Wells was content with my note of hand; this man requires security on my goods. It is a mere matter of form in my case, he says. As I am doing well, and there's no fear of ·my not keeping the interest paid up, I suppose it is. In two or three years from this, all being well, the debt itself will be wiped off."

"Oh yes; I hope so. The school. is prosperous."

Her tone was anxious, and Mr. Blair detected it. But for considering that she ought to know it, he would rather have kept this trouble to himself. And he was not sure upon another point : whether, in giving this bill of sale upon the furniture, Mr. Gavity might deem it essential to come in and take a list, article by article, bed by bed, table by table. If so, it would not have been possible to conceal it from her. He mentioned this. She, with himself, could not understand the necessity of their furniture being brought into the transaction at all, seeing that there could be no doubt as to their ability to repay. The one knew just as much about bills of sale and the rights they gave, as the other : and, that, was nothing.

And now that the communication to his wife was off his mind— for in that had lain the chief weight—Mr. Blair was more at ease. As they sat talking together, discussing the future in all its aspects, the shadow lifted itself, and things looked brighter. It did not seem to either of them so formidable a matter after all. It was only changing one creditor for another, and paying a little higher interest.

The transaction was accomplished. Gavity advanced the money, and took the bill of sale upon the furniture. He shot up the expenses—as money-lenders of his stamp generally do—and brought up the loan to a hundred and eighty, instead of a hundred and fifty. Still, taking things for all in all, the position was perhaps as fair and hopeful a one as can be experienced under debt. It was but a temporary clog; Mr. and Mrs. Blair both knew that. The school was flourishing; their prospects were good; they were young, and healthy, and hopeful. And though Mr. Gavity would of course exact his rights to the uttermost farthing, he had no intention of playing the rogue. In all candour let it be avowed, the gentleman money-lender did not see that it was a case affording scope for it.

I had to tell that much as well as I could, seeing that it only came to me by hearsay in the future.

And now to go back a little while, and to ourselves at Dyke Manor.

After their marriage the Squire did not lose sight of Mr. and Mrs. Blair. A basket of things went up now and then, and the second Christmas they were invited to come down; but Mary wrote to decline, on account of Joe, the baby. "Let them leave Joe at home," cried Tod; but Mrs. Todhetley, shaking her head, said the dear little infant would come to sad grief without its mother. Soon after that, when the Squire was in London, he took the omnibus and went to see them, and told us how comfortably they were getting on.

Years went round to another Christmas, when the exacting Joe would be some months over two years old. In the passing of time you are apt to lose sight of interests, unless they are close ones; and for some months we had heard nothing of the Blairs. Mrs. Todhetley spoke of it one evening.

"Send them a Christmas hamper," said the Squire.

The Christmas hamper went. With a turkey and ham, and a brace of pheasants in it; some bacon and apples to fill up, and sweet herbs and onions. Lena put in her favourite doll, dressed as a little mother, for young Joe. It had a false arm; and no legs, so to say: Hugh cut the feet off one day, and Hannah had to sew the stumps up. We hoped they would enjoy it all, including the doll, and drank good luck to them on Christmas Day.

A week and a half went on, and no news came. Mrs. Todhetley grew uneasy about the hamper, feeling sure it had been confiscated by the railway. Mary Blair had always written so promptly to acknowledge everything sent to them.

One January day the letter came in by the afternoon post. We knew Mary's handwriting. The Squire and Madam were at the Sterlings', and it was nine o'clock at night when they drove in. Mrs. Todhetley's face ached, which was quite usual she had a white handkerchief tied round it. When they were seated round the fire, I remembered the letter, and gave it to her.

"Now to hear the fate of the hamper!" she exclaimed, carrying it to the lamp. But, what with the face-ache, and what with her

eyes, which were not so good by candle-light as they used to be,
Mrs. Todhetley could not read the contents readily. She looked
at the writing, page after page, and then gave a short scream of
dismay. Something was wrong.

"Those thieves have grabbed the hamper!" cried the Squire.

"No; I think the Blairs have had the hamper. I fear it is
something worse," she said faintly. "Perhaps you will read it
aloud."

The Squire put his spectacles on as he took the letter. We
gathered round the table, waiting. Mrs. Todhetley sat with her
head aside, nursing her cheek; and Tod, who had been reading,
put his book down. The Squire hammered a good deal over the
writing, which was not so legible as Mary's was in general. She
appeared to have meant it for Mrs. Todhetley and the Squire
jointly.

"'My very Dear Friends,

"'If I have delayed writing to you it was not for want
of in-ingredients'"——

"Ingredients!" cried one of us.

"It must be gratitude," corrected the Squire. "Don't interrupt."

"'Gratitude for your most welcome and liberal present, but
because my heart and hands have alike shrunk from the ex—ex—
explanation it must entail. Alas! a series of very terrible mis-
fortunes have overwormed—overwhelmed us. We have had to
give up our school and our prospects together, and to turn out of
our once happy dome.'"

"Dome!" put in Tod.

"I suppose it's home," said the Squire. "This confounded lamp
is as dim as it can be to-night!" And he went on fractiously.

"'Through no fault of my husband's he had to borrow a hundred
and fifty pounds nearly twelve months ago. The man he had it
from was a money-lender, a Mr. Gavity; he charged a high rate of
interest, and brought the cost up to about thirty pounds; but we
have no reason to think he wished to act un—unfar—unfairly by
us. He required security—which I suppose was only reasonable.
The Reverend Mr. Lockett offered himself; but Gavity said parsons
were slippers.'"

"Good gracious!" said Mrs. Todhetley.

"The word's slippery, I expect," cried the Squire with a frown.
"One would think she had emptied the water-bottle into the ink-
pot."

"'Gavity said parsons were slippery; meaning that they were
often worth no more than their word. He took, as security, a bill
of sale on the furnace. Stay,—furniture. Our school was quite

prosperous; there was not the slightest doubt that in a short time
the whole of the debt could be cleared off; so we had no hesitation
in letting him have the bill of sale. And no harm would have come
of it, but for one dreadful misfortune, which (as it seems) was a
necessary part of the attendant proceedings. My husband got put
into *Jer—Jer—Jerry's Gazelle.'*"

"*Jerry's Gazelle?*"

"*Jerry's Gazette,*" corrected the Squire.

"*Jerry's Gazette?*"

We all spoke at once. He stared at the letters and then at us.
We stared back again.

"It *is Jerry's Gazette*—as I think. Come and see, Joe."

Tod looked over the Squire's shoulder. It certainly looked like
"*Jerry's Gazette,*" he said; but the ink was pale.

"'*Jerry's Gazette.*' Go on, father. Perhaps you'll find an explanation further on."

"'This *Jerry's Gazette*, it appears, is circulated chiefly (and I
think privately) amongst comical men—commercial men; mer-
chants, and tradespeople. When they read its list of names, they
know at once who is in difficulties. Of course they saw my
husband's name there, Pyefinch Blair; unfortunately a name so
peculiar as not to admit of any doubt. I did not see the *Gazette*,
but I believe the amount of the debt was stated, and that Gavity
(but I don't know whether he was mentioned by name) had a bill
of sale on our household furniture.'"

"What the dickens is *Jerry's Gazette?*" burst forth the Squire,
giving the letter a passionate flick. "I know but of one *Gazette*,
into which men of all conditions go, whether they are made lords
or bankrupts. What's this other thing?"

He put up his spectacles, and stared at us all again, as if expecting an answer. But he might as well have asked it of the moon.
Mrs. Todhetley sat with the most hopeless look you ever saw on
her face. So he went on reading again.

"'We knew nothing about *Jerry's Gazette* ourselves, or that
there was such a pub—pub—publication, or that the transaction
had appeared in it; and could not imagine why the school began
to fall off. Some of the pupils were taken away, *at once*, some at
Lady-day; and by Midsummer nearly every one had left. We
used to lie awake night after night, grieving and wondering what
could be the matter, searching in vain for any cause of offence,
given unwittingly to the boys or their parents. Often and often we
got up in the morning to go about our day's work, never having
closed our eyes. At last, a gentleman, whose son had been one of
the first renewed—removed, told Pyefinch the truth: that he had
appeared in *Jerry's Gazette*. The fathers who subscribed to

Jerry's Gazette had seen it for themselves; and they informed the others.'"

"The devil take *Jerry's Gazette*," interrupted Tod, deliberately. "This reads like an episode of the Secret Inquisition, sir, in the days of the French Revolution."

"It reads like a thing that an honest Englishman's ears ought to redden to hear of," answered the Squire, as he put the lamp nearer, for his outstretched arms were getting cramped.

"'Pyefinch went round to every one.of the boy's fathers. Some would not see him, some not hear him; but to those who did, he imported—imparted—the whole circumstances; showing how it was that he had had to borrow the money (or rather to re-borrow it, but I have not time in this letter to go so far into detail), and that it could not by any possibility injure the boys or touch their interests. Most of them, he said, were very kind and sympathizing, so far as words went, saying that in this case *Jerry's Gazette* appeared to have been the means of inflicting a cruel wrong; but they would not agree to replace their sons with us. They either declined point-blank, or said they'd consider of it; but you see the greater portion of the boys were already placed at other schools. All of them told Pyefinch one thing—that they were thoroughly satisfied with his treatment in every respect, and but for this interruption would probably have left their sons with him as long as they wanted intrusion—instruction. The long and short of it was this, my dear friends : they did not choose to have their sons educated by a man who was looked upon in the commercial world as next door to a bankrupt. One of them delicately hinted as much, and said Mr. Blair must be aware that he was liable to have his house topped—stripped—at any moment under the bill of sale. We said to ourselves that evening, as Pyefinch and I talked together, that we might have removed boys of our own from a school under the same circumstances.'"

"That's true enough," murmured Mrs. Todhetley.

"'My letter has grown very long and I must hasten to conclude it. Just before the rent was due at Michaelmas (we paid it half-yearly, by agreement) Gavity put the bill of sale into force. One morning several men came in and swept off the furniture. We were turned out next : though indeed to have attempted to remain in that large house were folly. The landlord came in a passion, and told Pyefinch that he would put him in prison if he were worth it ; as he was not, he had better go out of the pitch—place—forthwith, as another tenant was ready to take possession. Since then we have been staying here, Pyefinch vainly seeking to get some employment. What we hoped was, that he would obtain an under-mastership to some public fool—— "

"Fool, sir!"

"'School. But it seems difficult. He sends his best regards to you, and bids me say that the reason you have not heard from us so long is, that we could not bear to tell you the ill news after your former kindness to us. The arrival of the hamper leaves us no resource.

"'Thank you for that. Thank you very truly. The people at the old house have our address, and re-directed it here. We received it early on Christmas Eve. How good the things were, you do not need to be told. I stuffed the turkey—I shall make a famous cook in time—and sent it to the backhouse—bakehouse. You should have seen the pill—picture—it was when it came home. Believe me, my dear friends, we are both of us grateful for all your kindness to us, past and present. Little Joe is so delighted with the doll, he scarcely puts it out of his arms. Our best love to all, including Hugh and Lena. Thank Johnny for the beautiful new book he put in. I must apologize in conclusion for my writing; the ink we get in these penny bottles is pale; and baby has been on my lap all the time, never easy a minute. Do not say anything of all this, please, should you be writing to Wales.

"'Ever most truly yours,
"'MARY BLAIR.

"'13, *Difford's Buildings, Paddington.*'"

The Squire put the letter down and his spectacles on it, quite solemnly. You might have heard a pin drop in that room.

"This is a thing that must be inquired into. I shall go up to-morrow."

"And I'd go too, sir, but for my engagement to the Whitneys," said Tod.

"She must mean, in speaking of a baby, that there's another," spoke Mrs. Todhetley, in a frightened sort of whisper. "Besides little Joe. Dear me!"

"I don't understand it," stamped the Squire, getting red. "Turned out of house and home through *Jerry's Gazette!* Do we live in England, I'd like to ask?—under English laws?—enjoying English rights and freedom? *Jerry's Gazette?* What the deuce *is Jerry's Gazette?* Where does it come from? What issues it? The Lord Chamberlain's Office?—or Scotland Yard?—or some Patent society that we've not heard of, down here? The girl must have been imposed upon: her statement won't hold water."

"It looks as though she had been, sir."

"*Looks* like it, Johnny! It must be so," said the Squire, growing warmer. "I have temporary need of a sum of money, and I borrow it straightforwardly, honestly purposing and undertaking to pay it back with good interest, but not exactly wanting my neighbours to know about it; and you'd like me to believe that there's some association, or publication, or whatever else it may be, that won't allow this to be done privately, but must pounce upon the transaction, and take it down in print, and send it round to the public, just as if it were a wedding or a burying!"

The Squire had grown redder than a roost-cock. He always did when tremendously put out, and the matter would not admit of calling in old Jones the constable.

"Folly! Moonshine! Blair, poor fellow, has been slipping into some disaster, had his furniture seized, and so invents this fable to appease his wife, not liking to tell her the truth. *Jerry's Gazette!* When I was a youngster, my father took me to see an exhibition in Worcester called 'Jerry's Dogs.' · The worst damage you could get there was a cold, from the holes in the canvas roof, or a pitch over the front into the sawdust. But in *Jerry's Gazette*, according to this tale, you may be damaged for life. Don't tell me! Do we live in Austria, or France, or any of those places, where—as it's said—a man can't so much as put on a pair of clean stockings in a morning, but its laid before high quarters in black and white at mid-day by the secret police! No, you need not tell me that."

"I never heard of *Jerry's Gazette* in all my life; I don't know whether it is a stage performance or something to eat; but I feel convinced Mary Blair would not write this without having good grounds for it," said Tod, bold as usual.

And do you know—though you may be slow to believe it—the Squire had taken latterly to listen to him. He turned his red old face on him now, and some of its fierceness went out of it.

"Then, Joe, all I can say is this—that English honour and English notions have changed uncommonly from what they used to be. 'Live and let live' was one of our mottoes; and most of us tried to act up to it. I know no more of this," striking his hand on the letter, "than you know, boys; and I cannot think but that she must have been under some unaccountable mistake in writing it. Any way, I'll go up to London to-morrow: and if you like, Johnny, you can go with me."

We went up. I did not feel sure of it until the train was off, for Tod seemed three-parts inclined to give up the shooting at the Whitneys', and start for London instead; in which case the Squire might not have taken me. Tod and some more young fellows were invited to Whitney Hall for three days, to a shooting-match.

It was dusk when we reached London, and as cold as charity. The Squire turned into the railway hotel and had some chops served, but did not wait for a regular dinner. When once he was in for impatience, he *was* in for it.

"Difford's Buildings, Paddington," had been the address, so we thought it would not be far to go. The Squire held on in his way along the crowded streets, as if he were about to set things to rights, elbowing the people, and asking the road at every turn. Some did not know Difford's Buildings, and some directed us wrongly; but we got there at last. It was in a narrow, quiet street; a row of what Londoners call eight-roomed houses, with little gates opening to the square patches of smoky garden, and "Difford's Buildings" written up as large as life at the corner.

"Let's see," said the Squire, looking sideways at the windows. "Number thirteen, was it not, Johnny?"

"Yes, sir."

Difford's Buildings were not well lighted, and there was no seeing the numbers. The Squire stopped before the one he thought must be thirteen; when some one came out at the house-door, shutting it behind him, and met us at the gate. A youngish clergyman in a white necktie. He and the Squire stood looking at each other in the gathering darkness.

"Can you tell me if Mr. Blair lives here?"

"Yes, he does," was the answer. "I think—I think I have the pleasure of speaking to Mr. Todhetley."

The Squire knew him then—the Reverend Mr. Lockett. They had met when Blair first took to the school.

"What *is* all this extraordinary history?" burst forth the Squire, seizing him by the button of his great-coat, and taking him a few yards further on. "Mrs. Blair has been writing us a strange rigmarole, which nobody can make head or tail of; about ruin, and sales, and something she calls *Jerry's Gazette.*"

"Ay," quietly answered the clergyman in a tone of pain, as he put his arm inside the Squire's, and they paced slowly up and down. "It is one of the saddest histories my experience has ever had to do with."

The Squire was near coming to an explosion in the open street. "Will you be pleased to tell me, sir, whether there exists such a thing as *Jerry's Gazette*, or whether it is a fable? I have heard of Jerry's Performing Dogs; went to see 'em once: but I don't know what this other invention can be."

"Certainly there is such a thing," said Mr. Lockett. "It is, I fancy, a list of people who unfortunately get into difficulties; at least, people who fall into difficulties seem to get shown up in it. I am told it is meant chiefly for private circulation: which may imply, as I imagine (but here I may be wrong) what may be called secret circulation. Blair had occasion to borrow a little money, and *his* name appeared in it. From that moment he was a marked man, and his school fell off."

"Goodness bless my soul!" cried the Squire solemnly, completely taken aback at hearing Mary's letter confirmed. "Who gives *Jerry's Gazette* the right to do this?"

"I don't know about the right. It seems it has the power."

"It is a power I never heard of before, sir. We have a parson, down our way, who tells us every Sunday the world's coming to an end. I think it must be. I know it's getting too clever for me to understand. If a man has the misfortune (perhaps after years of struggling that nobody knows anything about but himself) to break up at last, he goes into the country's *Gazette* in a straightforward manner, and the public read it over their breakfast-tables, and there's nothing underhand about it. But as to this other thing—if I comprehend the matter rightly—Blair did not as much as know of its existence, or that his name was going into it."

"I am sure he did not; or I, either," said Mr. Lockett.

"I should like its meaning explained, then," cried the Squire, getting hotter and angrier. "Is it a fair, upright, honest thing; or is it a sort of Spanish Inquisition?"

"I cannot tell you," answered the parson, as they both stood still. "Mr. Blair was informed by the father of one of his pupils that he believed the sheet was first of all set up as a speculation, and was found to answer so well that it became quite an institution. I do not know whether this is true."

"I have heard of an institution for idiots, but I never heard of one for selling up men's chairs and tables," stormed the Squire. "No, sir, and I don't believe it now. I might take up my standing to-morrow on the top of the Monument, and say to the public, 'Here I am, and I'll ferret out what I can about you, and whisper it to one another of you;' and so bring a serpent's trail on the unsuspecting heads, and altogether play Old Gooseberry with the crowds below me. Do you suppose, sir, the Lord Chancellor would wink his eye at me, stuck aloft there at my work, and would tolerate such a spectacle?"

"I fear the Lord Chancellor has not much to do with it," said Mr. Lockett, smiling at the Squire's random logic.

"Then suppose we say good men—public opinion—commercial justice and honour? Come!"

He shook the frail railings, on which his hand was resting, until they nearly came to grief. Mr. Lockett related the particulars of the transaction from the beginning; the original debt, which Blair was suddenly called upon to pay off, and the contraction of the one to Gavity. He said that he himself had had as much to do with it as Blair, in the capacity of friend and adviser, and felt almost as though he were responsible for the turn affairs had taken; which had caused him scarcely to enjoy an easy moment since. The

Squire began to abuse Gavity, but Mr. Lockett said the man did
not appear to have had any ill intention. As to his having sold
off the goods—if he had not sold them, the landlord would have
done so.

"And what's Blair doing now?" asked Mr. Todhetley.

"Battling with illness for his life," said the clergyman. "I have
just been praying with him."

The Squire retreated towards the lamp-post, as if some one had
given him a blow. Mr. Lockett explained further.

It was in September that they had left their home. His own
lodging and the church of which he was curate were in Paddington,
and he found rooms for Blair and his wife in the same neighbourhood—two parlours in Difford's Buildings. Blair (who had lost
heart so terribly as to be good for little) spared no time or exertion
in seeking for something to do. He tried to get into King's
College; they liked his appearance and testimonials, but at present
had no vacancy: he tried private schools for an ushership, but did
did not get one: nothing seemed to be vacant just then. Then he
tried for a clerk's place. Day after day, ill or well, rain or fine,
feasting or fasting, he went tramping about London streets. At
last, one of those who had had sons at his school, gave him some
out-door employment—that of making known a new invention and
soliciting customers for it from shop to shop: Blair to be paid on
commission. Naturally, he did not let weather hinder him, and
would come home to Difford's Buildings at night, wet through.
There had been a great deal of rain in November and December.
But he got wet once too often, and was attacked with rheumatic
fever. The fever was better now; but the weakness it had left was
dangerous.

"She did not say anything about this in her letter," interrupted
the Squire resentfully, when Mr. Lockett had explained so far.

"Blair told her not to do so. He thought if their position were
revealed to the friends who had once shown themselves so kind, it
might look almost like begging for help again."

"Blair's a fool!" roared the Squire.

"Mrs. Blair has not made the worst of it to her family in Wales.
It would only distress them, she says, for they could not help her.
Mr. Sanker has been ill again for some time past, has not been
allowed, I believe, to draw his full salary, and there's no doubt they
want every penny of their means for themselves; and more too."

"How have they lived here?" asked the Squire, as we went
slowly back to the gate.

"Blair earned a little while he could get about; and his wife has
been enabled to procure some kind of wool-work from a warehouse
in the city, which pays her very well," said the clergyman, dropping

his voice to a whisper, as if he feared to be overheard. "Unfortunately there's the baby to take up much of her time. It was born in October, soon after they came there."

And I should like to know what business there has to be a baby?" cried the Squire, who was like a man off his head. "Couldn't the baby have waited for a more convenient season?"

"It might have been better; it is certainly a troublesome, crying little thing," said the parson. "Yes, you can go straight in : the parlour door is on the right. I have a service this evening at seven, and shall be late for it. This is your son, I presume, sir?"

"My son! law bless you! My son is a strapping young fellow, six feet two in his stockings. This is Johnny Ludlow."

He shook hands pleasantly, and was good enough to say he had heard of me. The Squire went on, and I with him. There was no lamp in the passage, and we had to feel on the right for the parlour door.

"Come in," called out Mary, in answer to the knock. I knew her voice again.

We can't help our thoughts. . Things come into the mind without leave or licence; and it is no use saying they ought not to, or asking why they do. Nearly opposite the door in the small room was the fireplace. Mary Blair sat on a low stool before it, doing some work with coloured wools with a big hooked needle, a baby in white lying flat on her lap, and the little chap, Joe, sitting at her feet. All in a moment it put me in mind of Mrs. Lease, sitting on her stool before the fire that day long ago (though in point of fact, as I discovered afterwards, hers had been a bucket turned upside down) with the sick child on her lap, and the other little ones round her. Why this, to-night, should have reminded me of that other, I cannot say, but it did; and in the light of an omen. You must ridicule me if you choose : it is not my fault; and I am telling nothing but the truth. Lease had died. Would Pyefinch Blair die?

The Squire went in gingerly, as if he had been treading on ploughshares. The candle stood on the mantel-piece, a table was pushed back under the window. Altogether the room was poor, and a small saucepan simmered on the hob. Mary turned her head, and rose up with a flushed face, letting the work fall on the baby's white nightgown, as she held out her hand. Little Joe, a sturdy fellow in a scarlet frock, with big brown eyes, backed against the wall by the fireplace and stood staring, Lena's doll held safely under his pinafore.

She lost her presence of mind. The Squire was the veriest old stupid, when he wanted to make-believe, that you'd see in a winter's day. He began saying something about "happening to be in town,

and so called." But he broke down, and blurted out the truth.
"We've come to see after you, my dear; and to learn what all this
trouble means."

And then *she* broke down. Perhaps it was the sight of us, recalling the old time at Dyke Manor, when the future looked so fair
and happy; perhaps it was the mention of the trouble. She put
her hands before her face, and the tears rained through her
fingers.

"Shut the door, will you, Johnny," she whispered. "Very
softly."

It was the other door she pointed to, one at the end of the
room, and I closed it without noise. Except for a sob now and
again, that she kept down as well as she could, the grief passed
away. Young Joe, frightened at matters, suddenly went at her, full
butt, and hid his eyes in her petticoats with a roar. I took him on
my knee and got him round again. Somehow children are never
afraid of me. The Squire rubbed his old red nose, and said he had
a cold.

But, was she not altered! Now that the flush had faded, and
emotion passed, the once sweet, fresh, blooming face stood out
in its reality. Sweet, indeed, it was still; but the bloom and fresh-
ness had given place to a haggard look, and to dark circles round
the soft brown eyes, weary now.

She had no more to tell of the past calamities than her letter
and Mr. Lockett had told. *Jerry's Gazette* was the sore point
with the Squire, but she did not seem to understand it better than
we did.

"I want to know one thing," said he, quite fiercely. "How did
Jerry's Gazette get at the transaction between your husband and
Gavity? Did Gavity go to it, open-mouthed, with the news?"

Mary did not know. She had heard something about a register
—that the bill of sale had to be registered somewhere, and thought
Jerry's Gazette might have obtained the information from that
source.

"Heaven bless us all!" cried the Squire. "Can't a man borrow
a bit of money but it must become known to his enemies, if he has
any, bringing them down upon him like a pack of hounds in full
cry? This used to be the freest land on earth."

The baby began to scream. She put down the wool-work, and
hushed it to her. I am sure the Squire had half a mind to tell
her to give it a gentle shaking. He looked upon screaming babies
as natural enemies: the truth is, with all his abuse, he was afraid of
them.

"Has it got a name?" he asked gruffly.

"Yes—Mary: he wished it," she said, glancing at the door.

" I thought we should have to call it Polly, in contradistinction to mine."

Polly! That was another coincidence. Lease's eldest girl was Polly. And what made her speak of things in the past tense? She caught me looking at her; caught, I fancy, the fear on my face. I told her hurriedly that little Joe must be a Dutchman, for not a word could I understand of the tale he was whispering about his doll.

What with Mary's work, and the little earned by Blair while he was about, they had not wanted for necessaries in a plain way. I suppose Lockett took care they should not do so: but he was only a curate.

The baby needed its supper, to judge by the squealing. Mary poured the contents of the saucepan—some thin gruel—into a saucer, and began feeding the little mite by teaspoonfuls, putting each one to her own lips first to test it.

"That's poor stuff," cried the Squire, in a half-pitying, half-angry tone, his mind divided between resentment against babies in general and sympathy with this one. As the baby was there, of course it had to be fed, but what he wanted to know was, why it need have come just when trouble was about. When put out, he had no reason at all. Mrs. Blair suddenly turned her face towards the end door, listening; and we heard a faint voice calling " Mary."

"Joe, dear, go and tell papa that I will be with him in one minute."

The little chap slid down, giving me his doll to nurse, and went pattering across the carpet, standing on tiptoe to open the door. The Squire said he should like to go in and see Blair. Mary went on first to warn him of our advent.

My goodness! *That* Pyefinch Blair, who used to flourish his cane, and cock it over us boys at Frost's! I should never have known him for the same.

He lay in bed, too weak to raise his head from the pillow, the white skin drawn tightly over his hollow features; the cheeks slightly flushing as he watched us coming. And again I thought of Lease; for the same look was on this face that had been on his when he was dying.

"Lord bless us!" cried the Squire, in what would have been a solemn tone but for surprise. And Mr. Blair began faintly to offer a kind of apology for his illness, hoping he should soon get over it now.

It was nothing but the awful look, putting one unpleasantly in mind of death, that kept the Squire from breaking out with a storm of abuse all round. Why could they not have sent word to Dyke Manor, he wanted to know. As to asking particulars about *Jerry's*

Gazette, which the Squire's tongue was burning to do, Blair was too
far gone for it. While we stood there the doctor came in; a little
man in spectacles, a friend of Mr. Lockett's. He told Blair he was
getting on all right, spoke to Mrs. Blair, and took his departure.
The Squire, wishing good night in a hurry, went out after the doctor,
and collared him as he was walking up the street.

"Won't he get over it?"

"Well, sir, I am afraid not. His state of weakness is alarming."

The Squire turned on him with a storm, just as though he had
known him for years: asking why on earth Blair's friends (meaning
himself) had not been written to, and promising a prosecution if he
let him die. The doctor took it sensibly, and was cool as iced water.

"We medical men are only gifted at best with human skill, sir,"
he said, looking the Squire full in the face.

"Blair is young—not much turned thirty."

"The young die as well as the old, when it pleases Heaven to
take them."

"But it doesn't please Heaven to take *him*," retorted the Squire,
worked up to the point when he was not accountable for his words.
"But that you seem in earnest, young man, probably meaning no
irreverence, I'd ask you how you dare bring Heaven's name into
such a case as this? Did Heaven fling him out of house and home
into *Jerry's Gazette*, do you suppose? Or did man? Man, sir:
selfish, hard, unjust man. Don't talk to me, Mr. Doctor, about
Heaven."

"All I wished to imply, sir, was, that Mr. Blair's life is not in
my keeping, or in that of any human hands," said the doctor, when
he had listened quietly to the end. "I will do my best to bring
him round; I can do no more."

"You must bring him round."

"There can be no 'must' about it: and I doubt if he is to be
brought round. Mr. Blair has not naturally a large amount of
what we call stamina, and this illness has laid a very serious hold
upon him. It would be something in his favour if the mind were at
ease: which of course it cannot be in his circumstances."

"Now look here—you just say outright he is going to die,"
stormed the Squire. "Say it and have done with it. I like people
to be honest."

"But I cannot say he is. Possibly he may recover. His life
and his death both seem to hang on the turn of a thread."

"And there's that squealing young image within earshot! Could
Blair be got down to my place in the country? You might come
with him if you liked. There's some shooting."

"Not yet. It would kill him. What we have to fight against
now is the weakness: and a hard fight it is."

The Squire's face was rueful to look at. "This London has a reputation for clever physicians: you pick out the best, and bring him here with you to-morrow morning. Do you hear, sir?"

"I will bring one, if you wish it. It is not essential."

"Not essential!" wrathfully echoed the Squire. "If Blair's recovery is not essential, perhaps you'll tell me, sir, whose is! What is to become of his poor young wife if he dies?—and the little fellow with the doll?—and that cross-grained puppet in white? Who will provide for them? Let me tell you, sir, that I won't have him die—if doctors can keep him alive. He belongs to me, sir, in a manner: he saved my son's life—as fine a fellow as you could set eyes on, six feet two without his boots. Not essential! What next?"

"It is not so much medical skill he requires now as care, and rest, and renovation," spoke the doctor in his calm way.

"Never mind. You take a physician to him, and let him attend him with you, and don't spare expense. In all my life I never saw anybody want patching up so much as he wants it."

The Squire shook hands with him, and went on round the corner. I was following, when the doctor touched me on the shoulder.

"He has a good heart, for all his hot speech," whispered he, nodding towards the Squire. "In talking with him this evening, when you find him indulging hopes of Blair's recovery, *don't encourage them:* rather lead him, if possible, to look at the other side of the question."

The surgeon was off before I recovered from my surprise. But it was now my turn to run after him.

"Do you know that he will not get well, sir?"

"I do not know it; the weak and the strong are alike in the hands of God; but I think it scarcely possible that he can recover," was the answer; and the voice had a solemn tone, the face a solemn aspect, in the uncertain light. "And I would prepare friends always to meet the worst when it is in my power to do so."

"Now then, Johnny! You were going to take the wrong turning, were you, sir! Let me tell you, you might get lost in London before knowing it."

The Squire had come back to the corner, looking for me. I walked on by his side in silence, feeling half dazed, the hopeless words playing pranks in my brain.

"Johnny, I wonder where we can find a telegraph office? I shall telegraph to your mother to send up Hannah to-morrow. Hannah knows what the sick need: and that poor thing with her children ought not to be left alone."

But as to giving any hint to the Squire of the state of affairs, I should like the doctor to have tried it himself. Before I had finished the first syllable, he attacked me as if I had been a tiger; demanding whether those were my ideas of Christianity, and if I supposed there'd be any justice in a man's dying because he had got into *Jerry's Gazette.*

In the morning the Squire went on an expedition to Gavity's office in the city. It was a dull place of two rooms, with a man to answer people. We had not been there a minute when the Squire began to explode, going on like anything at the man for saying Mr. Gavity was engaged and could not be seen. The Squire demanded if he thought we were creditors, that he should deny Gavity.

What with his looks and his insistence, and his promise to bring in Sir Richard Mayne, he got to see Gavity. We went into a good room with a soft red carpet and marble-topped desk in it. Mr. Gavity politely motioned to chairs before the blazing fire, and I sat down.

Not the Squire. Out it all came. He walked about the room, just as he walked at home when he was in a way, and said all kinds of things; wanting to know who had ruined Pyefinch Blair, and what *Jerry's Gazette* meant. Gavity seemed to be used to explosions: he took it so coolly.

When the Squire calmed down, he almost grew to see things in Gavity's own light—namely, that Gavity had not been to blame. To say the truth, I could not understand that he had. Except in selling them up. And Gavity said if he had not done it, the landlord would.

So nothing was left for the Squire to vent his wrath on but *Jerry's Gazette.* He no more understood what *Jerry's Gazette* really was, or whether it was a good or bad thing in itself, than he understood the construction of the planet Jupiter. It's well Dwarf Giles was not present. The day before we came to London, he overheard Giles swearing in a passion, and the Squire had pounced upon him with an indignant inquiry if he thought swearing was the way to get to heaven. What he said about *Jerry's Gazette* caused Gavity's eyes to grow round with wonder.

"Lord love ye!" said Gavity, "*Jerry's Gazette* a thing that wants putting down! Why, it is the blessedest of institutions to us City men. It is a public Benefactor. The commercial world has had no boon like it. Did you know the service it does, you'd sing its praises, sir, instead of abusing it."

"How dare you tell me so to my face?" demanded the Squire.

"*Jerry's Gazette's* like a gold mine, sir. It is making its fortune. A fine one, too."

"*I* shouldn't like to make a fortune out of my neighbours' tears, and blood, and homes, and hearths," was the wrathful answer. "If Pyefinch Blair dies in his illness, will *Jerry's Gazette* settle a pension from its riches on his widow and children? Answer me that, Mr. Gavity."

Mr. Gavity, to judge by his looks, thought the question nearly as unreasonable as he thought the Squire. He wanted to tell of the vast benefit *Jerry's Gazette* had proved in certain cases; but the Squire stopped his ears, saying Blair's case was enough for him.

"I do not deny that the *Gazette* may work mischief once in a way," acknowledged Mr. Gavity. "It is but a solitary instance, sir; and in all commercial improvements the few must suffer for the many."

No good. The Squire went at him again, hammer and tongs, and at last dashed away without saying good morning, calling out to me to come on, and not stop a moment longer in a nest of thieves and casuists.

Difford's Buildings had us in the afternoon. The baby was in its basket, little Joe lay asleep before the fire, the doll against his check, and Mary was kneeling by the bed in the back room. She got up hastily when she saw us.

"I think he is weaker," she said in a whisper, as she came through the door and pushed it to. "There is a look on his face that I do not like."

There was a look on hers. A wan, haggard, patiently hopeless look, that seemed to say she could struggle no longer. It was not natural; neither was the calm, lifeless tone.

"Stay here a bit, my dear, and rest yourself," said the Squire to her. "I'll go in and sit with him."

There could be no mistake now. Death was in every line of his face. His head was a little raised on the pillow; and the hollow eyes tried to smile a greeting. The Squire was good for a great deal, but not for making believe with that sight before him. He broke down with a great sob.

"Don't grieve for me," murmured poor Blair. "Hard though it seems to leave her, I have learnt to say, 'God's will be done.' It is all for the best—oh, it is all for the best. We must through much tribulation enter into the Kingdom."

And then *I* broke down, and hid my face on the counterpane. Poor old Blair! And we boys had called him Baked Pie!

I went to Paddington station to meet the train. Hannah was in it, and came bursting out upon me with a shriek that might have been heard at Oxford. Upon the receipt of the telegram, she and Mrs. Todhetley came to the conclusion that I had been run over, and was lying in some hospital with my legs off. That was through the Squire's wording of the message; he would not let me write it. "Send Hannah to London to-morrow by mid-day train, to nurse somebody that's in danger."

Blair lingered three days yet before he died, sensible to the last, and quite happy. Not a care or anxiety on his mind about what had so troubled him all along—the wife and children.

"Through God's mercy; He knows how to soothe the death-bed," said Mr. Lockett.

Whether Mary would have to go home to Wales with her babies, or stay and do what she could for them in London, depending on the wool-work, the clergyman said he did not know, when talking to us at the hotel. He supposed it must be one of the two.

"We'll have them down at the Manor, and fatten 'em up a bit, Johnny," spoke the Squire, a rueful look on his good old face. "Mercy light upon us! and all through *Jerry's Gazette!*"

I must say a word for myself. *Jerry's Gazette* (if there is such a thing still in existence) may be, as Mr. Gavity expressed it to us then, the "blessedest of institutions to him and commercial men." I don't wish to deny it, and I could not if I wished; for except in this one instance (which may have been an exceptional case, as Gavity insisted) I know nothing of it or its working. But I declare on my honour I have told nothing but the truth in regard to what it did for the schoolmaster, Pyefinch Blair.

XIII.

SOPHIE CHALK.

THE horses went spanking along the frosty road, the Squire driving, his red comforter wrapped round his neck. Mrs. Todhetley sat beside him; Tod and I behind. It was one of the jolliest days that early January ever gave us; dark blue sky, and icicles on the trees: a day to tempt people out. Mrs. Todhetley, getting to her work after breakfast, said it was a shame to stay indoors: and it was hastily decided to drive over to the Whitneys' place and see them. So the large phaeton was brought round.

I had not expected to go. When there was a probability of their staying anywhere sufficiently long for the horses to be put up, Giles was generally taken: the Squire did not like to give trouble to other people's servants. It would not matter at the Whitneys': they had a host of them.

"I don't know that I care about going," said Tod, as we stood outside, waiting for the others, Giles at the horses' heads.

"Not care, Tod! Anna's at home."

He flicked his glove at my face for the impudence. We laughed as him about Anna Whitney sometimes. They were great friends. The Squire, hearing some nonsense one day, took it seriously, and told Tod it would be time enough for him to get thinking about sweethearts when he was out of leading-strings. Which of course Tod did not like.

It was a long drive; I can tell you that. And as we turned in at the wide gravel sweep that led up to the house, we saw their family coach being brought round with some luggage on it, the postilion in his undress jacket, just laced at the seams with crimson. The Whitneys never drove from the box.

Whitney Hall was a long red-brick house with a good many windows and wide circular steps leading to the door, its park and grounds lying around it. Anna came running to meet us as we went in, dressed for a journey. She was seventeen; very fair; with a gentle face, and smooth, bright, dark auburn hair; one of the sweetest girls you could see on a summer's day. Tod was the

first to shake hands with her, and I saw her cheeks blush as crimson as Sir John's state liveries.

"You are going out, my dear," said Mrs. Todhetley.

"Oh yes," she answered, the tears rising in her eyes, which
were as blue as the dark blue sky. "We have had bad news.
William—— "

The dining-room door across the hall opened, and a host of them
came forth. Lady Whitney in a plaid shawl, the strings of her
bonnet untied; Miss Whitney (Helen), Harry, and some of the
young ones behind. Anna's quiet voice was drowned, for they all
began to tell of it together.

Sir John and William were staying at some friend's house at
Ombersley. Lady Whitney thought they would have been home
to-day: instead of which the morning's post had a brought
letter to say that an accident had occurred to William in hunting; some muff who couldn't ride had gone swerving right against
Bill's horse, and he was thrown. Except that Bill was insensible,
nothing further of the damage could be gathered from the letter;
for Sir John, if put out, could write no more intelligibly than the
Squire. The chief of what he said was—that they were to come off
at once.

"We are going, of course; I with the two girls and Harry; the
carriage is waiting to take us to the station," said poor Lady
Whitney, her bonnet pushed off. "But I do wish John had explained further: it is such suspense. We don't think it can be
extremely serious, or there would have been a telegram. I'm sure
I have shivered at every ring that has come to the door this
morning."

"And the post was never in, as usual, until nearly ten o'clock,"
complained Harry. " I wonder my father puts up with it."

"And the worst is that we had a visitor coming to-day," added
Helen. " Mamma would have telegraphed to London for her not
to start, but there was not time. It's Sophie Chalk."

"Who is Sophie Chalk?" asked Tod.

Helen told us, while Lady Whitney was finding plaecs for everyone at the table. They had been taking a scrambling luncheon;
sitting or standing: cold beef, mince-pies, and cheese.

"Sophie Chalk was a schoolfellow of mine," said Helen. "It
was an old promise—that she should come to visit us. Different
things have caused it to be put off, but we have kept up a corre-
spondence. At length I got mamma to say that she might come
as soon as Christmas was turned; and to-day was fixed. We don't
know what on earth to do."

"Let her come to us until you see how things turn out," cried the
Squire, in his hearty good-nature, as he cut himself a slice of beef.

"We can take her home in the carriage: one of these boys can ride back if you'll lend him a horse."

Mrs. Todhetley said he took the very words out of her mouth. The Whitneys were too flurried to affect ceremony, and very gladly accepted the offer. But I don't think it would ever have been made had the Squire and madam known what was to come of it.

"There will be her luggage," observed Anna; who usually remembered things for every one. And Lady Whitney looked round in consternation.

"It must come to us by rail; we will send for it from the station," decided Tod, always ready at a pinch. "What sort of a damsel is this Sophie Chalk, Anna?"

"I never saw her," replied Anna. "You must ask Helen."

Tod whispered something to Anna that made her smile and blush. "I'll write you my sentiments about her to Ombersley," he said aloud. "Those London girls are something to look at." And I knew by Tod's tone that he was prepared *not* to like Miss Sophie Chalk.

We saw them out to the carriage; the Squire putting in my lady; Tod, Helen and Anna. One of the housemaids, Lettice Lane, was wildly running in and out, bringing things to the carriage. She had lived with us once; but Hannah's temper and Letty's propensity for gossip did not get on together. Mrs. Todhetley, when they had driven away, asked her how she liked her place —which she had entered at Michaelmas. Oh, pretty well, Lettice answered: but for her old mother, she should emigrate to Australia. She used to be always saying so at Dyke Manor, and it was one of the things that Hannah would not put up with, telling her decent girls could find work at home.

Tod went off next, on horseback: and, before three o'clock, we drove to the station to meet the London train. The Squire stayed in the carriage, sending me and Mrs. Todhetley on the platform.

Two passengers got out at the small station; a little lady in feathers, and a butcher in a blue frock, who had charge of a calf in the open van. Mrs. Todhetley stepped up to the lady and inquired whether she was Miss Chalk.

"I am Miss Chalk. Have I the honour of speaking to Lady Whitney?"

While matters were being explained, I stood observing her. A very small, slight person, with pretty features white as ivory; and wide-open light blue eyes, that were too close together, and had a touch of boldness in them. It would take a great deal to daunt their owner, if I could read countenances: and that I was always doing so was no fault of mine, for the instinct, strong and irrepressible, lay within me—as old Duffham once said. I did not like her voice; it had no true ring in it; I did not much like her face. But the world in general no doubt found her charming, and the Squire thought her so.

She sat in front with him, a carpet-bag between them: and I, behind, had a great black box crowding my legs. She could not do without that much of her luggage: the rest might come by rail.

"Johnny," whispered Mrs. Todhetley to me, "I am afraid she is very grand and fashionable. I don't know how we shall manage to amuse her. Do you like her?"

"Well—she has got a stunning lot of hair."

"Beautiful hair, Johnny!"

With the hair close before us, I could only say so. It was brown; rather darker than Anna Whitney's, but with a red tinge in it, and about double the quantity. Nature or art was giving it a wonderful gloss in the light of the setting sun, as she turned her head about, laughing and talking with the Squire. Her dress was some bright purple stuff trimmed with white fur; her hands, lying in repose on her lap, had yellow gauntlets on.

"I'm glad I ordered a duck for dinner, in addition to the boiled veal and bacon, Johnny," whispered Mrs. Todhetley again. "The fish won't be much: it is only the cold cod done up in parsley sauce."

Tod, at home long before, was at the door ready for us when we arrived. I saw her staring at him in the dusk.

"Who was the gentleman that handed me out?" she asked me as we went in.

"Mr. Todhetley's son."

"I—think—I have heard Helen Whitney talk of him," she said in reflection. "He will be very rich, will he not?"

"Pretty well. He will have what his father has before him, Miss Chalk."

Mrs. Todhetley suggested tea, but she said she would prefer a glass of wine; and went up to her chamber after taking it. Hannah and the housemaid were hastily putting one in order for her. Sleepy with the frosty air, I was nodding over the fire in the drawing-room when the rustle of silk awoke me.

It was Miss Chalk. She came in gleaming like a fairy, her dress shining in the fire-light; for they had not been in to light the candles. It had a green-and-gold tinge, and was cut very low. Did she think we had a party?—or that dressing for dinner was the fashion in our plain country house—as it might have been at a duke's? Her shoulders and arms were white as snow; she wore a silver necklace, the like of which I had never seen, silver bracelets, and a thick cord of silver twisting in and out of her complicated hair.

"I'm sure it is very kind of your people to take me in," she said, standing still on the hearthrug in her beauty. "They have lighted a fire in my room; it is so comfortable. I do like a country house. At Lady Augustus Difford's——"

Her head went round at the opening of the door. It was Tod. She stepped timidly towards him, like a schoolgirl: dressed as now, she looked no older than one. Tod might have made up his mind not to like her; but he had to surrender. Holding out her hand to him, he could only yield to the vision, and his heart shone in his eyes as he bent them upon her.

"I beg your pardon for having passed you without notice; I did not even thank you for lifting me down; but I was frozen with the drive," she said, in low tones. "Will you forgive me, Mr. Todhetley?"

Forgive her! As Tod stood there with her hand in his, he looked inclined to eat her. Forgiveness was not enough. He led her to the fire, speaking soft words of gallantry.

"Helen Whitney has often talked to me about you, Mr. Todhetley. I little thought I should ever make your acquaintance; still less, be staying in your father's house."

"And I as little dreamt of the good fortune that was in store for me," answered Tod.

He was a tall, fine young fellow then, rising twenty, looking older than his age; she (as she looked to-night) a delicate, beautiful fairy, of any teens fancy might please to picture. As Tod stood over her, his manner took a gentle air, his eyes a shy light—quite unusual with him. She did not look up, except by a modest glance now and again, dropping her eyes when they met his own. He had the chance to take his fill of gazing, and used it.

Tod was caught. From the very first night that his eyes fell on Sophie Chalk, his heart went out to her. Anna Whitney! What child's play had the joking about her been to this! Anna might have been his sister, for all the regard he had for her of a certain sort; and he knew it now.

A looker-on sees more than a player, and I did not like one thing —she drew him on to love her. If ever a girl spread a net to entangle a man's feet, that girl was Sophie Chalk. She went about it artistically, too; in the sweetest, most natural way imaginable; and Tod did not see or suspect an atom of it. No fellow in a similar case ever does. If their heart's not engaged, their vanity is; and it utterly blinds them. I said a word or two to him, and

was nearly knocked over for my pains. At the end of the fortnight—and she was with us nearly that length of time—Tod's heart
had made its choice for weal or for woe.

She took care that it should be so; she did, though he cut my
head off now for saying it. You shall judge. She began on that
first night when she came down in her glistening silk, with the
silver on her neck and hair. In the drawing-room, after dinner, she
sat by him on the sofa, talking in a low voice, her face turned to
him, lifting her eyes and dropping them again. My belief is, she
must have been to a school where they taught eye-play. Tod
thought it was sweet, natural, shy modesty. I thought it was all
artistic. Mrs. Todhetley was called from the room on domestic
matters; the Squire, gone to sleep in his dinner-chair, had not
come in. After tea, when all were present, she went to the piano,
which no one ever opened but me, and played and sang, keeping
Tod by her side to turn the music, and to talk to her at available
moments. In point of execution, her singing was perfect, but the
voice was rather harsh—not a note of real melody in it.

After breakfast the next morning, when we were away together,
she came to us in her jaunty hat, all feathers, and her purple dress
with its white fur. She lured him off to show her the dyke and
goodness knows what else, leaving Lena, who had come out with
her, to be taken home by me. In the afternoon Tod drove her
out in the pony-chaise; they had settled the drive between them
down by the dyke, and I know she had plotted for it, just as surely
as though I had been behind the hedge listening. I don't say Tod
was loth; it was quite the other way from the first. They took a
two-hours' drive, returning home at dusk; and then she laughed
and talked with him and me round the fire until it was time to get
ready for dinner. That second evening she came down in a gauzy
sort of dress, with a thin white body. Mrs. Todhetley thought she
would be cold, but she said she was used to it.

And so it went on; never were they apart for an hour—no, nor
scarcely for a minute in the day.

At first Mr. and Mrs. Todhetley saw nothing. Rather were they
glad Tod should be so attentive to a stranger; for special politeness
had not previously been one of Tod's virtues; but they could only
notice as the thing went on. Mrs. Todhetley grew to have an
uneasy look in her eyes, and one day the Squire spoke out. Sophie
Chalk had tied a pink woollen scarf over her head to go out with
Tod to see the rabbits fed: he ran back for something, and the
Squire caught his arm.

"Don't carry that on too far, Joe. You don't know who the girl is."

"What nonsense, sir!" returned Tod, with a ready laugh; but he
turned the colour of a peony.

We did not know much about her, except that she seemed to be on the high ropes, talking a good deal of great people, and of Lord and Lady Augustus Difford, with whom she had been staying for two months before Christmas. Her home in London, she said, was at her sister's, who had married a wealthy merchant, and lived fashionably in Torriana Square. Mrs. Todhetley did not like to appear inquisitive, and would not ask questions. Miss Chalk was with us as the Whitneys' friend, and that was sufficient.

Bill Whitney's hurt turned out to be something complicated about the ribs. There was no danger after the first week, and they returned home during the second, bringing Bill with them. Helen Whitney wrote the same day for Sophie Chalk, and she said that her mamma would be happy also to see Tod and me for a short time.

We went over in the large phaeton, Tod driving, Miss Chalk beside him; I and Dwarf Giles behind. She had thanked Mrs. Todhetley in the prettiest manner; she told the Squire, as he handed her into the carriage, that she should never forget his kindness, and hoped some time to find an opportunity of repaying it.

Such kissing between Helen and Sophie Chalk! I thought they'd never leave off. Anna stood by Tod, while he looked on : a hungry light in his eyes, as if envying Helen the kisses she took. He had no eyes now for Anna. Lady Whitney asked if we would go upstairs to William : he was impatient to see us both.

" Halloa, old Johnny ! "

He was lying on his back on a broad flat sofa, looking just as well as ever in the face. They had given him up the best bedroom and dressing-room because he was ill : nice rooms, both—with the door opening between.

" How did it happen, Bill ? "

" Goodness knows ! Some fellow rode his horse pretty near over mine—don't believe he had ever been astride anything but a donkey before. Where's Tod ? "

" Somewhere.—I thought he was close behind me."

" I'm so glad you two have come. It's awfully dull, lying here all day."

" Are you obliged to lie ? "

" Carden says so."

" Do you have Carden ? "

" As if our folk would be satisfied without him in a surgical case, and one of danger ! He was telegraphed for on the spot, and came over in less than an hour. It happened near the Ombersley station. He comes here every other day, and Featherston between whiles as his locum tenens."

Tod burst in with a laugh. He had been talking to the girls in the gallery outside. Leaving him and Bill Whitney to have out their own chaffer, I went through the door to the other room—the fire there was the largest. "How do you do, sir?"

Some one in a neat brown gown and close white cap, sewing at a table behind the door, had got up to say this with a curtsey. Where had I seen her?—a woman of three or four and thirty, with a meek, delicate face, and a subdued expression. She saw the puzzle.

"I am Harry Lease's widow, sir. He was pointsman at South Crabb?"

Why, yes, to be sure! And she was not much altered either. But it was a good while now since he died, and she and the children had moved away at the time. I shook hands: the sight of her brought poor Harry Lease to my mind—and many other things.

"Are you living here?"

"I have been nursing young Mr. Whitney, sir. Mr. Carden sent me over from Worcester to the place where he was lying; and my lady thought I might as well come on here with them for a bit, though he don't want more done for him now than a servant could do. What a deal you have grown, sir!"

"Have I? You should see Joseph Todhetley. You knew me, though, Mrs. Lease?"

"I remembered your voice, sir. Besides, I heard Miss Anna say that you were coming here."

Asking after Polly, she gave me the family history since Lease's death. First of all, after moving to her mother's at Worcester, she tried to get a living at making gloves. Her two youngest children caught some disorder, and died; and then she took to go out nursing. In that she succeeded so well—for it seemed to be her vocation, she said—as to be brought under the notice of some of the medical gentlemen of the town. They gave her plenty to do, and she earned an excellent living, Polly and the other two being cared for by the grandmother.

"After the scuffle, and toil, and sorrow of the old days, nursing seems like a holiday to me, Master Ludlow," she concluded; "and I am at home with the children for a day or two as often as I can be."

"Johnny!"

The call was Bill Whitney's, and I went into the other room. Helen was there, but not Tod. She and Bill were disputing.

"I tell you, William, I shall bring her in. She has asked to come. You can't think how nice she is."

"And I tell you, Helen, that I won't have her brought in. What do I want with your Sophie Chalks?"

"It will be your loss."

"So be it! I can't do with strange girls here."

"You will see that."

"Now look here, Helen—*I won't have it.* To-morrow is Mr. Carden's day for coming, and I'll tell him that I can't be left in peace. He will soon give you a word of a sort."

"Oh, well, if you are so serious about it as that, let it drop," returned Helen, good-humouredly. "I only thought to give you pleasure—and Sophie Chalk did ask to come in."

"Who *is* this Sophie Chalk? That's about the nineteenth time I have asked it."

"The sweetest girl in the world."

"Let that pass. Who is she?"·

"I went to school with her at Miss Lakon's. She used to do my French for me, and touch up my drawings. She vowed a lasting friendship, and I am not going to forget it. Every one loves her. Lord and Lady Augustus Difford have just had her staying with them for two months."

"Good souls!" cried Bill, satirically. ·

"She is the loveliest fairy in the world, and dresses like an angel. Will you see her now, William?"

"No."

Helen went off with a flounce. Bill was half laughing, half peevish over it. Confinement made him fretful.

"As if I'd let them bring a parcel of girls in to bother me! *You*'ve had her for these past three weeks, I hear, Johnny."

"Pretty near it."

"Do you like her?"

"Tod does."

"What sort of a creature is the syren?"

"She'd fascinate the eyes out of your head, Bill, give her the chance."

"Then I'll be shot if she shall have the chance as far as I am concerned! Lease!"—raising his voice—"keep all strange ladies out of here. If they attempt to enter, tell them we've got rats about."

"Very well, sir."

Other visitors were staying in the house. A Miss Deveen, and her companion Miss Cattledon. We saw them first at dinner. Miss Deveen sat by Sir John—an ancient lady, active and upright, with a keen, pleasant face and white hair. She had on a worked-muslin shirt-front, with three emerald studs in it that glittered as bright as diamonds. They were beautiful. After dinner, when the four old ones began whist, and we were at the other end of the drawing-room in a group, some one spoke of the studs.

"They are nothing compared with some of her jewellery," said Helen Whitney. "She has a whole set of most beautiful diamonds. I hardly know what they are worth."

"But those emeralds she has on to-night must be of great value," cried Sophie Chalk. "See how they sparkle!"

It made us all turn. As Miss Deveen moved in throwing down her cards, the rays from the wax-lights fell on the emeralds, bringing out the purest green ever imagined by a painter.

"I should like to steal them," said Sophie Chalk; "they would look well on me."

It made us laugh. Tod had his eyes fixed on her, a strange love in their depths. Anna Whitney, kneeling on the ground behind me, could see it.

"I would rather steal a set of pink topaz studs that she has," spoke Helen; "and the opals, too. Miss Deveen is great in studs."

"Why in studs?"

"Because she always wears this sort of white body; it is her habitual evening dress, with satin skirts. I know she has a different set of studs for every day in the month."

"Who is she?" asked Sophie Chalk.

"A cousin of mamma's. She has a great deal of money, and no one in particular to leave it to. Harry says he hopes she'll remember, in making her will, that he is only a poor younger son."

"Just you shut up, Helen," interrupted Harry, in a whisper. "I believe that companion has ears at the back of her head."

Miss Cattledon glanced round from the whist-table, as though the ears were there and wide open. She was a wiry lady of middle age, quite forty, with a screwed-in waist and creaking stays, a piece of crimson velvet round her long thin neck, her scanty hair light as ginger.

"It is she that has charge of the jewel-box," spoke Helen, when we thought it safe to begin again. "Miss Deveen is a wonderful old lady for sixty; she has come here without a maid this time, and dresses herself. I don't see what use Miss Cattledon is to her, unless it is to act as general refrigerator, but she gets a hundred a year salary and some of the old satins. Sophie, I'm sure she heard what we said—that we should like to steal the trinkets."

"Hope she relished it!" quoth Harry. "She'll put them under double lock and key, for fear we should break in."

It was all jesting. Amid the subdued laughing, Tod bent his face over Sophie Chalk, his hand touching the lace on her sleeve. She had on blue to-night with a pearl necklace.

"Will you sing that song for me, Miss Chalk?"

She rose and took his arm. Helen jumped up and arrested them ere they reached the piano.

"We must not have any music just now. Papa never likes it when they are at whist."

"How very unreasonable of him!" cried Tod, looking fiercely at Sir John's old red nose and steel spectacles.

"Of course it is," agreed Helen. "If he played for guinea stakes instead of sixpenny, he could not be more particular about having no noise. Let us go into the study: we can do as we like there."

We all trooped off. It was a small square room with a shabby carpet and worn horse-hair chairs. Helen stirred up the fire; and Sophie sat down on a low stool and said she'd tell us a fairy tale.

We had been there just a week when it came out. The week was a good one. Long walks in the frosty air; a huge swing between the cedar trees; riding by turns on the rough Welsh pony for fun; bagatelle indoors, work, music, chatter; one dinner-party, and a small dance. Half my time was spent in Bill's room. Tod seemed to find little leisure for coming up; or for anything else, except Sophie Chalk. It was a gone case with Tod: looking on, I could see that; but I don't think any one else saw it, except Anna. He liked Sophie too well to make it conspicuous. Harry made open love to her; Sir John said she was the prettiest little lady he had seen for many a day. I dare say Tod told her the same in private.

And she? Well, I don't know what to say. That she kept Tod at her side, quietly fascinating him always, was certain; but her liking for him did not appear real. To me it seemed that she was *acting* it. "I can't make that Sophie Chalk out, Tod," I said to him one day by the beeches: "she seems childishly genuine, but I believe she's just as sharp as a needle." Tod laughed idly, and told me I was the simplest muff that ever walked in shoe-leather. She was no rider, and some one had to walk by her side when she sat on the Welsh pony, holding her on at all the turnings. It was generally Tod: she made believe to be frightfully timid with *him*.

It was at the end of the week that the loss was discovered: Miss Deveen's emerald studs were gone. You never heard such a commotion. She, the owner, took it quietly, but Miss Cattledon made noise enough for ten. The girls were talking round the study fire the morning after the dance, and I was writing a note at the table, when Lettice Lane came in, her face white as death.

"I beg your pardon, young ladies, for asking, but have any of you seen Miss Deveen's emerald studs, please?"

They turned round in surprise.

"Miss Deveen's studs!" exclaimed Helen. "We are not likely to have seen them, Lettice. Why do you ask?"

"Because, Miss Helen, they are gone—that is, Miss Cattledon says they are. But, with so much jewellery as there is in that case, it is very easy to overlook two or three little things."

Why Lettice Lane should have shaken all over in telling this, was a marvel. Her very teeth chattered. Anna inquired; but all the answer given by the girl was, that it had "put her into a twitter." Sophie Chalk's countenance was full of compassion, and I liked her for it.

"Don't let it trouble you, Lettice," she said kindly. "If the studs are missing, I dare say they will be found. Just before I came down here my sister lost a brooch from her dressing-table. The whole house was searched for it, the servants were uncomfortable——"

"And was it found, miss?" interrupted Lettice, too eager to let her finish.

"Of course it was found. Jewels don't get hopelessly lost in gentlemen's houses. It had fallen down, and, caught in the lace of the toilette drapery, was lying hid within its folds."

"Oh, thank you, miss; yes, perhaps the studs have fallen too," said Lettice Lane as she went out. Helen looked after her in some curiosity.

"Why should the loss trouble *her?* Lettice has nothing to do with Miss Deveen's jewels."

"Look here, Helen, I wish we had never said we should like to steal the things," spoke Sophie Chalk. "It was all in jest, of course, but this would not be a nice sequel to it."

"Why—yes—you did say it, some of you," cried Anna, who, until then, had seemed buried in thought; and her face flushed.

"What if we did?" retorted Helen, looking at her in some slight surprise.

Soon after this, in going up to Bill's room, I met Lettice Lane. She was running down with a plate, and looked whiter than ever.

"Are the studs found, Lettice?"

"No, sir."

The answer was short, the manner scared. Helen had wondered why the loss should affect her; and so did I.

"Where's the use of your being put out over it, Lettice? You did not take them."

"No, Master Johnny, I did not; but—but——" looking round and dropping her voice, "I am afraid I know who did; and it was through me. I'm a'most mad."

This was rather mysterious. She gave no opportunity for more, but ran down as though the stairs were on fire.

I went on to Bill's chamber, and found Tod and Harry with him: they were laughing over a letter from some fellow at Oxford. Standing at the window close by the inner door, which was ajar, I heard Lettice Lane go into the dressing-room and speak to Mrs. Lease in a half whisper.

"I can't bear this any longer," she said. "If you have taken those studs, for Heaven's sake put them back. I'll make some excuse—say I found them under the carpet, or slipped under the drawers—anything—only put them back!"

"I don't know what you mean," replied Mrs. Lease, who always spoke as though she had only half a voice.

"Yes, you do. You have got the studs."

By the pause that ensued, Nurse Lease seemed to have lost the power of speech. Lettice took the opportunity to put it more strongly.

"If you've got them about you, give them into my hand now, and I'll manage the rest. Not a living soul shall ever know of this if you will. Oh, do give them to me!"

Mrs. Lease spoke then. "If you say this again, Lettice Lane, I'll tell my lady all. And indeed, I have been wanting to tell her ever since I heard that something had gone. It was for your sake I did not."

"For my sake!" shrieked Lettice.

"Well, it was. I'm sure I'd not like to say it if I could help, Lettice Lane; but it did strike me that you might have been tempted to—to—you know."

So it was accusation and counter-accusation. Which of the two confessed first was uncertain; but in a short time the whole was known to the house, and to Lady Whitney.

On the previous night the upper housemaid was in bed with some slight illness, and it fell to Lettice Lane to put the rooms to rights after the ladies had dressed. Instead of calling one of the other servants she asked Mrs. Lease to help her—which must have been for nothing but to gossip with the nurse, as Lady Whitney said. On Miss Deveen's dressing-table stood her case of jewels, the key in the lock. Lettice lifted the lid. On the top tray glittered a heap of ornaments, and the two women feasted their eyes with them. Nurse Lease declared that she never put "a finger's end" on a single article. Lettice could not say as much. Neither (if they were to be believed) had observed the green studs; and the upper tray was not lifted to see what was underneath. Miss Cattledon, who made one at the uproar, put in her word at this, to say they were telling a falsehood, and her face had enough vinegar in it to pickle a salmon. Other people might like Miss Cattledon, but I did not. She was in a silent rage with Miss Deveen for having chosen to keep the jewel-case during their stay at Whitney Hall, and for carelessly leaving the key in it. Miss Deveen took the loss calmly, and was as cool as a cucumber.

"I don't know that the emerald studs were in the upper tray last night; I don't remember to have seen them," Miss Deveen said, as if bearing out the assertion of the two women.

"Begging your pardon, madam, they *were* there, stiffly corrected Miss Cattledon. "I saw them. I thought you would put them on, as you were going to wear your green satin gown, and asked if I should lay them out; but you told me you would choose for yourself."

Miss Deveen had worn diamonds; we had noticed their lustre.

"I'm sure it is a dreadful thing to have happened!" said poor Lady Whitney, looking flurried. "I dare not tell Sir John; he would storm the windows out of their frames. Lease, I am astonished at *you*. How could you dare open the box?"

"I never did open it, my lady," was the answer. "When I got round from the bed, Lettice was standing with it open before her."

"I don't think there need be much doubt as to the guilty party," struck in Miss Cattledon with intense acrimony, her eyes swooping down upon Lettice. And if they were not sly and crafty eyes, never you trust me again.

"I do not think there need be so much trouble made about it," corrected Miss Deveen. "It's not your loss, Cattledon—it is mine: and my own fault too."

But Miss Cattledon would not take the hint. She stuck to it like a leech, and sifted evidence as subtly as an Old Bailey lawyer. Mrs. Lease carried innocence on the surface; no one could doubt it: Lettice might have been taken for a seven-years' thief. She sobbed, and choked, and rambled in her tale, and grew as confused as a hunted hare, contradicting herself at every second word. The Australian scheme (though it might have been nothing but foolish talk) told against her now.

Things grew more uncomfortable as the day went on, the house being ransacked from head to foot. Sophie Chalk cried. She was not rich, she said to me, but she would give every shilling of money she had with her for the studs to be found; and she thought it was very wrong to accuse Lettice, when so many strangers had been in the house. I liked Sophie better than I had liked her yet: she looked regularly vexed.

Sir John got to know of it: Miss Cattledon told him. He did not storm the windows out, but he said the police must come in and see Lettice Lane. Miss Deveen, hearing of this, went straight to

Sir John, and assured him that if he took any serious steps while
the affair was so doubtful, she would quit his house on the instant,
and never put foot in it again.   He retorted that it must have been
Lettice Lane—common sense and Miss Cattledon could not be
mistaken—and that it ought to be investigated.

They came to a compromise.   Lettice was not to be given into
custody at present; but she must quit the Hall.   That, said Miss
Deveen, was of course as Sir John and Lady Whitney pleased.   To
tell the truth, suspicion did seem strong against her.

She went away at eventide.   One of the men was charged to
drive her to her mother's, about five miles off.   I and Anna, hastening home from our walk—for we had lost the others, and the stars
were coming out in the wintry sky—saw them as we passed the
beeches.   Lettice's face was swollen with crying.

"We are so sorry this has happened, Lettice," Anna gently said,
going up to the gig.   "I do hope it will be cleared up soon.   Remember one thing—I shall think well of you until it is.   *I* do
not suspect you."

"I am turned out like a criminal, Miss Anna," sobbed the girl.
"They searched me to the skin; that Miss Cattledon standing on
to see that the housekeeper did it properly; and they have searched
my boxes.   The only one to speak a kind word to me as I came
away, was Miss Deveen herself.   It's a disgrace I shall never get
over."

"That's rubbish, Lettice, you know,"—for I thought I'd put in
a good word, too.   "You will soon forget it, once the right fellow
is pitched upon.   Good luck to you, Lettice."

Anna shook hands with her, and the man drove on, Lettice
sobbing aloud.   Not hearing Anna's footsteps, I looked round and
saw she had sat down on one of the benches, though it was white
with frost.   I went back.

"Don't you go and catch cold, Anna.".

"Johnny, you cannot think how this is troubling *me*."

"Why you—in particular?"

"Well—for one thing I can't believe that she is guilty.   I have
always liked Lettice."

"So did we at Dyke Manor.   But if she is not guilty, who is?"

"I don't know, Johnny," she continued, her eyes taking a thoughtful, far-off look.   "What I cannot help thinking, is this—though
I feel half ashamed to say it.   Several visitors were in the house
last night; suppose one should have found her way into the room,
and taken them?   If so, how cruel this must be on Lettice Lane."

"Sophie Chalk suggested the same thing to me to-day.   But a
visitor would not do such a thing.   Fancy a lady stealing jewels!"

"The open box might prove a strong temptation.   People do

things in such moments, Johnny, that they would fly from at other times."

"Sophie said that too. You have been talking together."

"I have not exchanged a word with Sophie Chalk on the subject. The ideas might occur naturally to any of us."

I did not think it at all likely to have been a visitor. How should a visitor know there was an open jewel-box in Miss Deveen's room? The chamber, too, was an inner one, and therefore not liable to be entered accidentally. To get to it you had to go through Miss Cattledon's.

"The room is not easy of access, you know, Anna."

"Not very. But it might be reached."

"I say, are you saying this for any purpose?"

She turned round and looked at me rather sharply.

"Yes. Because I do not believe it was Lettice Lane."

"Was it Miss Cattledon herself, Anna? I have heard of such curious things. Her eyes took a greedy look to-day when they rested on the jewels."

As if the suggestion frightened her—and I hardly know how I came to whisper it—Anna started up, and ran across the lawn, never looking back or stopping until she reached the house.

XIV.

AT MISS DEVEEN'S.

THE table was between us as we stood in the dining-room at Dyke Manor—I and Mrs. Todhetley—and on it lay a three-cornered article of soft geranium-coloured wool, which she called a "fichu." I had my great coat on my arm ready for travelling, for I was going up to London on a visit to Miss Deveen.

It was Easter now. Soon after the trouble, caused by the loss of the emerald studs at Whitney Hall in January, the party had dispersed. Sophie Chalk returned to London; Tod and I came home; Miss Deveen was going to Bath. The studs had not been traced—had never been heard of since; and Lettice Lane, after a short stay in disgrace at her mother's cottage, had suddenly disappeared. Of course there were not wanting people to affirm that she had gone off to her favourite land of promise, Australia, carrying the studs with her.

The Whitneys were now in London. They did not go in for London seasons; in fact, Lady Whitney hardly remembered to have had a season in London at all, and she quite dreaded this one, saying she should feel like a fish out of water. Sir John occupied a bedroom when he went up for Parliament, and dined at his club. But Helen was nineteen, and they thought she ought to be presented to the Queen. So Miss Deveen was consulted about a furnished house, and she and Sir John took one for six weeks from just before Easter. They left Whitney Hall at once to take possession; and Bill Whitney and Tod, who got an invitation, joined them the day before Good Friday.

The next Tuesday I received a letter from Miss Deveen. We were very good friends at Whitney, and she had been polite enough to say she should be glad to see me in London. I never expected to go, for three-parts of those invitations do not come to anything. She wrote now to ask me to go up; it might be pleasant for me, she added, as Joseph Todhetley was staying with the Whitneys.

It is of no use going on until I have said a word about Tod. If ever a fellow was hopelessly in love with a girl, he was with Sophie

Chalk. I don't mean hopeless as to the love, but as to getting out of it. On the day that we were quitting Whitney Hall—it was on the 26th of January, and the icicles were clustering on the trees—they had taken a long walk together. What Tod said I don't know, but I think he let her know how much he loved her, and asked her to wait until he should be of age and could ask the question—would she be his wife? We went with her to the station, and the way Tod wrapped her up in the railway-carriage was as good as a show. (Pretty little Mrs. Hughes, who had been visiting old Featherston, went up by the same train and in the same carriage.) They corresponded a little, she and Tod. Nothing particular in her letters, at any rate—nothing but what the world might see, or that she might have written to Mrs. Todhetley, who had one from her on occasion—but I know Tod just lived on those letters and her remembrance; he could not hide it from me; and I saw without wishing to see or being able to help myself. Why, he had gone up to London now in one sole hope—that of meeting again with Miss Chalk!

Mrs. Todhetley saw it too—had seen it from the time when Sophie Chalk was at Dyke Manor—and it grieved and worried her. But not the Squire: he no more supposed Tod was going to take up seriously with Sophie Chalk, than with the pink-eyed lady exhibited the past-year at Pershore Fair.

Well, that's all of explanation. This was Wednesday morning, and the Squire was going to drive me to the station for the London train. Mrs. Todhetley at the last moment was giving me charge of the fichu, which she had made for Sophie Chalk's sister.

"I did not send it by Joseph; I thought it as well not to do so," she observed, as she began to pack it up in tissue paper. "Will you take it down to Mrs. Smith yourself, Johnny, and deliver it?"

"All right."

"I—you know, Johnny, I have the greatest dislike to anything that is mean or underhand," she went on, dropping her voice a little. "But I do not think it would be wrong, under the circumstances, if I ask you to take a little notice of what these Smiths are. I don't mean in the way of being fashionable, Johnny; I suppose they are all that; but whether they are nice, good people. Somehow I did not like Miss Chalk, with all her fascinations, and it is of no use to pretend that I did."

"She was too fascinating for ordinary folk, good mother."

"Yes, that was it. She seemed to put the fascinations on. And, Johnny, though we were to hear that she had a thousand a year to her fortune, I should be miserable if I thought Joe would choose her for his wife."

" She used to say she was poor."

" But she seemed to have a whole list of lords and ladies for her friends, so I conclude she and her connections must be people of note. It is not that, Johnny—rich or poor—it is that I don't like her for herself, and I do not think she is the one to make Joe happy. She never spoke openly about her friends, you know, or about herself. At any rate, you take down this little parcel to Mrs. Smith, with my kind regards, and then you'll see them for yourself. And in judgment and observation you are worth fifty of Joe, any day."

" Not in either judgment or observation; only in instinct."

" And that's for yourself," she added, slipping a sovereign into my pocket. " I don't know how much Mr. Todhetley has given you. Mind you spend your money in right things, Johnny. But I am not afraid; I could trust you all over the world."

Giles put in my portmanteau, and we drove off. The hedges were beginning to bud ; the fields looked green. From observations about the young lambs, and a broken fence that he went into a passion over, the Squire suddenly plunged into something else.

" You take care of yourself, sir, in London ! Boys get into all kinds of pitfalls there, if they don't mind."

" But I do not call myself a boy, sir, now."

" Not call yourself a boy ! " retorted the Squire, staring. " I'd like to know what else you are. Tod's a boy, sir, and nothing else, though he does count twenty years. I wonder what the world's coming to ! " he added, lashing up Bob and Blister. " In my days, youngsters did not think themselves men before they had done growing."

" What I meant was that I am old enough to take care of myself. Mrs. Todhetley has just said she could trust me all over the world."

" Just like her foolishness ! Take care you don't get your pockets picked : there's sure to be a thief at every corner. And don't you pick them yourself, Master Johnny. I knew a young fellow once who went up to London with tén pounds in his pocket. He was staying at the Castle and Falcon Hotel, near the place where the mails used to start from—and a fine sight it was to see them bowl out, one after another, with their lamps lighted. Well, Johnny, this young fellow got back again in four days by one of these very mails, every shilling spent, and his fare down not paid. You'd not think that was steady old Jacobson ; but it was."

I laughed. The Squire looked more inclined to cry.

" Cleaned out, he was ; not a rap left ! Money melts in London —that's a fact—and it is very necessary to be cautious. *His* went in seeing the shows; so he told his father. Don't you go in for too many of them, Johnny, or you may find yourself without funds to bring you home, and railways don't give trust. You might go to the Tower, now; and St. Paul's; and the British! Museum; they are steady places. I wouldn't advise a theatre, unless it's just once—some good, respectable play; and mind you go straight home after it. Some young men slink off to singing-shops now, they say, but I am sure such places can bring no good."

"Being with Miss Deveen, sir, I don't suppose I shall have the opportunity of getting into much harm."

"Well, it's right in me to caution you, Johnny. London is a dreadful place, full of sharpers and bad people. It used to be in the old days, and I don't suppose it has improved in these. You have no father, Johnny, and I stand to you in the light of one, to give you these warnings. Enjoy your visit rationally, my boy, and come home with a true report and a good conscience. That's the charge my old father always gave to me."

Miss Deveen lived in a very nice house, north-westward, away from the bustle of London. The road was wide, the houses were semi-detached, with gardens around and plenty of trees in view. Somehow I had hoped Tod would be at the Paddington terminus, and was disappointed, so I took a cab and went on. Miss Deveen came into the hall to receive me, and said she did not consider me too big to be kissed, considering she was over sixty. Miss Cattledon, sitting in the drawing-room, gave me a finger to shake, and did not seem to like my coming. Her waist and throat were thinner and longer than ever; her stays creaked like parchment.

If I'd never had a surprise in my life, I had one before I was in the house an hour. Coming down from the bedroom to which they had shown me, a maid-servant passed me on the first-floor landing. It was Lettice Lane! I wondered—believe me or not, as you will—I wondered whether I saw a ghost, and stood back against the pillar of the banisters.

"Why, Lettice, is it you?"

"Yes, sir."

"But—what are you doing *here?*"

"I am here in service, sir."

She ran on upstairs. Lettice in Miss Deveen's house. It was worse than a Chinese puzzle.

"Is that you, Johnny? Step in here?"

The voice—Miss Deveen's—came from a half-opened door, close at hand. It was a small, pretty sitting-room, with light blue curtains and chairs. Miss Deveen sat by the fire, ready for dinner. In her white body shone amethyst studs, quite as beautiful as the lost emeralds.

"We call this the blue-room, Johnny. It is my' own exclusively, and no one enters it except upon invitation. Sit down. Were you surprised to see Lettice Lane?"

"I don't think I was ever so much surprised in all my life. She says she is living here."

"Yes ; I sent for her to help my housemaid."

I was thoroughly mystified. Miss Deveen put down her book and spectacles.

"I have taken to glasses, Johnny."

"But I thought you saw so well."

"So I do, for anything but very small type—and that book seems to have been printed for none but the youngest eyes. And I see people as well as things," she added significantly.

I felt sure of that.

"Do you remember, Johnny, the day after the uproar at Whitney Hall, that I asked you to pilot me to Lettice Lane's mother's, and to say nothing about it?"

"Yes, certainly. You walked the whole four miles of the way. It is five by road."

"And back again. I am good for more yet than some of the young folk are, Johnny; but I always was an excellent walker. Next day the party broke up; that pretty girl, Sophie Chalk, departed for London, and you and young Todhetley left later. When you reached your home in the evening, I don't suppose you thought I had been to Dyke Manor the same day."

"No! Had you really, Miss Deveen?"

"Really and truly. I'll tell you now the reason of those journeys of mine. As Lettice Lane was being turned out of the Hall, she made a remark in the moment of departure, accidentally I am sure, which caused me to be almost certain she was not guilty of stealing the studs. Before, whilst they were all condemning her as guilty, *I* had felt doubtful of it ; but of course I could not be sure, and Miss Cattledon reproaches me with thinking every one innocent under every circumstance—which is a mistake of hers. Mind, Johnny, the few words Lettice said might have been used designedly, by one crafty and guilty, on purpose to throw me off suspicion : but I felt almost persuaded that the girl had spoken them in unconscious innocence. I went to her mother's to see them both ; I am fond of looking into things with my own eyes ; and I came away with my good opinion strengthened. I went next to Mrs. Todhetley's to hear what she said of the girl ; I saw her and your old nurse, Hannah, making my request to both not to speak of my visit. They gave the girl a good character for honesty ; Mrs. Todhetley thought her quite incapable of taking the studs ; Hannah. could not say what a foolish girl with roving ideas o

Australia in her head might do in a moment of temptation. In less than a fortnight I was back in London, having paid my visit to Bath. I had been reflecting all that time, Johnny, on the cruel blight this must be on Lettice Lane, supposing that she was innocent. I thought the probabilities were that she *was* innocent, not guilty; and I determined to offer her a home in my own house during the uncertainty. She seemed only too glad to accept it, and here she is. If the girl should eventually turn out to be innocent, I shall have done her a real service; if guilty, why I shall not regret having held out a helping hand to her, that may perhaps save her for the future."

"It was very kind and thoughtful of you, Miss Deveen!"

"My chief difficulty lay in keeping the suspicion lying on Lettice Lane a secret from my household. Fortunately I had taken no servants with me to Whitney Hall, my maid having been ill at the time; but Cattledon is outrageously virtuous, and of course proportionally bitter against Lettice. You saw that at Whitney."

"She would have been the first to tell of her."

"Yes. I had to put the thing rather strongly to Miss Cattledon—'Hold your tongue or leave me.' It answered, Johnny. Cattledon likes her place here, and acts accordingly. She picks up her petticoats from contamination when she meets the unfortunate Lettice; but she takes care to hold her tongue."

"Do you think it will ever be found out, Miss Deveen?"

"I hope it will."

"But who—could have taken them?" And the thought of what I had said to Anna Whitney, that it might be Miss Cattledon herself, flashed over me as I put the question.

"I think"—Miss Deveen glanced round as if to make sure we were alone, and dropped her voice a little—"that it must have been one of the guests who came to Whitney Hall that night. Cattledon let out one thing, but not until after we were at home again, for the fact seemed not to have made the least impression on her memory at the time; but it came back afterwards. When she was quitting her room after dressing that evening—I being already out of mine and downstairs—she saw the shawl she had worn in the afternoon lying across a chair just as she had thrown it off. She is very careful of her clothes; and hesitated, she said, whether to go back then and fold it; but, knowing she was late, did not do so. She had been downstairs about ten minutes, when I asked her to fetch my fan, which I had forgotten. Upon going through her room to mine, she saw the shawl lying on the floor, and picked it up, wondering how it could have come there. At that time the maids had not been in to put either her room or mine to rights. Now, what I infer, Johnny, is that my jewel-case was visited and

the studs were stolen *before* Lettice Lane and Mrs. Lease went near
the rooms, and that the thief, in her hurry to escape, brushed against
the shawl and threw it down."

"And cannot Miss Cattledon see the probability of that?"

"She will not see it. Lettice Lane is guilty with her and no one
else. Prejudice goes a long way in this world, Johnny. The
people who came to the dance that night were taking off their
things in the next room to Miss Cattledon's, and I think it likely
that some one of them may have found a way into my chamber,
perhaps even by accident, and the sight of the brilliant emerald
studs—they were more beautiful than any they were lying with—
was too much for human equanimity. It was my fault for leaving
the dressing-case open—and do you know, Johnny, I believe I left
it literally *open*—I can never forget that."

"But Lettice Lane said it was shut; shut but not locked."

"Well, it is upon my conscience that I left it open. Whoever
took the studs may have shut down the lid, in caution or forget-
fulness. Meanwhile, Johnny, don't you say anything of what I
have told you; at the Whitneys' or elsewhere. They do not know
that Lettice Lane is with me; they are prejudiced against her,
especially Sir John; and Lettice has orders to keep out of the way
of visitors. Should they by chance see her, why, I shall say that
as the case was at best doubtful, I am giving the girl a chance to
redeem her good name. We are going there after dinner. So
mind you keep counsel."

"To the Whitneys'?"

"It is only next door, as you may say. I did not mention that
you were coming up," she added, "so there will be a surprise for
them. And now we will go down. Here, carry my book for me,
Johnny."

In the drawing-room we found a grey-haired curate, with a mild
voice; Miss Cattledon was simpering and smiling upon him. I
gathered that he did duty in the church hard by, and had come to
dinner by invitation. He took in Miss Deveen, and that other
blessed lady fell to me. It was a very good dinner, uncommonly
good to me after my journey. Miss Deveen carved. And didn't
she make me eat! She said she knew what boys' appetites were.
The curate took his leave, but Miss Deveen sat on; she fancied to
have heard that the Whitneys were to have friends to dinner that
night, and would not go in too early.

About half-a-dozen houses lay between, and Miss Deveen put a
shawl over her head and walked the distance. "Such a mistake, to
have taken a place for them so near Hyde Park!" whispered Miss
Cattledon as we were following—and I'm sure she must have been
in a gracious mood to give me the confidence. "Neither Sir John

nor Miss Deveen has much notion of the requirements of fashionable society, Mr. Ludlow: as to poor Lady Whitney, she is a very
owl in all that relates to it."

Poor Lady Whitney—not looking like an owl, but a plain, good-
hearted English mother—was the first to see us. There was no
dinner-party after all. She sat on a chair just inside the drawing-
room, which was precisely the same in build and size as Miss
Deveen's, but had not her handsome furniture and appointments.
She said she was glad to see me, and would have invited me with
Joe, but for want of beds.

They were all grouped at the other end of the room, playing at
forfeits, and a great deal too busy to notice me. I had leisure to
look at them. Helen was talking very fast: Harry shouting; Anna
sat leaning her cheek on her hand; Tod stood frowning and angry
against the wall; the young ones were jumping about like savages;
and Bill Whitney was stuck on a stool, his eyes bandaged, and the
tips of a girl's white fingers touching his hands. A fairy, rather
than a girl, for that's what she looked like, with her small, light
figure and her gauze skirts floating: Miss Sophie Chalk.

But what on earth had come to her hair? It used to be brown;
it was now light, and gleaming with gold spangles. Perhaps it
belonged to her fairy nature.

Suddenly Bill shouted out "Miss Chalk," threw off the bandage,
and caught her hands to kiss her! It was all in the forfeits: he
had a right to do it, because he guessed her name. She laughed
and struggled, the children and Helen were as wild Indians with
glee, and Tod looked ready to bring the roof down. Just as Bill
gave the kiss, Anna saw me.

Of course it created an interlude, and the forfeits were thrown up.
Tod came out of his passion, feeling a little frightened.

"Johnny! Why, what in the world brings you here? Anything
wrong with my father?"

"I am only come up on a visit to Miss Deveen, Tod."

"Well, I'm sure!" cried Tod; as if he thought he ought to have
all the visiting, and I none of it.

Sophie put her hand into mine. "I am so glad to see you again,"
she said in her softest tone. "And dear Mrs. Todhetley, how is
she? and the sweet children?"

But she never waited to hear how; for she turned away at some
question put by Bill Whitney.

Sir John came in, and the four old ones sat down to their whist
in the small drawing-room opening from this. The children were
sent to bed. Sophie Chalk went to the piano to sing a song in
hushed tones, Tod putting himself on one side, Bill on the other.

"Are *both* of them going in for the lady's favour?" I asked of

Anna, pointing to the piano, as she made room for me on the sofa.

"I think Miss Chalk would like it, Johnny."

"How well Bill is looking!"

"Oh, he has quite recovered; he seems all the stronger for his accident. I suppose the rest and the nursing set him up."

"Is Sophie Chalk staying here?"

"No; there's hardly room for her. But she has been here every day and all day since we came up. They send her home in a cab at night, and one of the maids has to go with her. It is Helen's arrangement."

"Do you like London, Anna?"

"No. I wish I had stayed at home."

"But why?"

"Well—but I can't tell you every reason."

"Tell me one?"

Anna did not answer. She sat looking out straight before her, her eyes full of trouble.

"Perhaps it is all nothing, Johnny. I may be fanciful and foolish, and so take up mistaken notions. Wrong ones, on more points than one."

"Do you mean anything—*there?*"

"Yes. It would be—*I* think—a terrible misfortune for us, if William were to engage himself to Sophie Chalk."

"You mean Tod, Anna?" I said, impulsively.

She blushed like a rose. "Down at Whitney I did think it was he; but since we came here she seems to have changed; to be— to be——"

"Going in for Bill. I put it plainly you see, Anna."

"I cannot help fearing that it would be a very sad mistake for either of them. Oh, Johnny, I am just tormented out of my peace, doubting whether or not I ought to speak. Sometimes I say to myself, yes it would be right, it is my duty. And then again I fancy that I am altogether mistaken, and that there's nothing for me to say."

"But what could you say, Anna?"

Anna had been nervously winding her thin gold chain round her finger. She unwound it again before answering.

"Of course—what could I? And if I were to speak, and—and —find there was no cause," she dreamily added, "I should never forgive myself. The shame of it would rest upon me throughout life."

"Well, I don't see that, Anna. Just because you fancied things were serious when they were not so! Where would be the shame?"

"You don't understand, Johnny. *I* should feel it. And so I

wish I had stayed down at Whitney, out of the reach of torment. I wish another thing with all my heart—that Helen would not have Sophie Chalk here."

"I think you may take one consolation to yourself, Anna—that whatever you might urge against her, it would most likely make not the smallest difference one way or the other. With Tod I am sure it would not. If he set his mind on marrying Sophie Chalk, other people's grumbling would not turn him from it."

"It might depend a little on what the grumblings were," returned Anna, as if fighting for the last word. "But there; let it drop. I would rather say no more."

She took up a photograph book, and we began looking over it together.

"Good gracious! Here's Miss Cattledon? Small waist and all!"

Anna laughed. "She had it taken in Bath, and sent it to William. He had only asked her for it in joke."

"So those studs have never turned up, Anna?"

"No. I wish they would. I should pray night and morning for it, if I thought it would do no one an injury."

"Johnny!" called out Sir John.

"Yes, sir."

"Come you, and take my hand for five minutes. I have just remembered a note I ought to have written this afternoon."

"I shall be sure to play badly," I said to Lady Whitney, who had fallen to Sir John in cutting for partners.

"Oh, my dear, what does it matter?" she kindly answered. "I don't mind if you do. I do not play well myself."

———————

The next morning Miss Cattledon went out to ten-o'clock daily service. Miss Deveen said she had taken to the habit of doing so. I wondered whether it was for the sake of religion, or for that grey-haired curate who did the prayers. Sitting by ourselves, I told Miss Deveen of the commission I had from Mrs. Todhetley; and somehow, without my intending it, she gathered a little more.

"Go by all means, and learn what you can, Johnny. Go at once. I don't think you need, any of you, be afraid, though," she added, laughing. "I have seen very much of boy-and-girl love; seen that it rarely comes to anything. Young men mostly go through one or two such episodes before settling seriously to the business of life."

The omnibus took me to Oxford Street, and I found my way from thence to Torriana Square. It proved to be a corner house, its front entrance being in the square. But there was a smaller entrance on the side (which was rather a bustling street), and a sort of office window, on the wire blind of which was written, in white letters, "Mr. Smith, wine-merchant."

A wine-merchant! Well, I was surprised. Could there be any mistake? No, it was the right number. But I thought there must be, and stood staring at the place with both eyes. That *was* a come-down. Not but that wine-merchants are as good as other people; only Sophie Chalk had somehow imparted the notion of their living up to lords and ladies.

I asked at the front-door for Mrs. Smith, and was shown upstairs to a handsome drawing-room. A little girl, with a sallow face, thin and sickly, was seated there. She did not get up, only stared at me with her dark, keen, deep-set eyes.

"Do you know where your mamma is, Miss Trot?" asked the servant, putting a chair.

"You can go and search for her?"

She looked at me so intently as the maid left the room, that I told her who I was, and what I had come for. The child's tongue—it seemed as sharp a one as Miss Cattledon's—was let loose.

"I have heard of you, Johnny Ludlow. Mrs. Smith would be glad to see you. You had better wait."

I don't know how it is that I make myself at home with people; or, rather, that people seem so soon to be at home with me. I don't *try* to do it, but it is always so. In two or three minutes, when the girl was talking to me as freely as though I were her brother, the maid came back again.

"Miss Trot, I cannot find your mamma."

"Mrs. Smith's out. But I was not obliged to tell you so. I'll not spare you any work when you call me Miss Trot."

The maid's only answer was to leave the room: and the little girl—who spoke like a woman—shook her dark hair from her face in temper.

"I've told them over and over again I will not be called Miss Trot. How would you like it? Because my mamma took to say it when I was a baby, it is no reason why other people should say it."

"Perhaps your mamma says it still, and so they fall into it also."

"My mamma is dead."

Just at the moment I did not take in the meaning of the words. "Mrs. Smith dead!"

"Mrs. Smith is not my mother. Don't insult me, please. She came here as my governess. If papa chose to make a fool of him-self by marrying her afterwards, it was not my fault. What are you looking at?"

I was looking at her: she seemed so strange a child; and feeling slightly puzzled between the other Mrs. Smith and this one. They say I am a muff at many things; I am sure I am at understanding complicated relationships.

"Then—Miss Chalk is—*this* Mrs. Smith's sister?"

"Well, you might know that. They are a pair, and I don't like either of them. There are two crying babies upstairs now."

"Mrs. Smith's?"

"Yes, Mrs. Smith's"—with intense aggravation. "Papa had quite enough with me, and I could have managed the house and servants as well as *she* does. And because Nancy Chalk was not enough, in addition we must be never safe from Sophonisba! Oh, there are crosses in life!"

"Who is Sophonisba?"

"She is Sophonisba."

"Perhaps you mean Sophie Chalk?"

"Her name's not Sophie, or Sophia either. She was christened Sophonisba, but she hates the name, and takes care to drop it always. She is a deep one, is Sophonisba Chalk!"

"Is this her home?"

"She makes it her home, when she's not out teaching. And papa never seems to think it an encroachment. Sophonisba Chalk does not keep her places, you know. She thought she had got into something fine last autumn at Lord Augustus Difford's, but Lady Augustus gave her warning at the first month's end."

"Then Miss Chalk is a governess?"

"What else do you suppose she is? She comes over people, and gets a stock of invitations on hand, and goes to them between times. You should hear the trouble there is about her dresses, that she may make a good appearance. And how she does it I can't think: they don't tell me their contrivances. Mrs. Smith must give her some—I am sure of it—which papa has to pay for; and Sophonisba goes in trust for others."

"She was always dressed well down with us."

"Of course she was. Whitney Hall was her great-card place; but the time for the visit was so long before it was fixed, she thought it had all dropped through. It came just right: just when she was turned out of Lady Augustus Difford's. Helen Whitney had promised it a long while before."

"I know; when they were schoolfellows at Miss Lakon's."

"They were not schoolfellows. Sophonsiba was treated as the rest, but she was only improving pupil. She gave her services, learnt of some of the masters, and paid nothing. How old do you think she is?" broke off Miss Trot.

"About twenty."

"She was six-and-twenty last birthday; and they say she will look like a child till she's six-and-thirty. I call it a shame for a young woman of that age to be doing nothing for herself, but to be living on strangers: and papa and I are nothing else to her."

" How old are you ? " I could not help asking.

" Fifteen ; nearly sixteen. People take me to be younger, because I am short, and it vexes me. They would not think me young if they knew how I feel. Oh, I can tell you it is a sharpening thing for your papa to marry again, and to find yourself put down in your own home."

" Has Miss Chalk any engagement now ? "

" She has not had an engagement all this year, and now it's April ! I don't believe she looks after one. She pretends to teach me—while she's waiting, she says ; but it's all a farce ; I won't learn of her. I heard her tell Mr. Everty I was a horrid child. Fancy that ! "

" Who is Mr. Everty ? "

" Papa's head-clerk. He is a gentleman, you know, and Sopho-nisba thinks great things of him. Ah, I could tell something, if I liked ! but she put me on my honour. Oh, she's a sly one ! Just now, she is all her time at the Whitneys', red-hot for it. You are not going ? Stay to luncheon."

" I must go ; Miss Deveen will be waiting for me. You can deliver the parcel, please, with Mrs. Todhetley's message. I will call in to see Mrs. Smith another day."

" And to see me too ? " came the quick retort.

" Yes, of course."

" Now, mind, you can't break your word. I shall say it is me you are coming to call upon ; they think I am nobody in this house. Ask for *Miss* Smith when you come. Good-bye, Johnny Ludlow ! "

She never stirred as I shook hands ; she seemed never to have stirred hand or foot throughout the interview. But, as I opened the door, there came an odd sort of noise, and I turned to look what it was.

She. Hastening to cross the room, with a crutch, to ring the bell ! And I saw that she was both lame and deformed.

In passing down the side street by the office, some one brushed by, with the quick step of a London business man. Where had I seen the face before ? Whose did it put me in mind of ? Why —it came to me all in a minute—Roger Monk's ! He who had lived at Dyke Manor for a short time as head-gardener under false auspices. But, as I have not said anything about him before, I will not enter into the history now. Before I could turn to look, Monk had disappeared ; no doubt round the corner of the square.

" Tod," I said, as soon as I came across him, " Sophie Chalk's a governess."

" Well, what of that ? " asked Tod.

"Not much; but she might as well have been candid with us at Dyke Manor."

"A governess is a lady."

"Ought to be. But why did she make out to us that she had been a visitor at the Diffords', when she was only the teacher? We should have respected her just as much; perhaps made more of her."

"What are you cavilling at? As if a lady was never a teacher before!"

"Oh, Tod! it is not that. Don't you see?—if she had kept a chandler's shop, and been open about it, what should we have cared? It was the sailing under false colours; trying to pass herself off for what she is not."

He gave no answer to this, except a whistle.

"She is turned six-and-twenty, Tod. And she was not a school-girl at Miss, Lakon's, but governess-pupil."

"I suppose she was a schoolgirl once?"

"I suppose she was."

"Good. What else have you to say, wise Johnny?"

"Nothing."

Nothing; for where was the use? Sophie Chalk would have been only an angel in his eyes, though he heard that she had sold apples at a street-corner. Sophie, that very morning, had begged Lady Whitney to let her instruct the younger children, "as a friend," so long as they were in town; for the governess at Whitney was a daily one, and they had not brought her. Lady Whitney at first demurred, and then kissed Sophie for her goodness. The result was, that a bed was found for Miss Chalk, and she stayed with them altogether.

But I can't say much for the teaching. It was not Sophie Chalk's fault, perhaps. Helen would be in the schoolroom, and Harry would be there; and I and Anna sometimes; and Tod and Bill always. Lady Whitney looked upon this London sojourn as a holiday, and did not mind whether the children learnt or played, provided they were kept passably quiet. I told Sophie of my visit to take the fichu, and she made a wry face over the lame girl.

"That Mabel Smith! Poor morbid little object! What she would have grown into but for the fortunate chance of my sister's marrying into the house, I can't imagine, Johnny. I'll draw you her portrait in her night-cap, by-and-by."

The days went on. We did have fun: but war was growing up between William Whitney and Tod. There could no longer be a mistake (to those who understood things and kept their eyes open) of the part Sophie Chalk was playing: and that was trying to throw Tod over for William Whitney, and to make no fuss about it. I don't believe she cared a brass button for either: but Bill's future position in life would be better than Tod's, seeing that his father was a baronet. Bill was going in for her favour; perhaps not seriously: it might have been for the fun of the moment, or to amuse himself by spiting Tod. Sir John and my lady never so much as dreamt of the by-playing going on before their faces, and I don't think Helen did.

"I told you she'd fascinate the eyes out of your head, Bill, give her the chance," said I to him one day in the schoolroom, when Miss Chalk was teaching her pupils to dance.

"You shut up, Johnny," he said, laughing, and shied the atlas at me.

Before the day was out, there was a sharp, short quarrel. They were all coming for the evening to Miss Deveen's. I went in at dusk to tell them not to make it nine at night. Turning into the drawing-room, I interrupted a scene—Bill Whitney and Tod railing at one another. What the bone of contention was I never knew, for they seemed to have reached the end of it.

"You did," said Tod.

"I did not," said Bill.

"I tell you, you *did*, William Whitney."

"Let it go; it's word against word, and we shall never decide it. You are mistaken, Todhetley; but I am not going to ask your leave as to what I shall do, or what I shan't."

"You have no right to say to Miss Chalk what I heard you saying to-day."

"I tell you, you did not hear me say anything of the sort. Put it that you did—what business is it of yours? If I chose to go in for her, to ask her to be the future Lady Whitney—though it may be many a year, I hope, before I step into my father's place, good old man!—who has the right to say me nay?"

Tod was foaming. Dusk though it was, I could see that. They took no more account of my being present, than of Harry's little barking dog.

"Look here, Bill Whitney. If——"

"Are you boys quarrelling?"

The interruption was Anna's. Passing through the hall, she had heard the voices and looked in. As if glad of the excuse to get away, Bill Whitney followed her from the room. Tod went out and banged the hall-door after him.

I waited, thinking Anna might come in, and strolled into the little drawing-room. There, quiet as a mouse, stood Sophie Chalk. She had been listening, for certain; and I hope it gratified her: her eyes sparkled a little.

"Why, Johnny! was it *you* making all that noise? What was the matter? Anything gone wrong?"

It was all very fine to try it on with me. I just looked straight at her, and I think she saw as much. Saying something about going to search for Helen, she left the room.

"What was the trouble, Johnny?" whispered Anna, stealing up to me.

"Only those two having a jar."

"I heard that. But what was it about? Sophie Chalk?"

"Well, yes; that was it, Anna."

We were at the front window then. A man was lighting the street-lamps, and Anna seemed to be occupied in watching him. There was enough care on her face to set one up in the dismals for life.

"No harm may come of it, Anna. Any way, you can do nothing."

"Oh, Johnny, I wish I knew!" she said, clasping her hands. "I wish I could satisfy myself which way *right* lies. If I were to speak, it might be put down to a wrong motive. I try to see whether that thought is not a selfish one, whether I ought to let it deter me. But then—that's not the worst."

"That sounds like a riddle, Anna."

"I wish I had some good, judicious person who would hear all and judge for me," she said, rather dreamily. "If you were older, Johnny, I think I would tell you."

"I am as old as you are, at any rate."

"That's just it. We are neither of us old enough nor experienced enough to trust to our own judgment."

"There's your mother, Anna."

"I know."

"What you mean is, that Sir John and Lady Whitney ought to have their eyes opened to what's going on, that they may put an end to Miss Chalk's intimacy here, if they deem the danger warrants it?"

"That's near enough, Johnny. And I don't see my way sufficiently clearly to do it."

"Put the case to Helen."

"She would only laugh in my face. Hush! here comes some one."

It was Sophie Chalk. She looked rather sharply at us both, and said she could not find Helen anywhere.

And the days were to go on in outward smoothness and private discomfort, Miss Sophie exercising her fascinations on the whole of us.

But for having promised that lame child to call again in Torriana Square, I should not have cared to go. It was afternoon this time. The servant showed me upstairs, and said her mistress was for the moment engaged. Mabel Smith sat in the same seat in her black frock; some books lay on a small table drawn before her.

"I thought you had forgotten to come."

"Did you? I should be sure not to forget it."

"I am so tired of my lessons," she said, irritably, sweeping the books away with her long thin fingers. "I always am when *they* teach me. Mrs. Smith has kept me at them for two hours; she has gone down now to engage a new servant."

"I get frightfully tired of my lessons sometimes."

"Ah, but not as I do; you can run about: and learning, you know, will never be of use to me. I want you to tell me something. Is Sophonisba Chalk going to stay at Lady Whitney's?"

"I don't know. They will not be so very long in town."

"But I mean is she to be governess there, and go into the country with them?"

"No, I think not."

"She wants to. If she does, papa says he shall have some nice young lady to sit with me and teach me. Oh, I do hope she will go with them, and then the house would be rid of her. I say she will: it is too good a chance for her to let slip. Mrs. Smith says she won't: she told Mr. Everty so last night. He wouldn't believe her, and was very cross over it."

"Cross over it?"

"He said Sophonisba ought not to have gone there at all without consulting him, and that she had not been home once since, and only written him one rubbishing note that had nothing in it; and he asked Mrs. Smith whether she thought that was right."

A light flashed over me. "Is Miss Chalk going to marry Mr. Everty?"

"I suppose that's what it will come to," answered the curious child. "She has promised to; but promises with her don't go for much when it suits her to break them. Sophonisba put me on my honour not to tell; but now that Mr. Everty has spoken to Mrs. Smith and papa, it is different. I saw it a long while ago; before she went to the Diffords'. I have nothing to do but to sit and watch and think, you see, Johnny Ludlow; and I perceive things quicker than other people."

"But—why do you fancy Miss Chalk may break her promise to Mr. Everty?"

"If she meant to keep it, why should she be scheming to go away as the Whitneys' governess? I know what it is: Sophonisba does not think Mr. Everty good enough for her, but she would like to keep him waiting on, for fear of not getting anybody better."

Anything so shrewd as Mabel Smith's manner in saying this,
was never seen. I don't think she was naturally ill-natured, poor
thing; but she evidently thought she was being wronged amongst
them, and it made her spitefully resentful.

"Mr. Everty had better let her go. It is not I that would marry
a wife who dyed her hair."

"Is Miss Chalk's dyed? I thought it might be the gold dust."

"Have you any eyes?" retorted Mabel. "When she was down
in the country with you her hair was brown; it's a kind of yellow
now. Oh, she knows how to set herself off, I can tell you. Do
you happen to remember who was reigning in England when the
massacre of St. Bartholomew took place in France?"

The change of subject was sudden. I told her it was Queen
Elizabeth.

"Queen Elizabeth, was it? I'll write it down. Mrs. Smith says
I shall have no dessert to-day, if I don't tell her. She puts those
questions only to vex me. As if it mattered to anybody. Oh,
here's papa!"

A little man came in with a bald head and pleasant face. He
said he was glad to see me and shook hands. She put out her
arms, and he came and kissed her: her eyes followed him everywhere; her cheeks had a sudden colour: it was easy to see that
he was her one great joy in life. And the bright colour made her
poor thin face look almost charming.

"I can't stay a minute, Trottie; going out in a hurry. I think I
left my gloves up here."

"So you did, papa. There was a tiny hole in the thumb and
I mended it for you."

"That's my little attentive daughter! Good-bye. Mr. Ludlow,
if you will stay to dinner we shall be happy."

Mrs. Smith came in as he left the room. She was rather a plain
likeness of Miss Chalk, not much older. But her face had a
straightforward, open look, and I liked her. She made much of
me and said how kind she had thought it of Mrs. Todhetley to be
at the trouble of making a fichu for her, a stranger. She hoped—
she did hope, she added rather anxiously, that Sophie had not
asked her to do it. And it struck me that Mrs. Smith had not
quite the implicit confidence in Miss Sophie's sayings and doings
that she might have had.

It was five o'clock when I got away. At the door of the office in
the side street stood a gentleman—the same I had seen pass me the
other day. I looked at him, and he at me.

"Is it Roger Monk?"

A startled look came over his face. He evidently did not
remember me. I said who I was,

"Dear me! How you have grown! Do walk in." And he spoke to me in the tones an equal would speak, not as a servant.

As he was leading the way into a sort of parlour, we passed a clerk at a desk, and a man talking to him.

"Here's Mr. Everty; he will tell you," said the clerk, indicating Monk. "He is asking about those samples of pale brandy, sir: whether they are to go."

"Yes, of course; you ought to have taken them before this, Wilson," was Roger Monk's answer. And so I saw that *he* was Mr. Everty.

"I have resumed my true name, Everty," he said to me in low tones. "The former trouble, that sent me away a wanderer, is over. Many men, I believe, are forced into such episodes in life."

"You are with Mr. Smith?"

"These two years past. I came to him as head-clerk; I now have a commission on sales, and make a most excellent thing of it. I don't think the business could get on without me now."

"Is it true that you are to marry Miss Chalk?" I asked, speaking on a sudden impulse.

"Quite true; if she does not throw me over," he answered, and I wondered at his candour. "I suppose you have heard of it indoors?"

"Yes. I wish you all success."—And didn't I wish it in my inmost heart!

"Thank you. I can give her a good home now. Perhaps you will not talk about that old time if you can help it, Mr. Ludlow. You used to be good-natured, I remember. It was a dark page in my then reckless life; I am doing what I can to redeem it."

I dare say he was; and I told him he need not fear. But I did not like his eyes yet, for they had the same kind of shifty look that Roger Monk's used to have. He might get on none the worse in business; for, as the Squire says, it is a shifty world.

Sophie Chalk engaged to Mr. Everty, and he Roger Monk! Well, it was a complication. I went back to Miss Deveen's without, so to say, seeing daylight.

XV.

THE GAME FINISHED.

THE clang of the distant church bell was ringing out for the daily morning service, and Miss Cattledon was picking her way across the road to attend to it, her thin white legs displayed, and a waterproof cloak on. It had rained in the night, but the clouds were breaking, promising a fine day. I stood at the window, watching the legs and the pools of water; Miss Deveen sat at the table behind, answering a letter that had come to her by the morning post.

"Have you ever thought mine a peculiar name, Johnny?" she suddenly asked.

"No," I said, turning to answer her. "I think it a pretty one."

"It was originally French: De Vigne: but like many other things has been corrupted with time, and made into what it is. Is that ten o'clock striking?"

Yes: and the bell was ceasing. Miss Cattledon would be late. It was a regular penalty to her, I knew, to go out so early, and quite a new whim, begun in the middle of Lent. She talked a little in her vinegar way of the world's wickedness in not spending some of its working hours inside a church, listening to that delightful curate with the mild voice, whose hair had turned prematurely grey. Miss Deveen, knowing it was meant for her, laughed pleasantly, and said if the many years' prayers from her chamber had not been heard as well as though she had gone into a church to offer them up, she should be in a poor condition now. I went with Miss Cattledon one Monday morning out of politeness. There were nine-and-twenty in the pews, for I counted them: eight-and-twenty being single ladies (to judge by the look), some young, some as old as Cattledon. The grey-haired curate was assisted by a young deacon, who had a black beard and a lisp and his hair parted down the middle. It was very edifying, especially the ten-minutes' gossip with the two clergymen coming out, when we all congregated in the aisle by the door.

"My great-grandfather was a grand old proprietor in France,

Johnny; a baron," continued Miss Deveen. "I don't think I have much of the French nature left in me."

"I suppose you speak French well, Miss Deveen?"

"Not a word of it, Johnny. They pretended to teach it me when I was a child, but I'm afraid I was unusually stupid. Why, who can this be?"

She alluded to a ring at the visitors' bell. One of the servants came in and said that the gentleman who had called once or twice before had come again.

Miss Deveen looked up, first at the servant, then at me. She seemed to be considering.

"I will see him in two or three minutes, George"—and the man shut the door.

"Johnny," she said, "I have taken you partly into my confidence in this affair of the lost studs; I think I will tell you a little more. After I sent for Lettice Lane here—and my impression, as I told you, was very strongly in favour of her innocence—it occurred to me that I ought to see if anything could be done to prove it ; or at least to set the matter at rest, one way or the other, instead of leaving it to time and chance. The question was, how could I do it? I did not like to apply to the police, lest more should be made of it than I wished. One day a friend of mine, to whom I was relating the circumstances, solved the difficulty. He said he would send to me some one with whom he was well acquainted, a Mr. Bond, who had once been connected with the detective police, and who had got his dismissal through an affair he was thought to have mismanaged. It sounded rather formidable to my ears, 'once connected with the detective police;' but I consented, and Mr. Bond came. He has had the thing in hand since last February."

"And what has he found out?"

"Nothing, Johnny. Unless he has come to tell me now that he has—for it is he who is waiting. I think it may be so, as he has called so early. First of all, he was following up the matter down in Worcestershire, because the notion he entertained was, that the studs must have been taken by one of the Whitneys' servants. He stayed in the neighbourhood, pursuing his inquiries as to their characters and habits, and visiting all the pawnbrokers' shops that he thought were at available distances from the Hall."

"Did he think it was Lettice Lane?"

"He *said* he did not : but he took care (as I happen to know) to worm out all he could of Lettice's antecedents while he was inquiring about the rest. I had the girl in this room at his first visit, not alarming her, simply saying that I was relating the history of the studs' disappearance to this friend who had called, and desired her to describe her share in it to make the story complete. Lettice suspected nothing; she told the tale simply and naturally, without fear : and from that very moment, Johnny, I have felt certain in my own mind the girl is as innocent as I am. Mr. Bond '*thought* she might be,' but he would not go beyond that ; for women, he said, were crafty, and knew how to make one think black was white."

" Miss Deveen, suppose, after all, it should turn out to have been Lettice?" I asked. " Should you proceed against her?"

" I shall not proceed against any one, Johnny ; and I shall hush the matter up if I can," she answered, ringing for Mr. Bond to be shown in.

I was curious to see him also ; ideas floating through my brain of cocked-hats and blue uniform and Richard Mayne. Mr. Bond turned out to be a very inoffensive-looking individual indeed ; a little man, wearing steel spectacles, in a black frock-coat and grey trousers.

" When I last saw you, madam," he began, after he was seated, and Miss Deveen had told him he might speak before me, " I mentioned that I had abandoned my search in the country, and intended to prosecute my inquiries in London."

" You did, Mr. Bond."

" That the theft lay amongst Sir John Whitney's female servants, I have thought likely all along," continued Mr. Bond. " If the thief felt afraid to dispose of the emeralds after taking them—and I could find no trace of them in the country—the probability was that she would keep them secreted about her, and get rid of them as soon as she came to London, if she were one of the maids brought up by Lady Whitney. There were two I thought in particular might have done it ; one was the lady's maid ; the other, the upper-housemaid, who had been ill the night of their disappearance. All kinds of ruses are played off in the pursuit of plunder, as we have cause to learn every day; and it struck me the housemaid might have feigned illness, the better to cover her actions and throw suspicion off herself. I am bound to say I could not learn anything against either of these two young women ; but their business took them about the rooms at Whitney Hall; and an open jewel-case is a great temptation."

" It is," assented Miss Deveen. " That carelessness lay at my door, and therefore I determined never to prosecute in this case ; never, in fact, to bring the offender to open shame of any sort in regard to it."

" And that has helped to increase the difficulty," remarked Mr. Bond. " Could the women have been searched and their private places at Whitney Hall turned out, we might or might not have found the emeralds ; but——"

"I wouldn't have had it done for the Lord Chancellor, sir," interrupted Miss Deveen, hotly. "*One* was searched, and that was quite enough for me, for I believe her to be innocent. If you can get at the right person quietly, for my own satisfaction, well and good. My instructions went so far, but no farther."

Mr. Bond took off his spectacles for a minute, and put them on again. "I understood this perfectly when I took the business in hand," he said quietly. "Well, madam, to go on. Lady Whitney brought her servants to London, and I came up also. Last night I gleaned a little light on the matter."

He paused, and put his hand into his pocket. I looked, and Miss Deveen looked.

"Should you know the studs again?" he asked her.

"You may as well ask me if I should know my own face in the glass, Mr. Bond. Of course I should."

Mr. Bond opened a pill-box: three green studs lay in it on white cotton. He held it out to Miss Deveen.

"Are these they?"

"No, certainly not," replied Miss Deveen, speaking like one in disappointment. "*Those* are not to be compared with mine, sir."

Mr. Bond put the lid on the box, and returned it to his pocket. Out came another box, long and thin.

"These are my studs," quickly exclaimed Miss Deveen, before she had given more than a glance. "You can look yourself for the private marks I told you about, Mr. Bond."

Three brilliant emeralds, that seemed to light up the room, connected together by a fine chain of gold. At either end, the chain was finished off by a small square plate of thin gold, on one of which was an engraved crest, on the other Miss Deveen's initials. In shape the emeralds looked like buttons more than studs.

"I never knew they were linked together, Miss Deveen," I exclaimed in surprise.

"Did you not, Johnny?"

Never. I had always pictured them as three loose studs. Mr. Bond, who no doubt had the marks by heart before he brought them up, began shutting them into the box as he had the others.

"Anticipating from the first that the studs would most probably be found at a pawnbroker's, if found at all, I ventured to speak to you then of a difficulty that might attend the finding," said he to Miss Deveen. "Unless a thing can be legally proved to have been stolen, a pawnbroker cannot be forced to give it up. And I am under an engagement to return these studs to the pawnbroker, whence I have brought them, in the course of the morning."

"You may do so," said Miss Deveen. "I dare say he and I can come to an amicable arrangement in regard to giving them up later. My object has been to discover who stole them, not to bring trouble or loss upon pawnbrokers. How did you discover them, Mr. Bond?"

"In a rather singular manner. Last evening, in making my way to Regent Street to a place I had to go to on business, I saw a young woman turn out of a pawnbroker's shop. The shutters were put up, but the doors were open. Her face struck me as being familiar; and I remembered her as Lady Whitney's housemaid—the one who had been ill in bed, or pretended to be, the night the studs were lost. Ah, ah, I thought, some discovery may be looming up here. I have some acquaintance with the proprietor of the shop; a very respectable man, who has become rich by dint of hard, honest work, and is a jeweller now as well as a pawn-broker. My own business could wait, and I went in and found him busy with accounts in his private room. He thought at first I had only called in to see him in passing. I gave him no par-ticulars; but said I fancied a person in whom I was professionally interested, had just been leaving some emerald studs in his shop."

"What is the pawnbroker's name?" interrupted Miss Deveen.

"James. He went to inquire, and came back, saying that his assistant denied it. There was only one assistant in the shop: the other had left for the night. This assistant said that no one had been in during the last half-hour, excepting a young woman, a cousin of his wife's; who did not come to pledge anything, but simply to say how-d'ye-do, and to ask where they were living now, that she might call and see the wife. Mr. James added that the man said she occupied a good situation in the family of Sir John and Lady Whitney, and was not likely to require to pledge any-thing. Plausible enough, this, you see, Miss Deveen; but the coincidence was singular. I then told James that I had been in search for these two months of some emerald studs lost out of Sir John Whitney's house. He stared a little at this, paused a moment in thought, and then asked whether they were of unusual value and very beautiful. Just so, I said, and minutely described them. Mr. James, without another word, went away and brought the studs in. Your studs, Miss Deveen."

"And how did he come by them?"

"He won't tell me much about it—except that they took in the goods some weeks ago in the ordinary course of business. The fact is he is vexed: for he has really been careful and has managed to avoid these unpleasant episodes, to which all pawnbrokers are liable. It was with difficulty I could get him to let me bring them up here: and that only on condition that they should be in his hands again before the clock struck twelve."

"You shall keep faith with him. But now, Mr. Bond, what is your opinion of all this?"

"My opinion is that that same young woman stole the studs: and that she contrived to get them conveyed to London to this assistant, her relative, who no doubt advanced money upon them. I cannot see my way to any other conclusion under the circumstances," continued Mr. Bond, firmly. "But for James's turning crusty, I might have learned more."

"I will go to him myself," said Miss Deveen, with sudden resolution. "When he finds that my intention is to hold his pocket harmless and make no disturbance in any way, he will not be crusty with me. But this matter must be cleared up if it be possible to clear it."

Miss Deveen was not one to be slow of action, once a resolve was taken. Mr. Bond made no attempt to oppose her: on the contrary, he seemed to think it might be well that she should go. She sent George out for a cab, in preference to taking her carriage, and said I might accompany her. We were off long before Miss Cattledon's conference with the curates within the church was over.

The shop was in a rather obscure street, not far from Regent Street. I inquired for Mr. James at the private door, and he came out to the cab. Miss Deveen said she had called to speak to him on particular business, and he took us upstairs to a handsomely furnished room. He was a well-dressed, portly, good-looking man, with a pleasant face and easy manners. Miss Deveen, bidding him sit down near her, explained the affair in a few words, and asked him to help her to elucidate it. He responded frankly at once, and said he would willingly give all the aid in his power.

"Singular to say, I took these studs in myself," he observed. "I never do these things now, but my foreman had a holiday that day to attend a funeral, and I was in the shop. They were pledged on the 27th of January: since Mr. Bond left this morning I have referred to my books."

The 27th of January. It was on the night of the 23rd that the studs disappeared. Then the thief had not lost much time! I said so.

"Stay a minute, Johnny," cried Miss Deveen: "you young ones sum up things too quickly for me. Let me trace past events. The studs, as you say, were lost on the 23rd; the loss was discovered on the 24th, and Lettice Lane was discharged; on the 25th those of us staying at Whitney Hall began to talk of leaving; and on the 26th you two went home after seeing Miss Chalk off by rail to London."

"And Mrs. Hughes also. They went up together."

"Who is Mrs. Hughes?" asked Miss Deveen.

"Don't you remember?—that young married lady who came to the dance with the Featherstons. She lives somewhere in London."

Miss Deveen considered a little. "I don't remember any Mrs. Hughes, Johnny."

"But, dear Miss Deveen, you must remember her," I persisted. "She was very young-looking, as little as Sophie Chalk; Harry Whitney, dancing with her, trod off the tail of her thin pink dress. I heard old Featherston telling you about Mrs. Hughes, saying it was a sad history. Her husband lost his money after they were married, and had been obliged to take a small situation."

· Recollection flashed upon Miss Deveen. "Yes, I remember now. A pale, lady-like little woman with a sad face. But let us go back to business. You all left on the 26th; I and Miss Cattledon on the 27th. Now, while the visitors were at the Hall, I don't think the upper-housemaid could have had time to send off the studs by rail. Still less could she have come up herself to pledge them."

Miss Deveen's head was running on Mr. Bond's theory.

"It was no housemaid that pledged the studs," spoke Mr. James.

"I was about to say, Mr. James, that if you took them in yourself over the counter, they could not have been sent up to your assistant."

"All the people about me are trustworthy, I can assure you, ma'am," he interrupted. "They would not lend themselves to such a thing. It was a lady who pledged those studs."

"A lady?"

"Yes, ma'am, a lady. And to tell the truth, if I may venture to say it, the description you have now given of a lady just tallies with her."

"Mrs. Hughes?"

"It seems so to me," continued Mr. James. "Little, pale, and lady-like: that is just what she was."

"Dear me!" cried Miss Deveen, letting her hands drop on her lap as if they had lost their power. "You had better tell me as much as you can recollect, please."

"It was at dusk," said Mr. James. "Not quite dark, but the lamps were lighted in the streets and the gas indoors: just the hour, ma'am, that gentlefolk choose for bringing their things to us. I happened to be standing near the door, when a lady came into the shop and asked to see the principal. I said I was he, and retired behind the counter. She brought out these emerald studs"—touching the box—"and said she wanted to sell them, or pledge them for their utmost value. She told me a tale, in apparent confidence, of a brother who had fallen into debt at college, and she was trying to get together some money to help him, or frightful trouble might come of it. If it was not genuine," broke off Mr. James, " she was the best actor I ever saw in all my life."

" Please go on."

" I saw the emeralds were very rare and beautiful. She said they were an heirloom from her mother, who had brought the stones from India and had them linked together in England. I told her I could not buy them; she rejoined that it might be better only to pledge them, for they would not be entirely lost to her, and she might redeem them ere twelve months had passed if I would keep them as long as that. I explained that the law exacted it. The name she gave was Mary Drake, asking if I had ever heard of the famous old forefather of theirs, Admiral Drake. The name answers to the initials on the gold."

" ' M. D.' They were engraved for Margaret Deveen. Perhaps she claimed the crest, also, Mr. James," added that lady, sarcastically.

" She did, ma'am; in so far as that she said it was the crest of the Drake family."

" And you call her a lady?"

" She had every appearance of one, in tone and language too. Her hand—she took one of her gloves off when showing the studs—was a lady's hand; small, delicate, and white as alabaster. Ma'am, rely upon it, though she may not be a lady in deeds, she must be living the life of one."

" But now, who was it?"

Yes, who was it? Miss Deveen, looking at us, seemed to wait for an answer, but she did not get one.

" How much did you lend upon the studs?"

" Ten pounds. Of course that is nothing like their value."

" Should you know her again? How was she dressed?"

" She wore an ordinary Paisley shawl; it was cold weather; and had a thick veil over her face, which she never lifted."

" Should not that have excited your suspicion?" interrupted Miss Deveen. " I don't like people who keep their veils down while they talk to you."

The pawnbroker smiled. " Most ladies keep them down when they come here. As to knowing her again, I am quite certain that I should; and her voice too. Whoever she was, she went about it very systematically, and took me in completely. Her asking for the principal may have thrown me somewhat off my guard."

We came away, leaving the studs with Mr. James: the time had not arrived for Miss Deveen to redeem them. She seemed very thoughtful as we went along in the cab.

" Johnny," she said, breaking the silence, " we talk lightly enough about the Finger of Providence; but I don't know what else it can be that has led to this discovery so far. Out of the hundreds of pawnbroking establishments scattered about the metropolis, it is wonderfully strange that this should have been the one the studs were taken to; and furthermore, that Bond should have been passing it last night at the moment Lady Whitney's housemaid came forth. Had the studs been pledged elsewhere, we might never have heard of them; neither, as it is, but for the housemaid's being connected with Mr. James's assistant."

Of course it was strange.

"You were surprised to see the studs connected together, Johnny. That was the point I mentioned in reference to Lettice Lane. '*One* might have fallen down,' she sobbed out to me, in leaving Whitney Hall; 'even two; but it's beyond the bounds of probability that three should, ma'am.' She was thinking of the studs as separated; and it convinced me that she had never seen them. True, an artful woman might say so purposely to deceive me, but I am sure that Lettice has not the art to do it. But now, Johnny, we must consider what steps to take next. I shall not rest until the matter is cleared."

"Suppose it should never get on any further!"

"Suppose you are like a young bear, all your experience to come?" retorted Miss Deveen. "Why, Johnny Ludlow, do you think that when that Finger I ventured to speak of is directing an onward course, It halts midway? There cannot, I fear, be much doubt as to the thief; but we must have proof.

"You think it was——"

"Mrs. Hughes. What else can I think? She is very nice, and I could not have believed it of her. I suppose the sight of the jewels, combined with her poverty, must have proved the temptation. I shall get back the emeralds, but we must screen her."

"Miss Deveen, I don't believe it was Mrs. Hughes."

"Not believe it?"

"No. Her face is not that of one who would do such a thing. You might trust it anywhere."

"Oh, Johnny! there you are at your faces again!"

"Well, I was never deceived in any face yet. Not in one that I *thoroughly* trusted."

"If Mrs. Hughes did not take the studs, and bring them to London, and pledge them, who else could have brought them? They were taken to Mr. James's on the 27th, remember."

"That's the puzzle of it."

"We must find out Mrs. Hughes, and then contrive to bring her within sight of Mr. James."

"The Whitneys know where she lives. Anna and Helen have been to call upon her."

"Then our way is pretty plain. Mind you don't breathe a syllable of this to mortal ear, Johnny. It might defeat our aims. Miss Cattledon, always inquisitive, will question where we have been this morning with her curious eyes; but for once she will not be satisfied."

"I should not keep her, Miss Deveen."

"Yes you would, Johnny. She is faithful; she suits me very well; and her mother and I were girls together."

It was a sight to be painted. Helen Whitney standing there in her presentation dress. She looked wonderfully well. It was all white, with a train behind longer than half-a-dozen peacocks' tails, lace and feathers about her hair. The whole lot of us were round her; the young ones had come from the nursery, the servants peeped in at the door; Miss Cattledon had her eye-glass up; Harry danced about the room.

"Helen, my dear, I admire all very much except your necklace and bracelets," said Miss Deveen, critically. "They do not match: and do not accord with the dress."

The necklace was a row of turquoises, and did not look much: the bracelets were gold, with blue stones in the clasps. The Whitney family did not shine in jewels, and the few diamonds they possessed were on Lady Whitney to-day.

"But I had nothing else, Miss Deveen," said Helen, simply. "Mamma said these must do."

Miss Deveen took off the string of blue beads as if to examine them, and left in its place the loveliest pearl necklace ever seen. There was a scream of surprise; some of us had only met with such transformations in fairy tales.

"And these are the bracelets to match, my dear. Anna, I shall give you the same when your turn for making your curtsey to your queen comes."

Anna smiled faintly as she looked her thanks. She always seemed regularly down in spirits now, not to be raised by pearl necklaces. For the first time her sad countenance seemed to strike Tod. He crossed over.

"What is wrong, Anna?" he whispered. "Are you not well?"

"Quite well, thank you," she answered, her cheeks flushing painfully.

At this moment Sophie Chalk created a diversion. Unable to restrain her feelings longer, she burst into tears, knelt down outside

Helen's dress, and began kissing her hand and the pearl bracelet in a transport of joy.

"Oh, Helen, my dear friend, how rejoiced I am? I said upstairs that your ornaments were not worthy of you."

Tod's eyes were glued on her. Bill Whitney called out Bravo. Sophie, kneeling before Helen in her furbelows, made a charming tableau.

"It is good acting, Tod," I said in his ear.

He turned sharply. But instead of cuffing me into next week, he just sent his eyes straight out to mine.

"Do you call it acting?"

"I am sure it is. But not for you."

"You are bold, Mr. Johnny."

But I could tell by the subdued tone and the subdued manner, that his own doubts had been at last awakened whether or not it *was* acting.

Lady Whitney came sailing downstairs, a blaze of yellow satin; her face, with flurry, like a peony. She could hardly say a word of thanks for the pearls, for her wits had gone wool-gathering. When she was last at Court herself, Bill was a baby in long-clothes. We went out with them to the carriage; the lady's-maid taking at least five minutes to settle the trains: and Bill said he hoped the eyes at the windows all round enjoyed the show. The postillion—an unusual sight in London—and the two men behind wore their state liveries, white and crimson; their bouquets bigger than cabbages.

"You will dance with me the first dance to-night?" Tod whispered to Sophie Chalk, as they were going in after watching the carriage away.

Sophie made a slight pause before she answered; and I saw her eyes wander out in the distance towards Bill Whitney.

"Oh, thank you," she said, with a great display of gratitude. "But I think I am engaged."

"Engaged for the first dance?"

"Yes. I am so sorry."

"The second, then?"

"With the greatest pleasure."

Anna heard it all as well as I. Tod gave Sophie's hand a squeeze to seal the bargain, and went away whistling.

Not being in the world of fashion, we did not know how other people finished up Drawing-room days (and when Helen Whitney went to Court they *were* Drawing-rooms), but the Whitneys' programme was this: A cold collation in lieu of dinner, when Fate should bring them home again, and a ball in the evening. The ball was our joint invention. Sitting round the schoolroom fire one night we settled it for ourselves: and after Sir John and my

lady had stood out well, they gave in.   Not that it would be much
of a ball, for they had few acquaintances in London, and the house
was small.   .   .

But now, had any aid been wanted by Miss Deveen to carry out
her plans, she could not have devised better than this.   For the
Whitneys invited (all unconsciously) Mrs. Hughes to the ball.
Anna came into Miss Deveen's after they had been sending out the
invitations (only three days before the evening), and began telling
her the names as a bit of gossip.   She came at last to Mrs.
Hughes.

"Mrs. Hughes," interrupted Miss Deveen, "I am glad of that,
Anna, for I want to see her."

Miss Deveen's seeing her would not go for much in the matter
of elucidation; it was Mr. James who must see her; and the plan
by which he might do so was Miss Deveen's own.   She went down
and arranged it with him, and before the night came, it was all cut
and dried.   He and she and I knew of it; not another soul in the
world.

"You will have to help me in it a little, Johnny," she said.   "Be
at hand to watch for Mr. James's arrival, and bring him up to me."

We saw them come back from the Drawing-room between five
and six, Helen with a brilliant colour in her cheeks; and at eight
o'clock we went in.   London parties, which begin when you ought
to be in your first sleep, are not understood by us country people,
and eight was the hour named in the Whitneys' invitations.
Cattledon was screwed into a rich sea-green satin (somebody else's
once), with a water-lily in her thin hair; and Miss Deveen wore all
her diamonds.   Sir John, out of his element and frightfully dis-
consolate, stood against the wall, his spectacles lodged on his old
red nose.   The thing was not in his line.   Miss Deveen went up to
shake hands.

"Sir John, I am rather expecting a gentleman to call on me on
business to-night," she said; "and have left word for him to step in
and see me here.   Will you forgive the liberty?"

"I'm sure it's no liberty; I shall be glad to welcome him," replied
Sir John, dismally.'   "There'll not be much here but stupid boys
and girls.   We shall get no whist to-night.   The plague only knows
who invented balls."   .

It was a little odd that, next to ourselves, Mrs. Hughes should be
the first to arrive.   She was very pale and pretty, and her husband
was a slender, quiet, delicate man, looking like a finished gentleman.
Miss Deveen followed them with her eyes as they went up to
Lady Whitney.

"She does not look like it, does she, Johnny?" whispered Miss
Deveen to me.   No, I was quite sure she did not.

Sophie Chalk was in white, with ivy leaves in her spangled hair, the sweetest fairy to look at ever seen out of a moonlight ring. Helen, in her Court dress and pearls, looked plain beside her. They stood talking together, not noticing that I and Tod were in the recess behind. Most of the people had come then, and the music was tuning up. The rooms looked well; the flowers, scattered about, had come up from Whitney Hall. Helen called to her brother.

"We may as well begin dancing, William."

"Of course we may," he answered. "I don't know what we have waited for. I must find a partner. Miss Chalk, may I have the honour of dancing the first dance with you?"

That Miss Chalk's eyes went up to his with a flash of gratitude, and then down in modesty to the chalked floor, I knew as well as though they had been behind her head instead of before it.

"Oh, thank you," said she, "I shall be so happy." And I no more dared glance at Tod than if he had been an uncaged crocodile. She had told *him* she was engaged for it.

But just as William was about to give her his arm, and some one came and took away Helen, Lady Whitney called him. He spoke with his mother for a minute or two and came back with a cloud on his face.

"I am awfully sorry, Sophie. The mother says I must take out Lady Esther Starr this first time, old Starr's wife, you know, as my father's dancing days are over. Lady Esther is seven-and-thirty if she's a day," growled Bill, "and as big as a lighthouse. I'll have the second with you, Sophie."

"I am *afraid* I am engaged for the second," hesitated Miss Sophie. "I think I have promised Joseph Todhetley."

"Never mind him," said Bill. "You'll dance it with me, mind."

"I can tell him I mistook the dance," she softly suggested.

"Tell him anything. All right."

He wheeled round, and went up to Lady Esther, putting on his glove. Sophie Chalk moved away, and I took courage to glance sideways at Tod.

His face was white as death: I think with passion. He stood with his arms folded, never moving throughout the whole quadrille, only looking out straight before him with a fixed stare. A waltz came next, for which they kept their partners. And Sophie Chalk had enjoyed the luck of sitting down all the time. Whilst they were making ready for the second quadrille, Tod went up to her.

"This is our dance, Miss Chalk."

Well, she had her share of boldness. She looked steadily in his

face, assuring him that he was mistaken, and vowing through thick
and thin that it was the *third* dance she had promised him. Whilst
she was excusing herself, Bill came up to claim her. Tod put out
his strong arm to ward him off.

"Stay a moment, Whitney," he said, with studied calmness, "let
me have an understanding first with Miss Chalk. She can dance
with you afterwards if she prefers to do so. Miss Chalk, *you know*
that you promised yourself to me this morning for the second dance.
I asked you for the first: you were engaged for that, you said, and
would dance the second with me. There could be no mistake, on
your side or on mine."

"Oh, but *indeed* I understood it to be the third, dear Mr. Todhetley," said she. "I am dreadfully sorry if it is my fault. I will
dance the third with you."

"I have not asked you for the third. Do as you please. If you
throw me over for this second dance, I will never ask you for another
again as long as I live."

Bill Whitney stood by laughing; seeming to treat the whole as a
good joke. Sophie Chalk looked at him appealingly.

"And you certainly promised *me*, Miss Chalk," he put in.
"Todhetley, it is a misunderstanding. You and I had better draw
lots."

Tod bit his lip nearly to bleeding. All the notice he took of Bill's
speech was to turn his back upon him, and address Sophie.

"The decision lies with you alone, Miss Chalk. You have engaged
yourself to him and to me : choose between us."

She put her hand within Bill's arm, and went away with him,
leaving a little honeyed flattery for Tod. But Bill Whitney looked
back curiously into Tod's white face, all his brightness gone; for
the first time he seemed to realize that it was serious, almost an
affair of life or death. His handkerchief up, wiping his damp
brow, Tod did not notice which way he was going, and ran
against Anna. "I beg your pardon," he said, with a start, as if
waking out of a dream. "Will you go through this dance with me,
Anna?"

Yes. He led her up to it; and they took their places opposite
Bill and Miss Chalk.

Mr. James was to arrive at half-past nine. I was waiting for him
near the entrance door. He was punctual to time; and looked very
well in his evening dress. I took him up to Miss Deveen, and she
made room for him on the sofa by her side, her diamonds glistening. He must have seen their value. Sir John had his rubber then
in the little breakfast-parlour : Miss Cattledon, old Starr, and another
making it up for him. Wanting to see the game played out, I kept
by the sofa.

This was not the dancing-room: but they came into it in couples between the dances, to march round in the cooler air. Mr. James looked and Miss Deveen looked; and I confess that whenever Mrs. Hughes passed us, I felt queer. Miss Deveen suddenly arrested her and kept her talking for a minute or two. Not a word bearing upon the subject said Mr. James. Once, when the room was clear and the measured tread to one of Strauss's best waltzes could be heard, Lady Whitney approached. Catching sight of the stranger by Miss Deveen, she supposed he had been brought by some of the guests, and came up to make his acquaintance.

"A friend of mine, dear Lady Whitney," said Miss Deveen.

Lady Whitney, never observing that no name was mentioned, shook hands at once with Mr. James in her homely country fashion. He stood up until she had moved away.

"Well?" said Miss Deveen, when the dancers had come in again. "Is the lady here?"

"Yes."

I had expected him to say No, and could have struck him for destroying my faith in Mrs. Hughes. She was passing at the moment.

"Do you see her now?" whispered Miss Deveen.

"Not now. She was at the door a moment ago."

"Not now!" exclaimed Miss Deveen, staring at Mrs. Hughes. "Is it not *that* lady?"

Mr. James sent his eyes in half-a-dozen directions.

"Which lady, ma'am?"

"The one who has just passed in black silk, with the simple white net quilling round the neck."

"Oh dear, no!" said Mr. James. "I never saw that lady in my life before. The lady, *the* lady, is dressed in white."

Miss Deveen looked at him, and I looked. *Here*, in the rooms, and yet not Mrs. Hughes!

"This is the one," he whispered, "coming in now."

The one, turning in at that particular instant, was Sophie Chalk. But others were before her and behind her. She was on Harry Whitney's arm.

"Why don't you dance, Miss Deveen?" asked bold Harry, halting before the sofa.

"Will you dance with me, Master Harry?"

"Of course I will. Glad to get you."

"Don't tell fibs, young man. I might take you at your word, if I had my dancing-shoes on."

Harry laughed. Sophie Chalk's blue eyes happened to rest on Mr. James's face: they took a puzzled expression, as if wondering where she had seen it. Mr. James rose and bowed to her. She must have recognized him then, for her features turned livid, in spite of the powder upon them.

"Who is it, Johnny?" she whispered, in her confusion, loosing Harry's arm and coming behind.

"Well, you must ask that of Miss Deveen. He has come here to see her: something's up, I fancy, about those emerald studs."

Had it been to save my fortune, I could not have helped saying it. I saw it all as in a mirror. *She* it was who had taken them, and pledged them afterwards. A similar light flashed on Miss Deveen. She followed her with her severe face, her condemning eyes.

"Take care, Johnny!" cried Miss Deveen.

I was just in time to catch Sophie Chalk. She would have fallen on my shoulder. The room was in a commotion at once: a young lady had fainted. What from? asked every one. Oh, from the heat, of course. And no other reason was breathed.

Mr. James's mission was over. It had been successful. He made his bow to Lady Whitney, and withdrew.

Miss Deveen sent for Sophie Chalk the next day, and they had it out together, shut up alone. Sophie's coolness was good for any amount of denial, but it failed here. And then she took the other course, and fell on her knees at Miss Deveen's feet, and told a pitiable story of being alone in the world, without money to dress herself, and the open jewel-casket in Miss Deveen's chamber (into which accident, not design, had really taken her) proving too much in the moment's temptation. Miss Deveen believed it; she told her the affair should never transpire beyond the two or three who already knew it; that she would redeem the emeralds herself, and say nothing even to Lady Whitney; but, as a matter of course, Miss Chalk must close her acquaintance with Sir John's family.

And, singular to say, Sophie received a letter from some one that same evening, inviting her to go out of town. At least, she said she did.

So, quitting the Whitneys suddenly was plausibly accounted for; and Helen Whitney did not know the truth for many a day.

What did Tod think? For that, I expect, is what you are all wanting to ask. That was another curious thing—that he and Bill Whitney should have come to an explanation before the ball was over. Bill went up to him, saying that had he supposed Tod could mean anything serious in his admiration of Sophie Chalk, he should never have gone in for admiring her himself, even in pastime; and certainly would not continue to do so or spoil sport again.

"Thank you for telling me," answered Tod, with indifference. "You are quite welcome to go in for Sophie Chalk in any way you please. *I* have done with her."

"No," said Bill, "good girls must grow scarcer than they are before I should go in seriously for Sophie Chalk. She's all very well to talk and laugh with, and she is uncommonly fascinating."

It was my turn to put in a word. "As I told you, Bill, months ago, Sophie Chalk would fascinate the eyes out of your head, give her the chance."

Bill laughed. "Well she has had the chance, Johnny: but she has not done it."

Altogether, Sophie, thanks to her own bad play, had fallen to a discount.

'When Miss Deveen announced to the world that she had found her emerald studs (lost through an accident, she discovered, and recovered in the same way) people were full of wonder at the chances and mistakes of life. Lettice Lane was cleared triumphantly. Miss Deveen sent her home for a week to shake hands with her friends and enemies, and then took her back as her own maid.

And the only person I said a syllable to was Anna. I knew it would be safe: and I dare say you would have done the same in my place. But she stopped me at the middle of the first sentence.

"I have known it from the first, Johnny: I was nearly as sure of it as I could be; and it is that that has made me so miserable."

"Known it was Sophie Chalk?"

"As good as known it. I had no proof, only suspicion. And I could not see whether I ought to speak the suspicion even to mamma, or to keep it to myself. As things have turned out, I am very thankful to have been silent."

"How was it, then?"

"That night at Whitney Hall, after they had all come down from dressing, mamma sent me up to William's room with a message. As I was leaving it—it is at the end of the long corridor, you know—I saw some one peep cautiously out of Miss Cattledon's chamber, and then steal up the back stairs. It was Sophie Chalk. Later, when we were going to bed, and I was quite undressed, Helen, who was in bed, espied Sophie's comb and brush on the table—for she had dressed in our room because of the large glass —and told me to run in with them: she only slept in the next room. It was very cold. I knocked and entered so sharply that the door-bolt, a thin, creaky old thing, gave way. Of course I begged her pardon; but she seemed to start up in terrible fear, as if I had been a ghost. She had not touched her hair, but sat in her shawl, sewing at her stays; and she let them drop on the carpet and threw a petticoat over them. I thought nothing, Johnny; nothing at all. But the next morning when commotion arose and the studs were missing, I could not help recalling all this; and I quite hated myself for thinking Sophie Chalk might have taken them when she stole out of Miss Cattledon's room, and was sewing them later into her stays."

"You thought right, you see."

"Johnny, I am very sorry for her. I wish we could help her to some good situation. Depend upon it, this will be a lesson to her: she will never so far forget herself again."

"She is quite able to take care of herself, Anna. Don't let it trouble you. I dare say she will marry Mr. Everty."

"Who is Mr. Everty?"

"Some one who is engaged in the wine business with Sophie Chalk's brother-in-law, Mr. Smith."

XVI

GOING TO THE MOP.

" I NEVER went to St. John's mop in my life," said Mrs. Todhetley.

" That's no reason why you never should go," returned the Squire.

" And never thought of engaging a servant at one."

" There are as good servants to be picked up at a mop as out of it; and you have a great deal better choice," said he. " My mother has hired many a man and maid at the mop: first-rate servants too."

" Well, then, perhaps we had better go into Worcester to-morrow and see," concluded she, rather dubiously.

" And start early," said the Squire. " What is it you are afraid of?" he added, noting her doubtful tone. " That good servants don't go to the mop to be hired?"

" Not that," she answered. " I know it is the only chance farm-house servants have of being hired when they change their places. It was the noise and crowd I was thinking of."

" Oh, that's nothing," returned the Pater. " It is not half as bad as the fair."

Mrs. Todhetley stood at the parlour window of Dyke Manor, the autumn sun, setting in a glow, tingeing her face and showing up its thoughtful expression. The Squire was in his easy-chair, looking at one of the Worcester newspapers.

There had been a bother lately about the dairy-work. The old dairy-maid, after four years of the service, had left to be married; two others had been tried since, and neither suited. The last had marched herself off that day, after a desperate quarrel with Molly; the house was nearly at its wits' end in consequence, and perhaps the two cows were also. Mrs. Todhetley, really not knowing what in the world to do, and fretting herself into the face-ache over it, was interrupted by the Pater and his newspaper. He had just read there the reminder that St. John's annual Michaelmas Mop would take place on the morrow: and he told Mrs. Todhetley that she could go there and hire a dairy-maid at will. Fifty if she wanted them. At that time the mop was as much an institution as the fair or the wake. Some people called it the Statute Fair.

Molly, whose sweet temper you have had a glimpse or two of before, banged about among her spoons and saucepans when she heard what was in the wind. "Fine muck it 'ud be," she said, "coming out o' that there Worcester mop." Having the dairy-work to do as well as her own just now, the house scarcely held her.

We breakfasted early the next morning and started betimes in the large open carriage, the Squire driving his pair of fine horses, Bob and Blister. Mrs. Todhetley sat with him, and I behind. Tod might have gone if he would: but the long drive out and home had no charms for him, and he said ironically he should like to see himself attending the mop. It was a lovely morning, bright and sunny, with a suspicion of crispness in the air: the trees were putting on their autumn colours, and shoals of black-berries were in the hedges.

Getting some refreshment again at Worcester, and leaving the Squire at the hotel, I and Mrs. Todhetley walked to the mop. It was held in the parish of St. John's—a suburb of Worcester on the other side of the Severn, as all the country knows. Crossing the bridge and getting well up the New Road, we plunged into the thick of the fun.

The men were first, standing back in a line on the foot-path, fronting the passers-by. Young rustics mostly in clean smock-frocks, waiting to be looked at and questioned and hired, a broad grin on their faces with the novelty of the situation. We passed them : and came to the girls and women. You could tell they were nearly all rustic servants too, by their high colours and awk-ward looks and manners. As a rule, each held a thick cotton umbrella, tied round the middle after the fashion of Mrs. Gamp's, and a pair of pattens whose bright rings showed they had not been in use that day. To judge by the look of the present weather, we were not likely to have rain for a month : but these simple people liked to guard against contingencies. Crowds of folk were passing along like ourselves, some come to hire, some only to take up the space and stare.

Mrs. Todhetley elbowed her way amongst them. So did I. She spoke to one or two, but nothing came of it. Whom should we come upon, to my intense surprise, but our dairy-maid—the one who had taken herself off the previous day !

" I hope you will get a better place than you had with me, Susan," said the Mater, rather sarcastically.

" I hopes as how I shall, missis," was the insolent retort. "'Twon't be hard to do, any way, that won't, with that there overbearing Molly in yourn."

Johnny Ludlow.—I.   17

We went on. A great hulking farmer as big as a giant, and looking as though he had taken more than was good for him in the morning, came lumbering along, pushing every one right and left. He threw his bold eyes on one of the girls.

"What place be for you, my lass?"

"None o' yourn, master," was the prompt reply.

The voice was good-natured and pleasant, and I looked at the girl as the man went shouldering on. She wore a clean light cotton gown, a smart shawl all the colours of the rainbow, and a straw bonnet covered with sky-blue bows. Her face was fairer than most of the faces around; her eyes were the colour of her ribbons; and her mouth, rather wide and always smiling, had about the nicest set of teeth I ever saw. To take likes and dislikes at first sight without rhyme or reason, is what I am hopelessly given to, and there's no help for it. People laugh mockingly: as you have heard me say. "There goes Johnny with his fancies again!" they cry: but I know that it has served me well through life. I took a liking to this girl's face: it was an honest face, as full of smiles as the bonnet was of bows. Mrs. Todhetley noticed her too, and halted. The girl dropped a curtsey.

"What place are you seeking?" she asked.

"Dairy-maid's, please, ma'am."

The good Mater stood, doubtful whether to pursue inquiries or to pass onwards. She liked the face of the girl, but did not like the profusion of blue ribbons.

"I understand my work well, ma'am, please; and I'm not afraid of any much of it, in reason."

This turned the scale. Mrs. Todhetley stood her ground and plunged into questioning.

"Where have you been living?"

"At Mr. Thorpe's farm, please, near Severn Stoke."

"For how long?"

"Twelve months, please. I went there Old Michaelmas Day, last year."

"Why are you leaving?"

"Please, ma'am"—a pause here—"please, I wanted a change, and the work was a great sight of it; frightful heavy; and missis often cross. Quite a herd o' milkers, there was, there."

"What is your name?"

"Grizzel Clay. I be strong and healthy, please, ma'am; and I was twenty-two in the summer."

"Can you have a character from Mrs. Thorpe?"

"Yes, please, ma'am, and a good one. She can't say nothing against me."

And so the queries went on; one would have thought the Mater was hiring a whole regiment of soldiers. Grizzel was ready and willing to enter on her place at once, if hired. Mrs. Thorpe was in Worcester that day, and might be seen at the Hare and Hounds inn.

"What do you think, Johnny?" whispered the Mater.

"I should hire her. She's just the girl I wouldn't mind taking without any character."

"With those blue bows! Don't be simple, Johnny. Still I like the girl, and may as well see Mrs. Thorpe."

"By the way, though," she added, turning to Grizzel, "what wages do you ask?"

"Eight pounds, please, ma'am," replied Grizzel, after some hesitation, and with reddening cheeks.

"Eight pounds!" exclaimed Mrs. Todhetley. "That's very high."

"But you'll find me a good servant, ma'am."

We went back through the town to the Hare and Hounds, an inn near the cathedral. Mrs. Thorpe, a substantial dame in a long cloth skirt and black hat, by which we saw she had come in on horse-back, was at dinner.

She gave Grizzel Clay a good character. Saying the girl was honest, clean, hardworking, and very sweet-tempered; and, in truth, she was rather sorry to part with her. Mrs. Todhetley asked about the blue bows. Ay, Mrs. Thorpe said, that was Grizzel Clay's great fault—a love of finery: and she recommended Mrs. Todhetley to "keep her under" in that respect. In going out we found Grizzel waiting under the archway, having come down to learn her fate. Mrs. Todhetley said she should engage her, and bade her follow us to the hotel.

"It's an excellent character, Johnny," she said, as we went along the street. "I like everything about the girl, except the blue ribbons."

"I don't see any harm in blue ribbons. A girl looks nicer in ribbons than without them."

"That's just it," said the Mater. "And this girl is good-looking enough to do without them. Johnny, if Mr. Todhetley has no objection, I think we had better take her back in the carriage. You won't mind her sitting by you?"

"Not I. And I'm sure I shall not mind the ribbons."

So it was arranged. The girl was engaged, to go back with us in the afternoon. Her box would be sent on by the carrier. She presented herself at the Star at the time of starting with a small bundle: and a little birdcage, something like a mouse-trap, that had a bird in it.

"Could I be let take it, ma'am?" she asked of Mrs. Todhetley.

"It's only a poor linnet that I found hurt on the ground the last morning I went out to help milk Thorpe's cows. I'm a-trying, please, to nurse it back to health."

"Take it, and welcome," cried the Squire. "The bird had better die, though, than be kept to live in that cage."

"I was thinking to let it fly, please, sir, when it's strong again."

Grizzel had proper notions. She screwed herself into the corner of the seat, so as not to touch me. I heard all about her as we went along.

She had gone to live at her Uncle Clay's in Gloucestershire when her mother died, working for them as a servant. The uncle was "well-to-do," rented twenty acres of land, and had two cows and some sheep and pigs of his own. The aunt had a nephew, and this young man wanted to court her, Grizzel: but she'd have nothing to say to him. It made matters uncomfortable, and last year they turned her out: so she went and hired herself at Mrs. Thorpe's.

"Well, I should have thought you had better be married and have a home of your own than go out as dairy-maid, Grizzel."

"That depends upon who the husband is, sir," she said, laughing slightly. "I'd rather be a dairy-maid to the end o' my days—I'd rather be a prisoner in a cage like this poor bird—than have anything to say to that there nephew of aunt's. He had red hair, and I can't abide it."

Grizzel proved to be a good servant, and became a great favourite in the house, except with Molly. Molly, never taking to her kindly, was for quarrelling ten times a day, but the girl only laughed back again. She was superior to the general run of dairy-maids, both in looks and manners: and her good-humoured face brought sweethearts up in plenty.

Two of them were serious. The one was George Roper, bailiff's man on a neighbouring farm; the other was Sandy Lett, a wheelwright in business for himself at Church Dykely. Of course matters ran in this case, as they generally do run in such cases, all cross and contrary: or, as the French say, *à tort et à travers*. George Roper, a good-looking young fellow with curly hair and a handsome pair of black whiskers, had not a coin beyond the weekly wages he worked for: he had not so much as a chair to sit in, or a turn-up bedstead to lie on; yet Grizzel loved him with her whole heart. Sandy Lett, who was not bad-looking either, and had a good home and a good business, she did not care for. Of course the difficulty lay in deciding which of the two to choose: ambition and her friends recommended Sandy Lett; imprudence and her own heart, George Roper. Like the donkey between the two bundles of hay, Grizzel was unable to decide on either, and kept both the swains on the tenter-hooks of suspense.

Sunday afternoons were the great trouble of Grizzel's life. Roper had holiday then, and came: and Lett, whose time was his own, though of course he could not afford to waste it on a week-day, also came. One would stand at the stile in one field, the other at a stile in another field: and Grizzel, arrayed in one of the light print gowns she favoured, the many-coloured shawl, and the dangerous blue-ribboned bonnet, did not dare to go out to either, lest the other should pounce upon his rival, and a fight ensue. It was getting quite exciting in the household to watch the progress of events. Spring passed, the summer came round; and between the two, Grizzel had her hands full. The other servants could not imagine what the men saw in her.

"It is those blue ribbons she's so fond of!" said Mrs. Todhetley to us two, with a sigh. "I doubted them from the first."

"I should say it is the blue eyes," dissented Tod.

"And I the white teeth and laughing face. *Nobody* can help liking her."

"You shut up, Johnny. If I were Roper——"

"Shut up yourself, Joseph: both of you shut up: you know nothing about it," interrupted the Squire, who had seemed to be asleep in his chair. "It comes of woman's coquetry and man's folly. As to these two fellows, if Grizzel can't make up her mind, I'll warn them both to keep off my grounds at their peril."

One evening during the Midsummer holidays, in turning out of the oak-walk to cross the fold-yard, I came upon Grizzel leaning on the gate. She had a bunch of sweet peas in her hand, and tears in her eyes. George Roper, who must have been talking to her, passed me quickly, touching his hat.

"Good evening, sir."

"Good evening, Roper."

He walked away with his firm, quick stride: a well-made, hand-some, trustworthy fellow. His brown velveteen coat (an old one of his master's) was shabby, but he looked well in it; and his gaitered legs were straight and strong. That he had been the donor of the sweet peas, a rustic lover's favourite offering, was evident. Grizzel attempted to hide them in her gown when she saw me, but was not quick enough, so she was fain to hold them openly in her hand, and make believe to be busy with her milk-pail.

"It's a drop of skim milk I've got over; I was going to take it to the pigs," said she.

"What are you crying about?"

"Me crying!" returned Grizzel. "It's the sun a shinin' in my eyes, sir."

Was it! "Look here, Grizzel, why don't you put an end to this state of bother? You won't be able to milk the cows next."

"'Tain't any in'ard bother o' that sort as 'll keep me from doing my proper work," returned she, with a flick to the handle of the pail.

"At any rate, you can't marry two men: you would be taken up by old Jones the constable, you know, and tried for bigamy. And I'm sure you must keep *them* in ferment. George Roper's gone off with a queer look on his face. Take him, or dismiss him."

"I'd take him to-morrow, but for one thing," avowed the girl in a half whisper.

"His short wages, I suppose—sixteen shillings a week."

"Sixteen shillings a week short wages!" echoed Grizzel. "I call 'em good wages, sir. I'd never be afraid of getting along on them with a steady man—and Roper's that. It ain't the wages, Master Johnny. It is, that I promised mother never to begin life upon less than a cottage and some things in it."

"How do you mean?"

"Poor mother was a-dying, sir. Her illness lasted her many a week, and she might be said to be a-dying all the time. I was eighteen then. 'Grizzy,' says she to me one night, 'you be a likely girl and 'll get chose afore you be many summers older. But you must promise me that you'll not, on no temptation whatsoever, say yes to a man till he has a home of his own to take you to, and beds and tables and things comfortable about him. Once begin without 'em, and you and him 'll spend all your after life looking out for 'em; but they'll not come any the more for that. And you'll be at sixes-and-sevens always: and him, why perhaps he'll take to the beer-shop—for many a man does, through having, so to say, no home. I've seen the ill of it in my days,' she says, 'and if I thought you'd tumble into it I'd hardly rest quiet in the grave where you be so soon a-going to place me.' 'Be at ease, mother,' says I to her in answer, 'and take my promise, which I'll never break, not to set-up for marriage without a home o' my own and proper things in it.' That promise I can't break, Master Johnny; and there has laid the root of the trouble all along."

I saw then. Roper had nothing but a lodging, not a stick or stone that he could call his own. And the foolish man, instead of saving up out of his wages, spent the remnant in buying pretty things for Grizzel. It was a hopeless case.

"You should never have had anything to say to Roper, knowing this, Grizzel."

Grizzel twirled the sweet peas round and round in her fingers, and looked foolish, answering nothing.

" Lett has a good home to give you and means to keep it going. He must make a couple of pounds a week. Perhaps more."

" But then I don't care for him, Master Johnny."

" Give him up then. Send him about his business."

She might have been counting the blossoms on the sweet-pea stalks. Presently she spoke, without looking up.

" You see, Master Johnny, one does not like to—to lose all one's chances, and grow into an old maid. And, if I *can't* have Roper, perhaps—in time—I might bring myself to take Lett. It's a better opportunity than a poor dairy-maid like me could ever ha' looked for."

The cat was out of the bag. Grizzel was keeping Lett on for a remote contingency. When she could make up her mind to say No to Roper, she meant to say Yes to him.

" It is awful treachery to Roper ; keeping him on only to drop him at last," ran my thoughts. " Were I he, I should give her a good shaking, and leave—— "

A sudden movement on Grizzel's part startled me. Catching up her pail, she darted across the yard by the pond as fast as her pattens would go, poured the milk into the pig-trough with a dash, and disappeared indoors. Looking round for any possible cause for this, I caught sight of a man in light fustian clothes hovering about in the field by the hay-ricks. It was Sandy Lett ; he had walked over on the chance of getting to see her. But she did not come out again.

The next move in the drama was made by Lett. The following Monday he presented himself before the Squire—dressed in his Sunday-going things, and a new hat on—to ask him to be so good as to settle the matter, for it was " getting a'most beyond him."

" Why, how can I settle it ? " demanded the Squire. " What have I to do with it ? "

" It's a tormenting of me pretty nigh into fiddle-strings," pleaded Lett. " What with her caprices—for sometimes her speaks to me as pleasant as a angel, while at others her won't speak nohow ; and what with that dratted folk over yonder a-teasing of me "— jerking his head in the direction of Church Dykely—" I don't get no peace of my life. It be a shame, Squire, for any woman to treat a man as she's a-treating me."

" I can't make her have you if she won't have you," exploded the Squire, not liking the appeal. " It is said, you know, that she would rather have Roper."

Sandy Lett, who had a great idea of his own merits, turned his nose up in the air. " Beg pardon, Squire," he said, " but that won't wash, that won't. Grizzel couldn't have nothing serious to say to that there Roper ; nought but a day-labourer on a farm ; *she couldn't:* and if he don't keep his distance from her, I'll wring his ugly head round for him. Look at me beside him!—my good home wi' its m'hogany furniture in't. I can keep her a'most like a lady. She may have in a wench once a week for the washing and scrubbing, if she likes: I'd not deny her nothing in reason. And for that there Roper to think to put hisself atween us! No; 'twon't do: the moon's not made o' green cheese. Grizzel's a bit light-hearted, sir; fond o' chatter; and Roper he've played upon that. But if you'd speak a word for me, Squire, so as I may have the banns put up——"

"What the deuce, Lett, do you suppose I have to do with my women-servants and their banns?" testily interrupted the Squire. "I can't interfere to make her marry you. But I'll tell you thus much, and her too: if there is to be this perpetual uproar about Grizzel, she shall quit my house before the twelvemonth she engaged herself for is up. And that's a disgrace for any young woman."

So Sandy Lett got nothing by coming, poor unfortunate man. And yet—in a sense he did. The Squire ordered the girl before him, and told her in a sharp, decisive tone that she must either put an end to the state of things—or leave his service. And Grizzel, finding that the limit of toleration had come, but unable in her conflicting difficulties to decide which of the swains to retain and which discard, dismissed the two. After that, she was plunged over head and ears in distress, and for a week could hardly see to skim off the cream for her tears.

"This comes of hiring dairy wenches at a statty fair!" cried wrathful Molly.

The summer went on. August was waning. One morning when Mr. Duffham had called in and was helping Mrs. Todhetley to give Lena a spoonful of jam (with a powder in it), at which Lena kicked and screamed, Grizzel ran into the room in excitement so great, that they thought she was going into a fit.

"Why, what is it?" questioned Mrs. Todhetley, with a temporary truce to the jam hostilities. "Has either of the cows kicked you down, Grizzel?"

"I'm—I'm come into a fortin!" shrieked Grizzel hysterically, laughing and crying in the same breath.

Mr. Duffham put her into a chair, angrily ordering her to be calm—for anger is the best remedy in the world to apply to hysterics—and took a letter from her that she held out. It told her that her Uncle Clay was dead, and had left her a bequest of forty pounds. The forty pounds to be paid to her in gold whenever she should go and apply for it. This letter had come by the morning post : but Grizzel, busy in her dairy, had only just now opened it.

"For the poor old uncle to have died in June, and them never to ha' let me hear on't !" she said, sobbing. "Just like 'em ! And me never to have put on a bit o' mourning for him !"

She rose from the chair, drying her eyes with her apron, and held out her hand for the letter. As Mrs. Todhetley began to say she was very glad to hear of her good luck, a shy look and a half-smile came into the girl's face.

"I can get the home now, ma'am, with all this fortin," she whispered.

Molly banged her pans about worse than ever, partly in envy at the good luck of the girl, partly because she had to do the dairy work during Grizzel's absence in Gloucestershire : a day and a half, which was given her by Mrs. Todhetley.

"There won't be no standing anigh her and her finery now," cried rampant Molly to the servants. "She'll tack her blue ribbons on to her tail as well as her head. Lucky if the dairy some fine day ain't found turned all sour !"

Grizzel came back in time ; bringing her forty pounds in gold wrapped-up in the foot of a folded stocking. The girl had as much sense as one here and there, and a day or two after her arrival she asked leave to speak to her mistress. It was to say that she should like to leave at the end of her year, Michaelmas, if her mistress would please look out for some one to replace her.

"And what are you going to do, Grizzel, when you do leave? What are your plans?"

Grizzel turned the colour of a whole cornfield of poppies, and con-fessed that she was going to be married to George Roper.

"Oh," said Mrs. Todhetley. But she had nothing to urge against it.

"And please, ma'am," cried Grizzel, the poppies deepening and glowing, "we'd like to make bold to ask if the master would let to us that bit of a cottage that the Claytons have went out of."

The Mater was quite taken aback. It seemed indeed that Grizzel had been laying her plans to some purpose.

"It have a nice piece o' ground to grow pertaters and garden stuff, and it have a pigsty," said Grizzel. "Please, ma'am, we shall get along famous, if we can have that."

"Do you mean to set up a pig, Grizzel ?"

Grizzel's face was all one smile. Of course they did. With such a fortune as she had come into, she intended herself and her hus-band to have everything good about them, including a pig.

"I'll give Grizzel away," wrote Tod when he heard the news of the legacy and the projected marriage. "It will be fun ! And if

you people at home don't present her with her wedding-gown it
will be a stingy shame. Let it have a good share of blue bows."

"No, though, will he!" exclaimed Grizzel with sparkling eyes,
when told of the honour designed her by Tod. "Give me away!
Him! I've always said there's not such another gentleman in these
parts as Mr. Joseph."

The banns were put up, and matters progressed smoothly; with
one solitary exception. When Sandy Lett heard of the treason
going on behind his back, he was ready to drop with blighted love
and mortification. A three-days' weather blight was nothing to his.
Quite forgetting modesty, he made his fierce way into the house,
without saying with your leave or by your leave, and thence to the
dairy where Grizzel stood making-up butter, startling the girl so
much with his white face and wild eyes that she stepped back into
a pan of cream. Then he enlarged upon her iniquity, and wound
up by assuring her that neither she nor her "coward of a Roper"
could ever come to good. After that, he left her alone, making no
further stir.

Grizzel quitted the Manor and went into the cottage, which the
Squire had agreed to let to them : Roper was to come to it on the
wedding-day. A daughter of Goody Picker's, one Mary Standish
(whose husband had a habit of going off on roving trips and staying away until found and brought back by the parish), stayed
with Grizzel, helping her to put the cottage in habitable order, and
arrange in it the articles she bought. That sum of forty pounds
seemed to be doing wonders : I told Grizzel I could not have made
a thousand go as far.

"Any left, Master Johnny? Why of course I shall have plenty
left," she said. "After buying the bed and the set o' drawers and
the chairs and tables ; and the pots and pans and crockeryware for
the kitchen ; and the pig and a cock and hen or two ; and perviding
a joint of roast pork and some best tea and white sugar for the
wedding-day, we shall still have pounds and pounds on't left.
'Tisn't me, sir, nor George nether, that 'ud like to lavish away all
we've got and put none by for a rainy day."

"All right, Grizzel. I am going to give you a tea-caddy."

"Well now, to think of that, Master Johnny!" she said, lifting
her hands. "And after the mistress giving me such a handsome
gownd!—and the servants clubbing together, and bringing a roast-
ing oven and beautiful set o' flat irons. Roper and me 'll be set
up like a king and queen."

On Saturday, the day before that fixed for the wedding, I and
Tod were passing the cottage—a kind of miniature barn, to look
at, with a thatched roof, and a broken grindstone at the door—
and went in : rather to the discomfiture of Grizzel and Mrs. Stan-

dish, who had their petticoats shortened and their arms bare, scouring and scrubbing and making ready for the morrow. Returning across the fields later, we saw Grizzel at the door, gazing out all ways at once.

"Consulting the stars as to whether it will be fine to-morrow, Grizzel?" cried Tod, who was never at a loss for a ready word.

"I was a-looking out for Mary Standish, sir," she said. "George Roper haven't been here to-night, and we be all at doubtings about several matters he was to have come in to settle. First he said he'd go on betimes to the church o' Sunday morning; then he said he'd come here and we'd all walk together: and it was left at a uncertainty. There's the blackberry pie, too, that he've not brought."

"The blackberry pie!" said I.

"One that Mrs. Dodd, where he lodges, have made a present of to us for dinner, Master Johnny. Roper was to ha' brought it in to-night ready. It won't look well to see him carrying of a baked-pie on a Sunday morning, when he've got on his wedding-coat. I can't think where he have got to!"

At this moment, some one was seen moving towards us across the field path. It proved to be Mary Standish: her gown turned up over her head, and a pie in her hands the size of a pulpit cushion. Red syrup was running down the outside of the dish, and the crust looked a little black at the edges.

"My, what a big beauty!" exclaimed Grizzel.

"Do take it, Grizzel, for my hands be all cramped with its weight," said Mrs. Standish: who, as it turned out, had been over to Roper's lodgings, a mile and a half away, with a view to seeing what had become of the bridegroom elect. And she nearly threw the pie into Grizzel's arms, and took down her gown.

"And what do Roper say?" asked Grizzel. "And why have he not been here?"

"Roper's not at home," said Mary Standish. "He come in from work about six; washed and put hisself to rights a bit, and then went out with a big bundle. Mrs. Dodd called after him to bring the pie, but he called back again that the pie might wait."

"What was in the bundle?" questioned Grizzel, resenting the slight shown to the pie.

"Well, by the looks on't, Mother Dodd thought 'twas 'is working clothes packed up," replied Mary Standish.

"His working clothes!" cried Grizzel.

"A going to take 'em to the tailor's, maybe, to get 'em done up. And not afore they wanted it."

"Why, it's spending money for nothing," was Grizzel's comment. "I could ha' done up them clothes."

"Well, it's what Mother Dodd thought," concluded Mary Standish.

We said good night, and went racing home, leaving the two women at the door, Grizzel lodging the heavy blackberry pie on the old grindstone.

It was a glorious day for Grizzel's wedding. The hour fixed by the clerk (old Bumford) was ten o'clock, so that it might be got well over before the bell rang out for service. We reached the church early. Amongst the few spectators already there was cross-grained Molly, pocketing her ill-temper and for once meaning to be gracious to Grizzel.

Ten o'clock struck, and the big old clock went ticking on. Clerk Bumford (a pompous man when free from gout) began abusing the wedding-party for not keeping its time. The quarter past was striking when Grizzel came up, with Mary Standish and a young girl. She looked white and nervous, and not at all at ease in her bridal attire—a green gown of some kind of stuff, and no end of pink ribbons: the choice of colours being Grizzel's own.

"Is Roper here yet?" whispered Mary Standish.

"Not yet."

"It's too bad of him!" she continued. "Never to send a body word whether he meant to call for us, or not : and us a waiting there till now, expecting of him."

But where was George Roper? And (as old Bumford asked) what did he mean by it? The clergyman in his surplice and hood looked out at the vestry twice, as if questioning what the delay meant. We stood just inside the porch, and Grizzel grew whiter and whiter.

"Just a few minutes more o' this delay, and there won't be no wedding at all this blessed morning," announced Clerk Bumford for the public benefit. "George Roper wants a good blowing up, he do."

Ere the words were well spoken, a young man named Dicker, who was a fellow-lodger of Roper's and was to have accompanied him to church, made his appearance alone. That something had gone wrong was plainly to be seen : but, what with the publicity of his present position, and what with the stern clerk pouncing down upon him in wrath, the young man could hardly get his news out.

In the first place, Roper had never been home all night; never been seen, in short, since he had left Mrs. Dodd's with the bundle, as related by Mary Standish. That morning, while Dicker in his consternation knew not what to be at—whether to be off to church alone, or to wait still, in the hope that Roper would come—two notes were delivered at Mrs. Dodd's by a strange boy: the one addressed to himself, John Dicker, the other to "Miss Clay," meaning Grizzel. They bore ill news; George Roper had given up his marriage, and gone away for good.

At this extraordinary crisis, pompous Clerk Bumford was so taken aback, that he could only open his mouth and stare. It gave Dicker the opportunity to put in a few words.

"What we thought at Mother Dodd's was, that Roper had took a drop too much somewhere last evening, and couldn't get home. He's as sober a man as can be—but whatever else was we to think? And when this writed note come this morning, and we found he had gone off to Ameriky o' purpose to avoid being married, we was downright floundered. This is yours, Grizzel," added the young man in as gently considerate a tone as any gentleman could have used.

Grizzel's hand shook as she took the letter he held out. She was biting her pale lips hard to keep down emotion. "Take it and read it," she whispered to Mary Standish—for in truth she herself could not, with all that sea of curious eyes upon her.

But Mary Standish laboured under the slight disadvantage of not being able to read writing: conscious of this difficulty, she would not touch the letter. Mr. Bumford, his senses and his tongue returning together, snatched it without ceremony out of Grizzel's hand.

"I'll read it," said he. And he did so. And I, Johnny Ludlow, give you the copy verbatim.

"Der Grisl, saterdy evenin, this comes hoppin you be wel as it leves me at presint, Which this is to declar to you der grisl that our marage is at an end, it hav ben to much for me and praid on my sperits, I cant stand it no longer nohow and hav took my leve of you for ivir, Der Grisl I maks my best way this night to Livirpol to tak ship for Ameriky, and my last hops for you hearby xprest is as you may be hapy with annother, I were nivir worthey of you der grisl and thats a fac,'but I kep it from you til now when I cant kep it no longer cause of my conshunse, once youv red this hear letter dont you nivir think no mor on me agen, which I shant on you, Adew for ivir,

"your unfortnit friend George Roper.

"Ide av carred acros that ther blakbured pi but shoud have ben to late, my good hops is youl injoy the pi with another better nor you ivir could along with me, best furwel wishes to Mary Standish, G R."

What with the penmanship and what with the spelling, it took old
Bumford's spectacles some time to get through. A thunderbolt
could hardly have made more stir than this news. No one spoke,
however; and Mr. Bumford folded the letter in silence.

"I always knowed what that there Roper was worth," broke
forth Molly. "He pipe-clayed my best black cloak on the sly one
day when I ordered him off the premises. You be better without
him, Grizzel, girl—and here's my hand and wishing you better luck
in token of it."

"Mrs. Dodd was right—them was a change a' clothes he was a
taking with him to Ameriky," added Mary Standish.

"Roper's a jail-bird, I should say," put in old Bumford. "A
nice un too."

"But what can it be that's went wrong—what is it that have
took him off?" wondered the young man, Dicker.

The parson in his surplice had come down the aisle and was
standing to listen. Grizzel, in the extremity of mental bitterness
and confusion, but striving to put a face of indifference on the
matter before the public, gazed around helplessly.

"I'm better without him, as Molly says—and what do I care?"
she cried recklessly, her lips quivering. The parson put his hand
gravely on her arm.

"My good young woman, I think you are in truth better without
him. Such a man as that is not worthy of a regret."

"No, sir, and I don't and won't regret him," was her rapid
answer, the voice rising hysterically.

As she turned, intending to leave the church, she came face to
face with Sandy Lett. I had seen him standing there, drinking in
the words of the note with all his ears and taking covert looks at
Grizzel.

"Don't pass me by, Grizzel," said he. "I feel hearty sorry for
all this, and I hope that villain 'll come to be drowned on his way
to Ameriky. Let me be your friend. I'll make you a good one."

"Thank you," she answered. "Please let me go by."

"Look here, Grizzel," he rejoined with a start, as if some thought
had at that moment occurred to him. "Why shouldn't you and
me make it up together? Now. If the one bridegroom's been a
wicked runagate, and left you all forsaken, you see another here
ready to put on his shoes. Do, Grizzel, do!"

"Do what?" she asked, not taking his meaning.

"Let's be married, Grizzel. You and me. There's the parson
and Mr. Bumford all ready, and we can get it over afore church
begins. It's a good home I've got to take you to. Don't say nay,
my girl."

Now what should Grizzel do? Like the lone lorn widow in

"David Copperfield," who, when a ship's carpenter offered her marriage, "instead of saying, 'Thank you, sir, I'd rather not,' up with a bucket of water and dashed it over him," Grizzel "up" with her hand and dealt Mr. Sandy a sounding smack on his left cheek. Smarting under the infliction, Sandy Lett gave vent to a word or two of passion, out of place in a church, and the parson administered a reprimand.

Grizzel had not waited. Before the sound of her hand had died away, she was outside the door, quickly traversing the lonely churchyard. A fine end to poor Grizzel's wedding!

The following day, Monday, Mrs. Todhetley went over to the cottage. Grizzel, sitting with her hands before her, started up, and made believe to be desperately busy with some tea-cups. We were all sorry for her.

"Mr. Todhetley has been making inquiry into this business, Grizzel," said the Mater, "and it certainly seems more mysterious than ever, for he cannot hear a word against Roper. His late master says Roper was the best servant he ever had; he is as sorry to lose him as can be."

"Oh, ma'am, but he's not worth troubling about—my thanks and duty to the master all the same."

"Would you mind letting me see Roper's note?"

Grizzel took it out of the tea-caddy I had given her—which caddy was to have been kept for show. Mrs. Todhetley, mastering the contents, and biting her lips to suppress an occasional smile, sat in thought.

"I suppose this is Roper's own handwriting, Grizzel?"

"Oh, ma'am, it's his, safe enough. Not that I ever saw him write. He talks about the blackberry pie, you see; one might know it is his by that."

"Then, judging by what he says here, he must have got into some bad conduct, or trouble, I think, which he has been clever enough to keep from you and the world."

"Oh yes, that's it," said Grizzel. "Poor mother used to say one might be deceived in a saint."

"Well, it's a pity but he had given some clue to its nature: it would have been a sort of satisfaction. But now—I chiefly came over to ask you, Grizzel, what you purpose to do?"

"There's only one thing for me now, ma'am," returned poor crest-fallen Grizzel, after a pause: "I must get another place."

"Will you come back to the Manor?"

A hesitation—a struggle—and then she flung her apron up to her face and burst into tears. Dairy-maids have their feelings as well as their betters, and Grizzel's "lines" were very bitter just then. She had been so proud of this poor cottage home; she had grown to love it so in only those few days, and to look forward to years of happiness within it in their humble way : and now to find that she must give it up and go to service again !

"The Squire says he will consider it as though you and Roper had not taken the cottage; and he thinks he can find some one to rent it who will buy the furniture of you—that is, if you prefer to sell it," she resumed very kindly. "And I think you had better come back to us, Grizzel. The new maid in your place does not suit at all."

Grizzel took down her apron and rubbed her eyes. · "It's very good of you, ma'am—and of the master—and I'd like to come back only for one thing. I'm afraid Molly would let me have no peace in my life: she'd get tanking at me about Roper before the others. Perhaps I'd hardly be able to stand it."

"I will talk to her," said Mrs. Todhetley, rising to leave. "Where is Mary Standish to-day ?"

"Gone over to Alcester, ma'am. She had a errand there she said. But I think it was only to tell her folks the tale of my trouble."

Molly had her "talking to" at once. It put her out a little; for she was really feeling some pity for Grizzel, and did not at all intend to "get tanking" at her. Molly had once experienced a similar disappointment herself; and her heart was opening to Grizzel. After her dinner was served that evening, she ran over to the cottage, in her coarse cooking apron and without a bonnet.

"Look here," she said, bursting in upon Grizzel, sitting alone in the dusk. "You come back to your place if you like—the missis says she has given you the option—and don't you be afeard of me. 'Tisn't me as'll ever give back to you a word about Roper ; and, mind, when I says a thing I mean it."

"Thank you, Molly," humbly replied poor Grizzel, catching her breath.

"The sooner you come back the better," continued Molly, fiercely. "For it's not me and that wench we've got now as is going to stop together. I had to call the missis into the dairy this blessed morning, and show her the state it was in. So you'll come back, Grizzel—and we'll be glad to see you."

Grizzel nodded her head : her heart was too full to speak.

"And as to that false villain of a Roper, as could serve a woman such a pitiful trick, I only wish I had the doctoring of him ! He should get a—a—a——" Molly's voice, pitched in a high tone, died gradually away. What on earth was it, stepping in upon them? Some most extraordinary object, who opened the door softly, and came in with a pitch. Molly peered at it in the darkness with open mouth.

A cry from Grizzel. A cry half of terror, half of pain. For she had recognized the object to be a man, and George Roper. George Roper with his hair and handsome whiskers cut off, and white sleeves in his brown coat—so that he looked like a Merry Andrew.

He seemed three parts stupefied : not at all like a traveller in condition to set off to America. Sinking into the nearest wooden chair, he stared at Grizzel in a dazed way, and spoke in a slow, questioning, wondering voice.

" I can't think what it is that's the matter with me."

" Where be your whiskers—and your hair?" burst forth Molly.

The man gazed at her for a minute or two, taking in the question gradually; he then raised his trembling hand to either side his face—feeling for the whiskers that were no longer there.

" A nice pot o' mischief *you*'ve been a getting into!" cried sharp Molly. " Is that your own coat? What's gone of the sleeves?"

For, now that the coat could be seen closely, it turned out that its sleeves had been cut out, leaving the bare white shirt-sleeves underneath. Roper looked first at one arm, then at the other.

" What part of Ameriky be you bound for, and when do the ship sail?" pursued sarcastic Molly.

The man opened his mouth and closed it again; like a born natural, as Molly put it. Grizzel suddenly clung to him with a sobbing cry.

" He is ill, Molly ; he's ill. He has had some trick played on him. George, what be it?" But still George Roper only gazed about him as if too stupid to understand.

In short, the man *was* stupid. That is, he had been stupefied, and as yet was only partially recovering its effects. He remembered going into the barber's shop on Saturday night to have his hair cut, after leaving his bundle of clothes at the tailor's. Some ale was served round at the barber's, and he, Roper, took a glass. After that he remembered nothing : all was blank, until he woke up an hour ago in the unused shed at the back of the blacksmith's shop.

That the ale had been badly drugged, was evident. The question arose—who had played the trick? In a day or two, when Roper had recovered, an inquiry was set on foot : but nothing came of it. The barber testified that Roper seemed sleepy after the ale, and a joke went round that he must have been drinking some previously. He went out of the shop without having his hair cut, with several more men—and that was all the barber knew. Of course Sandy Lett was suspected. People said he had done it in hope to get himself substituted as bridegroom. Lett, however, vowed through thick and thin that he was innocent ; and nothing was traced home to him. Neither was the handwriting of the note.

They were married on the Thursday. Grizzel was too glad to get him back unharmed to make bones about the shorn whiskers. No difficulty was made about opening the church on a week-day. Clerk Bumford grumbled at it, but the parson put him down. And the blackberry pie served still for the wedding-dinner.

XVII

BREAKING DOWN.

" Have him here a bit."

" Oh! But would you like it?"

" Like it?" retorted the Squire. "'I know this: if I were a hard-worked London clerk, ill for want of change and rest, and I had friends living in a nice part of the country, I should feel it uncommonly hard if they did not invite me."

" I'm sure it is very kind of you to think of it," said Mrs. Todhetley.

"Write at once and ask him," said the Squire.

They were speaking of a Mr. Marks. He was a relation of Mrs. Todhetley's; a second or third cousin. She had not seen him since she was a girl, when he used sometimes to come and stay at her father's. He seemed not to have got on very well in life; was only a clerk on a small salary, was married and had some children. A letter now and then passed between them and Mrs. Todhetley, but no other acquaintanceship had been kept up. About a month before this, Mrs. Todhetley had written to ask how they were going on; and the wife in answering—for it was she who wrote—said her husband was killing himself with work, and she quite believed he would break down for good unless he had a rest.

We heard more about it later. James Marks was clerk in the great financial house of Brown and Co. Not particularly great as to reputation, for they made no noise in the world, but great as to their transactions. They did a little banking in a small way, and had mysterious money dealings with no end of foreign places : but if you had gone into their counting-house in London you'd have seen nothing to show for it, except Mr. Brown seated at a table-desk in a small room, and half-a-dozen clerks, or so, writing hard, or bending over columns of figures, in a larger one. Mr. Brown was an elderly little gentleman in a chestnut wig, and the "Co." existed only in name.

James Marks had been thrown on the world when he was seventeen, with a good education, good principles, and a great anxiety to get on in life. He had to do it; for he had only himself to look to --and, mind you, I have lived long enough to learn that that's not at all the worst thing a young man can have. When some friends of his late father's got him into Brown and Co.'s house, James Marks thought his fortune was made. That is, he thought he was placed in a position to work up to one. But no. Here he was, getting on for forty years of age, and with no more prospect of fortune, or competency either, than he had had at the beginning.

How many clerks, and especially bankers' clerks, are there in that City of London now who could say the same! Who went into their house (whatsoever it may be) in the hey-day of youth, exulting in their good luck in having obtained the admission for which so many others were striving. They saw not the long years of toil before them, the weary days of close work, with no rest or intermission, except Sunday ; they saw not the struggle to live and pay ; they saw not themselves middle-aged men, with a wife and family, hardly able to keep the wolf from the door. It was James Marks's case. He had married. And what with having to keep up the appearance of gentlepeople (at least to make a pretence at it) and to live in a decent-looking dwelling, and to buy clothes, and to pay doctors' bills and children's schooling, I'll leave you to guess how much he had left for luxuries out of his two hundred a year.

When expenses were coming upon him thick and fast, Marks sought out some night employment. A tradesman in the neigh-bourhood—Pimlico—a butterman doing a flourishing business, advertised for a book-keeper to attend two or three hours in the evening. James Marks presented himself and was engaged. It had to be done in secrecy, lest offence should be taken at head-quarters. Had the little man in the chestnut wig heard of it, he might have objected to his clerk keeping any books but his own. Shut up in the butterman's small back-closet that he called his counting-house, Mr. Marks could be as private as need be. So there he was! After coming home from his day's toil, instead of taking recreation, the home-sitting with his wife, or the stroll in the summer weather, in place of throwing work to the winds and giving his brain rest, James Marks, after snatching a meal, tea and supper combined, went forth to work again, to weary his eyes with more figures and his head with casting them up. He generally managed to get home by eleven except on Saturday ; but the day's work was too much for any man. Better for him (could he have pocketed pride, and gained over Brown and Co.) that he had hired himself to stand behind the evening counter and serve out the butter and cheese to the customers. It would at least have been a relief from the accounts. And so the years had gone on.

A portion of the wife's letter to Mrs. Todhetley had run as follows: " Thank you very much for your kind inquiries after my husband, and for your hope that he is not overworking himself. *He is.* But I suppose I must have said something about it in my last letter (I am ashamed to remember that it was written two years ago!) that induced you to refer to it. That he is overworking himself I have known for a long time: and things that he has said lately have tended to alarm me. He speaks of sometimes getting confused in the head. In the midst of a close calculation he will suddenly seem to lose himself—lose memory and figures and all, and then he has to leave off for some minutes, close his eyes, and keep perfectly still, or else leave his stool and take a few turns up and down the room. Another thing he mentions—that the figures dance before his eyes in bed at night, and he is adding them up in his brain as if it were daytime and reality. It is very evident to me that he wants change and rest."

"And what a foolish fellow he must have been not to take it before this!" cried the Squire, commenting on parts of the letter, while Mrs. Todhetley wrote.

" Perhaps that is what he has not been able to do, sir," I said.

" Not able! Why, what d'ye mean, Johnny ? "

" It is difficult for a banker's clerk to get holiday. Their work has to go on all the same."

"Difficult! when a man's powers are breaking down! D'ye think bankers are made of flint and steel, not to give their clerks holiday when it is needed? Don't you talk nonsense, Johnny Ludlow."

But I was not so far wrong, after all. There came a letter of warm thanks from Mr. Marks himself in answer to Mrs. Todhetley's invitation. He said how much he should have liked to accept it and what great good it would certainly have done him; but that upon applying for leave he found he could not be spared. So there seemed to be an end of it; and we hoped he would get better without the rest, and rub on as other clerks have to rub on. But in less than a month he wrote again, saying he would come if the Squire and Mrs. Todhetley were still pleased to have him. He had been so much worse as to be obliged to tell Mr. Brown the truth— that he believed he *must* have rest ; and Mr. Brown had granted it to him.

It was the Wednesday in Passion Week, and a fine spring day, when James Marks arrived at Dyke Manor. Easter was late that year. He was rather a tall man, with dark eyes and very thin hair ; he wore spectacles, and at first was rather shy in manner.

You should have seen his delight in the change. The walks he took, the enjoyment of what he called the sweet country. "Oh," he said one day to us, "yours must be the happiest lot on earth. No forced work ; your living assured; nothing to do but to revel in this health-giving air! Forgive my freedom, Mr. Todhetley," he added a moment after: " I was contrasting your lot with my own."

We were passing through the fields towards the Court: the Squire was taking him to see the Sterlings, and he had said he would rather walk than drive. The hedges were breaking into green: the fields were yellow with buttercups and cowslips. This was on the Monday. The sun shone and the breeze was soft. Mr. Marks sniffed the air as he went along.

" Six months of this would make a new man of me," we heard him say to himself in a low tone.

" Take it," cried the Squire.

Mr. Marks laughed, sadly enough. " You might as well tell me, sir, to--to take heaven," he said impulsively. " The one is no more in my power than the other.—Hark! I do believe that's the cuckoo ! "

We stood to listen. It was the cuckoo, sure enough, for the first time that spring. It only gave out two or three notes, though, and then was silent.

" How many years it is since I heard the cuckoo ! " he exclaimed, brushing his hand across his eyes. " More than twenty, I suppose. It seems to bring back my youth to me. What a thing it would be for us, sir, if we could only go to the mill that grinds people young again ! "

The Squire laughed. " It is good of *you* to talk of age, Marks ; why, I must be nearly double yours," he added—which of course was random speaking.

" I feel old, Mr. Todhetley : perhaps older than you do. Think of the difference in our mode of life. I, tied to a desk for more hours of the twenty-four than I care to think of, my brain ever at work; you, revelling in this beautiful, healthy freedom ! "

" Ay, well, it is a difference, when you come to think of it," said the Squire soberly.

" I must not repine," returned Marks. " There are more men in my case than in yours. No doubt it is well for me," he continued, dropping his voice, with a sigh. " Were your favoured lot mine, sir, I might find so much good in it as to forget that this world is not our home."

Perhaps it had never struck the Squire before how much he was to be envied; but Marks put it strongly. " You'd find crosses and cares enough in my place, I can tell you, Marks, of one sort or another. Johnny, here, knows how I am bothered sometimes."

" No doubt of it," replied Marks, with a smile. " No lot on

earth can be free from its duties and responsibilities; and they must of necessity entail care. That is one thing, Mr. Todhetley; but to be working away your life at high pressure—and to know that you are working it away—is another."

"You acknowledge, then, that you are working too hard, Marks," said the Squire.

"I know I am, sir. But there's no help for it."

"It is a pity."

"Why it should begin to tell upon me so early I don't know. There are numbers of other men, who work as long and as hard as I do, and are seemingly none the worse for it."

"The time will come though when they will be, I presume."

"As surely as that sun is shining in the sky."

"Possibly you have been more anxious than they, Marks."

"It may be so. My conscience has always been in my work, to do it efficiently. I fear, too, I am rather sensitively organized as to nerves and brain. Upon those who are so, I fancy work tells sooner than on others."

The Squire put his arm within Marks's. "You must have a bit of a struggle to get along, too, on your small salary."

"True: and it all helps. Work and struggle together are not the most desirable combination. But for being obliged to increase my means by some stratagem or other, I should not have taken on the additional evening's work."

"How long are you at it, now, of an evening?"

"Usually about two hours. On Saturdays and at Christmas-time longer."

"And I suppose you must continue this night-work?"

"Yes. I get fifty pounds a year for it. And I assure you I should not know how to spare one pound of the fifty. No one knows the expenses of children, except those who have to look at every shilling before it can be spent."

There was a pause. Mr. Marks stooped, plucked a cowslip and held it to his lips.

"Don't you think, Marks," resumed the Squire, in a confidential, friendly tone, "that you were just a little imprudent to marry?"

"No, I do not think I was," he replied slowly, as if considering the question. "I did not marry very early: I was eight-and-twenty; and I had got together the wherewithal to furnish a house, and something in hand besides. The question was mooted among us at Brown's the other day—whether it was wiser, or not, for young clerks to marry. There is a great deal to be urged both ways—against marrying and against remaining single."

"What can you urge against remaining single?"

"A very great deal, sir. I feel sure, Mr. Todhetley, that you can form no idea of the miserable temptations that beset a young fellow in London. Quite half the London clerks, perhaps more, have no home to go to when their day is over; I mean no parent's home. A solitary room and no one to bear them company in it; that's all they have; perhaps, in addition, a crabbed landlady. Can you blame them very much if they go out and escape this solitude?—they are at the age, you know, when enjoyment is most keen; the thirst for it well-nigh irrepressible—— "

"And then they go off to those disreputable singing places!" exploded the Squire, not allowing him to finish.

"Singing places, yes; and other places. Theatres, concerts, supper-rooms—oh, I cannot tell you a tithe of the temptation that meets them at every turn and corner. Many and many a poor young fellow, well-intentioned in the main, has been ruined both in pocket and in health by these snares; led into them at first by dangerous companions."

"Surely all do not get led away."

"Not all. Some strive on manfully, remembering early precepts and taking God for their guide, and so escape. But it is not the greater portion who do this. Some marry early, and secure themselves a home. Which is best?—I put the question only in a worldly point of view. To commit the imprudence of marrying, and so bring on themselves and wives intolerable perplexity and care: or to waste their substance in riotous living!"

"I'll be shot if I know!" cried the Squire, taking off his hat to rub his puzzled head. "It's a sad thing for poor little children to be pinched, and for men like you to be obliged to work yourselves to shatters to keep them. But as to those others, I'd give 'em all a night at the treadmill. Johnny! Johnny Ludlow!"

"Yes, sir."

"You may be thankful that *you* don't live in London."

I had been thinking to myself that I was thankful not to be one of those poor young clerks to have no home to go to when work was over. Some fellows would rather tramp up and down the streets, than sit alone in a solitary room; and the streets, according to Marks, teemed with temptations. He resumed.

"In my case I judged it the reverse of imprudence to marry, for my wife expected a fairly good fortune. She was an only child, and her father had realized enough to live quietly; say three or four hundred a year. Mr. Stockleigh had been a member of the Stock Exchange, but his health failed and he retired. Neither I nor his daughter ever doubted—no, nor did he himself—that this money must come to us in time."

"And won't it?" cried the Squire.

Marks shook his head. " I fear not. A designing servant, that they had, got over him after his daughter left—he was weak in health and weak in mind—and he married her. Caroline—my wife—resented it naturally; there was some recrimination on either side, and since then they have closed the door against her and me. So you see, with no prospect before us, there's nothing for me but to work the harder," he concluded, with a kind of plucked-up cheerfulness.

"But, to do that, you should get up your health and strength, Marks. You must, you know. What would you do if you broke down?"

"Hush!" came the involuntary and almost affrighted answer. "Don't remind me of it, sir. Sometimes I dream of it, and cannot bear to awaken."

We had got to like Marks very much only in those few days. He was a gentleman in mind and manners and a pleasant one into the bargain, though he did pass his days adding up figures and was kept down by poverty. The Squire meant to keep him for a month: two months if he would stay.

On the following morning, Tuesday, during breakfast-time, a letter came for him by the post—the first he had had. He had told his wife she need not write to him, wanting to have all the time for idle enjoyment: not to spend it in answering letters.

"From home, James?" asked Mrs. Todhetley.

"No," said he, smiling. "It is only a reminder that I am due to-morrow at the house."

"What house?" cried the Squire.

"Our house, sir. Brown and Co.'s."

The Squire put down his buttered roll—for Molly had graciously sent in hot rolls that morning—and stared at the speaker.

"What on earth are you talking of?" he cried. "You don't mean to say you are thinking of going back?"

"Indeed I am—unfortunately. I must get up to London to-night."

"Why, bless my heart," cried the Squire, getting up and standing a bit, "you've not been here a week!"

"It is all the leave I could get, Mr. Todhetley: a week. I thought you understood that."

"You can't go away till you are cured," roared the Squire. "Why didn't you go back the day you came? Don't talk nonsense, Marks."

"Indeed I should like to stay longer," he earnestly said. " I wish I could. Don't you see, Mr. Todhetley, that it does not lie with me?"

"Do you dare to look me in the face, Marks, and tell me this one week's rest has cured you? What on earth!—are you turning silly?"

"It has done me a great, great deal of good——"

"It has not, Marks. It can't have done it; not real good," came the Squire's interruption. "One would think you were a child."

"It was with difficulty I obtained this one week's leave," he explained. "I am really required in the office; my absence I know causes trouble. This holiday has done so much for me that I shall go back with a good heart."

"Look here," said the Squire: "suppose you take French leave, and stay?"

"In that case my discharge would doubtless arrive by the first post."

"Look here again: suppose in a month or two you break down and have to leave? What then?"

"Brown and Co. would appoint a fresh clerk in my place."

"Why don't Brown and Co. keep another clerk or two, so as to work you all less?"

Marks smiled at the very idea. "That would increase their expenses, Mr. Todhetley. They will never do that. It is a part of the business of Brown's life to keep expenses down."

Well, Marks had to go. The Squire was very serious in thinking more rest absolutely needful—of what service *could* a week be, he reiterated. Down he sat, wrote a letter to Brown and Co., telling them his opinion, and requesting the favour of their despatching James Marks back for a longer holiday. This he sent by post, and they would get it in the morning.

"No, I'll not trust it to you, Marks," he said: "you might never deliver it. Catch an old bird with chaff!"

To this letter there came no answer at all; and Mr. Marks did not come back. The Squire relieved his mind by calling Brown and Co. thieves and wretches—and so it passed. It must be remembered that I am writing of past years, when holidays were not so universal for any class, clerk or master, as they are at present. Not that I am aware whether financiers' clerks get them now.

The next scene in the drama I can only tell by hearsay. It took place in London, where I was not.

It was a dull, rainy day in February, and Mrs. Marks sat in her parlour in Pimlico. The house was one of a long row, and the parlour just about large enough to turn in. She sat by the fire, nursing a little two-year-old girl, and thinking; and three other children, the eldest a boy of nine, were playing at the table—building houses on the red cloth with little wooden bricks. Mrs. Marks was a sensible woman, understanding proper management, and had taken care to bring up her children not to be troublesome. She looked about thirty, and must have been pretty once, but her face was faded now, her grey eyes had a sad look in them. The chatter at the table and the bricks fell unheeded on her ear.

"Mamma, will it soon be tea-time?"

There was no answer.

"Didn't you hear, mamma? Carry asked if it would soon be tea-time. What were you thinking about?"

She heard this time, and started out of her reverie. "Very soon now, Willy dear. Thinking? Oh, I was thinking about your papa."

Her thoughts were by no means bright ones. That her husband's health and powers were failing, she felt as sure of as though she could foresee the ending that was soon to come. How he went on and did his work was a marvel: but he could not give it up, or bread would fail.

The week's rest in the country had set Mr. Marks up for some months. Until the next autumn he worked on better than he had been able to do for some time past. And then he failed again. There was no particular failing outwardly, but he felt all too conscious that his overtaxed brain was getting worse than it had ever been. He struggled on; making no sign. That he should have to resign part of his work was an inevitable fact: he must give up the evening book-keeping to enable him to keep his more important place. "Once let me get Christmas work over," thought he, "and as soon as possible in the New Year, I will resign."

He got the Christmas work over. Very heavy it was, at both places, and nearly did for him. It is the last straw, you know, that breaks the camel's back: and that work broke James Marks. Towards the end of January he was laid up in bed with a violent cold that settled on his chest. Brown and Co. had to do without him for eleven days: a calamity that—so far as Marks was concerned—had never happened in Brown and Co.'s experience. Then he went back to the city again, feeling shaken; but the evening labour was perforce given up.

No one knew how ill he was: or, to speak more correctly, how unfit for work, how more incapable of it he was growing day by day. His wife suspected a little. She knew of his sleepless nights, the result of overtaxed nerves and brain, when he would toss and turn and get up and walk the room; and dress himself in the morning without having slept.

"There are times," he said to her in a sort of horror, "when I cannot at all collect my thoughts. I am as long again at my work as I used to be, and have to go over it again and again. There have been one or two mistakes, and old Brown asks what is coming to me. I can't help it. The figures whirl before me, and I lose my power of mind."

"If you could only sleep well!" said Mrs. Marks.

"Ay, if I could. The brain is as much at work by night as by day. There are the figures mentally before me, and there am I, adding them up."

"You should see a clever physician, James. Spare the guinea, and go. It may be more than the guinea saved."

Mr. Marks took the advice. He went to a clever doctor; explained his position, the kind of work he had to do, and described his symptoms. "Can I be cured?" he asked.

"Oh yes, I think so," said the doctor, cheerfully, without telling him that he had gone on so far as to make it rather doubtful. "The necessary treatment is very simple. Take change of scene and perfect rest."

"For how long?"

"Twelve months, at least."

"Twelve months!" repeated Marks, in a queer tone.

"At least. It is a case of absolute necessity. I will write you a prescription for a tonic. You must live *well*. You have not lived well enough for the work you have to do."

As James Marks went out into the street he could have laughed a laugh of bitter mockery. Twelve months' rest for *him?* The doctor had told him one thing—that had he taken rest in time, a very, very much shorter period would have sufficed. "I wonder how many poor men there are like myself in London at this moment," he thought, "who want this rest and cannot take it, and who ought to live better and cannot afford to do it!"

It was altogether so very hopeless that he did nothing, except take the tonic, and he continued to go to the City as usual. Some two or three weeks had elapsed since then: he of course growing worse, though there was nothing to show it outwardly: and this was the end of February, and Mrs. Marks sat thinking of it all over the fire; thinking of what she knew, and guessing at what she did not know, and her children were building houses at the table.

The servant came in with the tea-things, and took the little girl. Only one servant could be kept—and hardly that. Mrs. Marks had made her own tea and was pouring out the children's milk-and-water, when they heard a cab drive up and stop at the door. A minute after Mr. Marks entered, leaning on the arm of one of his fellow-clerks.

" Here, Mrs. Marks, I have brought you an invalid," said the latter gaily, making light of it for her sake. " He seems better now. I don't think there's much the matter with him."

Had it come? Had what she had been dreading come—that he was going to have an illness, she wondered. But she was a trump of a wife, and showed herself calm and comforting.

" You shall both of you have some tea at once," she said, cheerfully. " Willy, run and get more tea-cups."

It appeared that Mr. Marks had been, as the clerk expressed it, very queer that day ; more so than usual. He could not do his work at all ; had to get assistance continually from one or the other, and ended by falling off his stool to the floor, in what he called, afterwards, a " sensation of giddiness." He seemed fit for nothing, and Mr. Brown said he had better be taken home.

That day ended James Marks's work. He had broken down. At night he told his wife what the physician had said ; which he had not done before. She could scarcely conceal her dismay.

A twelvemonth's rest for him! What would become of them? Failing his salary, they would have no means whatever of living.

" Oh, if my father had only acted by us as he ought!" she mentally cried. " James could have taken rest in time then, and all would have been well. Will he help us now it has come to this? Will *she* let him?—for it is she who holds him in subjection and steels his heart against us."

Mr. Stockleigh, the father, lived at Sydenham. She, the new wife, had taken him off there from his residence in Pimlico as soon as might be after the marriage ; and the daughter had never been invited inside the house. But she resolved to go there now. Saying nothing to her husband, Mrs. Marks started for Sydenham the day after he was brought home ill, and found the place without trouble.

The wife, formerly the cook, was a big brawny woman with a cheek and a tongue of her own. When Mrs. Marks was shown in, she forgot herself in the surprise; old habits prevailed, and she half dropped a curtsey.

" I wish to see papa, Mrs. Stockleigh."

" Mr. Stockleigh's out, ma'am."

" Then I must wait until he returns."

Mrs. Stockleigh did not see her way clear to turn this lady from the house, though she would have liked to do it. She made a show of hospitality, and ordered wine and cake to be put on the table. Of which wine, Mrs. Marks noticed with surprise, she drank *four* glasses. " Now and then we used to suspect her of drinking in the kitchen!" ran through Mrs. Marks's thoughts. " Has it grown upon her?"

The garden gate opened, and Mr. Stockleigh came through it. He was so bowed and broken that his daughter scarcely knew him. She hastened out and met him in the path.

"Caroline!" he exclaimed in amazement. "Is it really you? How much you have changed?"

"I came down to speak to you, papa. May we stay and talk here in the garden?"

He seemed glad to see her, rather than not, and sat down with her on the garden bench in the sun. In a quiet voice she told him all: and asked him to help her. Mrs. Stockleigh had come out and stood listening to the treason, somewhat unsteady in her walk.

"I—I would help you if I could, Caroline," he said, in hesitation, glancing at his wife.

"Yes, but you can't, Stockleigh," she put in. "Our own expenses is as much as iver we can manage, Mrs. Marks. It's a orful cost, living out here, and our two servants is the very deuce for extravigance. I've changed 'em both ten times for others, and the last lot is always worse than the first."

"Papa, do you see our position?" resumed Mrs. Marks, after hearing the lady patiently. "It will be a long time before James is able to do anything again—if he ever is—and we have not been able to save money. What are we to do? Go to the workhouse? I have four little children."

"You know that you can't help, Stockleigh," insisted Mr. Stockleigh's lady, taking up the answer, her face growing more inflamed. "You've not got the means to do anything: and there's an end on't."

"It is true, Caroline; I'm afraid I have not," he said—and his daughter saw with pain how tremblingly subject he was to his wife. "I seem short of money always. How did you come down, my dear?"

"By the train, papa. Third class."

"Oh dear!" cried Mr. Stockleigh. "My health's broken, Caroline. It is, indeed, and my spirit too. I am sure I am very sorry for you. Will you come in and take some dinner?"

"We've got nothing but a bit of 'ashed beef," cried Mrs. Stockleigh, as if to put a damper upon the invitation. "Him and me fails in our appetites dreadful: I can't think what's come to 'em."

Mrs. Marks declined dinner: she had to get back to the children. That any sort of pleading would be useless while that woman held sway, she saw well. "Good-bye, papa," she said. "I suppose we must do the best we can alone. Good morning, Mrs. Stockleigh."

To her surprise her father kissed her; kissed her with quivering lips. "I will open the gate for you, my dear," he said, hastening on to it. As she was going through, he slipped a sovereign into her hand.

"It will pay for your journey, at least, my dear. I am sorry to hear of your travelling third class. Ah, times have changed. It is not that I won't help you, child, but that I can't. She goes up to receive the dividends, and keeps me short. I should not have had that sovereign now, but it is the change out of the spirit bill that she sent me to pay. Hush! the money goes in drink. She drinks like a fish. Ah, Caroline, I was a fool—a ¦fool! Fare you well, my dear."

"Fare *you* well, dear papa, and thank you," she answered, turning away with brimming eyes and an aching heart.

After resting for some days and getting no better, James Marks had to give it up as a bad job. He went to the City house, saw Mr. Brown, and told him.

"Broken down!" cried old Brown, hitching back his wig, as he always did when put out. "I never heard such nonsense. At your age! The thing's incomprehensible."

"The work has been very wearing to the brain, sir; and my application to it was close. During the three-and-twenty years I have been with you I have never had but one week's holiday: the one last spring."

"You told me then you felt like a man breaking down, as if you were good for nothing," resentfully spoke old Brown.

"Yes, sir. I told you that I believed I was breaking down for want of a rest," replied Marks. "It has proved so."

"Why, you had your rest."

"One week, sir. I said I feared it would not be of much use. But—it was not convenient for you to allow me more."

"Of course it was not convenient; you know it could not be convenient," retorted old Brown. "D'you think I keep my clerks for play, Marks? D'you suppose my business will get done of itself?"

"I was aware myself, sir, how inconvenient my absence would be, and therefore I did not press the matter. That one week's rest did me a wonderful amount of service: it enabled me to go on until now."

Old Brown looked at him. "See here, Marks—we are sorry to lose you: suppose you take another week's change now, and try what it will do. A fortnight, say. Go to the sea-side, or somewhere."

Marks shook his head. "Too late, sir. The doctors tell me it will be twelve months before I am able to work again at calculations."

"Oh, my service to you," cried Mr. Brown. "Why, what are
you going to do if you cannot work?"

"That is a great deal more than I can say, sir. The thought of
it is troubling my brain quite as much as work ever did. It is never
out of it, night or day."

For once in his screwy life, old Brown was generous. He told
Mr. Marks to draw his salary up to the day he had left, and he
added ten pounds to it over and above.

During that visit I paid to Miss Deveen's in London, when Tod
was with the Whitneys, and Helen made her first curtsey to the
Queen, and we discovered the ill-doings of that syren, Mademoiselle
Sophie Chalk, I saw Marks. Mrs. Todhetley had given me two or
three commissions, as may be remembered: one amongst them was
to call in Pimlico, and see how Marks was getting on.

Accordingly I went. We had heard nothing, you must understand, of what I have told above, and did not know but he was
still in his situation. It was a showery day in April: just a twelvemonth, by the way, since his visit to us at Dyke Manor. I found
the house out readily; it was near Ebury Street; and I knocked.
A young lad opened the door, and asked me to walk into the
parlour.

"You are Mr. Marks's son," I said, rubbing my feet on the mat:
"I can tell by the likeness. What's your name?"

"William. Papa's is James."

"Yes, I know."

"He is ill," whispered the lad, with his hand on the door handle.
"Mamma's downstairs, making him some arrowroot."

Well, I think you might have knocked me down with a feather
when I knew him—for at first I did not. He was sitting in an
easy-chair by the fire, dressed, but wrapped round with blankets:
and instead of being the James Marks we had known, he was like
a living skeleton, with cheek-bones and hollow eyes. But he
was glad to see me, smiled, and held out his hand from the
blanket.

It is uncommonly awkward for a young fellow to be taken unawares like this. You don't know what to say. I'm sure I as much
thought he was dying as I ever thought anything in this world. At
last I managed to stammer a word or two about being sorry to see
him so ill.

"Ay," said he, in a weak, panting voice, "I am different from
what I was when with your kind people, Johnny. The trouble I
foresaw then has come."

"You used sometimes to feel then as though you would not long keep up," was my answer, for really I could find nothing else to say.

He nodded. "Yes, I felt that I was breaking down—that I should inevitably break down unless I could have rest. I went on until February, Johnny, and then it came. I had to give up my situation; and since then I have been dangerously ill from another source—chest and lungs."

"I did not know your lungs were weak, Mr. Marks."

"I'm sure I did not," he said, after a fit of coughing. "I had one attack in January through catching a cold. Then I caught another cold, and you see the result: the doctor hardly saved me. I never was subject to take cold before. I suppose the fact is that when a man breaks down in one way he gets weak in all, and is more liable to other ailments."

"I hope you will get better as the warm weather comes on. We shall soon have it here."

"Better of this cough, perhaps: I don't know: but not better yet of my true illness that I think most of—the overtaxed nerves and brain. Oh, if I could only have taken a sufficient rest in time!"

"Mr. Todhetley said you ought to have stayed with us for three months. He says it often still."

"I believe," he said, solemnly lifting his hand, "that if I could have had entire rest then for two or three months, it would have set me up for life. Heaven hears me say it."

And what a dreadful thing it now seemed that he had not!

"I don't repine. My lot seems a hard one, and I sometimes feel sick and weary when I dwell upon it. I have tried to do my duty: I could but keep on and work, as God knows. There was no other course open to me."

I supposed there was not.

"I am no worse off than many others, Johnny. There are men breaking down every day from incessant application and want of needful rest. Well for them if their hearts don't break with it!"

And, to judge by the tone he spoke in, it was as much as to say that his heart had broken. :

"I am beginning to dwell less on it now," he went on. "Perhaps it is that I am too weak to feel so keenly. Or that Christ's words are being indeed realized to me: 'Come unto me, all ye that labour and are heavy laden, and I will give you rest.' God does not forsake us in our trouble, Johnny, once we have learnt to turn to Him."

Mrs. Marks came into the room with the cup of arrowroot. The boy had run down to tell her I was there. She was very pleasant and cheerful: you could be at home with her at once. While he was waiting for the arrowroot to cool, he leant back in his chair and dropped into a doze.

"It must have been a frightful cold that he caught," I whispered to her.

"It was caught the day he went into the City to tell Mr. Brown he must give up his situation," she answered. "There's an old saying, of being penny wise and pound foolish, and that's what poor James was that day. It was a fine morning when he started; but rain set in, and when he left Mr. Brown it was pouring, and the streets were wet. He ought to have taken a cab, but did not, and waited for an omnibus. The first that passed was full; by the time another came he had got wet and his feet were soaking. That brought on a return of the illness he had had in January."

"I hope he will get well."

"It lies with God," she answered.

They made me promise to go again. "Soon, Johnny, soon," said Mr. Marks with an eagerness that was suggestive. "Come in the afternoon and have some tea with me."

I had meant to obey literally and go in a day or two; but one thing or other kept intervening, and a week or ten days passed. One Wednesday Miss Deveen was engaged to a dinner-party, and I took the opportunity to go to Pimlico. It was a stormy afternoon, blowing great guns one minute, pouring cats and dogs the next. Mrs. Marks was alone in the parlour, the tea-things on the table before her.

"We thought you had forgotten us," she said in a half-whisper, · shaking hands. "But this is the best time you could have come; for a kind neighbour has invited all the children in for the evening, and we shall be quiet. James is worse."

"Worse!"

"At least, weaker. He cannot sit up long now without great fatigue. He lay down on the bed an hour ago and has dropped asleep," she added, indicating the next room. "I am waiting for him to awake before I make the tea."

He awoke then: the cough betrayed it. She went into the room, and presently he came back with her. No doubt he was worse! my heart sank at seeing him. If he had looked like a skeleton before, he was like a skeleton's ghost now."

"Ah, Johnny! I knew you would come."

I told him how it was I had not been able to come before, going into details. It seemed to amuse him to hear of the engagements, and I described Helen Whitney's Court dress as well as I could— and Lady Whitney's—and the servants' great bouquets—and the ball at night. He ate one bit of thin toast and drank three big cups of tea. Mrs. Marks said he was always thirsty.

After tea he had a violent fit of coughing and thought he must lie down to rest for a bit. Mrs. Marks came back and sat with me.

"I hope he will get well," I could not help saying to her.

She shook her head. "I fear he has not much hope of it himself," she answered. "Only yesterday I heard him tell Willy—that—that God would take care of them when he was gone."

She could hardly speak the last words, and broke down with a sob. I wished I had not said anything.

"He has great trust, but things trouble him very much," she resumed. "Nothing else can be expected, for he knows that our means are almost spent."

"It must trouble you also, Mrs. Marks."

"I seem to have so much to trouble me that I dare not dwell upon it. I pray not to, every hour of the day. If I gave way, what would become of them?"

At dark she lighted the candles and drew down the blinds. Just after that, there came a tremendous knock at the front-door, loud and long. "Naughty children." she exclaimed. "It must be they."

"I'll go; don't you stir, Mrs. Marks."

I opened the door, and a rush of wind and rain seemed to blow in an old gentleman. He never said a word to me, but went banging into the parlour and sank down on a chair out of breath.

"Papa!" exclaimed Mrs. Marks. "Papa!"

"Wait till I get up my speech, my dear," said the old gentleman. "She is gone."

"Who is gone!" cried Mrs. Marks.

"*She.* I don't want to say too much against her now she's gone, Caroline; but she *is* gone. She had a bad fall downstairs in a tipsy fit some days ago, striking her head on the flags, and the doctors could do nothing for her. She died this morning, poor soul; and I am coming to live with you and James, if you will have me. We shall all be so comfortable together, my dear."

Perhaps Mrs. Marks remembered at once what it implied—that the pressure of poverty was suddenly lifted and she and those dear ones would be at ease for the future. She bent her head in her hands for a minute or two, keeping silence.

"Your husband shall have rest now, my dear, and all that he needs. So will you, Caroline."

It had come too late. James Marks died in May.

It was about three or four years afterwards that we saw the death of Mr. Brown in the *Times.* The newspapers made a flourish of trumpets over him; saying he had died worth two hundred thousand pounds.

"There must be something wrong somewhere, Johnny," remarked the Squire, in a puzzle. "*I* should not like to die worth all that money, and know that I had worked my clerks to the bone to get it together. I wonder how he will like meeting poor Marks in the next world?"

XVIII.

REALITY OR DELUSION?

THIS is a ghost story. Every word of it is true. And I don't mind confessing that for ages afterwards some of us did not care to pass the spot alone at night. Some people do not care to pass it yet.

It was autumn, and we were at Crabb Cot. Lena had been ailing; and in October Mrs. Todhetley proposed to the Squire that they should remove with her there, to see if the change would do her good.

We Worcestershire people call North Crabb a village; but one might count the houses in it, little and great, and not find four-and-twenty. South Crabb, half a mile off, is ever so much larger; but the church and school are at North Crabb.

John Ferrar had been employed by Squire Todhetley as a sort of overlooker on the estate, or working bailiff. He had died the previous winter; leaving nothing behind him except some debts; for he was not provident; and his handsome son Daniel. Daniel Ferrar, who was rather superior as far as education went, disliked work: he would make a show of helping his father, but it came to little. Old Ferrar had not put him to any particular trade or occupation, and Daniel, who was as proud as Lucifer, would not turn to it himself. He liked to be a gentleman. All he did now was to work in his garden, and feed his fowls, ducks, rabbits, and pigeons, of which he kept a great quantity, selling them to the houses around and sending them to market.

But, as every one said, poultry would not maintain him. Mrs. Lease, in the pretty cottage hard by Ferrar's, grew tired of saying it. This Mrs. Lease and her daughter, Maria, must not be confounded with Lease the pointsman: they were in a better condition of life, and not related to him. Daniel Ferrar used to run in and out of their house at will when a boy, and he was now engaged to be married to Maria. She would have a little money, and the Leases were respected in North Crabb. People began to whisper a query as to how Ferrar got his corn for the poultry: he was not known to buy much: and he would have to go out of his house at

Christmas, for its owner, Mr. Coney, had given him notice. Mrs.
Lease, anxious about Maria's prospects, asked Daniel what he
intended to do then, and he answered, "Make his fortune: he
should begin to do it as soon as he could turn himself round."
But the time was going on, and the turning round seemed to be as
far off as ever.

After Midsummer, a niece of the schoolmistress's, Miss Timmens,
had come to the school to stay: her name was Harriet Roe. The
father, Humphrey Roe, was half-brother to Miss Timmens. He
had married a Frenchwoman, and lived more in France than in
England until his death. The girl had been christened Henriette;
but North Crabb, not understanding much French, converted it into
Harriet. She was a showy, free-mannered, good-looking girl, and
made speedy acquaintance with Daniel Ferrar; or he with her.
They improved upon it so rapidly that Maria Lease grew jealous,
and North Crabb began to say he cared for Harriet more than for
Maria. When Tod and I got home the latter end of October, to
spend the Squire's birthday, things were in this state. James Hill,
the bailiff who had been taken on by the Squire in John Ferrar's
place (but a far inferior man to Ferrar; not much better, in fact,
than a common workman, and of whose doings you will hear soon
in regard to his little step-son, David Garth) gave us an account of
matters in general. Daniel Ferrar had been drinking lately, Hill
added, and his head was not strong enough to stand it; and he was
also beginning to look as if he had some care upon him.

"A nice lot, he, for them two women to be fighting for," cried
Hill, who was no friend to Ferrar. "There'll be mischief between
'em if they don't draw in a bit. Maria Lease is next door to mad
over it, I know; and t'other, finding herself the best liked, crows
over her. It's something like the Bible story of Leah and Rachel,
young gents, Dan Ferrar likes the one, and he's bound by promise
to the t'other. As to the French jade," concluded Hill, giving his
head a toss, "she'd make a show of liking any man that followed
her, she would; a dozen of 'em on a string."

It was all very well for surly Hill to call Daniel Ferrar a "nice
lot," but he was the best-looking fellow in church on Sunday morning—well-dressed too. But his colour seemed brighter; and his
hands shook as they were raised, often, to push back his hair, that
the sun shone upon through the south-window, turning it to gold.
He scarcely looked up, not even at Harriet Roe, with her dark eyes
roving everywhere, and her streaming pink ribbons. Maria Lease
was pale, quiet, and nice, as usual; she had no beauty, but her face
was sensible, and her deep grey eyes had a strange and curious
earnestness. The new parson preached, a young man just appointed
to the parish of Crabb. He went in for great observances of Saints'

days, and told his congregation that he should expect to see them
at church on the morrow, which would be the Feast of All
Saints.

Daniel Ferrar walked home with Mrs. Lease and Maria after
service, and was invited to dinner. I ran across to shake hands
with the old dame, who had once nursed me through an illness,
and promised to look in and see her later. We were going back to
school on the morrow. As I turned away, Harriet Roe passed, her
pink ribbons and her cheap gay silk dress gleaming in the sunlight.
She stared at me, and I stared back again. And now, the explanation of matters being over, the real story begins. But I shall have
to tell some of it as it was told by others.

The tea-things waited on Mrs. Lease's table in the afternoon;
waited for Daniel Ferrar. He had left them shortly before to go
and attend to his poultry. Nothing had been said about his coming
back for tea : that he would do so had been looked upon as a
matter of course. But he did not make his appearance, and the
tea was taken without him. At half-past five the church-bell rang
out for evening service, and Maria put her things on. Mrs. Lease
did not go out at night.

" You are starting early, Maria. You'll be in church before other
people."

" That won't matter, mother."

A jealous suspicion lay on Maria—that the secret of Daniel
Ferrar's absence was his having fallen in with Harriet Roe:
perhaps had gone of his own accord to seek her. She walked
slowly along. The gloom of dusk, and a deep dusk, had stolen
over the evening, but the moon would be up later. As Maria
passed the school-house, she halted to glance in at the little sitting-
room window : the shutters were not closed yet, and the room was
lighted by the blazing fire. Harriet was not there. She only saw
Miss Timmens, the mistress, who was putting on her bonnet before
a hand-glass propped upright on the mantel-piece. Without warning, Miss Timmens turned and threw open the window. It was only
for the purpose of pulling-to the shutters, but Maria thought she
must have been observed, and spoke.

" Good evening, Miss Timmens."

" Who is it ? " cried out Miss Timmens, in answer, peering into
the dusk. " Oh, it's you, Maria Lease! Have you seen anything
of Harriet ? She went off somewhere this afternoon, and never
came in to tea."

" I have not seen her."

" She's gone to the Batleys', I'll be bound. She knows I don't
like her to be with the Batley girls : they make her ten times
flightier than she would otherwise be."

Miss Timmens drew in her shutters with a jerk, without which they would not close, and Maria Lease turned away.

"Not at the Batleys', not at the Batleys', but with *him*," she cried, in bitter rebellion, as she turned away from the church. From the church, not to it. Was Maria to blame for wishing to see whether she was right or not?—for walking about a little in the thought of meeting them? At any rate it is what she did. And had her reward; such as it was.

As she was passing the top of the withy walk, their voices reached her ear. People often walked there, and it was one of the ways to South Crabb. Maria drew back amidst the trees, and they came on: Harriet Roe and Daniel Ferrar, walking arm-in-arm.

"I think I had better take it off," Harriet was saying. "No need to invoke a storm upon my head. And that would come in a shower of hail from stiff old Aunt Timmens."

The answer seemed one of quick accent, but Ferrar spoke low. Maria Lease had hard work to control herself: anger, passion, jealousy, all blazed up. With her arms stretched out to a friendly tree on either side,—with her heart beating,—with her pulses coursing on to fever-heat, she watched them across the bit of common to the road. Harriet went one way then; he another, in the direction of Mrs. Lease's cottage. No doubt to fetch her—Maria —to church, with a plausible excuse of having been detained. Until now she had had no proof of his falseness; had never perfectly believed in it.

She took her arms from the trees and went forward, a sharp faint cry of despair breaking forth on the night air. Maria Lease was one of those silent-natured girls who can never speak of a wrong like this. She had to bury it within her; down, down, out of sight and show; and she went into church with her usual quiet step. Harriet Roe with Miss Timmens came next, quite demure, as if she had been singing some of the infant scholars to sleep at their own homes. Daniel Ferrar did not go to church at all: he stayed, as was found afterwards, with Mrs. Lease.

Maria might as well have been at home as at church: better perhaps that she had been. Not a syllable of the service did she hear: her brain was a sea of confusion; the tumult within it rising higher and higher. She did not hear even the text, "Peace, be still," or the sermon; both so singularly appropriate. The passions in men's minds, the preacher said, raged and foamed just like the angry waves of the sea in a storm, until Jesus came to still them.

I ran after Maria when church was over, and went in to pay the promised visit to old Mother Lease. Daniel Ferrar was sitting in the parlour. He got up and offered Maria a chair at the fire, but she turned her back and stood at the table under the window, taking off her gloves.   An open Bible was before Mrs. Lease : 1 wondered whether she had been reading aloud to Daniel.

"What was the text, child?" asked the old lady.

No answer.

"Do you hear, Maria!   What was the text?"

Maria turned at that, as if suddenly awakened.   Her face was white; her eyes had in them an uncertain terror.

"The text?" she stammered.   "I—I forget it, mother.   It was from Genesis, I think."

"Was it, Master Johnny?"

"It was from the fourth chapter of St. Mark, 'Peace, be still.'"

Mrs. Lease stared at me.   "Why, that is the very chapter I've been reading.   Well now, that's curious.   But there's never a better in the Bible, and never a better text was taken from it than those three words.   I have been telling Daniel here, Master Johnny, that when once that peace, Christ's peace, is got into the heart, storms can't hurt us much.   And you are going away again to-morrow, sir?" she added, after a pause.   "It's a short stay?"

I was not going away on the morrow.   Tod and I, taking the Squire in a genial moment after dinner, had pressed to be let stay until Tuesday, Tod using the argument, and laughing while he did it, that it must be wrong to travel on All Saints' Day, when the parson had specially enjoined us to be at church.   The Squire told us we were a couple of encroaching rascals, and if he did let us stay it should be upon condition that we did go to church. This I said to them.

"He may send you all the same, sir, when the morning comes," remarked Daniel Ferrar.

"Knowing Mr. Todhetley as you do Ferrar, you may remember that he never breaks his promises."

Daniel laughed.   "He grumbles over them, though, Master Johnny."

"Well, he may grumble to-morrow about our staying, say it is wasting time that ought to be spent in study, but he will not send us back until Tuesday."

Until Tuesday!   If I could have foreseen then what would have happened before Tuesday!   If all of us could have foreseen!   Seen the few hours between now and then depicted, as in a mirror, event by event!   Would it have saved the calamity, the dreadful sin that could never be redeemed?   Why, yes; surely it would.   Daniel Ferrar turned and looked at Maria.

"Why don't you come to the fire?"

"I am very well here, thank you."

She had sat down where she was, her bonnet touching the curtain. Mrs. Lease, not noticing that anything was wrong, had begun talking

about Lena, whose illness was turning to low fever, when the house
door opened and Harriet Roe came in.

"What a lovely night it is!" she said, taking of her own accord
the chair I had not cared to take, for I kept saying I must go.
"Maria, what went with you after church? I hunted for you everywhere."

Maria gave no answer. She looked black and angry; and her
bosom heaved as if a storm were brewing. Harriet Roe slightly
laughed.

"Do you intend to take holiday to-morrow, Mrs. Lease?."

"Me take holiday! what is there in to-morrow to take holiday
for?" returned Mrs. Lease.

"I shall," continued Harriet, not answering the question: "I
have been used to it in France. All Saints' Day is a grand
holiday there; we go to church in our best clothes, and pay visits
afterwards. Following it, like a dark shadow, comes the gloomy
Jour des Morts."

"The what?" cried Mrs. Lease, bending her ear.

"The day of the dead. All Souls' Day. But you English don't
go to the cemeteries to pray."

Mrs. Lease put on her spectacles, which lay upon the open pages
of the Bible, and stared at Harriet. Perhaps she thought they
might help her to understand. The girl laughed.

"On All Souls' Day, whether it be wet or dry, the French
cemeteries are full of kneeling women draped in black; all praying
for the repose of their dead relatives, after the manner of the Roman
Catholics."

Daniel Ferrar, who had not spoken a word since she came in, but
sat with his face to the fire, turned and looked at her. Upon which
she tossed back her head and her pink ribbons, and smiled till all
her teeth were seen. Good teeth they were. As to reverence in her
tone, there was none.

"I have seen them kneeling when the slosh and wet have been
ankle-deep. Did you ever see a ghost?" added she, with energy.
"The French believe that the spirits of the dead come abroad
on the night of All Saints' Day. You'd scarcely get a French
woman to go out of her house after dark. It is their chief
superstition."

"What *is* the superstition?" questioned Mrs. Lease.

"Why, *that*," said Harriet. "They believe that the dead are
allowed to revisit the world after dark on the Eve of All Souls; that
they hover in the air, waiting to appear to any of their living
relatives, who may venture out, lest they should forget to pray on
the morrow for the rest of their souls." *

* A superstition obtaining amongst some of the lower orders in France.

"Well, I never!" cried Mrs. Lease, staring excessively. "Did you ever hear the like of that, sir?" turning to me.

"Yes; I have heard of it."

Harriet Roe looked up at me; I was standing at the corner of the mantel-piece. She laughed a free laugh.

"I say, wouldn't it be fun to go out to-morrow night, and meet the ghosts? Only, perhaps they don't visit this country, as it is not under Rome."

"Now just you behave yourself before your betters, Harriet Roe," put in Mrs. Lease, sharply. "That gentleman is young Mr. Ludlow of Crabb Cot."

"And very happy I am to make young Mr. Ludlow's acquaintance," returned easy Harriet, flinging back her mantle from her shoulders. "How hot your parlour is, Mrs. Lease."

The hook of the cloak had caught in a thin chain of twisted gold that she wore round her neck, displaying it to view. She hurriedly folded her cloak together, as if wishing to conceal the chain. But Mrs. Lease's spectacles had seen it.

"What's that you've got on, Harriet? A gold chain?"

A moment's pause, and then Harriet Roe flung back her mantle again, defiance upon her face, and touched the chain with her hand.

"That's what it is, Mrs. Lease: a gold chain. And a very pretty one, too."

"Was it your mother's?"

"It was never anybody's but mine. I had it made a present to me this afternoon; for a keepsake."

Happening to look at Maria, I was startled at her face, it was so white and dark: white with emotion, dark with an angry despair that I for one did not comprehend. Harriet Roe, throwing at her a look of saucy triumph, went out with as little ceremony as she had come in, just calling back a general good night; and we heard her footsteps outside getting gradually fainter in the distance. Daniel Ferrar rose.

"I'll take my departure too, I think. You are very unsociable to-night, Maria."

"Perhaps I am. Perhaps I have cause to be."

She flung his hand back when he held it out; and in another moment, as if a thought struck her, ran after him into the passage to speak. I, standing near the door in the small room, caught the words.

"I must have an explanation with you, Daniel Ferrar. Now. To-night. We cannot go on thus for a single hour longer."

"Not to-night, Maria; I have no time to spare. And I don't know what you mean."

"You do know. Listen. I will not go to my rest, no, though it were for twenty nights to come, until we have had it out. I *vow* I will not. There. You are playing with me. Others have long said so, and I know it now."

He seemed to speak some quieting words to her, for the tone was low and soothing; and then went out, closing the door behind him. Maria came back and stood with her face and its ghastliness turned from us. And still the old mother noticed nothing.

"Why don't you take your things off, Maria?" she asked.

"Presently," was the answer.

I said good night in my turn, and went away. Half-way home I met Tod with the two young Lexoms. The Lexoms made us go in and stay to supper, and it was ten o'clock before we left them.

"We shall catch it," said Tod, setting off at a run. They never let us stay out late on a Sunday evening, on account of the reading.

But, as it happened, we escaped scot-free this time, for the house was in a commotion about Lena. She had been better in the afternoon, but at nine o'clock the fever returned worse than ever. Her little cheeks and lips were scarlet as she lay on the bed, her wide-open eyes were bright and glistening. The Squire had gone up to look at her, and was fuming and fretting in his usual fashion.

"The doctor has never sent the medicine," said patient Mrs. Todhetley, who must have been worn out with nursing. "She ought to take it; I am sure she ought."

"These boys are good to run over to Cole's for that," cried the Squire. "It won't hurt them; it's a fine night."

Of course we were good for it. And we got our caps again; being charged to enjoin Mr. Cole to come over the first thing in the morning.

"Do you care much about my going with you, Johnny?" Tod asked as we were turning out at the door. "I am awfully tired."

"Not a bit. I'd as soon go alone as not. You'll see me back in half-an-hour."

I took the nearest way; flying across the fields at a canter, and startling the hares. Mr. Cole lived near South Crabb, and I don't believe more than ten minutes had gone by when I knocked at his door. But to get back as quickly was another thing. The doctor was not at home. He had been called out to a patient at eight o'clock, and had not yet returned.

I went in to wait: the servant said he might be expected to come in from minute to minute. It was of no use to go away without the medicine; and I sat down in the surgery in front of the shelves, and fell asleep counting the white jars and physic bottles. The doctor's entrance awoke me.

"I am sorry you should have had to come over and to wait," he said. "When my other patient, with whom I was detained a considerable time, was done with, I went on to Crabb Cot with the child's medicine, which I had in my pocket."

"They think her very ill to-night, sir."

"I left her better, and going quietly to sleep. She will soon be well again, I hope."

"Why! is that the time?" I exclaimed, happening to catch sight of the clock as I was crossing the hall. It was nearly twelve. Mr. Cole laughed, saying time passed quickly when folk were asleep.

I went back slowly. The sleep, or the canter before it, had made me feel as tired as Tod had said he was. It was a night to be abroad in and to enjoy; calm, warm, light. The moon, high in the sky, illumined every blade of grass; sparkled on the water of the little rivulet; brought out the moss on the grey walls of the old church; played on its round-faced clock, then striking twelve.

Twelve o'clock at night at North Crabb answers to about three in the morning in London, for country people are mostly in bed and asleep at ten. Therefore, when loud and angry voices struck up in dispute, just as the last stroke of the hour was dying away on the midnight air, I stood still and doubted my ears.

I was getting near home then. The sounds came from the back of a building standing alone in a solitary place on the left-hand side of the road. It belonged to the Squire, and was called the yellow barn, its walls being covered with a yellow wash; but it was in fact used as a storehouse for corn. I was passing in front of it when the voices rose upon the air. Round the building I ran, and saw—Maria Lease: and something else that I could not at first comprehend. In the pursuit of her vow, not to go to rest until she had "had it out" with Daniel Ferrat, Maria had been abroad searching for him. What ill fate brought her looking for him up near our barn?—perhaps because she had fruitlessly searched in every other spot.

At the back of this barn, up some steps, was an unused door. Unused partly because it was not required, the principal entrance being in front; partly because the key of it had been for a long time missing. Stealing out at this door, a bag of corn upon his shoulders, had come Daniel Ferrar in a smock-frock. Maria saw him, and stood back in the shade. She watched him lock the door and put the key in his pocket; she watched him give the heavy bag a jerk as he turned to come down the steps. Then she burst out. Her loud reproaches petrified him, and he stood there as one suddenly turned to stone. It was at that moment that I appeared.

I understood it all soon; it needed not Maria's words to enlighten me. Daniel Ferrar possessed the lost key and could come in and out at will in the midnight hours when the world was sleeping, and help himself to the corn. No wonder his poultry throve; no wonder there had been grumblings at Crabb Cot at the mysterious disappearance of the good grain.

Maria Lease was decidedly mad in those few first moments. Stealing is looked upon in an honest village as an awful thing; a disgrace, a crime; and there was the night's earlier misery besides. Daniel Ferrar was a thief! Daniel Ferrar was false to her! A storm of words and reproaches poured forth from her in confusion, none of it very distinct. "Living upon theft! Convicted felon! Transportation for life! Squire Todhetley's corn! Fattening poultry on stolen goods! Buying gold chains with the profits for that bold, flaunting French girl, Harriet Roe! Taking his stealthy walks with her!"

My going up to them stopped the charge. There was a pause; and then Maria, in her mad passion, denounced him to me, as representative (so she put it) of the Squire—the breaker-in upon our premises! the robber of our stored corn!

Daniel Ferrar came down the steps; he had remained there still as a statue, immovable; and turned his white face to me. Never a word in defence said he: the blow had crushed him; he was a proud man (if any one can understand that), and to be discovered in this ill-doing was worse than death to him.

"Don't think of me more hardly than you can help, Master Johnny," he said in a quiet tone. "I have been almost tired of my life this long while."

Putting down the bag of corn near the steps, he took the key from his pocket and handed it to me. The man's aspect had so changed; there was something so grievously subdued and sad about him altogether, that I felt as sorry for him as if he had not been guilty. Maria Lease went on in her fiery passion.

"You'll be more tired of it to-morrow when the police are taking you to Worcester gaol. Squire Todhetley will not spare you, though your father was his many-years bailiff. He could not, you know, if he wished; Master Ludlow has seen you in the act."

"Let me have the key again for a minute, sir," he said, as quietly as though he had not heard a word. And I gave it to him. I'm not sure but I should have given him my head had he asked for it.

He swung the bag on his shoulders, unlocked the granary door, and put the bag beside the other sacks. The bag was his own, as we found afterwards, but he left it there. Locking the door again, he gave me the key, and went away with a weary step.

"Good-bye, Master Johnny."

I answered back good night civilly, though he had been stealing. When he was out of sight, Maria Lease, her passion full upon her still, dashed off towards her mother's cottage, a strange cry of despair breaking from her lips.

"Where have you been lingering, Johnny?" roared the Squire, who was sitting up for me. "You have been throwing at the owls, sir, that's what you've been at; you have been scudding after the hares."

I said I had waited for Mr. Cole, and had come back slower than I went; but I said no more, and went up to my room at once. And the Squire went to his.

I know I am only a muff; people tell me so, often: but I can't help it; I did not make myself. I lay awake till nearly daylight, first wishing Daniel Ferrar could be screened, and then thinking it might perhaps be done. If he would only take the lesson to heart and go on straight for the future, what a capital thing it would be. We had liked old Ferrar; he had done me and Tod many a good turn: and, for the matter of that, we liked Daniel. So I never said a word when morning came of the past night's work.

"Is Daniel at home?" I asked, going to Ferrar's the first thing before breakfast. I meant to tell him that if he would keep right, I would keep counsel.

"He went out at dawn, sir," answered the old woman who did for him, and sold his poultry at market. "He'll be in presently: he have had no breakfast yet."

"Then tell him when he comes, to wait in, and see me: tell him it's all right. Can you remember, Goody? 'It is all right.'"

"I'll remember, safe enough, Master Ludlow."

Tod and I, being on our honour, went to church, and found about ten people in the pews. Harriet Roe was one, with her pink ribbons, the twisted gold chain showing outside a short-cut velvet jacket.

"No, sir; he has not been home yet; I can't think where he can have got to," was the old Goody's reply when I went again to Ferrar's. And so I wrote a word in pencil, and told her to give it him when he came in, for I could not go dodging there every hour of the day.

After luncheon, strolling by the back of the barn: a certain reminiscence I suppose taking me there, for it was not a frequented spot: I saw Maria Lease coming along.

Well, it was a change! The passionate woman of the previous
night had subsided into a poor, wild-looking, sorrow-stricken thing,
ready to die of remorse. Excessive passion had wrought its usual
consequences; a re-action: a re-action in favour of Daniel Ferrar.
She came up to me, clasping her hands in agony—beseeching that
I would spare him; that I would not tell of him; that I would give
him a chance for the future: and her lips quivered and trembled,
and there were dark circles round her hollow eyes.

I said that I had not told and did not intend to tell. Upon
which she was going to fall down on her knees, but I rushed off.

"Do you know where he is?" I asked, when she came to her
sober senses.

"Oh, I wish I did know! Master Johnny, he is just the man to
go and do something desperate. He would never face shame;
and I was a mad, hard-hearted, wicked girl to do what I did last
night. He might run away to sea; he might go and enlist for a
soldier."

"I dare say he is at home by this time. I have left a word for
him there, and promised to go in and see him to-night. If he will
undertake not to be up to wrong things again, no one shall ever
know of this from me."

She went away easier, and I sauntered on towards South Crabb.
Eager as Tod and I had been for the day's holiday, it did not seem
to be turning out much of a boon. In going home again—there
was nothing worth staying out for—I had come to the spot by the
three-cornered grove where I saw Maria, when a galloping policeman
overtook me. My heart stood still; for I thought he must have
come after Daniel Ferrar.

"Can you tell me if I am near to Crabb Cot—Squire Todhetley's?"
he asked, reining-in his horse.

"You will reach it in a minute or two. I live there. Squire
Todhetley is not at home. What do you want with him?"

"It's only to give in an official paper, sir. I have to leave one
personally upon all the county magistrates."

He rode on. When I got in I saw the folded paper upon the
hall-table; the man and horse had already gone onwards. It was
worse indoors than out; less to be done. Tod had disappeared
after church; the Squire was abroad; Mrs. Todhetley sat upstairs
with Lena: and I strolled out again. It was only three o'clock
then.

An hour, or more, was got through somehow; meeting one, talking to another, throwing at the ducks and geese; anything. Mrs.
Lease had her head, smothered in a yellow shawl, stretched out over
the palings as I passed her cottage.

"Don't catch cold, mother."

" I am looking for Maria, sir. I can't think what has come to her to-day, Master Johnny," she added, dropping her voice to a confidential tone. "The girl seems demented: she has been going in and out ever since daylight like a dog in a fair."

" If I meet her I will send her home."

And in another minute I did meet her. For she was coming out of Daniel Ferrar's yard. I supposed he was at home again.

" No," she said, looking more wild, worn, haggard than before; "that's what I have been to ask. I am just out of my senses, sir. He has gone for certain. Gone!"

I did not think it. He would not be likely to go away without clothes.

" Well, I know he is, Master Johnny; something tells me. I've been all about everywhere. There's a great dread upon me, sir; I never felt anything like it."

"Wait until night, Maria; I dare say he will go home then. Your mother is looking out for you; I said if I met you I'd send you in."

Mechanically she turned towards the cottage, and I went on. Presently, as I was sitting on a gate watching the sunset, Harriet Roe passed towards the withy walk, and gave me a nod in her free but good-natured way.

" Are you going there to look out for the ghosts this evening?" I asked: and I wished not long afterwards I had not said it. "It will soon be dark."

" So it will," she said, turning to the red sky in the west. "But I have no time to give to the ghosts to-night."

" Have you seen Ferrar to-day?" I cried, an idea occurring to me.

" No. And I can't think where he has got to; unless he is off · to Worcester. He told me he should have to go there some day this week."

She evidently knew nothing about him, and went on her way with another free-and-easy nod. I sat on the gate till the sun had gone down, and then thought it was time to be getting homewards.

Close against the yellow barn, the scene of last night's trouble, whom should I come upon but Maria Lease. She was standing still, and turned quickly at the sound of my footsteps. Her face was bright again, but had a puzzled look upon it.

" I have just seen him: he has not gone," she said in a happy whisper. "You were right, Master Johnny, and I was wrong."

" Where did you see him?"

" Here; not a minute ago. I saw him twice. He is angry, very, and will not let me speak to him; both times he got away before I could reach him. He is close by somewhere."

I looked round, naturally; but Ferrar was nowhere to be seen.
There was nothing to conceal him except the barn, and that was
locked up. The account she gave was this—and her face grew
puzzled again as she related it.

Unable to rest indoors, she had wandered up here again, and saw
Ferrar standing at the corner of the barn, looking very hard at her.
She thought he was waiting for her to come up, but before she got
close to him he had disappeared, and she did not see which way.
She hastened past the front of the barn, ran round to the back, and
there he was. He stood near the steps looking out for her; waiting
for her, as it again seemed; and was gazing at her with the same
fixed stare. But again she missed him before she could get quite
up; and it was at that moment that I arrived on the scene.

I went all round the barn, but could see nothing of Ferrar. It
was an extraordinary thing where he could have got to. Inside
the barn he could not be: it was securely locked; and there was
no appearance of him in the open country. It was, so to say, broad
daylight yet, or at least not far short of it; the red light was still
in the west. Beyond the field at the back of the barn, was a grove
of trees in the form of a triangle; and this grove was flanked by
Crabb Ravine, which ran right and left. Crabb Ravine had the
reputation of being haunted; for a light was sometimes seen dodging about its deep descending banks at night that no one could
account for. A lively spot altogether for those who liked gloom.

"Are you sure it was Ferrar, Maria?"

"Sure!" she returned in surprise. "You don't think I could
mistake him, Master Johnny, do you? He wore that ugly seal-skin
winter-cap of his tied over his ears, and his thick grey coat. The
coat was buttoned closely round him. I have not seen him wear
either since last winter."

That Ferrar must have gone into hiding somewhere seemed
quite evident; and yet there was nothing but the ground to receive
him. Maria said she lost sight of him the last time in a moment;
both times in fact; and it was absolutely impossible that he could
have made off to the triangle or elsewhere, as she must have seen
him cross the open land. For that matter I must have seen him
also.

On the whole, not two minutes had elapsed since I came up,
though it seems to have been longer in telling it: when, before we
could look further, voices were heard approaching from the direction
of Crabb Cot; and Maria, not caring to be seen, went away quickly.
I was still puzzling about Ferrar's hiding-place, when they reached
me—the Squire, Tod, and two or three men. Tod came slowly up,
his face dark and grave.

"I say, Johnny, what a shocking thing this is!"

" What is a shocking thing ? "

" You have not heard of it ?—But I don't see how you could hear it."

I had heard nothing. I did not know what there was to hear. Tod told me in a whisper.

" Daniel Ferrar's dead, lad."

" *What ?* "

" He has destroyed himself. Not more than half-an-hour ago. Hung himself in the grove."

I turned sick, taking one thing with another, comparing this recollection with that ; which I dare say you will think no one but a muff would do.

Ferrar was indeed dead. He had been hiding all day in the three-cornered grove : perhaps waiting for night to get away—perhaps only waiting for night to go home again. Who can tell ? About half-past two, Luke Macintosh, a man who sometimes worked for us, sometimes for old Coney, happening to go through the grove, saw him there, and talked with him. The same man, passing back a little before sunset, found him hanging from a tree, dead. Macintosh ran with the news to Crabb Cot, and they were now flocking to the scene. When facts came to be examined there appeared only too much reason to think that the unfortunate ap-pearance of the galloping policeman had terrified Ferrar into the act ; perhaps—we all hoped it !—had scared his senses quite away. Look at it as we would, it was very dreadful.

But what of the appearance Maria Lease saw ? At that time, Ferrar had been dead at least half-an-hour. Was it reality or delusion ? That is (as the Squire put it), did her eyes see a real, spectral Daniel Ferrar ; or were they deceived by some imagination of the brain ? Opinions were divided. Nothing can shake her own steadfast belief in its reality ; to her it remains an awful certainty, true and sure as heaven.

If I say that I believe in it too, I shall be called a muff and a double muff. But there is no stumbling-block difficult to be got over. Ferrar, when found, was wearing the seal-skin cap tied over the ears and the thick grey coat buttoned up round him, just as Maria Lease had described to me ; and he had never worn them since the previous winter, or taken them out of the chest where they were kept. The old woman at his home did not know he had done it then. When told that he died in these things, she protested that they were in the chest, and ran up to look for them. But the things were gone.

XIX

DAVID GARTH'S NIGHT-WATCH.

IT was the following year, and we were again at Crabb Cot. Fever had broken out at Dr. Frost's, and the school was dismissed. The leaves were falling late that year, for November was nearly half through, and they strewed the ground. But if the leaves were late, the frost was early. The weather had come in curiously cold. Three days before the morning I am about to speak of, the warm weather suddenly changed, and it was now as freezing as January. It is not often that you see ice mingling with the dead leaves of autumn. Both the ice and the leaves have to do with what happened : and I think you often find that if the weather is particularly unseasonable, we get something by which to remember it.

At the corner of a field between our house and North Crabb, stood a small solitary dwelling, called Willow Brook Cottage : but the brook from which it took its name was dry now. The house had a lonely look, and was lonely ; and perhaps that kept it empty. It had been unoccupied for more than a year, when the Squire, tired of seeing it so, happened to say in the hearing of James Hill, that new bailiff of ours, that he would let it for an almost nominal rent. Hill caught at the words and said he would be glad to rent it : for some cause or other he did not like the house he was in, and had been wanting to leave it. At least, he said so : but he was of a frightfully stingy turn, and we all thought the low rent tempted him. Hill, this working bailiff, was a steady man, but severe upon every one.

It was during this early frost that he began to move in. One morning after breakfast, I was taking the broad pathway across the fields to North Crabb, which led close by Willow Cottage, and saw Hill wheeling a small truck up with some of his household goods. He was a tall, strong man, and the cold was tolerably sharp, but the load had warmed him.

"Good morning, Master Johnny."

"Making ready for the flitting, Hill ? "

Hill wheeled the truck up to the door, and sat down on one of the handles whilst he wiped his face. It was an honest, though

cross face ; habitually red. The house had a good large garden at
its side, enclosed by wooden palings ; with a shed and some pigstys
at the back. Trees overshadowed the palings : and the fallen
leaves, just now, inside the garden and out were ankle-deep.

"A fine labour I shall have, getting the place in order !" cried
Hill, pointing to some broken palings and the overgrown branches.
" Don't think but what the Squire has the best of the bargain, after
all ! "

" You'd say that, Hill, if he gave you a house rent-free."

Hill took the key from his pocket, unlocked the door, and we
went in. This lower room was boarded ; the kitchen was at the
back ; above were two fair-sized chambers. One of them looked
towards Crabb Ravine ; the other was only lighted by a skylight in
the roof.

" You have had fires here, Hill ! "

" I had 'em in every room all day yesterday, sir, and am going
to light 'em again now. My wife said it must be done ; and she
warn't far wrong ; for a damp house plays the mischief with one's
bones. The fools that women be, to be sure !—and my wife's the
worst of 'em."

" What has your wife done ? "

" She had a bit of a accident yesterday, Master Johnny. A
coming out with a few things for this place, she stepped upon some
ice, and fell ; it gave her ankle a twist, and she had to be helped
home. I'm blest if she's not a-saying now that it's a bad omen !
Because she can't get about and help shift the things in here, she
says we shan't have nothing but ill-luck in the place."

I had already heard of the accident. Hill's wife was a little
shrinking woman, mild and gentle, quite superior to him. She was
a widow when he married her a short time ago, a Mrs. Garth, with
one son, David. Miss Timmens, the schoolmistress at North
Crab, was her sister. On the previous morning a letter had come
from Worcester, saying their mother, Mrs. Timmens, was taken
dangerously ill, and asking them to go over. Miss Timmens went ;
Hill refused for his wife. How could he get along at moving-time
without her, he demanded. She cried and implored, but Hill was
hard as flint. So she had to remain at home, and set about her
preparations for removal ; surly Hill was master and mistress too.
In starting with the first lot of movables—a few things carried in
her arms—the accident occurred. So that, in the helping to move,
she was useless ; and the neighbours, ever ready to take part in a
matrimonial grievance, said it served Hill right. Any way, it did
not improve his temper.

" When do you get in here, Hill ? "

" To-morrow, Master Johnny, please the pigs. But for the wife's awk'ardness we'd ha' been in to-day. As to any help Davvy could give, it's worth no more nor a rat's; he haven't got much more strength in him nor one neither. Drat the boy!"

Leaving Hill to his task, I went on; and in passing Mrs. Hill's dwelling, I thought I'd give a look in to inquire after the ankle. The cottage stood alone, just as this other one did, but was less lonely, for the Crabb houses were round about. Davy's voice called out, "Come in."

He was the handiest little fellow possible for any kind of house-work—or for sewing, either; but not half strong enough or rough enough for a boy. His soft brown eyes had a shrinking look in them, his face was delicate as a girl's, and his hair hung in curls. But he was a little bit deformed in the back—some called it only a stoop in the shoulders—and, though fourteen, might have been taken for ten. The boy's love for his mother was something wonderful. They had lived at Worcester; she had a small income, and he had been well brought up. When she married Hill—all her friends were against it, and it was in fact a frightful mistake— of course they had to come to North Crabb; but Davy was not happy. Always a timid lad, he could not overcome his first fear of Hill. Not that the man was unkind, only rough and resolute.

Davy was washing up the breakfast-things; his mother sat near, sorting the contents of a chest: a neat little woman in a green stuff gown, with the same sweet eyes as David and the same shrinking look in them. She left off when I went in, and said her ankle was no worse.

"It's a pity it happened just now, Mrs. Hill."

"I'd have given a great deal for it not to, sir. They call me foolish, I know; always have done; but it just seems to me like an omen. I had a few articles in my arms, the first trifles we'd begun to move, and down I fell on going out at this door. To me it seems nothing but a warning that we ought not to move into Willow Cottage."

David had halted in his work at the tea-cups, his brown eyes fixed on his mother. That it was not the first time he had listened to the superstition, and that he was every whit as bad as she, might plainly be seen.

"I have never liked the thought of that new place from the first, Master Johnny. It is as if something held me back from it. Hill keeps saying that it's a convenient dwelling, and dirt-cheap; and so it is; but I don't like the notion of it. No more does David."

"Oh, I dare say you will like it when you get in, Mrs. Hill, and David, too."

"It is to be hoped so, sir."

The day went on; and its after events I can only speak of from hearsay. Hill moved in a good many of his goods, David carrying some of the lighter things. Luke Macintosh was asked to go and sleep in the house that night as a safeguard against thieves, but he flatly refused, unless some one slept there with him. Hill ridiculed his cowardice; and finally agreed that David should bear him company.

He made the bargain without his wife. She had other views for David. Her intention was to send the lad over to Worcester by the seven-o'clock evening train; not so much because his bed and bedding had been carried off and there was nothing for him to sleep on, as that his dying grandmother had expressed a wish to see him. To hear then that David was not to go, did not please Mrs. Hill.

It was David himself who carried in the news. She had tea waiting on the table when they came in: David first, for his stepfather had stopped to speak to some one in the road.

"But, David, dear—you *must* go to Worcester," she said, when he told her.

"He will never let me, mother," was David's answer. "He says the things might be stolen if nobody takes care of them : and Macintosh is afraid to be there alone."

She paused and looked at him, a thought striking her. The boy was leaning upon her in his fond manner, his hand in hers.

"Should you be afraid, David ?"

"Not—I think—with Luke. We are to be in the same room, mother."

But Mrs. Hill noticed that his voice was hesitating; his small weak hand trembled in hers. There was not a more morally brave heart than David Garth's; he had had a religious training; but at being alone in the dark he was a very coward, afraid of ghosts and goblins.

"Hill," said she to her husband when he stamped in, the lad having gone to wash his hands, "I cannot let David sleep in the other house to-night. He will be too timid."

"Timid !" repeated Hill, staring at the words. "Why, Luke Macintosh will be with him."

"David won't like it. Macintosh is nothing but a coward himself."

"Don't thee be a fool, and show it," returned Hill, roughly. "Thee'll keep that boy a baby for his life. Davvy would as soon sleep in the house alone, as not, but for the folly put into his head by you. And why not? He's fourteen."

Hill—to give him his due—only spoke as he thought. That any one in the world, grown to fourteen and upwards, could be afraid of sleeping in a house alone, was to him literally incomprehensible.

"I said he must go over to Worcester to see mother, James," she meekly resumed ; "you know I did."

"Well, he can't go to-night; he shall go in the morning. There! He may stop with her for a week, an' ye like, for all the good he is to me."

"Mother's looking for him to-night, and he ought to go. The dying——"

"Now just you drop it, for he can't be spared," interrupted Hill. "The goods might be stole, with all the loose characters there is about, and that fool of a Macintosh won't go in of himself. He's a regular coward! Davvy must keep him company—it's not so much he does for his keep—and he may start for Worcester by daylight."

Whenever Hill came down upon her with this resolute decision, it struck her timid forthwith. The allusion to the boy's keep was an additional thrust, for it was beginning to be rather a sore subject. An uncle at Worcester, who had no family and was well to do, had partly offered to adopt the lad ; but it was not yet settled. Davy was a great favourite with all the relatives ; Miss Timmens, the schoolmistress, doted on him. Mrs. Hill, not venturing on further remonstrance, made the best of the situation.

"Davy, you are to go to Worcester the first thing in the morning," she said, when he came back from washing his hands. "So as soon as you've been home and had a bit o' breakfast, you shall run off to the train."

Tea over, Hill went out on some business, saying he should be in at eight, or thereabouts, to go with Davy to the cottage. As the hour drew near, David, sitting over the fire with his mother in pleasant talk, as they loved to do, asked if he should read before he went : for her habit was to read the Bible to him, or cause him to read to her, the last thing.

"Yes, dear," she said. "Read the ninety-first Psalm."

So David read it. Closing the book when it was over, he sat with it on his knee, thoughtfully.

"If we could only *see* the angels, mother! It is so difficult to remember always that they are close around, taking care of us."

"So it is, Davy. Most of us forget it."

"When life's over it will be so pleasant for them to carry us away to heaven! I wish you and I could go together, mother."

"We shall each go when God pleases, David."

"Oh yes, I know that."

Mrs. Hill, remembering this little bit of conversation, word for word, repeated it afterwards to me and others, with how they had sat, and David's looks. I say this for fear people might think I had invented it.

Hill came in, and they prepared to go to the other house.

David, his arms full—for, of course, with things to be carried, they did not go out empty-handed—came suddenly back from the door in going out, flung his load down, and clasped his mother. She bent to kiss him.

"Good night, my dear one! Don't you and Luke get chattering all night. Go to sleep betimes."

He burst into tears, clinging to her with sobs. It was as if his heart were breaking.

"Are you afraid to go?" she whispered.

"I must go," was his sobbing answer.

"Now then, Davvy!" called back Hill's rough tones. "What the plague are you lagging for?"

"Say good-bye to me, mother! Say good-bye!"

"Good-bye, and God bless you, David! Remember the angels are around you!"

"I know; I know!"

Taking up his bundles, he departed, keeping some paces behind Hill all the way; partly to hide his face, down which the tears were raining; partly in his usual awe of that formidable functionary who stood to him as a step-father.

Arrived at the house, Hill was fumbling for the key, when some one came darting out from the shadow of its eaves. It proved to be Luke Macintosh.

"I was a-looking round for you," said crusty Hill. "I began to think you'd forgot the time o' meeting."

"No, I'd not forgot it; but I be come to say that I can't oblige you by sleeping there," was Luke's reply. "The master have ordered me off with the waggon afore dawn, and so—I'm a-going to sleep at home."

Had I been there, I could have said the master had *not* ordered Luke off before dawn; but after his breakfast. It was just a ruse of his, to avoid doing what he had never relished, sleeping in the house. Hill suspected as much, and went on at him, mockingly asking if he was afraid of hobgoblins. Luke dodged away in the midst of it, and Hill relieved his anger by a little hot language.

"Come along, Davvy," said he at last; "we must put these here things inside."

Unlocking the door, he went in; and, the first thing, fell against something or other in the dark. Hill swore a little at that, and struck a light, the fire having gone out. This lower room was full of articles, thrown down out of hand; the putting things straight had been left to the morrow.

"Carry the match afore me, Davvy. These blankets must go upstairs."

By some oversight no candles had been taken to the house; only the box of matches. David lighted one match after the other, while Hill arranged the blankets on the mattress for sleeping. This room —the one with the skylight—was to be David's.

"There," said Hill, taking the box of matches from him, "you'll be comfortable here till morning. If you find it cold, you might keep on your trousers."

David Garth stood speechless, a look of horror struggling to his face. In that first moment he dared not remonstrate; his awe of Hill was too great.

"What's the matter now?" asked Hill, striking another match. "What ails you?"

"You'll not leave me here, all by myself?" whispered the unhappy boy, in desperate courage.

"Not leave you here by yourself! Why, what d'ye think is to harm you? Don't you try on your nonsense and your games with me, Master Davvy. I'm not soft, like your mother. Say your prayers and get to sleep, and I'll come and let you out in the morning."

By a dexterous movement, Hill got outside, and closed the door softly, slipping the bolt. The match in his fingers was nearly burnt out; nevertheless, it had shown a last faint vision of a boy kneeling in supplication, his hands held up, his face one of piteous agony. As Hill struck another match to light the staircase, a wailing cry mingled with the sound: entreaties to be let out; prayers not to be left alone; low moans, telling of awful terror.

"Drat the boy! This comes of his mother's coddling. Hold your row, Davvy," he roared out, wrathfully: "you'd not like me to come back and give you a basting."

And Mr. James Hill, picking his way over the bundles, locked the outer door, and betook himself home. That was our respectable bailiff. What do you think of him?

"Did you leave Davy comfortable?" asked Mrs. Hill, when he got back.

"He'll be comfortable enough when he's asleep," shortly answered Hill. "Of all hardened, ungrateful boys, that of yourn's the worst."

"Had Luke come when you got there?" she resumed, passing over the aspersion on Davy.

"He was waiting: he came right out upon us like an apparition," was Hill's evasive answer. And he did not tell the rest.

But now, a singular thing happened that night. Mrs. Hill was in a sound sleep, when a loud, agonized cry of "Mother" aroused her from it. She started up, wide awake instantly, and in terror so great that the perspiration began to pour off her face. In that moment the call was repeated. The voice was David's voice; it had appeared to be in the room, close to her, and she peered into every corner in vain. Then she supposed it must have come through the window; that David, from some cause or other, had come home from Willow Brook, and was waiting to be let in. A dread crossed her of Hill's anger, and she felt inclined to order the boy to go back again.

Opening the casement window, she called to him by name; softly at first, then louder. There was no answer. Mrs. Hill stretched out her head as far as the narrow casement allowed, but neither David nor any one else could she see; nothing but the shadows cast by the moonlight. Just then the old church clock struck out. She counted the strokes and found it twelve. Midnight. It was bitterly cold: she closed the window at last, concluding David had gone off from fear of being punished. All she could hope was that he would have the sense, that dangerously keen night, to run off to the brick kilns, and get warm there.

But the terror lay upon her yet; she was unable to tell why or wherefore; unless from the strangely appealing agony of the cry; still less could she shake it off. It seemed odd. Hill awoke with the commotion, and found her trembling.

"What have ye got to be affrighted on?" he asked roughly, when she had told her tale. And Mrs. Hill was puzzled to say what.

"You had been a-dreaming of him, that's what it was. You've got nothing else in your mind, day nor night, but that there boy."

"It was not a dream; I am quite positive it was himself; I could not mistake his voice," persisted Mrs. Hill. "He has come away from the cottage, for sure. Perhaps that Luke Macintosh might have got teasing him."

Knowing what Hill knew, that the boy was locked in, he might safely have stood out that he could not have come away from it; but he said no more. Rolling himself round, he prepared to go to sleep again, resentful at having been awakened.

Hill overslept himself in the morning, possibly through the interrupted rest. When he went out it was broad daylight. David Garth's being locked up half-an-hour more or less went for nothing with Hill, and he stayed to load the truck with some of the remainder of his goods.

"Send Davy home at once, James," called out the wife, as he began to wheel it away. "I'll give him his breakfast, and let him start off to the train."

For, with daylight, and the sight of the door-key, Mrs. Hill could only reverse her opinion, and conclude unwillingly that it might have been a dream. Hill showed her the key, telling her that he had locked the door "for safety." Therefore it appeared to be impossible that David could have got out.

:

The first thing Hill saw when he and his truck approached the cottage, was young Jim Batley, mounted on the roof and hammering away at the skylight with his freezing hands. Jim, a regular sailor for climbing, had climbed a tree, and thence swung himself on to the tiles. Hill treated him to some hard words, and ordered him to come down and get a licking. Down came Jim, taking care to dodge out of Hill's reach.

"I can't make David hear," said Jim. "I've got to go to Timberdale, and I want him to go along with me."

"That's no reason why you should get atop of my roof," roared Hill. "You look out for a sweet hiding, young Jim. The first time I get hold on you, you shall have it kindly."

"He sleeps uncommon hard," said Jim. "One 'ud think the cold had froze him. I've got to take a letter to my uncle's at Timberdale: we shall find a jolly good hot breakfast when we get there."

Hill condescended to abate his anger so far as to inform Jim Batley that David could not go to Timberdale; adding that he was going off by train to see his grandmother at Worcester. Ordering Jim to take himself away, he unlocked the door and entered the cottage.

Jim Batley chose to stay. He was a tall, thin, obstinate fellow, of eleven, and meant to wait and speak to David. Given to following his own way whenever he could, in spite of his father and mother, it occurred to him that perhaps David might be persuaded to take Timberdale first and the train after.

He amused himself with the dead leaves while he waited. But it seemed that David took a long time dressing. The truck stood at the door; Jim stamped and whistled, and shied a few stones at the topmost article, which was Mrs. Hill's potato saucepan. Presently Hill came out and began to unload, beginning with the saucepan.

"Where's Davy?" demanded Jim, from a safe distance. "Ain't he ready yet?"

"Now if you don't get off about your business I'll make you go," was Hill's answer, keeping his back turned to the boy. "You haven't got nothing to stop here for."

"I'm stopping to speak to Davy."

"Davy was away out o' here afore daylight and took the first train to Worcester. He's a'most there by now."

Young boys are not clever reasoners; but certain contradictory odds and ends passed through Jim's disappointed mind. For one thing, he had seen Hill unlock the door.

"I don't think he's gone out yet. I see his boots."

"What boots?" asked Hill, putting a bandbox inside the door.

" Davy's. I see 'em through the skylight; they stood near the mattress."

" Them was a pair of my boots as I carried here last night. I tell ye Davvy's *gone:* can't ye believe? He won't be home for some days neither, for his grandmother's safe to keep him."

Jim Batley went off slowly on his way to Timberdale : there was nothing to stay for, Davy being gone. Happening to turn round, he caught Hill looking after him, and saw his face for the first time. It had turned white as death. The contrast was very remarkable, for it was usually of a deep red.

" Well, I never!" cried Jim, halting in surprise. " Mayhap the cold have took him! Serve him right."

When Hill had got all the things inside he locked himself in, probably not to be disturbed while he arranged them. Mrs. Hill had been waiting breakfast ever so long when she heard the truck coming back.

" Whatever's become of David?" she began. " I expected him home at once."

" David has started for Worcester," said Hill.

" Started for Worcester? Without his breakfast ? "

" Now don't you worry yourself about petty things," returned Hill, crustily. " You wanted him to go, and he's gone. He won't starve; let him alone for that."

The notion assumed by Mrs. Hill was, that her husband had started the boy off from the cottage direct to the train. She felt thoroughly vexed.

" He had all his old clothes on, Hill. I would not have had him go to Worcester in that plight for any money. You might have let the child come home for a bit of breakfast—and to dress himself. There was not so much as a brush and comb at the place, to make his hair tidy."

" There's no pleasing you," growled Hill. " Last night you were a'most crying, cause Davvy couldn't be let go over to see your mother; and, now that he is gone, *that* don't please ye! Women be the very deuce for grumbling."

Mrs. Hill dropped the subject—there could be no remedy—and gave her husband his breakfast in silence. Hill seemed to eat nothing, and looked very pale; at moments ghastly.

" Don't you feel well ?" she asked.

" Well?—I'm well enough. What should ail me—barring the cold? It's as sharp a frost as ever I was out in."

" Drink this," she said, pouring him out another cup of hot tea. " It is cold; and I'm sorry we've got it so for our moving. What time shall we get in to-day, Hill?"

" Not at all."

"Not at all!" repeated the wife in surprise.

"No, not at all," was Hill's surly confirmation. "What with you disabled, and Davvy o' no use, things is not as forrard as they ought to be. I've got to be off to my work too, pretty quick, or the Squire'll be about me. We shan't get in till to-morrow."

"But nearly all our things are in," she remonstrated. "There's as good as nothing left here."

"I tell ye we don't go in afore to-morrow," said Hill, giving the table a thump. "Can't ye be satisfied with that?"

He went off to his work. Mrs. Hill, accepting the change as inevitable, resigned herself, and borrowed a saucepan to cook the potatoes for dinner. She might have spared herself the trouble; her husband did not come in for any. He bought a penny loaf and some cheese, and made his dinner of it inside our home barn, Molly giving him some beer. He had done it before when very busy: but the work he was about that day was in no such hurry, and he might have left it if he would.

"Who is to sleep in the house to-night?" his wife asked him when he got home to tea.

"I shall," said Hill. "I won't be beholden to nobody."

Mrs. Hill, remembering the experience of the past night, quaked a little at finding she should have to sleep in the old place alone, devoutly praying there might be no recurrence of the dream that had thrown her into such mortal terror. She and Davy were just alike—frightened at their own shadows in the dark. When Hill was safe off, she hurried into bed, and kept her head under the clothes.

Hill came back betimes in the morning; and they moved in at once; old Coney's groom, who happened to be out with the dog-cart, offering to drive Mrs. Hill. Though her ankle was better and the distance short, she could hardly have walked. Instead of finding the house in order, as she expected, it was all sixes and sevens; the things lying about all over it.

Towards evening, Hannah got me to call at Willow Brook and say she'd go there in the morning for an hour or two, to help put things in order—the mistress had said she might do so. The fact was, Hannah was burning for a gossip, she and Hill's wife being choice friends. It was almost dark; the front room looked tolerably straight, and Mrs. Hill sat by the fire, resting her foot and looking out at the window, the shutters not yet closed.

"I'd be very thankful for her to come, Master Johnny," she said eagerly, hardly letting me finish. "There's a great deal to do; and, besides that, it is so lonesome here. I never had such a feeling in all my life; and I have gone into strange homes before this."

" It does seem lonesome, somehow. The fancy may go off in a day or two."

" I don't know, sir: it's to be hoped it will. Master Johnny, as true as that we are sitting here, when I got out of Mr. Coney's dog-cart and put my foot over the threshold to enter, a fit of trembling took me all over. There was no cause for it : I mean I was not thinking of anything to give it me. Not a minute before, I was laughing; for the man had been telling me a joking story of something that happened yesterday at his master's. A strange fear seemed to come upon me all at once as I stepped over the threshold, and I began to shake from head to foot. Hill stared at me, and at last asked if it was the cold; I told him truly that I did not know what it was; except that it seemed like some unaccountable attack, for I was well wrapped up. He had some brandy in a bottle, and made me drink a drop. The fit went off; but I have had a queer lonesome feeling on me ever since, as if the house was not one to be alone in."

" And you have been alone, I suppose? "

" Every bit of the time, save when Hill came in to his dinner. I don't remember ever to have had such a feeling before in broad daylight. It's just as if the house was haunted."

Not believing in haunted houses, I laughed. Mrs. Hill got up to stir the fire. It blazed, and cast her shadow upon the opposite wall.

" When dusk came on, I could hardly bear it. But for your coming in, Master Johnny, I should have stood at the door in the cold, and watched for Hill: things don't feel so lonely to one out of doors as in."

So it seemed that I was in for a stay—any way, till Hill arrived. After this, it would not have been very kind to leave her alone ; she looked so weak and little.

" I've never liked the thought of moving here from the first," she went on; "and then there came the accident to my foot. Some people think nothing at all of omens, Master Johnny, but I do think of them. They come oftener than is thought for too; only, so few take notice of them. I wish Davy was back! I can't bear to be in this house alone."

" David is at Worcester, I heard Hill say."

" He went yesterday morning, sir. I expected a letter from him to-day; and it is very curious that none have come. Davy knew how anxious I was about mother; and he never fails to write when he's away from me. Somehow, all things are going crooked and cross just now. I had a fright the night before last, Master Johnny, and I am hardly quit of it yet."

" What was that?" I asked her.

She stared into the fire for a minute or two before she answered me. There was no other light in the room; I sat back against the wall beside the window—the shutters were still open.

"You might not care to hear it, sir."

"I should if it's worth telling."

Turning from the fire, she looked straight at me while she told it from beginning to end, exactly as I have written it above. The tale would have been just the thing for Mrs. Todhetley: who went in for marvels.

"Hill stood to it that it was a dream, Master Johnny; but the more I think of it, the less I believe it could have been one. If I had only heard the call in my sleep, or in the moment of waking, why of course it might have been a dream; but when I heard it the second time it was *after* I awoke. I heard it as plain as I hear my own voice now; and plainer, too."

"But what else, except a dream, do you fancy it could have been?"

"Well, sir, that's what is puzzling me. But for Hill's convincing me Davy could not have got out of here after he had locked him and Macintosh in for safety, I should have said it was the boy himself, calling me from outside. It sounded in the room, close to me: but the fright I was in might have deceived me. What's that?"

A loud rapping at the window. I am not ashamed to say that coming so unexpectedly it startled me. Mrs. Hill, with a shrill scream, darted forward to catch hold of my arm.

"Let me go. Some one wants to be let in. I dare say it's Hill."

"Master Johnny, I beg your pardon," she said, going back. "Hill ought to know better than to come frightening me at night like this."

I opened the door, and Miss Timmens walked in: not Hill. The knocking had not been intended to frighten any one, but as a greeting to Mrs. Hill—Miss Timmens having seen her through the glass.

"You know you always were one of the quaking ones, Nanny," she said, scoffing at the alarm. "I have just got back from Worcester, and thought you'd like to hear that mother's better."

"And it is well you are back, Miss Timmens," I put in. "The school has been in rebellion. Strangers, going by, have taken it for a bear garden."

"That Maria Lease is just good for nothing," said Miss Timmens, wrathfully. "When she offered to take my place I knew she'd not be of much use. Yes, sir; it was the thought of the school that brought me back so soon."

"And mother is really better!" cried Mrs. Hill. "I am so

thankful. If she had died and I not able to get over to her, I should never have forgiven myself. How is David?"

"Are you getting straight, Nancy?" asked Miss Timmens, looking round the room, and not noticing the question about David.

"Straight! and only moved in this morning! and me with this ankle!"

Miss Timmens laughed. She was just as capable as her sister was the contrary.

"About David?" added Mrs. Hill, "I was so vexed that he went over in his old clothes! It was Hill's fault. Have you brought me a letter from him?"

"How could I bring you a letter from him?" returned Miss Timmens. "A letter from where?"

It was a minute or two before elucidation was arrived at, for both were at cross-purposes. David Garth had not been at Worcester at all, so far as Miss Timmens knew; certainly not at his grandmother's.

To see Mrs. Hill sink back into her chair at this information, and let her hands fall on her lap, and gaze helplessly from her frightened eyes, was only to be expected. Miss Timmens kept asking what it all meant, and where David was, but she could get no answer. So I told her what Mother Hill had just told me —about Hill's sending him off to Worcester. She stared like anything.

"Why, where in the name of wonder can the boy have got to?"

"I see it all," spoke the mother then, in a whisper. "Davy did find his way out of this house; and it was his voice I heard, and not a dream. I knew it. I knew it at the time."

These words would have sounded mysterious to any one given to mystery. Miss Timmens was not. She was a long, thin female, with a chronic redness on her nose and one cheek, and she was as practical as could be. Demanding what Mrs. Hill meant by "not a dream," she stood warming her boots at the fire while she was enlightened.

"The boy is keeping away for fear of Hill tanning him," spoke Miss Timmens, summing up the question. "Don't you think so, Master Ludlow?"

"I should, if I could see how he got out of the cottage, after Hill had locked him in it."

"Luke Macintosh put him out at this window," said Miss Timmens, decisively. "Hill couldn't lock that up. They'd open the shutters, and Luke would pop him out : to get rid of the boy, no doubt. Mr. Luke ought to be punished for it."

I did not contradict her. Of course it might have been so ;

but knowing Luke, I did not think he would care to be left in the
house alone. Unless—the thought flashed over me—unless Luke
sent away David that he might be off himself. Amidst a good
deal of uncertainty, this view seemed the most probable.

"Where is David?" bemoaned Mrs. Hill; "where is he? And
with these bitter cold nights——"

"Now don't you worry.yourself, Nanny," interrupted strong-
minded Miss Timmens. "I'll see to David; and bring him home,
too."

Hill's cough was heard outside. Miss Timmens—who had been
in a dead rage at the marriage, and consequently hated Hill like
poison—hastened to depart. We went away together, passing Hill
by the dried-up brook. He looked stealthily at us, and threw back
a surly good night to me.

"I'm sure I don't know where I am to look for the boy first,"
began Miss Timmens, as we went along. "Poor fellow! he is
keeping away out of fear. It would not surprise me if Macintosh
is taking care of him. The man's not ill-natured."

"I don't understand why Hill should have told his mother
David was gone to Worcester, unless he did go." Neither did I.

"David never went to Worcester; rely upon that, Master Ludlow," was her answer. "He is well known at Shrub Hill Station,
and I could not have failed to hear of it, for one of the porters
lodges in mother's house; besides, David would have come down to
us at once. Good night, sir. I dare say he will turn up before
to-morrow."

She went on towards the school-house, I the other way to Crabb
Cot. Mrs. Todhetley and the Squire were talking together by the
blazing fire, waiting until old Thomas announced dinner.

"Where have you been lingering this cold evening, Johnny?"
began the Squire. "Don't you get trying the ponds, sir; the ice
is not wafer thick yet."

Kneeling on the rug between them, holding my hands to the
warmth, I told where I had been, and what I had heard. Mrs.
Todhetley, who seemed to have been born with a sympathy for
children, went into lamentation over—it was what she said—that
poor little gentle lamb, David.

"Macintosh is about somewhere," spoke the Squire, ringing the
bell. "We will soon hear whether he knows what has become of
the boy."

Thomas was ordered to find Macintosh and send him in. He
came presently, shy and sheepish, as usual. Standing just inside
the door, he blinked his eyes and rubbed his hands one over the
other, like an idiot. It was only his way.

"Do you know where David Garth is?" began the Squire, who

thought himself a regular Q.C. at cross-examining. Luke stared and said No. The fact was, he had not heard that David was missing.

"What time was it that you put him out of the window the night before last?"

Luke's eyes and mouth opened. He had no more idea what the Squire meant than the man in the moon.

"Don't stand there as if you were a born simpleton, but 'answer me," commanded the Squire. "When you and David Garth were put into Hill's new cottage to take care of the things for the night, how came you to let the boy out of it? Why did you do it? Upon what plea?"

"But I didn't do it, sir," said Luke.

"Now don't you stand there and say that to my face, Macintosh. It won't answer; for I know all about it. You put that poor shivering boy out at the window that you might be off yourself; that's about the English of it. Where did he go to?"

"But I couldn't do it, sir," was Luke's answer to this. "I was not in the place myself."

"You were not there yourself?"

"No, sir, I warn't. Knowing I should have to go off with the waggon pretty early, I went down and telled Hill that I should sleep at home."

"Do you mean to say you did not go into Hill's place at all?"

"No, sir, I didn't. I conclude Hill slept there hisself. I know nothing about it, for I don't happen to have come across Hill since. I've kept out of his way."

This was a new turn to the affair. Luke quitted the room, and a silence ensued. Mrs. Todhetley touched me on the shoulder.

"Johnny?"

"Yes!" I said, wondering at the startled look in her eyes.

"I hope Hill did not put that poor child into the house alone! If so, no wonder that he made his escape from it."

The matter could not rest. One talked, and another talked: and before noon next day it was known all over the place that David Garth had been put to sleep by himself in the empty cottage. Miss Timmens attacked Hill with her strong tongue, and told him it was enough to frighten the child to death. Hill was sullen. He would answer nothing; and all she could get out of him was, that it was no business of hers. In vain she demanded his reasons for saying the boy had gone to Worcester by the early train: whether he sent him—whether he saw him off. Hill said David did go; and then took refuge in dogged silence.

The schoolmistress was not one to be played with. Of a tena-
cious turn, she followed out things with a will. She called in the
police ; she harangued people outside her door ; she set the parish
in a ferment. But David could not be heard of, high or low.
Since the midnight hour, when that call of his awoke his mother,
and was again repeated, he seemed to have vanished.

There arose a rumour that Jim Batley could tell something.
Miss Timmens pounced upon him as he was going by the school-
house, conveyed him indoors, and ordered him to make a clean
breast of it. It was not much that Jim had to tell : but that
little seemed of importance to Miss Timmens, and he told it
readily. One thing Jim persisted in—that the boots he saw
through the skylight must have been David's boots. Hill had
called them his, he said, but they were not big enough—not men's
boots at all. Hill was looking "ghastly white," as if he had had
a fright, Jim added, when he told him David was gone off to
Worcester.

Perhaps it was in that moment that a fear of something worse
than had been yet suspected dawned upon Miss Timmens. Tying
on her bonnet, she came up to Crabb Cot, and asked to see the
Squire.

"It is getting more serious," she said, after old Thomas had
shown her in. "I think, sir, Hill should be forced to explain what
he knows. I have come here to ask you to insist upon it."

"The question is—what does he know?" rejoined the Squire.

"More than he has confessed," said Miss Timmens, in her
positive manner. "Jim Batley stands to it that those boots must,
from the size, have been David's boots. Now, Squire Todhetley, if
David's boots were there, where was David? That is what's lying
on my mind, sir."

"What did Jim Batley see besides the boots?" asked the
Squire.

"Nothing in particular," she answered. "He said the cupboard
door stood open, and hid the best part of the room. David would
not be likely to run away and leave his boots behind him."

"Unless he was in too great a fright to stop to put them on."

"I don't think that, sir."

"What is it you wish to imply?" asked the Squire, not seeing the
drift of the argument.

"I wish I knew myself," replied Miss Timmens, candidly. "I
am certain Hill has not told all he could tell : he has been deceitful
over it from the first, and he must be made to explain. Look here,
sir : when he got to Willow Cottage that morning, there's no doubt
he thought David was in it. Very well. He goes in to call him ;
stays a bit, and then comes out and tells young Jim that David has

gone to Worcester. How was he to know David had gone to Worcester?—who told him? The boy says, too, that Hill looked ghastly, as if he had been 'frightened."

"David must have gone somewhere, or he would have been in the room," argued the Squire. "He would not be likely to go back after quitting it, and his mother heard him call to her in the middle of the night."

"Just so, sir. But—if Hill did not find him, why should he come out and assert that David had started for Worcester?—Why not have said David had escaped?"

"I am sure I don't know."

"It's the boots that come over me," avowed Miss Timmens; "I can't come to the bottom of them. I mean to come to the bottom of Hill, though, and make him disclose what he knows. You are his master, sir, and perhaps he will tell you without trouble, if you will please to be so good as question him. If he won't, I'll have him brought up before the Bench."

Away went Miss Timmens, with a parting remark that the school must be rampant by that time. The Squire sat thinking a bit, and then put on his hat and great-coat, telling me I might come with him and hear what Hill had to say. We expected to find Hill in the ploughed field between his cottage and North Crabb. But Hill was in his own garden; we saw him as we went along. Without ceremony, the Squire opened the wooden gate, and stepped in. Hill was raking the leaves together by the shed at the end of the garden.

He threw down the rake when he saw us, as if startled, his red face turning white. Coming forward, he began a confused excuse for being at home at that hour of the day, saying there was so much to do when getting into a fresh place; and that he had not been well for two days, "had had a sickness upon him." The Squire, never hard with the men, told him he was welcome to be there, and began talking about the garden.

"It is as rich a bit of land, Hill, as any in the parish,' and you may turn it to good account if you are industrious. Does your wife intend to keep chickens?"

"Well, sir, I suppose she will. Town-bred women don't understand far about 'em, though. It may be a'most as much loss as profit."

"Nonsense," said the Squire, in his quick way. "Loss! when you have every convenience about you! This used to be the fowl-house in Hopton's time," he added, rapping the side of the shed with his stick. "Why! you've been putting a padlock on it, Hill!"

For the door was fastened with a padlock; a new one, to judge by its look. Hill made no comment. He had taken up the rake again and was raking vigorously at the dead leaves. I wondered what he was shaking for.

"Have you any treasures here, that you should lock it up?"

"Only the watering-can, sir, and a few o' my garden tools," answered Hill. "There's a heap of loose characters about, and nothing's safe from 'em."

Putting his back against the shed, the Squire suddenly called on Hill to face him, and entered on the business he had come upon. "Where was David Garth? Did he, Hill, know anything about him?"

Hill had looked pale before; I said so; but that was nothing to the frightful whiteness that took him now. Ears, lips, neck; all turned the hue of the dead. The rake shook in his grasp; his teeth chattered.

"Come, Hill," said the Squire; "I see you have something to say."

But Hill protested he had nothing to say: except that the boy's absence puzzled him. The Squire put some home questions upon the points spoken of by Miss Timmens, showing Hill that we knew all. He then told him he might take his choice; answer, or go before the magistrates.

Apparently Hill saw the futility of holding out longer. His very aspect would have convicted him, as the Squire said: if he had committed murder, he could not have looked more guilty. Glancing shudderingly around on all sides, as though the air had phantoms in it, he whispered his version of the morning's work.

It was true that he *had* gone to the house expecting to find David in it; and it was true that when he entered he found him flown. Not wishing to alarm the boy's mother, he told Jim Batley that David had gone by early train to Worcester: he told the mother so. As to the boots, Hill declared they were his own, not David's; and that Jim's eyes must have been deceived in the size. And he vowed and declared he knew no more than this, or where David could have got to.

"What do you think you deserve for locking the child in the house by himself?" asked the Squire, sternly.

"Everything that'll come upon me through it," readily acknowledged Hill. "I could cut my hands off now for having done it; but I never thought he'd be really frightened. It's just as if his ghost had been haunting me ever since; I see him a-following of me everywhere."

"His ghost!" exclaimed the Squire. "Do you suppose he is dead?"

" I don't know," said the man, passing his shaking hand across his damp forehead. " I wish to Heaven I had let him go off to his grandmother's that same blessed night ! "

" Then you wish me to understand, Hill, that you absolutely know nothing of where the boy may be ? "

" Nothing at all, sir."

" Don't you think it might have been as well if you had told the truth from the first ? " asked the Squire, rather sarcastically.

" Well, sir, one's mind gets confused at times, and I thought of his mother. I could not be off seeing that if anything had happened, it lay on my shoulders for having left him alone, in there."

Whether the Squire believed Hill could tell more, I don't know. I did. As we went on to the school-house, the Pater kept silence. Miss Timmens was frightfully disappointed at the result, and said Hill was a shifty scoundrel.

" I cannot tell what to think," the Squire remarked to her. " His manner is the strangest I ever saw ; it is just as though he had something on his conscience. He said the boy's ghost seemed to haunt him. Did you notice that, Johnny ? "

" Yes, sir. A queer idea."

" He—he—never could have found David dead in the morning ? " cried Miss Timmens, in a low tone, herself turning a little pale. " Dead of fright ? "

" That could not be," said the Squire. " You forget that David had made his escape before midnight, and was at his mother's, calling to her."

" True, true," assented Miss Timmens. " Any way, I am certain Hill is somehow or other deceiving us, and he is a born villain for doing it."

But Hill, deceiving us though he had been, could not hold out. In going back, we saw him leaning over the palings waiting for us. But that the man is living yet, I should have said he was going to die there and then, for he looked exactly like it.

It seemed that just after we left him, a policeman had made his appearance. Not as a policeman, but as a friend ; for he and Hill were cronies. He told Hill confidentially that there was " going to be a row over that there lost boy ; that folks were saying that he might have been murdered ; that unless Hill could tell something satisfactory about him, he and others might be in custody before the day was over." Whether Hill found himself brought to a point from which there was neither advance nor retreat, or that he inevitably saw that concealment could no longer be maintained, or that he was stricken to despair and felt helpless, I know not. There he stood, his head over the palings, saying he would tell all.

It was a sad tale to listen to. Miss Timmens's last supposition was
right—Hill, upon going up to release David Garth, had found him
dead. And, so far as the man's experience of death went, he must
have been dead for six or seven hours.

"I'd like you to come and see him, sir," panted Hill.

Gingerly stepped the Squire in Hill's wake across the garden to
the shed. Unlocking the door, Hill stepped back for us to
enter. On a mattress on the ground was David, laid straight in
his every-day clothes, and covered with a blanket; his pretty hair,
which his mother had so loved, carefully smoothed. Hill,—
rough, burly, cross-grained Hill,—burst into tears and sobbed like
a child.

"I'd give my life to undo it, and bring him back again, Squire; I'd
give my life twice over, Master Johnny; but I declare before Heaven,
I never thought to harm the boy. When I see him the next morning,
lying dead, I'd not have minded if the Lord had struck me dead too.
I've been a'most mad ever since."

"Johnny," said the Squire, in low tones, "go you to South Crabb,
and bring over Mr. Cole. Do not talk of this."

The surgeon was at home, and came back with me. I did not
quite understand why the Squire sent for him, seeing he could do no
good.

And the boots were David's, after all; the only things he had
taken off. Hill had brought him to this shed the next night; with
some vague idea of burying him in the ground under the leaves.
"But I couldn't do it," he avowed amid his sobs; "I couldn't
do it."

There was an examination, Cole and another making it; and they
gave evidence at the inquest. One of them (it was Cole) thought
the boy must have died from fright, the other from the cold; and a
nice muff this last must have been.

"I did not from the first like that midnight call, or the apparently
causeless terror the poor mother awoke in," said Mrs. Todhetley, to
me. "The child's spirit must have cried out to her in his death-
agony. I have known a case like this before."

"But——"

"Hold your tongue, Johnny. You have not lived long enough to
gain experience of these things."

And I held it.

XX.

DAVID GARTH'S GHOST.

"Is it true that she's going to marry him, Miss Timmens?"

"True! *I* don't know," retorted Miss Timmens, in wrath. "It won't be for lack of warning, if she does. I told her so last night; and she tossed her head in answer. She's a vain, heartless girl, Hannah Baber, with no more prudence about her than a female ostrich."

"There may be nothing in it, after all," said Hannah. "She is generally ready to flirt, you know."

"Flirt!" shrieked Miss Timmens in her shrillest tone. "She'd flirt with a two-legged wheelbarrow if it had trousers on."

This colloquy was taking place at the private door of the schoolhouse. And you must understand that we have gone back a few months, for at this time David Garth was not dead. Hannah, who had gone down from Crabb Cot on an errand, came upon Miss Timmens standing there to look out. Of course she stayed to gossip.

The object of Miss Timmens's wrath was her niece, Harriet Roe. A vain, showy, handsome, free-natured girl, as you have heard, with bright dark eyes and white teeth—who had helped to work the mischief between Maria Lease and Daniel Ferrar which had led to Ferrar's dreadful death. Humphrey Roe, Harriet's father, was half-brother to Miss Timmens and Mrs. Hill; he had settled in France, and married a Frenchwoman. Miss Harriet chose to call herself French, and politely said the English were not fit to tie that nation's shoes. Perhaps that was why she had now taken up with a cousin, Louis Roe. Not that Louis Roe was really French: he had been born in France of English parents, and so was next door to it. A fashionable-looking young man North Crabb considered him, for he wore well-cut coats and a moustache. A moustache was a thing to be stared at in simple country places then. It may have had something to do with Miss Timmens's dislike to the young man. Louis Roe was only a distant relative: a tenth cousin, or so; of whom Miss Timmens had heard before, but never seen. When he appeared unexpectedly one January day at the school-house (it was

the January after Daniel Ferrar's death), ostensibly to see Harriet,
whom he had known in France, Miss Timmens, between surprise
and the moustache, was less gracious than she might have been.
From that time to this—March—he had (as Miss Timmens put it)
haunted the place, though chiefly taking up his abode at Worcester.
Harriet had struck into a flirtation with him at once, after her
native fashion: and now it was reported that they were going to
be married. Miss Timmens could not find out that he was doing
anything for a living. He talked of his fine "affaires" over in
France: but when she questioned him of what nature the "affaires"
were, he either evaded her like an eel, or gave rambling answers
that she could make neither head nor tail of. The way in which
he and Harriet would jabber French in her presence, not a word
of which language could she comprehend, and the laughing that
went on at the same time, put Miss Timmens's back up worse than
anything, for she thought they were making game of her. She
could be tart when she pleased; and when that happened, the redness in the nose and cheek grew redder. Very tart indeed was she,
recounting these grievances to Hannah.

"My firm belief, Hannah Baber, is, that he wants to get hold of
Harriet for her two-hundred pounds. She has that much, you
know: it came to her from her mother. Roe·would rather play
the gentleman than work. It is the money he's after, not Harriet."

"The money may put him into some good way of business, and
they may live comfortably together," suggested Hannah.

"Pigs may fly," returned Miss Timmens. "There's something
in that young man, Hannah Baber, that I could not trust. Oh,
but girls are wilful!—and simple, at the best, where the men are
concerned! They can't see an inch beyond their noses: no, and
they won't let others, who have sight, see for them. Look there!"

Emerging into the spring sunshine from the withy walk, came
the gentleman in question; Harriet Roe in her gay ribbons at his
side. Miss Timmens gave her door a bang, regardless of good
manners, and Hannah·pursued her way.

The road thus paved for it, North Crabb church was not taken
by surprise when it heard the marriage banns read out one Sunday
morning between Louis Roe, of the parish of St. Swithin, Worcester
(he was staying there at the time), and Henriette Adèle Marie Roe.
Miss Timmens, who had not been taken into confidence, started
violently; Mademoiselle Henriette Adèle Marie, sitting by her side,
held up her head and her blooming cheeks with unruffled equanimity. It was said there was a scene when they got home: Miss
/Timmens's sister (once Mrs. Garth, but then our bailiff's wife,
James Hill) looking in at the school-house to assist at it. Neither
of them could make anything of Harriet.

"I'll tell you what it is, Aunt Susan and Aunt Nancy," said the girl passionately, when her temper got roused : "*my mind is made up to marry Louis;* and if you don't drop this magging now and for good; if you attempt to worry me any further, I'll go off to Worcester, and stay with him till the day arrives. There! how would you like that? I will, I declare. It would be thought nothing at all of in my country, with the wedding so near."

This shut them up. Mrs. Hill, a meek, gentle little woman, who had her sorrows, and habitually let Miss Timmens do all the talking when they were together, began to cry. Harriet ate her cold dinner standing, and went off for an afternoon promenade with Monsieur Louis. From that time, even Miss Timmens gave up all thought of opposition, seeing that events must take their course. Harriet's parents were dead; she was over age, and her own mistress in the eye of the law.

"Would you mind taking a turn with me in the withy walk, Harriet Roe?" asked Maria Lease, as they were coming out of church that same night.

Harriet was alone. Louis Roe had gone back to Worcester. The request surprised her considerably. Since Daniel Ferrar's death the past November, Maria had been very distant with her; averting her head if they happened to meet.

"So you have come to your senses, have you, Maria Lease?" was the half insolent, half good-natured answer. "I'll walk down it with you if you like."

"Come to my senses in what way?" asked Maria, in low, subdued, sad tones, as they went towards the withy walk.

"About—*you* know what. You blamed *me* for what happened. As good as laid his death at my door."

"Did you ever hear me say so?"

"Oh, I could see: your manner was enough. As if I either helped it on—or could have prevented it! We used to have just a bit of talking and laughing together, he and I, but that was all."

That's all! And the gold chain was still on Harriet's neck. Maria suppressed a sigh.

"Whether I blamed you for it, Harriet Roe, or whether I blamed myself, is of no moment now. The past can never be recalled or redeemed in this world—its remembrance alone remains. I want to do you a little service, Harriet. Nothing may come of it, but it is my duty to speak."

Amidst the shadows of the withy beds, under the silent stars, Maria spoke, dropping her voice to a whisper. In a sufficiently curious but accidental manner, she had heard something said the previous week about Louis Roe. A stranger, who had known him in France, spoke very much in his disfavour. He said that any girl,

if she cared for her future happiness and credit, would be mad to
unite herself to him. Maria had asked no particulars; they might
not have been given if she had; but the impression of Louis Roe
left on her mind was not a good one. All this she quietly repeated
to Harriet. It was received in anything but a friendly spirit.

"Thank you for nothing, Maria Lease. Because you lost your
own husband—that was to have been—you think you'll try what
you can do to deprive me of mine. A slice of revenge, I suppose:
but it won't succeed."

"Harriet, you are mistaken," rejoined Maria; and Miss Harriet
thought she had never in her life heard so mournfully sad a tone
as the words were spoken in. "So much self-reproach fell upon
me that bitter evening when he was found dead: reproach that can
never be lifted from me while time shall last: that I do not think
I can ever again do an ill turn in this life, or give an unkind word.
The whole world does not seem to be as sinful in its wickedness as
I was in my harsh unkindness; and there's no sort of expiation left
to me. If I pass my whole existence laying my hands under other
people's feet in humble hope to serve them, it cannot undo the
bitterness of my passion when I exposed him before Johnny Ludlow.
The exposure was more than he could bear; and he—he put an end
to it. I suffer always, Harriet Roe; my days are one prolonged
burning agony of repentance. Repentance that brings no relief."

"My goodness!" cried Harriet, her breath almost scared away at
hearing this, careless-natured though she was. "I'll tell you what,
Maria: I should turn Roman Catholic in your place; and let a
priest absolve me from the sin."

A priest absolve her from the sin! The strange anguish on her
compressed lips was visible as Maria Lease turned her face upwards
in the starlight. ONE Most High and merciful Priest was ever
there, who could, and would, wash out her sin. But—what of
Daniel Ferrar, who had died in his?

"If there is one person whom I would more especially seek in
kindness to serve, it is you, Harriet," she resumed, putting her hand
gently on Harriet's arm—and her fingers accidentally touched the
chain that Daniel Ferrar had hung round the girl's neck in his
perfidy. "Revenge!—from me!"

"The very idea of my giving up Louis is absurd," was Harriet's
rejoinder, as they came out of the withy walk. "Thank you all
the same, Maria Lease; and there's my hand. I see now that you
meant kindly: but no one shall set me against my promised
husband."

Maria shook the hand in silence.

"Look here, Maria—don't go and tell your beautiful scandal to
sharp Susan Timmens. Not that I care whether you do or not,

except on the score of contention. She would strike up fresh
opposition, and it might come to scratching and fighting. My
temper has borne enough : one can't be a lamb always."

The wedding came off on Easter Tuesday. Harriet wore a bright
silk dress, the colour of lilac, with a wreath and veil. When the
latter ornaments came home, Miss Timmens nearly fainted. Decent
young women in their station of life were married in bonnets, she
represented : not in wreaths and veils. But Harriet Roe, reared to
French customs, said bonnets could never be admissible for a bride,
and she'd sooner go to church in a coal-scuttle. The Batley girls,
in trains and straw-hats, were bridesmaids. Miss Timmens wore
a new shawl and white gloves; and poor little David Garth—who
was to die of fright before that same year came to an end—stood
with his hand locked in his mother's.

And so, in the self-same church where she had sat displaying
her graces before the ill-fated Daniel Ferrar, and by the same young
clergyman who had preached to her then,—Harriet became the wife
of Louis Roe, and went away with him to London.

The next move in the chain of events was the death of David
Garth in Willow Cottage. It occurred in November, when Tod
and I were staying at home, and has been already told of. James
Hill escaped without punishment : it was said there was no law to
touch him. He protested through thick and thin that he meant no
harm to the boy; to do him justice, it was not supposed he had : he
was finely repentant for it, and escaped with a reprimand.

Mrs. Hill refused to remain in the cottage. What with her innate
tendency to superstition, with the real facts of the case, and with
that strange belief—that David's spirit had appeared to her in the
moment of dying ; a belief firm and fixed as adamant—she passed
into a state of horror of the dwelling. Not another night could she
remain in it. The doctor himself, Cole, said she must not. Miss
Timmens took her in as a temporary thing; until the furniture
could be replaced in their former house, which was not let. Hill
made no objection to this. For that matter, he seemed afraid of
the new place himself, and was glad to get back to the old one.
All his native surliness had left him for the time : he was as a subdued man whose tongue has departed on an excursion. You see,
he had feared the law might come down upon him. The coroner's
inquest had brought in a safe verdict : all Hill received was a
censure for having locked the boy in alone : but he could not yet
feel sure that the affair would not be taken up by the magistrates :
and the parish said in his hearing that his punishment ought to be
transportation at the very least. Altogether, it subdued him.

So, as soon as David's funeral was over, and while his wife was still with Miss Timmens, Hill began to move back his goods in a sort of humble silence. Crowds collected to see the transport, much to Hill's annoyance and discomfiture. The calamity had caused intense excitement in the place; and Miss Timmens, who had a very long tongue, and hated Hill just as much as she had loved David, kept up the ball. Hill's intention was to lock up Willow Cottage until he could get Mr. Todhetley to release him from it. At present he dared not ask: all of us at Crabb Cot, from the Squire downwards, were bitterly against him for his wicked inhumanity to poor David.

Curious to say—curious because of what was to happen out of it—as Hill was loading the truck with the last remaining things, a stranger came up to the cottage door. Just at the first moment, Hill did not recognize him; he had shaved off his moustache and whiskers, and grown a beard instead. And that alters people.

"How are you, Hill? What are you up to here?"

' It was Louis Roe—who had married Mademoiselle Henriette the previous Easter. Where they had been since, or what they had done, was a sort of mystery, for Harriet had written only one letter. By that letter, it was gathered that they were flourishing in London: but no address was given, and Miss Timmens had called her a heartless jade, not to want to hear from her best relatives.

Hill answered that he was pretty well, and went on loading; but said nothing to the other question. Louis Roe—perceiving sundry straggling spectators who stood peering, as if the loading of a hand-barrow with goods were a raree-show—rather wondered at appearances, and asked again. Hill shortly explained then that they had moved into Willow Cottage; but his wife found it didn't suit her, and so they were moving back again to the old home.

He went off with the truck, before he had well answered, giving no time for further colloquy. Louis Roe happened to come across young Jim Batley amidst the tag-rag, and heard from him all that had occurred.

"He must be a cruel devil, to leave a timid child all night in a house alone!" was Mr. Roe's indignant comment; who, whatever his shortcomings might be in the eyes of Miss Timmens, was not thought to be hard-hearted.

"His mother, she sees his ghost," went on Jim Batley. "Leastways, heered it."

Mr. Roe took no notice of this additional communication. Perhaps ghosts held a low place in his creed—and he appeared to have plunged into a reverie. Starting out of it in a minute or two, he ran after Hill, and began talking in a low, business tone.

Hill could not believe his ears. Surely such luck had never

befallen a miserable man! For here was Louis Roe offering to take Willow Cottage off his hands: to become his, Hill's, tenant for a short time. The double rent; this, and that for the old house he was returning to; had been weighing upon Hill's mind as heavily as David weighed upon it. The man had saved plenty of money, but he was of a close nature. Squire Todhetley was a generous man; but Hill felt conscious that he had displeased him too much to expect any favour at present.

"What d'ye want of the cottage?" asked Hill, suppressing all signs of satisfaction. "Be you and Harriet a-coming to live down here?"

"We should like to stay here for a few weeks—say till the dead of winter's over," replied Roe. "London is a beastly dull place in bad weather; the fogs don't agree with Harriet. I had thought of taking two or three rooms at Birmingham: but I don't know but she'll like this cottage best—if you will let me have it cheap."

It would be cheap enough. For Hill named the very moderate rent he had agreed to pay the Squire. Only too glad was he, to get that. Roe promised to pay him monthly.

North Crabb was electrified at the news. Mr. and Mrs. Roe were coming to stay in the cottage where poor David Garth had just died. No time was lost over it, either. On the following day some hired furniture was put into it, and Harriet herself arrived.

She was looking very ill. And I'm sure if she had appeared with a beard as well as her husband, her face could not have seemed more changed. Not her face only, but her manners. Instead of figuring off in silks and ribbons, finer than the stars, laughing with every one she met, and throwing her handsome eyes about, she wore only plain things, and went along noticing no one. Some people called it "pride;" Miss Timmens said it was disappointment. The first time Tod and I met her, she never lifted her eyes at all. Tod would have stayed to speak; but she just said, "Good morning, gentlemen," and went on.

"I say, Johnny, there's some change there," was Tod's remark, as he turned to look after her.

They had been in the place about a week—and Roe seemed to keep indoors, or else was away, for no one ever saw him—when a strange turn arose, that was destined to set the neighbourhood in an uproar. I was running past the school-house one evening at dusk, and saw Maria Lease sitting with Miss Timmens by fire-light. Liking Maria very much—for I always did like her, and always shall—I went bolt in to them. James Hill's wife was also there, in her mourning gown with crape on it, sitting right back in the chimney corner. She had gone back to Hill then, but made no scruple of leaving him alone often: and Hill, who had had his lesson, put up with it. And you would never guess; no, not though you had tried from then till Midsummer; what they were whispering about, as though scared out of their seven senses.

David Garth's ghost was haunting Willow Cottage.

Miss Timmens was telling the story; the others listened with open mouths. She began at the beginning again for my benefit.

"I was sitting by myself here about this time last evening, Master Johnny, having dismissed the children, and almost too tired with their worry to get my own tea, when Harriet Roe came gliding in at the door, looking whiter than a sheet, and startling me beyond everything. 'Aunt Susan,' says she in so indistinct a tone that I should have boxed one of the girls had she attempted to use such, 'would you take pity on me and let me stay here till to-morrow morning? Louis went away this afternoon, and I dare not stop alone in the place all night.' 'What are you afraid of?' I asked, not telling her at once that she might stay; but down she sat, and threw her mantle and bonnet off—taking French leave. I never saw *her* in such a state before," continued Miss Timmens vehemently; "shivering and shaking as if she had an ague, and not a particle of her impudence left in her. 'I think that place must be damp with the willow brook, aunt,' says she; 'it gives me a sensation of cold.' 'Now don't you talk nonsense about your willow brooks, Harriet Roe,' says I. 'You are not shaking for willow brooks, or for cold either, but from fright. What is it?' 'Well then,' says she, plucking up a bit, 'I'm afraid of seeing the boy.' 'What boy?' says I—'not David?' 'Yes; David,' she says, and trembles worse than ever. 'He appeared to Aunt Nancy; a sign he is not at rest; and he is as sure to be in the house as sure can be. Dying in the way he did, and lying hid in the shed as he did, what else is to be expected?' Well, Master Johnny, this all seemed to me very odd—as I've just observed to Nancy," continued Miss Timmens. "It struck me, sir, there was more behind. 'Harriet,' says I, 'have you *seen* David Garth?' But at first no satisfactory answer could I get from her, neither yes nor no. At last she said she had not seen him, but knew she should if she stayed in the house by herself at night, for that he came again, and was *in* it. It struck me she was speaking falsely; and that she *had* seen him; or what she took for him."

"I know she has; I feel convinced of it," spoke up poor Mrs. Hill, tilting back her black bonnet—worn for David—to wipe the tears from her eyes. "Master Ludlow, don't smile, sir—though it's best perhaps for the young to disbelieve these solemn things. As surely as that we are talking here, my dear boy's spirit came to me in the moment of his death. I feared it might take to haunting the cottage, sir; and that's one reason why I could not stay in it."

"Yes; Harriet has seen him," interposed Maria Lease in low, firm tones. "Just as I saw Daniel Ferrar. Master Johnny, *you* know I saw *him*."

Well, truth to say, I thought she must have seen Daniel Ferrar. Having assisted at the sight—or if not at the actual sight, at the place and time and circumstance attending it—I did not see how else it was to be explained away.

"Where's Harriet now?" I asked.

"She stayed here last night, and went off by rail this morning to her grandmother's at Worcester," replied Miss Timmens. "Mother will be glad of her for a day or so, for she keeps her bed still."

"Then who is in the cottage?"

"Nobody, sir. It's locked up. Roe is expected back to-morrow."

Miss Timmens began to set her tea-things, and I left them. Whom should I come upon in the road, but Tod—who had been over to South Crabb. I told him all this; and we took the broad path home through the fields, which led us past Willow Cottage. The fun Tod made of what the women had been saying, was beyond everything. A dreary dwelling, it looked; cold, and deserted, and solitary in the dusky night, on which the moon was rising. The back looked towards Crabb Ravine and the three-cornered grove in which Daniel Ferrar had taken his own life away; and to the barn where Maria had seen Ferrar after death. In front was the large field, bleak and bare; and beyond, the scattered chimneys of North Crabb. A lively dwelling altogether!—let alone what had happened in it to David Garth. I said so.

"Yes, it is a lively spot!" acquiesced Tod. "Beautifully lively in itself, without having the reputation of being haunted. Eugh! Let's get home to dinner, Johnny."

Mr. and Mrs. Coney and Tom came in after dinner. Old Coney and the Squire smoked till tea-time. When tea was over we all sat down to Pope Joan. Mr. Coney kept mistaking hearts for diamonds, clubs for spades; he had not his spectacles, and I offered to fetch them. Upon that, he set upon Tom for being lazy and letting Johnny Ludlow do what it was his place to do. The result was, that Tom Coney and I had a race which should reach the farm first. The night was bright, the moon high. Coming back with the spectacles, a man encountered us, tearing along as fast as we were. And that was like mad.

"Halloa!" cried Tom. "What's up."

Tom had cause to ask it. The man was Luke Macintosh: and never in all my life had I seen a specimen of such terror. His face was white, his breath came in gasps. Without saying with your leave or by your leave, he caught hold of Tom Coney's arm.

"Master, as I be a living sinner, I ha' just seen Davy Garth."

"Seen David Garth?" echoed Tom, wondering whether Luke had been drinking.

"I see him as plain as plain. He be at that end window o' the Willow Cottage."

"Do you mean his ghost, or himself?" asked Tom, making game of it.

"Why, his ghost, in course, sir. It's well known hisself be dead and buried—worse luck! Mercy on us!—I'd ha' lost a month's wages rather nor see this."

Considering Luke Macintosh was so great a coward that he would not go through the Ravine after nightfall, this was not much from him. Neither had his conscience been quite easy since David's death: as it may be said that he, through refusing at the last moment to sleep in the house, had in a degree been the remote cause of it. His account was this: Passing the Willow Cottage on his way from North Crabb, he happened to look up at the end window, and saw David standing there all in white in the moonlight.

"I never see nothing plainer in all my born days, never," gasped Luke. "His poor little face hadn't no more colour in it nor chalk. Drat them ghosts and goblins, then! What does they come and show theirselves to decent folk for?"

He was trembling just as Miss Timmens, some three hours before, had described Harriet Roe to have trembled. An idea flashed into my mind.

"Now, Luke, just you confess—who is it that has put this into your head?" I asked. But Luke only stared at me: he seemed unable to understand.

"Some one has been telling you this to-night at North Crabb?"

"Telling me what, Master Ludlow?"

"That David Garth is haunting the cottage. It is what people are saying, Tom," I added to Coney.

"Then, Master Johnny, I never heered a blessed syllable on't," he replied; and so earnestly that it was not possible to doubt him. "Nobody have said nothing to me. For the matter o' that, I didn't stop to talk to a soul, but just put Molly's letter in the window slit —which was what I went for—and turned back again. I wish the woman had ha' been skinned afore she'd got me to go off to the post for her to-night. Plague on me, to have took the way past the cottage! as if the road warn't good enough to ha' served me!—and a sight straighter!"

"Were there lights in the cottage, Luke?" asked Coney. "Did you see the Roes about?"

"There warn't no more sign o' light or life a-nigh the place, Mr. Tom, no more nor if they'd all been dead and buried inside it."

"It is shut up, Tom," I said. "Roe and his wife are away."

"Lawk a mercy!—not a living creature in it but the ghost!" quaked Luke.

As I have said, this was not much from Luke, taking what he was into consideration; but it was to be confirmed by others. One of the Coneys' maid-servants came along, as we stood there, on her way from North Crabb. A sensible, respectable woman, with no nonsense about her in general; but she looked almost as scared as Luke now.

"You don't mean to say *you* have seen it, Dinah?" cried Tom, staring at her.

"Yes, I have, sir."

"What! seen David Garth?"

"Well, I suppose it was him. It was something at the window, in white, that looked like him, Mr. Tom."

"Did you go on purpose to look for it, Dinah?" asked Tom ironically.

"The way I happened to go was this, sir. James Hill overtook me coming out of North Crabb: he was going up to Willow Cottage to speak to Roe; and I thought I'd walk with him, instead of taking the road. Not but what he's a beauty to walk with, *he* is, after his cruelty to his wife's boy," broke off Dinah: "but company is company on a solitary road at night. When we got to the cottage, Hill knocked; I stayed a minute to say how-d'ye-do to Mrs. Roe, for I've not seen her yet. Nobody answered the door; the place looked all dark and empty. 'They must be out for the evening, I should think,' says Hill: and with that he steps back and looks up at the windows. 'Lord be good to us! what's that?' says he, when he had got round where he could see the end casement. I went to him, and found him standing like a pump, just as stiff and upright, his hands clutched hold of one another, and his eyes staring up at the panes in mortal terror. 'What is it?' says I. 'It's Davvy,' says he; but the voice didn't sound like Hill's voice, and it scared me a bit. 'Yes, it's him,' says Hill; 'he have got on the sheet as was wrapped round him to carry him to the shed. I—I lodged him again that there window to make the turning; the stairs was awk'ard,' went on Hill, as if he was speaking again the grain, but couldn't help himself.—And sure enough, Mr. Tom—sure enough, Master Ludlow, there was David."

"Nonsense, Dinah!" cried Tom Coney.

"I saw him quite well, sir, in the white sheet," said Dinah. "The moon was shining on the window a'most as bright as day."

"It were brighter nor day," eagerly put in Luke Macintosh. "You'll believe me now, Mr. Tom."

"I'd not believe it if I saw it," said Tom Coney.

"As we stood looking up, me laying hold of Hill's arm," resumed Dinah, as if she had not told all her tale, "there came a loud whistling and shouting behind. Which was young Jim Batley, bringing some message from them sisters of his to Harriet Roe. I bade him hush his noise, but he only danced and mocked at me; so then I told him the cottage was empty, except for David Garth. That hushed him. He came stealing up, and stood by me, staring. You should have seen his face change, Mr. Tom.

"Was he frightened?"

"Frightened is hardly the word for it, sir. His teeth began to chatter, as if he had a fit; and down he went at last like a stone, face first, howling fearful. We couldn't hardly get him up again to come away, me and Hill. And as to the ghost, Mr. Tom, it *was* still there."

"Well, it is a queer tale," acknowledged Tom Coney.

"We made for the road, all three of us then, and I turned on here—and I didn't half like coming by the barn where Maria Lease saw Daniel Ferrar," candidly added Dinah. "T'other two went on their opposite way, Jim never letting go of Hill's coat-tails."

There was no more Pope Joan that night. We carried the story indoors; and I mentioned also what had been said to Miss Timmens. The Squire and old Coney laughed.

With David Garth's ghost to be seen, it could not be supposed that I, or Tod, or Tom Coney, should stay away from the sight. When we reached the place, some twenty people had collected round the house. Jim Batley had told the tale in North Crabb.

But curious watchers had seen nothing. Neither did we. For the bright night had changed to darkness. A huge curtain of cloud had come up from the south, covering the moon and the best part of the sky, as a pall covers a coffin. If gazing could have brought a ghost to the window, there would assuredly have been one. The casement was at the end of the house; serving to light the narrow upstairs passage. A huge cherry-tree hid the casement in summer; very slightly its bare branches obscured it now.

A sound, as of some panting animal, came up beside me as I leaned on the side palings. I turned; and saw the bailiff. Some terrible power of fascination had brought him back again, against his will.

"So it is gone, Hill, you see."

"It's not gone, Mr. Johnny," was his answer. "For some of our sights, it'll never go away again. You look well at the right-hand side, sir, and see if you don't see some'at white there."

Peering steadily, I thought I did see something white—as of a face above a white garment. But it might have been fancy."

"Us as saw *him* couldn't mistake it for fancy," was Hill's re-joinder. "There was three on us : me, and Dinah up at Coney's, and that there imp of a Jim Batley."

"Some one saw it before you did, Hill. At least he says so. Luke Macintosh. He was scared out of his senses."

The effect of these words on Hill was such, that I quite believed he was scared out of *his*. He clasped his hands in wild emotion, and turned up his eyes to give thanks.

"It's ret'ibution a working its ends, Mr. Ludlow. See it first, did he ! And I hope to my heart he'll see it afore his eyes evermore. If that there Macintosh had not played a false and coward's game, no harm 'ud ha' come to Davvy."

The crowd increased. The Squire and old Coney came up, and told the whole assemblage that they were born idiots. Of course, with nothing to be seen, it looked as though we all were that. In the midst of it, making quietly for the back-door, as though he had come home through Crabb' Ravine from Timberdale, I espied Louis Roe. Saying nothing to any one, I went round and told him.

"David Garth's ghost in the place ! " he exclaimed. "Why, it will frighten my wife to death. Of course there's nothing of the sort ; but women are so foolishly timid."

I said his wife was not there. Roe took a key from his pocket, unlocked the back-door, and went in. He was talking to me, and I stepped over the threshold to the kitchen, into which the door opened. He began feeling on the shelf for matches, and could not find any.

"There's a box in the bedroom, I know," he said ; and went stumbling upstairs.

Down he came, after a minute or so, with the matches, struck one, and lighted a candle. Opening the front door, he showed himself, explained that he had just come home, and complained of the commotion.

"There's no such thing in this lower world as ghosts," said Roe. "Whoever pretends to see them must be either drunk or mad. As to this house—well, some of you had better walk in and re-assure yourselves. You are welcome."

He was taken at his word. A few came in, and went looking about for the ghost, upstairs and down. Writing about it now, it seems to have been the most ridiculous thing in the world. Nothing was to be found. The narrow passage above, where David had stood, was empty. "As if supernatural visitants waited while you looked for them ! " cried the superstitious crowd outside.

It is easier to raise a disturbance of this kind than to allay it, and the ghost-seers stayed on. The heavy cloud in the heavens rolled away by-and-by ; and the moon came out, and shone on the

casement again. But neither David Garth nor anything else was
then to be seen there.

The night's commotion passed away, but not the rumours. That
David Garth's spirit could not rest, but came back to trouble the
earth, especially that spot known as Willow Cottage, was accepted
as a fact. People would go stealing up there at night, three or four
of them arm-in-arm, and stand staring at the casement, and walk
round the cottage. Nothing more was to be seen—perhaps because
there was no moon to light up the window. Harriet Roe was at
home again with her husband; but she did not go abroad much :
and her face seemed to wear a sort of uneasy terror. "The fear of
seeing *him* is wearing her heart out; why does Roe stop in the
place?" said North Crabb : and though Harriet had never been
much of a favourite, she had plenty of sympathy now.

It soon came to be known in a gradual sort of way that a visitor
was staying at Willow Cottage. A young woman fashionably
dressed, who was called Mrs. James ; and who was said to be the
wife of James Roe, Louis Roe's elder brother. Some people
declared that a man was also there : they had seen one. Harriet
denied it. An acquaintance of her husband's, a Mr. Duffy, had
been over to see them from Birmingham, she said, but he went
back again. She was not believed.

What with the ghost, and what with the mystery attaching to
its inhabitants, Willow Cottage was a great card just then. If you
ask me to explain what mystery there could be, I cannot do so :
all I know is, an idea that there was something of the kind, apart
from David, dawned upon many minds in North Crabb. Miss
Timmens spoke it openly. She did not like Harriet's looks, and
said that something or other was killing her. And Susan Timmens
considered it her duty to try and come to the bottom of it.

At all sorts of hours, seasonable and unseasonable, Miss Timmens
presented herself at Willow Cottage. Rarely alone. Sometimes
Mrs. Hill would be with her ; or it would be Maria Lease ; or one
of the Batley girls ; or once it was young Jim. Louis Roe grew
to feel annoyed at this ; he told Harriet he would not have confounded people coming there, prying ; and he closed the door
against them. So, the next time Miss Timmens went, she found
the door bolted in the most inhospitable manner. Harriet threw
open the parlour window to speak to her.

"Louis says he won't have any more visitors calling here just
now ; not even you, Aunt Susan."

"What does he say that for?" snapped Miss Timmens.

"We came down here to be quiet : he has some accounts to go

over, and can't be disturbed at them. So perhaps you'll stay away, Aunt Susan. I'll come to the school-house sometimes instead."

It was the dusk of the evening, but Miss Timmens could see the fearful look of illness on Harriet's face. She was also trembling.

"Harriet, what's the matter with you?" she asked, in a kinder tone.

"Nothing."

"*Nothing!* Why, you look as ill as you can look. You are trembling all over."

"It's true I don't feel very well this evening, aunt, but I think it is nothing. I often feel as if I had a touch of ague."

Miss Timmens bent her face nearer; it had a strange concern in it. "Harriet, look here. There's some mystery about this place; won't you tell me what it is? I—seem—to—be—afraid—for—*you*," she concluded, in a slow and scarcely audible whisper.

For answer, Miss Timmens found the window slammed down in her face. An impression arose—she hardly knew whence gathered, or whether it had any foundation—that it was not Harriet who had slammed it, but some one concealed behind the curtain.

"Well I'm sure!" cried she. "It might have taken my nose off."

"It was so cold, aunt!" Harriet called out apologetically through the glass. "Good night."

Miss Timmens walked off in dudgeon. Revolving matters along the broad field-path, she liked their appearance less and less. Harriet was looking as ill as possible: and what meant that trembling? Was it caused by sickness of body, or terror of mind? Mrs. Hill, when consulted, summed it up comprehensively: "It is David about the place: *that's* killing her."

Harriet Roe did not make her appearance at the school-house, and the next day but one Miss Timmens went up again. The door was bolted. Miss Timmens knocked, but received no answer. Not choosing to be treated in that way she made so much noise, first at the door and then at the window, that the former was at length unclosed by Mrs. James, in list shoes and a dressing-gown, as if her toilette had been delayed that day. The chain was kept up—a new chain that Miss Timmens had not seen before—and she could not enter.

"I want to see Harriet, Mrs. James."

"Harriet's gone," replied Mrs. James.

"Gone! Gone where?"

"To London. She went off there yesterday morning."

Miss Timmens felt, as she would have said, struck into herself. An idea flashed over her that the words had not a syllable of truth in them.

"What did she go to London for?"

Mrs. James glanced over her two shoulders, seemingly in terror herself, and sunk her voice to a whisper. "She had grown afraid of the place, this dark winter weather. Miss Timmens—it's as true as you're there—nothing would persuade her out of the fancy that she was always seeing David Garth. He used to stand in a sheet at the end of the upstairs passage and look at her. Leastways, *she* said so."

This nearly did for Miss Timmens. It might be true; and she could not confute it. "Do *you* see him, Mrs. James?"

"Well, no; I never have. Goodness knows, I don't want to."

"But Harriet was not well enough to take a long journey," contended Miss Timmens. "She never could have undertaken one in her state of health."

"I don't know what you mean by 'state,' Miss Timmens. She would shake a bit at times; but we saw nothing else the matter with her. Perhaps *you* would shake if you had an apparition in the house. Any way, well or ill, she went off to London. Louis took her as far as the station and saw her away."

"Will you give me her address? I should like to write to her."

Mrs. James said she could not give the address, because she did not know it. Nothing more was to be got out of her, and Miss Timmens reluctantly departed.

"I should hope they've not murdered her—and are concealing her in the house as Hill concealed David," was the comment she gave vent to in her perplexity and wrath.

From that time, nothing could be heard of Harriet Roe. A week went on; nearly two weeks; but she never was seen, and no tidings came of her. So far as could be ascertained, she had not gone away by train: neither station-master nor porter remembered to have seen her. Miss Timmens grew as thin as a ghost herself: the subject worried her night and day. That some ill had happened to Harriet; or been *done* to her, she did not doubt. Once or twice she managed to see Roe; once or twice she saw Mrs. James: speaking to them at the door with the chain up. Roe said he heard from his wife nearly every other day; but he would not show the letters, or give the address: a conclusive proof to the mind of Miss Timmens that neither had any existence. *What had they done with Harriet?* Miss Timmens could not have been in much worse mental trouble had she herself made away with her.

One morning the postman delivered a letter at the school-house. It bore the London post-mark, and purported to be from Harriet. A few lines only—saying she was well and enjoying herself, and should come back sometime—the writing shaky and blotted, and bearing but a slight resemblance to hers. Miss Timmens dashed it on the table.

"The fools, to think they can deceive me this way! That's no more Harriet's writing than it is mine."

But Miss Timmens's passion soon subsided into a grave, settled, awful dread. For she saw that this had been written to delude her into the belief that Harriet was in health and life—when she might be in neither one nor the other. She brought the letter to Crabb Cot. She took it round the parish. She went with it to the police-station; imparting her views of it to all freely. It was a sham; a blind; a forgery: and *where* was she to look for poor lost Harriet Roe?

That same evening the ghost appeared again. Miss Timmens and others went up to the cottage, intending to demand an inter-view with Roe; and they found the house shut up, apparently deserted. Reconnoitring the windows from all points, their dis-mayed eyes rested on something at the end casement: a thin, shadowy form, robed in white. Every one of them saw it; but, even as they looked, it seemed to vanish away. Yes, there was no question that the house was haunted. Perhaps Harriet had died from fright, as poor David died.

Things could not go on like this for ever. After another day or two of discomfort, Mr. Todhetley, as a county magistrate, incited by the feeling in the parish, issued a private mandate for Roe to appear before him, that he might be questioned as to what had become of his wife. It was not a warrant; but a sort of friendly invitation, that could offend no one. Jiff the policeman was en-trusted with the delivery of the message, a verbal one, and I went with him.

As if she had scented our errand for herself, and wanted to make a third in it, who should meet us in the broad path, but Miss Timmens. Willow Cottage might or might not be haunted, but I am sure her legs were: they couldn't be still.

"What are *you* doing up here, Jiff?" she tartly asked.

Jiff told her. Squire Todhetley wanted Roe at Crabb Cot.

"It will be of no use, Jiff; the door's sure to be fast," groaned Miss Timmens. "My opinion is that Roe has left the place for good."

Miss Timmens was mistaken. The shutters were open, and the house showed signs of life. •Upon knocking at the door—Miss Timmens took off her patten to do it with, and you might have heard the echoes at North Crabb—it was flung wide by Mrs. James.

Mr. Roe? No, Mr. Roe was not at home. Mrs. Roe was.

Mrs. Roe was! "What, Harriet?" cried excited Miss Timmens.

Yes, Harriet. If we liked to walk in and see her, we could do so.

By the kitchen fire, as being biggest and hottest, in a chair stuffed about with blankets, sat Harriet Roe. Worn, white, shadowy, she was evidently just getting over some desperate illness. I stared; the policeman softly whistled; you might have knocked Miss Timmens down with a feather.

"Good patience, child—why, where have you been hiding all this while?" cried she. "And what on earth has been the matter with you?"

"I have been upstairs in my room, Aunt Susan, keeping my bed. As to the illness, it turned out to be ague and low fever."

"Upstairs where?"

"Here."

Jiff went out again; there was nothing to stay for. I followed, leaving Miss Timmens and Harriet to have it out together.

She had really been ill in bed all the time, Mrs. James and Roe attending on her. It did not suit them to admit visitors; for James Roe, who had fallen into some difficulty in London, connected with forged bills, was lying concealed at Willow Cottage. That's why people were kept out. It would not have done by any means for Miss Timmens and her sharp eyes to go upstairs and catch a glimpse of him; so they concocted the tale that Harriet was away. James Roe was safely away now, and Louis with him. Louis had been mixed up in the bill trouble in a lesser degree: but quite enough so to induce him to absent himself from London for a time, and to stay quietly at North Crabb.

"Was it fear or ague that caused you to shake so that last evening I saw you here?" questioned Miss Timmens.

"Ague. I never got out of bed after that night. I could hardly write that letter, aunt, that Louis sent to London to be posted to you."

"And—did you really see David Garth?"

"No, I never saw him," said Harriet. "But, after all the reports and talk, I was timid at being in the house alone—James and his wife had not come then—and that's why I asked you to let me stay at the school-house the night my husband was away."

"But it was told me that you did see him."

"I was always frightened for fear I should."

"It strikes me you have had other causes for fright as well, Harriet," cried shrewd Miss Timmens.

"Well, you see—this business of James Roe's has put me about. Every knock that came to the door seemed to me to be somebody coming for him. My husband says the ghost is all rubbish and fancy, Aunt Susan."

"Rubbish and fancy, does he?"

"He says that when he came in here with Johnny Ludlow, the

night there was that commotion, in going up for some matches, he fell over something at the top of the stairs by the end casement, and flung it behind the rafters. Next day he saw what it was. I had tied a white cloth over a small dwarf mop to sweep the walls with, and must have left it near the window. I remembered that I did leave it there. It no doubt looked in the moonlight just like a white face. And that's what was taken for David's ghost."

Miss Timmens paused, considering matters : she might believe just as much of this as she liked.

"It appeared again at the same place, Harriet, two or three days ago."

"That was me, aunt. I saw you all looking up, and drew away again for fear you should know me. Mrs. James was making my bed, and I had crawled there."

There it ended. So far the mystery was over. The explanation was confided to the public, who received it differently. Some accepted the mop version ; others clung to the ghost. And Hill never had a penny of his rent. Louis Roe was away ; and, as it turned out, did not come back again.

Mrs. James wanted to leave also ; and Maria Lease took her place as nurse. Tenderly she did it, too; and Harriet got well. She was going off to join her husband as soon as she could travel : it was said in France. No one knew ; unless it was Maria Lease. She and Harriet had become confidential friends.

"Which is the worse fate—yours or mine?" cried Harriet to Maria, half mockingly, half woefully, the day she was packing her trunk. "You have your lonely life, and your never-ending repentance for what you call your harsh sin : I have my sickness and my trouble—and I have enough of that, Maria." But Maria Lease only shook her head in answer.

"Trouble and repentance are our best lot in this world, Harriet. They come to fit us for heaven."

But North Crabb, though willingly admitting that Harriet Roe, in marrying, had not entered on a bed of lilies, and might have been happier had she kept single, would not, on the whole, be shaken from its belief that the ghost still haunted the empty cottage. Small parties made shivering pilgrimages up there on a moonlight night, to watch for it, and sometimes declared that it appeared. Fancy goes a long way in this world.

XXI.

SEEING LIFE.

THE Clement-Pells lived at Parrifer Hall, and were as grand as all the rest of us put together. After that affair connected with Cathy Reed, and the death of his son, Major Parrifer and his family could not bear to stay in the place. They took a house near London, and Parrifer Hall was advertised to be let. Mr. Clement-Pell came forward, and took it for a term of years.

The Clement-Pells rolled in riches. His was one of those cases of self-made men that have been so common of late years : where an individual, from a humble position, rises by perceptible degrees, until he towers above all, like a Jack sprung out of a box, and is the wonder and envy of the world around. Mr. Clement-Pell was said to have begun life in London as a lawyer. Later, circumstances brought him down to a bustling town in our neighbourhood where he became the manager of a small banking company ; and from that time he did nothing but rise. " There is a tide in the affairs of men, which, taken at the flood, leads on to fortune," says Shakespeare : and this was the tide in Mr. Clement-Pell's. The small banking company became a great one. Its spare cash helped to make railways, to work mines, and to do all kinds of profitable things. The shareholders flourished ; Mr. Clement-Pell was more regarded than a heathen deity. He established a branch at two or three small places ; and, amongst them, one at Church Dykely. After that, he took Parrifer Hall. The simple people around could not vie with the grandeur of the Pells, and did not try to do so. The Pells made much of me and Joseph Todhetley—perhaps because there was a dearth of young fellows near—and often asked us to the Hall. Mrs. Pell, a showy, handsome woman, turned up her nose at all but the best families, and would not associate with farmers, however much they might live like gentlefolk. She was decisive in manner, haughty, and ruled the house and everything in it, including her husband, with iron will. In a slight degree she and her children put us in mind of the Parrifers : for they held their heads in the clouds as the Parrifers had done, and the ostentation they displayed was just the least bit vulgar. Mr. Pell was a good-looking, gentlemanlike man, with a pleasant, hearty, straightforward manner that took with every one. He was neither fine nor stuck up : but his wife and daughters were ; after the custom of a good many who have shot up into greatness.

And now that's the introduction to the Clement-Pells. One year they took a furnished house in London, and sent to invite me and Tod up in the summer. It was not very long after we had paid that visit to the Whitneys and Miss Deveen. The invitation was cordially pressed ; but Squire Todhetley did not much like our going.

"Look here, you boys," said he, as we were starting, for the point was yielded, "I'd a great deal rather you were going to stay at home. Don't you let the young Pells lead you into mischief."

Tod resented the doubt. "We are not boys, sir."

"Well, I suppose you'd like to call yourselves young men," returned the Pater; "you in particular, Joe. But young men have gone up to London before now, and come home with their fingers burnt."

Tod laughed.

"They have. It is this, Joe : Johnny, listen to me. A young fellow, just launched on the world, turns out very much according to the companions he is thrown amongst and the associations he meets with. I have a notion that the young Pells are wild ; fast, as it is called now ; so take care of yourselves. And don't forget that though their purses may be unlimited, yours are not."

Three footmen came rushing out when the cab stopped at the house in Kensington, and the Pells made much of us. Mr. Pell and the eldest son, James, were at the chief bank in the country ; they rarely spared the time to come up; but the rest were in town. Mrs. Pell, the four girls, the two sons, and a new German governess. The house was not as large as Parrifer Hall, and Tod and I had a top room between us, with two beds in it. Fabian Pell held a commission in the army. Augustus was reading for the bar —he was never called at home anything but "Gusty."

We got there just before dinner, and dressed for it—finding dress was expected. A worn-looking, fashionable man of thirty was in the drawing-room when we went down, the Honourable Mr. Crayton : and Fabian brought in two officers. Mrs. Pell wore blue, with a string of pearls on her neck that were too big to be real : the two girls were in white silk and white shoes. Altogether, considering it was not a state occasion, but a friendly dinner, the dresses looked too fine, more suited to a duke's table ; and I wondered what Mrs. Todhetley would have said to them.

"Will you take Constance in to dinner, Mr. Todhetley?

Tod took her. She was the second girl : the eldest, Martha Jane, went in with one of the officers. The younger girls, Leonora and Rose, dined in the middle of the day with the governess. Gusty was not there, and Fabian and I went in together.

"Where is he?" I asked of Fabian.

"Gusty? Oh, knocking about somewhere. His getting home to dinner's always a chance. He has chambers in town."

Why the idea should have come over me, I know not, unless it was the tone Mrs. Pell spoke in, but it flashed across my mind that she was looking at Tod as a possible husband for her daughter Constance. He was not of an age to marry yet : but some women like to plot and plan these things beforehand. I hated her for it : I did not care that Tod should choose one of the Pells. Gusty made his appearance in the course of the evening ; and we fellows went out with him.

The Squire was right : it was fast life at the Pells', and no mistake. I don't believe there was a thing that cost money but Fabian and Gusty Pell and Crayton went in for it. Crayton was with them always. He seemed to be the leader : the Pells followed him like sheep ; Tod went with them. I sometimes : but they did not always ask me to go. Billiards and cards were the chief amusements ; and there'd be theatres and singing-halls. The names of some of the places would have made the Squire's hair stand on end. One, a sort of private affair, that the Pells and Crayton said it was a favour to gain admittance to, was called "Paradise." Whether that was only the Pells' or Crayton's name for it, we did not hear. And a paradise it was when you were inside, if decorations and mirrors can make one. Men and women in evening dress sang songs in a kind of orchestra ; to which you might listen sitting and smoking or lounging about and talking : if you preferred a rubber at whist or a hand at écarté in another room, there you had it. Never a thing was there, apparently, that the Squire could reasonably have grumbled at, except the risk of losing money at cards, and the sense of intoxicating pleasure. But I don't think it was a good place to go to. The Pells called all this "Seeing Life."

It would not have done Tod much harm—for he had his head on his shoulders the right way—but for the gambling. It is a strong word to use ; but the play grew into nothing less. Had the Squire said to us, Take care you don't learn to gamble up in London, Tod would have resented it as much as if he had been warned not to go and hang himself, feeling certain that there was no more chance of one than the other. But gambling, like some other things—drinking for instance—steals upon you by degrees, too imperceptibly to alarm you. The Pells and Crayton and other

fellows that they knew went in for cards and billiards wholesale.
Tod was asked at first to take a quiet hand with them ; or just play
for the tables—and he thought no more of complying than if the
girls had pressed him to make one at the round game of Old Maid,
or to while away a wet afternoon at bagatelle.

There was no regularity in Mrs. Pell's household : there was no
more outward observance of religion than if we'd lived in Heathen-
dom. It was so different from Tod's last London visit, when he
was at the Whitneys'. *There* you had to be at the breakfast-table
to the moment—half-past eight ; and to be in at bedtime, unless
engaged out with friends. Sir John read a chapter of the Bible
morning and night, and then, pushing the spectacles lower on his
old red nose, he'd look over them at us and tell us simply to be good
boys and girls. *Here* you might come down at any hour, from nine
or ten, to eleven or twelve, and ring for fresh breakfast to be
supplied. As to staying out at night, that was quite ad libitum ; a
man-servant sat up till morning to open the door.

I was initiated less into the card-playing than Tod, and never
once was asked to make one at pool, probably because it was taken
for granted that I had less money to stake. Which was true. Tod
had not much, for the matter of that : and it never struck me to
think he was losing wholesale.

I got home one night at twelve, having been dining at Miss
Deveen's and going to a concert with her afterwards. Tod was not
in, and I sat up in our room, writing to Mr. Brandon, which I had
put off doing until I felt ashamed. Tod came in as I was folding
the letter. It was hot weather, and he stretched himself out at the
open window.

"Are you going to stop there all night, Tod?" I asked by-and-
by. "It's one o'clock."

"I may as well stop here, for all the sleep I shall get in bed,"
was his answer, as he brought his head in. "I'm in an awful mess,
Johnny."

"What kind of mess?"

"Debt."

"Debt! What for?"

"Card-playing," answered Tod, shortly. "And betting at pool.",

"Why do you play?"

"I'll be shot if I would ever have touched one of their cards, or
their billiard balls either, had I known what was to come of it.
Let me once get out of this hole, and neither Gusty Pell nor Crayton
shall ever draw me in again. I'll promise them *that.*"

"How much is it?"

"That I owe? Twenty-five pounds."

"Twenty-five—what?" I cried, starting up.

"Don't wake up the next room, Johnny. Twenty-five pounds.
And not a stiver in my pocket to go on with. I owe it to Crayton."

Sitting on the edge of his bed, he told me how the thing had
crept upon him. At first they only played for shillings; one night
Crayton suddenly changed the stakes to sovereigns. The other
fellows playing took it as a matter of course, and Tod did not like
to make a fuss, and get up——

"I should, Tod," I interrupted.

"I dare say you would," he retorted. "I didn't. But I honestly
told them that if I lost much, my purse would not stand it. Oh
that need not trouble you, they said. When we rose, that night, I
owed Crayton nineteen pounds.

"They must be systematic gamblers!"

"No, not that. Gentlemen who play high. Since then I have
played, hoping to redeem my losses—they tell me I shall be sure to
do it. But the redemption has not come yet, for it is twenty-five
pounds now."

"Tod," I said, after a pause, "it would about kill the Pater."

"It would awfully vex him. And that's what is doing the mischief, you see, Johnny. I can't write home for the money without
telling him what I want it for; he'd never give it me unless I said:
and I can't cut our visit short to the Pells and leave Crayton in
debt."

"But—*what's* to be done, Tod?"

"Nothing until I get some luck, and win enough back to pay
him."

"You may get deeper into the mire."

"Yes—there's that chance."

"It will never do to go on playing."

"Will you tell me what else I am to do? I must continue to
play : or pay."

I couldn't tell him; I didn't know. Fifty of the hardest pro-
blems in Euclid were nothing to this. Tod sat down in his shirt-
sleeves.

"Get one of the Pells to let you have the money, Tod. A loan
of twenty or thirty pounds can be nothing to them."

"It's no good, Johnny. Gusty is cleaned out. As to Fabian, he
never has any spare cash, what with one expensive habit and
another. Oh, I shall win it back again : perhaps to-morrow. Luck
must turn."

Tod said no more. But what particularly struck me was this:
that, to win money from a guest in that way, and he a young fellow
not of age, whose pocket-money they knew to be limited, was not
at all consistent with the idea of their being "gentlemen."

The next evening we were in a well-known billiard-room.

Fabian Pell, Crayton, and Tod were at pool. It had been a levee day, or something of that sort, and Fabian was in full regimentals. Tod was losing, as usual. He was no match for those practised players.

"I wish you would get me a glass of water, Johnny," he said.

So I got it. In turning back after taking the glass from his hand, who should I see on the high bench against the wall, sitting just where I had been sitting a minute before, but my guardian and trustee, Mr. Brandon. *Could* it be he? Old Brandon in London! and in a billiard-room.

"It is never you, sir! Here!"

"Yes, it is I, Johnny Ludlow," he said in his squeaky voice. "As to being here, I suppose I have as much right to be here as you have: perhaps rather more. I should like to ask what brings *you* here."

"I came in with those three," I said, pointing towards the board.

He screwed up his little eyes, and looked. "Who are they?" he asked. "Who's the fellow in scarlet?" For he did not happen to know these two younger Pells by sight.

"That's Fabian Pell, sir. The one standing with his hands in his pockets, near Joseph Todhetley, is the Honourable Mr. Crayton."

"Who's the Honourable Mr. Crayton?"

"I think his father is the Earl of Lackland."

"Oh, ah; one of Lackland's sons, is he? There's six or eight sons, of them, Johnny Ludlow, and not a silver coin amongst the lot. Lackland never had much, but what little it was he lost at horse-racing. The sons live by their wits, I've heard: lords' sons have not much work in them. The Honourable Mr. Crayton, eh! Your two friends had better take care of themselves."

The thought of how Tod had "taken care" of himself flashed into my mind. I wouldn't have old Brandon know it for the world.

"I posted a letter to you to-day, sir. I did not know you were from home."

"What was it about?"

"Nothing particular, sir. Only I had not written since we were in London."

"How long are you going to stay here, Johnny Ludlow?"

"About another week, I suppose."

"I mean *here*. In this disreputable room."

"Disreputable, sir!"

"Yes, Johnny Ludlow, disreputable. Disreputable for all young men, especially for a very young one like you. I wonder what your father would have said to it!"

"I, at least, sir, am doing no harm in it."

"Yes, you are, Johnny. You are suffering your eyes and mind

to grow familiar with these things. So, their game is over, is it!"

I turned round. They had finished, and were leaving. In looking for me, Tod saw Mr. Brandon. He came up to shake hands with him, and told me they were going.

"Come in and see me to-morrow morning, Johnny Ludlow," said Mr. Brandon, in a tone of command. "Eleven o'clock."

"Yes, sir. Where are you staying?"

"The Tavistock; Covent Garden."

"Johnny, what the mischief brings *him* here?" whispered Tod, as we went downstairs.

"I don't know. I thought it must be his ghost at first."

From the billiard-rooms we went on to Gusty's chambers, and found him at home with some friends. He served out wine, with cold brandy-and-water for Crayton—who despised anything less. They sat down to cards—loo. Tod did not play. Complaining of a racking headache, he sat apart in a corner. I stood in another, for all the chairs were occupied. Altogether the party seemed to want life, and broke up soon.

"Was it an excuse to avoid playing, Tod?" I asked, as we walked home.

"Was what an excuse?"

"Your headache."

"If your head were beating as mine is, Johnny, you wouldn't call it an excuse. You'll be a muff to the end of your days."

"Well, I thought it might be that."

"Did you! If I made up my mind not to play, I should tell it out straightforwardly: not put forth any shuffling 'excuse.'"

"Any way, a headache's better than losing your money."

"Don't bother."

I got to the Tavistock at five minutes past eleven, and found Mr. Brandon reading the *Times*. He looked at me over the top of it, as if he were surprised.

"So you *have* come, Mr. Johnny!"

"Yes, sir. I turned up the wrong street and missed my way: it has made me a little late."

"Oh, that's the reason, is it," said Mr. Brandon. "I thought perhaps a young man, who has been initiated into the ways of London life, might no longer consider it necessary to attend to the requests of his elders."

"But would you think that of me, sir?"

Mr. Brandon put the newspaper on the table with a dash, and burst out with as much feeling as his weak voice would allow him.

"Johnny Ludlow, I'd rather have seen you come to sweep a crossing in this vile town, than to frequent one of its public billiard-rooms!"

"But I don't frequent them, Mr. Brandon."

"How many times have you been in?"

"Twice in the one where you saw me: once in another. Three times in all."

"That's three times too much. Have you played?"

"No, sir; there's never any room for me."

"Do you bet?"

"Oh no."

"What do you go for, then?"

"I've only gone in with the others when I have been out with them."

"Pell's sons and the Honourable Mr. Crayton. Rather ostentatious of you, Johnny Ludlow, to hasten to tell me he was the 'Honourable.'"

My face flushed. I had not said it in that light.

"One day at Pershore Fair, in a booth, the clown jumped on to the boards and introduced himself," continued Mr. Brandon: "'I'm the clown, ladies and gentlemen,' said he. That's the Honourable Mr. Crayton, say you.—And so you have gone in with Mr. Crayton and the Pells!"

"And with Joseph Todhetley."

"Ay. And perhaps London will do him more harm than it will you; you're not much better than a boy yet, hardly up to bad things. I wonder what possessed Joe's father to let you two come up to stay with the Pells! I should have been above it in his place."

"Above it? Why, Mr. Brandon, they live in ten times the style we do."

"And spend twenty times as much over it. Who was thinking about style or cost, Mr. Johnny? Don't you mistake Richard for Robert."

He gave a flick to the newspaper, and stared me full in the face. I did not venture to speak.

"Johnny Ludlow, I don't like your having been initiated into the iniquities of fast life—as met with in billiard-rooms, and similar places."

"I have got no harm from them, sir."

"Perhaps not. But you might have got it."

I supposed I might: and thought of Tod and his losings.

"You have good principles, Johnny Ludlow, and you've a bit of sense in your head; and you have been taught to know that this world is not the end of things. Temptation is bad for the best,

though. When I saw you in that place last night, looking on with
eager eyes at the balls, listening to the betting, I wished I had never
let your father make me your guardian."

"I did not know my eyes or ears were so eager, sir. I don't
think they were."

"Nonsense, boy: that goes as a matter of course. You have
heard of gambling hells?"

"Yes, sir."

"Well, a public billiard-room is not many degrees better. It is
crowded with adventurers who live by their wits. Your needy
'honourables,' who've not a sixpence of their own in their purses,
and your low-lived blackguards, who have sprung from the scum of
the population, are equally at home there. These men, the lord's
son and the blackguard, must each make a living: whether by turf-
betting, or dice, or cards, or pool—they must do it somehow. Is it
a nice thing, pray, for you honest young fellows to frequent places
where you must be their boon companions?"

"No, I don't think it is."

"Good, Johnny. Don't you go into one again—and keep young
Todhetley out if you can. It is no place, I say, for an honest man
and a gentleman: you can't touch pitch and not be defiled; neither
can a youngster frequent these billiard-rooms and the company he
meets in them, and come away unscathed. His name will get a
mark against it. That's not the worst: his *soul* may get a mark
upon it; and never be able to throw it off again during life. You
turn mountebank, and dance at wakes, Johnny, rather than turn
public billiard player. There's many an honest mountebank, dancing
for the daily crust he puts into his mouth: I don't believe you'd find
one honest man amongst billiard sharpers."

He dropped the paper in his heat. I picked it up.

"And that's only one phase of their fast life, these billiard-rooms,"
he continued. "There are other things: singing-halls, and cider
cellars—and all sorts of places. You steer clear of the lot, Johnny.
And warn Todhetley. He wants warning perhaps more than
you do."

"Tod has caught no harm, I think, except——"

"Except what?" asked he sharply, as I paused.

"Except that I suppose it costs him money, sir."

"Just so. A good thing too. If these seductions (as young fools
call them) could be had without money, the world would soon
be turned upside down. But as to harm, Johnny, once a young
fellow gets to feel at home in these places, I don't care how short
his experience may be, he loses his self-respect. He does; and it
takes time to get it back again. You and Joe had not been gone
five minutes last night, with your 'Honourable' and the other fellow

in scarlet, when there was a row in the room. Two men quarrelled about a bet; sides were taken by the spectators, and it came to blows. I have heard some reprobate language in my day, Johnny Ludlow, but I never heard such as I heard then. Had you been there, I'd have taken you by the back of the neck and pitched you out of the window, before your ears should have been tainted with it."

"Did you go to the billiard-room, expecting to see me there, Mr. Brandon?" I asked. And the question put his temper up.

"Go to the billiard-room, expecting to see *you* there, Johnny Ludlow!" he retorted, his voice a small shrill pipe. "How dare you ask it? I'd as soon have expected to see the Bishop of London there, as you. I can tell you what, young man: had I known you were going to these places, I should pretty soon have stopped it. Yes, sir: you are not out of my hands yet. If I could not stop you personally, I'd stop every penny of your pocket-money."

"We couldn't think—I and Tod—what else you had gone for sir," said I, in apology for having put the question.

"I don't suppose you could. I have a graceless relative, Johnny Ludlow; a sister's son. He is going to the bad, fast, and she got me to come up and see what he was after. I could not find him; I have not found him yet; but I was told that he frequented those rooms, and I went there on speculation. Now you know. He came up to London nine months ago as pure-hearted a young fellow as you are: bad companions laid hold of him, and are doing their best to ruin him. I should not like to see *you* on the downward road, Johnny; and you shan't enter on it if I can put a spoke in the wheel. Your father was my good friend."

"There is no fear for me, Mr. Brandon."

"Well, Johnny, I hope not. You be cautious, and come and dine with me this evening. And now will you promise me one thing: if you get into any trouble or difficulty at any time, whether it's a money trouble, or what not, you come to me with it. Do you hear?"

"Yes, sir. I don't know any one I would rather take it to."

"I do not expect you to get into one willingly, mind. *That's* not what I mean: but sometimes we fall into pits through other people. If ever you do, though it were years to come, bring the trouble to me."

And I promised, and went, according to the invitation, to dine with him in the evening. He had found his nephew: a plain young medical student, with a thin voice like himself. Mr. Brandon dined off boiled scrag of mutton; I and the nephew had soup and fish and fowl and plum pudding.

After that evening I did not see anything more of old Brandon.

Upon calling at the Tavistock they said he had left for the rest of the week, but would be back on the following Monday.

And it was on the following Monday that Tod's affairs came to a climax.

We had had a regal entertainment. Fit for regal personages— as it seemed to us simple country people, inexperienced in London dinner giving. Mrs. Pell headed her table in green gauze, gold beetles in her hair, and a feathered-fan dangling. Mr. Pell, who had come to town for the party, faced her; the two girls, the two sons, and the guests were dispersed on either side. Eighteen of us in all. Crayton was there as large as life, and of the other people I did not know all the names. The dinner was given for some great gun who had to do with railway companies. He kept it waiting twenty minutes, and then loomed in with a glistening bald head, and a yellow rose in his coat: his wife, a very little woman in pink, on his arm.

"I saw your father yesterday," called out Pell down the table to Tod. "He said he was glad to hear you were enjoying your-selves."

"Ah—yes—thank you," replied Tod, in a hesitating sort of way. I don't know what *he* was thinking of; but it flashed into my mind that the Squire would have been anything but "glad," had he known about the cards, and the billiards, and the twenty-five-pound debt.

Dinner came to an end at last, and we found a few evening guests in the drawing-room—mostly young ladies. Some of the dinner people went away. The railway man sat whispering with Pell in a corner: his wife nodded asleep, and woke up to talk by fits and starts. The youngest girl, Rose, who was in the drawing-room with Leonora and the governess, ran up to me.

"Please let me be your partner, Mr. Ludlow! They are going to dance a quadrille in the back drawing-room."

So I took her, and we had the quadrille. Then another, that I danced with Constance. Tod was not to be seen anywhere.

"I wonder what has become of Todhetley?"

"He has gone out with Gusty and Mr. Crayton, I think," answered Constance. "It is too bad of them."

By one o'clock all the people had left; the girls and Mrs. Pell said good night and disappeared. In going up to bed, I met one of the servants.

"Do you know what time Mr. Todhetley went out, Richard?"

"Mr. Todhetley, sir? He has not gone out. He is in the

smoking-room with Mr. Augustus and Mr. Crayton. I've just taken up some soda-water."

I went on to the smoking-room: a small den, built out on the leads of the second floor, that no one presumed to enter except Gusty and Fabian. The cards lay on the table in a heap, and the three round it were talking hotly. I could see there had been a quarrel. Some stranger had come in, and was standing with his back to the mantel-piece. They called him Temply; a friend of Crayton's. Temply was speaking as I opened the door.

"It is clearly a case of obligation to go on; of honour. No good in trying to shirk it, Todhetley."

"I will not go on," said Tod, as he tossed back his hair from his hot brow with a desperate hand. "If you increase the stakes without my consent, I have a right to refuse to continue playing. As to honour, I know what that is as well as any one here."

They saw me then: and none of them looked too well pleased. Gusty asked me what I wanted; but he spoke quite civilly.

"I came to see after you all. Richard said you were here."

What they had been playing at, I don't know: whether whist, écarté, loo, or what. Tod, as usual, had been losing frightfully: I could see that. Gusty was smoking; Crayton, cool as a cucumber, drank hard at brandy-and-soda. If that man had swallowed a barrel of cognac, he would never have shown it. Temply and Crayton stared at me rudely. Perhaps they thought I minded it.

"I wouldn't play again to-night, were I you," I said aloud to Tod.

"No, I won't; there," he cried, giving the cards an angry push. "I am sick of the things—and tired to death. Good night to you all."

Crayton swiftly put his back against the door, barring Tod's exit. "You cannot leave before the game's finished, Todhetley."

"We had not begun the game," rejoined Tod. "*You* stopped it by trebling the stakes. I tell you, Crayton, I'll not play again to-night."

"Then perhaps you'll pay me your losses."

"How much are they?" asked Tod, biting his lips.

"To-night?—or in all, do you mean?"

"Oh, let us have it all," was Tod's answer; and I saw that he had great difficulty in suppressing his passion. All of them, except Crayton, seemed tolerably heated. "You know that I have not the ready-money to pay you; you've known that all along: but it's as well to ascertain how we stand."

Crayton had been coolly turning over the leaves of a note-case, adding up some figures there, below his breath.

"Eighty-five before, and seven to-night makes just ninety-two. Ninety-two pounds, Todhetley."

I sprang up from the chair in terror. It was as if some blast had swept over me. "Ninety-two pounds! Tod! do you owe *that?*"

"I suppose I do."

"*Ninety-two pounds!* It cannot be. Why, it is close upon a hundred!" Crayton laughed at my consternation, and Temply stared.

"If you'll go on playing, you may redeem some of it, Todhetley," said Crayton. "Come, sit down."

"I will not touch another card to-night," said he, doggedly. "I have said it: and I am not one to break my word: as Johnny Ludlow here can testify to. I don't know that I shall play again after to-night."

Crayton was offended. Cool though he was, I think he was somewhat the worse for what he had taken—perhaps they all were. "Then you'll make arrangements for paying your debts," said he, in scornful tones.

"Yes, I'll do that," answered Tod. And he got away. So did I, after a minute or two: Gusty kept me, talking.

In passing upstairs, for we slept on the third floor, Mr. Pell came suddenly out of a room on the left; a candle in one hand and some papers in the other, and a look on his face as of some great trouble.

"What! are you young men not in bed yet?" he exclaimed. "It is late."

"We are going up now. Is anything the matter, sir?" I could not help asking.

"The matter?" he repeated.

"I thought you looked worried."

"I am worried with work," he said, laughing slightly. "While others take their rest, I have to be up at my books and letters. Great wealth brings great care with it, Johnny Ludlow, and hard work as well. Good night, my lad."

Tod was pacing the room with his hands in his pockets. It was a terrible position for him to be in. Owing a hundred pounds —to put it in round numbers—for a debt of honour. No means of his own, not daring to tell his father. I mounted on the iron rail of my little bed opposite the window, and looked at him.

"Tod, what *is* to be done?"

"For two pins I'd go and enlist in some African regiment," growled he. "Once over the seas, I should be lost to the world here, and my shame with me."

"Shame!"

"Well, and it is shame. An ordinary debt that you can't pay is bad enough ; but a debt of honour—— "

He stopped, and caught his breath with a sort of sob—as if there were no word strong enough to express the sense of shame.

" It will never do to tell the Pater."

" Tell *him !* " he exclaimed sharply. " Johnny, I'd cut off my right hand—I'd fling myself into the Thames, rather than bring such a blow on him."

" Well, and so I think would I."

" It would kill him as sure as we are here, Johnny. He would look upon it that I have become a confirmed gambler, and I believe the shock and grief would be such that he'd die of it. No : I have not been so particularly dutiful a son, that I should bring *that* upon him."

I balanced myself on the bed-rail. Tod paced the carpet slowly.

" No, never," he repeated, as if there had not been any pause. " I would rather die myself."

" But what is to be done ? "

" Heaven knows ! I wish the Pells had been far enough before they had invited us up."

" I wish you had never consented to play with the lot at all, Tod. You might have stood out from the first."

" Ay. But one glides into these things unconsciously. Johnny, I begin to think Crayton is just a gambler, playing to win, and nothing better."

" Playing for his bread. That is, for the things that constitute it. His drink, and his smoke, and his lodgings, and his boots, and his rings. Old Brandon said it. As to his dinners, he generally gets them at friends' houses."

" Old Brandon said it, did he ? "

" Why, I told you so the same day. And you bade me shut up."

" Do you know what they want me to do, Johnny ? To sign a post-obit bond for two hundred, or so, to be paid after my father's death. It's true. Crayton will let me off then."

" And will you do it ? " I cried, feeling that my eyes blazed as I leaped down.

" No, I *won't :* and I told them so to-night. That's what the quarrel was about. ' Every young fellow does it whose father lives too long and keeps him out of his property,' said that Temply. ' May be so ; I won't,' I answered. Neither will I. I'd rather break stones on the road than speculate upon the good Pater's death, or anticipate his money in that manner to hide my sins."

" Gusty Pell ought to help you."

" Gusty says he can't. Fabian, I believe, really can't ; he is in

difficulties of his own: and sometimes, Johnny, I fancy Gus is.
Crayton fleeces them both, unless I am mistaken. Yes, he's a
sharper; I see through him now. I want him to take my I O U
to pay him as soon as I can, and he knows I would do it, but he
won't do that. There's two o'clock."

It was of no use sitting up, and I began to undress. The
question reiterated itself again and again—what was to be done?
I lay awake all night thinking, vainly wishing I was of age.
Fanciful thoughts crossed my mind: of appealing to rich old Pell,
and asking him to lend the money, not betraying Gusty and the
rest by saying what it was wanted for; of carrying the story to
Miss Deveen, and asking her; and lastly, of going to old Brandon,
and getting *him* to help. I grew to think that I *would* do this,
however much I disliked it, and try Brandon; that it lay in my
duty to do so.

Worn and haggard enough looked Tod the next morning. He
had sat up nearly all night. When breakfast was over, I started
for the Tavistock, whispering a word to Tod first.

"Avoid the lot to-day, Tod. I'll try and help you out of the
mess."

He burst out laughing in the midst of his perplexity. " *You,*
Johnny! what next?"

" Remember the fable of the lion and the mouse."

" But you can never be the mouse in this, you mite of a boy!
Thank you all the same, Johnny: you mean it well."

"Can I see Mr. Brandon?" I asked at the hotel, of a strange
waiter.

"Mr. Brandon, sir? He is not staying here."

"Not staying here!"

"No, sir, he left some days ago."

"But I thought he was coming back again."

"So I believe he is, sir. But he has not come yet."

"Do you know where he is?"

"At Brighton, sir."

It was about as complete a floorer as I ever wished to get. All
the way along, I had been planning which way to break it to him.
I turned from the door, whistling and thinking. Should I go after
him to Brighton? I had the money, and the time, why should I
not do so? Heaven alone knew how much depended upon Tod's
being released from trouble; Heaven alone knew what desperate
course he might take in his shame, if not released from it.

Dropping a note to Tod, saying I should be out for the day, and
getting a porter to take it up, I made the best of my way to the
nearest Brighton station, and found a train just starting. Brighton
was a large place, and they could not tell me at the Tavistock what

hotel Mr. Brandon was staying at; except that one of the waiters "thought" it might be the Old Ship. And that's where I first went, on arrival.

No. No one of the name of Brandon was at the Old Ship. So there I was, like an owl in a desert, wondering where to go next.

And how many hotels and inns I tried before I found him, it would be impossible to remember now. One of the last was up Kemp Town way—the Royal Crescent Hotel.

"Is Mr. Brandon staying here?"

"Mr. Brandon of Warwickshire? Yes, sir."

It was so very unexpected an answer after all the failures, that I hardly believed my own ears. Mr. Brandon was not well, the waiter added: suffering from cold and sore throat—but he supposed I could see him. I answered that I must see him; I had come all the way from London on purpose.

Old Brandon was sitting in a long room, with a bow-window looking out on the sea; some broth at his elbow, and a yellow silk handkerchief resting cornerwise on his head.

"Mr. Ludlow, sir," said the waiter. And he dropped the spoon into the broth, and stared at me as if I were an escaped lunatic.

"Why!—you! What on earth brings *you* here, Johnny Ludlow?"

To tell him what, was the hardest task I'd ever had in my life. And I did it badly. Sipping spoonfuls of broth and looking hard at me whilst he listened, did not help the process. I don't know how I got it out, or how confused was the way I told him that I wanted a hundred pounds of my own money.

"A hundred pounds, eh?" said he. "You are a nice gentleman, Johnny Ludlow!"

"I am very sorry, sir, to have to ask it. The need is very urgent, or I should not do so."

"What's it for?" questioned he.

"I—it is to pay a debt, sir," I answered, feeling my face flush hot.

"Whose debt?"

By the way he looked at me, I could see that he knew as plainly as though I had told him, that it was not my debt. And yet—but for letting him think it was mine, he might turn a deaf ear to me. Old Brandon finished up his broth, and put the basin down.

"You are a clever fellow, Johnny Ludlow, but not quite clever enough to deceive me. You'd no more get into such debt yourself, than I should. I have a better opinion of you than that. Who has sent you here?"

"Indeed, sir, I came of my own free will. No one knows, even, that I have come. Mr. Brandon, I hope you will help me: it is almost a matter of life or death."

"You are wasting words and time, Johnny Ludlow."

And I felt I was. Felt it hopelessly.

"There's an old saying, and a very good one, Johnny—Tell the whole truth to your lawyer and doctor. I am neither a lawyer nor a doctor: but I promise you this much, that unless you tell me the truth of the matter, every word of it, and explain your request fully and clearly, you may go marching back to London."

There was no help for it. I spoke a few words, and they were quite enough. He seemed to grasp the situation as by magic, and turned me, as may be said, inside out. In five minutes he knew by heart as much of it as I did.

"So!" said he, in his squeaky voice—ten times more squeaky when he was vexed. "Good! A nice nest you have got amongst. Want him to give post-obit bonds, do they! Which *is* Todhetley—a knave or a fool?"

"He has refused to give the bonds, I said, sir."

"Bonds, who's talking of bonds?" he retorted. "For playing, *I* mean. He must have been either a knave or a fool, to play till he owed a hundred pounds when he knew he had not the means to pay."

"But I have explained how it was, sir. He lost, and then played on, hoping to redeem his losses. I think Crayton had him fast, and would not let him escape."

"Ay. Got him, and kept him. That's your grand friend, the Honourable, Johnny Ludlow. There: give me the newspaper."

"But you will let me have the money, sir?"

"Not if I know it."

It was a woeful check. I set on and begged as if I had been begging for life: saying I hardly knew what. That it might save Tod from a downhill course—and spare grief to the poor old Squire—and pain to me. Pain that would lie on my mind always, knowing that I possessed the money, yet might not use it to save him.

"It's of no use, Johnny. I have been a faithful guardian to you, and done well by your property. Could your dead father look back on this world and see the income you'll come into when you are of age, he would know I speak the truth. You cannot suppose I should waste any portion of it, I don't care how slight a one, in paying young men's wicked gambling debts."

I prayed him still. I asked him to put himself in my place and see if he would not feel as I felt. I said that I should never —as I truly believed—have an opportunity of spending money that would give me half the pleasure of this, or do half the good. Be-

sides, it was only a loan : Tod was sure to repay it when he could.
No : old Brandon was hard as flint. He got up] and rang the
bell.

"We'll drop it, Johnny. What will you take? Have you had
anything since breakfast?"

"No, sir. But I don't want anything."

"Bring up dinner for this young gentleman," he said, when the
waiter appeared. "Anything you have that's *good*. And be quick
about it, please."

They brought up a hastily prepared dinner : and very good it was.
But I could scarcely eat for sorrow. Old Brandon, nursing himself
at the opposite end of the table, the yellow handkerchief on his head,
looked at me all the while.

"Johnny Ludlow, do you know what I think—that you'd give
away your head if it were loose. It's a good thing you have me to
take care of you."

"No, sir, I should not. If you would let me have this hundred
pounds—it is really only ninety-two, though—I would repay it with
two hundred when I came of age."

"Like the simpleton you are."

"I think I would give half my money, Mr. Brandon, to serve Todhetley in this strait. We are as brothers."

"No doubt you would : but you've not got it to give, Johnny.
You can let him fight his own battles."

"And I would if he were able to fight them : but he is not
able; it's an exceptional case. I must go back to London, and try
there."

Old Brandon opened his eyes. "How?"

"I think perhaps Miss Deveen would let me have the money.
She is rich and generous—and I will tell her the whole truth.
It is a turning-point in Todhetley's life, sir : help would save
him."

"How do you know but he'd return to the mire? Let him have
this money, and he might go on gambling and lose another hundred.
Perhaps hundreds at the back of it."

"No, sir, that he never would. He may go deeper into the mire
if he does not get it. Enlist, or something."

"Are you going already, Johnny?"

"Yes, sir. I must catch the next train, and it's a good way to the
station."

"You can take a fly. Wait a few minutes."

He went into his bedroom, on the same floor. When he came back,
he held a piece of paper in his hand.

"There, Johnny. But it is my loan ; not yours."

It was a cheque for a hundred pounds. He had listened, after all! The surprise was so great that I am afraid my eyes were dim.

"The loan is mine, Johnny," he repeated. "I am not going to risk your money, and prove myself a false trustee. When Todhetley can repay it, it will be to me, not to you. But now—understand: unless he gives you a solemn promise never to play with that 'Honourable' again, or with either of the Pells, *you will not use the cheque*, but return it to me."

"Oh, Mr. Brandon, there will be no difficulty. He only wants to be quit of them."

"Get his promise, I say. If he gives it, present this cheque at Robarts's in Lombard Street to-morrow, and they'll pay you the money over the counter."

"It is made out to my order!" I said, looking at the cheque: "not to Crayton!"

"To Crayton!" retorted Mr. Brandon. "I wouldn't let a cheque of mine, uncrossed, fall into *his* hands. He might add an ought or two to the figures. I drew it out for an even hundred, you see: the odd money may be wanted. You'll have to sign your name at the back: do it at the bank. And now, do you know why I have let you have this?"

I looked at him in doubt.

"Because you have obeyed the injunctions I gave you—to bring any difficulty you might have to me. I certainly never expected it so soon, or that it would take this form. Don't you get tumbling into another. Let people take care of themselves. There: put it into your breast-pocket, and be off."

I don't know how I got back to town. There was no accident, and we were not pitched into next week. If we had been, I'm not sure that I should have minded it; for that cheque in my pocket seemed a panacea for all human ills. The Pells were at dinner when I entered: and Tod was lying outside his bed, with one of his torturing headaches. He did not often have them: which was a good thing, for they were rattlers. Taking his hand from his head, he glanced at me.

"Where have you been all day, Johnny?" he asked, hardly able to speak. "That was a short note of yours."

"I've been to Brighton."

Tod opened his eyes again with surprise. He did not believe it.

"Why don't you say Bagdad, at once? Keep your counsel, if you choose, lad. I'm too ill to get it out of you."

"But I don't want to keep it: and I have been to Brighton. Had dinner there, too. Tod, old fellow, the mouse has done his work. Here's a cheque for you for a hundred pounds."

He looked at it as I held it out to him, saw it was true, and then sprang off the bed. I had seen glad emotion in my life, even at that early period of it, but hardly such as Tod's then. Never a word spoke he.

" It is lent by Mr. Brandon to you, Tod. He bade me say it. I could not get any of mine out of him. The only condition is—that, before I cash it, you shall promise not to play again with Crayton or the Pells."

" I'll promise it now. Glad to do it. Long live old Brandon! Johnny, my good brother, I'm too ill to thank you—my temples seem as if they were being split with a sledge-hammer—but you have *saved* me."

I was at Robarts's when it opened in the morning. And signed my name at the back of the cheque, and got the money. Fancy *me* having a hundred pounds paid to me in notes and gold! The Squire would have thought the world was coming to an end.

XXII.

OUR STRIKE.

IT was September, and they were moving to Crabb Cot for a week or two's shooting. The shooting was not bad about there, and the Squire liked a turn with his gun yet. Being close on the Michaelmas holidays, Tod and I were with them.

When the stay was going to be short, the carriages did not come over from Dyke Manor. On arriving at South Crabb station, there was a fly waiting. It would not take us all. Mr. and Mrs. Todhetley, the two children, and Hannah got into it, and some of the luggage was put on the top.

"You two boys can walk," said the Pater. "It will stretch your legs."

And a great deal rather walk, too, than be boxed up in a crawling fly!

We took the way through Crabb Lane: the longest but merriest, for it was always lively with noise and dirt. Reports had gone abroad long before that Crabb Lane was "out on strike:" Tod and I thought we would take a look at it in this new aspect.

There were some great works in the vicinity—I need not state here their exact speciality—and the men employed at them chiefly inhabited Crabb Lane. It was setting-up these works that caused the crowded dwellings in Crabb Lane to be built—for where a number of workmen congregate together, habitations must of necessity follow.

You have heard of Crabb Lane before—in connection with what I once told you about Harry Lease the pointsman. It was a dingy, over-populated, bustling place, prosperous on the whole, its inhabitants as a rule well-to-do. A strike was quite a new feature, bringing to most of them a fresh experience in life. England had strikes in those past days, but they were not common.

Crabb Lane during working hours had hitherto been given over to the children, who danced in the gutters and cried and screamed themselves hoarse. Women also would be out of doors, idling away their time in gossip, or else calling across to each other from the windows. But now, as I and Tod went down it, things looked different. Instead of women and children, men were there. Every individual man, I believe, out of every house the lane contained; for there appeared to be shoals of them. They lounged idly against the walls, or stood about in groups. Some with pipes, some without; some laughing and jeering, apparently in the highest spirits, as if they had climbed the tree of fortune; some silent and anxious-looking.

"Well, Hoar, how are you?"

It was Tod who spoke. The man he addressed, Jacob Hoar, was one of the best of the workmen: a sober, steady, honest fellow, with a big frame and a resolute face. He had the character of being fierce in temper, sometimes savage with his fellow-men, if put out. Alfred Hoar—made pointsman at the station in poor Harry Lease's place—was his brother.

Hoar did not answer Tod at all. He was standing quite alone near the door of his house, a strangely defiant look upon his pale face, and his firm lips drawn in. Unless I was mistaken, some of the men over the way were taking covert glances at him, as though he were a kangaroo they had to keep aloof from. Hoar turned his eyes slowly upon us, took off his round felt hat, and smoothed back his dark hair.

"I be as well as matters 'll let me be, young Mr. Todhetley," he then said.

"There's a strike going on, I hear," said Tod. "Has been for some time."

"Yes, there's a strike a-going on," assented Hoar, speaking in a deliberate, sullen manner, as a man resenting some special grievance. "Has been for some time, as you say. And I don't know when the strike 'll be a-going off."

"How is Eliza?" I asked.

"Much as usual, Mr. Johnny. What should ail her?"

Evidently there was no sociability to be got out of Jacob Hoar that afternoon, and we left him. A few yards further, we passed Ford's, the baker's. No end of heads were at the shop door, and *they* seemed to be staring at Hoar.

"He must have been dealing out a little abuse to the public generally, Tod," said I.

"Very likely," answered Tod. "He seems bursting with some rage or other."

"Nay, I don't think it's rage so much as vexation. Something must have gone wrong."

"Well, perhaps so."

"Look here, Tod. If we had a home to keep up and a lot of mouths to feed and weekly rent to pay, and a strike stopped the supplies, we might be in a worse humour than Hoar is."

"Right, Johnny." And Tod went off at a strapping pace.

How it may be with other people, I don't know: but when I get back to a place after an absence, I want to see every one, and am apt to go dashing in at doors without warning.

"It won't take us a minute to look in on Miss Timmens, Tod," I said, as we neared the school-house. "She'll tell us the news of the whole parish."

"Take the minute, then, if you like," said Tod. "I am not going to bother myself with Miss Timmens."

Neither perhaps should I, after that, for Tod swayed me still ; but in passing the door it was opened wide by one of the little scholars. Miss Timmens sat in her chair, the lithe, thin cane, three yards long, raised in her hand, its other end descending, gently enough on the shoulders of a chattering girl.

"I don't keep it to beat 'em," Miss Timmens was wont to say of her cane, "but just to tap 'em into attention when they are beyond the reach of my hand." And, to give her her due, it was nothing more.

"It's you, is it, Master Johnny ? I heard you were all expected."

"It's me, safe enough. How goes the world with you, Miss Timmens ? "

"Cranky," was the short answer. "South Crabb's going out of its senses, I think. The parson is trying to introduce fresh ways and doings, in my school: new-fangled rubbish, Master Johnny, that will bring more harm than good. I won't have it, and so he and I are at daggers drawn. And there's a strike in the place ! "

I nodded. While she spoke, it had struck me, looking at the room, that it was not so full as usual.

"It's the strike does that," she said, in a sort of triumph. " It's the strike that works all the ill and every kind of evil "—and it was quite evident the strike found no more favour with her than the parson's fresh ways.

"But what has the strike to do with the children's absence from school ? "

"The strike has carried all the children's best things to the pawn-shop, and they've nothing decent left to come abroad in. That is one cause, Johnny Ludlow," she concluded, very tartly.

"Is there any other ? "

"Don't you think that sufficient? I am not going to let them appear before me in rags—and so Crabb Lane knows. But there is another cause, sir. This strike has so altered the course of things that the whole order of ordinary events is turned upside down. Even if the young ones' frocks were home again, it would be ten to one against their coming to school."

"I don't see the two little Hoars." And why I had been looking for those particular children I can't say, unless it was that Hoar and his peculiar manner had been floating in my mind ever since we passed him.

"'Liza and Jessy—no, but they've been here till to-day," was the reply, given after a long pause. "Are you going, Mr. Johnny?—I'll just step outside with you."

She drew the door close behind her, keeping the handle in her hand, and looked straight into my face.

"Jacob Hoar has gone and beat his boy almost to death this morning—and the strike's the cause of *that*," she whispered, emphatically.

"Jacob Hoar has!—Why, how came he to do it?"—I exclaimed, recalling more forcibly than ever the man's curious look, and the curious looks of the other men holding aloof from him. "Which of his boys is it?"

"The second of them; little Dick. Yes, he is black and blue all over, they say; next door to beat to death; and his arm's broken. And they have the strike to thank for it."

She repeated the concluding words more stingingly than before. That Miss Timmens was wroth with the strike, there could be no mistake. I asked her why the strike was to be thanked for the beating and the broken arm.

"Because the strike has brought misery; and *that* is the source of all the ill going on just now in Crabb Lane," was her reply. "When the men threw themselves out of work, of course they threw themselves out of wages. Some funds have been furnished to them, weekly I believe, from the Trades Union League—or whatever they call the thing—but it seems a mere nothing compared with what they used to earn. Household goods, as well as clothes, have been going to the pawn-shop; but they have now pledged all they've got to pledge, and are, it is said, in sore straits: mothers and fathers and children alike hungry. It is some time now since they have had enough to eat. Fancy that, Mr. Johnny!"

"But why should Dicky be beaten for that?" I persisted, trying to keep her to the point—a rather difficult matter with Miss Timmens at all times.

"It was in this way," she answered, dropping her voice to a lower key, and giving a pull at the door to make sure it had not opened. "Dicky, poor fellow, is half starved; he's not used to it, and feels it keenly: resents it, I dare say. This morning, when out in the lane, he saw a tray of halfpenny buns, hot from the oven, put on old Ford's counter. The sight was too much for him, the temptation too great. Dicky Hoar is naturally honest; has been, up to now, at all events: but I suppose hunger was stronger than honesty to-day. He crept into the shop on all fours, abstracted a bun with his fingers, and was creeping out again, when Ford pounced upon him, bun in hand. There was a fine outcry. Ford was harsh, roared out for the policeman, and threatened him with jail, and in the midst of the commotion Hoar came up. In his mortification at hearing that a boy of his had been caught pilfering, he seized upon a thick stick that a bystander happened to have, and laid it unmercifully upon poor Dick."

"And broke his arm?"

"And broke his arm. And covered him with weals beside. He'll be all manner of colours to-morrow."

"What a brutal fellow Hoar must be!"

"To beat him like that?—well, yes," assented Miss Timmens, in accents that bore rather a dubious sound. "Passion must have blinded him and urged him further than he intended. The man has always been upright; prided himself on being so, as one may say; and there's no doubt that to find his child could be a thief shook him cruelly. This strike is ruining the tempers of the men; it makes them feel at war with everything and everybody."

When I got home I found them in the thick of the news also, for Cole the doctor was there telling it all. Mrs. Todhetley, sitting on the sofa with her bonnet untied and her shawl unpinned, was listening in a kind of horror.

"But surely the arm cannot be *broken*, Mr. Cole!" she urged.

"Broken just above the wrist, ma'am. I ought to know, for I set it. Wicked little rascal, to steal the bun! As to Hoar, he is as fierce as a tiger when really enraged."

"Well, it sounds very shocking."

"So it does," said Cole. "I think perhaps it may be productive of one good—keep the boy from picking and stealing to the end of his life."

"He was hungry, you say."

"Famished, ma'am. Most of the young ones in Crabb Lane are so just now."

The Squire was walking up and down the room, his hands in his pockets. He halted, and faced the Doctor.

"Look here, Cole—what has brought this state of things about? A strike!—and prolonged! Why, I should as soon have expected to hear the men had thrown up their work to become Merry Andrews! Who is in fault?—the masters or the men?"

Cole lifted his eyebrows. "The masters lay the blame on the men, the men lay it on the masters."

"What is it the men are holding out for?"

"To get more wages, and to do less work."

"Oh, come, that's a twofold demand," cried the Pater. "Modest folk generally ask for one favour at a time. Meanwhile things are all at sixes-and-sevens, I suppose, in Crabb Lane?"

"Ay," said the Doctor. "At worse than sixes-and-sevens, indoors and out. There are empty cupboards and empty rooms within; and there's a good deal of what's bad without. It's the wives and children that suffer, poor things." ·

"The men must be senseless to throw themselves out of work!"

"The men only obey orders," cried Mr. Cole. "There's a spirit of disaffection abroad: certain people have constituted themselves rulers, and they say to the men, 'You must do this,' and 'You must not do that.' The men have yielded themselves up to be led, and *do* do what they are told, right or wrong."

"I don't say they are wrong to try to get more wages if they can; it would be odd if we were to be debarred from bettering ourselves," spoke the Squire. "But to throw up their work whilst they are trying, there's the folly; there's where the shoe must tighten. Let them keep on their work whilst they agitate."

"They'd tell you, I expect, that the masters would be less likely to listen then than they are now."

"Well, they've no right, in common sense, to throw up their wives' and children's living, if they do their own," concluded the Squire.

Cole nodded. "There's some truth in that," he said as he got up to leave. "Any way, things are more gloomy with us than you'd believe, Squire."

You may remember that I told you, when speaking of the Court and my early home, how, when I was a little child of four years old, Hannah my nurse, and Eliza one of her fellow-servants, commented freely in my hearing on my father's second marriage, and shook me well because I was wise enough to understand them. Eliza was then housemaid at the Court; and soon after this she had left it to marry Jacob Hoar. She was a nice sort of young woman (in spite of the shaking), and I kept up a great acquaintance with her, and was free, so to say, of her house in Crabb Lane, running in and out of it at will, when we were at Crabb Cot. A tribe of little Hoars arrived, one after another. Jacky, the eldest, over ten now, had a place at the works, and earned two shillings a week. "'Twarn't much," said Hoar the father, "but 'twas bringing his hand in." Dick, the second, he who had just had the beating, was nine; two girls came next, and there was a young boy of three.

Hoar earned capital wages—to judge by the comfortable way in which they lived: I should think not less than forty shillings a week. Of course they spent it all, every fraction; as a rule, families of that class never put by for a rainy day. They might have done it, I suppose; in those days provisions were nothing like as dear as they are now; the cost of living altogether was less.

Of course the Hoars had to suffer in common with the rest under the strike. But I did not like to hear of empty cupboards in connection with Eliza; no, nor of her boy's broken arm; and in the evening I went back to Crabb Lane to see her. They lived next door but one to the house that had been Lease the pointsman's; but theirs was far better than that tumble-down hut.

Well, it was a change! The pretty parlour looked half dismantled. Its ornaments and best things had gone, as Miss Timmens expressed it, to adorn the pawnshop. The carpet also. Against the wall, on a small mattress brought down for him, lay Dicky and his bruises. Some of the children sat on the floor: Mrs. Hoar was kneeling over Dicky and bathing his cheek, which was big enough for two, for it had caught the stick kindly.

"Well, Eliza!"

She got up, sank into a chair, flung her apron up to her face, and burst into tears. I suppose it was at the sight of me. Not knowing what to say to that, I pulled the little girls' ears and then sat down on the floor by Dicky. *He* began to cry.

"Oh come, Dick, don't; you'll soon be better. Face smarts, does it?"

"I never thought to meet you like this, Master Johnny," said Eliza, getting up and speaking through her tears. "'Twas hunger made him do it, sir; nothing else. The poor little things be so famished at times it a'most takes the sense out of 'em."

"Yes, I am sure it was nothing else. Look up, Dick. Don't cry like that." One would have thought the boy was going into hysterics.

I had an apple in my pocket and gave it to him. He kept it in his hand for some time, and then began to eat it ravenously, sobbing now and then. The left arm, the broken one, lay across him, bound up in splints.

"I didn't mean to steal the bun," he whispered, looking up at me through his tears. "I'd ha' give Mrs. Ford the first ha'penny for it that I'd ever got. I was a-hungered, I was. We be always a-hungered now."

"It is hard times with you, I am afraid, Eliza," I said, standing by her.

Opening her mouth to answer, a sob caught her breath, and she put her hand to her side, as if in pain. Her poor face, naturally patient and meek, was worn, and had a bright hectic spot upon it. Eliza used to be very pretty, and was young-looking still, with smooth brown hair, and mild grey eyes: she looked very haggard now and less tidy. But, as to being tidy, how can folk be that, when all their gowns worth a crown are hanging up at the pawn-broker's?

"It's dreadful times, Master Johnny. It's times that frighten me. Worse than all, I can't see when it is to end, and what the end is to be."

"Don't lose heart. The end will be that the men will go to work again : I dare say soon."

"The Lord send it!" she answered. "That's the best we can hope for, sir; and that 'll be hard enough. For we shall have to begin life again, as 'twere; with debts all around us, and our house-hold things and our clothes in pledge."

"You will get them out again then."

"Ay, but how long will it take to earn the money to do it? This strike, as I look upon it, has took at the rate of five years of pros-perity out of our lives, Master Johnny."

"The league—or whatever it is—allows you all money to live, does it not?"

"We get some, sir. It's not a great deal. They tell us that there's strikes a-going on in many parts just now; these strikes have to be helped as well as the operatives here ; and so it makes the allowance small. We have no means of knowing whether that's true or not, us women, I mean ; but I dare say it is."

"And the allowance is not enough to keep you in food?"

"Master Johnny, there's so many other things one wants, beside bare food," she answered, with a sigh. "We must pay our rent, or the landlord would turn us out: we must have a bit o' coal for firing : we must have soap; clothes must be washed, sir, and we must be washed: we must have a candle these dark evenings; shoes must be mended : and there's other trifles, too, that I needn't go into, as well as what Hoar takes for himself——"

"But does he take much?" I interrupted.

"No, sir, he don't : nothing to what some of 'em takes : he has always been a good husband and father. The men, you see, sir, must have a few halfpence in their pockets to pay for their smoke and that, at their meetings in the evening. There's not much left for food when all this comes to be taken out—and we are seven mouths to fill."

No wonder they were hungry!

"Some of the people you've known ought to help you, Eliza. Mrs. Sterling at the old home might: or Mrs. Coney. Do they?"

Eliza Hoar shook her head. "The gentlemen be all again us, sir, and so the ladies dare not do anything. As to Mrs. Sterling—

I don't know that she has so much as heard of the strike—all them miles off."

"You mean the gentlemen are against the strike!"

"Yes, sir; dead again it. They say strikes is the worst kind of evil that can set in, both for us and for the country; that it will increase the poor-rates to a height to be afraid of, and in the end drive the work away from the land. Sitting here with my poor children around me at dusk to save candle, I get thinking sometimes that the gentlemen may not be far wrong, Master Johnny."

Seeing the poor quiet faces lifted to me, from which every bit of spirit seemed to have gone, I wished I had my pockets full of buns for them. But buns were not likely to be there; and of money I had none: buying one of the best editions of Shakespeare had just cleared me out.

"Where's Hoar?" I asked, in leaving.

A hot flush overspread her face. "He has not shown himself here, Master Johnny, since what he did to *him*," was her resentful answer, pointing to Dick. "Afraid to face me, he is."

"I'd not say too much to him, Eliza. It could not undo what's done, and might only make matters worse. I dare say Hoar is just as much vexed about it as you are."

"It's to be hoped he is! Why did he go and set upon the child in that cruel way? It's the men that goes in for the strike; 'tisn't us: and when the worry of it makes 'em so low they hardly know where to turn, they must vent it upon us. Master Johnny, there are minutes now when I could wish myself dead but for the children."

I went home with my head full of a scheme—getting Mrs. Todhetley and perhaps the Coneys to do something for poor Eliza Hoar. But I soon found I might as well have pleaded the cause of the public hangman.

Who should come into our house that evening but old Coney himself. As if the strike were burning a hole in his tongue, he began upon it before he was well seated, and gave the Squire his version of it: that is, his opinion. It did not differ in substance from what had been hinted at by Eliza Hoar. Mr. Coney did not speak *for* the men or *against* them; he did not speak for or against the masters: that question of conflicting interests he said he was content to leave: but what he did urge, and very strongly, was, that strikes in themselves must be productive of an incalculable amount of harm; they brought misery on the workmen, pecuniary embarrassment on the masters, and they most inevitably would, if persisted in, eventually ruin the trade of the kingdom; therefore they should, by every possible means, be discouraged. The Squire, in his hot fashion, took up these opinions for his own and enlarged upon them.

· When old Coney was gone and we had our slippers on, I told them of my visit to Eliza, and asked them to help her just a little.

"Not by a crust of bread, Johnny," said the Squire, more firmly and quietly than he usually spoke. "Once begin to assist the wives and children, and the men would have so much the less need to bring the present state of things to an end."

"I am so sorry for Eliza, sir."

"So am I, Johnny. But the proper person to be sorry for her is her husband : her weal and woe can lie only with him."

"If we could help her ever so little!"

The Squire looked at me for a full minute. "Attend to me, Johnny Ludlow. Once for all, NO! The strike, as Coney says, must be discouraged by every means in our power. *Discouraged*, Johnny. Otherwise these strikes may come into fashion, and grow to an extent of which no man can foresee the end. They will bring the workmen to one of two things—starvation, or the workhouse. That result seems to me inevitable."

"I'm sure it makes me feel very uncomfortable," said the Mater. "One can hardly see where one's duty lies."

"Our poor-rates are getting higher every day ; what do you suppose they'll come to if this is to go on?" continued the Squire. "I'd be glad for the men to get better pay if they are underpaid now : whether they are or not, I cannot tell ; but rely upon it, striking is not the way to attain to it. It's a way that has ruined many a hopeful workman, who otherwise would have gone on contentedly to the end of his days ; ay, and has finally killed him. It will ruin many another. Various interests are at stake in this; you must perceive it for yourself, Johnny lad, if you have any brains ; but none so great as that of the workmen themselves. With all my heart I wish, for their own sakes, they had not taken this extreme step."

"And if the poor children starve, sir?" I ventured to say.

"Fiddlestick to starving! They need not starve while there's a workhouse to go to. And *won't;* that's more. *Can't* you see how all this acts, Mr. Johnny? The men throw themselves out of work ; and when matters come to an extremity the parish must feed the children, and we, the rate-payers, must pay. A pleasant prospect ! How many scores of children are there in Crabb Lane alone?"

"A few dozens, I should say, sir."

"And a few to that. No, Johnny ; let the men look to their families' needs. For their own sakes ; I repeat it ; for their own best interests, I'll have them left alone. They have entered on this state of things of their own free will, and they must themselves fight it out.—And now get you off to bed, boys."

"The Pater's right, Johnny," cried Tod, stepping into my room

as we went up, his candle flaring in the draught from the open staircase window; "right as right can be on principle; but it *is* hard
for the women and children——"

"It is hard for themselves, too, Tod: only they have the unbend-
ing spirit of Britons, to hold out to the death and make no bones
over it."

"I wish you'd not interrupt a fellow," growled Tod. "Look
here; I've got four-and-sixpence, every farthing I can count just
now. You take it and give it to Eliza. The Pater need know
nothing."

He emptied his trousers pocket of the silver, and went off with
his candle. I'm not sure but that he and I both enjoyed the state
of affairs as something new. Had any one told us a year ago that
our quiet neighbourhood could be disturbed by a public ferment
such as this, we should never have believed it.

The next morning I went over to South Crabb with the four-and-
sixpence. Perhaps it was not quite fair to give it, after what the
Squire had said—but there's many a worse thing than that done
daily in the world. Eliza caught her breath when I gave it to her,
and thanked me with her eyes as well as her lips. She had on a
frightfully old green gown—green once—shabby and darned and
patched, and no cap; and she was on her knees wiping up some
spilt water on the floor.

"Mind, Eliza, you must not say a word to any one. I should
get into no end of a row."

"You were always generous, Master Johnny. Even when a
baby——"

"Never mind that. It is not I who am generous now. The
silver was given me for you by some one else; I am cleared out,
myself. Where's Dicky?"

"He's upstairs in his bed, sir: too stiff to move. Mr. Cole, too,
said he might as well lie there to-day. Would you like to go up
and see him?"

As I ran up the staircase, open from the room, a vision of her
wan face followed me—of the catching sob again—of the smooth
brown hair which she was pressing from her temples. We have
heard of a peck of troubles: she seemed to have a bushel of them.

Dicky was a sight, as far as variety of colours went. There was
no mistake about his stiffness.

"It won't last long, Dick; and then you'll be as well as ever."

Dick's grey eyes—they were just like his mother's—looked up at
mine. I thought he was going to cry.

"There. You will never take anything again, will you?"

Dick shook his head as emphatically as his starched condition
allowed. "Father says as he'd kill me the next time if I did."

"When did he say that?"

"This morning; afore he went out."

Dicky's room had a lean-to roof, and was about the size of our jam closet at Crabb Cot. Not an earthly article was in it but the mattress he was lying on.

"Who sleeps here besides you, Dicky?"

"Jacky and little Sam. 'Liza and Jessy sleeps by father and mother."

"Well, good day, Dicky."

Whom should I come upon at the end of Crabb Lane, but the Squire and Hoar. The Squire had his gun in his hand and was · talking his face red : Hoar leaned against the wooden palings that skirted old Massock's garden, and looked as sullen as he had looked yesterday. I thought the Pater had been blowing him up for beating the boy; but it seemed that he was blowing him up for the strike. Cole, the surgeon, hurrying along on his rounds, stopped just as I did.

"Not your fault, Hoar!" cried the Squire. "Of course I know it's not your fault alone, but you are as bad as the rest. Come; tell me what good the strike has done for you."

"Not much as yet," readily acknowledged Hoar, in a tone of incipient defiance.

"To me it seems nothing less than a crime to throw yourself out of work. There's the work ready to your hands, *spoiling* for want of being done—and yet you won't do it!"

"I do but obey orders," said Hoar : who seemed to be miserable enough, in spite of the incipient defiance.

"But is there any sense in it?" reasoned the Squire. "If you men could drop the work and still keep up your homes and their bread-and-cheese, and their other comforts, I'd say nothing. But look at your poor suffering wives and children. I should be *ashamed* to be idle, when my idleness bore such consequences."

The man answered nothing. Cole put in his word.

"There are times when I feel *I* should like to run away from my work, and go in for a few weeks' or months' idleness, Jacob Hoar; and drink my two or three glasses of port wine after dinner of a day, like a lord; and be altogether independent of my station and my patients, and of every other obligation under the sun. But I can't. I know what it would do for *me*—bring me to the parish."

"D'ye think we throw up the work for the sake o' being idle?" returned Hoar. "D'ye suppose, sirs,"—with a burst of a sigh—"that this state o' things is a *pleasure* to us? We are doing it for future benefit. We are told by them who act for us, and who must know, that great benefit will come of it if we be only firm; that our rights be in our own hands if we only persevere long enough in standing out for 'em. Us men has our rights, I suppose, as well as other folks."

"Those who, as you term it, act for you, may be mistaken, Hoar," said the Squire. "I'll leave that point : and go on to a different question. Do you think that the future benefit (whatever that may be: it's vague enough now) *is worth the cost you are paying for it?*"

No reply. A look crossed Hoar's face that made me think he sometimes asked the same question of himself.

"It does appear to be a very *senseless* quarrel, Hoar," went on the Squire. Cole had walked on. "One-sided too. There's an old saying, 'Cutting off one's nose to spite one's face,' and your strike seems just an illustration of it. You see, it is only *you men* that suffer. The rulers you speak of don't suffer: while they are laying down rules for you, they are flourishing on the meat and corn of the land; the masters, in one sense, do not suffer, for they are not reduced to any extremity of any kind. But you, my poor fellows, *you* bear the brunt of it all. Look at your homes, how they are bared; look at your hungry children. What but hunger drove little Dick to crib that bun yesterday?"

Hoar took off his hat and passed his hand over his brow and his black hair. It seemed to be a favourite action of his when in any worry of thought.

"It is just ruin, Jacob Hoar. If some great shock—say a mountain of snow, or a thunderbolt—descended suddenly from the skies and destroyed everything there was in your home, leaving but the bare walls standing, what a dreadful calamity you would think it. How bitterly you'd bemoan it!—perhaps almost feel inclined, if you only dared, to reproach Heaven for its cruelty! But you—you bring on this calamity yourself, of your own free and deliberate will. You have dismantled your home with your own fingers; you have taken out your goods and sold or pledged them, to buy food. I hear you have parted with all."

"A'most," assented Hoar readily ; as if it quite pleased him the Squire should show up the case at its worst.

"Put it that you resume work to-morrow, you don't resume it as a free man. You'll have a load of debt and embarrassment on your shoulders. You will have your household goods to redeem— if they are then still redeemable: you will have your clothes and shoes to buy, to replace present rags : while on your mind will lie the weight of all this past time of trouble, cropping up every half-hour like a nightmare. Now—is the future benefit you hint at worth all this?"

Hoar twitched a thorny spray off the hedge behind the pales, and twirled it about between his teeth.

"Any way," he said, the look of perplexity clearing somewhat on his face, "I be but doing as my mates do ; and we are a-doing for the best. So far as we are told. and believe, it'll be all for the best."

"Then *do* it," returned the Squire in a passion ; and went stamping away with his gun.

"Johnny, they are all pig-headed together," he presently said, as we crossed the stile into the field of stubble whence the corn had been reaped. "One can't help being sorry for them : they are blinded by specious arguments that will turn out, I fear, to be all moonshine. Hold my gun, lad. Where's that dog, now? Here, Dash, Dash, Dash ! "

Dash came running up ; and Tod with him.

In a fortnight's time, Crabb Cot was deserted again. Tod and I returned to our studies, the Squire and the rest to Dyke Manor. As the weeks went on, scraps of news would reach us about the strike: There were meetings of the masters alone : meetings of the men and what they called delegates ; meetings of masters and men combined. It all came to nothing. The masters at length offered to concede a little : the men (inwardly wearied out, sick to death of the untoward state of things) would have accepted the slight concession and returned to work with willing feet ; but their rulers—the delegates, or whatever they were—said no. And so the idleness and the pinching distress continued : the men got more morose, and the children more ragged. After that (things remaining in a chronic state of misery, I suppose) we heard nothing.

"Another lot of faggots, Thomas ; and heap up the coal. This is weather ! Goodness, man ! Don't put the coal on gingerly, as if you were afraid of it. Molly's a fool."

We were in the cozy sitting-room again at Crabb Cot. The Squire was right : it *was* weather : the coldest I have ever felt in December. Old Thomas's hands were frozen with the drive from the station. Molly, who had come on the day before, had put about a handful of fire in the grate to greet us with. Naturally it put the Squire's temper up.

"That there strike's a-going on still, sir," began Thomas, as he waited to watch his wood blaze up.

"No ! " cried the Squire. For we had naturally supposed it to be at an end.

"It is, though, sir. Ford the driver told me, coming along, that Crabb Lane was in a fine state for distress."

"Oh dear! I wish I knew whose fault it is!" bewailed Mrs. Todhetley. "What more did the driver say, Thomas?"

"Well, ma'am, *he* said it must be the men's fault—because there the work is, still a-waiting for 'em, and they won't do it."

"The condition the poor children must be in!"

"Like hungry wolves," said old Thomas. "'Twas what Ford called 'em, and he ought to know: own brother to Ford the baker, as lives in the very thick of the trouble!"

Scarcely anything was talked of that evening but the strike. Its long continuance half frightened some of us. Old Coney, coming in to smoke his pipe with the Squire, pulled a face as long as his arm at the poor-rate prospect: the Squire wondered how much work would stay in the country.

It was said the weekly allowance made to the men was not so much as it had been at first. It was also said that the Society, making it, considered Crabb Lane in general had been particularly improvident in spending the allowance, or it would not have been reduced to its present distressed condition. Which was not to be wondered at, in Mr. Coney's opinion: people used to very good wages, he said, could not all at once pull up habits and look at every farthing as a miser does. Crabb Lane was reproachfully assured by the Society that other strikes had kept themselves quite respectable, comparatively speaking, upon just the same allowance, and had not parted with *all* their pots and pans.

That night I dreamt of the strike. It's as true as that I am writing this. I dreamt I saw thousands and thousands of red-faced men—not pale-faced ones—each tossing a loaf of bread up and down.

"I suppose I may go over and see Eliza," I said to Mrs. Todhetley, after breakfast in the morning.

"There is no reason why you should not, Johnny, that I know of," she answered, after a pause. "Excepting the cold."

As if I minded the cold! "I hope the whole lot, she and the young ones, won't look like skeletons, that's all. Tod, will you come?"

"Not if I know it, old fellow. I have no fancy for seeing skeletons."

"Oh, that was all my nonsense."

"I know that. A pleasant journey to you."

The hoar frost had gathered on the trees, the ice hung fantastically from their branches: it was altogether a beautiful sight. Groups of Miss Timmens's girls, coming to school with frozen noses, were making slides as they ran. As to Crabb Lane, it looked nearly deserted: the cold kept the men indoors. Knocking at Hoar's door with a noise like a fire-engine, I went in with a leap.

The scene I came upon brought me up short. Just at first I did not understand it. In the self-same corner by the fireplace where Dicky's bed had been that first day, was a bed now, and Eliza lay on it : and by her side, wedged against the wall, was what looked like a bundle of green baize with a calico nightcap on. The children—and really and truly they were not much better than living skeletons—sat on the floor.

"What's to do here, you little mites? Is mother ill?"

Dicky, tending the fire (I could have put it into a cocoa-nut), turned round to answer me. He had got quite well again, arm and all.

"Mother's *very* ill," said he in a whisper. "That's the new baby."

"The new what?"

"The new baby," repeated Dick, pointing to the green bundle. "It's two days old."

An old tin slop-pail, turned upside down, stood in the corner of the hearth. I sat down on it to revolve the news and take in the staggering aspect of things.

"What do you say, Dick? A baby—two days old?"

"Two days," returned Dick. "I'd show him to you but for fear o' waking mother."

"He came here the night afore last, he did, while we was all asleep upstairs," interposed the younger of the little girls, Jessy. "Mr. Cole brought him in his pocket : father said so."

"'Twasn't the night afore last," corrected 'Liza. "'Twas the night afore that."

Poor, pale, pinched faces, with never a smile on any one of them! Nothing takes the spirit out of children like long-continued famine.

Stepping across, I looked down at Mrs. Hoar. Her eyes were half open as if she were in a state of stupor. I don't think she knew me : I'm not sure she even saw me. The face was fearfully thin and hollow, and white as death.

"Wouldn't mother be better upstairs, Dick?"

"She's here 'cause o' the fire," returned Dick, gently dropping on a bit of coal the size of a marble. "There ain't no bed up there, neither ; they've brought it down."

The "bed" looked like a sack of shavings. From my heart I don't believe it was anything else. At that moment, the door opened and a woman came in ; a neighbour, I suppose ; her clothes very thin.

"It's Mrs. Watts," said Dick.

Mrs. Watts curtsied. She looked as starved as they did. It seemed she knew me.

" She be very bad, Mr. Ludlow, sir."

" She seems so. Is it—fever?"

"Law, sir! It's more famine nor fever. If her strength can last out—why, well and good; she may rally. If it don't, she'll go, sir."

"Ought she not to have things, Mrs. Watts? Beef-tea and wine, and all that."

Mrs. Watts stared a minute, and then her lips parted with a sickly smile. "I don't know where she'd get 'em from, sir! Beef-tea and wine! A drop o' plain tea is a'most more nor us poor can manage to find now. The strike have lasted long, you see, sir. Any way, she's too weak to take much of anything."

"If I—if I could bring some beef-tea—or some wine—would it do her good?"

"It might just be the saving of her life, Mr. Ludlow, sir."

I went galloping home through the snow. Mrs. Todhetley was stoning raisins in the dining-room for the Christmas puddings. Telling her the news in a heap, I sat down to get my breath.

"Ah, I was afraid so," she said quietly, and without surprise. "I feared there might be another baby at the Hoars' by this time."

"Another baby at the Hoars'!" cried Tod, looking up from my new Shakespeare that he was skimming. "How is it going to get fed?"

"I fear that's a problem none of us can solve, Joseph," said she.

"Well, folk must be daft, to go on collecting a heap more mouths together, when there's nothing to feed them on," concluded Tod, dropping his head into the book again. Mrs. Todhetley was slowly wiping her fingers on the damp cloth, and looking doubtful.

"Joseph, your papa's not in the way and I cannot speak to him —*do* you think I might venture to send something to poor Eliza under the circumstances?"

"Send and risk it," said Tod, in his prompt manner. "*Of course.* As to the Pater—at the worst, he'll only storm a bit. But I fancy he would be the first to send help himself. He wouldn't let her die for the want of it."

"Then I'll despatch Hannah at once."

Hoar was down by the bed when Hannah got there, holding a drop of ale to his wife's lips. Mr. Cole was standing by with his hat on.

"*Ale!*" exclaimed Hannah to the surgeon. "May she take *that?*"

"Bless me, yes," said he, "and do her good."

Hannah followed him outside the door when he was leaving.

"How will it go with her, sir?" she asked. "She looks dreadfully ill."

"Well," returned the Doctor, "I think the night will about see the end of it."

The words frightened Hannah. "Oh, my goodness!" she cried. "What's the matter with her that she should die?"

"Famine and worry have been the matter with her. What she will die of is exhaustion. She has had a sharpish turn just now, you understand; and has no stamina to bring her up again."

It was late in the afternoon when Hannah came home again. There was no change, she said, for the better or the worse. Eliza still lay as much like one dead as living.

"It's quite a picter to see the poor little creatures sitting on the bare floor and quiet as mice, never speaking but in a whisper," cried Hannah, as she shook the snow from her petticoats on the mat. "It's just as if they had an instinct of what is coming."

The Squire, far from being angry, wanted to send over half the house. It was not Eliza's fault, he said, it was the strike's—and he hoped with all his heart she'd get through it. Helping the men's wives in ordinary was not to be thought of; but when it came to dying, that was a different matter. In the evening, between dinner and tea, I offered to go over and see whether any progress had been made. Being curious on the point themselves, they said yes.

The snow was coming down smartly. My great-coat and hat were soon white enough for me to be taken for a ghost enjoying the air at night. Knocking at the Hoars' door gently, it was opened by Jacky. He asked me to go in.

To my surprise they were again alone—Eliza and the children. Mrs. Watts had gone home to put her own flock to bed; and Hoar was out. 'Liza sat on the hearthstone, the sleeping bundle on her lap.

"Father's a-went to fetch Mr. Cole," said Jacky. "Mother began a talking queer—dreams, like—and it frightened him. He told us to mind her till he run back with the Doctor."

Looking down, I thought she was delirious. Her eyes were wide open and glistening · a scarlet spot shone on her cheeks. She began talking to me. Or rather to the air: for I'm sure she knew no one.

· "A great bright place it is, up there; all alight and shining. Silvery, like the stars. Oh, it's beautiful! The people be in white, and no strikes can come in!"

"She've been a-talking about the strikes all along," whispered Jacky, who was kneeling on the mattress. "Mother! Mother, would ye like a drop o' the wine?"

Whether the word mother aroused her, or the boy's voice—and

she had always loved Jacky with a great love—she seemed to recognize him. He raised her head as handy as could be, and held the tea-cup to her lips. It was half full of wine; she drank it all by slow degrees, and revived to consciousness.

"Master Johnny!" she said then in a faint tone.

I could not help the tears filling my eyes as I knelt down by her in Jacky's place. She knew she was dying. I tried to say a word or two.

"It's the leaving the children, Master Johnny, to strikes and things o' that kind, that's making it so hard for me to go. The world's full o' trouble: look at what ours has been since the strike set in! I'd not so much mind *that* for them, though—for the world here don't last over long, and perhaps it's a'most as good to be miserable as easy in it—if I thought they'd all come to me in the bright place afterwards. But—when one's clammed with famine and what not, it's a sore temptation to do wrong. Lord, bring them to me!" she broke forth, suddenly clasping her hands. "Lord Jesus, pray for them, and save them!"

She was nothing but skin and bone. Her hands fell, and she began plucking at the blanket. You might have heard a pin drop in the room. The frightened children hardly breathed.

"I shall see your dear mamma, Master Johnny. I was at her death-bed; 'twas me mostly waited on her in her sickness. If ever a sainted lady went straight to heaven, 'twas her. When I stood over her grave I little thought my own ending was to be so soon. Strikes! Nothing but strikes—and famine, and bad tempers, and blows. Lord Jesus, wash us white from our sins, and take us all to that better world! No strikes there; no strikes there."

She was going off her head again. The door opened, and Hoar, the Doctor, and Mrs. Watts all came in together.

Mrs. Todhetley went over through the snow in the morning. Eliza Hoar had died in the night, and lay on the mattress, her wasted face calm and peaceful. Hoar and the children had migrated to the kitchen at the back, a draughty place hardly large enough for the lot to turn round in. The eldest girl was trying to feed the baby with a tea-spoon.

"What are you giving it, Eliza?" asked Mrs. Todhetley.

"Sugar and water, with a sup o' milk in't, please, ma'am."

"I hope you are contented, Jacob Hoar, now you have killed your wife."

Very harsh words, those for Mrs. Todhetley to speak: and she hastened to soften them. But, as she said afterwards, the matter altogether was a cruel folly and sin, making her heart burn with shame. "That is, Hoar, with the strike; for it is the strike that has killed her."

Hoar, who had been sitting with his head in the chimney, noticing no one, burst into a sudden flood of tears, and sobbed for a minute or two. Mrs. Todhetley was giving the children a biscuit apiece from her bag.

"I did it all for the best," said Hoar, presently. "'Twasn't me that originated the strike. I but joined in it with the rest of my mates."

"And their wives and families are in no better plight than yours."

"Nobody can say I've not done my duty as a husband and a father," cried Hoar. "I've not been a drunkard, nor a rioter, nor a spendthrift. I've never beat her nor swore at her, as some of 'em does."

"Well, she is lying *there;* and the strike has brought her to it. Is it so, or not?"

Hoar did not answer: only caught his breath with a sound of pain.

"It seems to me, Hoar, that the strikes cannot be the good things you think for," she said, her voice now full of pity for the man. "They don't bring luck with them; on the contrary, they bring a great deal of ill-luck. It is you workmen that suffer; mostly in your wives and children. I do not pretend to judge whether strikes may be good from a political point of view, I am not clever; but they do tell very hardly upon your poor patient wives and little ones."

"And don't you see as they tell upon us men, too!" he retorted with a sob that was half pitiful, half savage. "Ay, and worst of all: for if they should be mistaken steps stead of right ones, we've got 'em on our conscience."

"But you go in for them, Hoar. You, individually: and this last night's blow is the result. It certainly seems that there must be a mistake somewhere."

This has not been much to tell of, but it is *true;* and, as strikes are all the go just now, I thought I would write out for you a scrap of one of ours. For my own part, I cannot see that strikes do much good in the long run; or at best, that they are worth the outlay.

I do know, for I have heard and seen it, that through many a long day the poor wives and children can only cry aloud to Heaven to pity them and their privations.

In course of time the strike (it was the longest on record in our parts, though we have had a few since then) came to an end. Upon which, the men began life again with bare homes and sickly young ones ; and a few vacant chairs.

XXIII.

BURSTING-UP.

THERE have been fiery August days in plenty; but never a more fiery one than this that I am going to tell of. It was Wednesday: and we were sitting under the big tree on the lawn at Dyke Manor. A tree it would have done you good only to look at on a blazing day: a large weeping ash, with a cool and shady space within it, large enough for a dozen chairs round, and a small table.

The chairs and the table were there now. On the latter stood iced cider and some sparkling lemonade: uncommonly good, both, on that thirsty day. Mr. Brandon, riding by on his cob, had called in to see us; and sat between me and Mrs. Todhetley. She was knitting something in green shades of wool. The Squire had on a straw hat; Tod lay on the grass outside, in the shade of the laurels; Hugh and Lena stood at the bench near him, blowing bubbles and chattering like magpies.

"Well, I don't know," said old Brandon, taking a draught of the lemonade. "It often happens with me if I plan to go any-where much beforehand, that when the time comes I am not well enough for it."

Mr. Todhetley had been telling him that he thought he should take the lot of us to the seaside for a week or two in September; and suggested that he should go with us. It had been a frightfully hot summer, and everybody felt worn out.

"Where shall you go?" questioned Mr. Brandon.

"Somewhere in Wales, I think," said the Squire. "It's easiest of access from here. Aberystwith, perhaps."

"Not much of a sea at Aberystwith," cried Mr. Brandon, in his squeaky voice.

"Well, it's not quite a Gibraltar Rock, Brandon, but it does for us. The last time we went to the seaside; it is three years ago now——"

"Four," mildly put in Mrs. Todhetley, looking up from her wools.

"Four, is it! Well, it was Aberystwith we went to then; and we were very comfortably lodged. It was at a Mrs. Noon's, I remember; and——who's coming now?"

A dash in at the gate was heard—a little startling Mr. Brandon, lest whatever it was should dash over his cob, tied to the gate-post —and then came the smooth run of light wheels on the gravel.

"Look out and see who it is, Johnny.".

Putting the leaves aside, I saw a light, elegant, open carriage, driven by a groom in livery; a gentleman seated beside him in dainty gloves.

"Why, that's the Clement-Pells' little carriage!" exclaimed Mrs. Todhetley, who had been looking for herself.

"And that's Mr. Clement-Pell in it," said I.

"Oh," said Mr. Brandon. "I'll go then." But the Squire put up his arm to detain him.

Tod did the honours. Went to receive him, and brought him to us under the tree. The children stopped blowing bubbles to stare at Mr. Clement-Pell as he crossed the lawn. It struck me that just a shade of annoyance appeared in his face when he saw so many of us there. Shaking hands, he sat down by Mr. Todhetley, observing that it was some time since he had seen us. It was six weeks, or so: for we had not happened to meet him since that visit of mine and Tod's at his house in Kensington. All the family were back again now at Parrifer Hall: and we were going to a grand entertainment there on the following day, Thursday. An open-air fête, the invitations had said.

"You have been very busy lately, Mr. Clement-Pell," observed the Squire. "I've not been able to get to see you to thank you for the kindness of your folk to my boys in town. Twice I called at your chief Bank, but you were not visible."

"I have been unusually busy," was the answer. "Business gets worse; that is, more extensive; every day. I have had to be about a good deal besides; so that with one thing and another, my time has been more than fully occupied. I am very glad your young men enjoyed themselves with us in London," he added in hearty tones.

Mr. Brandon gave me such a look that for the life of me I could not say a word in answer. The London visit, taking it altogether, had not been one of enjoyment: but Clement-Pell had no suspicion of the truth.

"Rather a *rapid* life, that London life," remarked Mr. Brandon dryly. And I went hot all over, for fear he might be going to let out things to the company.

"Rapid?" repeated Mr. Clement-Pell. "Well, so it is; especially for us business men."

Mr. Brandon coughed, but said no more. The Squire pressed refreshment on Mr. Clement-Pell. He'd have nothing to say to the cider—it would make him hotter, he thought—but took some of the lemonade. As he was putting the glass down Mrs. Todhetley asked whether to-morrow's fête was to be as grand and large as was reported. And the annoyance, seen before, most certainly again crossed Clement-Pell's face at the question.

"I do not really know much about it," he answered. "These affairs are my wife's, not mine."

"And perhaps you don't much care for them," put in the Squire, who had noticed the expression.

"I should like them very much, if I had more time to spare for them," said Mr. Clement-Pell, playing with his handsome chain and seals. "We men of large undertakings must be content to work ourselves, and to let our wives and daughters do the playing. However, I hope I shall manage an hour or two for this one to-morrow."

"What are to be the amusements?" inquired Mrs. Todhetley.

"The question is, rather, what they are not to be," smiled Mr. Clement-Pell. "I heard the girls talking about it with one another last night. Dancing, music, archery, fortune-telling——"

"Something, I suppose, of what may be called a fancy-fair," she interrupted.

"Just so. A fancy-fair without charge. At any rate, I make no doubt it will be pleasant : and I sincerely hope to see you all at it. *You* will come, I trust, Mr. Brandon. These things are not in your usual way, I am aware, but——"

"I have neither the health nor the inclination for them," said Mr. Brandon, quite shrilly, stopping him before he could finish.

"But I trust you will make an exception in favour of us to-morrow, I was about to say. Mrs. Clement-Pell and the Miss Clement-Pells will be so pleased to see you."

"Thank you," said old Brandon, in a tone only just short of rudeness. "I must be going, Squire."

He got up as he spoke, shook hands with Mrs. Todhetley only, nodded to the rest of us, and set off across the lawn. Children liked him in spite of his voice and dry manner, and of course Hugh and Lena, pipes and soap-suds and all, attended him to the gate.

As the brown cob went trotting off, and the Squire was coming back again—for he had gone too—Mr. Clement-Pell met him half-way across the lawn , and then they both went indoors together.

"Clement-Pell must want something," said Mrs. Todhetley. "Johnny, do you notice how very aged and worn he is? It never struck me until to-day. He looks quite grey."

"Well, that's because he is getting so. I shall be grey some time."

"But I don't mean that kind of greyness, Johnny; grey hairs. His *face* looks grey."

" It was the reflection of these green leaves, good mother."

" Well—perhaps it might be," she doubtfully agreed, looking up. " What a grand fête it is to be, Johnny !"

" You'll have to put on your best bib-and-tucker, good mother. That new dress you bought for the Sterlings' christening."

" I should if I went. But the fact is, Johnny, I and Mr. Tod-hetley have made up our minds not to go, I fancy. We were talking together about it this morning. However—we shall see when to-morrow comes."

" I wouldn't be you, then. That will be too bad."

" These open-air fêtes are not in our way, Johnny. Dancing, and archery, and fortune-telling are not much in the way of us old people. You young ones think them delightful—as we did once. Hugh ! Lena ! what *is* all that noise about ? You are not to take her bowl, Hugh : keep to your own. Joseph, please part them."

Joe accomplished it by boxing the two. In the midst of the noise, Mr. Clement-Pell came out. He did not cross the lawn again to Mrs. Todhetley ; just called out a good day in getting into his carriage, and lifted his hat as he drove away.

" I say, father, what did he want with you ? " asked Tod, as the Squire came sauntering back, the skirts of his light coat held behind him.

" That's my business, Joe," said the Squire. " Mind your own."

Which was a checkmate for Tod. The truth was, Tod had been uneasily wondering whether it might not be his business. That is, whether Mr. Clement-Pell had obtained scent of that gambling of his up in London and had come to enlighten the Squire. Tod never felt safe upon the point : which, you see, was all owing to his lively conscience.

" What a beautiful little carriage that is !" said Mrs. Todhetley to the Pater. " It puts me in mind of a shell."

" Ay ; must have cost a pretty penny, small as it is. Pell can afford these fancy things, with his floating wealth."

In that city of seething crowds and wealth, London, where gigantic operations are the rule instead of the exception, and large fortunes are made daily, Mr. Clement-Pell would not have been thought much of ; but in our simple country place, with its quiet experiences, Clement-Pell was a wonder. His riches were great. His power of making money for himself and others seemed elastic ; and he was bowed down to as a reigning potentate—a king—an Olympian deity.

You have heard of him before. He had come to a neighbouring town some years back as manager of a small banking company, having given up, it was understood, a good law practice in London to undertake it. The small banking grew and grew under his management. Some of its superfluous hoards were profitably employed: to construct railroads; to work mines; to found colonies. All sorts of paying concerns were said to have some of Clement-Pell's money in them, and to bring him in cent. per cent. It was believed that if all the wealth of the East India Company and the Bank of England to boot had been poured into the hands of Clement-Pell, it could not have been more than he would be able to use to profit, so great were the resources at his command. People fought with one another to get their money accepted by Mr. Clement-Pell. No wonder. The funds gave them a paltry three per cent. for it; Mr. Clement-Pell doubled the amount. So the funds lost the money, and Mr. Clement-Pell gained it. He was worshipped as the greatest benefactor that had ever honoured the country by settling down in it.

I think his manner went for something. It was so pleasant. The world itself might have loved Mr. Clement-Pell. Deputations asked for his portrait to hang up in public buildings; individuals besought his photograph. Mrs. Clement-Pell was less liked: she was extravagant and haughty. It was said she was of very high family indeed, and she could not have looked down upon common people with more scorn had she been born a duchess. I'm sure no duchess ever gave herself the airs that Mrs. Clement-Pell did, or wore such fine bonnets.

When Mr. Clement-Pell opened a little branch Bank at Church Dykely (as he had already done at two or three other small places), the parish at once ascended a few feet into the air. As Church Dykely in its humility had never possessed a Bank before, it was naturally something to be proud of. The Bank was a little house near to Duffham's, the doctor, with a door and one window; no larger premises being obtainable. The natives collected round to gaze, and marvel at the great doings destined to be enacted behind that wire blind: and Mr. Clement-Pell was followed by a tail of admiring rustics whenever he stepped abroad.

Church Dykely only had its branch in what might be called the later years, dating from the beginning of the Clement-Pell dynasty, and when he had made a far and wide reputation, and was in the full tide of his prosperity. It was after its establishment that he took Parrifer Hall. This little branch Bank was found to be a convenience to many people. It had a manager and a clerk; and Mr. Clement-Pell would condescend to be at it occasionally, chiefly on Mondays. He was popular with all classes: county gentlemen and rich farmers asked him to dinner; the poor got from him many a kind word and handshake. Mrs. Clement-Pell dined with him at the gentlemen's tables, but she turned up her nose at the farmers, and would not go near them. In short, take them for all

in all, there was no family so grand in the county, or who made so
much noise as the Clement-Pells. Their income was something
enormous; and of course they might launch out if they liked. It
had grown to be a saying amongst us, "As rich as the Clement-
Pells."

Mrs. Todhetley had said she supposed the entertainment would
be something like a fancy-fair. We had not had a great experience of fancy-fairs in our county; but if they were all like this,
I shouldn't mind going to one twice a week. The sky was un-
clouded, the wind still, the leaves of the trees scarcely stirred. On
the lawn the sun blazed hot and brilliant: but the groves were cool
and shady. Since the place came into Mr. Clement-Pell's occu-
pancy, he had taken-in part of a field, and made the grounds
more extensive. At least, Mrs. Clement-Pell had done so, which
came to the same: spending money went for nothing with her.
And why should it, when they had so much? If you climbed to
the top of an artificial rockery you could see over the high hedge.
I did so: and took a look at the chimneys of George Reed's cottage. You've not forgotten him; and his trouble with Major
Parrifer. But for that trouble, the Clement-Pells might never have
had the chance of occupying Parrifer Hall.

It was as good as fairy-land. Flags hung about; banners
waved; statues had decked themselves in garlands. The lawns
and the walks were alive with company, the ladies sported gala
dresses all the colours of the rainbow. Dancing, shooting, flirting,
talking, walking, sitting; we were as gay as birds of paradise.
There was a tent for the band, and another for refreshments, and
no end of little marquees, dotted about, for anything. One was a
post-office; where love-letters might be had for the asking. When
I look back on that day now through the mist of years, it stands
out as the gayest and sunniest left to memory. As to refreshment—you may think of anything you like and know it was
there. There was no regular meal at all throughout the afternoon
and evening; but you could begin eating and drinking when you
went in if you chose, and never leave off till you left. The refreshment tent communicated with one of the doors of the house,
through which fresh supplies came as they were wanted. All was
cold. Besides this, there was a tea and coffee marquee, where the
kettles were kept always on the boil. No one could say the
Clement-Pells spared pains or expense to entertain their guests
right royally.

Tod and I strolled about, to take in the whole scene. The
Clement-Pell carriages (the big barouche and the small affair that

Mrs. Todhetley had called a shell) came dashing up at intervals, graciously despatched to bring relays of guests who did not keep carriages of their own. Mrs. Clement-Pell stood on the lawn to receive them; the Miss Clement-Pells with her. If I were able to describe their attire I would do so; it beat anything for gorgeousness I had ever seen. Glistening silk skirts under robes of beautiful lace; fans in their hands and gossamer veils in their hair.

"I say, Tod, here they come!"

A sober carriage was driving slowly in. We knew it well: and its steady old horses and servants too. It was Sir John Whitney's. Rushing round a side path, we were up with it when it stopped. Bill Whitney and his two sisters came tumbling out of it.

"It's going on to your house now, with the trunk," said Helen, to us. "William has been most awfully tiresome: he would put his every-day boots and coat in our box, instead of bringing a portmanteau for himself."

"As if a fellow wanted a portmanteau for just one night!" exclaimed Bill. "What you girls can have in that big trunk, amazes me. I should say you are bringing your bed and pillows in it."

"It has only our dresses for to-morrow morning in it, and all that," retorted Helen, who liked to keep Bill in order and to domineer over him. "The idea of having to put in great clumsy boots with *them*, and a rough coat smelling of smoke!"

"This is to be left here, I think, Miss Helen," said the footman, displaying a small black leather bag.

"Why, yes; it contains our combs and brushes," returned Helen, taking it and giving it to one of the Clement-Pell servants, together with two cloaks for the evening.

Tod went up to the postillion. "Look here, Pinner: the Squire says you had better stop at the Manor to rest the horses. You will find the groom there, I dare say."

"Thank you, sir," said Pinner. "They'll be a bit done up if we goes straight off back."

The girls and Bill went up to the Clement-Pell group, and were made much of. It was the first time they had visited the Pells, and their coming was regarded as a special honour. Sir John and Lady Whitney had declined: and it was arranged that Bill and his sisters should sleep at our house, and the carriage come for them the next day.

Escaping from the Pells, we all sat down on a bench. Helen Whitney began whispering about the Miss Pells' dresses.

"I never saw such beauties," she exclaimed. "I wonder what they cost?"

"Millions, I should say," cried Bill.

"These are plain ugly old things beside them," grumbled Helen.

She meant her own dress and Anna's. They wore white spotted muslins, and blue ribbons. One of those gorgeous robes was worth fifty times as much : but I know which set of girls looked the most lady-like.

"They are very beautiful," sighed Helen, with a spice of envy. "But too much for an affair like this."

"Not for them," said Bill stoutly. "The Clement-Pells could afford robes of diamonds if they liked. I'm not sure but I shall go in for one of the girls."

"Don't talk nonsense," reproved Helen.

We went into the fortune-telling tent. It was full of people, screaming and laughing. A real gipsy with a swarthy skin and black flowing locks was telling fortunes. Helen had hers told when she could make a place, and was promised a lord for a husband, and five-and-thirty grandchildren. At which the tent roared again, and Helen laughed too.

"And now it is your turn, my pretty little maid," said the sibyl to Anna Whitney. And Anna, always modest and gentle, turned as red as a rose, and said she already knew as much of her own fortune as she desired to know at present.

"What's in *this* hand ?" cried the gipsy, suddenly seizing upon Tod's big one, and devouring its lines with her eyes. "Nay, master; don't draw it away, for there's matter here, and to spare. You are not afraid, are you ? "

"Not of you, my gipsy queen," gallantly answered Tod, resigning his palm to her. "Pray let my fate be as good as you can."

"It is a smooth hand," she went on, never lifting her gaze. "Very smooth. You'll not have many of the cares and crosses of life. Nevertheless, I see that you have been in some peril lately. And I should say it was connected with money. Debt."

There were not many things could bring the colour to Joseph Todhetley's face : but it matched then the scarlet mantle the gipsy wore slung over her right shoulder. You might have heard a pin drop in the sudden hush. Anna's blue eyes were glancing shyly up through their long lashes.

"Peril of debt, or—perhaps—of—steeple-chasing," continued the sibyl with deliberation ; and at that the shouts of laughter broke out again through the tent, and Anna smiled. "Take you care of yourself, sir ; for I perceive you will run into other perils before you settle down. You have neither caution nor foresight."

"*That's* true enough, I believe," said Tod. "Any more?"

"No more. For you are just one of those imprudent mortals who will never heed a friendly warning. Were I you, I'd keep out of the world till I grew older."

"Thank you," said Tod, laughing as much as the rest of them : and he drew away his hand.

"Johnny, that was a near shave," he whispered, putting his arm within mine when we had pushed our way out. "Was it all guess-work? Who the deuce is the woman ? "

"I know who *I* think she is. The Pells' English governess, Miss Phebus."

"Nonsense ! "

"I do. She has got herself up in character and dyed her skin and hair."

"Then, by George, if it *is*, she must have gathered an inkling of that matter in London."

"I don't see how."

"Nor I. Johnny, some of these days I shall be bursting out . with it to the Pater, and so get the weight off my mind."

"I shouldn't wonder. She says you have no caution."

"It's not pleasant, I can tell you, youngster, to live in dread that somebody else will bring it out to him. I'll go in for this next dance, I think. Where's Anna ? "

Anna did not say no. She would never say no to anything *he* asked her, if I possessed the gift of divination. They joined the dancers ; Bill and Helen went to the archery.

"And how are *you* enjoying it, pray, Johnny Ludlow ? "

The voice nearly shot me off the arm of the bench. For it was Mr. Brandon's. I don't think there was any living man I should have been so surprised at seeing at the fête as he.

"Why ! is it you, sir ? "

"Yes, it is, Johnny. You need not stare as if you thought me an intruder. I was invited."

"Yes, of course, sir. But I—I fancied you never came to such parties."

"Never was at one like this—unless I went to it in my sleep," he said, standing with me before the bench, and casting his eyes around. "I came to-day to look after you."

"After me, sir ! "

"Yes, after you. And perhaps a little bit after your friend, Todhetley. Mr. Pell informed us the entertainments would include fortune-telling : I didn't know but there might be a roulette-table as well. Or cards, or dice, or billiards."

"Oh no, sir ; there's nothing of that sort."

"It's not the fault of the young Pells, I expect, then. That choice companion of yours, called Gusty, and the other, one in scarlet."

"Neither of them is here, Mr. Brandon. Gusty has gone to the Highlands for grouse-shooting; and 'Fabian sent word he couldn't get leave to come down. I have not seen the eldest son yet, but I suppose he is somewhere about."

"Oh," said Mr. Brandon—and whenever he spoke of the Pells his voice was thinner than ever, and most decidedly took a mocking sound—"gone grouse-shooting, is Gusty! And the other can't get leave. A lieutenant, is he not?"

"Yes, a lieutenant. His sister Constance has just told us she does not believe it is true that he could not get leave. She thinks he never asked for it, because he wanted to stay in London."

"Ah. It's fine to be the Pells, Johnny. One son off to shoot grouse; another living his fast London life; the rest holding grand doings down here that could hardly be matched by the first nobleman amongst us. Very fine. Wonder what they spend a year—taking it in the aggregate?"

"Have you been here long, sir?"

"Half-an-hour, or so—I've been looking about me, Johnny, and listening to the champagne corks popping off. Squire here?"

"No. He and Mrs. Todhetley did not come."

"Sensible people. Where's young Joe?"

"He is with the Whitneys. Dancing with Anna, I think."

"And he had better keep to that," said Mr. Brandon, with a little nod. "He'll get no harm there."

We sat down, side by side. Taking a side-glance at him, I saw his eyes fixed on Mrs. and the Miss Clement-Pells, who were now mixing with the company. He did not know much about ladies' dress, but theirs seemed to strike him.

"Showy, Johnny, is it not?"

"It looks very bright in the sun, sir."

"No doubt. So do spangles."

"It's real, sir, that lace. Helen Whitney says so."

"A great deal too real. So is the rest of it. Hark at the music and the corks and the laughter! Look at the people, and the folly!"

"Don't you like the fête, sir?"

"Johnny, I hate it with my whole heart."

I was silent. Mr. Brandon was always more queer than other people.

"Is it in *keeping* with the Pells, this upstart grandeur and profusion? Come, Johnny Ludlow, you've some sense in your head: answer me. They have both risen from nothing, Johnny. When he began life, Pell's ambition was to rise to a competency; an el dorado of three or four hundred a year: and that only when he had worked for it. I have seen her take in the milk for their tea from the milkman at the door; when they kept one servant to do everything. Pell rose by degrees and grew rich; so much the more credit due to his perseverance and his business talents—— "

"And would you not have them spend their riches, Mr. Brandon?"

"Spend their riches!—of course I would, in a proper way. Don't you interrupt your elders, Johnny Ludlow. Where would be the use of a man's getting money unless he spent some of it. But not in *this* way; not in the lavish and absurd and sinful profusion that they have indulged in of late years. Is it seemly, or right, or decent, the way they live in? The sons apeing the manners and company of their betters, of young fellows who are born to the peerage and their thousands a year? The mother holding her head in the air as if she wore an iron collar: the daughters with their carriages and their harps and their German governesses, and their costly furbelows that are a scandal on common sense? The world has run mad after these Pells of late years: but I know this much—I have been ashamed only to look on at the Pells' unseemly folly."

At that moment Martha Jane Pell—in the toilette that Bill Whitney said must have cost "millions"—went looming by, flirting with Captain Connaught. Mr. Brandon looked after them with his little eyes.

"They are too fine for their station, Johnny. They were not born to this kind of thing; were not reared to it; have only plunged into it of recent years, and it does not sit well upon them. One can only think of upstarts all the time. The Pells might have lived as gentlepeople; ay, and married their children to gentlemen and gentlewomen had they pleased: but, to launch out in this unseemly way, has been a just humiliation to themselves, and has rendered them a poor, pitiful laughing-stock in the eyes of all right-minded people. It's nothing less than a burlesque on all the proprieties of life. And it may be that we have not seen the end of it, Johnny."

"Well, sir, they can hardly be grander than——"

"Say more assuming, lad."

"I suppose I meant that, Mr. Brandon. Perhaps you think they'll be for taking the Marquis's place, Ragley, next, if it should come into the market. Or Eastnor Castle: or——"

"I did not mean exactly in that way, Johnny," he interrupted again, a queer look on his thin lips as he got up.

"Are you going into the eating tent, sir?"

"I am going away. Now that I have seen that you and Joe Todhetley are tolerably safe from gaming tables and the like, there's nothing further to keep me here. I feel a sort of responsibility in regard to you two, seeing that that unpleasant secret lies with me, and not with Joe's father."

"It is early to go, sir. The fun has hardly begun."

"None too early for me. I am a magistrate; looked up to, in a manner, in the neighbourhood, insignificant though I am. It is not I who will countenance this upstart foolery by my presence longer than I can help, Johnny Ludlow."

Mr. Brandon disappeared. The hours went on to twilight and then to dark. Once during the evening I caught sight of Mr. Clement-Pell: and what occurred as I did so was like a bit of romance. People crowded the side paths under the light of the Chinese lanterns. For lanterns were hanging on the trees and shrubs, and the whole scene was one of enchantment out of the Arabian Nights. One of the remote walks was not lighted; perhaps it had been forgotten. I had missed Bill Whitney and was at the end of the grounds hunting for him, when I saw, through the trees, a solitary figure pacing this dark walk with his arms folded. It was not very likely to be Bill: but there was no harm in going to see.

It turned out to be Mr. Clement-Pell. But before I got out of the trees into the walk—for it was the nearest way back to the lights and the company—some one pushed through the trees on the opposite side of the path, and stood in front of him. The moon shone as much as an August moon ever does shine; and I saw Clement-Pell start as if he had been told his house was on fire.

"I thought this might be a likely place to find you," said the stranger in a savage whisper. "You have kept out of my way for two days at the Bank—too busy to see me, eh?—so, hearing what was going on here, I took the train and came over."

"I'm sure I am—happy to see you, Mr. Johnson," cried Clement-Pell in a voice that seemed to tremble a little; and unless the moonlight was in fault, he had turned as pale as a ghost. "Would have sent you an invitation had I known you were down."

"I dare say you would! I did not come to attend festivals, Pell, but to settle business-matters."

"You must be aware I cannot attend to business to-night," interrupted Clement-Pell. "Neither do I ever enter upon it at my own residence. I will see you to-morrow morning at eleven at the Bank."

"Honour bright? Or is it a false plea, put forth to shuffle out of me now?"

"I will see you to-morrow morning at the Bank at eleven o'clock," repeated Clement-Pell, emphatically. "We are very busy just now, and I must be there the first thing. And now, Mr. Johnson, if you will go into the refreshment tent, and make yourself at home——"

"No refreshments for me, thank you: I must hasten away to catch the train. But first of all, I will ask you a question : and answer it you must, whether it is your habit of entering on business at home, or whether it is not. Is it true that——"

I did not want to hear more secrets, and went crashing through the trees. I should have gone before, but for not liking they should know any one was there. They turned round.

"Oh, is it you, Mr. Ludlow?" cried Pell, putting out his hand as I passed them.

"Yes, sir. I am looking for young Whitney. Have you seen him?"

"I think I saw him at the door of one of the tents, just now. You'll find him amongst the company, I dare say. The Squire and Mrs. Todhetley have not come, I hear."

"No, sir."

"Ah well—give my very kind regards to them, and say I am sorry. I hope you are taking care of yourself—in the way of refreshments."

The stranger and I had stood facing each other. He was a very peculiar-looking man with a wide stare; black hair, white whiskers, and very short legs. I thought it anything but good manners of him to come over, as he had confessed to have done, to disturb Clement-Pell at such a time.

At nine o'clock Giles arrived with the pony-carriage for the young ladies and two of us: the other and Giles were to walk. But we didn't see the fun of leaving so early. Giles said he could not wait long: he must be back to get old Jacobson's gig ready, who was spending the evening at the Manor. The Jacobsons, being farmers, though they were wealthy, and lived in good old style, had been passed over when Mrs. Clement-Pell's invitations went out. So Tod sent Giles and the carriage back again, with a message that we all preferred walking, and should follow shortly.

Follow, we did; but not shortly. It was past eleven when we got away. The dancing had been good, and no one was at hand to say we must leave. Helen and Anna Whitney came out with their cloaks on. What with the dancing and the sultriness of the weather, the night was about as hot as an oven. We were almost the last to leave: but did not mean to say so at home. It was a splendid night, though; very clear, the moon larger than usual. We went on in no particular order; the five of us turning out of the Parrifer gates together.

"Oh," screamed Helen, when we were some yards down the road, "where's the bag? Anna, have you brought the bag?"

"No," replied Anna. "You told me you would bring it."

"Well—I meant to do so. William, you must run back for it."

"Oh, bother the bag," said Bill. "You girls can't want the bag to-night. I'll come over for it in the morning."

"Not want it!—Why, our combs and brushes and thin shoes are in it," retorted Helen. "It is on a chair in that little room off the hall. Come, William, go for it."

"I'll go, Helen," I said. "Walk quietly on, and I shall catch you up."

The grounds looked quite deserted : the Chinese lanterns had burned themselves out, and the doors appeared closed. One of the side windows was open and gay with light ; I thought it would be less trouble to enter that way, and leaped up the balcony steps to the empty room. Empty, as I took it to be.

Well, it was a sort of shock. The table had a desk and a heap of papers on it, and on it all lay a man's head. The face was hidden in his hands, but he lifted it as I went in.

It was Clement-Pell. But I declare that at the first moment I did not know him. If ever you saw a face more haggard than other faces, it was his. He sat bolt upright in his chair then, and stared at me as one in awful fear.

"I beg your pardon, sir. I did not know any one was here."

"Oh, it is you," he said, and broke out into a smile—which somehow made the face look even more worn and weary than before. "I thought you had all left."

"So we have, sir. But Miss Whitney forgot her bag, and I have run back for it. She left it in the small room in the hall."

"Oh ay, all right," he said. "You can go and get it, and run out this way again if you like. I dare say the hall-door is closed."

"Good night, sir," I said, coming back with the bag. "We have had a most delightful day, Mr. Clement-Pell, and I'm sure we ought to thank you for it."

"I am glad it has been pleasant. Good night."

The trees were pretty thick on this side the house. In passing a grove a few paces from the window, I saw something that was neither trunks nor leaves; but Mr. Johnson's face with its black hair and white whiskers. He was hiding in the trees, his face peeping out to look at the room and at Clement-Pell.

It made me feel queer. It made me think of treachery. Though what treachery, or where, I hardly knew. Not a trace was to be seen of the face now: he drew it in; no doubt to let me pass. Ought I to warn Mr. Pell that he was being watched? I had distinctly heard the man say he was going away directly : why had he stayed? Yes, it would be right and kind. Walking a bit further, I quietly turned back.

Clement-Pell had a pen in his hand this time, and was poring over what seemed to be a big account-book, or ledger. He looked surprised again, but spoke quietly.

"Still left something behind you, Mr. Ludlow?"

"No, sir, not this time," I said, speaking below my breath. "I thought I would come back and tell you, Mr. Pell, that some one outside is watching this room. If——"

I broke off in sheer astonishment. He started up from his chair and came creeping to where I stood, to hide himself as it seemed from the watcher, his haggard cheeks white as death. But he put a good face on it to me.

"I could not hear you," he whispered. "What did you say? Some one watching?"

"It is the same man I saw you talking to in the dark walk to-night, with the black hair and white whiskers. Perhaps he means no harm, sir; he is hiding in the trees, and just peeping out to look in here."

"You are sure it is that same man?" he asked with a relieved air.

"Quite sure."

"Then it is all right. Mr. Johnson is an eccentric friend of mine. Rather—in fact, rather given to take at times more than is good for him. I suppose he has been going in for champagne. I—I thought it might be some bad character."

It might be "all right," as Mr. Pell said: I fancied, by the relieved tone, that it *was* so: but I felt quite sure that he had cause to fear, if not Mr. Johnson, some one else. At that moment there arose a slight rustle of leaves outside, and he stood, holding his breath to listen, his finger raised. The smell of the shrubs was borne freely on the night air.

"It is only the wind: there must be a little breeze getting up," said Mr. Clement-Pell. "Thank you; and good night. Oh, by the way, don't talk of this, Mr. Ludlow. If Johnson *has* been exceeding, he would not like to hear of it again."

"No fear, sir. Once more, good night."

Before I had well leaped the steps of the balcony, the window, a very heavy one, was closed with a bang, and the shutters being put to. Glancing back, I saw the white face of Clement-Pell through the closing shutters, and then heard the bolts shot. What could he be afraid of? Perhaps Johnson turned mad when he drank. Some men do.

"Have you been making that bag, Johnny?" they called out when I caught them up.

" No."

" I'm sure it was on the chair," said Helen.

" Oh, I found it at once. I stayed talking with Mr. Pell. I say, has the night grown damp?—or is it my fancy?"

" What does it matter?" returned Bill Whitney. " I wish I was in a bath, for my part, if it was only cold water."

The Squire stood at the end of the garden when we reached home, with old Jacobson, whose gig was waiting. After reproaching us with our sins, first for sending the carriage back empty, then for being so late, the Squire came round and asked all about the party. Old Jacobson drew in his lips as he listened.

" It's fine to be the Clement-Pells!" cried he. " Why, a Duke-Royal could not give a grander party than that. Real lace for gowns, had they! No wonder Madame Pell turns her nose up at farmers!"

" Did Clement-Pell send me any particular message?" asked the Pater.

" He sent his kind regards," I said. " And he was sorry you and Mrs. Todhetley did not go."

" It was a charming party," cried Helen Whitney. " Papa and mamma put it to us, when the invitation came—would we go, or would we not go. They don't much care for the Clement-Pells. I am glad we did go: I would not have missed it for the world. But there's something about the Clement-Pells that tells you they are not gentlepeople."

" Oh, that's the show and the finery," said Bill.

" No, I think it lies more in their tones and their manner of speaking," said Helen.

" Johnny, are you *quite* sure Clement-Pell sent me no message, except kind regards, and that?"

" Quite sure, sir."

" Well, it's very odd."

" What is very odd, sir?"

" Never you mind, Johnny."

This was after breakfast on the Saturday morning. The Squire was opening a letter that the post had brought, and looked up to ask me. Not that the letter had anything to do with Clement-Pell, for it only enclosed a bill for some ironmongery bought at Evesham.

On the Friday the Whitneys had gone home, and Tod with them. So I was alone: with nothing to do .but to wish him back again.

" I am going to Alcester, Jonnny," said the Pater, in the course of the morning. "You can come with me if you like."

"Then will you please bring me back some money?" cried Mrs. Todhetley. "You will pass the Bank, I suppose."

"It's where I am going," returned the Pater: and I thought his voice had rather a grumbling tone in it.

We took the pony-carriage, and he let me drive. It was as hot as ever; and the Squire wondered when the autumn cool would be coming in. Old Brandon happened to be at his gate as we went by, and the Pater told me to pull up.

"Going in to Alcester?" cried Mr. Brandon.

"Just as far as the Bank," said the Pater. "So I hear you went to the Clement-Pells' after all, Brandon."

"I looked in to see what it was like," said old Brandon, giving me a moment's hard stare: as much as to recall to my mind what had really taken him there.

"It was a dashing affair, I hear."

"Rather too much so for me," cried Mr. Brandon drily. "Where's your son, sir?"

"Oh, he's gone home with the Whitneys' young folk. How hot it is to-day!"

"Ay. Too hot to stand in it long. Drive on, Johnny."

The Squire went in to the Bank alone, leaving me with the carriage. He banked with the Old Bank at Worcester; but it was a convenience to have some little money nearer in case of need, and he had recently opened a small account at Alcester. Upon which Clement-Pell had said he might as well have opened it with him, at his Church Dykely branch. But the Squire explained that he had as good as promised the Alcester people, years ago, that if he did open an account nearer than Worcester it should be with them. He came out, looking rather glum, stuffing some notes into his pocket-book.

"Turn the pony round, Johnny," said he. "We'll go back. It's too hot to stay out to-day."

"Yes, sir. Is anything the matter?"

"Anything the matter! No. Why do you ask?"

"I thought you looked put out, sir."

"There's nothing the matter. Only I think men of business should not be troubled with short memories. Take care of that waggon. What's the fellow galloping his horses at that rate for? Now, Johnny, I say, take care. Or else, give me the reins."

I nearly laughed. At home they never seemed to think I could do anything. If they did let me drive, it was always Now take care of this, Johnny; or, Take care of that. And yet I was a more careful driver than Tod: though I might not have had so much strength as he to pull up a four-in-hand team had it run away.

"Go round through Church Dykely, Johnny, and stop at Pell's Bank," said the Squire, as I was turning off on the direct road home.

I turned the pony's head accordingly. It took us about a mile out of our way. The pavement was so narrow and the Bank room so small, that I heard all that passed when the Squire went in.

"Is Mr. Clement-Pell here?"

"Oh dear no, sir," replied the manager. "He is always at the chief Bank on Saturday. Did you want him?"

"Not particularly. Tell him I think he must have forgotten to send to me."

"I'll tell him, sir. He may look in here to-night on his return. If you wish to see him yourself, he will be here all day on Monday."

The Squire came out and got in again. Cutting round the sharp corner by Perkins the butcher's, I nearly ran into Mrs. and the Miss Clement-Pells, who were crossing the dusty road in a line like geese, the one behind the other; their muslins sweeping the high-way like brooms, and their complexions sheltered under point lace parasols.

"There you go again, Johnny! Pull up, sir."

I pulled up: and the heads came from under the parasols, and grouped round to speak to us. They had quite recovered Thursday's fatigue, Mrs. Clement-Pell graciously said, in answer to the Squire's inquiries; and she hoped all her young friends had done the same, Mr. Todhetley's young friends in particular.

"*They* felt no fatigue," cried the Pater. "Why, ma'am, they'd keep anything of that sort up for a week and a day, and not feel it. How's Mr. Clement-Pell?"

"He is as well as he allows himself to be," she answered. "I tell him he is wearing himself out with work. His business is of vast magnitude, Mr. Todhetley. Good day."

"So it is," acquiesced the Pater as we drove on, partly to himself, partly to me. "Of vast magnitude. For my part, I'd rather do less, although it involved less returns. One can forgive a man, like him, forgetting trifles. And, Johnny, I shouldn't wonder but his enormous riches render him careless of small obligations."

Part of which was unintelligible to me.

Sunday passed. We nodded to the Miss Clement-Pells at church (their bonnets making the pew look like a flower-garden); but did not see Mr. Clement-Pell or his wife. Monday passed; bringing a note from Tod, to say Lady Whitney and Bill would not let him leave yet. Tuesday morning came in. I happened to be seated under the hedge in the kitchen-garden, mending a fishing-rod, when a horse dashed up to the back gate. Looking through, I saw it was the butcher boy, Sam Rimmer. Molly, who was in one of her stinging tempers that morning, came out.

"We don't want nothing," said she tartly. "So you might have spared yourself the pains of coming."

"Don't want nothing!" returned the boy. "Why's that?"

"Why's that!" she retorted. "It's like your imperence to ask. Do families want joints every day; specially such weather as this? I a-going to cook fowls for dinner, and we've the cold round o' beef for the kitchen. Now you know why, Sam Rimmer."

Sam Rimmer sat looking at her as if in a quandary, gently rubbing his hair, which shone again in the sun.

"Well, it's a pity but you wanted some," said he, slowly. "We've gone and been and pervided a shop full o' meat to-day, and it'll be a dead loss on the master. The Clement-Pells don't want none, you see: and they took a'most as much as all the rest o' the gentle-folks put together. There's summat up there."

"Summat up where?" snapped Molly.

"At the Clement-Pells'. The talk is, that they've busted-up, and be all gone off in consekence."

"Why, what d'ye mean?" cried Molly. "Gone off where? Busted-up from what?"

But, before Perkins's boy could answer, the Pater, walking about the path in his straw hat and light thin summer coat, came on the scene. He had caught the words.

"What's that you are saying about the Clement-Pells, Sam Rimmer?"

Sam Rimmer touched his hair, and explained. Upon going to Parrifer Hall for orders, he had found it all sixes-and-sevens; some of the servants gone, the rest going. They told him their master had bursted-up, and was gone away since Sunday morning; and the family since Monday morning. And his master, Perkins, would have all the meat left on his hands that he had killed on purpose for the Clement-Pells.

You should have seen the Squire's amazed face. At first he did not know how to take the words, and stared at Sam Rimmer without speaking.

"All the Banks has went and busted-up too," said Sam. "They be a-saying, sir, as how there won't be nothing for nobody."

The Squire understood now. He turned tail and rushed into the house. And rushed against Mr. Brandon, who was coming in.

"Well, have you heard the news?" asked Mr. Brandon in his thinnest voice.

"I can't believe it; I don't believe it," raved the Squire.

"Clement-Pell would never be such a swindler. He owes me two hundred pounds."

Mr. Brandon opened his little eyes. "Owes it *you!*"

"That day, last week, when he came driving in, in his smart cockle-shell carriage—when you were here, you know, Brandon. He got a cheque for two hundred pounds from me. A parcel of money that ought to have come over from the chief Bank had not arrived, he said, and the Church Dykely branch might be run close; would I let him have a cheque for two or three hundred pounds on the Bank at Alcester. I told him I did not believe I had anything like two hundred pounds lying at Alcester: but I drew a cheque out for that amount, and wrote a note telling the people there to cash it, and I would make it right."

"And Pell drove straight off to Alcester then and there, and cashed the cheque?" said Mr. Brandon in his cynical way.

"He did. He had told me I should receive the money on the following day. It did not come, or on the Friday either; and on Saturday I went to Alcester, thinking he might have paid it in there."

"Which of course he had not," returned old Brandon. "Well, you must have been foolish, to be so taken-in."

"Taken-in!" roared the Squire, in a passion. "Why, if he had asked me for two thousand pounds he might have had it—a man with the riches of Clement-Pell."

"Well, he wouldn't have got any from me. One who launched out as he did, and let his family launch out, I should never put much trust in. Any way, the riches are nowhere; and it is said Pell is nowhere too."

It was all true. As Sam Rimmer put it, Clement-Pell and his Banks had bursted-up.

XXIV.

GETTING AWAY.

You have heard of the avalanches that fall without warning and crush luckless dwellers in the Swiss mountains; and of mälströms that suddenly swallow up vessels sailing jauntily along on a calm sea; and of railway trains, filled with happy passengers, that one minute are running smoothly and safely along, and the next are nowhere: but nothing of this sort ever created the consternation that attended the bursting-up of the Clement-Pells.

It was Saturday night.—For we have to trace back a day or two. —Seated in the same room where I had seen him when I went back for Helen Whitney's bag, was Clement-Pell. That the man had come to his last gasp, he knew better than any one else in the world could have told him. How he had braved it out, and fought against the stream, and still kept off the explosion since the night but one before—Thursday—when Mr. Johnson had intruded himself into the grounds and then stealthily watched him from the trees, and he knew all was over, it might have puzzled him to tell. How he had fought against all for months, ay, and years, turned him sick only to recall. It had been a fierce, continuous, secret battle; and it had nearly worn him out, and turned his face and his hair grey before their time.

On the day following this fête-night, Friday, Clement-Pell took the train and was at his chief Bank early. He held his interview with Mr. Johnson; he saw other people; and his manner was free and open as usual. On this next day, Saturday, he had been denied to nearly all callers at the Bank: he was too busy to be interrupted, he told his clerks: and his son James boldly made appointments with them in his name for the Monday. After dark on Saturday evening, by the last train, he reached home, Parrifer Hall. And there he was, in that room of his; the door and shutters bolted and barred upon him, alternately pacing it in what looked like tribulation, and bending over account-books by the light of two wax candles.

Leaning his forehead on his hand, he sat there, and thought it out. He strove to look the situation fully in the face; what it was,

and what it would be. Ruin, and worse than ruin. Clement-Pell
had possessed good principles once: so to say, he possessed them
still. But he had allowed circumstances to get the better of him
and of them. He had come from his distant home (supposed to
have been London) as the manager of an insignificant and humble
little Bank: that was years ago. It was only a venture: but a certain
slice of luck, that need not be recorded here, favoured him, and he
got on beyond his best expectations. He might have made an
excellent living, nay, a good fortune, and kept his family as gentlepeople, had he been prudent. But the luck, coming suddenly, turned
his head, you see. Since then, I, Johnny Ludlow, who am no longer
the inexperienced boy of that past time, have known it turn the
heads of others. He launched out into ventures, his family launched
into expense. The ventures paid; the undue expense did not pay.
When matters came to be summed up by a raging public, it was
said that it was this expense which had swamped the Pells. That
alone, I suppose, it could not have been: but it must have gone
some way towards it.

It lay on his mind heavily that Saturday night. Looking back,
he got wondering how much more, in round figures, his family had
cost him than they ought to have cost. There had been his wife's
different expenses. Her houses, and her staff of servants, her
carriages and horses, her dresses and jewels, and all the rest that
it would take too long to tell of; and the costly bringing-up of his
daughters; and the frightful outlay of his two younger sons.
Fabian and Gusty Pell ought to have had ten thousand a year
apiece, to have justified it. James had his expenses too, but in a
quieter way. Clement-Pell ran his nervous fingers through his
damp hair, as he thought of this, and in his bitter mind told
himself that his family had ruined him. Unlimited spending—
show—the shooting up above their station! He gave a curse to it
now. He had not checked it when he might have done so; and it
(or they) got the upper hand, and then he could not. Nothing is so
difficult as to put down such expenses as these when they have
become a habit.

And so the years had soon come that he found need for supplies.
Unlimited as his millions were supposed to be by a confiding public,
Clement-Pell in secret wanted money more than most people. His
operations were gigantic, but then they required gigantic resources
to keep them going. Money was necessary—or the smash must
have come two or three years earlier. But sufficient money was
not then conveniently attainable by Clement-Pell: and so—he
created some. He believed when all his returns from these gigantic
operations should flow in, that he could redeem the act; could
replace the money, and no one ever be the wiser. But (it is the

old story; one that has been enacted before and since), he found somehow that he could not replace it. Like Tod and that gambling affair when we were in London, in trying to redeem himself, he only got further into the mire. Tod, in playing on to cover his losses, doubled them; Clement-Pell's fresh ventures in the stream of speculation only sent him into deeper water. Of late, Clement-Pell had been walking as on a red-hot ploughshare. It burnt and scorched him everlastingly, and he could not get out of it. But the end had come. The thunder-cloud so long hovering in the air was on the very point of bursting, and he was not able to meet it. He must get away: he could not face it.

Get away for good, as he hoped, never to be tracked by friends or foes. What his future life was to be he did not attempt to consider : he only knew that he would give all he ever had been worth to be able to live on, no matter how quietly, with his fellow-men around him. The little moderate home that he and his wife had once looked to as the haven of their desires, would have been a harbour of safety and pride to him now.

Say what you will, men do not like to be shown up as black sheep in the eyes of their fellows ; especially if they have hitherto stood out as conspicuously white leaders of the flock. The contrast is so great, the fall so startling. The public gives them all sorts of hard names ; as it did in the case of Clement-Pell. A desperately hardened man he must be, said the world, with a brazen conscience ; unprincipled as—well, yes, as Satan. But we may be very sure of one thing—that upon none does the disgrace tell so keenly, the ruin so heavily, the sense of shame so cruelly, as on these men themselves. Put it, if you will, that they make a purse and carry it off to set up a new home in some foreign land—they carry their sense of humiliation with them also ; and their sun of happiness in this life has set. Men have tried this before now, and died of it.

That was the *best* that lay prospectively before Clement-Pell : what the worst might be, he did not dare dwell upon. Certain ugly possibilities danced before his mental vision, like so many whirling ballet girls. "If I can only get away !" he muttered ; "if I can only get away ! "

He tried to confine his whole attention to the ledgers before him, and he put on his spectacles again. Mental trouble and mental work will dim the sight as well as whiten the hair and line the face, and Clement-Pell could not see as he had seen a year before. He altered figures ; he introduced entries ; he tore out whole leaves, and made a bonfire of them in the grate—carefully removing from the grate first of all its paper ornament. One book he burnt wholesale, even to the covers ; and the covers made a frightful smell and daunted him.

Money was wanted here, there, everywhere. Snatching a piece
of paper he idly dotted down the large sums occurring to him at the
moment; and quite laughed as he glanced at the total. These
were only business liabilities. At his elbow lay a pile of bills:
domestic and family debts. House rent, taxes, horses, carriages,
servants' wages, bills for food, bills for attire: all running back a
long while; for no one had pressed Clement-Pell. The outlay for
the fête might well have been profuse, since none of it was ever paid
for. Beside the bills lay letters from Fabian and Gusty—wanting
money as usual. To all these he scarcely gave a thought: they
were as nothing. Even though he were made bankrupt upon them,
they were still as nothing: for they would not brand his brow with
the word felon. And he knew that there were other claims, of
which no record appeared here, that might not be so easily wiped
out.

Just for a moment, he lost himself in a happy reverie of what
might have been had he himself been wise and prudent. It was
Gusty's pressing letter that induced the reflection. He saw himself a prosperous man of moderate expenses and moderate desires,
living at his ease in his own proper station, instead of apeing the
great world above him. His daughters reared to be good and
thoughtful women, his sons to be steady and diligent whatever their
calling, whether business or profession. And what were they?
"Curse the money and the pride that deluded me and my wife
to blindness!" broke with a groan from the lips of Clement-Pell.

A sharp knocking at the door made him start. He looked about
to see if there were anything to throw over his tell-tale table, and
had a great mind to take off his coat and fling it there. Catching
up the ornamental paper of the grate to replace it if he could, the
knocking came again, and with it his wife's voice, asking what that
smell of burning was. He let her in, and bolted the door again.

How far Mrs. Clement-Pell had been acquainted with his position,
never came out to the world. That she must have known something of it was thought to be certain; and perhaps the additional
launching out lately—the sojourn at Kensington, the fête, and all
the rest of it—had only been entered upon to disarm suspicion.
Shut up together in that room, they no doubt planned together the
getting-away. That Mrs. Clement-Pell fought against their leaving
home and grandeur, to become fugitives, flying in secret like so
many scapegoats, would be only natural: we should all so fight;
but he must have shown her that there was no help for it. When
she quitted the room again, she looked like one over whom twenty
years had passed—as Miss Phebus told us later. And the whole
of that night, Mrs. Clement-Pell never went to bed; but was in
her room gathering things together barefooted, lest she should be

heard. Jewels—dresses—valuables! It must have been an awful night; deciding which of her possessions she should take, and which leave for ever.

At six in the morning, Sunday, Mr. Clement-Pell's bell rang, and the groom was summoned. He was bade get the small open carriage ready to drive his master to the railway station to catch an early train. Being Sunday, early trains were not common. Mr. Clement-Pell had received news the previous night, as was intimated, of an uncle's illness. At that early hour, and Sunday besides, Clement-Pell must have thought he was safe from meeting people: but, as it happened (things do happen unexpectedly in this world), in bowling out from his own gates, he nearly bowled over Duffham. The Doctor, coming home from a distant patient, to whom he had been called in the night, was jogging along on his useful old horse.

"Well!" said he to the banker. "You *are* off early."

"Drive on, don't stop," whispered Clement-Pell to the groom. "I had news last night of the dangerous illness of my poor old uncle, and am going to see him," he called out to Duffham as they passed. "We shall have it piping hot again to-day, Doctor!"

The groom told of this encounter afterwards—as did Duffham too, for that matter. And neither of them had any more suspicion that Clement-Pell was playing a part than a baby could have had. In the course of the morning the groom drove in again, having safely conveyed his master to a distant station. The family went to church as usual, chaperoned by Miss Phebus. Mrs. Clement-Pell stayed at home, saying she had a headache: and no doubt quietly completed her preparations.

About six o'clock at night a telegram was delivered. The uncle was dying: Mrs. Clement-Pell must come as soon as possible, to be in time to see him: as to bringing the children she must do as she pleased about that. In Mrs. Pell's agitation and dismay she read the telegram aloud to the governess and the servant who brought it to her. Then was confusion! Mrs. Pell seemed to have lost her head. Take the children?—Of course she should take them;—and, oh, when was the earliest time they could start?

The earliest time by rail was the following morning. And part of the night was again passed in preparation—openly, this time. Mrs. Clement-Pell said they should probably stay away some days, perhaps a week or two, and must take things accordingly. The boxes were all brought into her room, that she might superintend; the poor old uncle was so very particular as to dress, she said, and she trusted he might yet recover. On the Monday morning, she and her daughters departed in the large carriage, at the same early hour that her husband had gone, and for the same remote station. After all, not so much luggage went; only a box a-piece. In stepping into her carriage, she told the servants that it would be an excellent opportunity to clean the paint of the sitting-rooms and of the first-floor while she was away : the previous week she had remarked to them that it wanted doing.

The day went on ; the household no doubt enjoying their freedom and letting the paint alone. No suspicion was aroused amongst them until late in the afternoon, when a curious rumour was brought over of some confusion at the chief Bank—that it had stopped and its master had flown. At first the governess and servants laughed at this : but confirmation soon came thick and three-fold. Clement-Pell had burst-up.

And why the expression "bursting-up" should have been universally applied to the calamity by all people, high and low, I know no more than you ; but it was so. Perhaps in men's minds there existed some assimilation between a bubble, that shines brightly for its brief existence before bursting, like the worthless froth it is, and the brilliant but foundationless career of Mr. Clement-Pell.

The calamity at first was too great to be believed in. It drove people mad only to fancy it might be true : and one or two, alas ! subsequently went mad in reality. For the bursting-up of Mr. Clement-Pell's huge undertakings caused the bursting-up of many private ones, and of households with them. Means of living went : homes were desolated.

It would be easier to tell you of those who had not trusted money in the hands of Clement-Pell, than of those who had. Some had given him their all. Led away by the fascinating prospect of large interest, they forgot future safety in the dazzling but delusive light of immediate good. I should like it to be distinctly understood that I, Johnny Ludlow, am writing of a matter which took place years ago ; and not of any recent event, or events, that may have since occurred to shake public equanimity in our own local world.

Disbelief in the misfortune was natural. Clement-Pell had stood on a lofty pedestal, unapproachable by common individuals. We put greater trust in him—in his unbounded wealth, his good faith, his stability—than we could have put in any other man on the face of the globe. We should almost as soon have expected the skies to fall as Clement-Pell. The interests of so many were involved and the ruin would be so universal, that the terrified natives could only take refuge in disbelief : and Squire Todhetley was amongst them.

The news was brought to Dyke Manor on the Tuesday morning, as you have heard, by the butcher boy, Sam Rimmer ; and was confirmed by Mr. Brandon. When the first momentary shock had been digested by the Squire, he arrived at the conclusion that it must be false. But that Sam had trotted off, he might have heard the length of the Pater's tongue. Sam being gone, he turned his indignation on Mr. Brandon.

"One would have thought you had sense to know better, Brandon," said he, raging about the breakfast-room with the skirts of his light morning coat held out behind him. "Giving ear to a cock-and-bull story that *can't* be true! Take care Pell does not get to hear it. He'd sue you for defamation."

"He'd be welcome," nodded old Brandon, in his thin voice, as he stood, whip in hand, against the window.

"The grand fête of last Thursday," gasped Mrs. Todhetley—who had been puzzling her brains over Sam Rimmer's master's book, the writing in which could never be deciphered. "Surely the Clement-Pells would not have given that fête had things been going wrong with them."

"And poured iced champagne, unlimited, down folk's throats; and strutted about in point-lace and diamonds," added old Brandon. "Madam, I'd believe it all the more for that."

As he spoke, the remembrance of the scene I had witnessed in the grounds, and Clement-Pell's curious fear later when I told him of the same man watching him, flashed over me, bringing a conviction that the report was true.

"I heard it at the chief Bank yesterday," began Mr. Brandon. "Having some business to transact in the town, I went over by train in the afternoon, and chanced to meet Wilcox in High Street. He is a red-faced man in general——"

"Oh, I know Wilcox," impatiently interrupted the Squire. "Face as red as the sun in a fog. What has that to do with it?"

"Well, it was as pale yesterday as the moon on a frosty night," went on old Brandon. "I asked if he had an attack of bile—being subject to it myself—and he said No, it was an attack of fright. And then he told me there was a report in town that something was wrong with Pell's affairs, and that he had run away. Wilcox will lose every penny of his savings."

"All talk; all talk," said the Pater in his obstinacy.

"And for a man to come to Wilcox's age, which must be five-and-fifty, it is no light blow to lose a life's savings," calmly went on old Brandon. "I went to the Bank, and found it besieged by an excited and angry crowd fighting to get in, the door locked, and the porter vainly trying to put up the shutters. That was enough to show me what the matter was, and I left Wilcox to it."

The Squire stared in perplexity, rubbing up his scanty hair the wrong way while his senses came to him.

"It is all true," said Mr. Brandon, nodding to him. "Church Dykely is in an uproar this morning already."

"I'll go and see for myself," said the Squire, stripping off his
nankeen coat in haste so great that he tore one sleeve nearly out.
"I'll go and see; this is *not* credible. Clement-Pell would never
have swindled me out of two hundred pounds only a day or two
before he knew he was going all to smash."

"The most likely time for him to do it," persisted Mr. Brandon.
"People, as a rule, only do these things when they are desperate."

But the Squire did not stay to listen. Settling himself into his
other coat, he went driving on across the fields as though he were
walking for a wager. Mr. Brandon mounted his cob, and put up
his umbrella against the sun.

"Never embark any money with these beguiling people that
promise you undue interest, Johnny Ludlow," said Mr. Brandon, as
I kept by his side, and opened the gates for him. "Where would
you have been now, young man—or, worse, where should I have
been—had I, the trustee of your property, consented to risk it with
Pell? He asked me to do it."

"Clement-Pell did, sir? When?'

"A year or two ago. I gave him an answer, Johnny: and I
fancy he has not altogether liked me since. 'I could not think of
placing even a shilling of Johnny Ludlow's where I did not know
it to be safe,' I said to him. 'It will be safe with me,' says Pell,
sharply. 'Possibly so, Mr. Pell,' I answered; 'but you see there's
only your word as guarantee, and that is not enough for an honest
trustee.' That shut him up."

"Do you mean to say you have doubted Clement-Pell's stability,
Brandon?" demanded the Squire, who was near enough to hear
this.

"I don't know about doubting," was the answer. "I have
thought it as likely to come to a smash as not. That the chances
for it were rather better than half."

This sent the Squire on again. *He* had no umbrella; and his
straw hat glistened in the heat.

Church Dykely was in a commotion. Folk were rushing up to
the little branch Bank black in the face, as if their collars throttled
them; for the news was spreading like fire in dry turf. The Squire
went bolting in through every obstruction, and seized upon the
manager.

"Do you mean to tell me that it's true, Robertson?" he fiercely
cried.—"That things have gone to smash?"

"I am afraid it is, sir," said Robertson, who looked more dead
than alive. "I am unable to understand it. It has fallen upon me
with as much surprise as it has on others."

"Now, don't you go and tell falsehoods, Robertson," roared the
Squire, as if he meant to shake the man. "Surprise upon you,

indeed! Why, have you not been here—at the head and tail of everything?"

"But I did not know how affairs were going. Indeed, sir, I tell you truth."

"Tell a jackass not to bray!" foamed the Squire. "Have you been short of funds here lately, or have you not? Come, answer me that."

"It is true. We have been short. But Mr. Clement-Pell excused it to me by saying that a temporary lock-up ran the Banks short, especially the small branch Banks. I declare, before Heaven, that I implicitly believed him," added Robertson, "and never suspected there could be any graver cause."

"Then you are either a fool or a knave."

"Not a knave, Squire Todhetley. A fool I suppose I have been."

"I want my two hundred pounds," returned the Squire. "And, Robertson, I mean to have it."

But Robertson had known nothing of the loan ; was surprised to hear of it now. As to repayment, that was out of his power. He had not two hundred pence left in the place, let alone pounds.

"It is a case of swindle," said the Squire. "It's not one of ordinary debt."

"I can't help it," returned Robertson. "If it were to save Mr. Clement-Pell from hanging, I could not give a stiver of it. There's my own salary, sir, since Midsummer ; that, I suppose, I shall lose : and I can't afford it, and I don't know what will become of me and my poor little children."

At this, the Squire's voice and anger dropped, and he shook hands with Robertson. But, as a rule, every one began by brow-beating the manager. The noise was deafening.

How had Pell got off? By which route : road or rail? By day or night? It was a regular hubbub of questions. Mr. Brandon sat on his cob all the while, patiently blinking his eyes at the people.

Palmerby of Rock Cottage came up ; his old hands trembling, his face as white as the new paint on Duffham's windows. "It can't be true!" he was crying. "It can't be true!"

"Had you money in his hands, Palmerby?"

"Every shilling I possess in the world."

Mr. Brandon opened his lips to blow him up for foolishness : but something in the poor old face stopped him. Palmerby elbowed his way into the Bank. Duffham came out of his house, a gallipot of ointment in his hand.

"Well, this is a pretty go!"

The Squire took him by the buttonhole. "Where's the villainous swindler off to, Duffham?"

" I should like to know," answered the surgeon. " I'd be pretty soon on his trail and ask him to refund my money."

" But surely he has none of yours ? "

" Pretty nigh half the savings of my years."

" Mercy be good to us ! " cried the Pater. " He got two hundred pounds out of me last week. What's to become of us all ? "

" It's not so much a question of what is to become of us—of you and me, Squire," said Duffham, philosophically, " as of those who had invested with him their all. We can bear the loss : you can afford it without much hurt ; I must work a few years longer, Heaven permitting me, than I had thought to work. That's the worst of us. But what will those others do ? What will be the worst for them ? "

Mr. Brandon nodded approvingly from his saddle.

" Coming home last night from Duck Lane—by the way, there's another infant at John Mitchel's, because he had not enough before —the blacksmith accosted me, saying Clement-Pell was reported to be in a mess and to have run off. The thing sounded so preposterous that I thought at first Dobbs must have been drinking ; and told him that I happened to know Clement-Pell was only off to a relative's death-bed. For on Sunday morning, you see—— "

A crush and rush stopped Duffham's narrative, and nearly knocked us all down. Ball the milkman had come bumping amongst us in a frantic state, his milk-cans swinging from his shoulders against my legs.

" I say, Ball, take care of my trousers. Milk stains, you know."

" Master Ludlow, sir, I be a'most mad, I think. Folks is saying as Mr. Clement-Pell and his banks have busted-up."

" Well ? You have not lost anything, I suppose ? "

" Not lost ! " panted poor Ball. " I've lost all I've got. 'Twere a hundred pound, Mr. Johnny, scraped together hard enou', as goodness knows. Mr. Clement-Pell were a-talking to me one day, and he says, says he, Ah, says he, it's difficult to get much interest now ; money's plentiful. I give eight per cent., says he ; most persons gets but three. Would ye take nine, sir, says I ; my hundred pound ? If you like, he says. And I took it to him, gentlemen, thinking what luck I was in, and how safe it were. My hundred pound ! "—letting the cans down with a clatter. " My hundred pound that I'd toiled so hard for ! Gentlefolk, wherever be all the money a-gone ? "

Well, it was a painful scene. One we were glad to get out of. The Squire, outrageously angry at the way he had been done out of his money, insisted on going to Parrifer Hall. Mr. Brandon rode his cob ; Duffham stepped into his surgery to get his hat.

One might have fancied a sale was going on. The doors were

open: boxes belonging to some of the servants were lying by the side-entrance, ready to be carted away; people (creditors and curiosity-mongers) stood about. Sam Rimmer's master, the butcher, came out of the house as we went in, swearing. Perkins had not been paid for a twelvemonth, and said it would be his ruin. Miss Phebus was in the hall, and seemed to have been having it out with him. She was a light-haired, bony lady of thirty-five, or so, and had made a rare good gipsy that day in the tent. Her eyes were peculiar: green in some lights, yellow in others: a frightfully hard look they had in them this morning.

"Oh, Mr. Todhetley, I am so glad to see you!" she said. "It is a cruel turn that the Clement-Pells have served me? leaving me here without warning, to bear the brunt of all this! Have you come in the interests of the family?"

"I've come after my own interests, ma'am," returned the Pater. "To find out, if I can, where Clement Pell has gone to: and to see if I can get back any of the money I have been done out of."

"Why, it seems every one must be a creditor!" she exclaimed in surprise, on hearing this.

"I know I am one," was his answer.

"To serve *me* such a trick,—to behave to me with this duplicity: it is infamous," went on Miss Phebus, after she had related to us the chief events of the Sunday, as connected with the story of the dying uncle and the telegram. "If I get the chance, I will have the law against them, Mr. Todhetley."

"It is what a few more of us mean to do, ma'am," he answered.

"They owe me forty pounds. Yes, Mr. Duffham, it is forty pounds: and I cannot afford to lose it. Mrs. Pell has put me off from time to time: and I supposed it to be all right; I suspected nothing. They have not treated me well lately, either. Leaving me here to take care of the house while they were enjoying themselves up in Kensington! I had a great mind to give warning then. The German governess got offended while they were in town, and left. Some friend of Fabian Pell's was rude to her."

A little man looked into the room just then; noting down the furniture with his eye. "None of these here articles must be moved, you understand, mum," he said to Miss Phebus.

"Don't talk to me," she answered wrathfully. "I am going out of the house as soon as I can put my things together." And the man went away.

"If I had only suspected!" she resumed to us, her angry tone full of pain; "and I think I might have done so, had I exercised my wits. My room is next to Mrs. Pell's; but it's not much larger than a closet, and has no fireplace in it: she only gave it me because it was not good enough for any one else. Saturday night was very hot—as you must remember—and I could not sleep. The window was open, but the room felt like an oven. After tossing about for I don't know how long, I got up and opened the door, thinking it might admit a breath of air. At that moment I heard sounds below—the quiet shutting of a door, and advancing footsteps. Wondering who could be up so late, I peeped out and saw Mrs. Pell. She came up softly, a candle in her hand, and her face quite curious and altered—aged and pale and haggard. She must be afraid of the ghosts, I thought to myself, as she turned off into her chamber—for we had been telling ghost-stories that night up to bed-time. After that, I did not get to sleep ; not, as it seemed, for hours ; and all the time I heard drawers being opened and shut in her bed and dressing-room. She must even then have been preparing for flight."

" And the dying uncle was invented for the occasion, I presume," remarked Mr. Duffham.

"All I know is, I never heard of an uncle before," she tartly answered. "I asked Mrs. Clement-Pell on Sunday night where the uncle lived, and how long a journey they had to go : she answered shortly that he was at his country house, and bade me not tease her. Mr. Duffham, can my own boxes be stopped?"

" I should think no one would attempt to do it," he answered. " But I'd get them out as soon as I could, were I you, Miss Phebus."

" What a wreck it will be ! " she exclaimed.

" You have used the right word, ma'am," put in Mr. Brandon, who had left his horse outside. " And not only here. Wrecks they will be ; and many of them."

We stood looking at one another ruefully. The Pater had come to hunt up his two hundred pounds ; but there did not seem much chance of his doing it. " Look here," said he suddenly to the governess, " where was that telegram sent from ? "

" We have not been able to discover. It was only seen by Mrs. Pell. After she had read it aloud, she crushed it up in her hand, as if in frightful distress, and called out about the poor dear old uncle. She took care it should not be seen : we may be very sure of that."

" But who sent the telegram ? "

" I don't know," said Miss Phebus viciously. " Her husband, no doubt. Neither was the luggage that they took with them labelled : we have remembered the fact since."

" I think we might track them by that luggage," observed the Pater. " Five big boxes."

" If you do track them by it I'll eat the luggage wholesale," cried wise old Brandon. " Clement-Pell's not a fool, or his wife either. They'll go off just in the opposite direction that they appeared to go—and their boxes in another. As to Pell, he was probably unknown at the distant station the groom drove him to."

There was no end to be served in staying longer at the house, and we quitted it, leaving poor Miss Phebus to her temper. I had never much liked her; but I could not help feeling for her that unlucky morning.

"What's to be done now?" gloomily cried the Squire, while old Brandon was mounting. "It's like being in a wood that you can't get out of. If Clement-Pell had played an honest part with me: if he had come and said, 'Mr. Todhetley, I am in sore need of a little help,' and told me a bit about things: I don't say that I would have refused him the money. But to dupe me out of it in the specious way he did was nothing short of swindling; and I will bring him to book for it if I can."

That day was only the beginning of sorrow. There have been such cases since: perhaps worse; where a sort of wholesale ruin has fallen upon a neighbourhood: but none, to me, have equalled that. It was the first calamity of the kind in my experience; and in all things, whether of joy or sorrow, our earliest impressions are the most vivid. It is the first step that costs, the French tell us: and that is true of all things.

The ruin turned out to be wider even than was feared; the distress greater. Some had only lost part of their superfluous cash. It was mortifying; but it did not further affect their prosperity, or take from them the means of livelihood; no luxuries need be given up, or any servants dispensed with. Others had invested so much that it would throw them back years, perhaps cripple them for life. Pitiable enough, that, but not the worst. It was as nothing to those who had lost their all.

People made it their business to find out more about Mr. and Mrs. Clement-Pell than had been known before. Both were of quite obscure origin, it turned out, and he had *not* been a lawyer in London, but only a lawyer's clerk. So much the more credit to him for getting on to be something better. If he had only had the sense to let well alone! But she?—well, all I mean to say here, is this: the farmers she had turned up her nose at were far, far better born and bred, even the smallest of them, than she was. Let that go: other women have been just as foolishly upstart as Mrs. Clement-Pell. One fact came out that I think *riled* the public worse than any other: that his Christian name was Clement and his surname Pell. He had united the two when growing into a great man, and put a "J." before the Clement, which had no right there. Mr. Brandon had known it all along—at least he chanced to know that in early life his name was simply Clement Pell. The Squire, when he heard of this, went into a storm of reproach at old Brandon, because he had not told it.

"Nay, why should I have sought to do the man an injury?" remonstrated Mr. Brandon. "It was no business of mine, that I should interfere. We must live and let live, Squire, if we care to go through the world peaceably."

The days went on, swelling the list of creditors who came forward to declare themselves. The wonder was, that so many had been taken in. But you see, people had not made it their business to proclaim that their money lay with Clement-Pell. Gentlefolk who lived on their fortunes; professional men of all classes, including the clergy; commercial men of high and low degree; small trades-people; widows with slender incomes, and spinsters with less. If Clement-Pell had taken the money of these people, not intentionally to swindle them, as the Squire put it in regard to his own, but only knowing there was a chance that it would not be safe, he must have been a hard and cruel man. I think the cries of the defrauded of that unhappy time must have gone direct to heaven.

He was not spared. Could hard words injure an absentee, Clement-Pell must have come in for all sorts of harm. His ears burned, I should fancy—if there's any truth in the saying that ears burn when distant friends give pepper. The queerest fact was, that no money seemed to be left. Of the millions that Clement-Pell had been worth, or had had to play with, nothing remained. It was inconceivable. What had become of the stores? The hoards of gold; the chests, popularly supposed to be filled with it; the bank-notes; the floating capital—where was it all? No one could tell. People gazed at each other with dismayed faces as they asked it. Bit by bit, the awful embarrassment in which he had been plunged for years came to light. The fictitious capital he had created had consumed itself: and the good money of the public had gone with it. Of course he had made himself secure and carried off loads, said the maddened creditors. But they might have been mistaken there.

For a week or two confusion reigned. Accountants set to work in a fog; official assignees strove to come to the bottom of the muddy waters. There existed some of what people called securities; but they were so hemmed in by claims that the only result would be that there would not be anything for any one. Clement-Pell had done well to escape, or the unhappy victims had certainly tarred and feathered him. All that time he was being searched for, and not a clue could be obtained to him. Stranger perhaps to say, there was no clue to his wife and daughters either. The five boxes had disappeared. It was ascertained that certain boxes, answering to the description, had been sent to London on the Monday from a populous station by a quick train, and were claimed at the London terminus by a gentleman who did *not* bear any resemblance to Clement-Pell. I'm sure the excitement of the affair was something before unknown to the Squire, as he raged up hill and down dale in the August weather, and it must have been as good as a course of Turkish baths to him.

Ah me! it is all very well to write of it in a light strain at this distance of time; but God alone knows how many hearts were broken by it.

One of the worst cases was poor Jacob Palmerby's. He had saved money that brought him in about a hundred a year in his old age. Clement-Pell got hold of the money, doubled the interest, and Palmerby thought that a golden era had set in. For several years now he had enjoyed it. His wife was dead; his only son, who had been a sizar at Cambridge, was a curate in London. With the bursting up of Clement-Pell, Jacob Palmerby's means failed: he had literally not a sixpence left in the world. The blow seemed to have struck him stupid. He mostly sat in silence, his head down; his clothes neglected.

"Come, Palmerby, you must cheer up, you know," said the Squire to him one evening that we looked in at Rock Cottage, and found Mr. Brandon there.

"Me cheer up," he returned, lifting his face for a moment—and in the last fortnight it had grown ten years older. "What am I to cheer up for? There's nothing left. *I* can go into the workhouse—but there's poor Michael."

"Michael?"

"My son, the parson. The capital that ought to have been his after me, and brought him in his hundred a year, as it did me before I drew it from the funds, is gone. Gone. It is of him I think. He has been a good son always. I hope he won't take to cursing me."

"Parsons don't curse, you know, and Michael will be a good son still," said Mr. Brandon, shrilly. "Don't you fret, Palmerby. Fretting does no good."

"It 'ud wear out a donkey—as I tell him," put in the old woman-servant, Nanny, who had brought in his supper of bread-and-milk.

He did not lift his head; just swayed it once from side to side by way of general response.

"It's the way he goes on all day, masters," whispered Nanny when we went out. "His heart's a-breaking—and I wish it was that knave of a Pell's instead. All these purty flowers to be left," pointing to the clusters of roses and geraniums and honeysuckles within the gate, "and the chairs and tables to be sold, and the very beds to be took from under us!"

"Nay, nay, Nanny, it may turn out better than that," spoke the Squire.

"Why, how can it turn out better, sirs?" she asked. "Pell didn't pay the dividends this two times past: and the master, believing as all his excuses was gospel, never thought of pressing for it. If we be in debt to the landlord and others, is it our fault? But the sticks and stones must be sold to pay, and the place be given up. There be the work'us for me; I know that, and it don't much matter; but it'll be a crying shame if the poor master have to move into it."

So it would be. And there were others in a similar plight to his; nothing else but the workhouse before them.

"He won't never live to go—that's one consolation," was Nanny's last comment as she held the gate open. "Good evening to ye, sirs; good evening, Master Johnny."

What with talking to Dobbs the blacksmith, and staying with Duffham to drink what he called a dish of tea, it was almost dark when I set out home; the Squire and Mr. Brandon having gone off without me. I was vaulting over the stile the near way across the fields, expecting to catch it for staying, when a man shot into my path from behind the hedge.

"Johnny Ludlow."

Well, I did feel surprised. It was Gusty Pell!

"Halloa!" said I. "I thought you were in Scotland."

"I was there," he answered. And then, while we looked at one another, he began to tell me the reason of his coming away. Why it is that all kinds of people seem to put confidence in me and trust me with matters they'd never speak of to others, I have never found out. Had it been Tod, for instance, Gusty Pell would never have shown himself out of the hedge to talk to him.

Gusty, shooting the grouse on the moors, had found his purse emptied of its last coin. He wrote to his father for more money: wrote and wrote; but none arrived: neither money nor letter. Being particularly in want of supplies, he borrowed a sovereign or two from his friends, and came off direct to see the reason why. Arrived within a few miles of home he heard very ugly rumours; stories that startled him. So he waited and came on by night, thinking it more prudent not to show himself.

"Tell me all about it, Johnny Ludlow, for the love of goodness!" he cried, his voice a little hoarse with agitation, his hand grasping my arm like a vice. "I have been taking a look at the place outside"—pointing up the road towards Parrifer Hall—"but it seems to be empty."

It was empty, except for a man who had charge of the things until the sale could take place. Softening the narrative a little, and not calling everything by the name the public called it, I gave the facts to Gusty.

He drew a deep breath at the end, like a hundred sighs in one. Then I asked him how it was he had not heard these things—had not been written to.

" I don't know," he said. " I have been moving about Scotland : perhaps a letter of theirs may have miscarried; and I suppose my later letters did not. reach them. The last letter I had was from Constance, giving me an account of some grand fête here that had taken place the previous day."

" Yes. I was at it with Todhetley and the Whitneys. The—the crisis came three or four days after that."

" Johnny, where's my father ? " he asked, after a pause, his voice sunk to a whisper.

" It is not known where he is."

" Is it true that he is being—looked for ? "

" I am afraid it is."

" And, if they find him—what then ? Why don't you speak ? " he added impatiently.

" I don't know what. Some people say it will only be a bad case of bankruptcy."

" Any way, it is a complete smash."

" Yes, it's that."

" Will it, do you think, be ruin, Johnny ? Ruin utter and unmitigated ? "

" It is that already—to many persons round about."

" But I mean to my own people," said he, impatiently.

" Well, I should fear it would be."

Gusty took off his hat to wipe his brow. He looked white in the starlight.

" What will become of me ? I must fly too," he muttered, as if to the stars. " And what of Fabian ?—he cannot remain in his regiment. Johnny Ludlow, this blow is like death to me."

And it struck me that of the two calamities, Gusty Pell, nonreligious though he was, would rather have met death. I felt dreadfully sorry for him.

" Where's James ? " he suddenly asked. " Is he gone too ? "

" James disappeared on the Sunday, it is said. It would hardly have been safe for him to remain : the popular feeling is very bitter."

" Well, I must make myself scarce again also," he said, after a pause. " Could you lend me a pound or so, Johnny, if you've got it about you ? "

I told him I wished I had ; he should have been heartily welcome
to it. Pulling out my pockets, I counted it all up—two shillings and
fivepence. Gusty turned from it with disdain.

"Well, good evening, Johnny. Thank you for your good wishes
—and for telling me what you have. I don't know to whom else
I could have applied : and I am glad to have chanced to meet
you."

He gave another deep sigh, shook my hand, got over the stile,
and crept away, keeping close to the hedge, as if he intended to
make for Alcester. I stood and watched him until he was lost in
the shadows.

And so the Pells, one and all, went into exile in some unknown
region, and the poor duped people stayed to face their ruin at home.
It was an awful time, and that's the truth.

XXV.

OVER THE WATER.

WE had what they called the "dead-lights" put in the ladies' cabin at Gravesend: that will show what the weather was expected to be in the open sea. In the saloon, things were pitching about before we reached Margate. Rounding the point off Broadstairs, the steamer caught it strong and sharp.

"Never heed a bit of pitching: we've the wind all for us, and shall make a short passage," said the captain in hearty tones, by way of consolation to the passengers generally. "A bit o' breeze at sea is rather pleasant."

Pleasant it might be to him, Captain Tune, taking in a good dinner, as much at ease as if he had been sitting in his dining-room ashore. Not so pleasant, though, for some of us, his passengers.

Ramsgate and other landmarks passed, and away in the open sea it was just a gale. That, and nothing less. Some one said so to the man at the wheel: a tall, middle-aged, bronzed-faced fellow in shirt sleeves and open blue waistcoat.

"Bless y're ignorance! This a gale! Why, 'taint half a one. It'll be a downright fair passage, this 'un will, shorter nor ord'nary."

"What do you call a gale—if this is not one?"

"I ain't allowed to talk: you may see it writ up."

"Writ up," it was. "Passengers are requested not to talk to the man at the wheel." But if he had been allowed to talk, and talked till now, he would never have convinced some of the unhappy creatures around, that the state of wind then blowing was not a gale.

It whistled in the sails, it roared over the paddle-wheels, it seemed to play at pitch-and-toss with the sea. The waves rose with mountain force, and then broke like mad: the steamer rolled and lurched, and righted herself; and then lurched and rolled again. Captain Tune stood on the bridge, apparently enjoying it, the gold band on his cap glistening in the sun. We got his name from the boat bills; and a jolly, courteous, attentive captain he seemed to be. But for the pitching and tossing and general discomfort, it would have been called beautiful weather. The air was bright; the sun as hot as it is in July, although September was all but out.

"Johnny. Johnny Ludlow."

The voice—Mr. Brandon's—was too faint to be squeaky. He sat amidships on a camp stool, his back against the cabin wall—or whatever the boarding was—wrapped in a plaid. A yellow handkerchief was tied over his head, partly to keep his cap on, partly to protect his ears. The handkerchief hid most of his face, except his little nose; which looked pinched and about as yellow as the silk.

"Did you call me, sir?"

"I wish you'd see if you can get to my tail pocket, Johnny. I've been trying this ten minutes, and do nothing but find my hands hopelessly entangled in the plaid. There's a tin box of lozenges there."

"Do you feel ill, sir?" I asked, as I found the box, and gave it to him.

"Never was ill at sea in my life, Johnny, in the way you mean. But the motion always gives me the most frightful headache imaginable. How are you?"

The less said about how I was, the better. All I hoped was he wouldn't keep me talking.

"Where's the Squire?" he asked.

I pointed to a distant heap on the deck, from which groans came forth occasionally: and just managed to speak in answer.

"He seems uncommonly ill, sir."

"Well, he *would* come, you know, Johnny. Tell him he ought to take——"

What he ought to take was lost in the rush of a wave which came dashing over us.

After all, I suppose it was a quick and good, though rough passage, for Boulogne-sur-Mer was sighted before we thought for. As the stiller I kept the better I was, there was nothing to do but to sit motionless and stare at it.

You'll never guess what was taking us across the Channel. Old Brandon called it from the first a wild-goose chase; but, go, the Squire would. He was after that gentleman who had played havoc with many people's hearts and money, who had, so to say, scattered ruin wholesale—Mr. Clement-Pell.

Not a trace had the public been able to obtain as to the direction of the Pells' flight; not a clue to the spot in which they might be hiding themselves. The weeks had gone on since their departure: August passed into September, September was passing: and for all that could be discovered of them, they might as well never have existed. The committee for winding up the miserable affairs raged

and fumed and pitied, and wished they could just put their hands
on the man who had wrought the evil; Squire Todhetley raged and
fumed also on his own score; but none of them were any the nearer
finding Pell. In my whole life I had never seen the Squire so
much put out. It was not altogether the loss of the two hundred
pounds he had been (as he persisted in calling it) swindled out of;
it was the distress he had to witness daily around him. I do think
nothing would have given him more satisfaction than to join a mob
in administering lynch law to Clement-Pell, and to tar and feather
him first. Before this happened, the Squire had talked of going to
the seaside: but he would not listen to a word on the subject now:
only to speak of it put him out of temper. Tod was away. He
received an invitation to stay with some people in Gloucestershire,
who had good game preserves; and was off the next day. And
things were in this lively state at home: the Squire grumbling,
• Mrs. Todhetley driving about with one or other of the children in
the mild donkey-cart, and I fit to eat my head off with having
nothing to do: when some news arrived of the probable sojourning
place of the Clement-Pells.

The news was not much. And perhaps hardly to be relied on.
Mr. and Mrs. Sterling at the Court had been over to Paris for a
fortnight: taking the baby with them. I must say that Mrs.
Sterling was always having babies—if any one cares for the information. Before one could walk another was sure to arrive. And
not only the baby had been to Paris, but the baby's nursemaid,
Charlotte. Old Brandon, remarking upon it, said he'd rather
travel with half a score of mischievous growing boys than one
baby: and *they* were about the greatest calamity he could
think of.

Well, in coming home, the Sterling party had, to make the short
crossing, put themselves on board the Folkestone boat at Boulogne,
and the nursemaid was sitting on deck with the baby on her lap,
when, just as the steamer was moving away, she saw, or thought
she saw, Constance Pell, standing on the shore a little apart from
the people gathered there to watch the boat off. Mrs. Sterling told
the nurse she must be mistaken: but Charlotte held to it that she
was not. As chance had it, Squire Todhetley was at the Court
with old Sterling when they got home; and he heard this. It put
him into a commotion. He questioned Charlotte closely, but she
never wavered in her statement.

"I am positive it was Miss Constance Pell, sir," she repeated.
"She had on a thick blue veil, and one of them new-fashioned
large round capes. Just as I happened to be looking at her—not
thinking it was anybody I knew—a gust of wind took the veil
right up above her bonnet, and I saw it was Miss Constance Pell.

She pulled at the veil with both her hands, in a scuffle like, to get it down again."

"Then I'll go off to Boulogne," said the Squire, with stern resolution. And back he came to Dyke Manor full of it.

"It will be a wild-goose chase," observed Mr. Brandon, who had called in. "If Pell has taken himself no further away than Boulogne—that is, allowing he has got out of England at all—he is a greater fool than I took him for."

"Wild-goose chase or not, I shall go," said the Pater, hotly. "And I shall take Johnny: he'll be useful as an interpreter."

"I will go with you," came the unexpected rejoinder of Mr. Brandon. "I want a bit of a change."

And so we went up to London to take the steamer there. And here we were, all three of us, ploughing the waves *en route* for Boulogne, on the wild-goose chase after Clement-Pell.

Just as the passengers had come to the conclusion that they, must die of it, the steamer shot into Boulogne harbour. She was tolerably long swinging round; then was made fast, and we began to land. Mr. Brandon took off his yellow turban and shook his cap out.

"Johnny, I'd never have come if I had known it was going to be like this," moaned the poor Squire—and every trace of red had gone out of his face. "No, not even to catch Clement-Pell. What on earth is that crowd for?"

It looked about five hundred people; they were pushing and crushing each other, fighting for places to see us land and go through the custom-house. No need to tell of this: not a reader of you, but you must know it well.

The first thing, patent to my senses amidst the general confusion, was hearing my name shouted out by the Squire in the custom-house.

"Johnny Ludlow!"

He was standing before two Frenchmen in queer hats, who sat behind a table or counter, asking him questions and preparing to write down the answers: what his name was, and what his age, and where he was born, just as though he were a footman in want of a place. Not a word could he understand, and looked round for me helplessly. As to my French—well, I knew it pretty well, and talked often with our French master at Dr. Frost's: but you must not think I was as fluent in it as though I'd been a born Frenchman. It was rather the other way.

We put up at the Hôtel des Bains. A good hotel—as is well known—but nothing to look at from the street. Mr. Brandon had been in Boulogne before, and always used it. The *table d'hôte* restored the Squire's colour and spirits together: and by the time

dinner was over, he felt ready to encounter the sea again. As to
Mr. Brandon, he made his meal of some watery broth, two slices of
melon, and a bowlful of pounded sugar.

The great question was—to discover whether the Clement-Pells
were in the town; and, if so, to find them out. Mr. Brandon's
opinion never varied—that Charlotte had been mistaken and they
were not in the place at all. Allowing, for argument's sake, that
they were there, he said, they would no doubt be living partly in
concealment; and it might not answer for us to go inquiring about
them openly, lest they got to hear of it, and took measures to secure
themselves. There was sense in that.

The next day we went strolling up to the post-office in the Rue
des Vieillards, the wind blowing us round the corners sharply;
and there inquired for the address of the Clement-Pells. The
people were not very civil; stared as if they'd never been asked for
an address before; and shortly affirmed that no such name was
known *there*.

"Why, of course not," said old Brandon quietly, as we 'strolled
down again. "They wouldn't be in the town under their own name
—if they are here at all."

And there would lie the difficulty.

That wind, that the man at the wheel had scoffed at when called
a gale, had been at any rate the beginning of one. It grew higher
and higher, chopping round to the south-west, and for three days
we had it kindly. On the second day not a boat could get out or
in; and there were no bathing-machines to be had. The sea was
surging, full of tumult—but it was a grand sight to see. The waves
dashed over the pier, ducking the three or four venturesome spirits
who went there. I was one of them—and received a good blowing
up from Mr. Brandon for my pains.

The gale passed. The weather set in again calm and lovely;
but we seemed to be no nearer hearing anything of the Clement-
Pells. So far as that went, the time was being wasted: but I
don't think any of us cared much about that. We kept our eyes
open, looking out for them, and asked questions in a quiet way:
at the *établissement*, where the dancing went on; at the libraries;
and of the pew women at the churches. No; no success: and
time went on to the second week in October. On account of the
remarkably fine weather, the season and amusements were pro-
tracted.

One Friday morning I was sitting on the pier in the sunshine,
listening to a couple of musicians, who appeared there every day.
He had a violin; she played a guitar, and sang "Figaro." An old
gentleman by me said he had heard her sing the same song for
nearly a score of years past. The town kept very full, for the

weather was more like summer than autumn. There were moments, and this was one of them, that I wished more than ever Tod was over.

Strolling back off the pier and along the port, picking my way amidst the ropes of the fishing-boats, stretched across my path, I met face to face—Constance Pell. The thick blue veil, just as Charlotte had described it, was drawn over her bonnet: but something in her form struck me, and I saw her features through the veil. She saw me too, and turned her head sharply towards the harbour.

I went on without notice, making believe not to have seen her. Glancing round presently, I saw her cross the road and begin to come back on the other side by the houses. Knowing that the only chance was to trace her home, and not to let her see I was doing it, I stopped before one of the boats, and began talking to a fisherman, never turning my head towards her at all. She passed quickly, on to the long street, once glancing back at me. When she was fairly on her way, I went at the top of my speed to the port entrance of the hotel; ran straight through the yard and up to my room, which faced the street. There she was, walking onwards, and very quickly. Close by the chemist's shop at the opposite corner, she turned to look back; no doubt looking after me, and no doubt gratified that I was nowhere to be seen. Then she went on again.

Neither the Squire nor Mr. Brandon was in the hotel, that I could find; so I had to take the matter in hand myself, and do the best I could. Letting her get well ahead, I followed cautiously. She turned up the grande Rue, and I turned also, keeping her in view. The streets were tolerably full, and though she looked back several times, I am sure she did not see me.

Up the hill of the Grande Rue, past the Vice-Consulate, under the gateway of the Upper Town, through the Upper Town itself, and out by another gateway. I thought she was never going to stop. Away further yet, to the neighbourhood of a little place called Mâquétra—but I am not sure that I spell the word properly. There she turned into a small house that had a garden before it.

They call me a muff at home, as you have heard often: and there's no doubt I have shown myself a muff more than once in my life. I was one then. What I ought to have done was, to have gone back the instant I had seen her enter; what I really did was, to linger about behind the hedge, and try to get a glimpse through it. It skirted the garden: a long, narrow garden, running down from the side of the house.

It was only a minute or two in all. And I was really turning back when a maid-servant in a kind of short brown bedgown (so Hannah called the things at home), black petticoat, grey stockings and wooden sabots, came out at the gate, carrying a flat basket made of black and white straw.

"Does Monsieur Pell live there?" I asked, waiting until she had come up.

"Monsieur *Qui?*" said the girl.

"Pell. Or Clement-Pell."

"There is no gentlemans at all lives there," returned she, changing her language to very decent English. "Only one Madame and her young meesses."

I seemed to take in the truth in a minute: they were there, but he was not. "I think they must be the friends I am in search of," was my remark. "What is the name?"

"Brune."

"Brune?—Oh, Brown. A lady and four young ladies?"

"Yes, that's it. Bon jour, monsieur."

She hurried onwards, the sabots clattering. I turned leisurely to take another look at the hedge and the little gate in it, and saw a blue veil fluttering inwards. Constance Pell, deeper than I, had been gazing after me.

Where had the Squire and old Brandon got to? Getting back to the hotel, I could not find either of them. Mr. Brandon might be taking a warm sea-bath, the waiters thought, and the Squire a cold one. I went about to every likely place, and went in vain. The dinner-bell was ringing when they got in—tired to death; having been for some prolonged ramble over beyond Capécure. I told them in their rooms while they were washing their hands —but as to stirring in it before dinner, both were too exhausted for it.

"I said I thought they must be here, Brandon," cried the Squire, in triumph.

"He is not here now, according to Johnny," squeaked old Brandon.

After dinner more time was lost. First of all, in discussing what they should do; next, in whether it should be done that night. You see, it was not Mrs. Pell they wanted, but her husband. As it was then dark, it was thought best to leave it until morning.

We went up in state about half-past ten; taking a coach, and passing *en route* the busy market scene. The coach seemed to have no springs: Mr. Brandon complained that it shook him to pieces. This was Saturday, you know. The Squire meant to be distantly polite to Mrs. and the Miss Pells, but to insist upon having the address given him of Mr. Pell. "We'll not take the coach quite up to the door," said he, "or we may not get in." Indeed, the getting in seemed to be a matter of doubt: old Brandon's opinion was that they'd keep every window and door barred, rather than admit us.

So the coach set us down outside the furthermost barrier of the Upper Town, and we walked on to the gate, went up the path, and knocked at the door.

As soon as the servant opened it—she had the same brown bed-gown on, the same grey stockings, and wooden sabots—the Squire dexterously slipped past her into the passage to make sure of a footing. She offered no opposition: drew back, in fact, to make room.

"I must come in; I have business here," said he, almost as if in apology.

"The Messieurs are free to enter," was her answer; "but they come to a house empty."

"I want to speak to Madame Brown," returned the Squire, in a determined tone.

"Madame Brown and the Mees Browns are depart," she said. "They depart at daylight this morning, by the first convoi."

We were in the front parlour then: a small room, barely fur-nished. The Squire flew into one of his tempers: he thought the servant was playing with him. Old Brandon sat down against the wall, and nodded his head. He saw how it was—they had really gone.

But the Squire stormed a little, and would not believe it. The girl, catching one word in ten, for he talked very fast, wondered at his anger.

The young gentlemans was at the place yesterday, she said, glancing at me: it was a malheur but they had come up before the morning, if they wanted so much to see Madame.

"She has not gone: I know better," roared the Squire. "Look here, young woman—what's your name, though?"

"Mathilde," said she, standing quite at ease, her hands turned on her hips and her elbows out.

"Well, then, I warn you that it's of no use your trying to deceive *me*. I shall go into every room of this house till I find Madame Brown—and if you attempt to stop me, I'll bring the police up here. Tell her that in French, Johnny."

"I hear," said Mathilde, who had a very deliberate way of speak-ing. "I comprehend. The Messieurs go into the rooms if they like, but I go with, to see they not carry off any of the articles. This is the salon."

Waiting for no further permission, he was out of the salon like a shot. Mr. Brandon stayed nodding against the wall; he had not the slightest reverence for the Squire's diplomacy at any time.

The girl slipped off her sabots and put her feet into some green worsted slippers that stood in the narrow passage. My belief was she thought we wanted to look over the house with a view to taking it.

"It was small, but great enough for a salle à manger," she said, showing the room behind—a little place that had literally nothing in it but an oval dining-table, some matting, and six common chairs against the walls. Upstairs were four bedrooms, bare also. As to the fear of our carrying off any of the articles, we might have found a difficulty in doing so. Except beds, chairs, drawers, and wash-hand-stands, there was nothing to carry. Mrs. Brown and the Miss Browns were not there: and the rooms were in as much order as if they had not been occupied for a month. Mathilde had been at them all the morning. The Squire's face was a picture when he went down: he began to realize the fact that he was once more left in the lurch.

"It is much health up here, and the house fine," said the girl, leaving her shoes in the passage side by side with the sabots, and walking into the salon in her stockings, without ceremony; "and if the Messieurs thought to let it, and would desire to have a good servant with it, I would be happy to serve them, me. I sleep in the house, or at home, as my patrons please; and I very good to make the kitchen; and I——"

"So you have not found them," interrupted old Brandon, sarcastically.

The Squire gave a groan. He was put out, and no mistake. Mathilde, in answer to questions, readily told all she knew.

About six weeks ago, she thought it was—but no, it must be seven, now she remembered—Madame Brown and the four Mees Browns took this house of the propriétaire, one Monsieur Bourgeois, marchand d'épicerie, and engaged her as servant, recommended to Madame by M. Bourgeois. Madame and the young ladies had lived very quietly, giving but little trouble; entrusted her to do all the commissions at the butcher's and elsewhere, and never questioned her fidelity in, the matter of the sous received in change at market. The previous day when she got home with some pork and sausages, which she was going after when the young gentlemans spoke to her—nodding to me—Madame was all bouleversée; first because Mees Constance had been down to the town, which Madame did not like her to do; next because of a letter——

At this point the Squire interrupted. Did she mean to imply that the ladies never went out?

No, never, continued Mathilde. Madame found herself not strong to walk out, and it was not proper for the young demoiselles

to go walk without her—as the Messieurs would doubtless understand. But Mees Constance had ennui with that, and three or four
times she had walked out without Madame's knowing. Yesterday,
par exemple, Madame was storming at her when she (Mathilde)
came home with the meat, and the young ladies her sisters stormed
at her——

"There; enough of that," snapped the Squire. "What took them
away?"

That was the letter, resumed the girl in her deliberate manner.
It was the other thing, that letter was, that had contributed to
Madame's bouleversement. The letter had been delivered by hand,
she supposed, while she was gone to the pork-shop; it told Madame
the triste news of the illness of a dear relative; and Madame had
to leave at once, in consequence. There was confusion. Madame
and the young ladies packing, and she (Mathilde), when her dinner
had been cooked and eaten, running quick for the proprietaire,
who came back with her. Madame paid him up to the end of
the next week, when the month would be finished and—that
was all.

Old Brandon took up the word. "Mr. Brown?—He was not
here at all, was he?"

"Not at all," replied Mathilde. "Madame's fancy figured to her
he might be coming one of these soon days: if so, I refer him to
M. Bourgeois."

"Refer him for what?"

"Nay, I not ask, monsieur. For the information, I conclude, of
where Madame go and why she go. Madame talk to the proprietaire
with the salon door shut."

So that was all we got. Mathilde readily gave M. Bourgeois's
address, and we went away. She had been civil through it all, and
the Squire slipped a franc into her hand. From the profusion of
thanks he received in return, it might have been a louis d'or.

Monsieur Bourgeois's shop was in the Upper Town, not far from
the convent of the Dames Ursulines. He said—speaking from behind his counter while weighing out some coffee—that Madame
Brown had entrusted him with a sealed letter to Monsieur Brown
in case he arrived. It contained, Madame had remarked to him,
only a line or two to explain where they had gone, as he would
naturally be disappointed at not finding them; and she had confided the trust to him that he would only deliver it into M. Brown's
own hand. *He* did not know where Madame had gone. As M.
Bourgeois did not speak a word of English, or the Squire a word of
French, it's hard to say when they would have arrived at an explanation, left to themselves.

"Now look here," said Mr. Brandon, in his dry, but uncommonly

clear-sighted way, as we went home, "*Clement-Pell's expected here.*
We must keep a sharp watch on the boats."

The Squire did not see it. "As if he'd remain in England all
this time, Brandon!"

"We don't know where he has stayed. I have thought all along
he was as likely to be in England as elsewhere: there's no place a
man's safer in, well concealed. The. very fact of his wife and
daughters remaining in this frontier town would be nearly enough
to prove that he was still in England."

"Then why on earth *did* he stay there?" retorted the Squire.
"Why has he not got away before?"

"I don't know. Might fear there was danger perhaps in making
the attempt. He has lain perdu in some quiet corner; and now
that he thinks the matter has partly blown over and the scent is
less keen, he means to come over. That's what his wife has waited
for."

The Squire seemed to grasp the whole at once. "I wonder when
he will be here?"

"Within a day or two, you may be sure, or not at all," said
Mr. Brandon, with a nod. "She'll write to stop his coming, if she
knows where to write to. The sight of Johnny Ludlow has
startled her. You were a great muff to let yourself be seen, young
Johnny."

"Yes, sir, I know I was."

"Live and learn, live and learn," said he, bringing out his tin
box. "One cannot put old heads upon young shoulders."

Sunday morning. After breakfast I and Mr. Brandon were
standing under the porte-cochère, looking about us. At the banking house opposite; at a man going into the chemist's shop with
his hand tied up; at the marchand-de-coco with his gay attire and
jingling bells and noisy tra-la-la-la: at anything, in short, there
might be to see, and so while away the half-hour before church-
time. The Squire had gone strolling out, saying he should be back
in time for service. People were passing down towards the port,
little groups of them in twos and threes; apart from the maid-
servants in their white caps, who were coming back from mass.
One of the hotel waiters stood near us, his white napkin in his hand.
He suddenly remarked, with the easy affability of the French of his
class (which, so far as I know, and I have seen more of France
since then, never degenerates into disrespect), that some of these
people might be expecting friends by the excursion boat, and were
going down to see it come in.

"What excursion boat?" asked Mr. Brandon of the waiter, quicker than he generally spoke.

"One from Ramsgate," the man replied. "It was to leave the other side very early, so as to get to Boulogne by ten o'clock; and to depart again at six in the afternoon." Mr. Brandon looked at the speaker; and then at me. Putting his hand on my shoulder, he drew me towards the port; charging the waiter to be sure and tell Mr. Todhetley when he returned, that we had gone to see the Ramsgate boat come in. It was past ten then.

"*If Clement-Pell comes at all it will be by this excursion boat*, Johnny," said he impressively, as we hurried on.

"Why do you think so, Mr. Brandon?"

"Well, I do think so. The people who make excursion trips are not those likely to know him, or of whom he would be afraid. He will conceal himself on it amongst the crowd. It is Sunday also—another reason. What flag is that up on the signal-post by the pier house, Johnny? Your eyes are younger than mine."

"It is the red one, sir."

"For a steamer in sight. She is not in yet then. It must be for *her*. It's hardly likely there would be another one coming in this morning."

"There she is!" I exclaimed. For at that moment I caught sight in the distance of a steamer riding on close up to the harbour mouth, pitching a little in her course.

"Run you on, Johnny," said Mr. Brandon, in excitement. "I'll come as quickly as I can, but my legs are not as fleet as yours. Get a place close to the cords, and look out sharply."

It was a bright day, somewhat colder than it had been, and the wind high enough to make it tolerably rough for any but good sailors—as the sparkles of white foam on the blue sea betrayed. I secured a good place behind the cord, close to the landing-stage: a regular crowd had collected, early though it was, Sunday being an idle day with some of the French. The boat came in, was being moored fast below us, and was crowded with pale faces.

Up came the passengers, mounting the almost perpendicular gangway: assisted by the boatmen, below; and by two appariteurs, in their cocked hats and Sunday clothes, above. It was nearly low water: another quarter-of-an-hour and they'd have missed their tide: pleasant, that would have been, for the excursionists. As only one could ascend the ladder at once, I had the opportunity of seeing them all.

Scores came: my sight was growing half-confused: and there had been no one resembling Clement-Pell. Some of them looked fearfully ill still, and had not put up the ears of their caps or turned down their coat collars; so that to get a good view of these faces

was not possible—and Clement-Pell might have already landed, for
all I could be sure of to the contrary. Cloaks were common in those
days, and travelling caps had long ears to them.

It was quite a stroke of fortune. A lady with a little boy behind
her came up the ladder, and the man standing next to me—he was
vary tall and big—went at once into a state of excitement. "C'est
toi! c'est toi, ma sœur!" he called out. She turned at the voice,
and a batch of kissing ensued. A stout dame pushed forward
frantically to share the kissing: but a douanier angrily marched
off the passenger towards the custom-house. She retorted on him
not to be so *difficile*, turned round and said she must wait for her
other little one. Altogether there was no end of chatter and commotion. I was eclipsed and pushed back into the shade.

The other child was appearing over the top of the ladder then;
a mite of a girl, her face held close to the face of the gentleman
carrying her. I supposed he was the husband. He wore a cloak,
his cap was drawn well over his eyebrows, and very little could be
seen of him but his hands and his nose. Was he the husband?
The mother, thanking him volubly in broken English for his politeness in carrying up her little girl, would have taken her from him;
but he motioned as if he would carry her to the custom-house, and
stepped onward, looking neither to the left nor right. At that
moment my tall neighbour and the stout dame raised a loud greeting
to the child, clapping their hands and blowing kisses: the man put
out his long arm and pulled at the sleeve of the young one's pelisse.
It caused the gentleman to halt and look round. Enough to make
him.

Why—where had I seen the eyes? They were close to mine, and
seemed quite familiar. Then remembrance flashed over me. They
were Clement-Pell's.

It is almost the only thing about a man or woman that cannot
be disguised—the expression of the eyes. Once you are familiar
with any one's eye, and have learned its expression by heart; the
soul that looks out of it; you cannot be mistaken in the eye,
though you meet it in a desert, and its owner be disguised as a
cannibal.

But for the eyes, I should never have known him, got up, as he
was, with false red hair. He went straight on instantly, not sus-
pecting I was there, for the two had hidden me. The little child's
face was pressed close to Mr. Pell's as he went on: a feeling came
over me that he was carrying it, the better to conceal himself. As
he went into the custom-house, I pushed backwards out of the
crowd; saw Mr. Brandon, and whispered to him. He nodded
quietly; as much as to say he thought Pell would come.

"Johnny, we must follow him: but we must not let him see us on

any account. I dare say he is going all the way up to Mâquétra—
or whatever you call the place."

Making our way round to the door by which the passengers were
let out, we mixed with the mob and waited. The custom-house was
not particular with Sunday excursionists, and they came swarming
out by dozens. When Pell appeared, I jogged Mr. Brandon's
elbow.

The touters, proclaiming the merits of their respective hotels, and
thrusting their cards in Pell's face, seemed to startle him, for he
shrank back. Comprehending the next moment, he said, No, no,
passed on to the carriages, and stepped into one that was closed.
The driver was a couple of minutes at least, taking his orders:
perhaps there was some bother, the one jabbering French, the
other English. But the coach drove off at last.

"Now then, Johnny, for that other closed coach. We shall have
to do without church this morning. Mind you make the coachman
understand what he is to do."

"Suivez cette voiture qui vient de partir; mais pas trop près."
The man gave back a hearty "Oui, monsieur," as if he understood
the case.

It was a slow journey. The first coach did not hurry itself, and
took by-ways to its destination. It turned into the Rue de la
Coupe, opposite our hotel, went through the Rue de l'Hôpital, and
thence to regions unknown. All I knew was, we went up a hill
worse than that of the Grande Rue, and arrived circuitously at
Mâquétra. Mr. Brandon had stretched his head out as we passed
the hotel, but could not see the Squire.

"It's his affair, you know, Johnny. Not mine."

Clement Pell got out at his gate, and went in. We followed
cautiously, and found the house-door on the latch, Mathilde having
probably forgotten to close it after admitting Mr. Pell. They stood
in the salon: Mathilde in a handsome light chintz gown and white
stockings and shoes, for she had been to nine-o'clock mass; he with
a strangely perplexed, blank expression on his face as he listened
to her explanation.

"Yes, monsieur, it is sure they are depart; it is but the morning
of yesterday. The propriétaire, he have the letter for you that
Madame confide to him. He—Tiens, voici encore ces Messieurs!"

Surprise at our appearance must have caused her change of
language. Clement-Pell gave one look at us and turned his face
to the window, hoping to escape unrecognized. Mr. Brandon
ordered me to the English church in the Upper Town, saying I
should not be very late for that, and told Mathilde he did not want
her.

"I shall make the little promenade and meet my bon-ami,"

observed Mathilde, independently, as I proceeded to do as I was bid. And what took place between the two we left can only be related at second hand.

"Now, Mr. Pell, will you spare me your attention?" began Mr. Brandon.

Clement-Pell turned, and took off his cloak and cap, seeing that it would be worse than useless to attempt to keep up the farce. With the red wig on his head and the red hair on his face, no unobservant man would then have recognized him for the great ex-financier.

Mr. Brandon was cold, uncompromising, but civil; Clement-Pell at first subdued and humble. Taking courage after a bit, he became slightly restive, somewhat inclined to be insolent.

"It is a piece of assurance for you to come here at all, sir; tracking me over my very threshold, as if you were a detective officer. What is the meaning of it? I don't owe you money."

"I have told you the meaning," replied Mr. Brandon—feeling that his voice had never been more squeaky, but showing no sign of wrath. "The affair is not mine at all, but Squire Todhetley's, I was down on the port when you landed—went to·look for you, in fact; the Squire did not happen to be in the way, so I followed you up in his place."

"With what object?"

"Why, dear me, Mr. Pell, you are not deaf. I mentioned the object; the Squire wants his two hundred pounds refunded. A very clever trick, your getting it from him!"

Clement-Pell drew in his lips; his face had no more colour in it than chalk. He sat with his back to the wall, his hands restlessly playing with his steel watch-chain. What had come of the thick gold one he used to wear? Mr. Brandon had a chair near the table, and faced him.

"Perhaps you would like me to refund to you all my creditors' money wholesale, as well as Mr. Todhetley's?" retorted Clement-Pell, mockingly.

"I have nothing to do with them, Mr. Pell. Neither, I imagine, does Mr. Todhetley intend to make their business his. Let each man mind his own course, and stand or fall by it. If you choose to assure me you don't owe a fraction to any one else in the world, I shall not tell you that you do. I am speaking now for my friend, Squire Todhetley: I would a great deal rather he were here to deal with you himself; but action has accidentally been forced upon me."

"I know that I owe a good deal of money; or, rather, that a good many people have lost money through me," returned Clement-Pell, after a pause. "It's my misfortune; not my fault."

Mr. Brandon gave a dry cough. "As to its not being your fault, Mr. Pell, the less said about that the better. It was in your power to pull up in time, I conclude, when you first saw things were going wrong."

Clement-Pell lifted his hand to his forehead, as if he felt a pain there. "You don't know; you don't know," he said irritably,—a great deal of impatience in his tone.

"No, I'm thankful that I *don't*," said Mr. Brandon, taking out his tin box, and coolly eating a lozenge. "I am very subject to heartburn, Mr. Pell. If ever you get it try magnesia lozenges. An upset, such as this affair of yours has been, would drive a man of my nerves into a lunatic asylum."

"It may do the same by me before I have done with it," returned Clement Pell. And Mr. Brandon thought he meant what he said.

"Any way, it is rumoured that some of those who are ruined will be there before long, Mr. Pell. You might, perhaps, feel a qualm of conscience if you saw the misery it has entailed."

"And do you think I don't feel it?" returned Mr. Pell, catching his breath. "You are mistaken, if you suppose I do not."

"About Squire Todhetley's two hundred pounds, sir?" resumed old Brandon, swallowing the last of the lozenge. "Is it convenient to you to give it me?"

"No, it is not," was the decided answer. And he seemed to be turning restive again.

"But I will *thank* you to do so, Mr. Pell."

"I cannot do so."

"And not to make excuses over it. They will only waste time."

"I have not got the money; I cannot give it."

Upon that they set on again, hammer and tongs. Mr. Brandon insisting upon the money; Pell vowing that he had it not, and could not and would not give so much as a ten-pound note of it. Old Brandon never lost his temper, never raised his voice; but he said a thing or two that must have stung Pell's pride. At the end of twenty minutes, he was no nearer the money than before. Pell's patience gave signs of wearing out: Mr. Brandon could have gone quietly on till bed-time.

"You must be aware that this is not a simple debt, Mr. Pell. It is—in fact—something worse. For your own sake, it may be well to refund it."

"Once more I say I cannot."

"Am I to understand that is as much as to say you will not?"

"If you like to take it so. It is most painful to me, Mr. Brandon, to have to meet you in this spirit, but you force it on me. The case is this : I am not able to refund the debt to Squire Todhetley, and he has no power to enforce his claim to it."

"I don't know that."

"I do-though. It is best to be plain, as we have come to this, Mr. Brandon; and then perhaps you will bring the interview to an end, and leave me in peace. You have no power over me in this country; none whatever. Before you can obtain that, there are certain forms and ceremonies to be gone through in a legal court; you must make over the—— "

"Squire Todhetley's is not a case of debt," interrupted old Brandon. "If it were, he would have no right in honour to come here and seek payment over the heads of the other creditors."

"It is a case of debt, and nothing else. As debt only could you touch me upon it here—and not then until you have proved it and got judgment upon it in England. Say, if you will, that I have committed murder or forged bank-notes—you could not touch me here unless the French government gave me up at the demand of the English government. Get all the police in the town to this room if you will, Mr. Brandon, and they would only laugh at you. They have no power over me. I have committed no offence against this country."

"Look here," said old Brandon, nodding his head. "I know a bit about French law; perhaps as much as you: knew it years ago. What you say is true enough; an Englishman, whether debtor or criminal, in his own land, cannot be touched here, unless certain forms and ceremonies, as you express it, are first gone through. But you have rendered yourself amenable to French law on another point, Clement-Pell; I could consign you to the police this moment, if I chose, and they would have to take you."

Clement-Pell quite laughed at what he thought the useless boast. But he might have known old Brandon better. "What is my crime, sir?"

"You have come here and are staying here under a false name —Brown. That is a crime in the eyes of the French law; and one that the police, if they get to know of it, are obliged to take cognizance of."

"No!" exclaimed Clement-Pell, his face changing a little.

"Yes," said Mr. Brandon. "Were I to give you up for it to-day, they would put you on board the first boat leaving for your own country. Once on the opposite shore, you may judge whether Squire Todhetley would let you escape again."

It was all true. Mr. Pell saw that it was so. His fingers nervously trembled; his pale face wore a piteous aspect.

"You need not be afraid of me: I am not likely to do it," said Mr. Brandon: "I do not think the Squire would. But you see now what lies within his power. Therefore I would recommend you to come to terms with him."

Clement-Pell rubbed his brow with his handkerchief.   He was driven into a corner.

"I have told you truth, Mr. Brandon, in saying that I am not able to repay the two hundred pounds.   I am not.   Will he take half of it?"

"I cannot tell.   I have no authority for saying that he will."

"Then I suppose he must come up here.   As it has come to this, I had better see him.   If he will accept one hundred pounds, and undertake not to molest me further, I will hand it over to him.   It will leave me almost without means: but you have got me in a hole. Stay a moment—a thought strikes me.   Are there any more of my creditors in the town at your back, Mr. Brandon?"

"Not that I am aware of.   I have seen none."

"On your honour?"

Mr. Brandon opened his little eyes, and took a stare at Pell.   "My word is the same as my honour, sir.   Always has been and always will be."

"I beg your pardon.   A man, driven to my position, naturally fears an enemy at every corner.   And—if my enemies were to find me out here, they might be too much for me."

"Of course they would be," assented Mr. Brandon, by way of comfort.

"Will you go for Squire Todhetley?   What is done, must be done to-day, for I shall be away by the first train in the morning."

Shrewd old Brandon considered the matter before speaking.   "By the time I get back here with the Squire you may have already taken your departure, Mr. Pell."

"No, on my honour.   How should I be able to do it?   No train leaves the town before six to-night: the water is low in the harbour and no boat could get out.   As it has come to this, I will see Squire Todhetley: and the sooner the better."·

"I will trust you," said Mr. Brandon.

"Time was when I was deemed more worthy of trust: perhaps was more worthy of it,"—and tears involuntarily rose to his eyes. "Mr. Brandon, believe me—no man has suffered by this as I have suffered.   Do you think I did it for pleasure?—or to afford myself wicked gratification!   No.   I would have forfeited nearly all my remaining life to prevent the smash.   My affairs got into their awful state by degrees; and I had not the power to retrieve them. God alone knows what the penalty has been to me—and what it will be to my life's end."

"Ay.   I can picture it pretty tolerably, Mr. Pell."

"No one can picture it," he returned, with emotion.   "Look at my ruined family—the position of my sons and daughters.   Not one of them can hold up their heads in the world again without the consciousness that they may be pointed at as the children of Clement-Pell the swindler. What is to be their future?—how are they to get along? You must have heard many a word of abuse applied to me lately, Mr. Brandon: but there are few men on this earth more in need of compassion than I—if misery and suffering can bring the need. When morning breaks, I wish the day was done; when night comes, I toss and turn and wonder how I shall live through it."

"I am sorry for you," said Mr. Brandon, moved to pity, for he saw how the man needed it. "Were I you, I would go back home and face my debts. Face the trouble, and in time you may be able to live it down."

Clement-Pell shook his head hopelessly. Had it been debt alone, he might never have come away.

The sequel to all this had yet to come. Perhaps some of you may guess it. Mr. Brandon pounced upon the Squire as he was coming out of church in the Rue du Temple, and took him back in another coach. Arrived at the house, they found the door fast. Mathilde appeared presently, arm-in-arm with her sweetheart—a young man in white boots with ear-rings in his ears. "Was M. Brown of depart," she repeated, in answer to the Squire's impulsive question: but no, certainly he was not. And she gave them the following information.

When she returned after midday, she found M. Brown all impatience, waiting for her to show him the way to the house of Monsieur Bourgeois, that he might claim Madame's letter. When they reached the shop, it had only the fille de boutique in it. Monsieur the patron was out making a promenade, the fille de boutique said he might be home possibly for the shutting up at two o'clock.

Upon that, M. Brown decided to make a little promenade himself until two o'clock; and Mathilde, she made a further promenade on her own account: and had now come up, before two, to get the door open. Such was her explanation. If the gentlemans would be at the pains of sitting down in the salon, without doubt M. Brown would not long retard.

They sat down. The clock struck two. They sat on, and the clock struck three. Not until then did any thought arise that Clement-Pell might not keep faith with them. Mathilde's freely expressed opinion was that M. Brown, being strange to the town, had lost himself. She ran to the grocer's shop again, and found it shut up: evidently no one was there.

Four o'clock, five o'clock; and no Mr. Brown. They gave him up then; it seemed quite certain that he had given them the slip.

Starving with hunger, exploding with anger, the Squire took his wrathful way back to the hotel : Mr. Brandon was calm and sucked his magnesia lozenges. Clement-Pell was a rogue to the last.

There came to Mr. Brandon the following morning, through the Boulogne post-office, a note ; on which he had to pay five sous. It was from Clement-Pell, written in pencil. He said that when he made the agreement with Mr. Brandon never a thought crossed him of not keeping faith : but that while he was waiting about for the return of the grocer who held his wife's letter, he saw an Englishman come off the ramparts—a creditor who knew him well and would be sure to deliver him up, were it in his power, if he caught sight of him. It struck him, Clement-Pell, with a panic : he considered that he had only one course left open to him—and that was to get away from the place at once and in the quietest manner he was able. There was a message to Mr.-Todhetley to the effect that he would send him the hundred pounds later if he could. Throughout the whole letter ran a vein of despairing sadness, according with what he had said to Mr. Brandon ; and the Squire's heart was touched.

"After all, Brandon, the fellow *is* to be pitied. It's a frightful position : enough to make a man lose heart for good and all. I'm not sure that I should have taken the hundred pounds from him."

"That's more than probable," returned old Brandon, drily. "It remains a question, though, in my mind, whether he did see the creditor and did 'take a panic :' or whether both are not invented to cover his precipitate departure with the hundred pounds."

How he got away from the town we never knew. The probability was, that he had walked to the first station after Boulogne on the Paris railroad, and there taken the evening train. And whether he had presented himself again at Monsieur Bourgeois's shop, that excellent tradesman, who did not return home until ten on Sunday night, was unable to say. Any way, M. Bourgeois held the letter yet in safety. So the chances are, that Mr. and Mrs. Pell are still dodging about the earth in search of each other, after the fashion of the Wandering Jew.

And that's a true account of our visit to Boulogne after Clement-Pell. Mr. Brandon calls it to this hour a wild-goose chase : certainly it turned out a fruitless one. But we had a good passage back again, the sea as calm as a mill-pond.

XXVI.

AT WHITNEY HALL.

IT has often been in my mind to tell of John Whitney's death. You will say it is too sad and serious for a paper. But it is well to have serious thoughts brought before us at certain seasons. This is one of them: seeing that it's the beginning of a new year, and that every year takes us nearer to another life whether we are old or whether we are young. *

Some of them thought his illness might never have come on but for an accident that happened. It is quite a mistake. The accident had nothing to do with the later illness. Sir John and Lady Whitney could tell you so as well as I. John was always one of those sensitive, thoughtful, religious boys that somehow don't seem so fit for earth as heaven.

"Now mind, you boys," cried Sir John to us at breakfast. "There's just a thin coating of ice on the lake and ponds, but it won't bear. Don't any of you venture on it."

"We will not, sir," replied John, who was the most obedient son living.

There's not much to be done in the way of out-door sports when snow lies on the ground. Crowding round the children's play-room window later, all the lot of us, we looked out on a white landscape. Snow lodged on the trees, hid the grass in the fields, covered the hills in the distance.

"It's an awful sell," cried Bill Whitney and Tod nearly in a breath. "No hunting, no shooting, and no nothing. The ponds won't bear; snowballing's common. One might as well lie in bed."

"And what sort of a 'sell' do you suppose it is for the poor men who are thrown out of work?" asked Sir John, who had come in, reading a newspaper, and was airing his back at the fire. "Their work and wages are stopped, and they can't earn bread for their children. You boys are dreadfully to be pitied, you are!"

He tilted his steel spectacles up on his good old red nose, and nodded to us. Harry, the pert one of the family, answered.

* Written for the January number of *The Argosy*, 1872.

"Well, papa, and it is a settler for us boys to have our fun spoiled. As to the working-men—oh, they are used to it."

Sir John stared at him for a full minute. "If I thought you said that from your heart, Mr. Harry, I'd order you from my presence. No son of mine shall get into the habit of making unfeeling speeches, even in jest."

Sir John meant it. We saw that Harry's words had really vexed him. John broke the silence.

"Papa, if I should live to be ever in your place," he said, in his quiet voice, that somehow *always* had a tone of thoughtfulness in it, even when at play with the rest of us at old Frost's, "I shall make a point of paying my labourers' wages in full this wintry time, just the same as though they worked. It is not their fault that they are idle."

Sir John started at *him* now. "What d'ye mean by 'if you live,' lad?"

John considered. The words had slipped from him without any special thought at all. People use such figures of speech. It was odd though, when we came to remember it a long while afterwards, that he should have said it just that one day.

"I recollect a frost that lasted fourteen weeks, boys," said Sir John. "That was in 1814. They held a fair on the Thames, we heard, and roasted an ox whole on it. Get a frost to last all that time, and you'd soon tire of paying wages for nothing, John."

"But, father, what else could I do—or ought I to do? I could not let them starve—or break up their poor homes by going into the workhouse. I should fear that some time, in return, God might break up mine."

Sir John smiled. John was so very earnest always when he took up a serious matter. Letting the question drop, Sir John lowered his spectacles, and went out with his newspaper. Presently we saw him going round to the farm-yard in his great-coat and beaver gaiters. John sat down near the fire and took up a book he was fond of—"Sintram."

This was Old Christmas Day. Tod and I had come over to Whitney Hall for a week, and two days of it were already gone. We liked being there, and the time seemed to fly. Tod and Bill still stood staring and grumbling at the snow, wishing the frost would get worse, or go. Harry went out whistling; Helen sat down with a yawn.

"Anna, there's a skein of blue silk in that workbag behind you. Get it out and hold it for me to wind."

Anna, who was more like John in disposition than any of them, always good and gentle, got the silk; and they began to wind it. In the midst of it, Harry burst in with a terrific shout, dressed up as a bear, and trying to upset every one. In the confusion Anna dropped the silk on the carpet, and Helen boxed her ears.

John looked up from his book. "You should not do that, Helen."

"What does she drop the silk for, then—careless thing!" retorted Helen, who was quick in temper. "Once soil that light shade of blue, and it can't be used. You mind yourself John."

John looked at them both. At Helen, taking up the silk from the floor; at Anna, who was struggling to keep down her tears under the infliction, because Tod was present. She wouldn't have minded me. John said no more. He had a very nice face without much colour in it; dark hair, and large grey-blue eyes that seemed to be always looking out for something they did not see. He was sixteen then, upright and slender. All the world liked John Whitney.

Later on in the day we were running races in the broad walk, that was so shady in summer. The whole of us. The high laurel hedges on either side had kept the snow from drifting, and it hardly lay there at all. We gave the girls a third of the run, and they generally beat us. After an hour of this, tired and hot, we gave in, and dispersed different ways. John and I went towards the lake to see whether the ice was getting thicker, talking of school and school interests as we went along. Old Frost's grounds were in view, which naturally put us in mind of the past: and especially of the great event of the half year—the sad fate of Archie Hearn.

"Poor little Hearn!" he exclaimed. "I did feel his death, and no mistake. That is, I felt for his mother. I think, Johnny, if I could have had the chance offered me, I would have died myself to let him live."

"That's easier said than done—if it came to the offer, Whitney."

"Well, yes it is. She had no one but him, you see. And to think of her coming into the school that time and saying she forgave the fellow—whoever it was. I've often wondered whether Barrington had cause to feel it."

"She is just like her face, Whitney—good. I've hardly ever seen a face I like as much as Mrs. Hearn's."

John Whitney laughed a little. They all did at my likes and dislikes of faces. "I was reading a book the other day, Johnny—— See that poor little robin!" he broke off. "It looks starved, and it must have its nest somewhere. I have some biscuit in my pocket."

It came into my head, as he dived into his pocket and scattered the crumbs, that he had brought the supply out for these stray birds. But if I write for ever I could not make you understand the thoughtfulness of John Whitney.

"Hark, Johnny! What's that?"

Cries, screams, sobs. We were near the end of the walk then and rushed out. Anna met us in a dreadful state of agitation. Charley was in the lake! Whitney caught the truth before I did, and was off like a shot.

The nurse, Willis, was dancing frantically about at the water's edge; the children roared. Willis said Master Charles had slipped on to the ice "surreptitiously" when her back was turned, and had gone souse in. John Whitney had already plunged in after his little brother; his coat, jacket, and waistcoat were lying on the bank. William Whitney and Tod, hearing the noise, came rushing up.

"Mamma sent me to tell nurse they had been out long enough, and were to come in," sobbed Anna, shaking like a leaf. "While I was giving her the message, Charley fell in. Oh, what will be done?"

That was just like Anna. Helen would have been cool as a cucumber. Done? Why, John had already saved him. The ice, not much thicker than a shilling, and breaking whenever touched, hardly impeded him at all. Bill and Tod knelt down and lent hands, and they were landed like a couple of drowned rats, Charley howling with all his might. John, always thoughtful, wrapped his great-coat round the lad, and the other two went off with him to the house.

John caught a cold. Not very much of one. He was hot, you see, when he plunged in; and he had only his jacket to put on over his wet clothes to walk home in. Not much of a cold, I say; but he never seemed to be quite the same after that day: and when all was over they would date his illness back from it. Old Featherstone physicked him; and the days passed on.

"I can't think why John should be so feverish," Lady Whitney would remark. His hands would be hot, and his cheeks scarlet, and he did not eat. Featherstone failed to alter the state of things; so one day Sir John took him into Worcester to Mr. Carden.

Mr. Carden did not seem to think much of it—as we heard over at Dyke Manor. There was nothing wrong with the lungs or any other vital part. He changed the medicine that Featherstone had been giving, and said he saw no present reason why John should not go back to school. Sir John, standing by in his old spectacles, listening and looking, caught up the words "at present" and asked Mr. Carden whether he had any particular meaning in saying it. But Mr. Carden would not say. Sending his pleasant blue eyes straight into Sir John's, he assured him that he did not anticipate mischief, or see reason to fear it. He thought, he hoped, that, once

John was back with his studies and his companions, he would recover tone and be as well as ever.

And Mr. Carden's physic did good; for when Whitney came back after the holidays, he seemed himself again. Lady Whitney gave five hundred directions to Mrs. Frost about the extras he was to eat 'and drink, Hall being had in to assist at the conference. The rest of us rather wished for fevers ourselves, if they entailed beaten-up eggs and wine and jelly between meals. He did his lessons; and he came out in the playground, though he did not often join in play, especially rough play: and he went for walks with us or stayed in as inclination led him, for he was allowed liberty in all things. By Easter he had grown thinner and weaker: and yet there was no specific disease. Mr. Carden came over to Whitney Hall and brought Dr. Hastings, and they could not discover any: but they said he was not strong and wanted care. It was left to John to decide whether he would go back to school after Easter, or not: and he said he should like to go. And so the weeks went on again.

We could not see any change at all in him. It was too gradual, I suppose. He seemed very quiet, strangely thoughtful always, as though he were inwardly puzzling over some knotty question hard to solve. Any quarrel or fight would put him out beyond belief: he'd come up with his gentle voice, and stretch out his hands to part the disputants, and did not rest until he had made peace. Wolfe Barrington, with one of his sneers, said Whitney's nerves were out of joint. Once or twice we saw him reading a pocket-Bible. It's quite true. And there was something in his calm face and in his blue-grey eyes that hushed those who would have ridiculed.

" I say, Whitney, have you heard ? " I asked. " The Doctor means to have the playground enlarged for next half. Part of the field is to be taken in."

" Does he ? " returned Whitney. It was the twenty-ninth of May, and a half-holiday. The rest had gone in for Hare-and-Hounds. I stayed with Whitney, because he'd be dull alone. We were leaning over the playground gate.

" Blair let it out this morning at mathematics. By the way, Whitney, you did not come in to them."

" I did not feel quite up to mathematics to-day, Johnny."

" I am glad it's going to be done, though. Are not you ? "

" It won't make much difference to me, I expect. I shall not be here."

" Not here ! "

" I don't think so."

His chin rested on his hands above the gate. His eyes were

gazing out straight before him; looking—as I said before—for something they did not see.

"Do you think you shall be too ill to come next half, Whitney?"

"Yes, I do."

"Are you feeling worse?" I asked after a minute or two, taken up with staring at the sky.

"That's what they are always asking me indoors?" he remarked. "It's just this, Johnny; I don't feel worse from day to day; I could not say any one morning that I feel a shade worse than I did the previous one: but when I look back a few weeks or months; say, for example, to the beginning of the half, or at Easter, and remember how very well I was then, compared with what I am now, I know that I must be a great deal worse. I could not do now what I did then. Why! I quite believe I might have gone in for Hare-and-Hounds then, if I had chosen. Fancy my trying it now!"

"But you don't have any pain."

"None. I'm only weak and tired; always feeling to want to lie down and rest. Every bit of strength and energy has gone out of me, Johnny."

"You'll get well," I said hastily.

"I'm sure I don't know."

"Don't you want to?" It was his cool answer made me ask it.

"Why, of course I do.

"Well then?"

"I'll tell you, Johnny Ludlow; there is a feeling within me, and I can't say why it's there or whence it comes, that's always saying to me I shall *not* get well. At least, whenever I think about it. It seems just as though it were telling me that instead of getting well it will be—be just the opposite."

"What a dreadful thing to have, Whitney! It must be like a fellow going about with a skeleton!"

"Not at all dreadful. It never frightens me, or worries me. Just as the rest of you look forward naturally to coming back here, and living out your lives to be men, and all that, so I seem *not* to look to it. The feeling has nothing bad at all about it. If it had, I dare say it would not be there."

I stood on the small gate and took a swing. It pained me to hear him say this.

"I suppose you mean, Whitney, that you may be going to die?"

"That's about it, Johnny. I don't know it; I may get well, after all."

"But you don't think you will?"

"No, I don't. Little Hearn first; I next. Another ought to follow, to make the third."

"You speak as easily as if it were only going out to tea, Whitney!"

"Well, I feel easy. I do, indeed."

"Most of us would be daunted, at any rate."

"Exactly. Because you are not going to die. Johnny Ludlow, I am getting to *think* a great deal; to have a sort of insight that I never had before; and I see how very wisely and kindly all things are ordered."

If he had gone in for a bout of tumbling like the mountebanks, I could not have been as much surprised as to hear him say this. It was more in Mrs. Frost's line than in ours. It laid hold on me at once; and from that moment, I believed that John Whitney would die.

"Look here, Whitney. It is evident by what you say about failing strength, that you must be getting worse. Why don't you tell them at home, and go there and be nursed?"

"I don't want to be nursed. I am not ill enough for it. I'm better as I am: here, amongst you fellows. As to telling them —time enough for that. And what is there to tell? They see for themselves I am not as strong as I was: there's nothing else to tell."

"There's this feeling that you say lies upon you."

"What, and alarm them for nothing? I dare say. There *would* be a hullabaloo. I should be rattled home in the old family coach, and Carden would be sent for, post haste, Hastings also, and—well, you are a muff, Johnny. I've told you this because I like you, and because I thought you would understand me; which is more than the other fellows would. Mind you keep counsel."

"Well, you ought to be at home."

"I am better here, while I am as I am. The holidays will be upon us soon. I expect I shall not come back afterwards."

Now, if you ask me till next week, I could not give a better account of the earlier part of John Whitney's illness than this. He was ill; and yet no one could find out why he should be ill, or what was the matter with him. Just about this time, Featherstone took up the notion that it was "liver," and dosed him for it. For one thing, he said Whitney must ride out daily, good hard riding. So a horse would be brought over from the Hall by the old groom, and they would go out together. During the Whitsun week, when Sir John was away from Parliament, he came also and rode with him. But no matter whether they went slow or fast, Whitney would come back ready to die from the exertion. Upon that, Featherstone changed his opinion, and said riding must be given up.

By the time the Midsummer holidays came, any one might see
the change in Whitney. It struck Mrs. Frost particularly when
he went in to say good-bye to her.

"For the last time, I think," he said in a low tone, but with a
smiling countenance, as she stood holding his hand.

Mrs. Frost knew what he meant, and her face, always so pale,
and delicate, went red.

"I trust not," she answered. "But—God knows what is
best."

"Oh yes, and we do not. Farewell, dear Mrs. Frost. Thank
you truly for all your care and kindness."

The tears stood in her eyes. *She* was to be the next one to go
from us, after John Whitney.

Wolfe Barrington stood at the door as he passed. - "Good luck
to you, Whitney," said he, carelessly. "I'd throw all those nerves
of yours over, if I were you, before I came back again."

Whitney turned back and held out his hand. "Thank you,
Barrington," he replied in his kind, truthful voice; "you wish me
well, I know. Good luck to *you*, in all ways; and I mean it with
my whole heart. As to nerves, I do not think I possess any,
though some of you have been pleased to joke about it."

They shook hands, these two, little thinking that, in one sense,
the life of both would soon be blighted. In a short time, only a
few weeks, Wolfe was to be brought nearer to immediate death
than even John Whitney.

Not until he was at home and had settled down among them,
did his people notice the great change in him. Lady Whitney,
flurried and anxious, sent for Sir John from London. Mr. Carden
was summoned, and old Featherstone met him often in con-
sultation. Dr. Hastings came once or twice, but he was an invalid
himself then; and Mr. Carden, as every one knew, was equal to
anything. Still—it was a positive fact—there was no palpable
disease to grapple with in John, only weakness and wasting away.
No cough, no damaged lungs. "If only it were gout or dropsy,
one would know what to do," grumbled Featherstone; but Mr.
Carden kept his own counsel. They decided that John should go
to the seaside for change.

"As if it could do me any good!" he remonstrated. "*Change*
won't make any difference to me. And I'd a great deal rather stay
quietly at home."

"Why do you say it will not do you good?" cried Lady Whitney,
who happened to hear him.

"Because, mother, I feel nearly sure that it will not."

"Oh dear!" cried she, flurried out of her senses, "John's going
to turn rebellious now."

"No, I am not," said John, smiling at her. "I mean to go without any rebellion at all."

"There's my best lad," said she fondly. "Change of scene is all pleasure, John. It's not like going through a course of pills and powders."

Well, they all went to the seaside, and at the end of five weeks they all came back again. John had to be assisted out of the carriage, from fatigue. There could be no mistake now.

After that, it was just a gradual decay. The sinking was so imperceptible that he seemed to be always at a stand-still, and some days he was as well as any one need be. His folk did not give up hope of him: no one does in such cases. John was cheerful, and often merry.

"It can't be consumption," Sir John would say. "We've nothing of the kind in our family; neither on his mother's side nor on mine. A younger sister of hers died of a sort of decline: but what can that have to do with John?"

Why, clearly nothing. As every one agreed.

In one of Mr. Carden's visits, Sir John tackled him as he was going away, asking what it was. The two were shut up together talking for a quarter-of-an-hour, Mr. Carden's horses—he generally came over in his carriage—growing rampant the while. Sir John did not seem much wiser when the sitting was over. He only shuffled his spectacles about on his old red nose—as he used to do when perplexed. Talking of noses: you never saw two so much alike as his and the Squire's, particularly when they went into a temper.

Not very long after they were back from the seaside, and directly after school met, the accident occurred to Barrington. You have heard of it before: and it has nothing to do with the present paper. John Whitney took it to heart.

"He is not fit to die," Bill heard him say. "He is not fit to die."

One morning John walked over to see him, resting on stiles and gates between whiles. It was not very far; but he was good for very little now. Barrington was lying flat on his bed, Mrs. Hearn waiting on him. Wolfe was not tamed then.

"It's going to be a race between us, I suppose, Whitney," said he. "You look like a shadow."

"A race?" replied Whitney, not taking him.

"In that black-plumed slow coach that carries dead men to their graves, and leaves them there. A race which of us two will have the honour of starting first. What a nice prospect! I always hated clayey soil. Fancy lying in it for ever and a day!"

"Fancy, rather, being borne on angels' wings, and living with

God in heaven for ever and ever!" cried Whitney earnestly. "Oh Barrington, fancy *that.*"

"You'd do for a parson," retorted Barrington.

The interview was not satisfactory: Whitney so solemnly earnest, Wolfe so mockingly sarcastic: but they parted good friends. It was the last time they ever saw each other in life.

And thus a few more weeks went on.

Now old Frost had one most barbarous custom. And that was, letting the boys take the few days of Michaelmas holiday, or not, as the parents pleased. Naturally, very few did please. I and Tod used to go home: but that was no rule for the rest. We did not go home this year. A day or two before the time, Sir John Whitney rode over to Dyke Manor.

"You had better let the two boys come to us for Michaelmas," he said to the Squire. "John wants to see them, and they'll cheer us up. It's anything but a lively house, I can tell you, Todhetley, with the poor lad lying as he is."

"I can't see why he should not get well," said the Squire.

"I'm sure I can't. Carden ought to be able to bring him round."

"So he ought," assented the Squire. "It would be quite a feather in his cap, after all these months of illness. As to the boys, you may be troubled with 'em, and welcome, Sir John, if you care to be."

And so, we went to Whitney Hall that year, instead of home.

John had the best rooms, the two that opened into one another. Sometimes he would be on the bed in one, sometimes on the sofa in the other. Then he would walk about on some one's arm; or sit in the easy-chair at the west window, the setting sun full on his wasted face. Barrington had called him a shadow: you should have seen him now. John had talked to Barrington of angels: he was just like an angel in the house himself. And—will you believe it?—they had not given up hope of his getting well again. I wondered the doctors did not tell Lady Whitney the plain truth, and have done with it: but to tell more professional truth than they can help, is what doctors rarely put themselves out of the way to do.

And still—the shadow of the coming death lay on the house. In the hushed voices and soft tread of the servants, in the subdued countenances of Sir John and Lady Whitney, and in the serious spirit that prevailed, the shadow might be seen. It is good to be in such a house as this: for the lessons learnt may take fast hold of the heart. It was good to hear John Whitney talk : and I never quite made out whether he was telling of dreams or realities.

Tod was out of his element : as much so as a fish is out of water. He had plenty of sympathy with John, would have made him well at any sacrifice to himself : but he could not do with the hushed house, in which all things seemed to give way to that shadow of the coming presence. Tod, in his way, was religious enough ; more so than some fellows are ; but dying beds he did not understand, and would a great deal rather have been shooting partridges than be near one. He and Bill Whitney—who was just as uncomfortable as Tod—used to get off anywhere whenever they could. They did not forget John. They would bring him all kinds of things ; flowers, fruit, blackberries as big as Willis's thimble, and the finest nuts off the trees ; but they did not care to sit long with him.

John was awake one afternoon, and I was sitting beside him. He sat in his easy-chair at the window—as he liked to do at this hour when the evening was drawing on. The intensely serene look that for some time now had taken possession of his face, I had never seen surpassed in boy or man.

"How quiet the house is, Johnny!" he said, touching my hand. "Where are they all?"

"Helen and Anna went out to ask after Mrs. Frost and Barrington. And the boys—but I think you know it—have gone with Sir John to Evesham. You wouldn't call the house quiet, John, if you could hear the row going on in the nursery."

He smiled a little. "Charley's a dreadful Turk : none of us elder ones were ever half as bad. Where's the mother?"

"Half-an-hour ago she was shut up with some visitors in the drawing-room. It's those Miss Clutterbucks, John : they always stay long enough to hold a county meeting."

"Is Mrs. Frost worse—that the girls have gone to ask after her?" he resumed.

"I think so. Harry said Dr. Frost shook his head about her, when they saw him this morning."

"She'll never be strong," remarked John. "And perhaps the bother of the school is too much for her."

"Hall takes a good deal of that, you know."

"But Hall cannot take the responsibility ; the true care of the school. That must lie on Mrs. Frost."

What a beautiful sky it was ! The sun was nearing the horizon ; small clouds, gold and red and purple, lay in the west, line above line. John Whitney sat gazing in silence. There was nothing he liked so much as looking at these beautiful sunsets.

"Go and play for me, will you, Johnny?"

The piano was at the far end of the room in the shade. My

playing is really nothing. It was nothing to speak of then, it is nothing to speak of now : but it is soft and soothing ; and some people like it. John could play a little himself, but it was too much exertion for him now. They had tried to teach Bill. He was kept hammering at it for half a year, and then the music master told Sir John that he'd rather teach a post. So Bill was released.

"The same thing that you played the evening before last, Johnny. Play that."

"But I can't. It was only some rubbish out of my own head, made up as I went along."

"Make up some more then, old fellow."

I had hardly sat down, when Lady Whitney came in, stirred the fire—if they kept up much, he felt the room too warm—and took one of the elbow-chairs in front of it.

"Go on, my dear," she said. "It is very pleasant to hear you."

But it was not so pleasant to play before her—not that, as I believed, her ears could distinguish the difference between an Irish Jig and the Dead March in Saul—and I soon left off. The playing or the fire had sent Lady Whitney into a doze. I crossed the room and sat down by John.

He was still looking at the sunset, which had not much changed. The hues were deeper, and streaks of gold shot upwards in the sky. Toward the north there was a broad horizon of green, fading into gold, and pale blue. Never was anything more beautiful. John's eyes fixed on it.

"If it is so beautiful here, Johnny, what will it be *there ?*" he breathed, scarcely above a whisper. "It makes one long to go."

Sometimes, when he said these things, I hardly knew how to answer, and would let his words die off into silence.

"The picture of heaven is getting realized in my mind, Johnny —though I know how poor an idea of it it must needs be. A wide, illimitable space ; the great white throne, and the saints in their white robes falling down before it, and the harpists singing to their harps."

"You must think of it often."

"Very often. The other night in bed, when I was between sleep and waking, I seemed to see the end—to go through it. I suppose it was one part thought, and three parts dream. I was dead, Johnny : I had already my white robe on, and angels were carrying me up to heaven. The crystal river was flowing along, beautiful flowers on its banks, and the Tree of Life, whose leaves are for the healing of the nations. I seemed to see it all, Johnny. Such flowers ! such hues ; brighter than any jewels ever seen. These colours are lovely "—pointing to the sky—" but they are tame compared with those I saw. Myriads of happy people were flitting about in white, redeemed as I was; the atmosphere shone with a soft light, the most delicious music floated in it. Oh, Johnny, think of this world with its troubles and disappointments and pains; and then think of that other one!"

The sunset was fading. The pale colours of the north were blending together like the changing hues of the opal.

"There are two things I have more than loved here," he went on. "Colours and music. Not the clashing of many instruments, or the mere mechanical playing, however classically correct, of one who has acquired his art by hard labour: but the soft, sweet, dreamy touch that stirs the heart. Such as yours, Johnny. Stop, old fellow. I know what you would say. That your playing is no playing at all, compared with that of a skilled hand; that the generality of people would wonder what there is in it: but for myself, I could listen to you from night till morning."

It was very foolish of him to say this; but I liked to hear it.

"It is the sort of music, as I have always fancied, that we shall hear in heaven. It was the sort I seemed to hear the other night in my dream; soft, low, full of melody. That *sort*, you know, Johnny; not the same. *That* was this earth's sweetest music etherealized."

Hearing him talk like this, the idea struck me that it might be better for us all generally if we turned our thoughts more on heaven and on the life we may find there. It would not make us do our duty any the less earnestly in this world.

"Then take colours," he went on. "No one knows the intense delight I have felt in them. On high days and holidays, my mother wears that big diamond ring of hers—you know it well, Johnny. Often and often have I stolen it from her finger, to let the light flash upon it, and lost myself for half-an-hour—ay, and more—gazing entranced on its changing hues. I love to see the rays in the drops of the chandeliers; I love to watch the ever-varying shades on a wide expanse of sea. Now these two things that I have so enjoyed here, bright colours and music, we have the promise of finding in heaven."

"Ay. The Bible tells us so."

"And I saw the harpers harping with their harps," he repeated to himself—and then fell into silence. "Johnny, look at the opal in the sky now."

It was very soft and beautiful.

"And there's the evening star."

I turned my head. Yes, there it was, and it trembled in the sky like a point of liquid silver.

"Sometimes I think I shall see the Holy City before I die," he continued. "See its picture as in a mirror—the New Jerusalem.

Oh, Johnny, I should have to shade my eyes. Not a beautiful
colour or shade but will be there; and her light like unto a jasper
stone, clear as crystal. When I was a little boy—four, perhaps—
papa brought me home a kaleidoscope from London. It was really
a good one, and its bits of glass were unusually brilliant. Johnny,
if I lived to be an old man, I could never describe the intense joy
those colours gave me—any more than I can describe the joy I
seemed to feel the other night in that dream of heaven."

He was saying all this in a tender tone of reverence that thrilled
through one.

"I remember another thing about colours. The year that papa
was pricked for High Sheriff, mamma went over with him to Worcester for the March Assize-time, and she took me. I was seven,
I think. On the Sunday morning we went with the crowd to
service in the cathedral. It was all very grand and imposing to
my young mind. The crashing organ, the long procession of
white-robed clergy and college boys, the two majestic beings in
scarlet gowns, their trains held up by gentlemen, and the wigs that
frightened me! I had been told I was going to college to see the
judge. In my astonished mind I don't think I knew which was
judge and which was organ. Papa was in attendance on the
judges; the only one who seemed to be in plain clothes in the
procession. An impression remained on me that he had a white
wand in his hand; but I suppose I was wrong. Attending papa,
walked his black-robed chaplain who was to preach; looking like
a crow amongst gay-plumaged birds. And, lining the way all
along the body of the cathedral from the north entrance to the
gates of the choir, were papa's livery men with their glittering
javelins. You've seen it all, Johnny, and know what the show is to
a child such as I was. But now, will you believe that it was all as
nothing to me, compared with the sight of the many-coloured,
beautiful east window?* I sat in full view of it. We had gone in
rather late, and so were only part of the throng. Mamma with me
in her hand—I remember I wore purple velvet, Johnny—was stepping into the choir after the judges and clergy had taken their
places, when one of the black-gowned beadsmen would have rudely
shut the gates upon her. Upon that, a verger pushed out his silver
mace to stop him. 'Hist,' says he, 'it's the High Sheriff's lady—
my Lady Whitney;' and the beadsman bowed and let us pass.
We were put into the pew under the sub-dean's stall. It was
Winnington-Ingram, I think, who was sub-dean then, but I am
not sure. Whoever it was did not sit in the sub-dean's stall, but
in the next to it, for he had given that up, as was customary, to
one of the judges. With the great wig flowing down right upon

* The old East window : not the new one.

my head, as it seemed, and the sub-dean's trencher sticking over the cushion close to it, I was in a state of bewilderment; and they were some way through the Litany—the cathedral service at Worcester began with the Litany then, you remember, as they had early morning prayers—before I ventured to look up at all. As I did so, the colours of the distant east window flashed upon my dazzled sight. Not dazzled with the light, Johnny, though it was a sunny day, but with the charm of the colours. What it was to me in that moment I could never describe. That window has been abused enough by people who call themselves connoisseurs in art; but I know that to me it seemed as the very incarnation of celestial beauty. What with the organ, and the chanting, and the show that had gone before, and now this sight to illuminate it, I seemed to be in Paradise. I sat entranced; unable to take my fascinated eyes from the window: the pew faces it, you know; and were I to live for ever, I can never forget that day, or what it was to me. This will show you what colours have been to me here, Johnny. What, then, will they be to me in heaven?"

"How well you remember things!"

"I always did—things that make an impression on me," he answered. "A quiet, thoughtful child does so. You were thoughtful yourself."

True. Or I don't suppose I could have written these papers. The light in the sky faded out as we sat in silence. John recurred to his dream.

"I thought I saw the Saviour," he whispered. "I did indeed. Over the crystal river, and beyond the white figures and the harps, was a great light. There stood in it One different from the rest. He had a grand, noble countenance, exquisite in sweetness, and it was turned upon me with a loving smile of welcome. Johnny, I *know* it was Jesus. Oh, it will be good to be there!"

No doubt of it. Very good for him.

"The strange thing was, that I felt no fear. None. Just as securely as I seemed to lie in the arms of the angels, so did I seem secure in the happiness awaiting me. A great many of us fear death, Johnny; I see now that all fear will cease with this world, to those who die in Christ."

A sudden burst of subdued sobbing broke the stillness of the room and startled us beyond everything. Lady Whitney had wakened up and was listening.

"Oh, John, my darling boy, don't talk so!" she said, coming forward and laying her cheek upon his shoulder. "We can't spare you; we can't indeed."

His eyes were full of tears: so were mine. He took his mother's hand and stroked it.

"But it must be, mother dear?" he gently whispered. "God will temper the loss to you all."

"Any of them but you, John! You were ever my best and dearest son."

"It's all for the best, mother: it must be. The others are not ready to go."

"And don't you *care* to leave us?" she said, breaking down again.

"I did care; very much; but lately I seem to have looked only to the time when we shall meet again. Mother, I do not think now I would live if the chance were offered me."

"Well, it's the first time I ever heard of young people wanting to die!" cried Lady Whitney.

"Mother, I think we must be very close on death *before* we want it," he gently answered. "Don't you see the mercy?—that when this world is passing from us, we are led insensibly to long for the next?"

She sat down in the chair that I had got up from, and drew it closer to him. A more simple-minded woman than Lady Whitney never lived. She sobbed gently. He kept her hand between his.

"It will be a great blow to me; I know that; and to your father. He feels it now more than he shows, John. You have been so good and obedient, you see; never naughty and giving us trouble like the rest."

There was another silence. His quiet voice broke it.

"Mother, dear, the thought has crossed me lately, that it must be good to have one whom we love very much, taken on to heaven. It must make it seem more like our final home; it must, I think, make us more desirous of getting there. 'John's gone on to it,' you and papa will be thinking; 'we shall see him again when the end comes.' And it will cause you to look for the end, instead of turning away from it, as too many do. Don't grieve, mother! Had it been God's will, I should have lived. But it was not; and He is taking me to a better home. A little sooner, a little later; it cannot make much difference which, if we are only ready for it when it comes."

The distant church bells, which always rang on a Friday night, broke upon the air. John asked to have the window opened. I threw it up, and we sat listening. The remembrance of that hour is upon me now, just as vividly as he remembered the moment when he first saw the old east window in the cathedral. The melody of the bells; the sweet scent of the mignonette in the garden; the fading sky: I close my eyes and realize it all.

The girls returned, bringing word that Mrs. Frost was very ill, but not much more so than usual. Directly afterwards we heard Sir John come home.

"They are afraid Barrington's worse," observed Helen; "and of course it is worrying Mrs. Frost. Mr. Carden has not been there to-day either, though he was expected: they hope he will be over the first thing in the morning."

In they trooped, Sir John and the boys; all eagerly talking of the pleasant afternoon they had had, and what they had seen and done at Evesham. But the room, as they said later, seemed to have a strange hush upon it, and John's face an altered look: and the eager voices died away again.

John was the one to read the chapter that night. He asked to do so; and chose the twenty-first of Revelation. His voice was low, but quite distinct and clear. Without pausing at the end, he went on to the next chapter, which concludes the Bible.

"Only think what it will be, Johnny!" he said to me later, following up our previous conversation. "All manner of precious stones! all sorts of glorious colours! Better even" (with a smile) "than the great east window."

I don't know whether it surprised me, or not, to find the house in commotion when I woke the next morning, and to hear that John Whitney was dying. A remarkable change had certainly taken place in him. He lay in bed; not insensible, but almost speechless.

Breakfast was scarcely over when Mr. Carden's carriage drove in. He had been with Barrington, having started from Worcester at day-dawn. John knew him, and took his hand and smiled.

"What's to be done for him?" questioned Sir John, pointing to his son.

Mr. Carden gave one meaning look at Sir John, and that was all. Nothing more of any kind could be done for John Whitney.

"Good-bye, Mr. Carden; good-bye," said John, as the surgeon was leaving. "You have been very kind."

"Good-bye, my boy."

"It is so sudden; so soon, you know, Carden," cried poor Sir John, as they walked downstairs together. "You ought to have warned me that it was coming."

"I did not know it would be quite so soon as this," was Mr. Carden's answer—and I heard him say it.

John had visitors that day, and saw them. Some of the fellows from Frost's, who came over when they heard how it was; Dr. Frost himself; and the clergyman. At dusk, when he had been lying quietly for some time, except for the restlessness that often ushers in death, he opened his eyes and began speaking in a whisper. Lady Whitney, thinking he wanted something, bent down her ear. But he was only repeating a verse from the Bible.

"And there shall be no night there: and they need no candle, neither light of the sun, for the Lord God giveth them light : and they shall reign for ever and ever."

Bill, who had his head on the bolster on the other side, broke into a hushed sob. It did not disturb the dying. They were John's last words.

Quite a crowd went to his funeral. It took place on the following Thursday. Dr. Frost and Mr. Carden (and it's not so often *he* wasted his time going to a funeral !) and Featherstone and the Squire amongst them. Poor Sir John sobbed over the grave, and did not mind who saw and heard him, while they cast the earth on the coffin.

"*Earth to earth, ashes to ashes, dust to dust; in sure and certain hope of the Resurrection to eternal life.*"

That the solemn promise was applicable to John Whitney, and that he had most assuredly entered on that glorious life, I knew as well then as I know now. The corruptible had put on incorruption, the mortal immortality.

Not much of a story, you will say. But I might have told a worse. And I hope, seeing we must all go out at the same gate, that we shall be as ready for it as he was.

JOHNNY LUDLOW.

THE END.